Kilcaraig

Kilcaraig

Annabel Carothers

ST. MARTIN'S PRESS
NEW YORK

To the natives of the Island of Mull,
wherever they may be.

Part One
1913–1946

A BREEZE IN THE BARLEY

A breeze in the barley
And gossip is there,
A thousand heads whispering,
A secret laid bare.

A thousand wise heads,
A-nod in the sun;
The joy on their faces!
The shame on one!

> John Gawsworth

1

The torrential rain had turned the pot-holes in the rough road into pools, and now that the sun had made its first appearance of the day, it transformed the water into patches of shimmering nothingness.

Nicholas Danvers, who was already driving with extreme caution along this absurdly narrow highway, pulled at the reins and brought the mare almost to a standstill. Driving directly into the sun was a perilous feat for the natives of the island, but for him, a stranger, it was a terrifying ordeal. Presently, because there was no one to witness his timidity, he halted Maggie, mopped his brow, and decided that with the clouds tearing across the sky at their present rate it would not be long before deluge took the place of this dazzling brilliance.

If anything should come up behind him now, he would have to quicken his pace, for certainly no vehicle could pass him here, yet if he drove any faster he would end up in the ditch and be the laughing-stock of the neighbourhood. He had a shrewd idea of the way these blue-eyed, open-faced Highland people felt about him in their hearts. Although by virtue of his profession he was admitted into the most intimate knowledge of their private lives, and was accepted by them with their inherent courtesy, their spirits must rebel against an English stripling, whom Doctor MacFie had had the folly to appoint as *locum tenens* during his well-earned rest.

His thoughts were interrupted by the rumble of a carriage somewhere behind him. He glanced over his shoulder and could see nothing; but here, in this wild glen, sound carried far. He had not yet learned what twists and turns the road took, or what might be concealed behind the ominous boulders, which seemed at any moment liable to be dislodged and slip down the mountainside on top of his trap and himself. He clutched the reins, prayed for an eclipse, and continued his journey.

As he proceeded, Nicholas realized that Maggie knew the road better than he did. He relaxed, trusting the little mare to keep the wheels out of the ditch, while he absorbed the scent of a Hebridean autumn, which matched so well the tangle of bog-myrtle, fading heather and golden fronds of bracken. The rocks were grey, and the loch down there on his left was black and fearful. There had been trees behind him, but now nothing but desolation, with here and there a scrubby little willow, or an isolated mountain ash, which he had learnt in these parts was called rowan.

Maggie came to a standstill. They had reached another gate.

Nicholas opened the gate and Maggie trotted through. Then he was in a quandary. What was the etiquette of this gate-shutting business? Believing a carriage to be behind him, should he leave the gate open? To be on the safe side, he closed it and urged Maggie to increase her speed, in case he had incurred the wrath of the driver behind him who would have to climb down to open and shut it.

He continued his journey, which was easier now as the road sloped gently downhill towards the sea. There were no more gates, but there were a few cottages. There was no sound of a carriage behind him any more. His sense of guilt left him, and it was only then that he realized how guilty he had felt. That the opening and shutting of a gate should engender such extreme emotions was indicative of the compulsive atmosphere of the place. One had to know by instinct the right way to behave, for until one knew, one was an outsider. How would he ever learn!

There were twists and turns in the road, with Maggie plodding up and down little braes as they approached Craignure, with its church, its inn and its few houses spread along at the foot of the precipitous tree-covered hill that rose almost straight out of the sea. A few people were on the jetty, waiting for the arrival of the boat from Oban, but Nicholas decided to call at the inn, where he was known. He still felt oppressively shy and ill at ease, and was puzzled by this wholly uncharacteristic sensation.

"Come along, Doctor Danvers," he was greeted in the soft, lilting voice, with the accent that enchanted him. "Is it tea you'll be wanting? Effie will bring it to you in the parlour as soon as it's infused. Andy will see to Maggie. I'll give him a shout."

Nicholas obeyed and found himself in a diminutive room. A large, welcoming peat fire burned in the horse-shoe grate. He extended his hands to the flame and was startled by the voice behind him.

"I followed you here. On earth why did you not leave the gates?"

He turned round and found a girl with wind-blown hair, freckles, and a charming, candid smile. She was wearing neat but shabby clothes, and Nicholas tried to think who she could be. She held out her hand to him, and he shook it warmly. He was getting used to this hand-shaking business. One did it all day, every day, all the time.

4

"I'm very sorry," he said. "I didn't know what was expected of me. But I'd have waited if I'd known the carriage I could hear was being driven by you!"

She laughed. She had grey eyes and dimples and the whitest of teeth. "What a very courteous thing to say! I know who you are. You must be the English doctor." There was no malice in her remark, but Nicholas felt that in her eyes he could belong to the outback of Timbuctoo, if there were such a place.

"I'm only here for a few weeks," he said apologetically.

She gestured him to sit down, and he did so obediently, feeling like a courtier in the presence of a queen.

"I hope they'll be happy weeks," she said. "You must think we're shockingly rude to have allowed you to be here a whole fortnight without having you over to see us, but my sister Catriona has been in Italy, and we waited till she got back. She's on the *Lochinvar* now."

"Now I know who you are!" exclaimed Nicholas. "You're one of the Lamonts of Kilcaraig. I've tried to catch a glimpse of the castle till I've nearly broken my neck, but its useless – there are too many trees."

"In summer we wallow in glorious mystery," she laughed. "But in autumn the denouement gradually takes place, so that by winter the castle is revealed, not as something splendid with towers and battlements, but as a tumbledown country-house that isn't even water-tight!"

"You can see all that from the road?"

"You can hear it," she said solemnly. "The plink, plonk of rain dropping into every imaginable receptacle all over the house."

"Doesn't it give you rheumatism?"

"That's your medical mind," she said, and added confidentially, "Doctor MacFie told us you were young. He didn't tell us you were very good-looking." She spoke in such a practical way that Nicholas felt no embarrassment. He gave her a long, appraising look and said, "You are very beautiful."

She replied. "Wait till you see Catriona. Then you'll know what beauty really is."

When Effie bumped into the room with a tray of tea and scones, the doctor was looking out of the window and Marian Lamont was warming her hands by the fire. Mercy, what sticky creatures the English must be. On earth how did he manage to keep Miss Marian from talking! She bumped out of the room, and went off to report proceedings to the kitchen.

Nicholas watched the slender, well-manicured hand that poured out the tea, and the frayed cuff that surrounded the small wrist. He had heard that there was not much affluence about the hereditary landowners in these parts, and judging by the attire of this lovely young woman, the description fell far short of the truth. Here was the personification of proud poverty. Miss Lamont in silks and laces would be just another society beauty. Miss Lamont in well-worn tweeds was enchantment.

"Your tea."

He took the cup from her, and felt the penetrating look to which he was being subjected.

"What are you thinking about?" she asked.

"I was thinking what a wonderful setting this island would make for the book I would like to write."

"Just fancy! A book! What sort of a book? Detective story, romance, or a sombre epic about the Clearances?" From the way she spoke, he could sense that the dreadful things that had happened in the past were still painful to her, although they were all over decades before she was born.

"It will be a novel about a family who live in a castle, and the heroine will be more beautiful than day," he said.

"Then she must be Catriona because you'll never invent a heroine more beautiful than her. But you'll have to spell her name K.A.T.R.I.N.A so that your readers will pronounce it properly."

They discussed the possibilities of his novel as they drank their tea and ate the hot buttered scones. They could see from the window when the steamer from Oban sailed round the point. As she turned out of the choppy waters of the Sound of Mull into the relative calm of Craignure Bay, they left the inn and walked together towards the jetty.

There was no pier at Craignure, but a converted lifeboat acted as tender between ship and shore, and this was being rowed out to collect the passengers, luggage and mail-bags, which could now be seen through the opened port-side hatch of the *Lochinvar*.

"What happens if there's a swell?" Nicholas asked as he watched what appeared to be a perilous feat of transferring passengers and goods from one ship to another.

"Our seamen have great skill and perfect timing," Marian assured him. "Look, there's a wee calf being lowered. You can see its head sticking out of a sack! They're putting it beside my sister – she's the one in green. Are you meeting someone, Doctor Danvers?"

"No—a typewriter and a microscope."

"Symbols of your two professions?"

"That's right."

"I didn't thank you for the tea."

"You're welcome."

"You've picked that up already."

"What?"

"You're welcome."

He laughed. "I hear it so often! Maybe some day I'll even have the Gaelic." He used the local idiom, and they both laughed.

He watched, his eyes screwed up against the now brilliant sunshine as the steamer went its way and the tender made for the shore. To be conveyed with a calf for company was not a very auspicious way for his heroine to make her bow, yet as he awaited his first sight of her he felt a frisson of anticipation. An oarsman obscured his view of both Miss Lamont and the calf, but as the tender came alongside the jetty and the oarsman jumped out, Nicholas saw her.

Catriona Lamont was more beautiful than ever he could picture anyone, even in his wildest dreams. He saw the sisters greet one another, not with a kiss but with the inevitable handshake; then there was a lot more handshaking to be got through before the traveller was allowed to make her way up the jetty to where he was standing spellbound, too numbed to care if a typewriter and a microscope were among the parcels being ruthlessly hurled ashore by the ferryman.

"This is my sister, Doctor Danvers." Marian's voice sounded very far away, but he felt the softness of a delicious hand in his, and looked into the impenetrable depth of slate-grey, arrogant eyes.

"I've heard so much about you that I almost feel I know you," he said, flushing at the use of such an artless greeting.

"Doctor Danvers is doing *locum* for Doctor MacFie. He's going to write a novel, and you're to be the heroine," Marian explained.

Catriona coloured very slightly. She must be accustomed to compliments, and to her sister's exuberance, but in that moment Nicholas sensed an unexpected vulnerability about this cool, exquisite woman.

"Will you be with us for long, Doctor Danvers?" she asked, and before he could reply, she added "You will please come and see us at the castle." It was together a command and a welcome.

Her voice was gentle and low, just as it should have been, and presently he was helping her into her carriage, while Marian, at the reins, called over her shoulder, "You'll be following us, so we'll leave the gates open."

The ferryman was at his side. "Your things are sorted now," he said, noticing with satisfaction how the doctor's eyes dwelt on the tracks the Lamonts' carriage had left. Nicholas murmured thanks and fumbled in his pocket.

"You're very welcome," the ferryman said, with warmth.

Nicholas blew his nose, to give himself an excuse for that search in his pocket. He was beginning to understand these people. It would be an insult to offer a tip.

He did not overtake the Lamonts' carriage until he reached Kilcaraig village. It was standing outside the post office, and was surrounded by more people than he would have believed Kilcaraig would house. Everyone was laughing. It seemed that no one was in awe of Catriona Lamont except himself.

Self-consciously, feeling a complete outsider, he took the turning to the left before the post office, and in a few minutes Maggie was plodding up the brae, and had come to a halt outside the doctor's house. He had a good view of the village from here. The site must have been chosen by someone with an insatiable curiosity, but utter disregard for the prevailing winds. Soon he was in his room, using the binoculars with which Mrs. MacFadyen, his housekeeper, had thoughtfully provided him. This distance away, he could see Catriona Lamont in detail in her green coat and green hat. He had to imagine the slate-grey eyes, but he could see her graceful movements.

"Doctor Danvers, I'm wondering if you'll be ready for your tea." Mrs. MacFadyen was regarding him balefully from the doorway. Guiltily, he replaced the binoculars on the window-sill.

"I'll be down in a moment. I was trying to see if that was a motor-car coming over the glen road."

"A motor-car?" She shook her head. "I'll infuse the tea." She left him to his shame. If she had thought there was a motor-car to be seen on the glen road or anywhere else, she would certainly have joined him at the window.

When he reached the bottom of the stairs, a peep through the lobby window showed him all he needed to know.

The Lamont carriage had continued on its way to the castle, had crossed the bridge over the burn, and was lost from sight among the trees.

2

During the night, Nicholas was called out to see Mrs. Ames at Caraig Lodge. Mrs. MacFadyen, who had given him the note delivered by a frightened maid from the Lodge, pointed out that Mrs. Ames had a way of thinking herself ill at unearthly hours, and that Doctor MacFie would never stand such nonsense, but Nicholas, conscious of his inexperience, dressed quickly and walked the quarter mile to his patient's house. It was a large house, built on a hillside close to the gates of the castle. The short drive leading up to it was well kept, and even in the darkness it was discernible that the house, unlike the castle, was well maintained.

Mrs. MacFadyen had been right. What had seemed to be a heart-attack proved to be the result of too heavy a dinner, and an apologetic Mr. Ames insisted on the doctor having a whisky before returning home to bed.

So it was that Nicholas learnt a little more about the Lamonts.

Caraig Lodge had been the shooting-lodge on the Kilcaraig estate, but an impecunious Lamont had sold it to pay off accumulated debts some seventy years ago, and since then the house and several hundred acres of land had changed hands many times. The Ameses had bought it only a few months ago, and it was easy to see that Mr. Ames was finding difficulty in adjusting from his life as a mill-owner in the North of England to that of a landowner on Mull.

"My daughter Nancy is on holiday from her finishing-school in Germany, and my son Michael has just left Harrow. He's going to Oxford, and those distressed gentlefolks over at the castle are going to have to accept that I'm Ames of Caraig Lodge, whether they like it or not." He was belligerent because he was unsure of himself.

"There doesn't seem to be anything snobbish about the Lamonts," Nicholas said uncomfortably. "Everyone speaks well of them, and the two Misses Lamont were most friendly when I met them this afternoon."

"I heard you'd met them," Mr. Ames said, adding the warning, "Everything you do in this place is noted and reported. Watch yourself, Doctor. When our Michael walked back from the village with young Marian the other day, the way people talked you'd think their engagement was about to be announced! Not that I'd mind it at all, if they want it that way when they're older. She's a pretty lass and the Lamonts could do with one of the girls marrying into a bit of money."

A few days later, Nicholas was thinking over this conversation in broody discontent. It was Sunday evening and he had not been to church, but Mrs. MacFadyen had been, and when she brought him his oil lamp she was still wearing her best bonnet. She told him the church was packed, and it was a pleasure to have Miss Lamont back again at the harmonium, because Miss Marian always forgot that the Middle C stuck, and it sounded dolefully and inharmoniously throughout the metrical psalm. Miss Lamont never forgot. She was not the forgetting kind.

"She's forgotten to ask me to lunch," Nicholas thought dismally. It was five days since his encounter with the Lamonts and he had not caught another glimpse of them, although he made daily visits to the village post office, which was also the village store.

The valley lay before him, mystic and as yet unexplored. Stretching through the mountains were three lochs, linked together by a burn, like three jewels on a pendant. The backs of the houses in the village were turned to Loch Caraig, the last and largest of the three, and facing them on a hill was Kilcaraig Castle, the centre of his universe but hidden from sight, because a Lamont, generations back, had surrounded it with trees.

He cursed the unknown architect of his despair when a further effort with the binoculars failed to reveal even a corner of the Lamont stronghold, but gradually his aggravation was soothed by the beauty of the landscape, which was slowly becoming golden in the rays of the setting sun. He watched, enchanted, as the kaleidoscope changed from yellow to pink, from pink to vermilion until, leaving the valley dyed deep purple, the sun slid away behind the hills.

Sometimes the sound of the sea was carried like a murmur through the glen, but tonight all was quiet and calm, and Nicholas wrote in his diary – "I may travel far, but I shall never see greater beauty than the sunset over the glen, and the arrogant splendour of Catriona Lamont's slate-grey eyes."

He had found something lyrical to enter for five nights now. He returned the diary to the top drawer of his dressing-table, and camouflaged it carefully with his socks.

It was not until the following Friday that another chance of seeing Catriona was offered to him.

"You'll be going to the concert in the school tonight, Doctor?" The question, as always, was framed as a statement by Hughie MacIntyre, whose arm Nicholas was bandaging in the surgery. It was the first he had heard of a concert, and he said so.

"The notice is in the post office," Hughie said. "But you'll not be bothering to read the board, seeing you're only here for a wee while."

Nicholas tied the ends of the knot before replying. "I've read the notices every day, but I couldn't say what was in any of them."

"There are better things to think about," Hughie said portentously, and Nicholas stiffened, knowing instinctively what Hughie was getting at.

"That's fixed you for the time being. Come back on Monday and I'll see how it's healing," he said. But Hughie was not interested in his wound, and would not be so easily put off.

"The Lamonts will be there," he said boldly. "They're bonnie lassies. You should see them." He was staring wide-eyed at Nicholas, the personification of innocence, but Nicholas knew better.

"I've met them both," he said.

"Aye. So I've heard." If the doctor could be honest, so could Hughie.

"They're very pretty," Nicholas said, gaining confidence.

Hughie propped up against the surgery door, removed a cigarette from behind his ear, lit it, and settled himself for a gossip.

"Kilcaraig's a fine man," he said. "You'll do well to meet Kilcaraig. He's had a sad life. Mistress Lamont died having a baby. The children were all wee things, and there was a housekeeper until Miss Catriona was old enough to become mistress of the castle. She's Kilcaraig's favourite. There's a son – Ian. He's in India in the army. A fine boy, but he married an English girl." He remembered suddenly to whom he was speaking, and added hastily, "It's just that she'll be mistress of Kilcaraig one day, if she's spared, and it will be difficult altogether."

"Not suitable at all," Nicholas said.

Hughie nodded, relieved that no offence was taken, and Nicholas took advantage of the momentary silence to remark on the fact that neither of the Misses Lamont was married.

"Och, Miss Marian's only nineteen. She's not ready to settle down yet. And Miss Catriona – well, it was a sad business, but Kilcaraig was right. It wouldn't have done at all, at all." He took a long puff at his cigarette. Nicholas dared not prompt him, for he had taken Mr. Ames' warning to heart about everything being repeated in the village. However, after an agonizing wait, Hughie decided to complete his reminiscence. "She was friendly with Hector MacNeill of Ardcross, and a grand pair they made, laughing together, dancing together, not a care in the world. But MacNeill wanted to marry her and that was the end of it. There was a terrible row, and Kilcaraig forbade her to see him any more."

"But why?"

"He was a Roman Catholic." Hughie remembered that he had not seen Nicholas in church. "You wouldn't be a Roman Catholic, Doctor Danvers?" he asked anxiously.

Nicholas assured him that he was not, and Hughie registered relief with an understanding sigh. "Not that I have anything against them, but for Kilcaraig it just would not do."

"Miss Lamont is over twenty-one. She can marry whom she pleases." Curiosity had overcome Nicholas's caution.

"MacNeill went straight off in a rage and married another woman. They say Miss Catriona has never laughed from that day to this."

Nicholas was appalled. What a heroine for his book – what an incredible tale of bigotry and folly! "She must be wretchedly unhappy," he said.

"Och, she's not unhappy. She's not anything at all. She's just a beautiful woman – a Lamont of Kilcaraig. They're a fine family. You'll do well to meet Kilcaraig." Having brought the conversation back to where it started, Hughie picked up his cap.

"I'll need to get back to the castle," he said. "I'm helping with the harvest. And thank you for sorting my arm."

"You're welcome!" Nicholas smiled, and Hughie left the surgery with that light, rhythmic walk inherited from his kilt-clad ancestors.

Nicholas watched the retreating figure from his desk in the surgery window. Hughie's words still echoed in his mind. Kilcaraig – a fine man indeed! A monster, a viper, a tyrant! He picked up his pen, and his hand shook as he tried to make out the list of supplies he was needing from Oban.

In a little while, he had recovered himself sufficiently to be able to consider another aspect of his talk with Hughie. How did Hughie know that he was interested in the Lamonts? Could it be that Mrs. MacFadyen knew that men had a way of hiding documents under their socks? He resolved to lock up his diary in his instrument case in future, but he hoped fiercely that no eyes had seen those sentimental entries but his own. While he was thinking, he was writing "Katrina" over and over again on his blotting-paper. Then he wrote "Catriona", because that was the right way to spell it, as Marian had pointed out. He tore up the paper, but he did not trust his waste-paper basket. Instead, he took the pieces to the parlour and put them on the fire.

The concert had been advertised to start at eight, but Mrs. MacFadyen warned Nicholas not to leave for the schoolhouse before the half hour. Even so, he found when he arrived that the door had not been opened, but someone had gone along to find the blacksmith who, being the school caretaker, was in charge of the key.

The arrival of the key coincided with the arrival of a large portion of the audience. These were the wise ones who had watched from their windows to see how things were progressing at the school.

Nicholas paid his shilling and was soon sitting near the front of the room, cramped and self-conscious, in a desk designed to accommodate a child from the infant class. His isolation was not to last for long because soon the Ames family was shown to the same

12

bench. Mrs. Ames peered at him through thick-lensed spectacles, and when she recognized him, her face broadened into a smile.

"You mustn't look so miserable, Doctor Danvers," she said. "It's the privilege of the gentry to sit in the front seats. Soon we'll be joined by the Lamonts, and maybe some of their friends. They entertain a lot at the castle, though I don't know how they do it, seeing they haven't even the money to paint the rusty gates."

The Lamonts' poverty was evidently a matter of mingled regret and satisfaction to the Ameses. Mr. Ames squeezed himself into the desk beside his wife and murmured his agreement, but the rather angular girl, who must be their daughter, leaned across them and said to Nicholas–"We poor Sassenachs have a job to hold our own."

"My mother was a MacDougall," Nicholas said defensively. "I've been becoming more clannish every day since I arrived here."

"Just fancy! You'll be wearing the kilt before you go!"

The firm, low voice came from just behind him. He turned quickly and looked into those slate-coloured eyes he had been dreaming about. He tried desperately to hide his confusion at seeing her so close to him. He poured out his genealogy in a rambling, ungrammatical sentence, and then broke off, horrified at his loss of self-control. She smiled at him kindly.

"You must tell my father. He'll be very interested, for he has an expert knowledge of clan history. It's shameful that you haven't met him yet. We've been making the most of the weather, to get in the harvest," she said.

"They all work in the fields, even the Laird himself," interposed Mrs. Ames.

Catriona nodded her agreement. "It's amazing what an extra pair of hands can do. Or an extra pair of feet. I was tramping grapes in Italy. It was a glorious, intoxicating feeling. I can understand now why children enjoy making mud pies."

"I thought women didn't tramp grapes," Mrs. Ames said. She had travelled considerably and liked to display her knowledge. "I suppose English tourists are allowed to do as they like."

A flicker of amusement passed between Catriona and Nicholas, but Catriona merely said, "The odd ways of strangers anywhere are apt to be tolerated by the natives". Then she turned to greet a friend, whom she introduced to Nicholas as Andrew Sinclair, in the army and home on leave at Duff.

"Duff is at the Other End," she said, stressing the two words that were applied by the natives of South Mull to those who lived on the north end of the island. "Fancy him coming all this way just for a concert!"

Jealousy smote Nicholas as he shook hands with the dark-haired young man with the Highland blue eyes, but other people were claiming Andrew Sinclair's attention. He excused himself, crossed the aisle, and eventually settled somewhere at the back of the hall.

Catriona did not accompany him, but Nicholas could hear her voice, and he knew that she was sitting somewhere close behind him. He was determined not to glance round at her, and he stared instead at the portrait of Gladstone which hung behind the chairman's table.

Nicholas the writer could recognize emotions which Nicholas the doctor dismissed as imaginative nonsense, fruit of gossip.

"Doctor Danvers, is there room for me at your desk? I jumped out of the carriage straight into a puddle and my left foot's soaking wet." Marian scrambled into the seat beside him. "I hope I don't squidge when my foot touches the pedal, for I'll need to accompany Mr. MacNab. He's the schoolmaster, and he likes to sing like Caruso."

Nicholas was left to digest this extraordinary but evidently acceptable ambition while the rest of the audience assembled, greeting one another in Gaelic. One of the last to arrive was Michael Ames, who had been lingering outside in the rain. When he was introduced to Nicholas, his candid brown eyes indicated an inward serenity that set him apart from the other members of his family. He was a likeable young man, and as he sat on the front bench, which was the penalty of all latecomers, he turned round to talk to the people behind him, happy, obviously at ease. It seemed possible to Nicholas that the Ameses would depend on their son as their hope of acceptance by the local community.

The sound of bagpipes now filled the air, there was a murmur from the audience, and Kilcaraig, as was customary, opened the concert with a selection of regimental marches.

Nicholas had expected him to be tall and strapping, and of course to be clad in a kilt, but he had not pictured the majesty of this bearded, broad-shouldered man. There was dignity in every inch of that fine, straight figure, and arrogance in the blue eyes that faced the audience, yet when the music ended and the applause had died down, Kilcaraig addressed the people with an informality that was as warm as it was unexpected; there was no trace of the oppressor, the iconoclast, the breaker up of dreams. Puzzled, Nicholas listened to the announcement of the first item, and watched a red-haired, red-faced young girl bound up to the platform.

She sang unaccompanied in Gaelic. Her voice was plaintive and clear. Nicholas began to tap his foot in rhythm. Marian took it up, and soon the schoolhouse vibrated with the rhythmic tapping of feet. Everyone joined in the chorus, and as Nicholas could not manage the Gaelic, he sang "Ho Ro", which sounded better than "Tra La".

The applause was terrific. Instantly the red-headed girl, whom Marian had whispered was a house-maid at the castle, obliged with an encore. Nicholas found that this was the pattern, and soon was growing hoarse with his ho-ros to songs and encores alike.

When the would-be Caruso's name was called, someone shouted from the back that Mr. MacNab had been summoned to Dalmally, where his aunt had died. There was a respectful murmur of sympathy and conjecture about when the funeral would take place; then the concert continued until Kilcaraig brought the first half to an end with a further selection on the pipes.

It had stopped raining and most of the men went outside to stretch their legs and to fortify themselves with a quick swig from the bottles they carried in their pockets. Nicholas, suspecting this would happen, and not being sure what his position as a doctor would be in such a matter, stayed in the schoolroom.

"I've sung till I'm hoarse and I've tapped until my feet ache," he said to Marian. "This is the most marvellous music I'll ever hear."

"You must come to our Highland dancing classes. We hold them every winter." Marian had been touched by Nicholas's enthusiasm.

"I won't be here," he said glumly.

"How lucky you are, Doctor Danvers. I dread the dreariness of winter here." It was Nancy Ames, and she had seen how downcast he looked. She wanted to be kind.

"It's the best time of year. A bronze landscape. Blazing fires. A quiet Christmas, but the New Year's Eve dance is splendid, and the fun goes on for weeks. Doctor Danvers, you must come and stay with us, just to see how we vibrate with life, when the world outside is dark."

He could scarcely believe it. He turned his head, and sure enough, it was she.

"Thank you, Miss Lamont. Some day indeed I will."

She bowed at him gravely. "You'll be very welcome," she said.

He managed to sit next to her during the second half of the programme. Whenever he dared, he glanced sideways at her. Her skin was so pale and her hair so dark that she might be a study in black and white, were it not for the red of her lips, and the green silk scarf draped loosely round her throat.

The concert was brought to an end by Kilcaraig's own choir. He conducted it himself, beautifully, making the best of every cadence. Nicholas knew not a word of what they were singing, but he was stirred to the depth of his soul. The music was of purple heather and lochs and mountains. Catriona leaned across to whisper. "*An T-Eilean Muileach. The Isle of Mull*. It's our own island song."

It was dark outside now. The paraffin lamps cast weird shadows across the room. A sheep dog at Nicholas' feet stirred and wagged a sleepy tail. Mr. Ames glanced surreptitiously at his watch.

As the music died away, Nicholas knew that he must escape from here quickly, before anyone could disturb the magic of his tranquillity. Catriona allowed him to push past her, through the desks and out of the hall. He walked slowly up the hillock to his house.

Far into the night, he sat by his window, watching the gleam of light that marked the schoolhouse. He could hear the sound of the bagpipes, hear the thudding rhythm of the dance. He could have been there with Catriona, could have touched her hand, perhaps even put his arm about her waist. Yet he was glad he had not stayed, for he would never forget or ever recapture that ecstasy of lamplight and music and Catriona, never for as long as he lived.

The untimely arrival of a MacPhail baby prevented him from going to church on Sunday, and when he returned home, having safely delivered Mary MacPhail of her third son, Mrs. MacFadyen told him that the sermon had been unusually long, and that Miss Marian, at the harmonium, had missed out two verses of a psalm. Miss Catriona had not been there.

When Hughie came to have his arm examined the following morning, he brought a message from the castle. Would Doctor Danvers kindly call there sometime? Seemingly Miss Catriona was ill.

With an effort Nicholas resisted the temptation to question Hughie, who showed surprising reticence over a subject which must consume him with curiosity, but as soon as he had dealt with his last patient, he closed the surgery, harnessed Maggie to the trap, and set off for the castle at a perilous rate. The post mistress, who had already heard of his summons, watched from her window, and waited for him to capsize at the bumpy bridge over the burn. She was disappointed, as miraculously he kept his balance. Soon he was hidden from view by the plantation of young firs at the bottom of the hill. Regretfully, she returned to her place behind the counter. There was not so much as a postcard in the box for her to read.

3

After crossing the bridge over the burn, Nicholas had to curb his anxiety to reach his patient, for once through the rusty gates the drive to the castle twisted steeply upward. Looking over his shoulder he could see the road that led to the MacPhails' farm at the south end of Loch Caraig, and here and there were scattered heaps of stones, all that remained of the cottages that had once housed Highland families. In the middle of a field of half-reaped barley were the ruins of a church. This was typical of the many scenes of desolation which showed in patches everywhere in Mull, sometimes due to natural causes, but more often the result of those inhuman acts which he had once written about in his history note-books under the heading "Highland Clearances". It was then that he had learnt of the many landowners throughout the Highlands who had evicted their tenants by setting fire to their thatched cottages and bricking up their wells, thus forcing them to settle overseas – all this in order that sheep could graze the land and bring wealth to the proprietors. It had meant nothing to him then, but since he came to Mull he could feel its heartbreak. After the farm, that road led to nowhere. Caraig village was dead.

He drove through a tunnel of trees and shrubs, unkempt, some of them almost meeting in the middle of the drive so that their branches obscured the sun and flicked at his face. He blinked as he came out of their shade and into the September sunshine. The gravelled forecourt was free of moss and weeds, and the castle was a graceful and well-proportioned house, built of red granite which showed, warm and welcoming, from among the patches of ivy that covered it.

To his right, green turf swept downhill to the trees that hid the road, and to his left was the boundary fence of Caraig Lodge, with its plantation of young fir trees. On the far side of the castle was the high wall of a vegetable and flower garden. The mountains rose behind it, purple with heather, the lower slopes black in patches where peat had been cut. In a nearby field of barley, men were at work, tying up the stooks, stretching, stopping now and again to strain their eyes in his direction.

"The doctor's trap," they would say, and wonder – if they did not know already – why it had come.

Marian appeared as soon as he had brought Maggie to a standstill.

"You didn't waste any time," she said.

"I thought it might be urgent." He climbed down from his seat and shook her hand.

"If it were urgent, I would have said so." She called over her shoulder and a man came out of the house. She introduced him as Willie who would look after the mare, and then she asked Nicholas to come with her as Catriona was in the dairy.

This was the last place he would have expected his patient to be, but he followed Marian round the back of the house, across a flagged yard to a spick and span out-house.

"Catriona's making butter," she explained. "I did it while she was away, but I haven't the knack and my arms ached dreadfully."

He could hear the rhythmic chug-chug of the churn as they approached an open door at the end of the building. The patient was standing by the churn, her sleeves rolled up to the elbow, and her cheeks pink with exertion. He had never seen anyone look in better health.

"I can't shake hands," she said, "for the butter's coming and if I stop, I'll spoil it."

Nicholas leaned against the door-post. It was a moment before he became aware that Marian had left them. He was alone with Catriona, and he felt more embarrassed than he had ever been before in all his life.

She lifted the lid of the churn and viewed its contents with admiration. He stepped forward, and peered over her shoulder at the little lumps of butter in the milky fluid.

"I'll give you some to take home with you," she said. "Or don't you like fresh butter?"

"I love it."

He watched her separate the butter from the butter-milk, slap it into pats which she stamped with a thistle design, and place it on a shelf. Then she turned her back on him and washed her hands under the tap at the back of the dairy. It occurred to him suddenly that she was at a loss, wanting to delay whatever it was she meant to say to him. In normal circumstances, he had no difficulty in helping a patient to relax. His professional instincts overcame his personal feelings.

"What is it I can do for you?" he said briskly, matter-of-fact,

18

tapping his fingers on his instrument case, just as if he could whip out a stethoscope there and then.

She dried her hands on a roller-towel. "I'm going to have a baby," she said.

Nicholas tightened his grip on his case. "Are you sure?"

She nodded. She was biting her lip.

He gave her a moment in which to recover herself; then he asked: "Does your father know?"

She nodded again. "I'm sorry. I didn't think I'd be so . . . foolish . . . about telling you." She turned round and her head was held high. She met his eyes with dignity, almost with defiance.

Nicholas smiled. "Suppose you sit down and tell me about it."

She sank on to a three-legged stool by the churn, her hands clasped very tightly on her lap.

"It happened in Italy, in July. As soon as I returned to London, I went to a friend of my father's, a Doctor Carson. His wife has asked me to stay with them until it's all over. But I must produce a reason for leaving Kilcaraig again, and for so long. That's where you can help me." She looked up at him. Her eyes were anxious rather than appealing.

"Will you help me, Doctor Danvers? Will you put about some story of a mysterious illness that you've ordered me to London for. For treatment or something?"

"Do you expect it to be believed?"

She smiled wryly. "It depends how well it's done."

Nicholas watched a lame spaniel cross the yard and enter the castle by the back door. He wondered why it was lame. He must find out. He ought to be able to do something for it. He turned to Catriona.

"I'll do anything I can to help you," he said.

She stood up. "Thank you," she said gravely, and held out her hand. He took it in his. It was very cold from the icy water.

"Do you want to examine me or anything?"

He released her hand. "I'll look after you until I hand you over to Doctor Carson. But it needn't necessarily be now."

"Very well. But you will stay to lunch?" It was not so much an invitation as a command. "Come, we'll walk a little, and I'll tell you my plans."

They walked along the mossy path towards the tangle of rhododendron bushes at the bottom of the hill.

"I'm taking Chrissie to England with me," Catriona said. "You heard her singing at the concert last night. She's utterly reliable, and the people will believe her version of my illness, even if they don't believe you." She smiled up at him. "You know how suspicious we all are of foreigners in those parts! I've written to my sister-in-law, Evelyn. She'll come home from India, and when my baby is born, I'll hand it over to her. If it's a boy, she'll be thankful to have an heir. If not – well, she is now a Lamont and she would sooner have another daughter than have the family put to shame."

"You mean you have made these arrangements without consulting her?" Nicholas was incredulous.

"Evelyn Lamont is blessed – you may think cursed – with a strong sense of duty."

"Do you consider it her duty to saddle herself with a child she doesn't want?"

"How callous you make me appear."

"And aren't you?"

She shrugged. "I don't really know. I've rather lost touch with myself these last few weeks."

"Are you going to enjoy seeing your own child being brought up by somebody else? Would it not be better to have it adopted by a stranger?"

She coloured. "I want my baby to belong to Kilcaraig."

"Sentimental folly!" They had reached the bottom of the hill. Nicholas plucked a leaf and tore it neatly down each vein.

"Now look what a mess you've made of it, and it was such a lovely thing."

"Symbolic," he said, and tossed it away.

"I hope not." She was watching where it fell, among a bed of nettles. "Shall we walk back through the big field? I want to see how they're getting on with the harvest."

She walked on a little ahead of him. She must want to show that their discussion was closed, and he was left to follow her, his mind in a whirl over what had been said, and even more, over what had not been said. He had committed himself to her outrageous plans without so much as asking her if her brother would consent to the deception, or if there was likely to be any interference from the baby's father. Why could she not marry him? Who was the father? Had he a wife? Was he an Italian and another Roman Catholic! Perhaps she didn't know who he was. Women could lose their heads, even women like Catriona Lamont of Kilcaraig.

Sickened, he knew that whatever the consequences might be, he was committed to play his part. He had been manipulated into accepting a situation which was repugnant to him, yet having placed herself in his hands Catriona would become dependent on him.

Imagination leapt ahead of reason. He might contrive to win both mother and baby for himself.

She turned round suddenly to wait for him. He caught up with her, panting, pushing the absurd thoughts out of his head.

There was a rough stile over a dyke, which separated the lawns from the field. The barley had not yet been reaped, and it quivered in the light September breeze. Catriona plucked an ear here and there and ate it as she climbed the footpath up the hill.

When they reached the men at work, Catriona stopped to speak to them. She was sorry not to be helping them. Perhaps tomorrow. Here Nicholas intervened, and shook his head. "You must take things easy – very easy – for a while," he said.

The men eyed Catriona with sympathy and awe. Just fancy, and she had never been ill in her life!

Nicholas was thankful to escape from these blue-eyed, intuitive people. When they reached the front door, Catriona threw away her piece of barley, and sighed with relief.

"So that's started that!" she said.

4

Nicholas followed Catriona across a square hall, past a wide spiral staircase and into a drawing-room which smelled of flowers and of damp. The green Axminster carpet had seen better days, so had the chintz covers on the sofa and chairs, but all were in keeping with the quiet dignity he had come to associate with the Lamonts.

There were three windows, two of them overlooking the loch, which was visible behind the trees, and one overlooking the drive, but darkened by the branches of a sycamore tree. The lame spaniel Nicholas had seen earlier that day was sitting on the window-seat, and Marian was inspecting his paw.

"He can't resist hedgehogs," she said. "That's why he's lame. He will try to play with them. I've never known a dog like him! Catriona – Chrissie's in a flurry. She thinks she's put the cooking sherry in the decanter. Will you taste it and see? I've no palate. Cooking, family, and guests. They're all graded, but they're all the same to me."

"Marian, it's most improper to disclose such secrets to strangers, though maybe that's not the way to describe Doctor Danvers any more," and Catriona went off in search of Chrissie and the decanter.

"I'm thinking of keeping bees, Doctor Danvers. Do you know anything about them? And is it true that their sting is good for rheumatism? What? You don't know, and you a doctor! Don't sit there, the springs are broken. Sit here."

She knew what had been said in the dairy, but it was only the speed at which she spoke that betrayed her nervousness. The great deception had begun, and she would play her unrehearsed part as well as she could. Nicholas tried to help by asking questions about the village, which she could answer easily, and without awkward pauses, until Catriona returned with the tray of drinks.

"Doctor Danvers, if you listen to Marian, you'll be both ill-informed and deaf!" Kilcaraig had entered behind Catriona, and was holding out his huge hand. "Welcome here at last. And I'm told you are the grandson of Isabel MacDougall. Well, well, well."

Nicholas had dreaded this encounter, but he was instantly at ease, realizing that there was to be no immediate family conference about the conspiracy. That would come later, when he knew them all better, but it struck him that it probably had never occurred to any of them that he might have refused Catriona's request.

The dining-room, with its large mahogany table, deer-skin rugs, open fireplace, and walls covered in hunting trophies was a sure reminder that however much custom and conduct might change, Kilcaraig Castle was rooted in the past.

Nicholas sat opposite to Marian, and Catriona, at the far end of the table, seemed to be a very long distance away. Kilcaraig said grace in Gaelic, and Chrissie served them with trout, followed by roast lamb with jacket potatoes and cauliflower that had been growing in the garden an hour before. After that, there was fruit dumpling, steaming hot from the cloth. Nicholas knew all about dumpling now.

Whenever he went to a cottage on a Sunday there was sure to be a dumpling bubbling on the range in an enormous pot, unless the patient belonged to a family who allowed no work at all to be done on the Sabbath day.

Catriona had been right when she said her father was an expert on clan history, and Nicholas learnt a great deal from him about the family. Then he was drawn onto the subject of the ruined village south of Loch Caraig, which fascinated Nicholas so much.

"The wells began to dry up," Kilcaraig said. "It was a long time before it was realized that the Lamont who had planted trees at the foothills of the mountains, believing that he had planted future prosperity, had sealed the fate of his own village. As the trees grew, they absorbed more and more water, so that less and less got through to the village. Then a dam was built, up here behind the castle, creating an artificial loch. It provided a grand water supply, but it meant the end of Caraig village, because in those days it was easier to build a house on a new site than to fetch water all the way from Loch Caraig. The row of cottages was built first, then the church and the manse, with the house that is now the post office somehow separating the two. The school followed, and the doctor's house on the brae, and Caraig Lodge. Caraig village paid the price of progress. Maybe some day progress will restore it again."

"So it wasn't the Clearances?"

Three pairs of startled eyes were turned upon him, and Chrissie dropped some knives with a clatter.

"Doctor Danvers, the Lamonts never did such things. Nobody ever left their homes, except of their own free will. So it has always been and so it must remain." Said by Kilcaraig, this was a reassurance rather than a rebuke.

Catriona, at her end of the table, turned crimson, perhaps hearing in his words an echo of the scene there must surely have been when she told him of her condition, but only Nicholas saw her discomfort, and a few minutes later she murmured grace, and they all went to the library for coffee.

This was obviously the room they occupied most. A peat fire burned in the grate. "We always have a fire in here. Even on the hottest days there are times when one's heart can do with the sight of a flame," Kilcaraig said, leaning back in a chair which must have been designed to accommodate his bulk.

The shelves which lined the walls were filled with books which were evidently read and re-read. There were dog-baskets in three corners of the room, and a puppy was chewing a glove, its eyes darting round for further articles to destroy. A hen had come in by an open window and was pecking around on the carpet. It was only when Marian saw it and pursued it, cackling, out that Nicholas realized there was anything unusual about having a hen in the room.

Some plaster had come off the ceiling, showing the lathes underneath. There was mildewed wall-paper beside the door, but the chair in front of it was Hepplewhite, and the vase on the table was unmistakeably Meissen.

"The Ameses are going to buy a motor-car," Marian said. She had been digging in a settle, and she brought out her knitting which consisted of a pair of needles and a great many balls of wool.

"Away! How will they get it up the brae to the Lodge?"

"They'll push it, Papa," Catriona said. "And it'll run backwards into the burn, and they'll all perish." She turned to Nicholas. "I'm sorry – we're talking about your patients. I'd forgotten you aren't one of the family."

It was the most unexpected compliment Nicholas had ever heard until its significance dawned on him. He was part of their plot, one of themselves.

"It must be very difficult for you to tolerate newcomers so close to the castle, Miss Lamont," he said. "But I think you'll find that they will mellow with time."

"When you've written your novel and made lots and lots of money, you'll buy it from them." Marian had been counting stitches, which had kept her quiet for a few minutes.

It was the first Kilcaraig had heard about the novel, and as Nicholas told him about it, he found it taking shape in his mind. He would have to write it some day, if only to save his face, but now it helped to pass the time pleasantly, make-believe taking the place of painful reality that was on the minds of each one of them.

When he got up to go, the tartan sock that Marian was knitting for her brother was no lengthier than it had been when he arrived, and Catriona had dropped out of the conversation in her efforts to help disentangle the nineteen balls of wool that were involved.

Kilcaraig saw him to the door, and they waited in the porch for Willie to bring round Maggie and the trap.

"Thank you for what you are doing for my daughter," Kilcaraig said.

"It's my privilege," Nicholas replied. "You're welcome" would hardly be suitable in the circumstances.

"She will be all right."

Nicholas, forgetting the customary manner of speech, took this as a statement, not as a question. It was only later, when he returned to the surgery and thought about the events of the day that he recognized the anguish behind the words. She would be all right. Of course she would. Nobody would ever find out. Somehow her secret must be kept, even in this place, where one's very thoughts seemed to be carried around by the breeze.

He wrote "call at the castle" in his engagement diary and added "to see Miss Lamont", in case somebody should happen to see it lying on his desk. He had to start them talking on the right lines, right away.

The door bell rang. That would be Archie Livingstone coming to have his boil *sorted*, that wonderful word, which covered every aspect of care, be it for stomach, reaper, motor-car or horse.

The sorting of Archie Livingstone's boil gave him an opening for his deception. Archie sank heavily onto a chair. "They say Miss Lamont's not so well," he said. "They say you went over there to see her. I hope it's not serious."

Nicholas boiled a pair of forceps and sighed over Miss Lamont's complaint. A germ perhaps from the south of Italy. Malaria. He warmed to the subject, only to be deflated when Archie said sagely, "Well, she's in the very place to get over it here."

As he tossed and turned in bed that night, Nicholas took stock of his situation, and the more he thought about it, the more horrified he became. He had been bewitched up there at the castle, but here in his bedroom, with the west wind whistling down the chimney and rattling his window, he had to face reality.

When his parents had scraped and saved to enable him to study medicine at Edinburgh University, he had determined that he would be a credit to them. He had succeeded far beyond his expectations, and had emerged as one of the most promising graduates of his year. There had followed post-graduate courses, and the post of registrar at one of the large provincial hospitals. That was a temporary job, which gave him the confidence to set up in practice on his own, but he had worked so hard that after a prolonged bout of influenza he was advised to take a break in some less demanding area. Doctor MacFie's advertisement had been the answer to that problem, and here he was on Mull, yet now he had a worrying weight on his mind.

He got up and dressed and crept downstairs. There was time for a walk before breakfast and the start of the day's work.

There was a light showing in a front bedroom at the manse, and activity in the post office, but there was no sign of life in the row of cottages. The natives of Kilcaraig rose late, because they spent so much of the night entertaining one another with cups of tea and lavish baking, gossip, songs, and sometimes a tune on the bagpipes.

He walked through the village on the road that led to the MacPhails' farm and after that to nowhere. Across a field on his right Loch Caraig shimmered in the rising sun, and on his left, high up and through the trees, was the castle, invisible, frightening now that he was enmeshed in the lives of the Lamonts.

"Doctor Danvers!"

He was startled, but it was Marian who stepped forward from behind a dry-stone wall. Dileas, the spaniel, was at her heels, absorbed in sniffing the excitements hidden on the ground.

"You're very early," he said.

"I've hardly slept a wink. Doctor Danvers, is the Great Deception going to work?"

"You can assess that better than I can. I don't know your brother. I don't know your sister-in-law. As for your sister, she's an enigma. She seems to take success for granted, but self-deception is often nature's compensation for unbearable distress."

Marian whistled under her breath. "I didn't know doctors understood about minds."

"We're learning," he said, wondering how her mind worked. She wasn't going to enlighten him about her brother or her sister-in-law, he was convinced of that.

They walked on, their silence broken by the snuffles of Dileas.

"Have you any idea who the father is?" he asked, hoping to surprise her into an admission.

"Catriona would have told me, if she wanted me to know," she said evasively.

He felt snubbed.

"It's very important," he said. She didn't reply. He tried again. "Does your father know?"

"I haven't asked."

He turned suddenly and caught her by the shoulders, looking straight into her eyes. "Marian, I'm in a frightful predicament. You must help me to sort things out. You're the only person who can."

She wriggled free of him. "Catriona knows all the answers. It doesn't do to treat a patient at second-hand. We'd better go back. The village will be waking up, and people will think we've had an assignation!"

Mrs. Ross, watching from behind the lace curtains in her cottage parlour, saw the doctor and Miss Marian part company at the bumpy bridge. They had looked very serious as they walked along the road. She decided that it must be something to do with Miss Catriona's illness, because seemingly Miss Marian had eyes only for Andrew Sinclair, and would never look at a doctor many years older than herself.

When Nicholas returned home, Mrs. MacFadyen scolded him for standing around talking in the chilly morning air. He should have put on his overcoat. It was different for Miss Marian. She was accustomed to the autumn climate, and was as strong as an ox.

"Unlike her sister," Nicholas mumbled, aware that his every movement had been observed through the binoculars.

"Aye, it's a pity about her," Mrs. MacFadyen said. "They say she's to go to London for X-rays."

"That's right."

26

Nicholas sat down to his breakfast. The rumours were spreading, and fast. He was caught in the vortex of his deception, and even Marian had denied him a helping hand.

A few days later, Catriona gave a dramatic demonstration of her ill-health. On the night of the festivities that marked the end of the harvest, the whole neighbourhood had gathered at the castle. The last of the corn was reaped, and a sheaf was tied up with ribbon. This was the harvest maiden, and the following year it would be tied to the first horse in the plough, and would assure a good harvest. Afterwards, it would be given to the horse to eat.

There had been dancing in the barn, and now as many as could squeeze into the dining-room were standing around, drinking whisky and eating the inevitable dumpling. The overflow were in the hall and in the kitchen, and even in the drawing-room, where a *ceilidh* had already begun. Marian was banging out an accompaniment, while a shepherd was singing a very long Gaelic song.

Catriona, assisted by Michael Ames, who had been invited to these harvest ceremonials, was handing round cookies. Young Angus, the newly-appointed gillie, had just helped himself from her laden tray when she collapsed neatly, even elegantly, into a heap on the floor. There was instant pandemonium. Nicholas pushed his way through the agitated crowd, and carried his jewel up to her bedroom.

She recovered quickly, horrified at this display of weakness. Nicholas pushed her back as she tried to sit up.

"You're a silly little fool," he told her. "They tell me you were dancing a quadrille?"

Catriona gave a gurgle that might have been a laugh. "Such a form of address! I ought to have the delicacy to swoon again." She closed her eyes. Her lips were smiling.

Nicholas sighed. "I'll be thankful to hand you over to Doctor Carson," he said. He turned away from her and looked out of the window, onto the moonlit lawn, where he could hear the sound of the accordion playing for "Strip the Willow".

A heavy sigh from under the door reminded him that Dileas had followed them upstairs. Nicholas admitted him. Grumbling, he jumped onto Catriona's bed. Her hand fondled his silky muzzle.

"Well, I'll leave you to rest," Nicholas said, his eyes resting enviously on the dog. He spoke too soon, for Marian, pale faced and wide-eyed, peeped round the door.

"Mercy, what a fright you gave me! I've only just heard about it. Would you like some brandy? A hot-water bottle? Some smelling-salts?"

Nicholas slipped away, remembering, as he reached the foot of the stairs, to look anxious and grave.

There were no more protestations when he spoke of treatment in London, for it was accepted that a Lamont who fainted must indeed be seriously ill, and what had been contracted in foreign parts was maybe best treated far from home.

During the weeks that followed, Nicholas called regularly at the castle, and recorded his patient's temperature, pulse and respirations. More than that was not expected of him, but it was enough to establish his professional attitude towards her, one he would maintain until she was safely in London under the care of Doctor Carson.

5

Nicholas was invited to spend his last evening in Kilcaraig at the castle. He had packed away his instruments, torn up any superfluous documents, outlined to Doctor MacFie the condition of the patients in his care, and told innumerable lies to prevent the stocky little doctor from paying an instant visit to the castle, to ascertain for himself the nature of the obscure malady from which Catriona was suffering.

When Chrissie showed him into the drawing-room, he found Marian kneeling on the hearth-rug, holding a newspaper against the grate to create a draught.

"It keeps belching smoke," she said. "It always does in an easterly wind." As she spoke, the paper caught fire, and she stuffed it into the grate. "There goes the *Oban Times*, and I've not read the advertisements yet." She stood up, rubbing her hands on her handkerchief.

"Now, admire my dress! My very best, in your honour!" She swung round, to show him the graceful folds of her skirt. "I won't have you go away thinking I'm always in rags."

"You always look lovely, both of you." He fondled the material between finger and thumb. "Silk," he said. "And in just the right shade of blue for you. Andrew Sinclair will love this dress."

"What makes you say that?" she asked quickly.

"You're not immune from the whispering of the breeze! When I first came here, I was told you were an unattached young lady. Now they say there will soon be an engagement announcement in the *Oban Times*."

She smiled and coloured. "We've always been friends. It only recently flared up into something more. Andrew wants it announced next time he's on leave. I would rather wait until this affair is over, but he knows nothing about it, though I suppose some day he'll have to be told."

She sounded doubtful. She had not fully grasped the enormity of the situation, which was not going to be resolved in a matter of months, or even of years. It would be part of her life for the whole of her life, but this was not time to issue words of warning. Nicholas offered her his good wishes, and heard a little of her plans for the future. There would be army life at first, and later, when Andrew's parents grew older, there would be the management of Duff.

"It's smaller than Kilcaraig, more of a farm than an estate, and there's not a lot of help available," she said. "Andrew is the only son, so we'll have to have lots and lots of children to ensure its future prosperity!" She lowered her voice and looked towards the door. "When will Catriona be leaving here? Her waist line is beginning to show."

"I wanted her to leave before Doctor MacFie came back, but she wouldn't. I can't understand why."

"It's because she hates dragging herself away from here. She seems to think the heather will die and the lochs dry up if she isn't here to see them flourish."

"I'm surprised, then, that she went to Italy for all those weeks."

"Oh, that was different," Marian said, and changed the subject with a subtle twist.

When Catriona entered the room, she was wearing a black velvet dress, with a Celtic cross at her throat. Her hair was swept up instead of rolled into a bun in the fashion of the day. She always did her hair that way – it showed her lovely neck to perfection. She swept past him and picked up the tongs. "You'll have the chimney on fire," she said to Marian as she rearranged the peats. "And what about giving Nicholas a drink? You really are a shocking hostess!"

Her use of his Christian name made Nicholas feel ecstatic. It must have slipped out. She could not have meant it. But it betrayed that she must think of him by that name.

When Kilcaraig joined them, he was surrounded, as always, by his dogs. He had been over to the MacPhails' farm, visiting a sick cow. Nicholas had discovered long ago that Kilcaraig was the deputy vet, lawyer, minister and doctor in these parts, as well as the laird. The parish minister had pointed this out to him when he first arrived, and as the weeks passed by, it was proved to him time and time again.

Everyone was determined to make this a gala evening, and after dinner, Nicholas found himself singing "Ho, Ro My Nutbrown Maid", while Marian played his accompaniment. After that, Kilcaraig fetched his pipes, and paced up and down the room, while Marian explained the rudiments of the Reel of Tulloch to Nicholas. He had been to several of the dances in the schoolhouse during these last weeks, but had never had the temerity to take the floor, although his feet had itched to dance, as the floor-boards vibrated beneath him, and the yells of "hooch" at times almost drowned the music.

Finally, Catriona was prevailed upon to sing. Her voice was low, and it occurred to Nicholas that she was nervous. He accompanied her himself, and although she sang in Gaelic, the English translation was there on the music before him, *An Gille Dubh Ciar-Dubh* – "The Dark-haired Lad".

"That's always been your favourite," Marian remarked, after the first verse, "I wonder why?" Catriona coloured and went on.

> "And now that together
> *Dubh ciar-dubh, dubh ciar-dubh,*
> We face the rude weather
> On hills black and blue,
> Some peaceful spot near me
> I'd choose and there cheer me
> No grey-beard to fear me
> And thou in my view."

Nicholas wondered if a dark-haired young man was on her mind. He fumbled the next few bars. Marian's eyes twinkled at him from across the room. Then Catriona sang.

> "My bonnie *dubh ciar-dubh*
> Let sharp tongues assail thee,
> One heart will not fail thee
> That knows to be true.
> *Dubh ciar-dubh! Dubh ciar-dubh*
> Though poor, poor thou be,
> No rich man can please me
> Like thee, love, like thee."

She leaned across and removed the music from the stand. He could see her name written on it as she folded it. Catriona M. Lamont. He wondered what the "M" stood for and she smiled and said "Martha", which he thought did not suit her at all. Then he remembered that tomorrow at this time he would be away from this bewitching place, and from the people he had come to love.

"Have another wee dram, it will cheer you up," Marian said, sensing his depression immediately. She jumped up quickly and there was a tearing sound as she caught her heel in the hem of her dress. Catriona silently handed her a pin, as if she carried one in readiness for such an occasion, and the breach was speedily repaired.

"I wonder if I'll ever be elegant like Catriona," Marian sighed, as she handed him his glass.

"If I were you, I wouldn't want to be in any way like me," Catriona said, tossing the remark over her shoulder as she looked through the pile of sheet-music on the piano. It was the first time she had made even a veiled reference to her dilemma in front of her family, but Kilcaraig ignored what could have been a challenge, and turning to Nicholas, asked him about his travelling arrangements for the next day.

Nicholas accepted unwillingly that there was to be no last-minute counselling, no detailed plan of action. When he reached London, he would be able to contact the people who were most closely involved, Ian and Evelyn Lamont in India, and Doctor Carson. Letters that could not fail to catch the eye of the post-mistress at Kilcaraig would pass unnoticed in London. That was an inescapable fact of life.

It was beginning to rain when he left the castle. Kilcaraig and his daughters stood in the doorway to wave him goodbye, and he could see them there in the lamplight, as the trap turned into the tunnel of trees. Maggie moved carefully downhill, and the rain was falling heavily as they left the shelter of the trees, stinging his face and forming little rivulets that dropped off the brim of his hat. The burn was roaring under the bridge, and he registered that he had felt that sharp rise and fall beneath the trap for the last time.

He turned right, leaving the manse and the cottages and the post office behind him, but knowing that there would be eyes peering from behind the curtains, and here and there a pair of binoculars would be trained on him despite the darkness. They would know that it was the doctor's trap, and that he had been dining at the castle. He would like to hear their remarks. But he would never hear them. And very soon he would be forgotten by them and the activities of some other stranger would be the cynosure of their eyes.

He stabled Maggie and went into the house. Doctor MacFie was waiting up for him.

"I've been thinking about Catriona Lamont," the doctor said. "It's heart trouble that's the matter with her, but not the sort that you or I or any other doctor can cure." He sucked his pipe thoughtfully.

"She's agreed to come to London for X-rays," Nicholas said uncomfortably.

Doctor MacFie gave him a shrewd look. "It's wasting your time. That's all it is. Wasting your time," he said regretfully, and he pushed forward his spectacles and picked up his copy of the *Oban Times*.

Nicholas drank the tea which Mrs. MacFadyen had left for him in pensive silence. It was no good trying to deceive these people, Catriona should realize that. It was no good at all.

A gust of wind blew down the chimney, spreading smoke and the white powdery peat-ash into the room.

6

The front of 7, Cranston Terrace, Islington, where Nicholas both lived and worked, made a brave attempt to keep up the respectability of bygone days. The woodwork was freshly painted, the brass door-knob was polished meticulously, the steps were scrubbed daily and whitened with pipe-clay.

Nicholas was proud of his home. It had been given to him by his Aunt Elvira when Uncle Donald died and she went off to live with her sister in Cornwall. "You might as well have it now as after I'm gone," she had said. "Mrs. Tibbetts will stay on to look after you, and all you need to do is to put up your plate."

Nicholas obeyed. Up went the brass plate bearing his name and medical qualifications and, amazingly, along came the patients. It was a very satisfactory arrangement indeed.

Today he was standing at his bedroom window, watching the rain spattering down upon the slate roof of his consulting-room. It projected beyond the main building, and occupied almost the whole of the backyard so that all Nicholas had room for was a few square yards of concrete, where he kept his two dustbins.

Next door, at number 8, someone had made a valiant attempt to achieve a garden, although a few bits of crazy paving, and a large number of puddles were all that was visible at present. On the left, at number 6, a cluster of snowdrops showed brave faces, amid a sea of mud, and bits of furniture and kitchen utensils.

In Kilcaraig, the whin, which Nicholas had always known as gorse, would be blossoming into patches of yellow among the bronze and gold of last year's bracken, and the mountains would still be capped with snow. He had never been in Mull in springtime, but Catriona had described it to him in vivid detail, when he visited her at the Carsons' home in St. John's Wood, or walked with her in one of London's parks.

She yearned for home, yet she prepared for the birth of her baby in a state of evident tranquillity. Nicholas found this strange and in some ways disturbing. In January, soon after her twenty-third birthday, she had been threatened with a miscarriage. A woman in her circumstances would be forgiven for welcoming such an event as a merciful relief, but not so Catriona. She obeyed scrupulously the orders given to her by Doctor Carson, and she rested so quietly in bed that she would not allow even Nicholas to visit her. As soon as she recovered, she seemed to be glowing with new health and vitality.

"I was never so anxious in all my life," she said to Nicholas. "I've set my heart now on having this baby."

"You won't be able to enjoy it for long," Nicholas replied, brutal because he wanted to impress upon her that her emotions, as well as her body, were going to be lacerated by the ordeal that lay ahead.

"He'll belong to Kilcaraig. And some day, Kilcaraig will belong to him."

She was obsessed by this idea, and when Nicholas received Ian Lamont's reply to his letter of enquiry about plans for the future, he concluded that the whole Lamont family was incapable of grasping the gravity of the situation. He would have hoped for better from an army officer who had reached the rank of captain, but Ian Lamont was adamant. He would accept his sister's child as his own. His wife, Evelyn, was sailing home from India on the P. & O. liner *Plassy*, and she would call on Doctor Danvers as soon as she arrived in London.

Nicholas was expecting her now.

He changed his tie, brushed his hair, and had just reached the drawing-room when the door-bell rang.

He saw Mrs. Tibbetts marching through the hall, wearing her new black dress and her most voluminous apron; long white streamers flowed from her cap. Mrs. Tibbetts was a snob. When she heard that

Doctor Danvers was expecting a visitor whose husband was the son of a Highland landowner, she had got busy with the blue-bag and the starch, but as she announced Mrs. Ian Lamont, Nicholas knew at once that Evelyn Lamont, in her crisp, white blouse, well-tailored navy blue suit, and smart but uninteresting hat, would take an immaculately dressed servant for granted.

When he had greeted her, and had settled her in an armchair, he noticed that the fire, newly lit, was threatening to go out. There would be a blazing fire in the library at Kilcaraig. He remarked on the fact, apologetically, and Evelyn Lamont surprised him by kneeling on the hearth, picking up the poker, and administering a deft blow onto a piece of coal. It broke and instantly burst into flame.

She looked up and smiled, and the severe and formidable woman who had entered the room melted in that instant into someone human, someone capable of being loved. She rubbed her hand against her skirt and sat down. Then she spoke.

"Doctor Danvers, you don't have to explain anything to me. I married into the Lamont family eight years ago. I know their idiosyncrasies and I know the inestimable worth of my husband and my father-in-law. They are the people who matter to me, and what I have undertaken to do I am doing for them, and for them alone. Do I make myself clear?"

"Very clear." His heart was thundering in his chest. His first impression had been the right one. This was the New Woman. He could picture her marching in protesting processions, chaining herself to railings, dying for the Cause.

"I have two daughters. Diana is six and Helen is four," Evelyn Lamont said. "As the result of an unavoidable operation I'll never have another child. I want a son. When the child is born, I'll take him to Kilcaraig. We will remain there until the autumn, then I'll return with him to India. My children are too young to ask questions, and they will accept him as their brother. They're at a hill station just now, Dalhousie, with their governess and an *ayah*. The governess is a bovine woman who already believes that I've come home to have a baby. The *ayah* is different. These people are intuitive." She frowned, staring into the now cheerful fire. "The Kilcaraig people are intuitive too. Nothing escapes them. I'm going to have to act a very difficult part, but I will deceive them, as I propose to deceive everyone else. It's my duty."

"And if it is a girl?"

"I have promised. There's nothing more to say."

But there was a great deal more to say, and Nicholas said it, after

Mrs. Tibbetts had brought in tea and cucumber sandwiches and slices of Dundee cake, which she arranged on a small table, covered in a white lace cloth.

Eveyln Lamont refused to eat anything, but she drank her tea while Nicholas put before her the problems that must be overcome. She raised her hand to stop him when she had heard enough.

"I understand the difficulties over the birth certificate, and I have no intention of breaking the law. My husband will see that the necessary document is concealed from all eyes but our own," she said, ignoring the many other factors he had raised. "As for the possibility that Catriona might change her mind, Doctor Carson must be accustomed to dealing with the whims of newly-delivered women. She must not be allowed to see the baby. She will convalesce in Switzerland, and by the time she returns to Kilcaraig I'll be back in India with my family."

"Marian and Andrew Sinclair are planning to marry in the autumn."

She raised a brow. "How does that affect the issue? If Marian wants to be with Catriona when she first returns home, she can perfectly well postpone her wedding until the spring."

She stood up, and Nicholas tried to imagine her holding a baby lovingly in her arms. He failed.

"Thank you for sparing me your time, and on a Sunday, too, when you should be able to relax." She carefully pulled on her kid gloves. He touched her arm as he opened the drawing-room door.

"Are you going to allow your mother to believe that she has a new grandchild?" he asked.

She tilted up her chin and surveyed him through narrowed eyes. "I should have told you that since my father died my mother has lived in a residential hotel in Bath. She devotes her life to playing bridge, to make up for the years she had to waste being a wife and a mother. She isn't interested in the grandchildren she owns already. She probably forgets how many there are."

As he helped her into the cab, Nicholas the physician, who was becoming fascinated by the ideas of Jung and Freud, longed to know more about this woman, who had unwittingly revealed in a few sentences how she had become the woman she was today. He returned to the house, steeped in a deep melancholy; then he went to his study and settled down to write the next chapter of his novel. The heroine was not a beautiful woman called Katrina, and the plot was a scorching love story set on an island in the South Seas. Through it, Nicholas could escape from the distressing realities of life.

Marian came to London a week later. She was admitted to Cranston Terrace by Mrs. Tibbetts just as Nicholas was clearing up after evening surgery. He found her standing on tiptoe in front of the overmantel in the drawing-room, re-arranging her hat-pins.

"Mercy, Nicholas, but you need a woman in the house to see that looking-glasses are put in the right place! This one's far too high!" She turned round and embraced him. The letters they had exchanged during the past few months had established a relationship between them which was one of close friendship, wholly devoid of the restrictions which had been imposed upon Nicholas by his profession.

"How far have you walked?" Nicholas was viewing the bedraggled hem of her skirt and the mud on her shoes with dismay.

"I set off from St. John's Wood, but I had no idea of the distance, or of the hardness of London pavements. So I ended up in a cab." She sat on the sofa and pushed off her shoes.

"What do you think of Catriona?" He had called her by her Christian name for a long time now.

"She says she's very well and very happy and that you are a good and faithful friend. Nicholas, how I wish that some day she would love you."

"So do I." He sat beside her, and took hold of her left hand. "Sapphires and diamonds. It's a beautiful ring, and I cut out the announcement in the *London Times*." There was only one *Times* recognized on Mull, and that was the *Oban Times*.

"A photographer came all the way from London to take pictures. We had a great time, hanging paintings over the patches of damp on the walls. We've put the Kilcaraig tapestry in the hall – that's the big one of the house with some of the family outside it, that used to hang in the library. It's incomplete as my mother was working on it, and it's scarcely been touched since she died. The portrait of my father is completed now, and although he grumbled all through the sittings, it's great altogether, the very image of himself!"

He relaxed, listening to Marian's prattle, putting in a word now and then, and being transported in spirit back to Kilcaraig, with its beauty and comfort and timelessness, for when all this was over, surely the old pattern would return.

"Evelyn made a great impression. She didn't stuff herself up with cushions or anything, but she wore very drapey clothes, and managed to walk like a woman who is soon going to have a baby. What did you think of her?"

"She interested me. I'd like to know her better."

36

"She interested Ian. He has never got to know her better. He doesn't say so, but I'm afraid it's true. Her father was in the I.C.S. and she and Ian met in Kashmir. I suppose it was the Ganges, and moonlight over the Taj Mahal and all that sort of thing that made them fall in love. I don't think they're as unhappy together as one would expect them to be."

Nicholas understood that the initials meant the Indian Civil Service, and he forbore to point out that neither the Ganges nor the Taj Mahal would be found in Kashmir.

"I hope she returns to London in time for the confinement. Babies are unpredictable, and nothing could explain the presence of a mother in Kilcaraig, while her baby was being born in London!"

"She'll be here. She's coming as soon as I get home, and I've only come for a few days. I had to see Catriona before . . . before." She shook her head. "Mother died having a baby, so did the baby. Doctor Carson wants Catriona to have her baby in a nursing home, but of course she won't hear of it. Nicholas, do you think he's afraid something might go wrong?"

"He would have told me if he thought so. I'm sure of that."

She looked relieved. "I'll tell my father. He worries as much as I do, although he never says so. He adores Catriona. He's like a lost soul when she's not about the place."

"It's a pity he didn't adore her enough to let her marry the man she loves, then this would never have happened."

He felt Marian stiffen. She would not allow criticism of her father.

"He could see that religious differences would lead to complications."

"I can't imagine greater complications than this present deceit."

When Marian left, he drove her home in his motor-car, his new and most proud possession. He spent a pleasant evening in the house at St. John's Wood. Catriona laughingly assured him that she had never felt better, but that she would be glad when she had her body to herself.

"It's so difficult to turn round in bed," she said. "Only two more weeks to go, then a summer in Switzerland, with Chrissie writing her wonderful compositions about the state of my health. For an eighteen-year-old, with only rudimentary education, she has the vivid imagination of the Brontë sisters!"

As he drove home, Nicholas decided that physical discomfort was the worst thing Catriona had to suffer. The emotional side of the transaction worried her not at all.

Marian returned to Mull, and Evelyn returned to London.

Nicholas took her to a concert one evening. The influence of the music failed to encourage her to confide in him, but as he saw her into the small hotel, close to the Carsons' house, where she would be hiding until the event took place, she clasped his hand, and assured him that he need have no fear. She would perform her duty faultlessly, no matter what her personal feelings were towards Catriona's child.

Chilled rather than comforted, Nicholas drove home. During the night, Doctor Carson telephoned, and Nicholas was soon at the house in St. John's Wood where Catriona struggled to bring her child into the world.

Afterwards, Nicholas was unable to recall the events of the next fourteen hours. He could remember only the anguish of waiting, and sometimes helping, but mostly of waiting and waiting, until the thin wail replaced the controlled whimpering of the agonized Catriona.

Chrissie, white as a ghost, leaned over the banisters, and called him upstairs. "See to the baby," she said. "They're trying to stop the bleeding."

The midwife was standing at the bedroom door, and he could see Doctor Carson leaning over the bed. It was Mrs. Carson who handed him the little, crumpled bundle, now crying strongly. No need for resuscitation here, but he took the baby in his arms, and looked at its battered, distorted face. He followed Chrissie to the room which had been prepared as a nursery, and he watched as she deftly carried out the duties the midwife would normally do. Watching the baby kept his mind off what was happening in that other room.

Silence, broken occasionally by a command from Doctor Carson. They would do what they could.

At last, Doctor Carson himself came into the nursery. "She wants to see the baby," he said, and, seeing Nicholas hesitate, he added gently "We can't wait for the bruises to disappear. There isn't time."

Nicholas picked up the now quiet little bundle, trying to drape as much shawl as possible over the bruised head.

Catriona was lying back on her pillows, white as chalk. A blood-stained sheet had been pushed hastily, almost out of sight, under the bed.

Nicholas approached her, kissed her gently on the brow, and saw the flicker of a smile in her slate-grey eyes. Then he held the baby close to her. Slightly, she shook her head, not in rejection, but with understanding, with love.

"*Grannda*," she whispered, and closed her eyes. It was the last word she would ever say.

Nicholas turned away from the bed, the baby held close to him, soft, tiny, hideous comfort in his moment of crushing grief.

"Grania," he murmured. "Grania. Grania."

Then he placed Grania Lamont of Kilcaraig in her cot.

1924

7

Robert Dutton cursed under his breath as the chauffeur brought the car to a halt in front of yet another of these infernal gates. He had expected the roads of Mull to be designed for carts and traps, rather than for a motor-car of the dimension of his Daimler, but the mentality of a people who put gates at frequent intervals across the roads, rather than fence their fields properly in an orderly way, bewildered him.

They should be compelled to arrange their fencing so that the road was left free – the practice of embracing a vast area of land in a single boundary was absurd. And what gates these were! Held together with pieces of string, they required a maximum amount of patience before they could be opened, and the weight of them, as they were rusted and had to be lifted into position, was enough to rupture any normal being.

"Don't shut it," he ordered. "If these damned people can't take better care of their property, they deserve to lose their cattle."

The chauffeur knew better than to argue, and the car slid forward once more, only to be brought to a halt a few yards further on by a child, clad in an oilskin coat, a sou'wester, and Wellington boots, who stood in the middle of the road in sullen defiance of all four-wheeled vehicles.

Robert leaned out of the car. "Get out of the way," he said.

"You haven't shut the gate."

"Do it for us."

"I can't lift it. And it's polite to say please."

"Get out of the way this instant, or we'll run you over!"

"Don't be silly!" The childish scorn was even more biting than an adult remonstrance would have been.

Since defeat was inevitable, the chauffeur jumped quickly out of the car and closed the offending gate. When he returned to his seat, the small assailant had already moved to the side of the road, and was eyeing Robert with antagonistic interest.

"Hurry!" Robert ordered, with some embarrassment, and once

again they were on their way, leaving behind them four foot six of victorious childhood, who was indicating her displeasure in a way that was anything but dignified.

The village of Kilcaraig was visible now, and Robert leaned forward to get a good view of the place. A gaunt and gabled house, a combined post office and shop, a church, a school, a row of cottages. Out of sight would be the farm, scattered dwelling-houses, and the castle. They would all be his, his own, his kingdom! How they would prosper under his care. A man in a field had stopped to sharpen his scythe. A scythe indeed! He would provide the crofters with mechanical cutters and threshers. The golden age lay ahead of them. His people. His gold.

He sank back in his seat, and noted how rusted was the big iron gate at the entrance to the castle, how mossy was the drive. The rhododendrons were out of control, rambling everywhere, forming a canopy over the car. They must be beautiful when they were in flower, but they were neglected, like everything else in this shabby place. He liked order, and he would have it here. A regiment of gardeners would transform it. He was planning how the lawns would be arranged when the car drew up at the studded door. This would not change. This was the perfect entrance to the baronial hall.

Marian Lamont had been watching the progress of the car through her binoculars. Since some of the trees had been thinned, and the sycamore had blown down, the road was visible from her bedroom window, and now that the rain had stopped her vision was less blurred. She could see the splashes the wheels made as the car plunged through the overflow from the burn; then she lost sight of it as it approached the drive at the foot of the hill.

She went to the top of the stairs, listening as the engine laboured up to the castle. There was a moment of silence before the rusty bell announced that the visitor had arrived.

She ran down the stairs and pulled open the heavy door. It creaked on its hinges. "I must remember to oil it . . . He'll think I'm a servant," she thought, all in a second. She held out her hand to the tall, ginger-haired man on the doorstep. He was younger than she had expected, probably not more than forty. When Evelyn had written from India about him, she had said nothing about his age.

"Welcome to Kilcaraig," Marian smiled. "Just fancy driving all the way from Tobermory on a dirty day like this! Come in and get warm."

She led the way into the library. "My father will join us presently. He's been helping to get a cow out of a ditch, and he's soaked to the skin." She prodded a peat with her foot, and the fire blazed up the chimney. Robert noticed that she had very neat ankles. This must be Marian, whose fiancé had been killed at the beginning of the war, in the battle of the Marne. He should have asked Evelyn more about her. She was a very pretty woman indeed.

"I hope the cow is all right," he said, feeling that some comment was expected of him.

"She was quite exhausted with trying to struggle out, but she's had a good rub down, and she's been given oatmeal and whisky. Oh dear, how thoughtless I am!" She went to a corner cupboard, brought out a tumbler, half filled it with whisky, and handed it to him. He accepted it because there was nothing else he could do. "She has a lovely disposition. Do you know anything about cows, Mr. Dutton?"

He sat by the fire, drinking the neat whisky, while they talked about the character of cows, Marian with animation, Robert in some bewilderment, until Kilcaraig joined them. Robert felt oddly uncomfortable in the presence of this bearded, kilt-clad giant of a man. Those blue eyes smiled a welcome, yet Robert felt that they concealed contempt. The big hand shook his own warmly, yet it made him conscious of inferiority.

"So you met my son and daughter-in-law in Kashmir?" Kilcaraig said. "It was good of you to come to Mull to tell us about them."

Robert murmured that it was a pleasure to call at the castle, about which Mrs. Lamont had told him so much. It had been so easy, as he drove through Mull, to compose the speech he would make, offering a fabulous sum of money for the purchase of the estate. Evelyn Lamont had told him that it was a white elephant, and a weight on Kilcaraig's mind and on his bank account. Her husband would not be able to afford it, and as they had no son to inherit it, there was no sense in hanging on to it while it fell into ruins before their eyes.

"If you're set on having an estate in the Highlands, make an offer for it," she had said. "The old man has never got over the death of his eldest daughter. He's surrounded by memories of her. I'm sure he'll part with it to the highest bidder."

Although Evelyn's words had been convincing enough, this contact with Kilcaraig himself filled Robert with alarm. But he had never allowed his courage to fail over a business transaction, and he was determined not to be intimidated now.

He talked politely about Ian and Evelyn, while his eyes were on Marian and his mind sought an opportunity to broach the purpose of his visit.

"I've never seen such acres of rushes and bracken as I've seen on this island," he said cautiously, feeling his way. "Money is needed, and up-to-date methods of farming, and an end to primitive forms of transport. Do you know that my Daimler had to be driven onto the boat at Oban, and off it when she arrived in Tobermory, over a couple of planks arranged like precarious see-saws!"

"They're careful to put them the right distance apart to take the wheels," Kilcaraig said reassuringly, but Marian jumped up from her stool by the fender with an exclamation of distress. "Your poor driver – he's out there in the car. I'll take him along for a cup of tea."

She hurried out of the room and closed the door behind her. Then she leaned against it in sudden panic. Robert Dutton had come to buy Kilcaraig! She knew it as surely as if he had told her so himself. And only last night, she'd been discussing ways and means with her father, and they had wondered how on earth they could carry on.

"Is something wrong, Aunt Marian? Why has that simply horrible man come here?"

Marian braced herself and smiled. "You've no reason to think he's horrible, Grania. I told you about him. He's Mr. Dutton, your parents' friend. Just look at these pools around you. Why do you come into the hall in your wet things?"

"Would you have me take them off outside and catch my death? Pull off my Wellingtons, Auntie – they're dreadfully much too small." Grania sat at the bottom of the stairs and held onto the banisters, while Marian tugged off her boots. Between "oohs" and "aahs" of discomfort, she told Marian that she had already taken the chauffeur to the servants' hall, and had been given a packet of aniseed balls as a gratuity.

"Have one," she offered. "Angus says they're grand things for taking away the smell when you've been drinking."

"The very idea!" But Marian took the sweet, and lodged it in her cheek. "You're getting too old to hang around so much in the kitchen. Diana and Helen don't make a nuisance of themselves to the servants when they're at home."

"They're only here during the holidays. They don't belong here like I do."

"That's just a lot of nonsense," Marian said, but she knew that it was true. Ian's children had been in India all through the war, and Evelyn had left the infant Grania in the safety of Kilcaraig when she went out to join them there. After it was over, and Ian, almost unscathed, had returned to Rawalpindi from service in Mesopotamia, Grania had been despatched in a troop-ship, under the care of a governess, to meet the family she had never known. Six months later, she was back at Kilcaraig, emaciated after a bout of sand-fly fever, and an almost lethal attack of jaundice. So it was that the castle had become her home. Diana and Helen who had accompanied her, found themselves in a new and strange environment, homesick for India, not caring whether they were at Kilcaraig or at boarding-school.

"That's just a lot of nonsense," Marian repeated. "Now, off you go and give Chrissie a hand. She's clearing up the rubbish you've collected in the nursery cupboard. And wear a decent dress when you come downstairs. I've warned cook that Mr. Dutton may stay for lunch."

Grania paused halfway up the stairs. "You won't marry that horrible man, will you? Not even if he's made of gold?"

"On earth what gave you that idea?"

"I heard them saying in the kitchen that unless you married money Grandpa would have to sell Kilcaraig. But I asked him about that, and he promised not to, so there's no need for you to do anything so drastic."

"I've often told you not to listen to silly gossip. You're becoming a precocious brat. It's time you went to boarding-school."

"When you talk like that, you sound just like Mummy!"

Marian opened her mouth to speak, but Grania had disappeared and the floor-boards creaked as she crossed the landing in her stockinged feet. Marian picked up the discarded Wellington boots and the oilskin, and took them to the cloakroom.

She was glad of the chance to be alone, to recover from the two shocks she had received, one after the other. First, there was the premonition that Robert Dutton meant to buy Kilcaraig, then the revelation that people who had known her all her life could think that anyone would take Andrew's place in her heart. The news that the Scots Guards had been decimated on the banks of the Marne had come through before the first Christmas of the war, that war which so many had believed would end by Christmas. Andrew Sinclair's name was among those in the long lists of the fallen, and Andrew Sinclair's memorial service was held in the little Kilcaraig church, where he was to have married her during the following spring. Ten years ago, and it seemed like yesterday. Ten years, and today's events had stirred up memories that were always just beneath the surface of her mind.

She washed her hands and tidied her hair, and tried to recall what Evelyn had said about Robert Dutton in her letter. "He's a director of Carnsworth, Prior and Dutton, and appears to have a finger in every financial pie. He's particularly interested in property." A typical businessman, Marian had thought, until understanding dawned upon her so suddenly, there in the library.

Carnsworth, Prior and Dutton. Armaments, no doubt. War profiteers. Was Robert Dutton making his millions while millions were dying in the mud? He was a guest in her home. He must not sense her hostility.

She looked at her watch and saw that she had been out of the room for nearly ten minutes. He would be using those minutes to manipulate and outmanoeuvre her father, for men who made millions must be both clever and ruthless. She hurried back to the library and pushed the door open.

Robert Dutton was standing by the window, staring through the mist at what little could be seen of Ben Caraig. He was drumming his fingers on the pane, petulantly, like a spoilt child who had been refused a toy.

"Raining again," Marian said brightly. "The weather in these parts is most unreliable, and you must find it very chilly after your holiday in Kashmir."

"I don't mind wet weather. I find extremes of climate very dull."

We've covered the weather, now we'll start on crops, Marian thought, amused because she suspected that Robert Dutton had tried to take Kilcaraig by storm, instead of by stealth, and in doing so, had lost all hope of success.

"Marian, Mr. Dutton is wanting to buy this place. I have told him that there has been a misunderstanding. It is not for sale." Kilcaraig had risen from his chair, and was standing beside the portrait of himself, so that it looked as if there were two Kilcaraigs in the room.

"Your father says he has promised his granddaughter that he will never part with her home!" Robert Dutton's voice shook with frustration.

"It's as good a reason as any for not selling something that one wants to keep," Marian said soothingly. "Besides, if we were to leave here, where else would we go?"

"I'll pay any price you ask, and I'll allow you to build a house on any site you choose!"

Marian thought that her father would explode with anger. Instead, he smiled and said, "Well, well, well, and what site could there be better than the one we have already?"

"You can think about it. I'm prepared to wait for your decision." Robert refused to accept defeat at the hands of these stubborn, impractical people. Then he saw the child who had come silently into the room. There were black curls where there had been a sou'wester, and a blue dress had replaced the oilskin coat, but the slate-coloured eyes and the defiant mouth were the same.

"This is my granddaughter, Grania," Kilcaraig said.

"So you are the young lady who makes a habit of barring my way?" Robert felt awkward with children. He disliked them because they embarrassed him.

Grania shook hands with him and said gravely, "You won't need to know about shutting gates behind you if you're not going to live here." She pulled a crumpled packet out of her pocket and held it out to him. "Have an aniseed ball."

He took one, as he had taken the whisky, because it was impossible to refuse. Marian asked him to stay for lunch, and he accepted that too. He felt trapped by these people, whom he had thought he could so easily bend to his will.

As he ate venison, liberally drenched in rowan jelly, on a plate which he recognized as Sèvres, he tried to ignore the brass pot near the window into which the rain dripped with a monotonous plink-plonk. The paper was peeling off the wall on his left, and he noticed that at one time it had been kept in place with nails, for a few rusty heads remained in the stained plaster.

A dog began to scratch itself vigorously at his feet.

"Mr. Dutton, if you pick up any fleas, wait until they're gorged, then catch them with a piece of soap." Grania smiled at him delightfully.

"Pay no attention. Our dogs have no fleas. I expect it's a tick," Marian said.

He was left to puzzle over this sinister remark, afraid to ask questions in case the explanation proved to be too revolting to contemplate. These people were the oddest mixture of elegance and barbarism that he had ever come across.

"I'm going to see your big sisters in Gloucestershire," he said to Grania, who was sitting opposite to him, across the wide mahogany table.

"Diana is sixteen and Helen is fourteen," she said, because she could think of nothing else to say, and the conversation turned to the charm of the Cotswolds, which carried them through until Chrissie came in and removed their plates. The dogs followed her to the kitchen, and did not return when she brought in the pudding.

Robert visualized rows of Sèvres dishes spread upon the kitchen floor being licked clean by dirty, doggie tongues. That was what had happened when he was in his uncle's house in Norfolk, when he was a boy. The uncle who was a farmer, not the one who made a fortune out of steel.

"Bramble and apple," Grania said, passing him a jug of cream. "We pick brambles by the ton. We'll give you a pot of jelly to take away with you. Uncle Nicholas says it's a very good tonic."

47

"Who is Uncle Nicholas?"

"He's not a real uncle – he's a very special friend. He used to be a doctor, but now he writes books."

Robert had little time for light reading. He had little time for anything but work, even when he was supposed to be on holiday.

"He got blown up in the war. He still has tiny black spots of shrapnel on his arms and legs. He showed them to me. He was with a field ambulance. Mr. Dutton, what did you do in the war?"

"Grania, you're talking too much. Run along and tell Chrissie that we're ready for coffee. Then you can take the eggs across to the Ameses, but don't stay there all afternoon." Marian knew that she had cut in too quickly, and that Robert Dutton would guess the reason why.

Grania laid her napkin on the table, and Kilcaraig rose and opened the door for her.

Robert Dutton, still seated, felt like an ill-mannered lout.

He turned to Marian. "I was in the Royal Engineers," he said. "I was one of the lucky ones. My three cousins didn't get through. My uncle needed me to take their place in the firm. I suppose you could say I was lucky in that, too."

Kilcaraig returned to his chair and said, "Our neighbour, Michael Ames, was in the R.E.s. He was blinded at Passchendaele. He was at St. Dunstan's for some time, where he learnt to do almost everything for himself, and a great deal for other people, too."

Robert knew about Michael Ames, because he had been briefed by Evelyn about the people who lived at Kilcaraig. He thought it wiser not to say so; instead he returned to the subject of travel, which brought them back to their only common ground, Ian and Evelyn and Kashmir.

Later, when his car was summoned, Marian and her father stood at the door and waved him off.

"I hope I'll never see him again," Marian said, turning into the house.

Kilcaraig paused in the hall and examined the grandfather clock. "We've got some beautiful things," he said. "Antiques, paintings, silver, glass, and china."

There was no need for him to say more. Marian knew what he was thinking, and she knew that he had no idea how to set about selling such things. Neither had she. Mr. Ames, whose Bible was *The Financial Times*, would be able to advise them, but one didn't speak of money matters outside the family.

Grania, breathless, flung herself into the house. "I waited with Michael until we saw him go. I hope he never comes back." Grania always spoke about Michael Ames as if he could see. She couldn't remember him before he became blind.

That night, when she was undressing for bed, she told Chrissie what she thought of Mr. Dutton. "He's got ginger hair, and he talks with a very grand accent, and he's horrible."

It summed up what Chrissie thought of him, or of anyone else who had the effrontery to fancy himself laird of Kilcaraig.

The visitor was soon forgotten in the battle to disentangle Grania's hair. "We'll need to grow it and put it into plaits," Chrissie said, tugging fiercely at the locks in her hand.

"Diana and Helen have nice smooth hair. That's why they look so orderly. But I don't like plaits. They make people look so prim. Like Mummy."

Chrissie administered a gentle tap with the hair brush. "Your father should never have chosen to go into the Indian Army. So much separation doesn't give a family a chance. Now, say your prayers, *mo chridhe*, and put a wee one up for me while you're at it."

She withdrew to the day-nursery, for she considered that Grania should be allowed ten minutes, night and morning, on her own. Grania dutifully mumbled some prayers, and read through the Bible verses appointed for the day. She disliked these formal sessions she spent with God, preferring to send up fervent little messages for help, or of thanks, as the occasions arose during the day.

When Chrissie returned, she was sitting on the big bed, cutting her toe nails.

Chrissie drew back the heavy curtains, and the pink glow of the sunset filled the room. Grania got out of bed and pattered over to the window. Chrissie ignored the fact that her bare feet were on the cold boards, for she knew that the sunset came to Grania as a benediction.

They watched together, as the sky slipped through its phases of gold, of pink, and of smoke and flame, until the summits of the mountains seemed themselves to have caught fire, before the final fading into night.

"Where *is* the sunset?" Grania asked.

"In the Land of Heart's Desire," Chrissie laughed. "Away to bed. You'll catch your death."

Grania obeyed thoughtfully. "It doesn't look so very far away," she said.

"Och, I would say it's in Tormore Bay, on the right hand side, on the way to Iona."

"Tormore Bay, on the way to Iona," Grania repeated. "Just fancy! The Land of Heart's Desire." Her eyes shone. "I can go there some day."

"Of course you can, it's not hard to find." Chrissie tucked in the bed clothes with her firm, plump hands.

She made a pretence of tidying the room, until she had assured herself that Grania was really drowsy and ready to go to sleep. Then she crept onto the landing, and leaned over the banisters. The dining-room door was open and she could hear Kilcaraig murmur a Gaelic blessing on the food.

A surge of tranquillity overcame her. She walked down the spiral staircase, past the Kilcaraig tapestry, and joined the others in the servants' hall.

8

The autumn was Grania's favourite season. The landscape was brown now, and the heather was springy under her feet as she bounded across the hills with the dogs, or learnt the intricacies of deer-stalking from Angus, the gillie. On wet days, she could sit by the kitchen fire, eating raw carrots, while Chrissie told her tales of the heroic past; of that Niall Lamont who slew a monster there, right at the foot of Ben Caraig, or of Grania Lamont, torn between passion for her lover and loyalty to the family, who had thrown herself into the inky blackness of the loch because an alliance between a Lamont and a Campbell was unthinkable.

Grania would listen, wide-eyed, to Chrissie's soft voice, and at night she would cuddle close under the smooth, home-laundered bed clothes, re-living the fierce, unfaltering devotion to Kilcaraig that had burned in the breasts of her ancestors.

There were cosy afternoons, too, when with a large apron wrapped around her, she would help cook to bake scones, kneading the dough on the huge kitchen table, or spooning out the golden pancake mixture on to the girdle. The pride, when she set a plateful of her own cookies on the table before grandpapa! And the joy when he smacked his lips and turned to Aunt Marian – "My, but these are grand! And who can have made them?"

Marian was busy these days with her sewing-machine, making down her own garments to fit her rapidly growing niece. Then, a few weeks ago there was excitement, when Marian had written to a shop in Edinburgh, ordering patterns of material. "Look," she said, when the intriguing parcel was delivered by Johnnie, the postman. "These are for you, Grania. Choose your colour for yourself." And Grania had pored over the swatches, fingering them lovingly, because it was seldom that she had anything new. She decided on a green and grey check, Marian sent off the order, and when the parcel arrived and the material was unfurled in all its splendour, Grania watched reverently as it took shape before her eyes.

At last it was ready, and she wore the new dress to the little Kilcaraig church, taking off her coat so as to be sure that everyone would see her in her finery. She shivered all through the long service. Never had she felt so stiff and cramped as she leaned forward in her seat, for Marian had taught her that only Papists and their kind knelt in prayer.

It was a relief to sit back and listen to Grandpapa reading the lesson from the plain, pitch pine lectern, but the new minister preached at such length that she was chilled to the bone, and had pins and needles by the time he had finished. A metrical psalm, the Old Hundredth, and the simple service was over. Grania slipped thankfully into her coat.

"On earth, what did you take it off for?" Marian asked, when they were outside amongst the tombstones. "You'll catch your death." But it was Kilcaraig and not Grania who was confined to bed on the following day.

Doctor MacFie was grave faced when he left the sick-room. "I'll send nurse along to help you. And maybe you should get someone from the mainland as well. It's pneumonia," he told Marian. Chrissie, leaning over the banisters, caught the words and burst into tears.

During the days that followed, nobody had time for Grania. The Ameses had friends staying at Caraig Lodge for the deer-stalking, and she never sought out Michael when there were other people about. She preferred to have him to herself. She was wretchedly aware of the calamity that hung over them all, and she wandered around on the moors, or sat disconsolately by the dark waters of the loch, praying fervently that Grandpa would get well. Heaven was a long way away now. God seemed to have forgotten all about her. Perhaps, like Aunt Marian and Chrissie, He was busy making Grandpa better.

At night she could hear the death-watch beetle ticking in the walls. It was a sound that had accompanied her all her life, but now it had a new significance. Willie had said that it meant someone would die. She buried her face in the pillow, sobbing hopelessly. Night after night it was the same, but on the fifth evening, about the time Johnnie was due to arrive with the mail, the battered taxi from

Craignure snorted up to the door, and a tall figure jumped quickly out. Grania, watching from the nursery window, didn't wait to hear the door-bell clang through the house. She ran downstairs and pulled open the door. "Uncle Nicholas," she sobbed. "Uncle Nicholas, you're just in time to save Grandpa."

Nicholas gathered her in his arms. Her slate-coloured eyes were swimming in tears, and her dark curls tumbled over a face wizened with anxiety. "Marian wrote to me, and I came at once. But I'm here as a friend, not as a doctor. I haven't touched a medical instrument for years!"

Grania never gave Doctor MacFie the credit for her grandfather's recovery, a fact which amused the old doctor enormously.

"When you had the measles, it was Chrissie you said pulled you through. Now you impute a healing touch to a man who writes books," he told her, as he snapped the stethoscope back into its case. "You've no faith in me at all! But for all that, I'll let you have a wee peep at Himself – just a wee peep, mind you."

Grania hugged him gratefully, and took immediate advantage of his decree. She was up in Kilcaraig's bedroom before the doctor had time to get into his great-coat.

She was shocked at the change in the old man. He was propped up against a mass of pillows in his huge bed, and his eyes seemed to have sunk away, deep into his gaunt face. A Lamont tartan plaid was around his shoulders, a New Testament in Gaelic lay between his limp hands.

"Come here," he said faintly to her, in Gaelic.

Grania drew a chair up to his bedside, and making no reference to his illness, she gave an account of herself, and of the animals, and of the snatches of gossip she had picked up on the estate. She spoke in Gaelic, purely, perfectly, as she had spoken it all her life. Kilcaraig's eyes glowed with pride.

"You're a real Lamont," he told her. "A real Kilcaraig. Grania of Kilcaraig, that's who you are."

After that, Grania was given free access to the sickroom. She knew when to talk and when to be silent, so she never worried the invalid, and often he would feign sleep while watching her through his eye-lashes, as she sat, still and calm, keeping a silent vigil by his bedside, her restlessness drained from her in her eagerness to give him strength.

She was Catriona all over again, Catriona in her beauty and selflessness and utter devotion. Sometimes Kilcaraig close his eyes to shut out the vision of his own darling child.

But for his blindness and interference, Catriona would be living over there at Ardcross, not a day's journey from Mull, instead of rotting in the graveyard by the church. All through the years he re-lived the anguish he had experienced when Catriona returned from Italy, and broken, terrified, had told him of her shameful predicament. He had prostrated her with his verbal chastisement, while inwardly his conscience had screamed at him -- "It's all my fault". Grania would be just as lovable if she had been brought up on "Aves" instead of the Shorter Catechism. He should never have forbidden Catriona's marriage to Hector MacNeill.

"When you grow up, see that you are broad-minded," he said to Grania one day after these musings.

"I'll try to," she said. He often spoke to her about this. She wondered why. But she never asked him, for he closed his eyes and gave her to know that this was one of the subjects she must not pursue. It was part of that mystery of which Grania was becoming increasingly aware, but she kept her awakening recognition of it locked up in her heart.

Diana and Helen would be coming home for the Christmas holidays, and Marian began to prepare for their arrival long before they were due. Marian always did things that way, which meant that the beds had to be aired over and over again, instead of just once. She was well ahead with her preparations before Nicholas left the castle. He sucked at his pipe and watched her bustling movements with amusement.

"The whole house drips with water, and all this fuss over the beds," he said. "You really are a most inconsistent person."

Marian tossed back her chestnut hair, which had been cut fashionably short during her last visit to Edinburgh. "It doesn't matter how many novels you write, you're still a doctor at heart. And a fussy one at that! Here, take this side of the bed. I've promised Grania I'll give her some help with her practice. She's found a piano transcription of *The Hebrides Overture*, and it's far too difficult for her. But she'll go on trying until she gets it right. Once she's set her heart on something she never gives up."

"She's getting more beautiful every day," Nicholas said, tucking in the blankets with deft hands. "She's also very intelligent, and she's going to ask questions about herself. She has the right to know the truth. Who's going to tell her?"

Marian arranged a white counterpane over the bed, then she sat on the ottoman in front of the window. The winter landscape was bleak, and there was a scattering of snow on the top of the mountains.

Nicholas pulled his pipe out of his pocket and sat beside her.

"I can't tell her anything," Marian said. "I'm not free to do so. Besides, we don't know the whole truth. We've only guessed at it."

It was the grief-stricken Kilcaraig who had insisted that the only man Catriona would ever have as a lover was the man she loved, and during those first dreadful weeks that followed her death, both Marian and Nicholas had found some consolation in this belief. Catriona would at least have experienced a brief interlude of joy.

It was Nicholas who stumbled upon a clue to the truth. He found that Hector MacNeill had been on a diplomatic mission to Rome during the summer of 1913, and Catriona Lamont had spent a few days there during July. Only some very strong magnet could have drawn her from the sea and the countryside into the scorching heat of the city.

"I believe your father knows the truth," Nicholas said now. "I believe he knows it because Catriona told it to him. It's strange how one can work these things out in retrospect. The war, following so soon, blotted out all other dilemmas. I don't suppose we'd be giving much thought to it now if Grania were not the image of Catriona. Other people must see how different she is from her sisters."

"You'd never think Diana and Helen had a drop of Lamont blood in their veins, yet they're Ian's all right. Nobody would doubt that at all. Grania's likeness to Catriona is easily explained, especially by the people here, who are obsessed with genealogy, as all Highland people are."

"I suppose we'd have more cause for concern if she was the image of Hector MacNeill," Nicholas said.

"One thing is sure. Hector MacNeill believes, like everyone else, that Catriona died suddenly of heart failure. He had no idea that she was expecting a baby."

"What makes you so sure?"

"Why, he came to her funeral. He'd have stayed away if he thought he had anything to do with her death." Having made the point which evidently settled the matter, Marian told Nicholas to stay where he was and enjoy his pipe. "The smoke may get rid of the moths I'm always chasing away," she said, and as he opened the door for her, he heard Grania practising her scales.

He watched Marian walk along the corridor, then he returned to the ottoman, and re-lit his pipe. This was Diana Lamont's bedroom. The heavy, Victorian furniture had been painted white, and there were little chips where the mahogany showed underneath.

"Vandalism!" he had exclaimed to Marian when he first saw it, but she had replied, "No, no, just homesickness. The furniture was white in her bedroom in Rawalpindi. I hadn't the heart to refuse when she asked if she could give it a lick of paint."

Helen's room, across the corridor, was painted a drab shade of blue, reflecting, possibly, her mood at the time she chose it. Nicholas had met the two girls soon after they arrived in Britain, and had been struck by their resemblance to their mother; the soft brown hair, the hazel eyes, and the mouth that rarely smiled. Only once had he seen Evelyn Lamont lose her composure, and that was when she came from her hotel to take charge of the infant she was to bring up as her own. She had taken one look at the baby, and had recoiled, saying, "I can't take her! I can't put the child of his dead daughter into Kilcaraig's arms."

"You promised."

He had said the words gently, but firmly, struggling against his own misgivings and distress, and her emotions were released in a torrent of tears. When she had recovered herself, she picked up the baby and stared into the crumpled face.

"Grania," she said.

"*Grannda*," Chrissie corrected her, Chrissie who had acted with incomparable fortitude during that unforgettable time.

"Grania," Evelyn Lamont repeated. "Isn't that the name she chose, Doctor Danvers?"

Nicholas nodded and Chrissie was silent. It was years later that she told him he had mis-heard that murmured word. *Grandda* was the Gaelic for ugly, and the infant could certainly be described as that, but Grania was the name conferred upon her when she was baptised in the little Kilcaraig church, and Grania she had remained, for *grannda* she would never, never be.

Nicholas walked round Diana's room, thinking his thoughts, wondering what the Gaelic word for beautiful could be, wondering what the Lamont girls would feel about their little sister as she grew more dazzling day by day, year by year.

He paused in front of a photograph, a group of self-consciously smiling girls wearing gym-tunics. Some were standing, some were seated, and Diana in the middle was holding a silver cup. She had talked about hockey the last time he had been to Cambray College to take her out to lunch. Helen had been there, too, and had jeered at her sister's aptitude for games.

"You'll be all muscle and sunburn, and you'll look awful in evening-dress. Isn't that so, Uncle Nicholas?"

"I'm not going to wear evening-dress. I'm going to Dartford to learn to be a games-mistress."

"Mummy won't let you – she hates hearty women." And Helen tucked into the chicken à la kiev on her plate.

Mummy won't let you. That Evelyn was the one who made decisions for the family had been apparent to Nicholas from the first moment that he met her, and he had looked forward with misgiving to meeting Ian Lamont, Younger of Kilcaraig, who must be so ineffectual, despite his background.

That meeting had not taken place for years, because the war had intervened, but when at last Marian summoned Nicholas to Kilcaraig because her brother was home on leave, he was not prepared for the man who greeted him on the jetty at Craignure.

Ian Lamont was not as tall as his father, but he was almost as broad-shouldered, his features were startlingly the same, as was the warmth of his handshake. Nicholas had been only a few minutes in the car with him when he realized that this was a man who allowed his wife to command only those areas over which he felt a woman should have control.

During the days that followed, his liking for Ian grew and grew. A kindly and courteous husband, he was also a devoted father and a willing worker when help was needed with various tasks on the estate. Kilcaraig, that benevolent despot, had deliberately faded into the background, concentrating on his fishing and shooting, but covertly watching how his son deputized for him.

Had it been possible, Ian would have followed in the tradition of the Lamonts, and would have joined the Argyll and Sutherland Highlanders, with a view to an early retirement and the sort of life he was leading now, but necessity had compelled him to choose the higher pay and faster promotion offered by the Indian Army.

"Evelyn enjoys life in India," he said one day to Nicholas as they were fishing on Loch Caraig. "Diana and Helen see no beauty in this place, unless the sun is shining. They weren't brought up here, like Grania. I don't think they'll ever want to live here, and I don't think Grania will ever want to live anywhere else."

From that moment Nicholas realized that a special bond existed between Ian and Grania, but it was not until two years later that Ian put his feelings into words. It happened when he was again home on leave and Nicholas was spending a few days at the castle.

Grania had been lost for hours. Nobody was particularly worried, because it never occured to them that she could come to any harm. She was found eventually, dusty and dishevelled, sitting in the attic surrounded by an assortment of old books, drawings, and sheets of music which she had found in a trunk. She was glowing with happiness.

"There are diaries here about Kilcaraig. And there are drawings of Caraig village and other places that are a heap of ruins now. And music written out by hand, pipe tunes I think, and they have Kilcaraig names."

"You've no right to open boxes without permission," Evelyn scolded, but Ian turned to Nicholas and said softly, "She's so like her mother. She's a dream daughter. I wish to God she was my own."

He had not been thinking of Grania's appearance. Nicholas knew that it was Catriona's love of all things that concerned Kilcaraig which Ian recognized had somehow been passed on to her child.

Someone opened the drawing-room door, and Nicholas was roused from his memories by the sound of Grania putting her heart into an inaccurate and fortissimo rendering of *The Hebrides Overture*.

He opened the window to rid the room of the smell of his pipe. It was pitch dark outside. He went downstairs to the glow of the lamp-light and the warmth of the fire.

9

Kilcaraig never fully regained his strength. By the following spring, he was able to walk along the paths by the house, and sometimes Willie drove him in the trap to the village, but his days of shooting and fishing were over. He entrusted Angus with the task of teaching Grania to fish, and he would watch her lessons on the loch through his binoculars, as he sat at the drawing-room window. He gave her a 4.10 gun for her eleventh birthday, and he erected a miniature range near the front-door, so that he could sit on a bench, wrapped closely in his plaid, and see how every day she became a more and more accurate shot.

"It's a bull's-eye every time, now," he told Marian. "She's a good shot!"

It was not long before she shot her first rabbit. It was a moment of triumph, until she saw the little creature twitching on the ground; then she wept with remorse.

"It's all right to kill for the pot," Kilcaraig assured her. "And if you mean to live here, lassie, you'll need to kill for the pot!"

After that, she went out with her gun regularly, always returning with two or three rabbits. Then one day she came home with a curlew. Kilcaraig was impressed. "If you can shoot that, you can shoot anything," he said.

"On earth, where did you find it?" Marian asked. "You'll be bringing us a golden eagle next. You'll need to watch out with that gun of yours."

It was not a golden eagle that Grania brought home next, it was a coot. She had taken so much trouble to retrieve it from the rushes in the loch that Kilcaraig sent it away to be stuffed, so that her efforts would not be wasted.

The Ameses had spent the cold months following Christmas in Malta, and when they returned Nancy was displaying a diamond ring, and was to be married to a naval officer before the end of the year. Grania thought that Nancy was very old to be getting married; she was older than Aunt Marian. She confided her views to Michael, careful not to say anything about his sister that might be offensive.

"But your aunt is a young woman, and a very attractive one," he said, "Don't be too sure that you'll have her at Kilcaraig forever."

"She's never got over Andrew Sinclair being killed," Grania said, because that was what Chrissie had told her. It was one of the things she thought about during the two minutes' silence every Armistice day, when she wore a poppy in her button hole, and stood among the people who had gathered round the pink granite War Memorial. It had been built beside the burn, across the road from the church, and it bore a frightening number of names – Lamonts, Campbells, Camerons, MacCormicks, MacPhails, the list went on and on.

"People do get over things," Michael said.

"I wouldn't. If Aunt Marian left here, it would be the most dreadful, awful calamity I can imagine. It would break my heart."

"It takes a lot to break a heart. People are very resilient, as I'm afraid you'll probably discover for yourself one day." Michael leaned forward and felt the material of her dress, then he smiled. "The green and grey check. How nice of you to put it on to come and see me."

"I always try to look my best for you."

She settled down to talk to him, always content with him, because he never allowed his blindness to be a burden to anyone, and he would listen patiently to all the silly things she said, and would treat them with interest and respect.

It was a while before she could call at the Lodge again, because she was busy helping to lift the peats which Angus and Willie had cut in May, and which lay on the peat-moss not far from the castle, ready to be made into stooks to dry.

These were the glad days, with the sun blazing down on them as they worked, with the scent of bog-myrtle to exhilarate, and with long draughts of oatmeal water to drink, ice-cold because they put the tin cans containing it into the burn that raced down to Loch Caraig.

They had all the peats up before the weather broke, and then there was the rush, between showers, to transport them in cart-loads to the castle, where Willie built them into huge stacks in the yard.

Diana and Helen were to come home in the middle of August, because they were spending the first fortnight of their holidays with friends.

Grania was puzzled to think that anyone would want to stay with someone else when they could be at Kilcaraig, but there were a number of things about her sisters that she couldn't understand. They were very old, in her eyes, and the prospect of the approaching years all the more undesirable, for her twelfth birthday loomed ahead of her, and with it the dreaded ordeal of boarding-school.

She consoled herself with the thought that her grandfather would never force her to leave Kilcaraig. Her mother would talk a lot, but her grandfather would have his way, and if need be, she would appeal to her father, who was her friend and ally. She wrote a brief letter to her parents every Sunday before church, but it was always her father she was thinking about, as the handwriting with which she was experimenting straggled across the page.

Marian, who acted as governess, helped at times by the minister's wife, taught her the three Rs and gave her a vivid account of Scottish history. She learnt only a smattering of Latin, but she knew the name of every flower on the island, and there were wonderful excursions to the Nuns' Cave at Carsaig, to Moy Castle at Lochbuie, and of course to Iona. Marian's stories brought Saint Columba and the Celtic saints and the ruins of the monastery to pulsating life.

> "Iona of my heart, Iona of my love,
> Instead of monks' voices shall be lowing of cattle,
> But ere the world shall come to an end
> Iona shall be as it was."

Grania copied the prophecy carefully into her note-book after one of her visits to the Cathedral.

"I can see it all," she told Marian one night. "Candles on the marble altar, flowers in the sanctuary, and the granite walls echoing to the chant of the psalms."

"Candles in a Scottish church! And flowers, too, and chanting!

Don't talk such nonsense," Marian said, outraged. "Now, get you along, and say your prayers, and ask God to make you a good Protestant."

Grania hugged her delightedly. "Grandpa says I must be broad-minded. And there were no Protestants when Saint Columba was alive!"

Marian kept her lips tightly shut, determined not to be drawn on the subject any more. *What's bred in the bone will come out in the flesh.* Had she not been taught that saying since early childhood, but surely being a Papist wasn't inherited in any way!

Diana arrived home with her hair put up in a bun, and Helen's hair had been bobbed.

"Well, well, well, and aren't you the grown-up ladies now!" Kilcaraig said admiringly. "In another year, Diana, you'll be going to the Oban Ball."

The ball which followed the Argyllshire Gathering was the occasion on which many young girls made their debut, for although some of them had been presented at Court, and had been invited to the Royal Garden Party which marked the end of the London season, a private dance was beyond the means of the majority of post-war Highland landowners. To take a party to the Oban ball had become an accepted substitute, and already, in her imagination, Diana was picturing herself in a white dress with a Lamont tartan sash across her breast, held in place by a diamond brooch on her shoulder. She would have partners galore, and they would be wearing full Highland dress, and she would be pronounced the belle of the ball.

"Mummy wrote to me about that," she said, glowing with pleasure. "After it's over, I'm to spend a winter in India, and possibly a summer in Kashmir."

"By which time you'll have given up silly ideas about taking a course at a Physical Training College," Helen said, quoting from Evelyn's letter.

Diana shrugged. "I don't think I'm really so keen about training for a career. It's a waste, when I want to get married."

Helen giggled, but Grania said, "You might not fall in love with the right man, or he mightn't fall in love with you. I'm going to have a career. Uncle Nicholas has given me his old typewriter, and I'm learning how to type; then I'll write books, like him, and I'll be rich and keep Kilcaraig in good repair, and we'll all live here and be happy ever after."

"That'll be just lovely, but first you'll have to learn how to spell properly!" Aunt Marian said. "Now off you go and help your sisters to unpack. After dinner, we'll see what came in that big crate

Willie's opening now. I expect it's the coot. Nothing else could be so bulky."

It was the coot, and it looked very handsome in its glass case. Kilcaraig placed it on the dining-room mantelpiece, and Grania gazed proudly at the electro-plate engraving, admiring her own name written in neat lettering. Her trophy had taken the place of the Meissen clock and no greater honour could have been conferred upon it than that.

"Where are we going to put the clock?" Helen asked, but she saw the quick exchange that passed between her aunt and her grandfather, so she turned her attention back to the coot.

Afterwards, she said to Diana, "Every time we come home, something else has gone. The Raeburn from the library, the Sheraton table from behind the drawing-room door, and now it seems the clock is doomed."

"They must have found some inconspicuous way of smuggling things off the island, and let's hope Uncle Nicholas organized it. At least he'll see that the things are handled by a reputable firm like Sotheby's or Christie's."

"What happens when our movable assets run out?"

"There's always Mr. Dutton and his cheque book, I suppose. Mother won't let him disappear from her life, even if she only keeps in touch once a year through a Christmas card!"

On the following day, there was a letter from Evelyn. Her mother, who was becoming more difficult as the years went by, had to be transferred to a nursing home, and Evelyn had decided that she must supervise the move herself. She would spend the winter at Kilcaraig and would arrive at the end of September.

Grania tried to make herself believe that the news was as welcome to her as it was to Diana and Helen, but she could see that with her mother at the castle she would have to forego many of the things which she took for granted. There would be no more going to concerts in the village school and staying for a while afterwards to watch the start of the dance which always followed. In short, there would be no more fun. While the formidable grandmother who lived in Bath was undoubtedly the principle reason for this unexpected homecoming, during the weeks ahead there would be ample opportunity to organize that long-dreaded event – boarding-school.

"I'll be twelve in April," Grania told herself, staring out of the nursery window onto the golden hill behind Caraig Lodge, for the autumn bracken had caught the gleam of the sinking sun. Tears pricked her eyes. She never used to have these attacks of melancholy, but now she could feel riotously happy at one moment, and then for no reason at all she wanted to weep. Questions rose in her mind which she dismissed quickly, shocked that they should ever have occurred to her, and changes were taking place in her body that made her feel awkward and shy. There was nobody she could ask about these conflicts, not even Aunt Marian, not Michael Ames, and least of all her mother. For the first time, she wanted to talk to girls of her own age.

The evening before Evelyn's arrival, Kilcaraig was sitting in the high-backed chair in the drawing-room, playing his chanter, which had long lain in its case, for he no longer had the breath to blow it. But tonight he felt festive, and he put all he had into *The Barren Rocks of Aden*. Marian watched anxiously, not daring to suggest that he was over-straining himself.

Diana and Helen bickered in undertones about which of them was to cross to Oban to meet their mother's train. Grania, weary of their arguments and sharing Marian's anxiety, suggested that they practise for a welcome-home concert for tomorrow night. Diana jumped at the idea, as it gave her a chance to sing. Beaming, Kilcaraig laid the chanter aside and watched Marian seat herself at the piano.

Diana sang in a true but unmusical voice of Colin calling the cattle home, and of the banks and braes of bonnie Doune. Helen followed, sight-reading MacDowell's *To A Wild Rose*, stopping frequently to correct her mistakes. Marian played a reel, which brought Kilcaraig to his feet, clapping his hands in rhythm, and pacing up and down, longing to break into a dance.

"Come, Grania, I want a song from you," he said. "You can surely manage something."

Grania chose a sheet of music from the pile on top of the piano, looked at it for a moment, then cleared her throat. "I know it," she said. "It doesn't need an accompaniment."

Her voice was small, low and clear.

"Once o'er the wide moor wending,
Or round the green hill bending,
Gay words and wild notes blending,
Spread for my good cheer.
For this my heart light-leaping
In waking, in sleeping,
Had no *dubh ciar-dubh* keeping
His joys from here."

When she had come to the end of the first verse, Marian went to the piano and turned over the pages of the music. "Give us something we can all join in," she said. Unprotesting, Grania played

An T-Eilean Muileach, but it was Kilcaraig who sang it, remembering every one of its innumerable verses, while the others joined in the chorus. They had almost exhausted their repertoire when Chrissie came in with a tray of tea, and reminded Grania that it was long past time for bed. Grania was so full of good humour towards everyone that she even kissed Diana and Helen goodnight.

Out in the hall, she could hear the servants having a *ceilidh* of their own. Angus was singing in his strong, true baritone voice. Grania listened for a moment, before going upstairs. A few months ago, she would have joined them, and Chrissie would scold her for doing so, and at the same time make no move to send her to bed. But it was different now. She was growing up. Saddened at the realization that even without Evelyn's interference, her world was already changing, she picked up her lamp from the hall table by the dining-room, and watched the ghostly spiral of the banisters as she went upstairs.

The rain was beating against the window pane when she reached her bedroom. It had been drizzling all day, but now it was coming down in earnest. Tomorrow evening, they would put a lamp in every window of the house to greet Evelyn on her return home. It was the traditional Highland welcome, and Grania loved to follow Chrissie round the house, as she lit the lamps and grumbled about all the glass funnels she would have to clean in the morning. Yet, Chrissie enjoyed the ritual as much as anyone. Besides, it was usually Marian who trimmed the lamps and cleaned the funnels, using screws of newspaper that achieved a glimmering cleanliness in a matter of seconds.

A long time after she had slipped into bed, Grania was still awake. She heard Diana and Helen come upstairs, and then there was silence, except for an occasional giggle to prove that Helen was in Diana's room, and would be likely to stay there gossiping for half the night, unless Marian heard her and turned her out. Then there was a rustle on the stairs and whispering voices. That would be Marian and Chrissie helping Grandpapa upstairs. They had tried to make him convert the library into a bedroom, to save him the toil of the stairs, but he would have none of it.

On an impulse, Grania got out of bed and pattered on her bare feet onto the landing to give him a final kiss. She felt the warmth and love of his embrace as he whispered, "Good night, Grania of Kilcaraig".

She shivered as she crept back under the bed clothes, but after a while she was cosy and completely happy. She woke up the next morning to the beginning of a new life.

Kilcaraig had died in his sleep.

10

The funeral procession wound its way through the mist and down the hill. A farm cart acted as hearse, and the coffin was covered with Kilcaraig's plaid. The two pipers were out of sight, but the strains of the lament were carried through the rain before being lost in the mountains. Marian and Chrissie were walking behind the cart, for although it was not the custom for women to be present at a Highland funeral, Marian had insisted that she should take Ian's place as head of the family, and Chrissie was there to give her support.

Grania watched it all from her bedroom window. She had been at the simple service held outside the house, and she was wet to the skin with the mist that hung over them like a shroud. Evelyn was directing operations in the kitchen, because all the gathered company must be fed on their return from the burial ground. Diana and Helen were shut in their respective rooms, helpless with grief. Grania shivered and leaned forward, straining to see the coffin before it vanished round the bend at the burn.

The last of the stragglers disappeared. Grania wriggled off the chair on which she had been kneeling. Her knees were painful with the imprint of the basket-seat. Her brain was numb; she had cast out grief so resolutely, so thoroughly, that she had nothing left but a vacuum, a limbo, dividing the golden memories of the past which she dared not recall, from the blank space of the future which she feared to consider.

Instinctively, she made her way to the library. The fire was out, and the unprecedented sight of the empty grate brought her sorrow to the surface. She dropped on to her grandfather's chair and wept unrestrainedly, until the tramp of feet outside reminded her of the need for self-control. It was Lachie MacPhail with a box of scones as a contribution towards the food for refreshments. The kitchen was piled high with the offerings of people who had loved Kilcaraig, and who showed their love by sending something, made with their own hands, that would lessen the need for cooking at the castle.

Grania put the scones in the kitchen, then went to the drawing-room. There was a fire there, but it was burning low. She flung some peats on it, and then turned her attention to the music on top of the piano.

Most of the sheets were dog-eared and yellow with age. Many of them had "Catriona M. Lamont" written on them. Grandpapa had loved Catriona better than anyone else in the world, and Chrissie had said this often, explaining that it was the reason her name was hardly ever mentioned. People couldn't talk about her because it made them miserable, and she thought this was strange. She wanted to talk about Grandpapa, to keep him in mind, so that he would always be a person to other people, and not just a name.

Perhaps she should not have sung Catriona's song that last night with Grandpapa. Marian had stopped her, yet she had sung it many times before. She picked up the sheet of music.

Evelyn bustled into the room, and Grania quickly pushed the music to the bottom of the pile.

"I hope you don't mean to play the piano, Grania," she said in sepulchral tones.

"There's nothing else to do."

"I think you might show a little respect for the dead."

"I'm sure Grandpapa would hate to leave a mournful hush behind him!" Grania said, two pink spots appearing in her cheeks. "And the minister's just been telling us of victory over the grave."

"What a way to talk. You're a horrid, callous little girl!" Evelyn's voice shook. She might have guessed that this ill-begotten hybrid would be without feeling or scruples.

Grania who had not for a moment intended to play the piano, put her foot on the loud pedal and struck a chord; then she closed the lid with a bang, so that all the strings twanged. Evelyn stared at her in impotent dismay before turning and leaving the room.

Grania was trembling, yet exhilarated. She knew that after this Evelyn would have no mercy on her, and would pack her off to boarding-school, where she would learn to play hockey, and to giggle, and to have passions on girls older than herself. She would not be any better educated than she had been by Aunt Marian, and by Mrs. MacLeod, who was very patient and interesting, although she knew so much about Latin and was the minister's wife.

She could hear the cars returning to the house, so she went into the hall in time to see Marian and Chrissie being helped out of Kilcaraig's modest car by Angus. They were followed by the Sinclairs, who had not been to Mull since they sold Duff after their son was killed. They had been kind and gentle, saying all the right, comforting things to Grania, which made her understand with an aching heart the sort of person Andrew must have been, and the sort of happiness Marian had missed.

Marian was soaking wet, and Grania went upstairs with her to see that she changed into dry clothes. "Mr. Baker has brought a crate of whisky!" Marian said. "He's so generous, but I just can't introduce him to people the way he wants – Mr. Baker of Duff! Imagine! It would stick in my throat." Mr. Baker had bought Duff, which was always changing hands, two years ago. He was a large man, who possessed a large car and a large voice, and a burning but unfulfilled ambition to be accepted socially by the established landowners of Mull.

"I wish Uncle Nicholas was here."

"He'll get our cable when he arrives in Buenos Aires. What a man he is for travelling! But I think when he hears this he'll come tearing home. There, do I look all right?" She was wearing a grey dress, prim, suitable for the occasion.

"Mummy will approve. She thinks I'm heartless." Grania's lips quivered. "She thought I was going to play the piano . . . Aunt Marian, why does Mummy not love me the same as Diana and Helen? I often think she doesn't like me at all!"

Marian was so shocked that she forgot for a moment that this was her father's funeral, and that she should be downstairs among the vast number of mourners who were now assembling at the house for tea.

"Grania, you mustn't think anything so silly. Your mother was very much upset that she couldn't keep you with her in India because you were so ill there. It's been very hard for her . . ." Her voice tailed off, because Grania would not be deceived, and she must remember, if only vaguely, how unhappy she had been during that winter in India, just after the war. "Come!" she said, "we have work to do. And I'll tell you this. I'm much happier about Grandpapa, now that I've seen him buried in the graveyard beside Catriona. It's made me feel that he is where he was longing to be."

There were people in the hall, there were people in the drawing-room and dining-room and library, and everywhere. They had come from all over Mull, and from Morvern, and from Iona, and their gentle good manners conveyed so forcibly their love and respect for Kilcaraig, that the whole atmosphere was pervaded by a sense of shared grief, and with it, consolation.

Michael Ames, with the special insight with which the blind become endowed, remarked on this to Grania, who was standing by his side, afraid he might be jostled. He had a cup of tea in his hand, and she was sharing his plate of sandwiches with him.

"Did you know my Aunt Catriona?" she asked him, quietly, so that nobody else would hear.

"Only slightly," he replied. "She was away from Mull during most of the year before the war. That's when we came here."

"Why did she die?"

"I think she developed some illness in Italy." Michael had never believed this, and he found it difficult to say it now.

"What did she look like?"

"She had soft curly black hair, and slate-grey eyes, and she was the loveliest woman I ever saw." He paused for a moment, then he added "A few years later, I never saw anyone again."

Grania did not make a sympathetic sound, or pat his arm, or do anything that would make him feel he had invited pity. Instead, she said, "I think there's a mystery about her. And I think it's something to do with me."

Michael, knowing the feel of Grania's silky curls, was at a loss for words. Suddenly he understood what he had never understood before – Kilcaraig's devotion to the infant whose birth had so closely followed the death of his daughter. Marian's marriage tragically postponed, so that she could be at home to comfort her father and help to care for the baby. Evelyn Lamont, dutiful but unmotherly towards her youngest child.

"Children of your age like to concoct mysteries," he said. Someone should be warned of the question that was clearly teasing Grania's mind. It was too intimate a matter for him to mention, even to Marian.

"I'll remove your cup." Grania had taken his words as a rebuff. He felt her disappear into the crowd. And he knew that he had somehow let her down.

When the last of the mourners had gone, Grania went to the kitchen to see if she could help, but it was full of women washing up, and she could hear Evelyn's voice, high-pitched and commanding, in the scullery. She fled upstairs, and she was crossing the landing to her room when she noticed that Grandpapa's bedroom door was ajar. She slipped into the room, closing the door behind her. It was so much as it had always been that it was difficult to believe that he was not downstairs, sitting in his big chair, reading his Gaelic Bible. Even the clock on the bureau was ticking. It was an eight-day clock and he would have wound it up himself.

She examined it carefully, loving it because it had been a present from the people on the estate, and he had loved it too. She replaced it and pulled open the drawer of the bureau, the one where he kept the cards she was allowed to play with except on Sundays, and the chess-men and the tin of sweets. They were all there, neatly arranged, ready for her as they had been for as long as she could remember, but now that her grandfather was dead, she felt as if she was prying, and she shut the drawer with a feeling of inexplicable guilt.

The Lamont plaid lay on the bed, and the Gaelic Bible was on the table beside it. She stroked the bible, then held it close to her, almost in an embrace. Something heavy fell out of it, onto the floor. It was a photograph, yellowed with age, and mounted on cardboard.

She picked it up and looked at it. It was of a woman, wearing a pre-war evening-dress, sitting on a Chippendale chair, holding a rose, a woman whose beauty, even in this faded photograph, was alive and startling. Grania put down the picture, and pushing her hair up from the nape of her neck, she held it piled on her head. She could see herself in the looking-glass above the bureau, and she could see the photograph before her. Trembling, she put the photograph back in the bible, and had returned it to the bedside table when Evelyn came into the room.

"You're always where you shouldn't be, Grania," she said. "Diana and Helen are helping to clear up the rooms downstairs. You really must be more responsible, like they are."

She waited until Grania had sullenly obeyed her, then she, too, opened the bible. She had found the photograph of Catriona among Kilcaraig's private papers, which duty had compelled her to check through before the lawyers arrived. She had meant to dispose of it immediately, but Marian had come into the room, and not wanting to draw attention to it, she had pushed the picture into the bible as a temporary hiding place.

Catriona had hated being photographed, but she had allowed Ian to try his skill with his new camera. That was during his last leave before the war, the year before Catriona went to Italy, and the whole horrible deception had begun.

She looked at Catriona, smiling that inscrutable smile captured by the camera. Catriona, adored by her family, but copulating in a vineyard, like any peasant woman. And they had all covered up for her. Evelyn remembered vividly the letter she had received in India. "*You will pretend the child is your own. You will realize that this must not happen to a Lamont. I know you can be relied upon to do your duty to the family, to the child.*" It was not a request, it was a command, and Evelyn had despised herself for entering so readily into the conspiracy. It was true what the contemptible, arrogant Catriona had said. She would not allow her husband's family to be disgraced.

She could not know, in those early days, that Catriona's child was going to usurp Ian's love, not only for herself, but for their children.

Ian idolized Grania, as he had idolized his sister. In sudden fury, she tore the picture in half, and had soon reduced it to fragments which she hid in her pocket. She would burn them when she went downstairs. Nobody knew about the photograph. Nobody would know what she had done.

That night, Grania returned to Kilcaraig's room. She had decided to take the picture, and ask Marian afterwards if she might keep it. Perhaps Marian would tell her why she had never been shown it before. Michael had said girls of her age concocted mysteries. Perhaps he was right. But she had opened the bible and found that the picture had gone. Unbelieving, she leafed through the pages. There were some texts, and a sprig of pressed white heather, flimsy and light. Nothing more.

Then she noticed a fragment of cardboard at her feet. It was a tiny piece, but she recognized it. Choking with rage, she picked it up and ran with it to her bedroom. Only Mummy had been in that room.

"I hate her, I hate her, I hate her!" Grania sobbed into her pillow. "I hate her so much."

Evelyn paused outside the door, hearing sobs, uncertain what to do about them. Perhaps she had misjudged Grania. Perhaps the poor child had some feelings after all. Tomorrow she must try to handle her with better understanding. It was what Ian would want. It was her duty to Kilcaraig's memory to do so.

With a renewed sense of obligation, she retired resolutely to bed.

11

Ian Lamont was granted compassionate leave, and he arrived three months after Kilcaraig's funeral. He was now Kilcaraig himself, but he could not think of himself in that way, and neither, obviously, could the people of Kilcaraig, many of whom among the elder ones still addressed him as Ian.

There must have been a time when his father experienced the bewilderment of filling an hereditary position of some importance. He, too, must have had to adapt. He, too, must have been called by his Christian name, yet there came a day when he emerged with all the qualities that the great name of Kilcaraig implied, at least to the people who inhabited the estate.

Like his father, Ian was more comfortable in a kilt than in trousers, he played the pipes and he had not forgotten one word of Gaelic, yet, as he walked over his land with Angus, or talked to the people in their homes, he was conscious of a feeling of inadequacy. Soon he must return to the army, and somehow he must keep Kilcaraig, tumbledown castle and all.

"You look very serious, Daddy." It was Grania, propped up against her bicycle at the end of the mossy drive. He no longer felt at ease with Grania, who had become shy and moody. Catriona, whom she resembled to the point of absurdity, had never been like this. He had tried to gain Grania's confidence, believing that her change of attitude had been brought about by the death of her grandfather, whom she adored, but Evelyn had mocked the suggestion that the child was deeply unhappy. "She's a spoilt brat," she insisted. "The only cure for her is boarding-school."

He realized that Grania was asking a question, not making a statement. He decided suddenly to try a new method of approach.

"I'm feeling very serious," he said. "And very worried, and I wonder if you can help."

Grania let her bicycle slide to the ground. She pushed it off the drive with her foot, and held out her hand to him. "Let's walk and talk away from the house. Out of sight, so's they don't ask us what we've been talking about."

They left the drive and followed a path through the trees.

"I know it's very difficult for you, Daddy, so I'm going to say it for you. You're going to send me to boarding-school, and you're wishing Mr. Dutton would buy the castle for acquisity, and Aunt Marian would marry him, so that we could go on living here."

"Acquisity?" he asked, playing for time.

"It's my name for the sort of money ordinary people like us can't even think about."

"And what makes you think that Mr. Dutton would be prepared to accommodate us all, even if he were married to Marian?" He tried to smile, but he was shaken that Grania had so accurately assessed his shameful thoughts about the part Marian might be expected to play in solving their financial problems.

"He'd do it to please Aunt Marian," Grania said. "Of course it won't happen like that. It's just a day-dream. Even if he were still around, Aunt Marian wouldn't have him."

They walked in silence while he pondered over what she had said. She obviously had no idea that Evelyn and Robert Dutton were still in touch.

"You're right about boarding-school," he said at last, for this was the moment of truth, and she would have to face it. "But you'll come here for your holidays, because it is your home and Marian's for as long as I live. But never, never would I allow a Lamont to be handed over to a new owner of Kilcaraig, as part of the furniture and fittings, not even for acquisity." He glanced down at her. She was giving serious consideration to his words.

"I take your point," she said, sounding like a learned member of a committee, and not like a child at all.

They separated before returning to the house. Grania retrieved her bicycle, so she arrived at the big studded door first, and brushed past Evelyn, who was waiting for her in the hall. Evelyn called to her as she ran upstairs, but by then Ian was on the doorstep, wiping his feet, and hoping to imply that he had been a long way walking on his own.

"Grania is insufferable," Evelyn hissed at him.

He caught at her arm, and led her into the drawing-room, where he hoped to discuss future plans without betraying that he had already made his decision known to Grania. Diana and Helen were sitting by the west window, playing chess and looking bored. Both of them had individually complained to him that while their school friends went to theatres and parties during the holidays, they were always stuck at Kilcaraig.

Evelyn stood by the fire, waiting for him to speak, sensing that this was to be a family consultation, but Ian merely picked the chanter from a pile of music that was lying on the piano, and started to practise some tunes. Exasperated, Evelyn turned on her heel and went in search of Marian, who would almost certainly be in the kitchen, talking in Gaelic to Chrissie and Angus and Willie and cook. But it wasn't Marian she found there, it was Grania, tear-stained but composed, who was telling the servants, in English, that not even for acquisity would her father sell Kilcaraig.

"And during the holidays we'll make up for the lost days when I'm at school," she said. "Then, when I grow up, there'll be an extra pair of hands to help look after things, so we'll manage somehow . . ." She broke off, seeing her mother standing there in the doorway, not looking angry, but hurt, deeply hurt.

Grania realized that she, and even the servants, knew what her father had planned, before he had told his wife. Impulsively, she jumped down from the kitchen table where she had been sitting, and went over to kiss her mother. "I've worked it all out, and now I'm going to tell you and Daddy the way I want it to be."

Evelyn knew it was a lie, and knew that the servants knew it, but to admit so now would stir up resentment and embarrassment, and would enhance the reputation she knew she already possessed of being a hard woman, whose burning jealousy of Grania could only be controlled by her equally burning determination to observe, at all times, her duty towards the child.

And so it was that a new way of life was introduced to Kilcaraig. Ian saw Grania installed at Cambray College with her sisters before he returned, with Evelyn, to India. Marian took over the management of the estate, aided by Angus, who knew more about it than any living soul, and cook and Willie and the people of Kilcaraig settled down to the way of life they had always known.

The rain dripped into the strategically placed bowls in the castle, as it had always done, and in some winds water poured under the window-sills, making it necessary to put towels on the floor to soak up the pools that gathered, menacing the carpets.

Grania's letters from school were not the miserable affairs that Marian had expected, for she enjoyed learning and was proud that she excelled in English, languages, and music. But always there ran through them a theme, a theme of homesickness for Kilcaraig. "I was watching the moon last night, I was thinking it is the same moon that you are seeing at Kilcaraig . . . The daffodils are lovely and make me think of the bright yellow acres of them at Kilcaraig . . . There are lilies now, but they call them narcissus. Kilcaraig must be laden with the scent of them, and I think of them covering Grandpapa's and Aunt Catriona's graves."

At the start of the holidays, she looked prim as she arrived in the ferry-boat, wearing her school uniform, her dark curls somehow kept under control, but in a matter of hours, she reverted to the Grania they had always known, tangled hair, often barefoot, chattering lightly to everyone she knew.

Michael Ames was the person she relied upon most to keep her abreast of what had happened while she was away. His knowledge was not confined to Kilcaraig, for ever since the war there had been constant changes on the island, as newcomers bought crumbling estates, some to settle down and adapt to the special way of life that was Mull, others to depart disenchanted, so that another displenishing sale would take place, and another new inhabitant take over for a while. The islanders themselves were also undergoing change. Of the few who returned from the war, many had found it impossible to scratch a living from the soil, and had found work on the mainland, so that their cottages became deserted, then derelict, and nettles grew where once their gardens had been. Time, too, was taking its toll, and the little Kilcaraig burial ground would soon need to have an adjacent field incorporated into it.

Diana left school and was presented at Court by Evelyn. She wore a beautiful white dress which Marian made for her, using a Vogue paper pattern, and later it was adapted so that it was suitable for the Oban Ball. After that, she and Evelyn went to India for the winter, to join her father, and returned to Mull for the summer, Diana bemoaning the fact that her friends would be enjoying themselves in Kashmir while she had to be content with a few private dances which were a feature of the social life of Mull.

Evelyn, to appease her, gave a dance at the castle, and after a day of furniture removing to clear a space in the drawing-room, Grania leaned over the banisters, and watched the guests arriving, most of them old friends but almost unrecognizable in their formal dress. At thirteen she was deemed to be too young to be at the party, a ruling which she accepted with equanimity, for it was the standard etiquette of the day.

The pattern was repeated when Helen made her debut. This was followed by a wonderful winter, with Ian home on leave and the family bringing in the New Year together. As the grandfather clock in the hall chimed the hour, their glasses were raised to greet the start of a new decade; then they went to the village school, where 1929 was already forgotten in a mist of whisky, bagpipe music and the clatter of dancing feet.

By now, Grania's resemblance to Catriona was so startling that Marian knew, beyond any shadow of doubt, that not a living soul would believe that she was anyone other than Catriona's daughter. The loyalty and good manners of the local people were Grania's safeguard. Never, by word or deed, would they betray the Lamont secret, least of all to Grania herself.

For Marian, the years had passed in contented monotony. Occasionally she went to Edinburgh, seldom to London, and there had appeared tints of grey in her chestnut hair. No man had replaced Andrew Sinclair in her life, nor it seemed ever could, but her friendship with Nicholas Danvers remained constant and secure. He was so much a member of the family, visiting the castle for long periods, even writing his books there, that no breath of gossip was ever uttered about his relationship with Marian. Tucked away in many a mind was the memory of the young doctor who had come to do *locum tenens* for Doctor MacFie, and who had ordered Catriona to London for tests for an obscure illness. An illness that had killed her. And Grania Lamont, whom Nicholas idolized, was the living image of Catriona. They thought their thoughts, but they said nothing, even to one another.

Then one day came a cablegram from India. Ian Lamont was

dead, killed by a sniper's bullet during a skirmish on the North-West frontier of India. Evelyn was at Kilcaraig at the time with Diana and Helen. Grania was in school.

Marian, who had taken the cablegram from the postman, whose face showed that he knew what news it contained, thought first of Grania, far away in England, perhaps playing hockey and looking at the sun and thinking it was the same sun shining at Kilcaraig.

She turned into the house, to break the news to Evelyn. She knew, as sure as if it were written there before her, that now Kilcaraig, the castle, the acres and all they contained, would be put up for sale.

"*Ne parcas, ne spernas.*" The Lamont motto was still readable, engraved on the stone over the front-door. "Neither spare nor dispose."

Evelyn took the cablegram from Marian's hand, as she sank, almost fainting, on to the settle in the hall.

1932

12

Grania eyed the contents of the sink with distaste. The porridge pot had been left to soak, and lumps of porridge had got among the egg-shells and tea leaves in the strainer. There was a horrid glob of something blocking up the drain, so that a greasy pool of water covered the bottom of the sink.

Gingerly, she scraped the mess from the drain and ran the hot-water tap to clear the residue, but, as she had expected, the hot water wasn't hot, and a glance at the boiler showed the reason why. She would have to re-light it, but meanwhile, the dishes must be washed. She put a kettle on the gas, and set about cleaning the kitchen. Then, when the kettle had boiled, she made herself a cup of tea. There was nothing better than tea to cheer the prospect of a load of greasy dishes.

With her saucerless cup placed on the ledge before her, she was soon busy with the dish-mop and the plates. The sink was in the window, so that as she worked she had a splendid view of backyards and of the net curtains that screened the occupants of the houses from view. She supposed that their own house, with its chipped stucco, must look as dreary as the rest, but she hoped that the curtains looked less grimy.

When they had moved to London, the house-agent pointed out the advantages of occupying two top floors, when he recommended the flat in Ladbroke Place. It improved the view, he had told them. He forgot to mention the stairs they must toil up to achieve the aspect of chimneys and cat-walks. He forgot, also, to hint that maisonette was the attractive name for two flats, inconvenient in every respect, and partitioned off as an entity, because he could not hope to induce anyone to take the top flat by itself. The final flight of stairs would be more than a prospective tenant could endure.

The move from Kilcaraig had taken place almost a year ago, during term time, so that Grania had not been there to see the castle stripped of furniture, and the crowds of people tramping over the lawns as the displenishing sale took place. She hadn't asked about that, or read about it in the *Oban Times*. She had closed her mind to the misery of it all from the moment she knew that the estate was to be sold.

When she came to London for the holidays, she had found that some of the familiar furniture had been brought to the maisonette. Her own bed, and her dressing-table and wardrobe had somehow been fitted into the small room which was allotted to her. The fitted carpet, the curtains and the wallpaper were of a kind she had once admired in an advertisement. Evelyn had done her best.

Marian, who had taken a long lease of a flat in Kensington, had furnished it almost entirely from the castle, so that the well-worn carpets covered the floors. Chrissie, too, had come to share her exile, and when Grania visited them, she had moments of believing she was still at home, so thoroughly had the atmosphere of Kilcaraig been transported into the London flat.

When she left school at the end of the Easter term, shortly before her eighteenth birthday, the typing she had taught herself at Kilcaraig made it possible for her to get a job in the Letting Office of a block of flats. She had been working there for three months now, proud of her independence and her pay packet, consisting of three pounds a week, one of which she put aside in her post office account in preparation for the day she dreamed of, when she would buy back Kilcaraig. Evelyn refused to accept payment from her for board and lodging, but Diana and Helen enjoyed the extra hair-dressing sessions, and the make-up they could buy out of her munificence. Generosity came as naturally to Grania as the air she breathed.

She had finished her tea and had almost finished the dishes when Evelyn came into the kitchen.

"How often must I tell you to wear an apron when you do the washing up?" Evelyn said, handing her the checked cotton one, which hung on the back of the door.

"I'm not a messy worker."

"That's nonsense – you're bound to get splashed."

Evelyn glanced swiftly round the room. The dishes were neatly stacked, the cutlery polished and placed on a tray, and the draining-board scrubbed as clean as its discoloured wood could be. "Where's Helen? Why isn't she helping you?"

"She's manicuring her nails and setting her hair for the party tonight. And anyway, it's my turn to do the chores."

"You should be free on Saturdays. You're the only one who works."

Grania fiddled in the sink, hoping that Evelyn would go before she

76

noticed that the boiler had gone out. Cleaning and re-lighting it was something she would prefer to do without an overseer.

"I hope Diana doesn't stay out too long. If Meredith brings her home, we'll have to ask him to stay for tea," Evelyn said.

Diana had talked about her lunch date with Meredith Jones for days. He was a Chartered Accountant who owned a house in Fulham, and a two-seater car. She saw him as the husband of her dreams, a role in which she had cast many who had shown an interest in her. It was her eagerness to be married that invariably drove them away.

"I'll make sandwiches. There's an un-opened packet of short-bread and the remains of a ginger cake in the tin. Diana will have to get rid of him in time to dress for the party." Grania was trying to clean her nails with the scrubbing brush.

Evelyn winced. "You'll ruin your hands," she said, starting to leave the room. She paused at the door. "Mrs. Vandon-Stewart would have invited you to the party if she knew you'd left school. It's not a formal affair – just a buffet supper for a few friends. Would you like to go in my place?"

Grania swung round, horrified. "Mother, you can't inflict three sisters on a hostess! Two are bad enough. Besides, it's good for you to go out sometimes yourself."

Evelyn went back to the sitting-room, and sat at the bureau with the household account book in front of her. She would never admit that she hated going to parties, now that she was a widow. Her self-confidence had deserted her after Ian's death, although she kept up appearances as best she could. Grania was right about the embarrassment of being saddled with three unmarried daughters and no male escort. It was a situation which could make any hostess blench. It was no longer necessary for her to accompany Diana and Helen to parties, but Grania would be on her hands for at least another year. Foolish Grania, who had so resolutely refused the invitations to stay with friends, and go to the Oban Ball.

"I'll never go back to Mull as a visitor. Never, never," she had said with such vehemence that Evelyn had not dared to raise the subject again.

She turned the pages of the account book. Because of the taxes she had to pay, the acquisity which Grania had talked about did not produce as much income as she had expected. After a struggle, she had prevailed upon Marian to accept her share from the sale of the estate, and now Marian was settled in the Kensington flat with Chrissie acting more as a companion than as a servant. Everything had been arranged as Ian would have wished, had he foreseen the absolute necessity of disposing of Kilcaraig.

As Ian would have wished! Her temple throbbed. She had always faced up to the vicissitudes of life with courage, but now she had to resort to self-deception, to excuse herself for acting as she had done.

Her eyes flickered further down the page. The monthly account from St. Clare's Nursing Home at Epsom was a further drain on her resources. She had to subsidize her mother, if she was to remain in the comfort to which she was accustomed, and the move from Bath to Epsom had made it possible for visits from family and friends to be more frequent. The old lady's memory had failed, but her health was perfect. It seemed that she would live for ever. Evelyn pushed back her hair, and held her hand against her throbbing head. It was wicked, it was inconceivable, that she should sit here at her writing bureau wishing her mother dead. But it was true.

Grania, in the kitchen, had re-lit the boiler, and had removed the charred pieces of paper with which it had been choked. She recognized the writing. Helen must have quarrelled with Claud Simons, and had stuffed his letters into the boiler in a fit of pique. Grania hoped she wouldn't regret it. Like Diana, Helen saw marriage as the only escape from the monotony of her life in London, where it was expected that ladies of leisure had the wherewithal to enjoy that leisure.

The water was heating up when Evelyn returned to the kitchen. "I've got a headache," she said. "I've just rung up Mrs. Vandon-Stewart to tell her I can't be there tonight. She asked about you, and I told her you're free."

"No!" Grania exclaimed, her eyes wide with indignation.

"She asked about you," Evelyn repeated. If there were any histrionics from Grania now, she would break down and scream.

The door-bell rang. Grania turned on her heel and went to answer it. It was Diana, who had forgotten her key. Meredith wasn't with her.

"Mother's going to make me go to the party in her place," was Grania's greeting.

Diana pulled off her hat and her gloves. "And why not? She usually ducks out of things at the last minute. It'll make a change for you to be with civilized people, instead of with those young friends of yours, who sit on stools queueing up for cheap seats at the theatre!" She pushed past Grania and went into the kitchen. Evelyn was standing as Grania had left her, staring across the backyards and the chimney pots. "Another headache, Mother? Go and lie down. I'll bring you a couple of aspirins and some eau-de-cologne. Grania, ring Aunt Marian and ask her if she can come round this evening. We don't want to leave Mother alone here, as she's not feeling well."

In appearance, in voice, Diana was like her mother, and Grania automatically obeyed her. As she dialled Marian's number, she heard Evelyn protesting, but going willingly enough to bed.

Grania delivered her message, and added "Aunt Marian, I've never been to a grown-up party. What on earth shall I wear?"

"The navy-blue woollen dress I made you for your birthday. It's a copy of a Molyneux model, I'll have you know!" Marian, as always, sounded cheerful. "I'll come round in time to see you all in your finery. You're a lucky girl. Mrs. Vandon-Stewart is full of American warmth and hospitality. I wish she'd invited me! Go along and enjoy yourself. It'll be a night to remember."

By the time Grania could claim the bathroom, the water was tepid, the floor was swamped, and all the towels were damp. None of the family seemed to be capable of using their allotted towels. She had a quick, cool bath and was rubbing herself vigorously with someone's discarded towel, when she heard Marian arrive. She had forgotten her dressing-gown, so she wrapped herself up in the towel and called to her from the top of the stairs.

"I'll just have a look at the patient," Marian called back, and went to Evelyn's bedroom which was next door to the kitchen.

She found Evelyn sitting up in bed, her long hair let down over her shoulders. She looked pinched and pale, and without make-up, touchingly vulnerable.

Marian sat on the edge of the bed. "Genuine headache, or an excuse to push Grania into high society?" she asked.

"A bit of both. I can't bear the thought of party noises, and Grania's going to have a raw deal, compared with her sisters. I've always been determined that her chances would be the same as the others in every respect."

"Evelyn, *mo chridhe*, you don't have to worry about Grania. She doesn't need chances. She's got it all built in, brains, beauty, and charm."

"That's what Catriona had. And look where it landed her!" She hadn't mentioned Catriona's name for years.

Marian leaned forward and patted her hand. "If you'd accept that Catriona's only fault was loving too recklessly, you'd stop believing that Grania's going to develop into a loose-living little horror."

Evelyn smiled wanly. "I wish I could see people through rose-coloured spectacles, as you do. And I hope that Diana and Helen aren't going to suffer now that Grania is being precipitated into their parties, because if that happens, it'll be all my fault."

"You're determined on martyrdom! We'll talk about your worries when the girls have gone."

She went upstairs to the bedroom which Diana and Helen shared, and did some tidying up for them, as neither of them had been able to make up their minds what to wear, and discarded clothes were lying in heaps all over the floor. Diana had finally chosen a yellow chiffon cocktail dress, which suited her well, creating a Grecian effect because of the way she had pinned up her hair. Helen wore pink crêpe, a little too tight, but Marian didn't comment on that, as it would make her feel self-conscious. Helen was preening in front of the long looking-glass when Grania came into the room.

She was wearing the plain, navy-blue dress, and she had fastened a Celtic cross round her neck. Her make-up was subdued, her dark curls gleaming.

"Do I look like Deirdre of the Sorrows?" she asked.

"You look like Grania of Kilcaraig," Marian said admiringly. "And wouldn't your grandfather be proud of you if he could see you now!"

Diana and Helen were proud of her when they arrived at Mrs. Vandon-Stewart's flat in Bryanston Square. It didn't matter that Grania was wearing a woollen dress and was looking different from the others. She would always look different, because her loveliness was unique.

Mrs. Vandon-Stewart received her with obvious delight. A connoisseur of beauty, she could see in this young girl an asset which would enhance her parties for many years to come.

The room was full of people and flowers and waiters. Evelyn had described this as a small informal party. She must have made a mistake. Grania stared round, awestruck by the magnificence of it all. She had only seen rooms like this in American films, and hadn't thought they could ever be real. Soon she was standing by the open french window, which led onto a small balcony, sipping champagne, and finding it easy to talk to the young men who gathered round her.

A tall, ginger-haired man was leaning against the Adam chimney-piece, listening to Sir Brian Thorn talking about the stock-market. He knew Sir Brian was hoping to get some helpful hints from him, but he wasn't going to give anything away. He seldom went to parties, and so was determined tonight not to mix business with pleasure.

His eyes were fixed on the girl across the room, the girl with the silken, curly hair, large expressive eyes, and the most beautiful face and figure he had ever seen. She must be young, very young. The plain, navy-blue dress displayed her slim body to perfection, and her gestures were as pretty and arresting as a ballerina's.

Sir Brian had stopped talking about the stock exchange. He too looked across the room and said softly to his companion, "Too young for us, more's the pity".

As he said the words, Grania saw the ginger-haired man, and looked at him in hostile recognition. She freed herself from her group of admirers, and walked purposefully up to him.

"I know who you are," she said. "You're Mr. Dutton, who didn't shut the gates. And I'm Grania. Grania Lamont of Kilcaraig. You bought Kilcaraig. You bought my home."

13

Robert Dutton hated Sir Brian for smirking there beside him, and he hated his forty-nine years of life, which must be twice the age of this bewitching girl.

Grania, seeing the expression on his face, hastened to explain herself. "It was most dreadful of me to say that. It isn't true any more, but it's what my grandfather used to call me. I'm truly sorry – you must think I have no manners."

Timidly, she held out her hand. Robert took it in his, and held it, frozen into position, not wanting to let it go.

"You may not believe it, but I understand the way you feel," he said, as his heart raced and hammered within him. *I must have her, I must have her, if it costs me everything I possess.*

Grania, unaware of the profound effect she was having upon him, drew him towards a sofa.

"Tell me about it," she said. "Tell me about Kilcaraig."

He spent the whole evening with her, and when he went to bed that night he tossed and turned.

Grania was scolded all the way home by Diana and Helen, who told her that it was her duty to move around at parties, and not corner the one guest who was known to be a multi-millionaire, who was old enough to be her father and, worst of all, was the owner of Kilcaraig.

"You made a dead set at him. It was so blatant. You're *uncouth*," Diana told her. "We won't say much of this to mother, but there'll be plenty of gossip about it. You've disgraced us all!"

Grania, in her corner of the taxi, let the words wash over her. She felt in her body the first stabbing urgency of desire, not desire for the ginger-haired man, but for the castle and the land and the people he owned. A desire for Kilcaraig. She had never really believed anything could be achieved through her ridiculous post office account, but now that she had met him, Robert Dutton could be the means of fulfilling her dreams.

When they arrived at Ladbroke Place, Marian had gone, but Evelyn was still awake. Grania said primly that she had enjoyed herself, kissed her goodnight, and left her sisters to give whatever account they chose about the party.

In her room, she sat in front of the looking-glass and considered her reflection. Grania Dutton of Kilcaraig. How silly it sounded! She laughed and prepared for bed, unfastening the dress which Marian had made so beautifully and so effectively for her. Marian, who could restore the family link with Kilcaraig, if only she could be prevailed upon to marry Robert Dutton! She snuggled between the sheets, her thoughts leaping ahead to the campaign she must launch with tact and skill. Robert Dutton had asked her where she lived. He would be in touch with her again, and when she had prepared Marian to look upon him favourably, she would effect the introduction which would in time restore her own happiness, and bring security back to them all.

Diana and Helen overslept, and while Evelyn and Grania had breakfast together, little was said about the party. Evelyn had heard all that she wanted to know the night before, and she was no longer interested. After she had helped with the washing-up, she set out for St. Clare's Home at Epsom, for this was the last Sunday of the month, the Sunday on which she visited her mother.

Meredith Jones collected Diana, and said that he was to drive her down to Brighton for the day. When they had gone, Helen appeared and announced casually that she was going to the Criterion to meet Claud Simons for lunch. Afterwards, they were going to a cinema. That reconciliation must have taken place over the telephone while everyone was too busy preparing for the party to notice. She had just banged the front door behind her when Marian telephoned to ask after Evelyn and to find out if Grania had enjoyed herself.

"I had a wonderful time. Mr. Dutton was there. He's mellowed over the years." Grania hadn't meant to blurt it out like that, but she couldn't help herself.

"You mean *our* Mr. Dutton?" Marian said, incredulity carrying over the telephone line.

"Yes, the one who bought Kilcaraig." Grania allowed a silence for the information to sink in.

82

"Tell me about the other people. I don't want to hear anything about *him*."

Grania told her what little she had taken in about the other people. When she rang off, she felt dismally sure that Marian wasn't going to co-operate in her project, which she had thought so feasible as she lay in bed last night.

She looked at the clock. A quarter past twelve. She had a whole day ahead of her with the house to herself. There were letters to write, one to Margaret Erskine, who was her best friend and was still at school, and one to her pen-friend Marie-Claire, who lived in Paris. This correspondence had been inaugurated years ago by Marian, and Grania had learnt more French from it than she had absorbed in any other way. Some day she would go to Paris and she would meet Marie-Claire. Some day she would travel and see the world.

She put her writing materials on the bureau, on top of the fat book containing the household accounts, then she hauled her portable gramophone from the wall cupboard. It was covered in red rexine and had been a present from her father for her fifteenth birthday.

Some of her records had been put away carelessly without their paper covers. There was a chip out of *You Are My Heart's Delight*, sung by Richard Tauber. It didn't matter, for the record was worn thin from being played so often. She snapped it in half and put it in the wastepaper basket. Damaged records weren't worth keeping, but this one must be replaced.

On the left of the cupboard were the records she only listened to when she was alone. Classical records, especially opera. She chose carefully the few she wanted, then she made herself scrambled eggs for lunch. She was eating it in the sitting-room when the door-bell rang. She opened the door, and took a step back into the flat, shocked because she had no make-up on, and was wearing an old pullover, an even older skirt, and a pair of well-worn bedroom slippers.

"Mr. Dutton!"

"I should have telephoned," he said. "I happened to be passing. I'm afraid I've come at a most inconvenient time." The plate of half-eaten scrambled egg was clearly visible on the arm of her chair in the sitting-room.

"Please come in. I'm having an early lunch. I'll make you some – it won't take a minute." She was the smiling, unruffled hostess she had been brought up to be, showing no sign of the mortification she felt.

She settled Robert Dutton in an arm-chair by the fire, and gave him a newspaper. Then she removed her plate and ate the remains of her lunch in the kitchen while she prepared some for him.

Robert could hear her moving about as he pretended to read. He had never for a moment expected to find her alone, for he had chosen to call at a time when Evelyn Lamont used to expect friends to drop in for a pre-lunch drink when she was in India. He had meant to make his meeting with her three daughters his excuse for renewing his acquaintance with her, for their friendship had petered out after his abortive attempt to buy Kilcaraig. She had, however, remembered him, and her lawyers had contacted him when it genuinely came up for sale several years later after Ian's death.

He had said nothing about that to Grania last night. He had been very careful about what he had said to her, but he had discovered from her questions how little he knew about the people of Kilcaraig, who had received him with a deadly courtesy that only thinly disguised their contempt.

Grania had looked young last night. Today she looked like a child, and he was a dirty old man to be coveting her in the way that he did. He had won Kilcaraig because he was prepared to play a waiting game, but now time was against him, and nothing could alter the gulf that separated him from her – over thirty unbridgeable years.

When she returned to the room, she carried a laden tray. He took it from her and held it while she opened the flap of a table, and pushed it close to the chair where he had been sitting. She had set the tray with a white linen cloth, and the heavy silver tableware bore the Kilcaraig crest. Besides the scrambled eggs, there were biscuits and cheese, and what looked like a treble whisky. She handed him a napkin, then knelt on the hearthrug in front of the fire.

"My sisters say I monopolized you last night," she said. "They say people should move around at parties. I didn't know that. I'm not yet officially Out."

"Lucy Vandon-Stewart never makes people circulate. That's why her parties are so agreeable. I liked being monopolized." He smiled at her. He had a very attractive smile. "What sort of parties do you usually go to?"

"A few of us eat in Soho, or in Lyons Corner House. We set the world to rights over coffee."

"I expect you do that more effectively than I do in boardroom meetings."

"You couldn't always have been old enough to be on a board. What did you do when you were young, Mr. Dutton?"

It must be difficult for her to imagine that he had ever been her age. He could scarcely believe it himself.

"My father was the youngest of three sons. He and his eldest brother worked in an engineering firm which had been established

84

by my grandfather in Manchester. I went to the Grammar School there, and won a scholarship to Oxford. I came out with a First, and wanted to study law, but my father persuaded me to go into the firm. By then, his eldest brother was the Managing Director, and had sent his three sons to Harrow, which gave me a mighty chip on the shoulder."

"You've overcome it very conspicuously!"

"I overcame it because of the war. By the time that was over, my mother and my two sisters were dead, wiped out by the Spanish flu epidemic that swept the country. Two of my cousins had been killed in action, and the third one died of wounds shortly after the Armistice. I was trapped into taking their place in the firm from which I had hoped to escape."

"What happened to your other uncle?"

He was surprised that she had listened so attentively.

"He was a farmer. Not the sort that you find on Mull! He specialized in growing potatoes and in producing eggs. The war proved to be a bonanza for him. He never married, and he died young."

"So you acquired his bonanza?"

"I sold the farm for a considerable profit, if that's what you mean." He had finished the scrambled eggs. She removed the plate and took it to the kitchen; then she returned to her place on the rug.

"I've often wondered how people make millions. I suppose it's a mixture of hard work and luck." She considered this for a while, her head tilted slightly, so that the flames from the fire played on her cheek. "What happened to your father?"

"He left the firm, and later remarried. I never cared for his second wife and lost touch with her after he died. That's my life history. What about yours?"

"You know mine. Yours is a success story. Mine's a tragedy." She sounded as if she meant it.

"People don't have tragedies at eighteen."

"People have tragedies much younger than that." She was thinking of her father's death, and of her mother's relentless determination to tear her from Kilcaraig. But it was not a subject she wanted to pursue. "Tell me about Michael Ames. I write to him through his mother, but he never has much to say about himself."

"His parents called on me soon after I arrived. I've not been at Kilcaraig very much, you know. There were things that had to be done . . ." The roof had been repaired and the granite walls re-pointed. The castle had been covered in scaffolding for months, but it was better that she shouldn't know that.

"You must have met Michael," she persisted.

"I went up there once. I'm afraid I'm not much good with handicapped people. It's difficult to talk naturally to a blind man."

"Michael sees right into people. He reads their minds!"

"Then it's just as well I've given him a wide berth!" He saw that she was not amused, and decided that he should change the subject. "Were you going to have a record recital?" he asked, indicating her gramophone.

"I adore opera," she said eagerly. "I expect you've been to Covent Garden and La Scala, and have heard people like Flagstad sing!" He had, and he had been infinitely bored. He did not tell her so. "Play me something," he said.

She wound up the gramophone, inserted a new needle, and after some initial hissing, the intermezzo from *Cavalleria Rusticana* filled the room.

"It's not my favourite. It was on the top of the pile," she said when it was over.

"What is your favourite?"

"I haven't got one. I've seen several operas at Sadlers Wells." She wound up the gramophone again. This time it was Gigli, singing *On With the Motley*. "I've got a friend who's a law student, and he's educating me. He knows a tremendous lot, and he often takes me in quite expensive seats."

"I expect you have lots of friends." Anger, jealousy, mounted in Robert.

"Quite a few, but they're mostly undergraduates, and they're only around during their vacations. Adrian Ferguson's different. He's around all the time."

"Is he special?"

"Oh yes, very special. We have lots in common. Now I'll get rid of the dishes while you listen to Melba singing *Caro Nome*. It's a bit scratchy, but she has such a pure and wonderful voice. She's like a choir boy."

Robert listened to *Caro Nome*, which had finished before Grania rejoined him. The automatic switch didn't work, so he had to let the record hiss on and on until he discovered the way to stop it by hand.

He had heard all her records, and she made him tea before he got up to go. At the front door, he held her gently by the shoulders. "I don't know when I've had such a happy afternoon."

"I hope I haven't bored you, Mr. Dutton."

"Robert. Can you bring yourself to call me Robert?"

"I'd like that, Robert. I call Nicholas Danvers 'Nicholas' now, instead of Uncle, and he's every bit as old as you!" She smiled enchantingly. He ached to take her in his arms, but he must not frighten her away.

"There'll be a taxi on the rank," she called to him as he descended the stairs, then she went to the sitting-room and leaned out of the window. His car and his chauffeur were waiting for him. She might have known that he never moved without his latest Daimler.

Half exultant, half afraid, she made up the fire, and tried to think what she would say about her visitor when the family came home. She decided to admit that she had given him a drink, nothing more.

On the following morning, twelve red roses were delivered to the maisonette. Grania was at work, and they were waiting for her when she got home.

"You seem to have made an impression," Evelyn said, while Diana and Helen teased her about her conquest. Two days later he telephoned her at the office and asked her out to lunch.

"I only have an hour," she said.

"That's all right. I know about punctuality. I'll see that we're served at once."

He took her to an exclusive restaurant, one of which she had never heard, and he returned her to her office five minutes before she was due back. When he parted from her, he kissed her on the cheek and asked if he could collect her again, on the following day. She refused, pleading a previous engagement. This onslaught was something she had not expected, and she had to think of some way in which to deal with it.

She telephoned Marian, who had been strangely silent for the last few days. She would have heard about Robert Dutton, and would be registering her disapproval by keeping off the telephone, and away from Ladbroke Place.

"Marian, may I bring him round to you for drinks? Try to make Nicholas come too. I want you both to meet him. He's really very nice, so long as one tries to forget that he owns Kilcaraig."

"You know very well that you wouldn't look at him twice, if he didn't own Kilcaraig!" Marian said. "Keep your flirtations for boys of your own age, and remember that a human heart beats in that gold-plated breast!" But she issued the invitations, and on the following Sunday, one week after Robert Dutton had rung the door bell of the maisonette, he was in Marian's flat, immaculate, suave, impressing Nicholas with his knowledge of what was happening in the world, but at the same time keeping the conversation light enough to be entertaining for Grania, who was watching with the analytical eye of a skilful stage director.

The first hurdle had been cleared. Marian had accepted Robert, in spite of the acquisity that had deprived her of her home, but she showed no sign that she was prepared to be conquered by him, and Robert showed nothing more than a polite interest in Marian.

By Christmas, Grania had been to dinner and to the theatre several times with him, and Evelyn had given up protesting about the wholly unsuitable friendship. Diana was giving trouble, indignant because Meredith had stopped asking her out; moreover, he had been seen at the Café Royal with another girl, an incident reported to her by Helen, who had slipped into a prolonged courtship with Claud Simons.

"There's nothing I can do about any of them!" Evelyn told Marian, who was spending the evening with her. "Robert Dutton is going to take them all to the Chelsea Arts Ball. Not only Grania, but her sisters as well, will get it into their heads that all the best things in life can be bought by this gold-plated Santa Claus!"

"Grania's too young to understand that men of that age aren't to be trifled with," Marian said.

"Grania's not so young that she doesn't realize the conquest she's made and what she's going to get out of it!" Evelyn retorted.

Grania, sitting with Robert in his Daimler, watched the lights of the Haymarket flicker past as they were driven away from His Majesty's Theatre. She was holding Robert's hand. Last night, for the first time, he had kissed her on the lips, and she had recoiled, for she had never been kissed in such a way before. Robert, recognizing her inexperience, hadn't tried to kiss her again, but now, with the thrill of the performance and the applause of the audience still ringing in her ears, she knew he must be tensed up, as she was, and the glass partition which separated them from the chauffeur was no protection against an amorous assault.

"Grania, do you like me?" he asked after a while.

"Yes. Yes, you know that I do."

"Because of me, or because of Kilcaraig?"

She hadn't expected such a direct question, but it was useless to dissemble. "First because of Kilcaraig. But you come a very close second." She was astonished. Although she would never claim to love him, it was true. She liked him very much.

His hand was on her jaw, then his fingers fondled her lips. By the time they reached Ladbroke Place, they were both sitting far apart in their separate corners, but Grania's theatre programme had been crumpled into a ball.

Evelyn and Marian were at the sitting-room window, watching out for them.

"Cinderella in her coach. The spell will break at midnight," Marian said as the Daimler drew up at the kerb.

Evelyn sighed. "Or at some time or other. God help them! God help us all!"

They heard Grania's key in the door.

"Robert will run you home, Marian," Grania said. A few weeks ago, she would have thought it a splendid ruse to get Marian and Robert together. Now it could be too late.

Robert refused the drink that Evelyn offered him, and he and Marian went out into the night.

"Was it a good play?" Evelyn asked, indicating the mangled programme.

"Anny Ahlers in *The Dubarry*. She's the most gorgeous red-head I've ever seen, and she sings so beautifully." Grania sang a few bars of Millocker's *I Give My Heart*.

Evelyn, who was unmusical, was satisfied. Grania was mesmerized by music, and this would account for the state to which she had reduced her programme.

Grania, in bed, could not get the words of that song out of her head.

She gave her heart all right, but not to one man. She gave her heart to Kilcaraig, but in order to win it for herself, there was a price that she would have to pay. Was it worth it?

At last she fell into a fitful sleep. When she awoke to the sight of clouds over the chimney pots, she had made up her mind.

She could not endure being mauled about by a man who was old enough to be her father. Not even when the prize was Kilcaraig.

14

When Chrissie heard that Mr. Dutton was courting Grania Lamont, she was at first disbelieving, then raging. She raged so much that it had to be in Gaelic, for, as Marian pointed out, flats in London are not entirely soundproof, and the neighbours would be calling the police if such invective in English were to penetrate their ears.

"Him an old man, and her just a child," Chrissie said, as she had done, over and over again. "It would be dreadful if it were you, Miss Marian, though you're a more suitable age. But Grania!"

Marian left her to keen, knowing that there would come a time when Chrissie would bow to the inevitable, just as she herself had been compelled to do. Grania had made up her mind to marry Robert from the first moment she saw him at the party – Marian was sure of it. She might have made up her mind years ago, and needed only the opportunity of meeting him again to put her plans into action.

Evelyn had often confessed that she found Grania difficult to handle. She seemed to be such an extrovert personality, yet underneath, there were unfathomable depths. Marian realized that Evelyn had good reason to assess Grania more objectively than she would assess Diana and Helen. The circumstances by which she had acquired Grania excused her for her apprehensiveness over the way she would shape her life. Ian and Evelyn had hoped for a boy, an heir. They had got a girl who had proved to be a living reminder of the woman who had established this cuckoo in their nest.

Her thoughts worried her. Marian had always loved Grania so dearly, loved her as if she were her own, as if she were more than her own, for she was Catriona's. Now that Grania was relentlessly heading for marriage with Robert, Marian recognized that she herself was in the grip of a whole host of conflicting emotions, for whereas she had originally written off Robert as a boorish young man not worth a second thought, now he had emerged as a man of culture, and of a considerable degree of charm. Her sort of man. Ashamed, she tried to banish the thought. Her sort of man, and Grania was bringing him to dinner tonight.

She went to the kitchen, where Chrissie was sullenly peeling potatoes and murmuring that she never thought she would see the day when a Lamont would marry for money.

"They aren't even engaged yet," Marian pointed out. "And perhaps we're all making fools of ourselves, and he's just being nice to Grania while he looks around for someone else."

"*Tuigidh bean bean eile,*" retorted Chrissie, and translated it, as if Marian did not already know it. "One woman understands another." And she added – "And we both understand what that silly child is doing."

The silly child was, at that moment, explaining to Evelyn that she and Robert Dutton were dining with Aunt Marian tonight. "It makes a change from restaurants," she said.

90

"And gives your poor aunt a nightmare of a meal to prepare. It's most thoughtless of you."

"I thought it would be more homey . . ."

"You never thought of asking him to come here for a nice, quiet homey evening with us.'

Evelyn had not found out about Robert eating scrambled eggs beside the fire. Her small, informal dinner parties were beautifully produced and served in the corner of the sitting-room that was set apart as the dining area, but Grania could not think of Robert sitting at the table, while Diana and Helen exchanged meaningful looks and conversation froze on their lips.

"I want him to hear Aunt Marian's Prokofiev records. You don't like modern music yourself."

"Nor, I am sure, does Robert Dutton, but he'll put up with anything to please you! If Marian had any sense, instead of encouraging you, she'd be thinking of him for herself."

"That's what I intended," Grania said angrily, unaware that she had used the past tense.

During the last two weeks, Robert had been in Zurich, and she had not seen him since he had smothered her with his kisses in the car. That her revulsion had been accompanied by an almost over-whelming physical delight was a revelation she could only think about with shame. She pushed it to the back of her mind, along with the other unacceptable experiences of her life.

Evelyn picked up her embroidery and sat on the Chippendale chair by the bureau. The rose-coloured threads she was using were bunched together on her lap. Grania, watching her, had the im-pression that she had lived through this moment before. That bureau, that chair, a photograph of a woman holding a rose in her hand.

"There was a photograph of Catriona Lamont in grandfather's bible," she said. "I found it on the day of his funeral. Why did you destroy it?"

The question surprised her as much as it surprised Evelyn, who looked up, colour flooding into her cheeks.

"I don't know what you're talking about."

"Yes you do. You tore it to pieces because you didn't want me to see it. But you were too late. I know how much I look like her, and I know the reason why. She was my mother."

In an instant, Evelyn was on her feet, and had slapped Grania across the face. Grania reeled back, and Evelyn slapped her again.

"How long have you known? And who told you? Not Marian, who gave up everything for Catriona and for you. Not Chrissie, surely. You were always prying into things – those diaries in the attics – the contents of your dead grandfather's room!" She broke off, trying to control herself, but the sight of Grania standing there with scarlet weals on her pale cheeks goaded her on. "Ian and I had to struggle to keep up the deception that was forced upon us. It nearly wrecked our marriage, you were so much more important to him than the girls or me! There – now you know it all! I was sworn to secrecy, and I would never have told you – never. And I didn't tell you. It was you who told me."

She sank onto the sofa. Her embroidery had slipped onto the floor. Grania picked it up and handed it to her, a small, automatic action which reduced the heat of the moment.

She stood in front of Evelyn. "I'm sorry – I shouldn't have said anything. It's so pointless, after all these years." Her voice was shaking so that she could hardly speak. "Nobody told me. And I never read the diaries – they were written before it all happened anyway. Call it instinct. I just guessed."

Helen was moving about in the room above. She had been washing her hair and would be coming down to dry it by the fire.

"If you were only guessing, then it was I who told you!" Evelyn said. "I'll never forgive myself. Marian will discover what I've done."

"I'd rather be sure than indulge in fantasies." This wasn't true, but she would have to think about that later. "There's no need for you to worry. It's in my own interest to keep this to myself."

Evelyn's bowed head filled Grania with pity. She felt that it was she herself who had provoked this degrading scene. But there was one more question to ask.

"Who is my father? Obviously he wasn't Daddy, I mean Ian, because Catriona was his sister."

Evelyn shook her head. "I don't know."

"You must have some idea."

There was the smallest hesitation before Evelyn repeated, "I don't know."

"Nicholas?"

The same shake of the head.

Grania went to the kitchen, splashed some cold water on her forehead and on her burning cheeks, and then she switched on the electric kettle. While she waited for it to boil, she set the tray. She heard Helen thumping downstairs, but Helen wasn't sensitive to atmosphere, and her presence would be useful during the next half-hour. The crisis was over, and somehow she and Evelyn must behave as if it had never occurred, if they were to continue to live

92

together under the same roof. She had to steady herself before she returned to the sitting-room with the tea.

"A cup of comfort." She pushed open the flap of the small table with her foot, and put down the tray. Evelyn was working at her embroidery, a pink rose developing as she stitched, a scene of domestic harmony, Grania thought wryly as she poured out the tea.

When Helen had gone back to her room to set her hair, Grania risked making a final reference to that harrowing episode. "Please let's have no apologies or explanations or reconciliations," she said. "There's just one thing I want to say. Thank you for all you've done for me all these years. I think my mother would want me to say that, too."

Tears welled into Evelyn's eyes. The words *thank you* had been like a voice from the grave, and she knew in her heart that she deserved them.

"Go and have your bath," she said briskly. "The water's hot and I want you to be ready to go the minute Robert Dutton comes to fetch you. We haven't any whisky in the house."

"I think he can live without it for half an hour!"

"And Grania, don't let anything that has happened this evening make you do something you may regret later."

Grania was ready when the door-bell rang. She was wearing a scarlet dress, and the defiant colour gave her an air of resolution. She kissed Evelyn quickly, and said "Goodbye, Mummy" quite naturally, then Evelyn heard her say to Robert – "We can't have you in for a drink because there isn't any whisky." The door banged. It was easy to see why the hard-headed businessman was captivated by Grania; her frankness must be a refreshing change for Robert Dutton, golden target of so many well-aimed darts.

There was plenty of whisky in Marian's flat, but Robert refused it and won reluctant approval from Chrissie, who noted the glass of sherry in his hand when she announced that dinner was ready.

They dined, just the three of them, because Grania had stressed that this was to be a musical evening. The only suitable man to make up a foursome was Nicholas, who could not be produced every time a man was needed about the place.

Robert noticed again the silver bearing the Kilcaraig crest. When the family had chosen what they wanted from the castle, they must have divided things very fairly between them. He recognized much of the furniture that he had seen in the dining-room at Kilcaraig eight years ago. The dining-room table was still at the castle, too large to be moved anywhere else, and too valuable to be put into the displenishing sale which he had held shortly after the deeds of the estate were safely in his hands.

"Grania, your coot is in the attic," he said when they had reached the stage of biscuits and cheese.

"I'm offended. It had a place of honour in the dining-room!"

"I only found it recently. It must have been forgotten when the junk you left behind was put up for auction."

"Are you suggesting that the castle was furnished with junk!" Grania's eyes wandered round the room. The grandfather clock, the Chinese screen, the cupboard in the corner that the dealers had implored them to sell. Then she laughed, remembering the chairs with broken springs, and the sofa which had lost a leg and had to be propped up with a copy of *Debrett*. "I suppose you have a point! But I want my coot back where it belongs, even if it looks out of place with all that furniture you bought at Maples and Harrods."

"I'm sure you have made Kilcaraig look very beautiful," Marian said. Grania had scarcely touched her wine, but all the evening her eyes had been bright and her cheeks unusually pink. "Grania's very conservative. She hates change even more than I do. But I expect you understand that – you've been seeing her quite a lot."

Robert looked at Grania across the table. She nodded in reply to his silent question, then she kept her eyes downcast, fixed on her empty plate.

"Grania's going to marry me," Robert said. "I asked her when we were on our way here, and we thought we'd keep it to ourselves for a few days, but obviously it's not going to be possible . . ."

Marian had jumped up and was embracing Grania, and congratulating Robert, while tears streamed down her cheeks.

"I thought there was something unusual about Grania. I should have guessed, after knowing her all her life. There's a bottle of champagne in the larder, left over from Christmas. I must tell Chrissie. And please telephone Evelyn, or she'll be very hurt. I hope it'll be all right, Grania. You're terribly young. What if she won't give her consent?"

"She'll give it all right," Grania said with an emphasis which hid a tiny element of doubt. *Grania, don't let anything that has happened this evening make you do something you may regret later.*

Robert went to the telephone, while Marian broke the news to Chrissie, and searched in the refrigerator for the ice cubes.

There were no Prokofiev records played in Marian's flat that night. Instead, there was a Kilcaraig style of celebration, with Chrissie singing Gaelic songs and Robert's chauffeur joining in the chorus. He had been sent to collect the Lamont family from Ladbroke

Place, and he had brought Meredith Jones too, because he happened to be there at the time. He had also called at Robert Dutton's flat in Albany for a crate of champagne.

Evelyn Lamont showed just the right degree of parental concern as she asked Robert the few questions she felt she should ask, and bestowed kisses upon Grania and Marian, whose face still showed the stain of tears.

During the evening, fragments of conversation indicated that the weeks ahead would be too full for Evelyn or Grania to concentrate on anything which did not concern the wedding – when it was to be and where; the number of guests, and should grandmother be brought from Epsom for the occasion – the questions and suggestions whirled round Evelyn, like the smoke from the cigarettes and the bubbles from the champagne.

As the clock struck midnight, Robert turned to Grania. "Yesterday you promised to marry me, Grania, Future of Kilcaraig," he said and kissed her on the lips.

Everyone laughed, and everyone cheered, and somebody opened another bottle of champagne.

"The comedy has started!" Grania told herself, with a deep sense of foreboding, and of subterfuge and shame.

15

The sun did not shine on Grania's wedding day. Not that it mattered, because there would be awnings and carpets at the church, and cameramen could take photographs even if there was a fog.

She stared across the chimney pots as Marian fastened the multitude of tiny buttons at the back of her dress. She was using Evelyn's bedroom because her own was too small, and Evelyn had changed early into the lilac-coloured dress and the pretty hat that had such a softening effect upon her face. Robert's chauffeur was driving her to Epsom, so that she could fetch her mother and take her to the church.

Grania thought about Kilcaraig, where the willows would be covered in catkins, and the daffodils in bloom. Springtime was lovely there, but she had always pictured herself being married in autumn, with berries and bronzed leaves decorating the little church.

The bridegroom would have black hair and would be wearing the kilt, and after the ceremony, the bride and groom would be piped all the way to the castle by Angus and Willie, and the people would follow in procession.

"You're a long way away," Marian observed.

"Yes. I'm getting married in Kilcaraig."

"Just as you should have done. I can't think on earth why you chose a London wedding, and in an English church too!"

Grania smiled. "Can you imagine Robert being married anywhere else, unless it was in a registry office! He'd set his heart on St. Margaret's, and besides, there are so many guests."

The number of invitations that had had to be sent had dismayed Evelyn, as it had dismayed many a bride's mother before her. It seemed impossible that people who lived as quietly as she and her daughters did could have so many friends. When Robert handed her his own guest-list, the sight of it had broken her resolution not to allow him to pay for the reception, as he had offered to do. She had to pocket her pride and tell him that she would accept his help.

"The people who mean most to you aren't here," Marian said, handing Grania her head-dress. She was thinking of the farmers, the crofters, the cotters who lived at Kilcaraig, and could not be expected to make the journey to London. A few had come, the MacPhails, the postmaster, the minister's wife, and cook, who worked in Edinburgh now. Other friends had come from Mull, but not Michael Ames, who Grania would particularly have wanted to be there,

"It's going to be a motley congregation," Grania said. "Robert's friends, who are captains of industry, and have never set eyes on a stag, except in a Landseer painting – and ours, who are happier in country clothes than in morning dress."

"You'll have to learn not to despise Robert's friends," Marian said quietly. During the crowded weeks of preparation for the wedding, she had been unable to issue the advice and warnings she would like to have given to Grania. Evelyn, busy making so many arrangements, had left it to Marian to take care of the bride, and this she had done in a practical way, helping to choose the trousseau and the wedding dress. She had not been able to discover what Grania really felt about Robert, or if she had grasped what it would be like to be mistress of Kilcaraig in such changed circumstances. It was too late to speak of that now. Instead, she said, "Now you may see what you look like."

She pulled away the dressing gown which she had draped over the cheval mirror, and Grania gasped with pleasure at the sight of herself.

Her white satin dress, cut on princess lines, had been designed to emphasise the smallness of her waist. The neck line was high, and the long sleeves were buttoned at the wrist with little satin buttons, the same as those on the back of the bodice. The full skirt formed a train, which was exquisitely embroidered with pearls and diamanté, and lined with tiny frills of lace. The tulle veil flowed from the pearl, diamanté and orange-blossom head-dress down to the tip of the train.

"It won't date," Grania said, studying herself. "I won't look silly when my grandchildren see photographs of my wedding." Her grandchildren. First there must be children, Robert's children.

Marian wiped her eyes. The sight of that lovely young bride had reduced her to the tears which she had struggled against all day. "Don't forget to put on your pearls," she said.

Robert's present to Grania had been a triple row of pearls. "Too large to be real," Helen had commented, but they were real all right, and Grania fastened them round her neck, regretting that she must wear them, for she would have preferred the simple, platinum cross given to her by Evelyn for her birthday several years ago.

"I'm ready," Grania said, casting a last, lingering look at her reflection. She picked up her train with the elegance of an Edwardian who was accustomed to handling such things, and the lace frills frothed across the white satin as she crossed the hall to the sitting-room.

Diana and Helen, in their bridesmaids' dresses of pale pink lace, were waiting there with Chrissie, who had helped them to dress. Clever make-up had masked their mousy colouring and because of their radiance they were pretty. Chrissie, wearing a bright blue dress and an almost-matching hat, was putting the final touches to their short, pink veils when Grania entered the room. She stopped what she was doing and greeted Grania in a flow of Gaelic, for in a moment of high tension she reverted to her native tongue.

"Translate that!" Nicholas turned away from the window. Grania had been too much absorbed in the business of dressing to hear his arrival at the house. He looked strangely unfamiliar in his morning dress, with his hair sleek and smooth, not pushed back and shaggy, as it usually tended to be.

"She says I'm pretty," Grania smiled.

"You've abbreviated it a little, I think!" Nicholas took her by the hand. "I feel so honoured, acting as your father today." He saw her wet her lips nervously and suck in her cheeks. Brides tended to cry on their wedding days, and Grania would be missing Ian Lamont, who had loved her so much during his short life.

"What I feel about her can't be said in English. It's not an expressive language at all," Chrissie said, and then continued to pour out her admiration upon Grania.

It was Marian who managed to stop her. She placed her hand on Chrissie's shoulder and addressed Grania. "When I gave you that dull travelling rug I told you that your real wedding present from me would follow later. Well, I'm giving it to you now." She gave Chrissie a little push forward. "I'm giving you Chrissie as your very willing caretaker, for you've never really grown up, and you'll need her for many years to come."

"Chrissie!" Now there was no holding back the tears. Grania was in Chrissie's arms, whispering words of affection in Gaelic.

Nicholas gently pulled them apart, and Diana, remembering her role as chief bridesmaid, handed Grania a powder compact. "We don't want a blotchy bride," she said, sounding just like her mother.

Chrissie straightened her hat. "I've got my passport and everything," she said. "Mr. Dutton has fixed it all up, but I won't be setting off on your honeymoon with you – you'll need a wee bit of time together before I join you. Now, *mo chridhe*, I'm going off to the church – the taxi will be waiting. Mrs. Lamont needs me there to look after her mother, who won't be able to take in much of what's happening, the poor soul." She carried out a quick, final inspection of the bridesmaids, kissed Grania and gave her a little, reassuring pat, and then she went.

Marian and Nicholas made desultory conversation, restlessly looking one moment at the clock, then out of the window, to see if the cars had arrived. Diana and Helen spoke in undertones to Grania, both of them awed by her, and Diana envious as well.

"It was awfully decent of Robert to have Meredith and Claud as ushers," she said. "It'll be such a relief to have some younger men at the Café de Paris tonight."

"I think you'll find several young ushers," Grania said, embarrassed by the implication that all Robert's friends were old.

"Then perhaps I'll meet someone new," Diana said hopefully. "I don't think Meredith will ever come up to scratch!"

Marian asked Helen to fetch the bouquets, which had been left in the coolness of the kitchen. By the time this was done, the cars had arrived, and Marian had put on the green hat she had made for herself. It looked like an Aage Thaarup model, for she had discovered that she had a flair for millinery. She whispered a few words of love and encouragement to Grania, then she herded the bridesmaids down the stairs.

Nicholas drew a watch from his waistcoat pocket. "We'll give them ten minutes to get ahead of us," he said.

"Yes." Grania was fiddling with the spray of moss roses and lily-of-the-valley which Diana had handed to her. Nicholas had placed roses and lily-of-the-valley on the shrouded body of Catriona as she lay in that room in St. John's Wood. At the moment, Grania looked almost as deathly pale as Catriona had done then.

"Would you like a tot of brandy?" he asked.

She shook her head. On countless occasions she had tried to find the courage to ask him the question which surely must be answered some day. Never had her need been so urgent as now, and she had been rehearsing all morning what she would say. "Are you giving me away because you are a special friend, or because you are my father?" Now, faced with him, she knew it was impossible. Instead, she said "You don't look like a famous author. The crowds will be dreadfully disappointed!"

"I'll mess up my hair and loosen my tie as we come out of the church," he said, wanting to make her smile. "Meantime, I think you'll find the crowds will only have eyes for you." Catriona's daughter, and all he could do was talk rubbish to her, when surely there must be questions he could have answered, advice he could have given. He had always found her a little reserved, not with other people, but with him.

Grania turned to the door. "I think we should go. Robert is so scrupulously punctual. I can't keep him waiting."

Nicholas offered her his arm. *For God's sake, don't arrive late,* Robert had said to him. *I'll think she isn't coming, I'll think the dream I'm dreaming isn't true after all.* It had been a touching and unexpected outburst, coming from a man who was always so precise and unruffled, and whose brain controlled the empire of Carnsworth, Prior and Dutton, which circled the globe.

Grania hadn't expected such a large crowd to have gathered outside the church. There were murmurs of admiration and approval as Nicholas helped her out of the car, and a group of people somewhere began to applaud.

She greeted the two friends from her office, and Margaret Erskine and Alison MacLean, who had come from Scotland to join her retinue. Diana re-arranged her train, and Helen put the final touches to her veil. Then the organist stopped improvising and burst into Wagner's bridal march. Grania placed her hand on Nicholas's arm, and was half way up the aisle before she saw Robert.

She had not realized how ginger-haired he looked, or how bald. She would look silly when she reached him and stood up there beside him at the altar. It wasn't too late, even now, to turn back.

"Dearly beloved, we are gathered together here in the sight of

God . . ." In the sight of God. She had read it so carefully, but now it was real and terrifying. Perhaps it was perjury to promise the things she was about to say. She could see Evelyn from the corner of her eye, and Evelyn's mother, asleep. And Marian. Marian looking lovely in green. So elegant.

". . . for the mutual society, help and comfort that one ought to have for the other, both in prosperity and in adversity . . ."

Yes, she could be Robert's comfort. She couldn't love him, but she could help and comfort him.

She made her vows in a clear, cool voice that betrayed nothing of her fears . . . "and thereto I give thee my troth." ("Please God, I mean it. I am going to be a good wife.") The ring was on her finger. They were declared man and wife, and the choir led the singing of a hymn about love.

Everyone was laughing in the vestry when they signed the register. Grania tried to laugh too, but she felt solemn, very solemn. She had made a very earnest private dedication of herself to Robert. She felt as if she were a nun, wedded to the church, instead of being a woman with a new name and a fabulous amount of money. Kilcaraig. At what price?

There was the Mendelssohn Wedding March, and rose petals, and photographs, and afterwards champagne and a four-tier wedding-cake, with hundreds of people kissing and complimenting her, all in a dizzy whirl. She felt she had no part in it herself. It was happening in a fast-moving film, and she was watching from a remote seat at the back of the auditorium.

At last she came to the time she had dreaded. She was alone with Robert in the new Rolls Royce, on their way to Hendon airport, where a chartered plane awaited them to take them to Paris on the first stage of their honeymoon.

"I hope you won't get air-sick," Robert said in a matter-of-fact voice, settling himself in the corner of the seat.

"I don't know. I've never flown before."

"I have some barley-sugar in my pocket if you do."

"How very thoughtful of you. I'm sure I'll be all right."

Robert turned and smiled at her. "Why are you so subdued? Are you regretting that you've become Mrs. Robert Dutton?"

"For goodness sake, don't get silly ideas about me already," she said, blushing deeply.

"I'm jealous. I don't say much, but I brood over things."

"There's nothing about me that can make you jealous yet," she said. She wished she had left out the "yet". It sounded all wrong.

A 52 bus passed them on its way to Victoria. She used to catch it when she worked in the office, and she had hated the mad scramble at the bus stop, the proximity of human bodies, the frequent necessity to strap-hang or be stepped on. Now the 52 bus spelt escape back to the familiar, happy things she had left behind.

"If you want to stop and take the bus back home, you can, you know. You'll surprise everyone, but they'll get over it."

She was startled by Robert's voice, cool and calm – like he must sound at a company directors' meeting.

"How did you know?" she said, never dreaming of a denial.

"Because I have an instinct for knowing things. That's how I made my money!"

"Too much knowledge can be an uncomfortable thing," she said. Someone had said this to her at some time, at some place. The terror of what was to happen to her tonight had been nagging at her for weeks. She had tried to comfort herself with the thought that it was an experience all brides had to endure. Her mother must have liked it, because there had been no need for her to do it at all.

She was back to the old anxiety that had haunted her for years. She had thought that marriage would be an instant cure, for, as Mrs. Robert Dutton, she would be a real person, not the mis-begotten daughter of an unknown father and of a mother she had never met.

"Robert," she said. "There's something I positively must ask you. I should have asked you long ago, right at the start."

"This is the start. The start of our lives together. So ask me now."

She sighed deeply and swallowed. Then she said, "Would it upset you dreadfully if you knew that I was a bastard?"

He smiled. His eyes were kind. "I knew about that. And it doesn't matter at all."

She turned to him, astonished. "On earth how did you know?"

"Your mother, that is, Evelyn told me shortly after we became engaged. She felt it was her duty. In fact, it was plain commonsense. I'd be bound to see your birth certificate sooner or later."

"I've never seen it." She bit her lip and sank back in her corner. She dared not ask her husband if he knew the name of her father. It was somehow indecent that she didn't know the name herself.

The car had reached the airport. In a short time, they were flying over London, with its myriads of lights, and the pink glow of the West End clearly visible from the air.

Down there below them, the bridesmaids and the ushers would be dancing the night away. Grania would give up everything she possessed, even Kilcaraig, just to be with them now.

16

Grania wrote from Paris: "I've seen the Eiffel Tower, and the Tuileries and Versailles and the Louvre and Notre Dame. We went to the *Folies Bergère* on my birthday. It's true that they don't wear any clothes." It was her nineteenth birthday, and she had been married for a week.

From Rome she wrote: "I've been to St. Peter's, and I've seen the Pope on his balcony, and the Colosseum and the catacombs, and I've thrown coins into the Trevi Fountain, so I'll come back here some day."

The letter from Athens was about the Parthenon, with a postscript that she wanted to see the pyramids, so Robert was taking her to Egypt.

"She'll get spoilt," Evelyn observed, and she reiterated this many times, as letters arrived from Tahiti, Buenos Aires, San Francisco, New York. It seemed that Grania's honeymoon would never come to an end, but one evening at the end of October, Marian's telephone rang. It was Grania, speaking from New York. "We're sailing on the *Aquitania* tomorrow. There's no reply from Ladbroke Place, so warn the family for me. And be a darling and see if there's a sign of life in the flat in Lowndes Square. Robert's arranged everything, so it's sure to be all right, but just in case . . ." She had a great deal more to say, which Marian didn't take in, because she was counting every second and calculating the cost of the call.

Marian telephoned Evelyn the next morning, and then she went to Lowndes Square and was shown over the flat which was to be the Duttons' London home. Robert had put it into the hands of an interior decorator, and it was ready for occupation. That night, Marian again telephoned Evelyn. "It's beautiful – like a show house in an exhibition."

"How ghastly," Evelyn said, with feeling. "But Grania will soon put an end to that!"

Grania presented herself without warning at Marian's flat. She was wearing the same sober suit that had been her going-away outfit over six months ago, but she was also wearing a mink coat.

"Just imagine Robert being a Sir!" she said, ladling jam onto Marian's newly-baked scones. "I'm thrilled about being a Lady. It'll be lovely giving my name when I put things on account!"

Robert had been knighted in the Birthday Honours, a fact which had amazed Marian, although she told herself that she supposed the King must know what he was about.

When Grania left her, she felt unusually depressed. Perhaps it was the quiet of the flat after Grania's exuberance. She still missed Chrissie, although Mrs. Lowe came in regularly, and was kind and always had plenty to say. Grania had promised that she would give Chrissie a whole day off, which she could spend with Marian and account for all she had done during the last few months.

Marian washed up the tea things and put them away. She was becoming too careful, too methodical. In another year, she would be forty, reaching that milestone pointing to old age. Life would have been so different if Catriona hadn't died. She would have married Andrew as soon as war was declared, and somehow that might have made a difference when he set out for the Front. She could have had a child of her own and be living now at Duff, perhaps looking forward to having grandchildren. But mercy! She must control her imagination! Grania was as dear to her as any child could be, and Grania's children would be as precious as those grandchildren of her dreams. Grania's and Robert's children. She just couldn't picture them at all. No, not at all.

As she passed through the hall, she noticed that there was something in the wire letter-box. It was a circular. "Best prices paid for old clothes, household linen, jewellery, artificial teeth." She read it and tore it up. She had nothing to sell, not even a tooth. The idea made her smile. All her life she had lived on the brink of poverty, and sometimes she and Nicholas laughed about the difficulties they had encountered when he smuggled those art treasures out of the castle and delivered them to the London auction rooms. Yet, even then, the New Year was brought in at Kilcaraig with a banquet fit for a king, though the very next day could see them without the where-withal to buy a bit of putty for a loose window pane.

There would be no loose window panes in the castle now. Everything would be in order; not a creaking hinge, not even at the front gate. And now there was electric light! Perhaps the lamp-room had been turned into a bathroom, as Ian's little bedroom had been. Strange to think there were six bathrooms, when there had only been one. Yet they had managed to keep clean!

Grania, who had stormed and wept that time Willie pruned the ivy, would be horrified at the number of alterations Robert had made. She never could abide change. Silly little ostrich that she was, in spite of what Robert had told her she would still be picturing it as it used to be. Anyhow, it was Chrissie who would be there to comfort her when she discovered the truth. Poor Chrissie. That homecoming to Kilcaraig would not be such a happy one at all.

"On earth, what am I standing here for!" She pulled herself up with a start. The pieces of the circular were still in her hand. All this train of thought arising out of a tooth she didn't have for sale! The very idea!

She went into the sitting-room, but it still seemed frightening and lonely. There was nothing for it but to go out. Soon she was in her hat and coat. She would go to the Metropole to see that thriller which had curdled her blood in the trailer last week. She locked the door carefully behind her, and walked down the three flights of stairs. She never trusted herself in the lift. She was halfway down, when she heard the telephone ring. She had seen Grania, and there was no one else she wanted to talk to, with Nicholas out of town. She was always answering the telephone lately, and there was nobody there.

While Marian was ignoring the telephone, Grania was being received by Helen at Ladbroke Place.

"Why didn't you tell us you were coming?" Helen said, examining with awe the label inside Grania's mink coat, which had been tossed over a chair. "Mother's at Epsom with Granny, but she'll soon be back. Diana's in the north of England, being interviewed for a job as under-matron in a boys' school. She's decided Meredith will never come up to scratch."

"And you?" Grania asked. She was sitting on the hearth-rug in front of the fire, where she had sat watching Robert eating scrambled eggs on that Sunday, a whole year ago.

"After your wedding I longed to be a lovely white bride," Helen said. "But I decided that a lifetime with Claud would be a high price to pay for one day of glamour. It's not as if he were rich, like Robert." She gave Grania a quick, quizzical look. "I wonder if you realize how lucky you are to have landed so smartly on your feet!"

"Nobody could be kinder than Robert is to me," Grania said, painfully ill at ease. She opened her hand bag and brought out some snapshots.

"A pictorial record of your travels," Helen said. She took the folder and looked at the pictures, one by one. Grania photographed beside all the predictable tourist attractions, the Arc de Triomphe, the Bridge of Sighs, the Trevi Fountain, Niagara Falls.

"There's some at the end, of Robert and me. Chrissie took them, and they aren't very good," Grania said.

Helen studied them in silence, and Grania guessed what she was thinking. Robert looked like a proud father showing his daughter the wonders of the world.

They had just finished with the snapshots when Evelyn came in, and after greetings and embraces, the wretched ordeal had to be gone through again. Grania felt humble now, almost apologizing for the splendour of her honeymoon.

"The trouble about being married to a captain of industry is that everything seems to have a business angle," she said. "He did a wonderful transaction while we were in Mexico."

Helen giggled. "You used to say that a good businessman meant a clever swindler!"

Grania coloured. "I used to talk a lot of rubbish. Now I know it simply isn't true."

"Robert's business methods are very much admired," Evelyn said, casting a look of cold rebuke at Helen. "His knighthood proves that."

"It proves he's successful, which is different," Helen persisted. "But I'm not calling Robert's integrity into question. His firm is a flourishing testimony to his enterprise and efficiency. That's more or less what was said in *The Times* and in other papers when the Honours List was published. I've kept the cuttings for you to glue into your Golden Memory book!"

Grania wasn't sure whether Helen was being serious or sarcastic. Moreover, the subject was one which secretly distressed her, for there had been times during the tour when Robert had boasted of some triumph, and she had squirmed inwardly. She knew he could be ruthless and would overlook the fact that his business acumen was sometimes responsible for failure and heartbreak in other parts of the world.

When he met with competition, he had only one policy. "We'll buy them out," he would murmur into a telephone, and from that moment, a new game would begin, carefully planned, brilliantly played, spectacularly won. It had happened in Mexico. Robert had smiled at her across the breakfast table. "Perado has caved in. I knew it. I knew it! *I just can't lose!*"

"You'll stay to supper?" Evelyn was asking. Grania jolted herself back to earth. She wondered what they had been talking about. She had been talking herself. She hoped she had made sense.

"I'd love to stay. Robert's business associates were on to him like a flight of locusts. He said he'd be out until fairly late."

"Just fancy! And on your first night home!" Helen said. Surprisingly, she didn't giggle.

"Lowndes Square isn't home, and after six months of honeymoon, we're like a staid married couple."

"When do you go to Kilcaraig?"

"In about ten days' time. There's things I have to do. I must get fitted for a new coat, and visit grandmother. How is she, by the way?"

"She won't know who you are," Evelyn said. "You can spare yourself the journey. It's a waste of time."

"All the same, I'll go," Grania said. Evelyn must think sadly of her mother as she used to be, playing cards and caring for little else. The family had grumbled then, grudging her this pleasure. "I'll go," she repeated. "Somewhere, deep inside, she may know more than we think."

There was a casserole for supper, prepared in advance, so Grania being there did not mean extra work. While they ate, Grania told them about Chrissie, who would be going to Kilcaraig a few days ahead of them, to help prepare the homecoming. "I can't imagine how she'll settle. She's been to a bull-fight, and she's literally been swept off her feet by a gaucho at a fiesta in the Argentine. She speaks Italian and Spanish muddled up together, and she calls a lift an elevator, and a biscuit a cracker. I think she's lost her soul!"

"She'll feel like a lost body among all the servants Robert seems to have imported," Helen said.

"So shall I!" Grania managed to laugh, but she knew that this was true. She felt like a stranger in Robert's world, just as she felt like a stranger now in this flat. In time she would learn how to adjust herself to living two different lives, one as the wife of a successful businessman, the other as a member of a family that poured scorn on ostentation of any kind.

She helped with the washing up, and made the tea. She had forgotten how many spoonfuls should go into the pot, but she dared not ask Helen, who would think her ignorance was affectation.

When they were drinking their tea, which was very black, she brought out the gold cigarette case, with her initials in diamonds, which Robert had given her in New York. Helen refused a cigarette, but they admired the case, weighing it in their hands, examining the diamonds. They didn't notice that Grania's lighter matched it. She lit her cigarette quickly, and her hand was trembling. She had to blink, because the smoke got in her eyes.

Helen returned the case. She didn't say, "Isn't it a bit too much of a good thing", as Grania had expected, but she asked if it was insured.

"Robert will have seen to that," Grania said; then she added what she had dreaded saying ever since she arrived at the flat. "When the heavy luggage is unpacked there will be presents for all of you. It was such fun choosing them."

She shuddered at the thought of it. Robert's presents had been embarrassingly lavish. She could picture how, when they had undone their parcels, and when their natural excitement had worn off, they would think, and quite likely would even say to one another, "How magnificent. But how vulgar!"

She stubbed out her cigarette on the china ashtray Diana had bought in Oban. She mustn't entertain these thoughts about Robert. She was being neurotic. Other people saw him as the kindly, thoughtful person she knew him to be.

"I must go," she said. "Or Robert will be home before I am."

As she spoke, the telephone rang. Evelyn went to answer it, and they could hear her voice, high-pitched, almost shouting, for she could never speak naturally on a telephone. She was commiserating with someone and looked agitated when she returned to the room.

"It's Marian," she said. "Her flat was ransacked while she was at the cinema. Everything of any value has been taken. She's dreadfully upset."

Grania remembered the polished sideboard, laden with silver from Kilcaraig, the battered leather jewellery case, containing the few things Marian's mother had left her – a pearl necklace, diamond earrings, an assortment of amethysts, cairngorms and amber.

"I'll ring Robert," she said. "He'll see to everything. I'll tell him we'll meet him at Marian's flat."

When they arrived, Robert was already in possession, reassuring Marian, interviewing the police, drawing up a careful description of the missing articles. There was nothing for Grania and Evelyn to do but make the customary cups of tea, and even this proved to be unnecessary, as Marian had already been fortified with brandy, which Robert had had the foresight to bring with him.

"He thinks of everything," Grania said to Marian, proud that Robert was giving visible proof of his ability to command a situation. "You needn't worry – you'll get everything back. There isn't anything that he can't do."

Evelyn, overhearing her, was considerably relieved. Earlier in the evening she had thought that Grania seemed to be nervous and edgy, and she blamed herself for consenting so readily to this most unsuitable marriage. That Grania was determined to marry Robert in order to acquire Kilcaraig was obvious from the start, but while Evelyn could not have prevented the engagement, she could have opposed the marriage. By the time she was twenty-one, Grania might have seen the absurdity of it for herself. It had been that terrible scene about the photograph of Catriona that had changed everything. Grania's marriage offered an easy way out of an intolerable situation, and Evelyn had permitted what in conscience she should have prevented.

"Evelyn, you haven't got a drink." Robert was speaking to her, but his eyes were on Grania, who was at the other side of the room. She was leaning on a bookcase and talking to a detective, dazzling him with her smile.

"I don't drink brandy," Evelyn said, but Robert handed her a glass, so she took it obediently. He hadn't heard what she said. He was gazing at the detective, and his eyes were pools of hatred. He crossed the room, and without a word drew Grania away, leaving the detective, pen and note-book in hand, gaping after her.

Evelyn drank her brandy quickly, although it burnt her throat. She had never before witnessed such a display of jealousy. It was electrifying in its intensity, and she was afraid. "I'll have to go," she said to Robert. "I must get home to Helen."

"My car will take you. You needn't send it back. Grania can drive me home." He let go of Grania's arm, and told her to take care of Marian for a few minutes, then he turned to the detective. "I think you've asked enough questions for tonight. Thank you for your help. I'm sure we can leave the matter safely in your hands, and that we'll shortly hear of your success."

The detective departed without so much as a glance at Grania. He had seen Robert's expression, and as a trained observer, he knew the deadly meaning of that look. Grania, unconcerned, was sitting on the sofa talking to Marian, but when she saw that Evelyn was leaving, she stood up and kissed her goodnight. She must by now be accustomed to Robert's reactions when she talked to other men, and she accepted his possessiveness as naturally as she accepted his gifts.

Robert took Evelyn down in the creaking lift. "You're looking tired," he said. "Don't spend the rest of the night describing everything to Helen. Take a couple of aspirins and another brandy, and go to bed."

It was years since any man had told her how to take care of herself. In spite of what had just happened, her heart warmed towards Robert. He was basically kind, and that made up for many, many faults.

The chauffeur was waiting with the Rolls Royce, and there was a

Citroen four-seater parked behind it, which presumably was the car which Grania was using. It was Adrian Ferguson who had taught her how to drive. She would have had the sense not to tell her husband about that.

Evelyn stepped into the Rolls, and the chauffeur tucked a rug round her. She closed her eyes, wallowing in the luxury that was now part of Grania's daily life. Whatever happened, she would never allow herself to worry about Grania any more. What was done was done, and all would be well, so long as the silly child never allowed herself to fall in love.

She was almost asleep and had to be roused by the chauffeur when the car drew up at Ladbroke Place.

17

Robert would not allow Marian to spend the night in her flat. "You'll feel nervous until the shock wears off. You must come to Lowndes Square with us."

"Mercy, not on your first night at home! I wouldn't dream of it. But I'll go to Evelyn – she did ask me. Ring her now, Grania, and you'll catch her before she goes to bed. Tell her I've changed my mind."

She could hear Grania making the arrangement. She had been appalled at the prospect of a night in Lowndes Square, not only for the reason she had given, but because her feelings towards Robert remained ambivalent. Tonight she was filled with gratitude towards him, but tomorrow she could resent being beholden to him. At times he attracted her, and at times he repelled her. She would never feel at ease with him, as she did with Nicholas, yet that in itself added to his fascination for her in an odd way.

Grania drove them to Ladbroke Place, Marian's suitcase on the seat beside her, Marian and Robert together on the back seat. She could see them reflected in her driving-mirror, which she had tilted in their direction, and she thought that although Marian's age made her a more suitable companion for Robert than herself, he still looked out of place, sitting there at Marian's side. From the crown of his ginger head to the sole of his hand-made shoes, Robert was unmistakeably a well-dressed Londoner, whereas Marian's beret and ancient Jaeger coat stamped her as a country woman, more accustomed to walking on the moors than on London pavements. How these two would get on together in the future remained to be seen. The close family ties which now existed between them could draw them closer together, or could snap under pressure, so that they drifted far, far apart.

While Robert took Marian and her suitcase up to the maisonette, Grania waited in the car. She was tired, and looked forward to getting to bed. It was that time of the month which she used to hate, but now she welcomed its inconvenience, because it meant that she had a rest from Robert's attentions. She found him far too demanding, but she would never deny him his rights. She had promised to comfort him, and she believed it was submission that the Prayer Book meant.

The front door slammed, and Robert joined her in the car. "If you're clever, you'll get her to agree to come to Kilcaraig for a while," he said. "You'll be alone a lot and it would be nice for both of you."

And so it was arranged. Grania and Robert were to drive to Edinburgh, where they would spend a couple of days with friends, before going on to Oban by train. Grania wanted the train journey, because that was how it had always been. Marian agreed to join them after two or three weeks. By then, she was assured, her stolen property would have been recovered, so she could enjoy her holiday and return to London without imagining there was a burglar hidden under the bed. In the meantime, she would remain with Evelyn, in the bedroom Grania used to occupy.

It rained the morning that Grania and Robert left Edinburgh, but by the time the train had passed through Stirling, the gateway to the Highlands, the sun shone and Grania stood in the corridor, drinking in the scenery, while Robert dozed in his corner seat. After three years of exile, Grania found the magnificence of the view almost overpowering. The sunlight lit the bracken with a pale gold flame, and the mist hung like vapour over the summit of the mountains. She was right never to have come back here on holiday. She could never have come as a visitor to the Highlands. She had to come only when she was coming home.

Robert woke up when they reached Connel Ferry, and he stood beside her as the train wound downhill, round the back of Oban, with sight of the strip of sea between the mainland and the island of Kerrera. And behind, the mountains of Mull. Robert put his arm round Grania's shoulders because she was in tears. "I'm so happy," she whispered. "I'm home."

"Not yet," he said, thinking of the surprise he had in store for her when they reached Kilcaraig. There was to be a homecoming that Grania would cherish as a wonderful, magical memory for the rest of her life.

Grania was out of the train almost before it had stopped. Oban railway station, with the seagulls screaming overhead, and the smell of tar and fish. The porter, who had always piled her luggage on his barrow, was waiting, all moustache and smiles, to trundle their possessions to the North Pier, where they would board the Mull boat. Grania shook his hand, and almost hugged him, and there were others there, the ticket collector, the station master, all old friends, and greeting her as if she were royalty.

Robert followed her, shaking hands too, and thinking that any strangers must suppose that he was her father, or an elderly uncle, or a plain-clothes policeman, guarding the life of this fabulous fairy-princess. "She's mine," he thought. "I bought her. I'll never let her go."

Grania, who had been walking ahead of him with the porter, turned back suddenly, accusingly. "Robert, it's Wednesday, the late day. We won't get to Kilcaraig until after dark."

Robert had remembered that the boat today would not sail until three o'clock, and then it would do a detour to Lismore, making the crossing to Mull in two hours instead of one.

"I thought lunch in an hotel would be better than on the boat," he said, thereby depriving Grania of another treat, mince and mashed potatoes, with rice pudding and jelly to follow. Lunch on the Mull boat. Ambrosia! Fighting back her chagrin, she managed to smile. "You think of everything," she said.

Robert recognized the effort for what it was, and was touched. "I wouldn't disappoint you for anything on earth," he said, and he thought – "Just you wait" – excitement coursing through his veins.

They arrived half an hour late at Craignure, because the boat was delayed at Lismore. Grania watched the mail-bags, luggage, and some tiny calves that were tied up in sacks with only their heads protruding, being lowered on to the ferry-boat, which had come alongside the ship in the bay.

Once the goods were packed on to the boat, the passengers were allowed to join them. They were all jammed together, as they chugged towards the shore, and Grania's eyes eagerly sought the old familiar signs, the inn, the church, the few cottages. It had not changed at all. She was the first to jump ashore, and she ran up the jetty, the flagstones under her feet slippery from the sea and the rain, and there was Angus, his rugged face glowing with joy at the sight of her.

Her hand was in his strong grip as he welcomed her in Gaelic, and she found that her reply was faltering. She would not have believed that she could forget so soon.

There were others there to greet her in the dark. The mail-bus driver, farmers, road-workers, shepherds, all sorts of old friends, from miles around. She loved them all, but did not know that they loved her so much.

At the top of the jetty, parked beside the Fionnphort ferry bus, was a gleaming Daimler with a liveried chauffeur, awaiting her. For a moment, she did not realize that this was to be her car, her chauffeur. Robert hadn't told her. It was the first of his surprises. Instinctively she held out her hand, and in some surprise the chauffeur took it. He had been in Mull for three days, and was learning some of the islanders' ways already.

"What's your name?" she asked.

"Farnborough, my lady."

How grand, she thought! "And your Christian name?"

"Roy."

She smiled. "I hope you'll be happy with us, Roy. And I hope sometime you'll let me drive your car."

Robert, standing behind her, felt that this episode had not gone quite as he had planned. Farnborough, whom he had chosen for this particular job for many reasons besides the fact that he was a good driver and mechanic, would not understand the odd familiarity with which the Lamonts treated their servants.

Soon he was in the car with Grania, with Angus in the front with Farnborough, a glass window firmly sealing them off from taking part in the conversation.

As the car moved luxuriously forward, Grania sighed. "It'll be the very devil if this monster gets ditched."

"Farnborough won't ditch it," Robert said, with the emphasis on the name Farnborough, thus rebuking her, although he knew it would not stop Grania calling the man "Roy".

"I was thinking about me driving it," Grania said. Robert took her hand and pressed it. He could not tell her now, while he wanted her to be so happy, that she must not drive this car herself.

They drove on through the darkness, Grania remembering by the feel of the bends in the road how they were progressing. The few houses they passed had lamps in every window, a Highland welcome, with still some miles to go before they reached the boundaries of Kilcaraig.

The car slowed down almost to a stop, and with a sharp half turn, the Glen road was behind them. Grania waited for them to stop at the first of the road gates. There was no gate – there was a cattle grid, and as they rumbled over it Grania exclaimed, "What's happened?" She had never heard of a grid.

Robert explained what it was, and why, and how in daylight she would see the fencing which now surrounded Kilcaraig. By the time the car reached the village, they had rumbled over three grids.

Three gates were gone. Progress. Grania swallowed hard, but was mollified when she saw the gleaming village. The lights were in the windows, and the people were in the street, and the car stopped at the post office, where Grania left it to be embraced and kissed and embraced again. Robert remained in his seat. This was a Lamont homecoming, and nothing to do with him.

"Look!" Grania said, as they resumed their journey and drove past Caraig Lodge. "Michael Ames will be in the window, and he'll hear us, and he'll wave. We must wave back. The darkness makes no difference to him, and he'll know."

Sheepishly, Robert waved, but Grania leaned over to the window and waved with enthusiasm, just as if her eagerness could be communicated to Michael in the darkness of his world. Her action kept her head turned from what would be her first glimpse of the castle, but she became suddenly aware of a glowing light there, behind the trees. Not the sunset, that was long past. Floodlights. The castle was floodlit.

They had passed over the bumpy bridge, through the iron gates, and were climbing up the smooth drive. And there it was, shining like a castle in the transformation scene of a fairy tale. Grania remembered the flickering lamp-light in every window, the newspapers used to clean the glass funnels. Her eyes pricked. It was beautiful and it was awful. Robert was waiting for her exclamations of delight, but if she tried to speak she would cry. She managed to press his hand, and swallow hard, and to pray that he would think she was overcome with emotion.

Robert helped her out of the car. The servants were lined up to greet them in the hall. They wore plum-coloured uniform to match the close-fitting pile carpet on the floor and on the stair. Chrissie was not among them. Chrissie would have avoided witnessing Grania's reaction to this display.

She managed to smile, and to say suitable words of appreciation and greeting. Automatically, she went into the drawing-room. It was magnificently furnished, and was illuminated by concealed electric lights. Like the exterior of the castle, this was a stage-set, beautifully designed, but absolutely unreal. Then she saw her coot, in its glass case on the mantelpiece, and she burst out laughing. This was not a tragedy, it was a farce.

Robert was standing beside her, pale and tired and anxious, knowing how near she had been to tears. She put her arms round him and kissed him. "I wish I could deserve all you do for me," she said. "I wish I didn't cry when things are lovely, it so messes up my face."

She could sense Robert's thankfulness and relief. He was happy because of a lie. If she could keep him happy, it would always be through lies.

"I want to see my bedroom," she said. It was only when they were going upstairs that she realized she should have said "our bedroom". But she hoped he hadn't spotted her mistake.

Chrissie was waiting for them on the landing. She hugged Grania as if they had been parted for years, instead of for a few days. Grania knew that Chrissie understood exactly what she was thinking about it all.

Robert opened the door that had once led to Kilcaraig's bedroom. "This is your room," he said. Grania stepped inside and looked around. It was beautifully, tastefully furnished, but before her was Kilcaraig's bed – her bed, the bed she would share with Robert. Again tears pricked her eyes, and she could feel the blush spreading down her neck.

Robert had opened another door, one that had not been there before. It led into the room that had been Ian's, and was now a bathroom, a beautiful bathroom, with mirrors and showers and a bidet.

"My room is through here," Robert said, and smiled indulgently. "It's only a dressing-room, of course, but there's a bed in it! I think you'll appreciate the right to some privacy, but please regard this as a corridor, not a barricade."

She went into Robert's room. It had been Catriona's bedroom, but now the furniture was wholly masculine, the built-in cupboards, the teak wood dressing-table, the trouser press. Beside the single bed there was a photograph, not of herself but of a group of people. She picked it up and looked at it.

"Myself when young," Robert said. "It was taken one autumn when we were digging up potatoes on my uncle's farm. My other uncle is there, and my cousins. I must have been about twelve years old at the time."

It was the first time she had seen a picture of him, or had even thought of him as a child. "I don't know him," she thought. "I don't know him, and I never will."

She returned to her bedroom, her eye avoiding the bidet as she passed through the bathroom. Whatever must the Kilcaraig people have thought when they heard about that! She paused beside the big bed where her grandfather had died.

"Our baby will be born in this," she said.

Robert put his arm round her, and pressed her shoulder. "Your grandmother died in childbirth, so did your mother. There must be no babies for you, Grania. I'll take care of that."

Grania's whole body seemed to freeze. She knew that Robert meant precisely what he said, and that if she tried to question his decision now, the dreadful disappointment of her homecoming would erupt into a torrent of tears and of rage.

"As you wish," she said. "I won't mention it any more."

She changed for dinner, attended by Chrissie, who sensed that something was terribly wrong, but she had been prepared to help Grania to accept the changes that had taken place in the castle. Gradually, between the two of them, some of its splendour would be subdued, and some of its more homely features restored.

The dining-room, except for the new carpet, was much as it had always been, but instead of using the large mahogany table, she and Robert sat at a small folding-table, an innovation which she appreciated. She could not bear to see Robert occupying her grandfather's seat at the head of the table tonight.

They were waited on by a butler and a parlour-maid, and afterwards they went to the library and played chess in front of an electric fire.

"Where does the electricity come from?" Grania asked, removing one of Robert's white knights from the board. His mind wasn't on the game, and she knew it.

"A generator," he said, "I'd like to install a few for the village, and some of the out-lying farms and crofts, but these people are so conservative – they say they prefer their paraffin lamps."

"I like lamp-light too. And tomorrow I want a peat fire lighted. We always kept one burning in this room."

"You must please yourself, but the servants aren't going to take to it very much. Peat produces such a very fine ash – the room will have to be dusted several times a day."

"Chrissie will see to it."

"Be careful – we don't want trouble in the kitchen. Chrissie has come here to be your personal maid."

They played on in silence, Grania simmering with indignation,

Robert belatedly concentrating on the game, which he eventually won.

After that, there was bed, with Robert claiming his rights as her husband, and Grania responding with her body, while her mind dwelt on the babies that would never be born, and on the futility of it all.

She remained awake long after Robert had fallen asleep. She was back at Kilcaraig, but she had not, after all, come home.

18

Michael Ames was sitting in the sun-room at Caraig Lodge, listening to the wireless. He had been reading, but had dropped his Braille book and could not be bothered to grope about for it on the floor. The dance-band programme was at any rate more in keeping with his mood.

Last night, Grania had come home, and today she would almost certainly come to see him, as she always used to do on the first day of her holidays. Because the sale of Kilcaraig had taken place during term-time, and the move to London had swiftly followed, she had been unable to say her farewells to the people she loved, but Michael still had the letter she had sent to him when the blow had fallen. It was scrawled across a piece of graph paper torn from a geometry book.

"That awful Mr. Dutton has bought Kilcaraig," she had written. "He's been waiting like a vulture to swoop, and mother says she's done the right thing for us all as he's paid acquisity for it. But Marian says she'd rather the castle fell to pieces over our heads than have someone else owning it. Some day, somehow, I'm going to get it back, if I have to go through hell to do so."

Other letters had followed sporadically, at first full of grief and anger, but developing gradually into accounts of the people she had met and the places she had seen; the Tower of London, Windsor Castle, Buckingham Palace. ("I'll be presented at Court one day, if I'm ever allowed to leave school!")

When she did leave school there was no mention of coming-out formalities, but this did not appear to worry her. The names of her school friends were replaced by the names of new friends; Simon,

116

who was an undergraduate at Oxford, Adrian who was an opera enthusiast. ("He's opened up a new and wonderful world for me.") Then came the letter which made Mrs. Ames, who read it to him, gasp.

"I'm going to marry Robert Dutton. I met him at a party a little while ago. I know what you'll be thinking but it's not really like that at all. It's something I can't explain. I hope you'll come to our wedding. It's to be in April."

Michael dictated a letter of good wishes, which his mother agreed was suitably vague, but he did not go to the wedding, although his parents did. Now he would be seeing the bride, and his joy at the prospect was mingled with intense embarrassment. He had disliked Robert Dutton's patronizing attitude on the only occasion on which he had met him, and he hated him for having made Grania his bartered bride. That Evelyn Lamont had allowed this to happen came as no surprise at all. Grania had never again referred to her doubts about her parentage, but from the day of her grandfather's funeral Michael had been convinced that instinct had led her to discover the truth about herself. From then on, she had been just a little more reticent, a little less self-assured, for in his darkness he could discern undertones which would pass unobserved by ordinary people.

"*I'll see you in my dreams.*" The dance music faded from the air and was followed by a programme about gardening. Michael switched it off. A few minutes later, he heard footsteps on the gravel drive and he identified them with ease, even after three long years. A gust of wind whirled into the room as the door opened.

"Michael!"

He stumbled over his book as he rose to greet Grania, but her hand steadied him, and then she was in his arms, half laughing, half crying, as he felt her hair, her face, her shoulders.

"You've grown," he said.

"And you've thickened, Michael. And you're silver around the temple. It suits you very well." She pushed him gently back into his chair, and drew up a chair for herself. "I hope you aren't thinking dreadful things about me. There was an awkward silence when I went into the post office just now. I would never have believed that my homecoming could cause anything like that. I'd expected laughter and welcome and lights."

He might have known that she would plunge into the subject, which could otherwise have hung like a curtain between them. "You had plenty of lights last night," he said. "And you must realize that your marriage has caused a bit of a stir."

"Oh Michael, it was idiotic of me to expect there would still be paraffin lamps, and it wasn't as if Robert hadn't told me about what he calls his improvements! But floodlighting was more than I'd bargained for, and the generator sounded like a car engine that's left running all night."

"You'll get used to it," Michael said. There had been electricity supplied by a generator at Caraig Lodge for years.

"And Kilcaraig will get used to me being married to Robert, I suppose. I'm almost used to it myself!" She laughed lightly. She sounded genuinely happy. She told him about her travels, and about Marian's burglary.

"It was a blessing in disguise. It's made her agree to come up here, and she's terribly grateful to Robert for getting all her property back."

"I thought the police did that."

"Of course they did. But it was Robert who gave her confidence in their success. There's a lot to be said for being able to rely on someone. I think that's what she understands now about me."

"So it wasn't just the lure of Kilcaraig that made you marry him?" She had virtually invited the question, and Michael had no hesitation in asking it.

"It put the idea into my head," she admitted. "But something else cropped up which upset me very much, and Robert was there, all safe and secure and wanting me to marry him. After seven months I haven't had any regrets." She had said what she wanted to say, had explained her marriage, but clearly had no intention of explaining what that something else had been. Michael scarcely heard her as she chattered on, telling him about the servants whom she had interviewed separately that morning. She had told the housekeeper, Mrs. Denny, who was homesick for Surbiton, that she could have her full pay in lieu of notice.

"She leaves tomorrow, thank goodness. I was scared stiff of her. I think the cook will follow, and I'll get our Mrs. Beaton back. She came to my wedding, and she hasn't settled in Edinburgh. The other maids are sure to be driven out by our winter weather. Robert never managed to dislodge Willie from being gardener-handyman, or Angus from being gillie, so we'll all be back as we were – except for Farnborough, who alarms me most of all."

"Isn't he the chauffeur?"

"He is, and although the Daimler is supposed to be mine, I'm not allowed to drive it. So I'd be a prisoner when Robert's away. But I think he's also my bodyguard and gaoler, under orders to report my every movement to Robert."

"How can you assume that, when you only arrived here last night!"

"I've been married long enough to know that Robert thinks every man who claps eyes on me will try to seduce me."

"So he feels you're safe with me?" Michael had not meant to reveal how sensitive he had become.

Grania, who had never given his blindness a thought, was astonished. "I suppose that's so," she admitted, for she couldn't withdraw her words. "I suppose we should be glad. It means we can be alone together, and we've always enjoyed that."

"Until you left, I didn't realize how much I depended on you to be not only my eyes, but my ears." He knew he had distressed her, and he was sorry.

"But that's nonsense. You were always the miracle man for knowing what's happening on Mull! Tell me what's been going on while I've been away."

He thought for a while. He would have to be careful. This Grania was no longer a child.

"Do you remember your Land of Heart's Desire?" he asked.

"Of course I do. At Tormore Bay where the sun sets. I never went there. Marian rebelled when she found that one had to follow a soggy sheep-track and scramble over a disused quarry to reach it. What about it?"

"A kinsman of yours has come to live there. That is, his name is Lamont, though I know, with you bewildering people, he could be the wrong branch of the family, or no relation at all."

"A Lamont at Tormore? There are Lamonts all over Mull, but the only cottages at Tormore have been uninhabited since the quarries closed in 1906. They must be ruins by now." She considered this. "Chrissie did say that one or two have been restored as holiday homes. There are no amenities at all. That's what makes it so magical, so out-of-this-world attractive."

"Now another has been built up, and by the very man himself, Roderick Lamont. Tall, dark, handsome, blue Highland eyes, plays the pipes like a pipe-major, and is in the pew in the kirk every Sunday."

"Away!" Grania used the exclamation beloved by the islanders to express incredulity. "What brought this tall, dark, handsome stranger to Tormore Bay?"

"Therein lies a mystery. He's very friendly and forthcoming, but what he does and where he comes from nobody can discover."

"I'll go to Tormore Bay, and I'll find out for myself."

"You'll do no such thing. If you race off there now, you'll have the whole island talking, and you'll have your bodyguard at your heels!"

Grania giggled, sounding like a child again. "A Daimler can't get to Tormore," she said, and added "Don't worry, I never really wanted to go there. Dream places are better left to the imagination. Besides, the dark-haired young man is probably a remittance-man, or an alcoholic. What else is going on? Is it true that Duff is on the market again?"

Mrs. Ames came into the room followed by her husband, who carried the tray of coffee. Grania had spoken to them in the garden on her way to see Michael, but now, over coffee, she was telling them more about her travels when the outer door burst open, and Robert was almost blown through it. He was breathless after coming up the brae in the high wind, and although he accepted a cup of coffee, he remained standing, his eyes moving from the wide windows to Grania.

"They told me in the post office that I'd find you here," he said to her. "You should have let me know where you were going. Dochy Campbell's chimney is on fire, and no one in the village shows the slightest concern, although the smoke is blowing towards the castle."

"They set fire to their chimneys on purpose. It's their way of cleaning them," Mrs Ames said.

"But Dochy's cottage is thatched." Grania had stood up in alarm. Black smoke was belching out of a chimney which was hidden from sight.

"It's not thatched now. I had it properly roofed. He was most ungrateful."

Grania laughed, relieved. "Then this is his protest! Whenever he sets fire to his chimney, he'll choose a day when the wind is blowing towards the castle, just to taunt us. The smuts can't reach us, we're too far away."

"I don't find insolence amusing." Robert was trying to control his anger. "And I won't have my tenants resorting to primitive ways of cleaning their chimneys. They must learn to do things correctly. Why, they could burn the whole place down."

"There's no need to worry," Mr. Ames said soothingly. "When we first came here, I thought what a slap-happy lot the people were and I'd teach them to mend their ways. Instead, they've taught me that they know what they're about, and no damned incomer is going to change them. And of course they're right."

"But you're a shining example of an incomer who has become one of ourselves." Grania laughed, and leaning over his chair, hugged him.

120

"It's time we went home. You have other visits to make, if you aren't going to cause offence." Robert opened the door, and the wind screamed through the room as she said her farewells. As soon as they were outside, he said "I think you should calm your exuberance. You aren't a schoolgirl any more. Mr. Ames is a man, and you are my wife."

"Why, he's old enough to be my grandfather!"

"He's not very many years older than I am."

Chastened, she walked silently beside him, taking the short cut to the castle through a field in which young fir trees had been planted.

The sunset was spectacular that night, as it so often was in November. Seeing it, Grania thought of her Land of Heart's Desire, and of Roderick Lamont who had come out of nowhere to make his home there. Whatever his name was, she resented him. He was an intruder who threatened her privacy, for when life was difficult she had always found sanctuary in her flights of fancy to Tormore Bay.

By the end of the week, she had become accustomed to the splendour of the castle, and to hearing the rain pouring down without having to go in search of receptacles to catch the drips. The cook departed, and so did the kitchen-maid, and Chrissie had a humanizing effect upon Hunter, the butler, when she called him by his Christian name, which was Jim.

Visits were made to every household in Kilcaraig, and Grania found that she was greeted warmly. She was driven sedately in her Daimler to the MacPhails' farm, and to some of the out-lying croft cottages, but when she was settled beside a kitchen range, and was plied with cups of tea, and with scones dripping with fresh butter, she found that she could relax and forget about the big car and the liveried chauffeur waiting outside for her, surrounded by cows and hens and mud.

When Marian was due to arrive, Robert decided that Farnborough should meet her at Craignure, for it was fitting that she should be greeted by Grania and himself at the castle. Grania, who had looked forward to waiting at the jetty for the arrival of the tough little *Lochinvar*, submitted without a murmur. Physically and mentallly, she was subject to Robert, and he had achieved his dominion over her almost without a struggle. On the rare occasions when she had been roused to anger, he had exulted in her snapping eyes and scarlet cheeks, and his remedy was simple. She soon found that the only passion she knew was the passion of fury coupled with a sensual delight in being taken against her will.

When Farnborough drove the Daimler up to the castle, Marian was out of it before he could walk round to open the door for her.

"I was held up at the post office," she said. "The whole place seemed to be out to greet me." There was nothing but delight in her exclamation as she entered the castle. "Robert, it's gorgeous! And it doesn't smell of damp any more!"

Eating pancakes and honey in the library in front of a blazing peat fire, with the two labradors snoring at their feet, Grania and Marian felt as if they had never been away from the castle. Robert sat on Kilcaraig's chair, happy that he, the provider, had made this contentment possible for the two people who mattered most to him – Grania, his most treasured possession, and Marian, indebted to him for his help.

"Will you be coming with us, Robert?" Grania's question broke into his thoughts. "Marian would like to go to Iona tomorrow. We should do it soon – before the weather breaks."

Robert thought of the long drive on the narrow, pot-holed road, the twenty-minute crossing in the chilly little ferry-boat, and the even chillier picnic on the island at this time of year.

"I have letters I must attend to. Farnborough will take you," he said.

Grania moved over to him, and sat on the arm of his chair. She caressed his ear gently. "Please Robert, may I drive the car?" Her voice was almost a purr.

Robert pictured the Daimler sliding into a ditch, and Grania loose on Iona, with no Farnborough to report to whom she had spoken, and why. But Marian would be there. She wouldn't allow Grania's high-spirits to spill into conversation with strangers, should there be any around at this time of year. The touch of her hand, the gentle, pleading eyes were irresistible.

"Very well. Take the car. If you scratch it, you'll be answerable to Farnborough!"

"No Robert, I'll be answerable only to you." Grania had won her point and with it a return of her self-confidence. If she gave her mind to it, she would always have her way with Robert. She had been too submissive, too anxious to please. "I'll be terribly careful. I expect we'll be home before dark."

They set off immediately after breakfast, Grania at the wheel, trying to look jaunty, and Marian beside her, feeling apprehensive, with a basket containing a picnic at her feet. "I like it there," she had said firmly to Farnborough, who had tried to stow it away in its proper place. He stood aside, watching from the bushes as the car moved slowly down the drive.

"I think he has the Evil Eye," Grania hissed, as she ground the gears before crossing the bumpy bridge.

"He's not very suitable for Mull," Marian said. When Farnborough had driven her from Craignure, she had pushed aside the glass partition which separated the front seat from the back, but she had been unable to induce him to talk to her.

Grania stopped the car outside the post office, and Marian went inside and bought some cinnamon balls, and a slab of milk chocolate. She told the post-mistress that they were bound for Iona, and was warned to watch the weather, and to tell Grania to drive carefully, or they'd end up in a ditch.

"They'll be happy now that they know where we're going," Marian said, as the car left the village behind, passed the brae where the doctor's house stood on its windy ridge, and rattled over the first of the three cattle-grids.

The road followed a circuitous route between the lochs and the mountains. The glen was as stark and wild as it had been centuries ago when warring clansmen had struggled for supremacy over the island. Then sword had met sword, battle-axe had met battle-axe, and the din of the affrays had echoed through the mountains.

Here, Ewen of the Small Head, only son of MacLaine, Chief of Lochbuie, had fought against his father in a bid to win yet more land to satisfy his greedy wife. He had been vanquished by the allied armies of Lochbuie and MacLean of Duart, and seeing that all was lost, he had spurred his black charger into the midst of his foes. A claymore gleamed in the sunshine, and Ewen's head rolled to the ground, but his horse galloped on bearing his body through the glen. The phantom, it was said, could be seen as a portent of disaster to the present day.

"We must get home before dark," Grania said. Steeped in the legends of Mull, she half believed them and certainly respected them.

"It won't be easy at this time of year," Marian said. She, too, was thinking of the horseman, and of the daylight that failed by tea-time, and she felt a little shiver run down her spine.

A hind jumped across the road, a few yards in front of the car, to join the herd of deer which stood motionless as statues, barely discernible against the peat and russet shades of the mountain side. A hare, its brown coat changing into winter white, disappeared behind a lichen covered boulder, and a buzzard kept patient watch from a telegraph pole overhead.

A sharp turn left brought them on to the main road to Iona and the long climb up the shoulder of Ben More. The rushes which grew in the middle of the single-track road brushed against the bottom of the Daimler, and Grania found that she was clutching tightly at the wheel, as if by doing so she could prevent the small miscalculation which could easily tip them into the ditch.

She pulled up at the top of the hill. The three lochs now glimmered in the valley below them, and from this vantage point Kilcaraig Castle could be seen among its trees. Grania handed Marian a handkerchief. "Open your window and wave," she said. "Robert will be watching us through his binoculars."

Marian did as she was told, feeling rather foolish. She handed back the handkerchief and said, "If you sometimes find Robert rather over-anxious about you, remember that he's thirty years older than you. Try not to forget it – he never does."

"I'm not allowed to forget," Grania said. She switched on the ignition and they moved forward on the downward stretch which would take them to Loch Scridain, that arm of the Atlantic which almost divided Mull into two islands.

The scenery became more gentle as they headed west, the twisting road following close beside the seashore. At the horse-shoe shaped village of Bunessan, some people were leaning against the sea wall. Grania waved at them and they waved back.

"They didn't recognize us," Grania said.

"Would you expect them to, in this great car!"

The ferry boat had just left the jetty when they reached the hamlet of Fionnphort at the end of the road. Grania parked the Daimler carefully on the wide, grassy verge, beside a beaten-up little Ford which had been home-painted navy-blue. They stayed in the car, watching the trail of white foam following the ferry-boat as it crossed the mile or so of sea to Iona. The austere, beautifully proportioned Cathedral stood out against its green background on this sunny autumn day. It was a few fields apart from the row of houses that formed Iona village, and behind these were the ruins of the nunnery, flower-drenched in summer, and now offering useful protection against the breeze.

"We'll have our picnic there," Marian said, but Grania wasn't looking at Iona. She had seen a little motor-boat emerging from behind the pink granite rocks. These protruded across the far side of the white sands of Fionnphort beach, and behind them was the disused pier of the granite quarry, and Tormore Bay.

As the motor-boat approached the jetty, Grania felt her pulse racing. This had happened before, over and over again; a dark-haired young man whose features, whose very movements she knew, for he had lived in her imagination for years. But even in her daydreams he had not worn a Lamont tartan kilt.

She watched him jump ashore and tie up his boat, then he swung round, shading his eyes against the sun and looking up the road as if he were expecting someone. He paid no attention to the Daimler at all.

"Our tartan! Who is he?" Marian had also been struck by the compelling good looks of the dark-haired young man.

"I don't know," Grania said. She couldn't say more. She could not explain. Her lips felt dry, her voice husky. She tied on a headscarf and prepared to get out of the car. Had she been alone, she would have reversed and driven it away. This encounter was too improbable, too disturbing to be endured.

A small bus rattled down the road and came to a halt close to the jetty, blocking the view from the Daimler, so Grania and Marian got out, and Grania paused to make much ado of locking the doors, a wholly unnecessary precaution on Mull. By the time they reached the jetty, the people from the bus had gathered there, clutching their maps and cameras and other tourist paraphernalia. They were chattering and laughing and pointing out the Cathedral to one another, some speaking broken English, others speaking in assorted different languages. Grania remembered now that this was a special international students' tour of the Hebrides. She had read about it in the *Oban Times*.

"Pretend we belong to them," she whispered to Marian, who laughed and nodded. The ferry-boat was returning from Iona, and the man in the kilt chatted to some of the tourists while they waited for it to arrive. When it did, he helped to make it fast, and then he stood aside, only a few feet from Grania. She could see the laughter lines round the deep blue Highland eyes.

Someone in uniform, obviously the courier, stepped forward. He said a few words in French, then in Spanish, then in German, then in Italian, and finally he spoke in English. "This is a friend of mine who will act as interpreter for those who don't speak English. He will tell you anything you want to know about St. Columba and Iona."

"But first I will greet you all in Gaelic," Roderick Lamont said, his voice warm, just as Grania had known it would be. "*Ceud mile failte.*"

He smiled and held out his hand; then he helped each one of them into the boat.

19

The grip on her arm had been firm but gentle, and Grania tried to impress the feel of it on her memory as she scrambled across a pile of life-rafts to the far side of the boat. She had become separated from Marian, who was at the helm, talking to the ferryman, and was likely to remain there until they reached Iona.

When everyone was packed on board and the engine was coaxed into action, it was Roderick Lamont who climbed round the passengers collecting the fares. He switched with ease from one language to another as he addressed each individual, guessing which language he should use, and providing much laughter when his guesses were wrong.

Grania, avoiding his eye, handed him a pound note, and he said "*Grazie*", and counted out her change in Italian. But she resembled Catriona, who didn't look Italian at all. Again the question came to her mind – who am I? She knew she should have laughed, as the others were doing, or she should have surprised him by speaking in Gaelic. She wanted to attract the attention of this man, and at the same time she wanted to avoid him. Instinct warned her to beware.

When they came alongside the jetty at Iona, she managed to jump ashore unaided, and it was the ferryman who helped Marian to land. They made straight for the ruins of the nunnery, which were only a few hundred yards from the shore, and they found that there were still the straggling remains of flowers growing at the foot of the tumbledown granite walls which had once divided the rooms from the refectory and the chapel.

They chose a patch of grass close to the memorial stone of the Prioress Anna as their picnic place.

"Our poor shipmates are shivering there on the jetty being briefed about Iona," Marian said, pouring coffee from the thermos flask. "It will be interesting to hear what they are told about this nunnery – so little is known that there's practically nothing to tell."

Grania unwrapped the sandwiches. She could hear approaching

footsteps and the voice of the courier giving information in English, then that other voice, translating rapidly into French and German.

"They'll be coming here on the way to the Cathedral," she said, in panic.

"Just pay no attention to them. They'll soon pass by." They ate their picnic, feeling like waxworks in Madame Tussaud's, while the group stood around and watched them from over the low, ruined wall, and Marian saw that it was not the Prioress Anna they were thinking about, but the lovely girl, whose hair, no longer covered by a headscarf, was dancing in the breeze.

The voices receded, fading away towards the Cathedral. Grania's thoughts were still on Roderick Lamont, and the Italian he had spoken on the boat.

"Was Nicholas a very good friend of Catriona's?" she asked.

"He was in love with her." Marian wondered why, after all these years, she should be asked this question now.

"How long did he know her?"

Marian had to think. "He met her in October, after she came back from Italy. It may even have been November. Why?"

"I just wondered." And I've wondered for years, thought Grania, and my birthday is in the middle of April, so he can't be my father. But an Italian could. A Neapolitan or a Sicilian! Her imagination began to take hold of her, but Marian was packing up the remains of their picnic, and scrutinizing the ground to make sure that no sign of their presence was left behind.

They met the tourists leaving the Cathedral as they arrived there. Roderick Lamont was not with them.

"I forgot to say, I asked the ferryman about that young man," Marian said. "He's built up a cottage at Tormore, and he was at Grenoble and at Oxford. He's connected with Mull somehow, but I don't think he can be one of us. He sounds a bit of a mystery, so take care!"

Grania knew that Marian had wanted to say this all through the picnic, but had delayed until their entry into the Cathedral prevented her from asking questions. They both tied on their headscarves as they entered by the West Door. There were steps down to the nave, and the green marble altar under the East window was characteristically austere. They tiptoed round, with the reverence that can overpower on entry into a place with years of sanctity behind it, and both were aware that, sitting on a seat in the middle of the church was Roderick Lamont. He was not meditating, he was drawing.

Grania was reading the guide book she had collected from a table by the side door, and Marian drew near to the artist, leaning over his shoulder, making no pretence about what she wanted to see. He looked up, his eyes were smiling, and deliberately he held up the drawing for her inspection. It was not of the interior of the Cathedral, it was of Grania, sitting there on a low stone wall by the Prioress Anna's tomb, the movement of her curly hair cleverly implied by his pencil. It was an exact, almost uncannily accurate picture of the way she looked. But underneath it he had written, in bold print – "Lady Dutton of Kilcaraig!"

Outraged, Marian took the eraser from the seat by his side, and rubbed out the offending exclamation mark.

"I think you are very unkind," she said, as she handed the drawing back to him; he tore it to shreds, there and then, in front of her. The delightful sketch had gone forever, but that did not appear to matter to him. "You weren't meant to see it. I scribble for my own amusement." He stood up now, easing his way through the rows of chairs. "I live at the back of beyond, but I know a *Tatler* beauty when I see one. Especially when she's a Lamont."

They left the Cathedral together. There was no sign of Grania, whom Marian thought would be exploring the ruined cloisters where she used to play hide and seek when she was a child. They stood by the West Door, close to a low, circular wall which surrounded a disused well. Visitors sometimes threw coins into it, thinking it was a wishing well.

Marian had taken off her coat in the Cathedral and she carried it over her arm. She was wearing a tweed jacket and a Lamont tartan skirt.

"I heard you were on the *Lochinvar* yesterday, Miss Lamont. News travels fast in Mull," he said.

She laughed, and they shook hands. She was surprised by the roughness of his hand. When she had watched him drawing, she had been struck by its shapeliness, thinking it was an artist's hand. But he had been doing manual work. He had built up his cottage himself. He offered her a cigarette from a crumpled packet. She refused it. He lit one for himself.

"Mr. Lamont, you've lived on Mull for a year. You'll understand that when I ask you what brought you here I'm not doing so out of mere curiosity. Family ties are strong. We share the same tartan. Have you any ties with Kilcaraig?"

"Only a tenuous one," he said, pulling on his cigarette. "My great-grandfather left home to set himself up in Sutherland, of all places! He did quite well, but then came the Clearances. His family were dispossessed, burnt out of their homes, and the only one who seems to have survived was my grandfather. He came back to Mull and worked in the granite quarries."

"Why didn't he go home to Kilcaraig?"

"The link had been broken before he was born." He stubbed out his cigarette. Marian cast a side-long look at him. His profile showed his even features and his determined chin. The fluctuating fortunes of Highland people were part of their history. An artisan might hesitate to claim relationship with the laird of Kilcaraig.

She had done some quick calculations while he talked. Robert Dutton often teased her about the complications of Highland relationships, with their first and second cousins, so many times removed, and the further distinction of their being "by marriage" or "of blood".

"An Ian Lamont left Kilcaraig some hundred years ago," she said. "Records weren't kept in those days, and all trace of him was lost. We must get together sometime, and fill in our family tree. Roderick is one of the names that crops up quite often. Why on earth didn't you come to Kilcaraig and make yourself known to us?" Then she gave a little laugh. "How silly I am! I still forget that I don't live there any more."

Grania was walking towards them slowly, reluctantly. She had not been in the cloisters. She had been in the Cathedral and had come out of it by the South Door.

"Grania, I think we've found a long lost cousin!" Marian called to her.

Roderick waited for her to reach them. "I hardly think I can claim that, Lady Dutton. But it's good to know that a Lamont is back at Kilcaraig, even if it's on the distaff side." There was no sting in his words. He had said exactly what he meant.

"You'll be very welcome at Kilcaraig," she said and held out her hand to him, wondering what sort of reception this man would receive from Robert, if he ever came near the place.

Roderick clasped her hand between both of his. The physical contact with him came not as a thrill but as a warm sensation of security, such as she had never experienced before. He released her almost immediately, but the feel of his touch lingered on.

"I've been talking to your courier friend," she said. "He tells me that he was at Grenoble with you, but never had your flair for languages. He couldn't believe his good luck when he discovered you were here in Mull."

"There's no escaping from one's friends," Roderick said.

"But why would you want to escape?"

"Mr. Lamont has already undergone an inquisition, Grania. Leave the poor soul alone."

"I'm sorry, Mr. Lamont, but you know what Mull is. We aren't filled with curiosity, it's just that we like to know."

She sat on the edge of the well, but he remained standing beside her. "I was brought up in South Africa, on my father's fruit farm," he said. "It had been started by my grandfather, who emigrated there after the Tormore quarries closed down in 1906. Like all expatriates, he revelled in the legends and language of the place he had loved. His passion was passed on to me, and I made up my mind that I'd come here as soon as I could. Well, I've managed it, and I've not been disappointed. Tormore Bay's still what I always imagined it would be – my Land of Heart's Desire. There – call me a sentimental idiot! I've answered your question. And I can see the ferryboat coming for us. Shall we go?"

He picked up Marian's coat and flung it over his shoulder, like a plaid. Grania rose to her feet, feeling that this must all be part of a dream. They cut through the Relig Oran, once the burial ground of the kings of Scotland and of France, and still the final resting-place of the people of Iona.

When he held open the little gate which led onto the sandy, pebbly track that was the road, Roderick said "Would you like to come and see where I live? It's only a few minutes by motor boat, when we get to Mull."

Grania fully expected Marian to refuse, but in fact she accepted with alacrity. The name of Lamont was the open sesame to her heart.

When they arrived back on Mull, they quickly transferred to Roderick's little motor boat, and were chugging across the bay, round the pink granite rocks to the small pier at Tormore, where once granite had been shipped to all parts of the world. When she had lived in London, Grania had made frequent pilgrimages to the Albert Memorial, to gaze at it in awe, because it was hewn out of Mull granite.

They were helped ashore, and in front of them was the steep hill, where the remains of the narrow gauge railway lines were still visible. Here the truck loads of cut granite had been brought from the top of the hill to the boat which would be waiting to receive it at the pier.

Roderick led them to his cottage, which was on the hillside, overlooking the bay. A collie dog greeted them, and at once Roderick had opened the door, which he never locked, and they were inside his cottage.

130

"It's like being on a ship!" Grania exclaimed, and so it was. Neatly lined with wood, its windows looked straight on to the sea, and it had the practicality and orderliness of a wardroom. There was even a telescope in a window, and charts on the wall. The chairs were upholstered in real leather, and beside the chimney piece was a crucifix, most beautifully carved.

"A friend did that for me," Roderick said. "We started out to discover the perfect way of life. He found it in a Trappist monastery, and I in Tormore Bay." He turned to Grania. "And you at Kilcaraig Castle." Then he addressed Marian. "And how about you?"

Marian was obviously puzzled and at a loss with this strange young man.

"I don't think perfection can be found this side of the grave. When you are older, you'll be reaching out for a different sort of perfection. But you won't find it because it doesn't exist." She sank into the chair he offered her, but Grania, unthinking, had gone through an open door, before finding that it led to his bedroom. Here was the simplicity she expected to find. She backed out, feeling that she was an intruder, but he called to her, "Do look round. There's a bathroom through there, and even a plug that pulls!" He added, "I'm sorry, I should have shown you that first."

He turned to Marian. "You must think I'm very naive to believe one can live in a constant state of perfection. I suppose what I mean is that it's something to relish to the full while it lasts, just because one knows it can't last forever."

Grania washed her hands in the neat little bathroom, and was glad not to have to pull the plug, which might have reverberated through this peaceful haven of a cottage. Back in the bedroom, she looked quickly at the books he had chosen to keep beside his bed. A Bible, *Hebridean Altars*, Palgrave's *Golden Treasury*, and a battered and much read copy of *Pride and Prejudice*. There were other books, but she couldn't linger. Over his bed was an icon, a magnificent thing. She examined it closely, feeling its beauty with her hands as well as with her eyes. Then she called to him, "Mr. Lamont, where did you get this?"

He was beside her at once, almost touching her. Her head was only a little above his shoulder. She could sense the strength of him and she wondered if he was aware of the effect he had upon her.

"That was a present from a Russian friend my father helped after the war," he said. "I'm glad you approve of it. You must have good taste . . ." He broke off.

"After all," Grania said. "You were going to say I must have good taste after all!"

131

She could not avoid his eyes. He was staring at her, willing her to look at him. For a long moment they held one another's gaze, then they turned and rejoined Marian in the sitting-room, where the kettle was boiling and a tea pot was warming by the fire. The dog, lying on the hearth rug, thumped his tail like a welcoming drum beat.

They dipped ginger biscuits into their tea as they delved deeper into the ever fascinating subject of genealogy, and they talked of Mull legends, and of the headless horseman riding through Glen More.

"We'll meet him on our way home. We'll never get there before dark," Grania said. The daylight was fading fast.

"I'll see that you're safe," Roderick assured her. "I won't be with you, but I'll see that you're safe."

The lamps were glowing in the few dwellings when they approached the jetty at Fionnphort. Roderick insisted on tying up his boat and seeing them to the car. He exclaimed when he saw its size and its grandeur, and he was able to locate the light switches for Grania.

"That's mine," he said, indicating the navy-blue Ford. "She gets over to Craignure and back with a very visible effort." He laid his hand on Grania's shoulder. "Don't be tempted to hurry home. Stick to a safe crawl, and you'll be sure you'll arrive."

He stood aside, was caught for a moment by the headlights, then he was behind them, invisible in the dark.

"Robert will be furious," Grania repeated periodically, but she drove slowly and carefully. Rabbits skittered in front of them, dazzled by the lights, and she had to watch for cattle on the road, and for deer. "Aunt Marian, don't let's tell him about going to Tormore."

Marian knew that Grania must be very agitated to address her as "aunt". She had dropped that courtesy long ago.

"He'll likely know before we reach home," she said, with the wisdom of her years. "And if he doesn't, he'll soon find out. And what was wrong about it? There's nothing shameful about a cup of tea! Tell the truth and shame the devil!"

"Roderick's a man," Grania said. "That's enough. He's a man."

Robert was waiting for them on the steps when they reached the castle. He had seen the approaching lights, even as far back as the road at the top of the glen. He was not angry at all.

"Andy brought a message from the post office, telling me that you had been delayed," he said. "It was most thoughtful of your cousin to contact me. We must invite him over to lunch one day. I suppose he has a car?"

132

Grania left Marian to tell him about their day out. She went upstairs to the room which had been her nursery. It was a guest room now, furnished in the style which she would expect to find in a good hotel. She stood by the window and stared out into the night. From here she used to watch the sunset which she had always believed would sink into Tormore Bay.

Roderick Lamont was unusually thoughtful and resourceful to have sent a message through to Robert. Maybe he knew about the careful watch that Robert Dutton kept on his wife.

"*I can't be with you, but I'll see you're safe,*" he had said. Safe from being received at home by a husband whose anxiety would have whipped him into a state of ungovernable rage.

She heard Robert go to his room to change for dinner. She stayed still, frozen like the deer upon the mountain side, until she heard him close his dressing-room door; then she tiptoed to her room, and found to her relief that Chrissie had come upstairs to run her bath.

In the library, Marian played a game of solitaire. She had given Robert a fairly accurate account of what they had done, but she had not admitted that Roderick Lamont was quite outstanding both in appearance and in charm, and far from being of her generation, he could only be older than Grania by a few years.

"He's too good to be true," she thought, looking reproachfully at the few marbles left in isolation on the board. "What sort of an end will there be to the beginning that's happened today?"

20

A few days after the visit to Iona, history was made at Kilcaraig. The telephone was installed in the castle. Two instruments were allotted to it, the one being put in Robert's study, and the other in the library, where Grania spent the whole of the first day telephoning her friends.

"Gossip won't be a breeze in the barley any more," she remarked at dinner. "It'll be a hurricane raging along all the telephone wires, and there won't be a good character left on the island!"

Robert gave her a long look. "You've been enjoying this innovation. I thought you hated progress."

"I'll hate it all right when people realize they can telephone us, as well as we them. And if your awful business pals ring up about filthy lucre in the small hours, I'll sue for divorce!" She turned her attention to the roast duck on her plate, unaware that her husband was staring at her in ill-concealed rage.

Marian, watching, thought "She must want to torment him. She can't be as insensitive as she pretends."

During the momentary silence which followed Grania's remark, Hunter appeared, like a stage butler in a well-rehearsed play. Robert, too, resumed eating, and Marian said that the weather forecast had been good. The stilted conversation dragged on through dinner, and they were about to leave the dining-room when Robert asked, "Did you invite your cousin to lunch, Grania?"

"My cousin?" She looked up, feigning surprise. "I forgot about it, with the telephone engineers being here, and all that upheaval. Say when, and I'll write."

"Not telephone?"

"There isn't one at Tormore."

"How do you know?"

She stood up, impatient, and tossed her napkin on to the table. "Because there aren't any wires there, and everyone knows there's no telephone nearer to him than Iona Ferry, and I think you want to pick a quarrel, but I'm not playing," and she moved over to him, rubbing her cheek against his cheek. He smiled, and put his arm round her waist.

Marian averted her eyes. She was a silly old maid, she thought, and would not understand marital relationships. What she was witnessing was perhaps a commonplace situation between two people who were adjusting to one another. Yet, what she believed she was witnessing was a young woman being deliberately provocative, and an elderly man being made to look a fool. Grania had never forgotten about that invitation, had never for a moment allowed her supposed cousin to be out of her thoughts.

They had brandy with their coffee, and soon Marian felt more at ease, more her own self, while Grania talked away about all the people she had contacted on the telephone, and all the things they had said.

"I feel like a fly on the wall," Marian thought. "I feel I shouldn't be here. I should get back to London."

The next morning, Grania wrote a letter beginning, "Dear Mr. Lamont", and continuing with a friendly, yet formal invitation to luncheon on Saturday. She walked to the village to post her letter, and noted the interested look the post mistress gave it as she tossed it into the mail-bag.

Grania next went to Caraig Lodge, and found Mr. and Mrs. Ames having coffee with Michael. She invited them all to luncheon on Saturday, and explained who she hoped would be there. When his parents left him alone with Grania, Michael said "Tell me about him. How did you meet him?"

She told him exactly as it had happened, mentioning even the icon on the wall, and the plug that pulled. When she had finished, Michael held out his hand. She took it in hers.

"Take care," he said. "Of all people in the whole wide world, you are the last I want to get hurt."

"But how could I be hurt? I'm a married woman, and I take my vows very seriously, and I don't share Robert's idea that every man who meets me is going to fall madly in love with me. It's just that it's so amazing to meet a gorgeous man who is well-read and intelligent and does all the things I admire, and who lives at Tormore Bay – why, it's like a dream come true! And there's something about the cottage that I can't explain. It's a haven because it isn't contaminated by human emotions. Do you understand what I mean?" Her eagerness, with its youth and innocence and folly, was pitiful and touching.

"I understand," he said. "But I don't think you do. He's a man, with all the instincts that go with being male. Something has driven him to seek the peace of a simulated hermit's cell. Discover that something and you could expose both him and you to great temptation and distress."

"You make a pleasant little excursion on an autumn day into a curtain-raiser for a melodrama!"

"Yes," Michael said. "That's exactly what I'm afraid it could be."

Roderick had to telephone his reply to Grania's letter, because he had spent a couple of days in Inverary and there was no time for him to write. Robert took the call, and he liked the voice of this kinsman of Grania's, but he had reservations about the wisdom of issuing the invitation. He had made the suggestion in attempt to conform to Grania's code of hospitality, as he understood it – food and drink must be offered, especially to kinsfolk and to strangers. He would never fathom her strange Highland ways, and she would never realize how hard he tried to do so. In honesty he had to admit that he wanted to see for himself this man who had come so unexpectedly into their lives. It hadn't occurred either to Marian or to Grania that he might be a rogue and an impostor.

When Saturday came, the Ameses were the first to arrive, having been urged by Grania to be punctual, so that she and Marian would not be alone with Robert when their very far distant cousin arrived. During the winter, Grania used the library rather than the drawing-room for small parties, and she had settled Michael and his parents beside the fire with a drink when the Wrights arrived. They had bought a house near Tobermory at about the same time as Robert had bought Kilcaraig, and this forged some sort of a link with him. Grania had invited them to the castle because she was worried that Robert had no Mull friends of his own.

Mrs. Wright, mentally costing everything in the room, tried to give her dutiful attention to Michael Ames. Marian, always reliably talkative, was doing well with the taciturn Mr. Wright, Mrs. Ames was unashamedly examining the books which lined the walls, and Robert and Mr. Ames stood by the table of drinks, exchanging views on the latest monetary crisis. Grania, over near the window, heard the roaring approach of a car that had lost its silencer. She turned away quickly, not wanting to look as if she had been keeping a watch for Roderick Lamont, and a moment later, Hunter announced him, and there he was, wearing his kilt and green tweed jacket.

It was Mrs. Wright who pointed out the astonishing resemblance between the newcomer and the portrait of Niall Lamont of Kilcaraig which hung on the wall behind him. The eyes, the nose, the colouring were the same, but the man in the painting had a long, dark beard.

"I'll have to grow one," Roderick said, touching his chin. Robert, who had received him most cordially, handed him a whisky. Roderick added water, which surprised Robert, who thought he would have preferred it neat.

"The portrait came back to Kilcaraig on the day I married my wife," Robert said. "It had been on loan to the MacArthur art galleries as it was too large for a London flat. The family likeness is almost uncanny. How lucky it was that you all converged on Iona last week."

Grania saw that Mrs. Wright was listening with interest. She was well-known for her skill in speading information, good or bad, through the island, and this snatch of conversation had given her just what Grania wanted her to hear. Hers was no clandestine friendship with Roderick Lamont, and she wanted the islanders to know it. Mrs. Wright would see that they did.

Later, sitting at the head of the wide mahogany table with Mr. Ames on one side of her and Mr. Wright on the other, Grania couldn't keep track of what the others were saying, but there were bursts of laughter, and at one point Marian and Roderick conducted a brief exchange in Gaelic. They were sitting opposite to one another, and their argument concerned which region spoke the best Gaelic.

Grania leaned forward and joined in. It was all over in a moment, but it left Mrs. Wright almost speechless for the rest of the meal. She

136

had thought Gaelic was the language of the peasants, yet here were the Lamonts speaking it as if it were their mother tongue, and the blood in their veins was as blue as ink. It must be possible to understand the culture of these Highland people. The Ameses had managed to do so. So could she.

There had been a sprinkling of snow during lunch, and the Wrights felt that they should set out for Tobermory as soon as they had finished their coffee.

"We don't want to be caught in a snowdrift," Mrs. Wright said to Grania, buttoning up her coat. "It's been so delightful to meet your cousin. Your husband couldn't have given him a warmer welcome if it had been your brother who had appeared out of obscurity after all these years!"

Grania felt stunned by her words. Her brother! Was this a piece of guesswork, or had Mrs. Wright picked up something and stored it in her gossip-hungry mind!

After they had gone, Robert offered to show Roderick round the estate. It was a surprising honour to confer upon a stranger, and Grania, watching them set off together, wondered what they would find to say to one another. So far as she knew, Robert's only interest in his property lay in seeing that the people who were paid to run it for him did so efficiently.

It began to snow again, and Grania, plying the Ameses and Marian with more coffee, found herself worrying about Robert more than she had been worried about Mrs. Wright's disturbing words, but in less than an hour the Labradors, wet and wagging, bounced into the room, followed by Roderick and by Robert, who looked pale and tired.

Roderick refused the invitation to stay for tea. "I've had a wonderful time, but I don't trust my headlights to see me home," he said to Grania. "Your husband has told me I may fish on Loch Caraig whenever I like. He says you're a dab hand at catching trout, so I hope you'll join me sometimes."

"I've not fished for years. I'd have to learn all over again." It would be months before the trout fishing began. Robert's words could have been a warning to keep away for a while, rather than an invitation to come to the castle at will.

Robert linked arms with her as they saw Roderick into his battered navy-blue Ford. Grania knew that this was one of her husband's ways of indicating that she was his property. The gravel crunched as the wheels gripped, and the car was off down the drive. Grania waited for Robert to comment on this new acquaintance, but he said nothing, and together they returned to the house, where the others had begun tea. By the silence which met them as they entered the room, Grania was sure that they had the subject of Roderick under discussion. Michael would tell her later. Not Marian. Marian had somehow changed towards her. Then she looked at Marian and realized why. She was handing a cup of tea to Robert, and was telling him he looked weary, and her expression showed the degree of her concern.

Perhaps, as her fortieth birthday drew near, she was regretting that it was Grania and not herself that was the mistress of Kilcaraig.

"She didn't want him," Grania thought bitterly, her mind still dwelling on Mrs. Wright's reference to Roderick as her half-brother. It was the sort of truth that everyone could know except herself. A chance remark by a notorious gossip shouldn't upset her so much. It was proof of her desperate insecurity that the matter milled through her mind while she poured out tea and handed out pancakes and helped Michael to cope with an awkward slice of creamy chocolate cake.

When the Ameses left and the debris had been removed by a maid, Robert and Marian began working out dates, because Marian was returning to London, and Robert had decided that he would have to resume responsibility for the Carnworth, Prior and Dutton empire. It had been in the hands of his deputy since his marriage nearly eight months ago.

"Shall I be coming?" Grania asked.

"Of course."

"For how long?"

"Until Christmas, if you like." Robert was watching her hard.

"Yes, I would like," she said, because she knew he would want her to say it. "I'll do the Christmas shopping."

"And I'm going to buy you a car."

She looked at Robert in astonishment. He continued, "I died a thousand deaths when you went to Iona last week. The Daimler's too big for you, and I can see that I can't expect you always to be under escort! So you must have something small and manageable of your very own."

Her arms were round him, and there were tears in her eyes. "You're the most surprising man I've ever known," she said. "And I don't deserve you at all – indeed I don't." He returned her embrace, stroked her curls, and quietly left the room.

"Could you not, just for once, have said 'I love you'," Marian asked.

Grania felt the colour creeping into her cheeks, and down her neck. "I'll leave that to you," she said and saw that Marian winced, just as if she had been hit. Immediately she was sorry, but it was too important a matter to be dismissed easily.

"Marian," she said. "It was the most utterly idiotic thing that it was me he chose, he'd be so much happier with you. But it's terrible that, of all people in the world, it should be you who is feeling about him the way I ought to do."

Marian looked at Grania, remembering Robert's first visit to the castle. The contempt she had felt for him, the hostility he had engendered in the child Grania.

"I have no envy for you at all, Grania. I know that there are difficult months – and perhaps years – ahead of you, because marrying for money is never a good thing to do. But he has bought you, and you owe it to him to give him his money's worth. I've heard a bit about Robert the past few days. He longs to be loved." Marian bit her lip. "I think something in me responds to that need. It's a ridiculous situation. I wouldn't like anyone to know about it except you."

Grania felt that this called for the sort of wisdom she did not yet possess. Nicholas would know what to say, so would Michael. All she knew was that she loved Marian so much that she would do anything in the world to stop her from feeling ridiculous and unhappy, for she must feel both.

"I think what you are really feeling is a very deep gratitude," she said. "About the burglary and all that. It's so dependable to have a man about the place. One who knows how to give orders, and have them obeyed." She felt the inadequacy of her words, but could see that Marian accepted the explanation gratefully. It was a clumsy effort, but it provided the necessary cover-up.

"I believe you're right," Marian said. "Times of crisis can have odd, emotional repercussions." Then, to dismiss the awkward subject she said, "It's funny how none of us noticed that Roderick resembles my father, and until today it never occurred to me to ask Donald MacBean if he knows anything about our family that isn't on record."

Donald MacBean was the oldest inhabitant of Kilcaraig. He was bedridden and lived in the cottage which his family had occupied for centuries. His daughter looked after him, and she refused to let anyone provide modern amenities which might spoil the peace of his home. The thatch remained on the roof, so did the slanted wooden chimney, and water had to be brought in buckets from the well. Donald, who was mentally alert although physically infirm, enjoyed holding court, propped up against a pile of pillows, their unpressed cases sparkling white as snow.

"If Donald knows anything disturbing, he won't tell," Grania said.

"What could be disturbing about Roderick Lamont?"

Grania bit her lip, thinking. Then she said, "Today Mrs. Wright hinted that he might be my illegitimate brother." She had to say it. She could not keep this new and crushing anxiety to herself.

Surprisingly, Marian laughed. "How absurd. Of course that isn't true. But maybe the old gossip has given you some sound advice. If you think of him as your brother, you won't get any silly notions about him. He's a very attractive young man. Take care, Grania. You're the last person in the world I would want to see hurt."

She had used almost the same words as Michael had used.

"I won't get involved with Roderick Lamont. Robert will see to that," Grania said.

"You're right there. He's done it already. Roderick isn't the sort of man who will abuse hospitality. You have a very astute husband, Grania, and one with a pretty complicated mind. He plans his moves in advance, and he's making very sure that the knight isn't going to take his queen."

Robert came into the room. He had changed for dinner, but was wearing bedroom slippers, as he often did when he was tired. The sight of the two women sitting together in the firelight was heart-warming and wonderful. His women. His family.

"Are you talking about chess?" he asked.

"Yes," Grania said. "Yes, we were talking about chess."

In a sort of a way she supposed that it was true.

21

During her first few days in London, Grania found that the noise and the pace were frightening, and that the pressure of being charming at luncheon parties and attentive during long after-dinner speeches was almost unbearable.

"I'm a country bumpkin at heart," she said to Adrian Ferguson, whom she had met for a drink while Robert was at a board meeting.

"You don't look like one," Adrian said. He had managed to meet her in the Opera Tavern, just off the Strand, which had been one of their favourite haunts before her marriage. Now, in her mink coat and matching hat, he wished he had chosen a place where she would be less conspicuous – the Waldorf or the Savoy.

Very soon he had forgotten her appearance, which had made him feel a little shy of her at first, as he told her about his first visit to Bayreuth.

"I couldn't believe it was true as I sat there in the Festspielhaus, actually hearing the prelude to *Das Rheingold*," he said. "You must get your Robert to take you there. With money no object, you can go every year!"

"I can't see Robert sitting through one Wagner opera, let alone four of them. I'm afraid hearing *The Ring* will be one of my unfulfilled ambitions."

But that night she told Robert about Bayreuth, although she implied that her companion had been a woman and their rendezvous an hotel.

"Of course I'll take you," he said. "There's nothing on earth I won't do for you. You should know that by now."

She thought about the baby she was not allowed to bear, but this was neither the time nor the place to say anything about it. Instead, she resolved never to inflict Wagner on Robert. In her own way she, too, tried to please.

The maisonette at Ladbroke Place was up more stairs than she had remembered, but it was cosy and homely after the artificial splendour of what was meant to be her London home in Lowndes Square. She found that Helen was peevishly undecided about what she wanted to do with her life, while Diana was preparing herself for the job of under-matron in a boys' school. She had bought First Aid manuals, and booklets on how to patch jacket elbows and how to knit new heels into old socks. Grania felt sorry for her. It must be dreadful to be excited about the prospect of dosing little boys with cough mixture, but it was probably the thought of the school masters she would meet that made Diana so light-hearted.

Farnborough drove Grania and Evelyn to Epsom one day, and they spent the afternoon listening to Evelyn's mother talking about her first visit to Kilcaraig. Her mind was crystal clear. She could describe it in every detail, just as it must have been, but she constantly addressed Grania as "Catriona".

"She's living in the past. She's not really with us any more," Evelyn said on the way home. She kept looking at her watch, because she had joined a bridge club, and she was afraid of being late. Grania remembered how her grandmother used to plan her life round her bridge parties, and it seemed that Evelyn was set to follow the same dismal pattern. There was nothing she could do about it, but she did ask her family to spend Christmas at Kilcaraig.

Evelyn accepted, and Diana and Helen, torn between the Christmas parties they would miss in London, and their curiosity about what had been done to Kilcaraig, decided to go there with her. Marian refused at first, because she had been there so recently, but in the end she agreed to a compromise and said she would arrive in time to bring in the New Year.

Nicholas Danvers had been in Havana during the ten days that the Duttons were in London, but he returned to Cranston Terrace to find that Mrs. Tibbetts had written out Grania's telephone message inviting him for Christmas. He rang her and caught her just before she was due to set off for the north.

"It's impossible," he said. "My novel isn't finished, and my publishers are breathing down my neck."

"You'll finish it at Kilcaraig. You'll have the room you used when you were a struggling and impecunious author. You'll be left strictly alone, and if you wish, you'll have your meals brought to you on a tray!"

Nicholas, hearing Grania's eager voice, succumbed. She might need his help during this, her first Christmas as mistress of Kilcaraig. He tipped his tropical clothes out of his suitcase and piled onto the bed the woollies he would need for Mrs. Tibbetts to pack.

Diana and Helen reacted to the changes in Kilcaraig much as Grania had thought they would. Nobody could fault the improvements that had been carried out by Robert, not only to the castle but throughout the whole estate. Equally, nobody could deny that they were out of keeping with the rest of Mull. Not a single gate was tied up with string, not a single fence was in a state of decay, and every cottage in the village was neat and painted, with windows which would stay open when one wanted them open, instead of having to prop them with a book or with a lump of peat. There were no broken sash-cords in Kilcaraig.

Evelyn sadly watched the calendar, longing for the holiday to be over, so that she could get back to the familiarity of her own home, and to her bridge club. Grania had become a stranger to her, and she never had been able to think of anything to say to Robert. Nicholas, aware of all that they were feeling, realized how wise he had been to accept the invitation to be here. Grania needed him.

There was a Christmas Eve party at the castle for all the children in the district, with Mr. Ames acting as Santa Claus, because Robert, having done so when he first arrived in Mull, had been so overcome with stage-fright that he never could repeat the ordeal. Then the

142

children left, clutching the toys they had been given, the drawing-room was in a mess with cracker papers and pine needles from the Christmas tree, and Diana and Helen exchanged looks as the plum-clad servants rapidly restored the room to order, and Hunter came in with a tray of drinks.

They were sitting round the fire, talking about the party and sipping their drinks, when the dogs unanimously barked the presence of a stranger, and Roderick Lamont was shown into the room. He had not been to the castle since that luncheon party in November and although he had been much on Grania's mind, she knew better than to try to contact him in any way.

He accepted a drink, explaining that he could not wait for long, as he was playing the pipes at the Creich Christmas party, down near Iona ferry. He had come to deliver a hamper which he had found on the jetty at Craignure, and which had somehow been forgotten by the carrier.

Diana and Helen studied him, almost gaping with fascination; Grania had said nothing to them about this gorgeous young man. Nicholas was watching too. Since her marriage, Grania had acquired a self-assurance that made it impossible to guess what her feelings might be, but Robert had an air of uncertainty about him, as if he might either hurl the intruder out of the room, or force him to settle down and become one of the family.

Michael Ames, in his darkness, could have described where everyone was sitting, as well as how they looked. Conversation flowed easily, with the talk of Christmas, which for most people on the island was merely a prelude to the festivities of the New Year.

Roderick got up to go, as abruptly as he had arrived. "See you all next year," he said, swinging out of the room, and leaving them with the feeling that the principal actor had left the stage, and it was the cue for the final curtain.

Marian arrived at Craignure on the same day that Evelyn and the two girls left. Grania waited for the arrival of the boat from Oban, and when it came, the ferry boat was packed with people making their way home to the island for the New Year; among them a very smart Marian who extricated herself from the crowd and kissed Grania.

"You've had your hair tinted," was Grania's greeting.

"I've got a job in a grand hat shop," Marian told her. "So I've changed my appearance and personality! I'm a very elegant lady. I hardly know myself!"

Grania had driven to Craignure in her new little grey car, which had been delivered at Tobermory just before the Christmas holidays.

She had been driven by Farnborough in the Daimler to meet it, and had watched with some apprehension as it was brought ashore across the planks on the MacBrayne's boat. Soon it was on the pier, sparkling and unscratched, and she set off for Kilcaraig, painfully conscious that Farnborough, following in the Daimler, was watching her every move, and noting if she put her foot on the brake too often. He would make a full report to Robert. Somehow she had brought her treasured Christmas present home.

Today it was different. She had already become used to the car, and she drove a little faster and with more confidence. She could hear the rushes which grew in the middle of the road brushing its under-body. No wonder Farnborough thought the Mull roads were not designed for anything more sophisticated than a cart. Despite her claim that she was a changed personality, Marian was as talkative as ever, and scarcely drew breath until they arrived at the castle, which was fully lighted, but not floodlit, for its last welcome of the year so soon to pass.

The New Year's Eve dance was held in the school house. Everyone was there, and as Grania danced and laughed with the people she had known all her life, she could see that Robert and Marian and Nicholas were dancing and laughing too. Michael Ames was sitting in a corner near the Christmas tree, clapping in time to the music, and tapping with his feet.

At midnight, they all sang *Auld Lang Syne*, some of them with tears on their cheeks, because they remembered the old acquaintances that would never be forgot especially those whose names were engraved on the War Memorial, and they thought of the names that could be added to that memorial, unless the statesmen managed to do something about the growing threat to peace in the world.

"We'll have to go," Grania said to Michael. "Can you come back with us for a drink?"

"I can't. Mother says she's tired; I think we should go home." He held up his hand to her. "There wouldn't be a wee bit of mistletoe just over my head, would there?"

Grania laughed, and as she kissed him, she put her arms round his neck. Robert tapped her on the shoulder. "It's time we went."

Michael released her immediately, but as she turned, Robert was already half way across the room to the door. He was very pale, and his lips were pressed tightly together. Grania followed him, saying "goodnights" and waving her hand, but her heart seemed to contract with fear. Thank God Nicholas and Marian were here! They were at the car, talking to Robert, who answered them in monosyllables.

144

Grania sat on the back seat, arranging Marian as a buffer between Robert and herself.

When they reached the castle, nobody suggested drinks. Grania kissed Marian, shook hands with Nicholas, and crept fearfully off to bed. Robert followed her, and as she opened the bedroom door, he caught at her wrist.

"If you must kiss Michael Ames, will you in future choose a less public place," he said. "I won't have you making a laughing stock of me."

His words were such an anti-climax after the threats she had expected, that she wanted to laugh.

"It's when I don't kiss in public that you'll need to start worrying," she said. "Don't ever look like Dracula over trifles. You gave me quite a scare, you silly old thing." She smiled, and kissed his chin, which was the nearest she could get to his lips. A moment later, she had closed the door, leaving him there on the landing, staring at where she had been, biting his lip because he wanted to cry, like a hurt child.

Inside the room, he could hear her singing. She often sang while she undressed.

> "*Dubh ciar-dubh, dubh ciar-dubh*,
> Though poor, poor thou be,
> No grey-beard can please me,
> Like thee, love, like thee."

Robert flung open the door. Her clothes were in a circle at her feet, and she was reaching out her hand for her nightdress.

He caught her by the shoulders, and pushed her on to the bed.

✻   ✻   ✻

In the library, Marian put more peat on the embers of the fire, and Nicholas foraged in a corner cupboard, where he knew some drinks were kept. He poured out a brandy for Marian and a whisky for himself. He had noticed Marian's involuntary shivers. Like himself, she would have preferred to witness a fierce marital row, rather than the icy calm of Robert's disapproval.

"*Slainte!*" Marian said, raising her glass.

"*Slandya*," Nicholas replied. Gaelic pronunciation had defeated him.

"I suppose she'll be all right?" Marian said.

"He won't strangle her, if that's what you mean. I think you can take it that she's used to this sort of display. She'll accept it as a normal aspect of married life."

The house was quiet, but the floor-boards creaked when, a little while later, they crept upstairs to their rooms.

Nicholas was up early on the following morning. He had slept very little, and he sat at his desk staring at the blank sheet of paper in front of him, his inventive train of thought severed by the frivolities of the past day, and by the distressing episode of last night.

There was a tap on the door, and the rattle of a tray. It wasn't a maid who entered, it was Grania.

"I saw the light shining from your room when I looked out of my window to see what the weather is up to. It's so silent, and yet there isn't frost or snow," she said.

Nicholas took the tray from her and put it on his desk.

"Are you all right?" he asked.

"I slept like a log, but I always wake early. The staff will have hangovers, and Chrissie spent last night at the MacPhails. She went to them after the dance, and I don't suppose anyone was in a fit state to drive her home!" She lifted the cover from the plate. The bacon and eggs were still hot and sizzling. "I cooked them myself. Don't touch the plate, it's scorching. When you've eaten your breakfast, I want to talk to you. I've brought a cup for myself, so I'll have coffee while I wait."

She poured out her coffee and sat on the window seat drinking it. Nicholas did as he was told. He ate what she had prepared, and followed it with a slice of toast and marmalade. Then he, too, poured out coffee.

She had spoken quickly, nervously, but there was something soothing about her silence. She had come here for a purpose, and he waited for what it was she wanted to say.

"I've got a terribly embarrassing question to ask you," she said.

"Yes?" One word, but it conveyed the cool, professional encouragement of those old days when he was a doctor, and his patient was finding difficulty in describing a symptom.

"Please will you tell me the name of the best gynaecologist in London. That isn't the embarrassing part – we'll come to that later."

"Do you mean a gynaecologist or an obstetrician?"

"I don't know. I'm not expecting a baby. I just want to be positively sure that I can have one without dying, like my mother and my grandmother did."

So she had been told about Catriona. He and Marian had thought she must have been. Evelyn had performed the necessary duty after all.

"It would be wise to take advice," he said. "There was nothing abnormal about your mother's confinement. She suffered an ordinary mischance of childbirth, which nowadays is dealt with easily." His thoughts were back in that room in St. John's Wood in the spring of 1914. This beautiful girl was the battered little *Grannda* he had held in his arms, close to his heart.

"You were in love with her, weren't you?"

"Yes."

"Until a little while ago, I thought you might be my father. But I know now that you can't be. You didn't know her at the time I was conceived."

"Grania, what put such an idea into your head?" He was appalled. He had known her all her life, and she had thought this.

"Because you're so special, I suppose. I wish you were my father. I wish someone was. I wish I knew." It was a cry from the heart, and he could not tell her. He could only guess at the truth. She waited, and seeing that there was no answer, she said nervously "Someone, somewhere, must know."

"I think not, Grania. I think that the secret went with your grandfather to the grave."

"May I have some more coffee?" She leaned over and handed him her cup. Sitting with her back to the window, he had been unable to see how pale she was. There was dark lines under her eyes. She couldn't have slept like a log. Under the surface, her whole life was a sham and she knew it.

"Grania, are you happy?"

"I'm not unhappy. You mustn't worry too much about last night. Robert is very kind to me. I mean that. I'd dreaded the physical side of marriage, but he understood that and he made it all right. Now I don't mind it any more." She had resumed her seat by the window and was stirring her coffee.

"But love isn't a matter of not minding it – it's a matter of joy, of the ultimate, the most sublime in human relationships."

"Who's talking about love?" She said it without any feeling. She stated it as a plain fact.

She was right of course. They weren't talking about love. Baffled, Nicholas said. "About that doctor. There's Adams, whose consulting room is in Queen Anne Street. When can Robert take you to London?"

She gave a little gasp. "I didn't tell you – Robert mustn't know anything about this."

"He'll have to know. He's your husband."

"He'll have to know if I start a baby, but at present he won't let me have one. He thinks it will kill me. He won't even talk about it – he's made up his mind. But he's not unreasonable. If I know beyond doubt that there's nothing to fear, he may listen. But he won't let me go through the indignity of finding out."

"There's nothing undignified about these tests, they're commonplace. There's nothing for you to be shy about."

She held up her hand to stop him. "I'm not worried about that side of it, Robert is. What worries me – and this is the dreadfully embarrassing thing I have to ask you – what worries me is that I can't pay for the consultation unless you lend me some money. Robert grudges me nothing, but I haven't a penny of my own, not even enough to buy a postage stamp."

Nicholas could see another task ahead of him. He would have to hint to Robert that women liked to have a degree of independence, and that lavish gifts were not enough. His pity for Grania was so great that his only way of dealing with it lay in hiding his concern.

"I'd be delighted to lend you money. You needn't worry at all about that. But how can all this happen without Robert knowing? You'll have to get to London for a start!"

"I've only got to say I want some new clothes, or to go to the theatre. I've told you – he doesn't mind what's spent on me, so long as it's not spent directly by me. He doesn't realize it, but it's one of the ways he keeps a leash fixed to my pearly collar." She touched the string of pearls which gleamed against her cashmere pullover. "He'll be awake now, so I'd better show up for breakfast. Don't tell him I've been here – he'll think I've been complaining about last night."

She took the tray and refused to let him carry it downstairs for her. "If I meet him, I'll say it's Marian's," she said. He opened the door for her, and closed it quietly after her. He had committed himself to another Lamont plot.

It had been just the same during that autumn before the outbreak of war. He had been trapped then, as he was trapped now. He returned to his desk and wrote a page about the mental anguish of his heroine; then he tore it into shreds and threw it into his waste-paper basket.

Anything he concocted was a poor substitute for the real thing that was happening here, under this roof.

22

Doctor MacColl put away his stethoscope, and addressed the prone form of Lachlan MacLachlan, who occupied the examining couch in the surgery where once Nicholas Danvers had dreamed his dreams.

"If you don't obey my orders, it will be you who will inhabit the first layer cut in the new burial ground," he said.

"That's a terrible threat you are giving me, doctor," sighed Lachlan, wondering how soon he could get out of the surgery, and back to his peat moss. He had never taken care of himself in all his life, and he had no intention of doing so now.

Doctor MacColl knew very well the thought processes of his patients. He had been on the island since Doctor MacFie left, and that was a long time ago.

"I talked to Lady Dutton," he said. "And she has arranged that your peats will be cut, and your cow milked, and your dog cared for at the castle itself, while you take that wee holiday with your cousin in Glasgow."

Lachlan pondered this. Without the worry of his peats and his cow and his dog, he could enjoy a holiday. It would be lonely to be the occupant of the first grave in the new burial ground.

"I'll consider it," he said, and Doctor MacColl knew he had won. He wrote out a prescription while Lachlan buttoned up his jacket. "I'll send the bottle along, and you'll take it as directed," he said. "And don't forget to take it with you when you go to Glasgow."

When surgery was over, Doctor MacColl drove up to the castle to tell Grania that her offer of assistance had been accepted, with the result that the MacLachlan cottage would be likely to house its present tenant for many years to come. A little bit of a rest could mean the difference between life and death, but the number of people in responsible positions who recognized this was dwindling. Sir Robert had been too busy to concern himself with the lives of those who worked for him, but his wife was different. The people as well as the place were important to her.

Grania was picking daffodils at the side of the drive. She looked tired. Only one year married, and the bloom was fading from her. Perhaps one day she would come to his surgery, and he would give her the news everyone in the village was hoping to hear. They wanted an heir for Kilcaraig.

"You look as if you could do with a rest yourself."

"Me, a rest?" She had just come back from London, where everything had gone according to plan. She had bought some clothes and had been to several theatres, and she had crept off to Queen Anne Street while Robert was at a board meeting. Mr. Adams, who examined her, had been very reassuring, and his secretary had not demurred when she was given a cash payment, instead of sending the customary bill. It had all been a strain, but it had also been a relief.

"Yes, you need a rest," Doctor MacColl was saying. He had said more than that, but she wasn't listening. "You tire yourself in London, with all those late nights, and you'll be going back there soon, to tire yourself all over again."

This was true. She was to be presented at Court on her marriage, having been on her honeymoon during the London season last year. There would also be the races at Ascot, and the tennis championships at Wimbledon, and a number of important balls, which she would be expected to attend.

She found that she was blushing. Doctor MacColl was thinking that she had started a baby, but no one could have found out about her visit to Queen Anne Street – no one at all.

"Robert's going away next week – just for a few days. I'll have a rest then." Suddenly she wasn't blushing, she was laughing. "I hope you don't misunderstand me, Doctor, I'll miss my husband very much. I don't much care for the idea of being alone."

During lunch, she said to Robert – "I've been thinking, why don't you drive south next week? Roy Farnborough wants the Daimler sorted. It would suit you both."

"Grania, the car may need servicing, but not sorting."

"Don't be so stuffy. You know what I mean." Her eyes were snapping. "And Doctor MacColl says I could do with a rest. So I could. A rest from being tailed by Farnborough every time I leave the house, even when I'm in my own car." She had to stop while Hunter removed their plates, and brought in the biscuits and cheese. She could see that Robert was white and furious, but when they were alone again, he said nothing. He just looked tired. At once she was sorry, but she dreaded that she would incur his usual remedy for any kind of quarrel with her, so she looked at her watch.

"I must go to Lachlan MacLachlan and talk about his trip to

Glasgow." She was halfway to the door before Robert could stop her. "I'll be back for tea," she said over her shoulder. She shut the door, and paused for a moment in case he called to her in that peremptory voice that she dared not disobey. There was silence. She ran out of the house, and soon she was heading for the village in her little grey car, alarmed at her own panic.

That night, Robert came to her room, and sat on her bed. He looked troubled, but she was calm now. She had settled everything with old Lachlan, and it had soothed her nerves to feel that she had done something useful.

"I've been thinking about what you said at lunch," Robert said. "Your idea is a good one – I'll get Farnborough to drive me south and have the car sorted." He glanced at her, hoping she would show pleasure that he had used that word. She registered nothing. She just lay staring straight ahead of her.

"We'll probably be away for about a week," he continued. "And during that week, I'll make up my mind about bringing Farnborough back. We need a chauffeur, but if you feel he's spying on you, I expect you would be happier if someone else drove the Daimler."

Still no response. She could have no idea how difficult it had been for him to muster up the courage to talk to her like this. It was his apology to her for his jealousy, for his mistrust of her, for all that he had done to make her unhappy. He stood up, and ended lamely – "I just wanted you to know".

He went to the door leading to the corridor, not the one to the bathroom, as if he wanted to establish that he no longer regarded the bathroom as a link between their bedrooms, but as a barrier. Before he closed the door, she had reached him, her satin nightdress clinging to her body, her arms flung round him. She was crying, he could feel her tears on his chest.

"I've been feeling like a bird in a gilded cage," she sobbed. "And I don't want Farnborough back because there are islanders who can drive the car. We don't need such a great big car anyway. We don't need prestige."

"You don't," he said, stroking her hair. "But I do. Come now, back to bed. You'll catch cold."

That night, they slept together for the first time since their honeymoon. Because there had been no love-making, Grania felt nearer to loving him than she had ever felt. Some day, perhaps, she would be able to lie like this in his arms, and talk to him about important things, like explaining why she so much wanted a baby, why she yearned to know who was her father, why she wanted just a little bit of money that would be unquestioned and her own. To talk about God and poetry and all the things lovers talked about. Or so they said. She lay awake, thinking about these things, listening to his breathing, glad that he was peacefully asleep, instead of working out how to make more money and how to keep his wife faithful to him. Perhaps he had other thoughts besides these. Like her, he might want to talk of all sorts of things – God, and poetry. One year married, and they hardly knew one another at all.

Farnborough and the Daimler left Kilcaraig the day before Robert, because the car would have to be loaded onto the boat at Tobermory. Grania said goodbye to him, casually, as if he were coming back, but she could see by the luggage he took with him that Robert had already decided what to do, and had acted on this decision.

She drove Robert to Craignure, and waved him off as he was ferried to the waiting boat. Farnborough and the car would be on board that boat. Grania felt a flood of relief that she would be unlikely to see either of them ever again.

When she walked up the jetty to her car, she saw that Roderick Lamont was talking to the bus driver and some others on the little pier. He waved to her, but otherwise showed no interest in her. "He despises me," she thought, as she got into her little car. It lurched forward and came to a standstill, because she mis-timed pressing the clutch when she engaged the gear. She pressed the starter. The engine spluttered and stopped. She tried again crimson with vexation. Trying to start a car that would not respond was a shaming experience. She could feel that someone was coming to help her, and she knew who it was.

"You've got the choke out," he said. "All you need is to push it in, and exercise a little patience. It will be all right in a few minutes."

She had wound down the window so that she could hear what he said, but she could not bring herself to look at him, as if he had caught her committing a misdemeanour. She pushed in the choke.

"Idiotic, isn't it, how silly one feels if one's car won't start," he said, apparently disposed to stay with her until she was able to drive away. "Like falling off a horse. You just hope nobody has noticed!"

Such a trivial thing to say, but it was exactly what she needed to hear. She looked at him gratefully. "I'm usually a very competent driver," she said, and thought how stilted that sounded.

"So I've noticed."

This surprised her. "I haven't seen you around."

"I've seen you. I was fishing on Loch Caraig twice last week. Remember? I'm allowed to."

"Why didn't you come and see us?"

"I came to fish, not to be a nuisance. Try the starter again."

The engine fired immediately.

"Off you go, before it stops! And next time, don't pull out the choke when the engine is hot. It floods it."

She nodded, not understanding what he meant, and she was past Torosay Castle before she could calm down after her brief, but somehow exciting encounter.

It had not occurred to her to see what was happening on Loch Caraig. Robert often gave people permission to fish, and to use the boat if they wished to do so, provided he could trust their competence to handle it. There was no charge for fishing on this loch, for that was part of the tradition of the estate.

The following afternoon, she took her gun and set off over the hills with Angus and her dogs. She was humming *The Road to the Isles* when Angus remarked that she sounded very cheerful.

"I am," she said, and managed not to add, "I'm free."

"Yes, you're terrible cheerful," Angus said reprovingly. "And they're surprised that you were at the dance in the school last night."

"I only stayed for half an hour, and hardly danced at all!" She had gone to be a spectator, but had been "lifted" by Willie for the eightsome reel. Nothing scandalous about that.

"You'll be missing Sir Robert." A statement of course, not a question.

"He's only away for a week. Surely I'm not meant to be in mournings because of that!" She used the plural, because that was the way Angus would say the word. Now he was clearly shocked.

"I've known you all your life, Miss Grania, and I don't need to tell you that you must be careful what you do. People talk."

She picked up a stone and threw it with all her might into the heather. The dogs bounded after it. "Angus," she said. "When people throw stones, they should always throw them into the heather."

"That's right," Angus said, frowning, because he couldn't understand why anyone should want to throw stones anywhere. "Or into a pool," he added, deep in thought.

Grania laughed. "That's right. Or into a pool." She patted his arm affectionately, then raised her gun. A white tail turned a somersault, then lay still, as the shot rang in her ears. "I don't like doing this at all," she said. "I don't know why it's supposed to be a sport."

Angus had picked up the rabbit brought to him by the Labrador. The spaniel was still searching in the heather for the stone.

"Miss Catriona always said the very same thing," he told her. "But she knew, like you do, that people and dogs have to eat. God knew what He was doing when He made the Universe."

Grania was impressed, not knowing if it were Angus or her mother who had put the thought into words, but she wondered if walking over the hills with her had reminded him of the days when he walked with Catriona, and if somehow the two of them had merged into one. She was sure he knew the truth about her. She was sure he knew who was her mother. She raised her gun again, and shot a hare.

"I hope it wasn't someone's grandmother," she said, as Angus picked it up. "Chrissie says they always are."

"So they say. So they say." They had turned down towards Loch Caraig, and Grania saw the familiar green of the Lamont tartan. She thought what a wonderful camouflage it was, blending as it did with the colour of the surroundings. He was fishing from the bank. She and Angus stood and watched, Grania thinking how graceful were his movements.

He was landing a trout as they approached him.

Angus looked in the basket. "Five," he said. "And you weren't here for long."

Roderick addressed Grania. "You told me you would try fishing again. I forgot to ask you yesterday why you didn't come last week."

"I told you. I didn't know you were here."

"Sir Robert came. He said you preferred to see Lachlan MacLachlan about going to Glasgow!"

"I had to do that," she said in a small voice. Robert had never mentioned fishing. She had left him to finish his lunch alone, because she had been afraid he would want a bedroom reconciliation of their quarrel.

"Have a go now." Roderick handed her his rod. "See if you can still cast."

She tried, and caught the heather behind her. It was black because the heather-burning had taken place in the area a short time ago, so that the new growth would be tender and sweet for the sheep to eat.

"It'll come back to you. You don't forget. It's like riding a bicycle – you can't forget." He came close to her, indicating what the movement of her hands, of her arms, should be.

"Now try – that's beautiful! Now, again. And you've caught one! Steady – steady!" He was as excited as she was, and after a moment she landed it. It must have weighed nearly three pounds.

"Angus, I'll stay here for a while. Take the dogs and my gun. And tell Chrissie that Mr. Lamont will bring me home." Grania handed him her gun. He looked doubtfully from her to Roderick, then he whistled and the dogs followed at his heels as he trudged away.

They took turns with the rod, but to no avail. After a while, Grania went and sat on a boulder, and almost immediately Roderick caught another trout. She watched him land it and cast again; then gradually she became aware of something that was unusual, and she stood on her boulder, shading her eyes from the sun.

"What's the matter?" Roderick asked. She thought he had forgotten she was there.

She pointed in the direction of a cottage which stood stark and isolated some distance from the loch. Its rounded granite corners, thatched roof, and tilted wooden chimney made it look as if it had been built for an exhibition, a typical Highland homestead of a former age.

"The chimney isn't smoking."

Roderick understood the smoke signals of rural life. A chimney that should be smoking and was not needed investigation. It could mean that the inhabitant of the cottage was ill.

"Old Donald MacBean lives there," Grania said. "He's not alone – his daughter Morag lives with him, but she's old too." She set off for the cottage. She wasn't leaving anything to chance.

Roderick put down his rod and followed her. She cut across the marshy ground, knowing by the colour of the moss where it was safe to tread. She jumped nimbly from hummock to hummock. Roderick, because of his weight, was in greater peril of landing knee-deep in the peaty water, but they arrived safely at the grassy patch which surrounded the cottage. There was a well-made peat stack beside a shed, and some old pots and pans, tins, and unidentifiable rusting objects were lying around in the usual Highland fashion.

The door of the cottage was ajar. A clock ticked noisily on a bright blue distempered wall. A table was spread with a sheet of newspaper, and there was one place set for a meal. The dresser was stacked with clean dishes, several biscuit tins, a pile of old newspapers, and some paraffin lamps. There were four kitchen chairs, and two sagging upholstered armchairs on either side of the shining black kitchen range. A large kettle was pushed aside on the hob, and the fire had gone out.

A firm old voice called from a room off the kitchen, "*Co tha sin? Thig a stigh.*"

Roderick stayed in the kitchen while Grania, with a gesture of relief that there was life in the cottage, went into the bedroom. He heard her explain in Gaelic about there being no smoke from the chimney; then he heard his own name, and the voices were lowered. He was about to back out of the door when Grania beckoned him into the room.

He found the old man propped up in a double bed which had brass bed-ends and a patchwork quilt. There was a text hung on a nail on the wall beside him, and a lithograph of a lighthouse. The beams in the roof were exposed, as they had been in the kitchen. It was a poor room, but it was comfortable and well-kept.

Grania made the introductions, and the old man bowed in acknowledgement with the dignity of an elder statesman.

"So it is you who is a direct descendant of Kilcaraig Mor, he who fathered twelve children, five of them daughters and seven of them sons. Now, there was a man!"

Roderick took the gnarled old hand in his and felt the scrutiny of the blue eyes. He thought of replying in Gaelic, but his courage failed him. He would be talking to a man who would scorn the flawed accent which he knew he must possess.

"Morag MacBean has gone to Doctor MacColl to have a tooth out," Grania said. "I'll get the fire going and I'll put the kettle on, and then she can have a cup of tea when she gets home. The fire isn't out – it's *smalled*."

Roderick knew what she meant. Live peats, covered in peat ash, would stay hot for days. He pulled a chair up by the bedside, and soon he was hearing tales of his forebears, spoken in the beautiful lilting words that made music of the English language when it was translated from the Gaelic.

It was some time before Grania reappeared. When she did, old Donald broke off in the middle of a story he had been telling, and spoke to her in Gaelic, thanking her for what she had done. The kettle had begun to boil when Morag came home, her face swathed in a woollen scarf, but she insisted on making tea for the visitors, providing scones and shortbread and cakes from the tins on the dresser.

"I'm glad you've met Donald," Grania said, as she and Roderick left the cottage. "He has a quite remarkable memory, and knows every detail of our family history, going back even further than our written records. Whenever he tells a story, he always uses exactly the same phrases. When you see him again, you'll notice that. I'm sure that's what happened with the bible. Accurate repetition from age to age ensured that what was handed on was true."

"I suppose you're right."

"I don't have to tell him much about you. As soon as I said your name, he could place you. Everyone in Mull knows you've renovated a cottage at Tormore, but he knows all the rest."

"What do you mean by that?"

"About Kilcaraig Mor's youngest son going off to Sutherland, and the dispersion of his family. What else could I mean?"

They were picking their way back over the bog. Grania, more

accustomed to the terrain than he was, chattered on about Kilcaraig Mor, the Great Kilcaraig, who had brought prosperity to the Lamonts, and had not lived to see his family dwindle away.

Roderick was glad to remain silent. He had been hearing about the beautiful Catriona Lamont, who had been forbidden to marry Hector MacNeill of Ardcross, and who was said to have died of a broken heart.

"It was not a broken heart that killed her," old Donald had said. "It was bearing Hector MacNeill's baby that killed her, and there is that baby, a woman now, and she is with you today." Then Grania had come into the room, and the old man had switched quickly to another subject.

"You're very quiet," Grania said. They had reached the loch. He retrieved his rod and began to dismantle it.

"I've been given a great deal to think about," he said. He fumbled with the fastening of the canvas cover for his rods. He could feel her grey eyes watching him, could see her shadow and the way the breeze ruffled her curls. "How reliable is Donald MacBean?" he asked.

"Very reliable. Like I said about the bible, what he says is gospel true."

"How does he know so much about your family?"

"*Our* family," she corrected him. "He knows, because he used to be a lighthouse-keeper. That meant living on remote lighthouses, Skerryvore or Dhuheartach, miles out in the Atlantic, for six weeks at a time. My grandfather gave him access to our archives, and he would take great files away with him to study them. He became devoted to our family, and my grandfather came to rely on his wisdom and discretion. He was one of ourselves."

"Have you kept a record of the things he told you?"

"He doesn't tell me important things, like he will tell you. It's not unusual in clan history for confidential matters to be entrusted only to the males. Call it feudalism if you like! The Appin murder is a typical example. The male Stewarts are believed to know the truth about that to this day. But we have nothing so historical, so important, to protect and treasure. All the same, see Donald whenever you can. So much will be lost to us when he dies."

Roderick would have liked to encourage her to talk some more, but he had no idea whether she knew the astonishing tale he had just heard. He didn't want to rouse her curiosity.

The car was parked on a rough track only a field away. It was quite close to the village, and in a matter of minutes he had driven her up to the castle, had helped her out of her seat, and was back

157

in the car and down the drive before she could invite him in for a drink.

She stared indignantly after him. She had never before failed to awaken a man's interest in her. She went into the castle, banging the heavy, studded door behind her. Symbolically she had shut Roderick Lamont out of her life.

23

During the next few days, Grania kept an eye on Loch Caraig, but there was no sign of Roderick, nor of his blue car.

On the evening before Robert was due to come home she went to see Michael.

"I've been a spectacular unsuccess with my kinsman, Roderick," she said, coming to the point at once, as she often did with Michael. She told him about the loch-side encounter and the visit to Donald MacBean. "It's established now, beyond doubt, that he's part of our family. He doesn't seem to want to be involved with us at all. Does he ever talk about us when he's alone with you?"

From their first meeting, Roderick had called on Michael from time to time. Grania had sometimes been offended that he could get as far as Caraig Lodge in his unreliable car, but not cover the few hundred yards which would bring him to the castle.

"There are times, Grania, when you can be tiresomely obtuse. How would a presentable young man dare to strike up anything like a friendship with Robert Dutton's wife! Besides, although he hasn't ever said so, I imagine he's come to Mull to escape from some sort of entanglement."

"Do you mean he's been crossed in love?" Her sense of outrage was as intense as it was unreasonable.

"I have no idea. He doesn't talk about himself. But the death of his parents, however tragic, couldn't be responsible for his withdrawing from normal life in the way that he has done."

"What happened to his parents?"

"Didn't you know? They were killed in an avalanche, during a ski-ing holiday. It was splashed in the newspapers a few years ago. You would have been in school at the time. It wasn't he who reminded me of it – I heard it in the post office when conjecture was rife after his first visit to me."

Grania returned to the castle, disconsolate, which was unusual after she had been with Michael. She had reached the porch when the telephone began to ring. She went into the library and picked up the receiver. It was Robert, asking her to meet him at Tobermory on the following day and to bring Duncan MacPhail with her. She asked no questions, but she guessed what this meant. Robert had bought a new car, and Duncan was to be promoted from being the estate lorry driver to being chauffeur. Kilcaraig was gradually being staffed by the people who loved it and who regarded it as their own.

As they drove to Tobermory, Duncan told Grania of his intention to be not only a first class driver, but also a good mechanic, so that if there was trouble he would be accepted for service in the Royal Air Force. He read the newspapers, and he knew about Adolf Hitler and the grave threat of war.

The boat from Oban appeared on a dead calm sea, and Grania waved to it from the pier at Tobermory, as she knew she was expected to do. Robert was the first passenger down the gangway, and she thought how old and tired he looked. He could not have changed so much in a single week. People must think them a very odd pair.

The new car was skilfully driven by Duncan down the planks from the boat. It was dark green and not large at all. There was no glass partition between the back and front seats, and in every way it was a more suitable car for Mull. They set off in convoy, Duncan in the new car, and Grania driving hers with Robert beside her. He, too, was worried about what was happening in Europe. He ignored the glorious view of mountains and sea, and tried to talk to Grania of his fears, but as he had expected, she dismissed the subject with her characteristic lack of interest in foreign affairs.

"Michael's a bit gloomy," she said. "He knows everything because he has the wireless on so much." Then she went on to tell him about Morag MacBean having a tooth out, and about the trout she had caught, and how Lachlan MacLachlan was enjoying his holiday in Glasgow, and had sent her a picture postcard of the Kelvin Hall.

Robert did not cross-examine her, as she had thought he would. He didn't mention Roderick, and that night after dinner he told her that he had been talking to Nicholas Danvers and had been assured that a baby was what Grania needed at Kilcaraig.

"When you go to London, you will be examined by whoever is the leading gynaecologist, and if the reports are good, I'll let you have your baby," he said, as if he were offering her a prize if she did well at school.

So it was that the London season was punctuated for Grania by visits to not one but several gynaecologists, and eventually Robert was convinced that he must accept their unanimous verdict. Grania was a perfectly normal woman and could expect to give birth to a perfectly normal baby.

Marian had to restrain her from buying a cot and layette before returning to Kilcaraig. "Wanting a baby doesn't mean having one," she said. Since working in her elegant hat shop, Marian had taken to dressing very smartly and had adopted a different style of living. Her flat had been redecorated, and thick pile carpets replaced the faded Axminster which she had brought from Kilcaraig. Grania, hating change, secretly grieved for the loss of both Marian's out-of-date fashion, and for the shabbiness of the South Kensington flat.

Evelyn's life was centred round her bridge club, but her visits to her mother were performed with the regularity of clockwork. Diana wrote enthusiastic letters about the little boys who had whooping-cough, and the schoolmasters who took her to cinemas, or to the local palais de danse. Grania gave a few dinner parties in the hope that she would provide Helen with a more rewarding social life, and she was unexpectedly successful. Helen ended the season by becoming engaged to an architect.

Robert and Grania returned to Mull in August for the usual round of luncheons, cocktail parties and dinner parties, and the occasional dances held in some of the larger houses. Grania invited friends to stay but their guests tended to be Robert's friends, more interested in talking business than in trying their luck with a rod on Loch Caraig or a gun on the moors.

Roderick called in one day, a courtesy visit to welcome them back from London. Robert showed him the studio portraits of Grania in Court dress, carefully posed to show to full advantage the regulation feathered head-dress and the train.

"This isn't a suitable subject for a man," Grania protested, but Roderick was amused.

"Is there any more suitable subject for a man than a beautiful woman?" he said, and Robert, much to Grania's surprise, agreed but he instantly collected the photographs and put them away in a drawer.

Roderick stayed for only about an hour, and when he was leaving Robert asked him if he would like to come over when the deer stalking began. Roderick thanked him, but said that he was to be away from Mull for a while. Typically, he didn't say where or when.

He drove off in his noisy car, and Grania was left with the blank feeling that she would not see him again until the spring.

During the winter Robert went to London fairly often, and sometimes Grania went with him. She had found that her life had become a series of monthly disappointments because, as Marian had warned her, wanting a baby didn't mean that she would have one.

When the Christmas and New Year festivities were over, Robert succumbed to the particular brand of influenza which was circulating on Mull. Doctor MacColl called daily, and Grania demonstrated that she had all the necessary qualities that made a good nurse. In April, she would celebrate her twenty-first birthday, and she hoped that Robert would decide that she had proved herself to be sensible and reliable, and that he would let her have a little bit of money of her very own.

Robert did not give her an allowance on her twenty-first birthday. He gave her Kilcaraig. He handed over the title deeds when they were leaving the breakfast table, and she had wondered how he had forgotten her birthday, with all the cards and presents that had been arriving at the castle.

She turned over the leaves of the document, silent, unable even to express her thanks. Robert watched her, knowing how she felt, knowing that this was the moment she had lived all her life dreaming about. She possessed Kilcaraig, and only she could now dispose of it. That was something she would never do. "*Ne parcas ne spernas.*" The Lamont motto, "Neither spare nor dispose".

At last, in a small, subdued voice, she said "Robert, you won't regret what you've given me today. I'll never be able to thank you enough."

"It saves me death duties," he said brusquely, because she was near to tears and so was he. "It would be better if you don't tell people about this. I don't want adventurers pursuing you when I'm not around to protect you."

"I never met an adventurer."

"I wouldn't like to be sure about that."

She looked up at him, surprised. He mustn't spoil this moment with silly, jealous thoughts, but he just added "You'll learn!" and kissed her before going to his study to begin the innumerable telephone calls that formed part of his daily routine.

Grania spent the morning receiving the friends who came to wish her a happy birthday, and the afternoon helping to decorate the village hall for the dance that was to take place that night. The hall had been Robert's gift to the people of Kilcaraig, an idea which came to him when, cramped up in a desk in the village school, he had watched a performance of *The Glen is Mine*, and had concluded that if, as Grania had said, he must be present at all local functions, he must find the means of doing so in comfort.

As the hall took shape before their eyes, the village people marvelled at his generosity to his face, and behind his back reminded one another that the poor soul had always looked the picture of misery when he attended concerts in the school. They were grateful to him, but had correctly assessed the situation.

"Maybe when the new organ is installed, he'll even come to church", Michael had overheard one day when he was in the post office. He hoped this would prove to be true, for Grania had said on a number of occasions that she wished her husband would accompany her every Sunday, and not just at Easter and Christmas. "He isn't Kirk," she had said defensively. "But he won't even go to the English church."

Michael was in the hall now, liking to mingle with the people, enjoying the scent of the daffodils which were being arranged around the platform, and listening to an altercation in Gaelic, emanating from the kitchen. He recognized that one of the upraised voices was Grania's. He loved to hear her speaking in Gaelic. He loved everything about her. He loved her, but he was blind, and he wasn't rich, and he was only a few years younger than her husband, who was too old for her by far.

"What was the row about?" he asked. She always remembered to come to him from time to time, to tell him what was going on.

"The same old argument about whether or not to cut the crusts off the sandwiches."

"Which won?"

"Crusts. People are hungry by midnight. In fact, there's mountains of food. It was wonderful of the Women's Guild to take on the catering for tonight."

As she spoke, he could tell that something had caught her attention.

"Roderick Lamont's here," she said. "I didn't know he was back in Mull."

Roderick greeted Michael first, to identify himself, then he said to Grania "I've been sent here to fetch you. There are surprises waiting for you at the castle, and your husband wants you to have a rest before dancing your way through the night."

He had not wished her a happy birthday, as everyone else had done. He must know it was her birthday, or he wouldn't be here now. Michael, in his puzzled darkness, heard his footsteps retreating beside the click of Grania's heels.

Her car was parked on the other side of the road, near the War

162

Memorial. Roderick held open the door for her, then settled beside her. "I walked down from the castle," he said. "I left my car up there as it's full of my paraphernalia for tonight."

"Are you coming to the party?"

"I've been asked to play the pipes at the dance."

"How lovely, that means you'll be having dinner with us." She was greatly relieved. Robert had told her to leave all the arrangements entirely to him, and she had been afraid that he would have planned an intimate dinner for just the two of them alone. Asking Roderick meant that other people must be coming. Cook, entrusted with the catering, had banned her from the kitchen during the past few days.

She drove along the village street, over the bumpy bridge, and had almost reached the castle, when Roderick asked her to stop.

"Let's walk the rest of the way – the daffodils are so lovely," he said.

She backed into a grassy patch between the rhododendrons, and he helped her to extricate herself from behind the driving wheel. They walked through the trees until they reached a glade which was golden with daffodils. She stood still. She was ahead of him. He came up behind her and caught at her wrists, holding her closely against him. "A happy birthday, Grania," he said and he kissed the nape of her neck. She wriggled free and turned to face him. His right hand was on her chin then it moved to her lips, parting them, and his mouth was on hers.

Somehow she managed to stay on her feet. She wanted to sink to the ground and consummate this delirious passion here, among the daffodils.

She clung to him, held by the strength of his embrace, then he released her, very gently. She caressed his lips, wanting more, but he placed the palm of his hand across her mouth. "We'll try not to do that again," he said. We. In that instant a bond had united them, stronger than any shared pledge or legal tie. Neither of them had planned it. Both knew it must not be revealed to any living soul.

They walked slowly hand in hand through the daffodils and under the trees which had screened them from the castle. By the time they reached the cobbled yard at the back of the castle they were a little apart and Grania signed to him to follow her to the front door. She knew that her cheeks were flushed, her eyes shining. The servants, even more than Robert, would misconstrue what had occurred.

As soon as they were inside, they resumed their normal attitude to one another, that of acquaintances rather than friends.

163

"Just go straight to the drawing-room," Roderick said, as he had been asked to do.

She found Robert there, with Marian and Nicholas, sitting by the fire. In the excitement of her greeting, Grania's pink cheeks and bright eyes were easily accounted for. "How did you get here? How didn't I find out?"

Marian explained that they had been smuggled to the castle during the afternoon, while Grania was lured to the village hall. "Robert was inspired to ask Roderick to meet us at Craignure, as you'd have noticed if a car had set off from Kilcaraig. It all went without a hitch."

"And so it should," Nicholas said. "We've both had plenty of practice. You won't remember how we used to smuggle art treasures out of here, to pay the rates and taxes and grocery bills!"

Robert, standing by the fireplace, with his arm across Grania's shoulders, looked proud and happy. Roderick both envied and pitied him. He knew that he should feel guilty, but instead he felt exhilarated. He had won a battle which he had been fighting for years, and the rigid discipline which he had imposed upon himself had not failed. His haven at Tormore Bay had often been his prison but the time spent there had not been wasted time. He had been able to master his own passion, and had controlled Grania's. He could leave his past behind him at last.

Grania dispensed tea from a silver tea pot, while Robert told her about the dinner-party he had arranged for that night.

"Just a family party," he said. "Nicholas is included because he brought you into the world."

She looked up, surprised. "No one has ever told me that," she said.

"I didn't do anything," Nicholas said. "I just happened to be there."

Roderick, stirring his tea, tried to think why he had been invited. Family ties, however slight, meant a great deal to Grania, but nothing at all to Robert. Moreover, it was assumed that he himself knew the circumstances of Grania's birth, circumstances which he had not thought Grania knew herself. He felt foolish, and rather angry, the ecstasy of such a short time ago resolving into the slough of despond which had blighted him for years.

As if reading his thoughts, Robert said to him "You, Roderick, are here as a member of Grania's family, and also, I hope, as my friend." There was no hint of suspicion or malice in Robert's voice. He turned to Grania. "You'd better lie down and sleep, if you can. You have an energetic night ahead of you."

When she left the room Roderick expected Robert to follow her. He didn't. He sat where she had been sitting and poured himself out another cup of tea.

Roderick was given the bedroom which had once been Grania's nursery to use as a dressing-room. When he had changed for dinner, he remembered the present he had brought for her. It was wrapped in blue crepe paper, and was in his suitcase. He had wanted to give her the icon she had admired so much, but its value rendered it unsuitable, for it would give rise to comment. Instead, he had bought the Hatchard edition of Shakespeare's Sonnets. It too was probably unsuitable – he had no idea of her literary tastes – but it was neat and decorous, and he had written her name on it, and the date, April 19th 1935. He had not written his own name, and was glad of that because of what had happened in the afternoon.

Wearing his dress kilt, and his velvet jacket, its silver buttons shining, he went downstairs. There was no one in the drawing-room, for the others had said they wanted to rest before they changed, so he went to the library to look at the books, which almost entirely lined the walls. He found Grania curled up in a chair, telephoning. She had no makeup on, and she was wearing a black silk wrap. She looked like a schoolgirl pretending to be a grown-up.

She signed to him to help himelf to a drink from the corner cupboard, but he shook his head and wandered round looking at the books, until he heard her put the receiver down.

"That was more birthday greetings," she said. "A telephone in the bedroom would save a lot of running downstairs. Do borrow any books you want."

"When the castle was sold, were these books sold with it?"

"Most of them were. There wasn't room for anything like all of them in London, and Robert liked their substantial, been-here-forever look."

He could imagine that. He could imagine Robert Dutton wondering how he could fill up all the empty shelves.

"Do you like reading?" It was a pointless question. She must have seen the shape of the parcel in its blue crepe paper, and known that it was for her.

"One of the loveliest things about coming back here was finding that the books hadn't changed," she said.

He smiled and handed her the parcel. Then he stood by the fire and watched, enchanted, the movements of her hands, the tilt of her head as she unwrapped it. Her thanks were warm, and sounded genuine. She examined the edition with the affection of someone who really did love books.

"I'll keep this always by my bedside. It'll be my very special reminder of today," she said. One of the sonnets had caught her eye, and she was reading it. He didn't like to ask her which one it was.

"Grania," he said when she had finished reading it. "Will you come over here? There's something I want to talk to you about, and the fireside is the right place to do it."

She hesitated, but she was accustomed to obeying Robert's orders. She pulled her wrap tightly round her as she tucked herself into one of the armchairs by the fire.

"Please don't tell me that you're sorry about what happened among the daffodils. I don't want you to be sorry, although I suppose we should be," she said.

"I wasn't going to talk about the daffodils. That's sacrosanct." He left that to sink in, hoping that she understood what he meant, then he said "When we were talking during tea, it was obvious that you knew about the unusual circumstances of your birth."

"So?"

"I'm not asking this out of curiosity, but I wonder how much you were told."

"I wasn't told anything. I discovered it for myself."

He thought she was not going to say anything more, but after considering it, she poured out her story, scarcely stopping to draw breath.

"I pretended that I didn't know. Then one day I lost my temper, and I told Mummy – I mean Evelyn – that I knew who my real mother was. It was horrible, but we patched it up, the way families do. Then I got engaged to Robert, and somehow everyone assumed that she'd told me about it gently. It wouldn't have made any difference if she had. Shattering news can never be broken gently, as I'm sure you know from your own experience." She sat there, biting at her knuckles and staring into the fire. "Nobody knows who my father is. If they do, they won't tell me. The secret died when Daddy was killed. I'll always think of him by that name. He was wonderful to me."

She had made it easy for him to tell her the rest.

"The family secret angle has been rather exaggerated," he said. "It was important to your mother that your father must not know of your existence. She confided in her father, and things might have gone very differently, had she lived." Then he told her what he had been told by Donald MacBean, adding the little extra that he had found out for himself about Hector MacNeill of Ardcross. "He died a few years ago, his wife re-married, and the estate was broken up and sold. Only Ardcross House remains, and I believe it's some kind of a school."

"Hector MacNeill," Grania repeated. "Not a Neapolitan or a Sicilian, but a native of Argyll. I know you must think I'm neurotic to care about it so much, but with all the talk that goes on about family ties I always wondered so much where I really fitted in."

Footsteps on the stairs brought her to her feet. "That's Robert," she said. "Go along to the drawing-room and keep him talking. He'll be furious if he finds me here with you, especially as I'm in this state of *déshabillé*!" She caught at his hand, and held it to her cheek. "Thank you, thank you. You've given me the best birthday present of all." Then she was gone, having first peeped cautiously round the door.

Roderick found that Marian was with Robert in the drawing-room. She was showing off her dress, which she said she had bought through an advertisement in *Vogue*. It was very distinctive and in a lovely shade of blue. "It had to be substantial, or I'd be torn to ribbons by the end of the night," she said, swirling round to show off her full skirt. "I hope I get lifted for every dance. I've never been a wallflower in all my life."

Nicholas came in, wearing a plum-coloured jacket, which made him look like the popular conception of a famous author. Robert was getting restive, looking at his watch, when Grania at last joined them. She was wearing a simple dress of Lamont tartan, which had been specially designed for the occasion by Molyneux.

"There's showing off for you," Marian said. "Robert – Grania was a nice, simple girl until she got into your hands. Her pearls came from Woolworths!"

"These came from Cartier's," Grania laughed. "Tonight I'm worth a million, and I mean to look it, at least until after supper, when the dancing gets really wild."

She sparkled all through dinner, and in the flickering candle-light which illuminated the table Roderick thought that he would never in his life see anyone lovelier. He remembered the sketch he had drawn of her in Iona. "*Lady Dutton of Kilcaraig!*" Despising her because she had traded her body for an estate. Now he would write "Grania of Kilcaraig, my heart's delight?" and the question mark would have to be there for he loved the look of her and he loved the feel of her, but he had no idea what the woman was like at all.

He played the pipes for a while after dinner, walking up and down in the hall, so that the sound in the dining-room would not be too deafening. Grania, drinking her coffee, which she hoped would counteract the effect of a little too much champagne, pictured him looking just as if he belonged in the castle. He was playing one of her favourites, *Mo Dhachaidh*, my home. Truly this was her home, for she owned the title deeds, and truly she had every right to be here, for every drop of her blood was Highland, and her roots were deep in Argyll.

"Wake up, little dreamer. It's time to go to the village hall." Robert's hands were on her shoulders, and she thought of Roderick's hands, holding her close to him, there among the daffodils. She left the table, and as she went through the hall her heart echoed the groan of the wind sinking out of the bagpipes, as Roderick put them back in their box.

It was a wonderful evening. Dancing and laughter, with Angus and Willie to play the pipes, as well as Roderick Lamont. There was a three-tiered birthday cake, just like a wedding, but the most surprising part of the evening happened at the beginning of the dance, when Robert Dutton led the Grand March with his wife, and faultlessly did the foursome reel.

"I did a crash course in London," he admitted. "And I hope I haven't made myself look like a silly old fool!"

Grania flung her arms round him, there in the hall, in front of all the people. Roderick, watching from beside the platform, where he was surrounded by the huge arrangement of daffodils, thought of that moment during the afternoon, and with sheer, primitive fury, he bent down and fingered the blade of the *sgian dubh* which was, as always, pushed into his sock.

24

When Marian returned to London two days after the party, Grania and Robert went with her. The arrangement had been made many months ago, under strong protest from Grania, who had looked forward to the Jubilee Bonfire for King George V and Queen Mary, and felt it outrageous that the owners of Kilcaraig should not be present at so important an occasion. She had not known then that by the sixth of May she would be the owner of Kilcaraig, and now it seemed inappropriate to renew her objections to going away. Nicholas, who had proofs to correct, agreed to remain, and to see that the blaze on the top of Ben Caraig was at least as big as anywhere else on the island.

He wrote to Grania to describe what a beautiful night it had been, with tea and dumpling round the bonfire, and other bonfires visible for miles around. He also told her that he was seeing a great deal of Michael Ames, who could talk about politics and music, and even about books. He did not add that mostly, when they were alone together, he and Michael talked about Grania.

"I've watched it all," Michael said, an expression which he often used. When Nicholas first heard it, he had felt real distress, but now he knew better.

"I've watched Grania as a child, and I've watched her during early adolescence. Then she came back here as a woman, but she still does the child act, especially when she's with her husband."

"She must know he likes it."

"I think she has made a habit of concealing the person she really is. When I've been alone with her, I've often been surprised by her. She comes out with ideas her husband would never think had entered her head. She has assessed, I think correctly, the situation in Europe, and she's very perceptive about foreign affairs. Yet I think if Robert asked her any question about such things she would imply that she never gave them a thought."

"He's bought himself a living doll. She's giving him value for money."

"At what cost to herself?"

"I suspect that she's beginning to find that out." Nicholas had thought that Robert Dutton had made serious errors of judgement when he invited Roderick Lamont to the intimacy of the family birthday gathering. Marian had explained his theory that friendship was the surest safeguard against treachery, but Nicholas was not convinced. When human passions were sufficiently aroused morals, ethics, everything tended to snap under the strain. "What do you make of her long-lost cousin from Tormore?" he asked.

"I think he could be the spark that starts the fire that ignites the fuse that blows up the dream-world that Grania built."

"Or that Robert built?"

"Yes, or for that matter, that Roderick built. Something more than sentiment has brought him to Mull. I enjoy his company, because like you and like Grania, and like only a very few other people, he doesn't treat me like a half-wit because I'm blind. He gives me bits of local gossip, and he's a mine of information about Mull's history and legends, but his references to Grania are so rare that their very absence indicates how much she occupies his mind.

He managed to describe her birthday party without saying a word about her! You were once a doctor with an interest in psychology. What do you make of that?"

"Even a has-been doctor doesn't diagnose at second-hand! I think as in all problems affecting personal relationships we'll just have to wait and see."

While Michael and Nicholas were talking about Grania in Mull, Grania was trying to make Evelyn Lamont see sense in London.

"Helen's always wanted a glamorous wedding," she said. "Robert's ready and willing to foot the bill, and nobody need know that he's paid for it. It won't be such a costly affair as mine was, because you won't have to have droves of industrial empire-builders and their mink-clad wives cluttering up the church."

"Helen will be married quietly at St. Stephen's, and we'll have a luncheon party at the Hyde Park Hotel," Evelyn said in her that's-the-end-of-the-argument voice. "And don't forget that you yourself wear mink and that your husband is building an empire which will flourish like a green bay tree if there's a war."

Grania returned to Lowndes Square, angry because her offer of help had been rejected, and humiliated because what Evelyn had said about her was true. She had spent ten horrible days in London, and all she wanted to do was to go home.

She had called in at her old office, but there had been staff changes, and Lola, who had been one of her bridesmaids, was married now herself. Cicely, another bridesmaid, and some new girls whom Grania had never met, took her out to lunch in a nearby café, where she had eaten baked beans on toast and had drunk indifferent coffee. She hadn't understood the office jokes and references to personalities whom she had either forgotten or hadn't known. Just as she no longer belonged to her family at Ladbroke Place, the ties with her job were broken. Most disappointing of all had been Adrian Ferguson, who had come to one of her cocktail parties, and instead of talking about the recent productions of operas he had seen, he told her about a girl called Alison, whom he obviously hoped to marry, and of his ambition some day to write K.C. after his name. Marian, because of her work in the hat shop, was only available for hurried lunch hour snacks, and at night Grania had to give dinner parties, or go to them, with occasional evenings at a theatre, to see a musical, or a slapstick comedy, which was Robert's form of relaxation.

All the time, in waking or in sleeping, like the words of the song *An Gille Dubh Ciar-Dubh* the dark-haired young man haunted her. A stranger, yet an integral part of herself because of a kiss among

170

the daffodils, and a shared desire which was too precious to have been wantonly fulfilled. "That's sacrosanct," he had said. Now her yearning heart understood what he had meant.

She helped herself to a gin and tonic, and when Robert came home he found her asleep, curled up in a chair. He picked up the glass and sniffed its contents. She opened her eyes. "I'm not drunk," she said.

"I didn't think you were. But don't you know the effect gin's supposed to have on women? I thought you wanted a baby too much to take silly risks."

"One slug of gin isn't going to bring on a miscarriage, and I haven't started a baby anyhow, as I have good reason to know!" She was blushing. Even after all this time she was shy about intimate personal matters. "If we don't have one, we don't. There's no point in blaming anything, when the reason lies somewhere in ourselves."

He knew the depression she felt at these times, and he had long ago discovered that his words of consolation or encouragement merely irritated her. "Don't forget the dinner at the Mansion House tonight, seven-thirty for eight," he said, and went to his room to change.

She would not have forgotten. She never failed him. She would be the loveliest woman present, and she would sparkle like the jewels she wore. His pearl beyond price. There was nothing in the world he wouldn't do to make her happy.

He turned the pages of his engagement diary, with its list of meetings and functions which he must attend. Somehow he would scrap the lot and take her away for a holiday in Italy. He picked up the telephone and asked his secretary to make the necessary arrangements, then he turned on the wireless to listen to the news.

Roderick Lamont was also listening to the news, which kept fading because the accumulator in his wireless set needed charging. He was sitting at the writing desk in his cottage and composing a letter asking for information about the territorial army. He could see that the time had come for him to loosen his ties with Tormore. This refuge, which he had built up with his own hands, had been his fortress, his citadel, his security. When he first arrived in Mull, he had been treated with suspicion, but his name had helped him to overcome the first barrier to acceptance. Then there were other names he could produce, MacCormicks, and MacLachlans, and MacLeans, whom he knew about, and he could talk about the quarries in the days when blasting was a familiar sound in the neighbourhood, and he could speak the Gaelic, even if it was not the best Gaelic as spoken on Mull.

His final triumph had been the Armistice service at the little War Memorial, which listed a heartbreaking number of names. He had taken his pipes with him in his car, and on an impulse, after the service, he stood by the memorial and played *The Flowers of the Forest*. The people knew well the lament, and they knew that they had an exceptionally gifted piper come into their midst. They asked him to stay. They never asked him why he had come at all. The true reason for that could be revealed some day, and meantime the legends that were circulating were harmless, and gave satisfaction to those that believed them. He was content to leave it at that.

He wrote his letter. He had no idea what the demands of the territorial army would be, but it made a start, and it would mean that when the time came he would be equipped to do what was required of him. That the time was coming he had no doubt at all.

It was a beautiful evening. He walked to the village to post his letter. It meant a sharp climb up the hill, using the old railway tracks as a footpath. There at the top were the piles of pink granite, cut like giant bricks, and left there to be carried downhill in trucks, but, because suddenly there were no more trucks, no more boats, and no more men, the granite remained as it was, as if a magic wand had cast a spell, immediately immobilizing everything in sight.

On leaving the top of the quarry, he walked down the sheep track at the back of the hill. From here he could see the island of Erraid, with its neat row of houses which were the homes of the lighthouse keepers and their families. From Erraid two of the most remote lighthouses in the Atlantic were manned, Dhuheartach and Skerryvore, where at one time Donald MacBean had studied the family history of the Lamonts of Kilcaraig, and had become deeply involved in their affairs.

Across the strip of sea on his right was Iona, green and peaceful with its restored Cathedral and its ancient ruins, now for him an ever-present reminder of that first but fatal encounter with Grania.

His path skirted the granite walls of a small burial ground, then he crossed a burn and was on the grassy slope that took him to the main road, with its few scattered houses and the combined post office and village store. He posted his letter, read the notices displayed in the window, and noted the date of the church sale-of-work. Then he returned to his cottage by the route he had come. He saw nobody. Everybody saw him.

Back at the cottage, he found his collie-dog, Fraoch, waiting for him. Fraoch had been out rabbiting when Roderick set out, and he realized that he had been all the way to the village and back without even noticing that his dog wasn't with him. There were other things weighing too much on his mind.

He sat by his window watching the sunset and thinking about Grania, who would want to be watching it too. Some day, before the world was torn apart by war, he must somehow watch the sunset with her, that was, if she ever wanted to do anything with him again. He had not seen her since her birthday dance.

It was growing dark. He lit his lamps and went into his bedroom. His icon was gleaming, the gold paint catching the light. He caressed it, as Grania had done. He had been fascinated then by her appearance because as a connoisseur of women, he had never seen one lovelier than she. A romantic chord was struck, too, in the blood-tie that existed between them, for he knew more about his family history than she had done at the time. That he would feel physical desire for her came as no surprise, but that she could both attract and repel him introduced a new dimension into his emotional life.

He despised her for becoming Robert Dutton's wife, a flagrant act of cupidity for all the world to see. But was it? For her, Kilcaraig could fulfil a basic need for the security she unconsciously craved for, as the truth dawned on her that she was not the person she had supposed herself to be.

He lit a cigarette and returned to his living-room. Two rooms, and a bathroom and a plug that pulled. A glorious view. A peaceful life away from the temptations and the torments of the past. An income of one thousand pounds a year. A talent for writing trite little articles, and illustrating them with thumbnail sketches, which people seemed to like. His idea of perfection, his safeguard from further anguish. But was it?

And Grania. A castle and several thousand acres of land. An adoring husband who was a millionaire and who could indulge her every whim. Insulation from the cares of the world. But was it?

Each of them had found an escape from life which was not an escape at all. Their illusions had been shattered by that one kiss.

He had thought her an adorable, feather-brained sham. The little he had seen of her had shown him her easy tears, her teasing, and the light-hearted kisses bestowed upon her husband with her childish patter. The poor man seemed to relish it, but did not see in it what surely everyone else must see, that she was giving a performance, play-acting.

That kiss among the daffodils had not been play-acting. Her instinct to yield to him had been real, although she knew she was close to the house, that anyone could have come along at any moment. It was he, of all people, who had kept her under control.

He had wanted to give her his icon, but he had given her Shakespeare's Sonnets. The one would amount to doing her homage, the other assumed an intellectual capacity he had, ever since he met her, believed she did not possess.

The thoughts, the inconsistencies, turned over and over in his mind, and when he settled in bed, with Fraoch curled up at his feet, he had come to a decision. He must see her soon, discover for himself if she was a wanton trollop, or a woman he could love and respect. Either way, the result would be the same. He would have to clear out of her life. Whether Robert Dutton was to be envied or pitied, the fact remained that Grania was his wife, and he had the right to keep her for himself.

Two weeks later, he received a postcard from her. It was a picture of the Leaning Tower of Pisa, and she had written, in her neat, childish writing, which he presumed she practised for the benefit of Robert – "We decided suddenly to fly to Italy. It was a very bumpy journey. Tomorrow we go to Capri. We will be back in Mull next month. Grania." He had read the postcard in the post office, where he collected it, along with several other letters, one of them obviously being a reply to his letter about the territorial army.

Today he had come to the village by boat, because he wanted to take home his supplies of butter, sugar, tea, and other necessities, collectively referred to in this part of the world as "the messages". Fraoch was with him, and jumped into the little boat, waiting, tail thumping, while the messages were piled around him.

As soon as the boat reached Tormore pier, and Roderick had loaded his trolley with his purchases, he went up to his cottage, and made himself stow away each item in its proper place before re-reading Grania's postcard. He was about to put it in the drawer where he kept the invitation to luncheon he had received from her over eighteen months ago. He had been ashamed of keeping that formal little note, but he could not have put it on the fire, with the other bits and pieces of rubbish that accumulated in his cottage. This note was special because it had been handled by Grania. He thought about her silky curls and the exquisite nape of her neck – he would always regret having torn up that sketch of her. He had done dozens of others since, but none had measured up to that one.

She was coming back to Mull in June, so this year she would not be doing the whole London season. They could fish together, they were safe out there on Loch Caraig in a boat. They could talk and he could get to know her.

He put a red ring round the word "June" on his calendar, then remembered his other letters, and settled down to read them. When he had done so, he propped up the picture of the Tower of Pisa on the mantelpiece, against the clock, and beside the application form he had received from the headquarters of the Argyll and Sutherland Highlanders.

25

There were no more postcards, but Roderick heard in the village that the Duttons were back in Mull. He knew, by the way he was told, that he was expected to react in some sort of way, but could only manage a disinterested "so I believe", which he felt was noted with greater satisfaction than would have been wild exclamations of delight.

He had been to see Michael Ames a few times while Grania was away, and had spent several days fishing on Loch Caraig. He had hoped to establish a routine, which he could keep up after her return, but found that he could not put into practice what he had so carefully planned.

Grania had either forgotten that kiss, among the many kisses she had given and received while she had been away, or she had remembered it as vividly as he did, and was afraid, or shy of making any show of friendship towards him.

She had been back for about a week, when he went to spend a few days in Edinburgh. He returned to Oban in time to catch the one-fifteen boat to Mull, and he followed the usual practice of going straight to the tiny dining-saloon, where, surrounded by murals depicting the story of the Young Lochinvar coming out of the West, he was served with the customary plate of mince, mashed potato and cabbage.

He saw Grania's legs first, as, laden with parcels, she climbed down the companion-way leading into the saloon. When he had settled her beside him and ordered her some mince, he noticed that there was only one other person having lunch, a man, deep in a book, as far from them as he could get. He was virtually alone with her, and had nearly an hour in which they could talk.

"Robert went south today, so I crossed to Oban with him. I've done some shopping," she indicated her parcels. "I'm glad you're here. I wanted to see you and didn't know how to set about contacting you without the whole of Mull thinking I was tracking you down."

"Thank you for your postcard. It was nice of you to think of me. I'd have sent you one of Iona Cathedral if I'd known your address."

"We were travelling around. The Tower of Pisa really does lean! We saw Mussolini addressing the crowd from his balcony at the Palazzo Venezia. It was all very theatrical, with people shouting *Duce, Duce, Duce,* and doing the fascist salute."

She prattled on about the unexpected holiday in Italy as the steward put the food in front of her. Roderick was sure that she was playing for time, trying to think how to express whatever it was that she wanted to say. He could feel it as surely as if she had told him so. He did not want to help her. He wanted to see whether the woman or the child would emerge from the struggle.

For a while, she gave her full attention to eating. Then she said, "I haven't seen you since my birthday. You lifted such a load off my mind when you told me about my father, and you gave me the Shakespeare Sonnets – I've read them so often that I almost know them by heart. And your kiss made me feel that I'd never been kissed before. I think you realized that. You could have done anything you wanted with me. Why didn't you; Roderick? Why, after a lifetime of conquests, were you so gallant over me?"

He felt his skin prickle. He sat motionless beside her.

'We were in Capri for a few days," she said. "I met people who had known you at Kitzbuhel, and they told me about your reputation with women, and about the girl who was killed. Then they told me about the avalanche and your parents, and I knew it wasn't just sentimental yearnings that had brought you to Tormore. Some day, if it doesn't distress you too much, I want you to tell me about it yourself."

"Nemesis," he said, hopelessly, helplessly.

"No, it's only me," she said. "They only told me, and that makes a difference. I think you know that."

She watched him, pushing the mince and potatoes around his plate. He wasn't eating. "I'm sorry, I must have spoken very clumsily. Perhaps bad news can be broken gently, after all. But this news isn't bad. I'm asking you to share something with me. That isn't bad at all. Like you sharing the secret of my father's name, it comes as a relief."

There was still no response. "It was because they found my maiden name was Lamont that they asked about you," she said. "I didn't tell them where you are, but it wouldn't matter if I did. They were nice people. They weren't being censorious. They were being kind."

As she spoke, he realized that she was right. It made all the difference that it was she who had stumbled upon this revelation of that dark, most dreadful, most hidden period of his life.

Grania signed to the steward and ordered pudding for both of them, pears and rice, and then coffee. "And be a dear and bring me two large malt whiskies. Tell the barman I'll come up and pay."

While they waited, she coaxed him to finish his first course. He felt the comfort of her nearness, of her concern, and he knew that she held him in the hollow of her hand.

The steward brought the whisky. "*Slainte!*" Grania said, and he responded with a wan smile. The sea was rough here. They must be near Lismore Lighthouse. Soon they would be at Craignure.

"I would like to tell you sometime," he said, his voice stiff and forced. "Tonight, when you are at Kilcaraig, will you think of me a little, because I'm going to have a battle with myself to think through what I have so long hoped to forget. I do want to tell you. I don't know how – we're never alone."

"We know it wouldn't do for us to meet alone." She used the plural, as he had once done.

The change in the sounds from the engine room showed that they were turning in towards Craignure Bay. Roderick gathered up Grania's parcels.

"There's something I want you to know before we get jammed into that ferry boat," he said.

"Yes?"

"Your knowing about me, and showing me that you are willing to talk to me again – you make me feel somehow absolved."

Her eyes lighted up. "That's a lovely thing to say, because it was a grisly sort of thing to have to tell you." There was a faint suggestion of childishness in her voice. She was back on Mull, where the woman gave way to the little girl, as of habit. Robert Dutton, who had bought her, liked her that way.

Roderick knew he could understand her now, and that he could better understand himself. He helped her to pack her parcels into the car, as she set off for home. Then he got into the Iona Ferry bus, because he had not wanted to leave his car overnight at Craignure, and therefore had made his way to the boat by public transport. He could have had a lift with Grania as far as the Kilcaraig cross road. He could have been alone with her for twenty minutes more; twenty minutes, when he yearned to be with her for all his life.

That night he wound up his portable gramophone, and put on a record. It was scratchy, nearly worn through, and he had not played it for years. A night on the Riviera. *What is this thing called love?* Culmination of a way of life he had entered into at the age of seventeen, at home in Cape Town. Relentlessly, he made himself recall the memories of those hidden, horrible years, while the record played on and he started it over again.

He had been preparing to leave South Africa to spend a year at Grenoble before going on to Oxford University, that was, if he passed the right examinations, and he was very sure of himself. At seventeen, he knew he was a success. He recognized his own good looks, and it amused him to see the admiring glances he got from women, young and old.

His father, during the past few years, had given him enlightening talks about life, each one more confusing than the last. He believed he knew a lot more than his father, because he had talked so much with other boys in school, some of whom claimed to have first-hand experience of that thing called love. Sometimes he invented romantic encounters, which he related to his friends. Then he met Caroline Vickers.

She was twenty-eight years old, sophisticated, charming, utterly amoral. Her husband, finding it impossible either to satisfy her, or to part with her, left her to her own devices. Soon she had devised that the fascinating young Roderick Lamont, whom she had met at a party, had found his way into her bedroom. Her husband was away. There was a whole night before her in which to initiate her conquest into the art of love-making.

The romance did not last long. Caroline's romances never did, but for Roderick that night with her surpassed the experiences, real or imaginary, with which his friends had regaled him. Any woman meant only one thing to him – a prize to be wooed and won, the more seemingly unattainable, the more desirable.

By the time he left for Grenoble, he had gained a reputation for being the Casanova of South Africa. He wasted no time in repeating his successes in France. He was not vain, but he knew he was irresistible to women of all ages. Unfortunately, one of the older ones turned out to be a friend of his parents. A prudently worded letter, denying any immediate knowledge of their son's sexual activities was duly delivered to his home in Cape Town. The Lamonts at once flew to France. They had a long and stormy interview with their son, impressing upon him not only their shock at his depravity, but their fears for his health. The life he had chosen to lead could have only one end.

Roderick was not worried about depravity, but he did fear the gruesome physical possibilities, which he had so far never taken into account. He agreed to accompany his parents to Kitzbuhel, where he would spend a holiday with them, and would lead an exemplary life, at least until he went to Oxford.

His parents' grief did distress him. He loved them, and his whole upbringing had inculcated in him a high sense of moral values. His escapades had not been without their nagging, dragging, often painful disturbance of his conscience. To renounce the lusts of the flesh was not difficult. To put the renunciation into practice was, he found, impossible.

At their hotel in Kitzbuhel, they met an English family, the Barretts. It was their only daughter, Veronica, to whom Roderick attached himself. She was very much an outdoor girl, excelling at skating and skiing, yet managing to look feminine and lovely when they danced together in the evenings. She was Roderick's sort of girl to the extent that he wished there had not been all those other girls before her.

When the time came for the Barretts to move on to the second part of their holiday, in the South of France, Roderick decided to go with them. His parents were apprehensive. They did not expect their son to become a reformed rake in so short a time, but they had arranged to do some climbing, and Roderick, who preferred skiing, would anyhow be left on his own in the Kitzbuhel hotel. Perhaps he was safer with the Barretts. He set off for Nice.

Once installed in their hotel, it soon became evident that Veronica, without the thrill of skiing, looked elsewhere for excitement and found it in speed. She hired a sports car, and she and Roderick enjoyed tearing round the roads of the Corniche with a recklessness that would have appalled her parents. One evening, in a state of high excitement, Veronica offered the wheel to Roderick. "I'm not up to your standard," he said. "I'll have us off the road."

"Call yourself a man!" she had scoffed. That settled it. They tore along the hill road, Roderick experiencing for the first time the delirium of another kind of possession – the possession of skill and speed and omnipotence. They were laughing and singing as the kilometres flew by. "*What is this thing called love?*" they sang together, and love for Roderick was not having a sensuous yielding woman, but a vibrant one, commanding him, full of promise of further excitements to come.

He had no recollection how it happened. Afterwards he was told it was a burst tyre. He was thrown clear, losing consciousness for a minute or so. When he sat up, dazed, on a bank by the roadside, he

179

saw the car. It had hurtled down the bank and was a blazing inferno. There was no sign at all of Veronica.

With the speed at which these things happen the police, the ambulance, the fire-fighters, were on the spot. Roderick was taken to hospital, suffering from shock. He was able to give his own and the girl's names and the name of the hotel where they were staying. Then he collapsed completely. It was days later that he opened his eyes, and knew that he was in a hospital. He could not remember how, or why he had got there.

When he was fully conscious, the nurse who was sitting quietly by his bed, fetched a doctor who examined him with care. Then he was told in good English, as they did not know that he could speak fluent French, that an avalanche had wiped out a party of British tourists who were climbing near Kitzbuhel.

He was able to leave the hospital and to return to Kitzbuhel to make the necessary identifications. His older brother, who was looking after the fruit farms near Cape Town, asked him to return to South Africa. He refused, but he saw the coffins containing his parents' bodies loaded onto an aeroplane, before he flew to London.

He was soon regarded as a misogynist at Oxford, where he worked hard and passed his examinations with brilliance. He did not know what to do with the remains of his life, and he did not care. Then he remembered Tormore Bay, and the disused quarries, and the Hebridean island which he had never been allowed to forget in Cape Town. He sent for his bagpipes, and for all his possessions, which his brother was glad to send to him, fearing, from past experience, what could happen if Roderick Lamont returned to work in the family business.

When he arrived at Mull, Roderick had not touched a woman for over three years, and was resolved never to touch one again. He was given permission to renovate one of the ruined cottages at Tormore, and he had found himself accepted by the islanders. Then he met Grania Dutton, and he had kissed her on her twenty-first birthday, rousing all his old passions, all his needs of a woman to love. And she knew about him, of all people in the world, she knew about his sordid past.

"Nemesis," he said, and she had replied. "No, it's only me."

What is this thing called love? The record, which he had put on over and over again, scratched itself to a halt.

He broke it in two and put the pieces in the fire.

26

"Would you say I use you as a confidante?" asked Grania. She and Michael were walking together to the village. They had met on the bridge, the water thundering under them, because it had rained heavily during the night.

"I would like to think you do," Michael replied, wondering what was coming next. He could always feel when Grania was finding it difficult to put her thoughts into words.

"When people have been married as long as Robert and I have been, there should be more tells and tolds," she said. "I wonder which of us is at fault that there isn't."

"What do you want to tell him? Or what do you want to be told?"

"I want to tell him more important things than that I've been fishing, or that I've seen the MacInneses' new baby. I want to tell him my thoughts as well as my deeds."

"Then why don't you?"

"He wouldn't understand." They walked more slowly because they were approaching the village. "And I expect he wants to tell me more important things than that he has brought off a big deal in Peru. If he thinks anything is more important than that!" There was an edge of contempt in her voice that Michael had never heard before. "It's somehow disloyal to talk to you like this, and it's disloyal to talk about things to other people that I don't talk about to Robert. It implies disloyalty, anyhow."

"Even married people have friends who share interests outside the bond of marriage. There's nothing disloyal in that."

"There is, when there aren't any interests within the bond of marriage. Michael, I've not talked like this before, and please try to forget it when you get home. But I've been most dreadfully burdened with very deep and catastrophic thoughts, so much so that I sometimes think I'll end up in a strait-jacket." She was trying to lighten the weight of feeling behind her words. They had reached the post office.

"More of this when we walk back," Michael said to her, as they entered and found a little group of people had gathered to commiserate with one another about the effects of last night's cloud burst.

Michael bought stamps, and Grania sent off a parcel of eggs to Marian. Then she read the notices and told Michael there was to be a bring-and-buy sale at the hall on Friday, followed by a dance.

Rob MacPhail heard her, and gave up his description of three sheep he had found drowned in the burn, to tell her that Roderick Lamont was to play the pipes at the dance.

"We have people staying," Grania said. "And I don't think they are dancing sort of people."

"Och, they'll like to watch us just the same." During the silence that followed, they were all thinking the same thought. The Duttons' English friends must find considerable entertainment in the weird ways of the islanders.

"We'll be at the bring-and-buy anyway," Grania said. "And I'll send something for the raffle." She explained to Michael, "It's in aid of the Red Cross."

They were leaving the post office when Roderick drew up in his car. He had come to Kilcaraig to see Michael, and finding him here with Grania was an unexpected embarrassment. He had wanted to talk to Michael about her.

"We may join you for a bit of the dance on Friday," Grania told him. "Lord and Lady Bronson are staying with us, and that awful, facetious Sir Brian Thorn, who was best man at our wedding."

"High society!"

"Big business! I've just told Michael that I think I'm going mad."

But nothing to do with that, Michael thought. Nothing to do with these people at all. He pitied her with all his heart. Always she must transfer her thoughts into light patter about trivialities. She needed her "tells" and "tolds", but they would always be denied to her.

Roderick drove them up to the castle, as Grania said she must get back to her guests. Michael knew she had been disposed to spend the whole morning with him. For once, he regretted Roderick's arrival. Grania could so easily retire into her private world of thoughts, and more thoughts, and the self-imposed barrier she erected between herself and her friends.

"She doesn't look well," Roderick said as he drove towards Caraig Lodge.

"I think she's very, very unhappy." Michael had been prepared to hear Grania's faltering attempt to explain her worries to him. Instead, he would listen to Roderick, and this seemed as good an opening as any.

"She's probably discovering how horrible people are, even the ones she had admired," Roderick said.

"What's happened between you?" Michael's words struck him so unexpectedly and fiercely that Roderick scraped the car, very slightly, on the low wall of the bridge over the burn. He did not reply until they had reached the house, and Michael, with his usual alacrity, had alighted from the car and preceded him to the sun-room. When they were settled, he repeated the question.

"Nothing," Roderick said. "Nothing at all." The silence was that of an empty room. If he had been Michael, he would have believed that he was sitting here alone, but he could see Michael, although Michael could not see him. He was not alone, and this curious sensation was the manifestation of Michael's unbelief at his reply. He could hear that scratchy record in his ear – *What is this thing called love?* Grania had met someone in Capri, and those memories must haunt him all over again.

"What has happened between us?" he said eventually. "I think everything. You see, Grania knows about me things I hoped would never be discovered."

Michael recognized the pain in his voice. Whatever Grania knew must be serious indeed. "Of all people in the world, isn't she the best one to know?" he said. "I, who have trusted her so much, have never regretted anything I've told her. She is to me the personification of the word solace. Concealed behind that façade of childishness, there is hidden a woman mature beyond her years. I've never said this to anyone but you, because I've wanted to assess her in the way she wants to be assessed. But you are different, and I don't need to tell you why, because you know that yourself."

Roderick was pacing up and down the room. "I am in love with her," he said, in a flat, factual voice. "She's totally out of my reach. Her husband is old, and will die. She will be a millionairess with a castle and an estate, and that would deter any decent-thinking man from considering marriage with her. I despised her for being Robert Dutton's wife in order to get Kilcaraig. I would despise myself if I became Grania's husband, her gigolo, to be given pocket money for cigarettes and for petrol for my car."

"That's being absurd. You wouldn't be marrying so as to own Kilcaraig. You'd be marrying Grania because you want her for your wife, and want her, I hope, enough to overlook the fact that you would also be saddled with what she is pleased to call her filthy lucre. As for pocket money, I notice that you already buy cigarettes and petrol, and other things besides, and are not beholden to anyone for that. Or is that the murky secret Grania has discovered? Is it something very serious indeed?"

He felt sudden alarm. Grania's faltering and frustrated attempt to talk to him this morning – perhaps she had to tell him something she could not bear to endure alone.

Roderick suddenly laughed, and sat down, relaxed. "I'm not living on blackmail," he said, realizing how very much more grave could have been the charges against him. Other young men had sown wild oats. Other young men had driven cars recklessly, had even killed a companion in so doing. "It's a strange thing," he said. "But I think you have summed up Grania very well. She is solace."

"And here we are, deciding what to do about her when her husband, who loves her in his own way, dies. Poor man, I expect he wonders himself what sort of adventurer is going to pursue her when she's a merry widow!"

"He's deep, that one. If he could find a way of separating Grania from Kilcaraig, he would ensure that whoever takes his place loves her for herself alone."

Roderick, as he spoke, tried to visualize what Grania really wanted out of life. Did Kilcaraig really mean as much to her as she had thought it did? Was the new Kilcaraig, with its neat fences and landscaped gardens merely a daily reminder to her that the life she had loved was a thing of the past? One thing he was certain about. The cottage at Tormore could be no substitute for Kilcaraig. He had much to think about that day as he drove home, but he felt better because he had been able to talk so candidly, so fully, about Grania.

On Friday evening, the party from the castle did come to the bring-and-buy sale. They listened to the minister's wife opening it, reading from the notes she had scribbled down on the back of an envelope.

Roderick, watching from a corner near the door, could understand why Grania thought her guests would not fit into a Mull dance. Lady Bronson, her stiffly corsetted figure squeezed into an exquisitely-tailored tweed suit, could hardly be swung round in "Strip the Willow", and her husband's complexion indicated that he would probably have a heart attack if expected to take his place on the dance floor. Sir Brian Thorn, eyeing some of the local girls, would perhaps have enjoyed himself more than Grania would have done in intervening to protect them from his advances. Robert, as always, looked tired. Roderick wondered if Michael, at the other side of the hall, was sharing his feeling of guilt that they had talked so blandly about what would happen to Grania when Robert was in his grave.

Surprisingly, when the stalls had been cleared, and tea, sandwiches and cakes eaten, and the hall prepared for the dance, Grania came up to Roderick.

"Robert says I can stay," she said. "He says he wants to talk business tonight, and that includes Esmeralda – believe it or not, that's her name – and he says I need young company. Do you mind if I stay?"

He was astounded. She really meant it. She really wondered if what she had heard about him made him too much embarrassed to be with her any more. He wanted to take her hands and hold them, pressed in his. "I shall be providing the music. I'll enjoy watching you dancing." He could see by her face that she understood. Not even in an eightsome reel was he going to put his arm round her waist.

At midnight, supper was served and as was usual, after it Grania, and the Ameses, and the minister and his wife, and the doctor all left. The dance would now get rowdier, for many of the men had half-bottles of whisky in their pockets, and these were handed round for quick swigs in the darkness outside the hall. Roderick waved his farewell from the platform. He had shared the piping for the dances with Angus and Willie, and although he had danced, he had not danced with Grania. Everyone noticed this. Most guessed the reason why.

Grania found Robert waiting for her in her bedroom, when she got home. He was sitting on the bed, wearing his dressing-gown, and he had been chain-smoking. She could tell by the atmosphere of the room.

"Undress in here, not in the bathroom," he said. "I want to talk to you."

She fumbled with the buttons of her blouse, took it off, and put it aside. Then she unfastened her skirt, let it fall in a circle at her feet, then picked it up, folded it neatly and put it with her blouse. In brassiere and panties, she felt both ridiculous and indecent. She wanted her nightdress, but it would mean going close to Robert. He saw her look at her pillow, and he understood her meaning. He put his hand under the pillow and tossed the nightdress at her, then he watched what she would do. She turned her back on him, and took off her brassiere, but she knew he could see her reflection in the dressing-table mirror. Thankfully, she pulled on her nightdress, and slipped out of her little pants. She heard his laugh, and he was behind her, holding her shoulders and kissing her hair.

"You will enchant me until the day I die," he said. "All the things we've done together, and you squirm over this!"

She could not smile. "You make me feel like a tart," she said.

He shook her, suddenly angry. "And what are you? A woman who gives her body for money – aren't you that?"

She stood frozen to the spot, like an animal from a foe.

"Did you dance with Roderick Lamont?"

"No."

"Why not?"

"He didn't ask me to."

"He's going to advertise to all who see you – and that is everyone – that you are forbidden fruit. Surely he can be more subtle than that."

She went into the bathroom and washed. She looked at herself in the long mirror. She tried to see herself as Robert saw her, his property, and as Roderick saw her, but he had never seen her like this, in a nightdress clinging to her body, enhancing every contour. She thought – "I wish I were dead". She returned to her bedroom. Robert was standing by the dressing-table, and he studied her as she got into bed and pulled the bedclothes round her.

"What I waited up to tell you was this. I had a talk with Edward and Esmeralda and Brian. I have decided to transfer forty thousand pounds to your name. You will keep the capital, I hope, but do what you like with the interest. It's not so much as it sounds. I have to think about death duties." He added that, fearing that if he did not, she would be emotionally grateful. He did not want that tonight.

Grania lay, her head on the pillow, her eyes closed, trying to take in what she had heard. Then she pushed down the bedclothes and pulled up her nightdress.

"Come on," she said. "I've cost a lot. Forty thousand pounds."

He took advantage of her invitation.

27

Robert was sitting at his bedrom window, his binoculars trained on Loch Caraig. Grania and Roderick were fishing all right, but they were doing a great deal of talking as well. He wished he had some device to fix on the boat, to record what they were saying. Some day someone would invent something like that.

Grania was rowing. She would take the boat to the head of the loch, then let it drift back. She would not have to concentrate on what she was doing, but now, at this moment, Roderick had caught a fish, and displayed the activity necessary to land it. Next week he would be going to a training camp with the Argyll and Sutherland Highlanders, for he had joined their territorial battalion. That would keep him out of the way for a couple of weeks. Perhaps he would even decide to join the regiment as a regular soldier.

Robert watched as Grania rowed the boat to the shore. Angus was there to tie it up and look after it. Walking at a reasonable pace, it would take twelve minutes to reach the castle from the loch. After ten minutes, he went downstairs, and settled hmself in the library, arranging himself to look as if he had been there all afternoon. Twenty-one minutes passed before Grania came into the house. He heard her go to the cloakroom. She was alone.

He called to her. She took her time, but she did hear him and come.

"How many?" he said.

"Only two. We weren't trying very hard. We were talking."

Did she know about the binoculars, or was she really as ingenuous as she appeared to be?

"What were you talking about?"

"Oh, shoes and ships and sealing-wax," she said lightly, and saw, to her surprise, that he looked bewildered. "And cabbages and kings," she added, feeling foolish, and wondering if she should explain that it was a quotation from *Alice Through The Looking Glass*.

"Grania Through The Looking Glass." He wanted her to think he had known what she meant. "Why didn't you bring Roderick here for a drink?"

"He didn't bring Fraoch, so he had to go home."

"Surely his neighbours at Tormore always look after Fraoch?"

"They're away." She hesitated. "I've said we can have Fraoch while he's at camp. Is that all right?"

"Love me, love my dog," he said. "Yes, we can have him. But he's not to share your bed."

"I suppose you're referring to Fraoch, not to Roderick!" she snapped, colouring and turning on her heel to leave the room.

"Come here." She came. She knew better than to refuse. He took her by the hand and said, quite kindly, "Grania, I'm sorry. I seem to goad you into saying revolting things."

She waited, wondering if he would say any more, but he released her, and she went up to her bedroom, ran the bath, and soon was lying in it, getting the fishy smell out of her hands, and the confused thoughts out of her mind.

She had fished Loch Caraig frequently with Roderick. It was almost a habit now. They met there once or twice a week. He had told her all he could recall of his life before he met her, every little detail of it. He answered her questions, too, and sometimes she had questioned him in the sort of detail she would never have believed herself able to express. It was not a one-sided revelation. She told him about her own life, her life with Robert – its extraordinary mixture of what was prosaic and what was obscene. She spoke without embarrassment and without a sense of disloyalty, for Roderick was not as other men, he was the man of her dreams.

They never talked of love. They never touched, yet they were wholly at ease with one another. It was as if they were bound up in a silken veil, so flimsy that it could easily be torn apart, yet so sacred that to damage it would be iconoclasm.

Grania had wanted to talk about things that were important to her – poetry and God. Now she could talk of these things, and of everything else besides. She would ask for nothing more from life than the bliss of being Roderick's friend.

By the end of September, the trout fishing was over, the boat laid up, and Roderick had spent his last evening at the castle, for he often ended the day by staying on for a drink, and sometimes for dinner.

"He'll be coming over for the stalking, I presume?" Robert said to Grania after they had waved him off in his car. "That is, unless sleuthing round the moors, rifle in hand, inhibits the kind of confidence you pour out to one another."

"I'm not very keen on stalking, as you know. I prefer to shoot deer with a camera." But what Robert had said was perfectly true. During the next few months she would rarely see Roderick, and then only when other people were present. They had both agreed about that.

Helen's wedding took place quietly in October, as Evelyn had planned, and it was a happy affair, attended only by members of the family, and a few of Evelyn's bridge-playing friends. The bride, glowing as all brides should, wore a blue dress and matching coat, and a very pretty hat from Marian's shop. She was attended by Diana, who had become engaged, not to a schoolmaster, as everyone had predicted, but to an Imperial Airways pilot. They were to be married in the Kensington registry office at Christmas. They had decided against a church wedding as neither ever went to church.

During the luncheon party which followed the service, Grania thought how lucky Helen had been to marry a man who was successful at his job and who was the right age for her. She looked across the table at her own husband, whose appearance was very distinguished now that his ginger hair had turned grey, but strangers must think he was her father.

Robert was sitting next to Evelyn's mother, who was slumped in a chair, in a world of her own, and he could feel Grania's eyes upon him, for he was always aware of her, whatever they did, wherever they were.

At St. Stephen's Church, hearing Helen and Charles Maitland exchanging vows had reminded him of his own marriage when he had been too much overcome to consider what either he or Grania were saying. At other people's weddings the full beauty and solemnity of the pledges always filled him with awe, but at his own he could think only "she's mine, she's mine," and his lips had spoken words, while his heart had exulted in the joy of acquisition. He was to learn later, and bitterly, that while she was physically submissive to him he could not win her heart. She would never know the mortification he felt when he used her body, just as he would use the body of a prostitute. He had paid dearly for her, but it was not with the filthy lucre which she so much despised that he had paid, it was in disappointment, frustration and grief.

The Maitlands left for their honeymoon in Ireland from Euston Station, and Robert and Grania left from the adjoining platform on the night train to Oban. The day after they arrived at Kilcaraig, Hunter handed in his notice.

"But I thought you had settled here. I thought you were happy with us," Grania said, genuinely distressed.

"And so I was, my lady," Hunter said, thinking of the concerts and the *ceilidhs*, and of how he had learnt to dance the eightsome reel. "I have personal reasons for wishing to find another post. Christina Cameron will explain what they are."

Christina Cameron was Chrissie. Grania found her ironing the gossamer-thin underwear which she had brought back from London.

"Jim asked me to marry him, the poor soul. The very idea!" Chrissie said, carefully separating some folds of lace. "We're better without a butler here. He doesn't suit the place."

"But Chrissie, he's a nice man. If you marry him, we'll have a house built for you that will be your very own."

"What would I be doing living in a home of my own, with you needing me here in the castle? It wouldn't do at all, at all. Now, just get you off to see Donald MacBean. He's wanting to know how the wedding went, and all the other things you can tell him about London."

Grania capitulated because she knew Chrissie too well to argue. She tramped across the fields to the thatched cottage on the far side of the loch, and Morag MacBean, apple-cheeked but now totally toothless, was waiting for her at the door, for she had seen her coming.

"I've put the kettle on, and I'll bring yous tea in a wee minute," she said, opening the door of Donald's bedroom. The old man was sitting up in bed, pipe in hand, and Roderick Lamont was sitting on the chair beside him.

"I didn't see your car," Grania said. Roderick usually parked his car near the village when he came to see Donald.

"I left it at the top of the glen. Fraoch hasn't had a decent walk for days, and neither have I."

He fetched two more chairs from the kitchen, and the four of them had tea, with oatcakes which were Morag's speciality, and they talked in Gaelic, which Donald spoke more easily than English.

When Grania left, Roderick went with her as far as the south bank of Loch Caraig. They paused at the boat house for a while, as one of the screws on the door-hinge had worked loose, and Roderick was able to fix it with the point of his *sgian dubh*; then he went his own way, up to the glen road, with Fraoch quartering the ground for rabbits, while Grania returned to the castle.

She met Robert on the stairs. "Where have you been?" he asked.

She told him about Donald MacBean and Morag. She didn't mention Roderick.

Four weeks later, she was driving home from a visit to the MacPhails' farm when she felt the yawning queasiness which used to precede car-sickness when she was a child. She pulled onto the grass verge and was out of the car before the retching began. There wasn't a soul in sight to witness her shame. She had eaten the usual scones at the MacPhails, and she decided that she had spread the fresh butter on too thickly. She had fully recovered by dinner-time, but the next morning the queasiness returned, and without having to check her diary she guessed the cause of her trouble. She had always imagined that starting a baby would be an experience of unqualified joy, and that she would run to Robert with the good news. Instead, she found that she viewed the prospect of motherhood with considerable apprehension. She wanted a baby, but she didn't want Robert's baby. She pictured the long, angular limbs and the ginger hair of the Dutton child who would some day be heir to Kilcaraig. The founding of a Dutton dynasty just didn't make sense.

Chrissie was the first to notice that all was not well with Grania. "You're pale and tired and irritable, not at all yourself. You'll need to ask Doctor MacColl to come round and have a look at you and prescribe a tonic."

"I don't need a tonic," Grania said. "I just want to be left alone in peace." Whereupon, she ran into the bathroom and was sick.

It was Chrissie who convinced her that Robert must be told about her baby, and without delay. "It's early days yet, only six weeks, but you'll need to keep him out of your bed for a wee while, just to let things settle. And that's no old wives' tale," she said.

Grania had never thought of that aspect of her condition, but that night, when Robert showed signs of becoming amorous round about bedtime, she playfully tried to ward him off. Unaccustomed to being rejected by her, he became more persistent. She sensed that what she had to tell him must be told at least with tenderness, but her rising anger added impetus to his desire. He had his way with her that night, and the next, and the next, until finally she refused him in a torrent of tears. Perplexed, for this had never happened before, he demanded an explanation.

She told him.

"Why on earth didn't you tell me before?"

"I wanted to be sure."

"Sure of what? Sure that you're having a baby, or sure that it's my baby?" He was furious.

She sat in bed, the bedclothes pulled up to her chin, as if for protection. "Whose could it be, if not yours?"

"Roderick Lamont's of course. What were you doing with him in the boat house as soon as you came back from London? You didn't waste any time getting into touch with him did you! And your rendezvous was at Donald MacBean's cottage. I saw you together. I saw you walking down to the loch, and vanishing into the boat-house. But you didn't tell me you had seen him. Why not? What had you to hide?"

She was so outraged that her only defence was to take his accusation as a joke. She tried to laugh. "What could possibly occur in a damp and draughty boat-house at the end of October?"

"I'm glad you see the comic side of it, for that's how it must have been. We all know what music-hall comedians say about the convenience of wearing a kilt!"

"You're a filthy-minded old ram!" She hurled the words at him and jumped out of bed, snatching her wrap, but he caught her and held her, struggling, against him.

"Don't you dare say that – don't you dare!" He shook her and pushed her back onto the bed. She lay there, stupefied, her heart pounding, then he was upon her, not trying to make love to her, but sobbing out his remorse and his shame.

Wordlessly, she stroked his heaving shoulders, and when he was calmer she indicated that he could get into bed beside her. It was always the same at the end of a quarrel, her gesture of forgiveness, but the bitterness or hurt that she felt was tucked away to fester in her mind, and he knew it.

He slept the sleep of exhaustion, but she spent most of the night awake, her teeming brain turning over and over what he had said. He had debased what was beautiful in her relationship with Roderick. She would never forget his mockery. It was so much more damaging than his physical attack upon her. The problems facing her in the future appeared to be insurmountable, but by the morning one of them was solved. She felt the warm stickiness of blood between her thighs, and there was a pain in her stomach and in her back which was far worse than anything she had experienced before. She managed to get to the bathroom without waking Robert, and there in the first-aid cupboard were pain-killing drugs, and rolls of cotton-wool. She was back in bed and pretending to be asleep when he woke up.

He knew she was pretending, but he had a bath and went down-stairs to breakfast, which he ate quickly; then he asked Chrissie to tell Grania that he had to go to Tobermory and would be back by tea-time.

When Chrissie delivered his message, she found Grania up and dressed but looking like a ghost. Chrissie was full of kindness and comfort, assuring her that such mishaps were common in early pregnancy. "Maybe I shouldn't have told you to tell Sir Robert," she said. "He'll be very disappointed, but next time it'll be all right, *mo chridhe*."

Grania flatly refused to ask Doctor MacColl to call, but she spent the day quietly, and when Robert came home she told him that her pregnancy had been a false alarm after all.

"Are you sure? Are you sure it wasn't my fault?" He was pitifully abject. She reassured him as a mother might reassure an anxious child, and he believed her, because in self-deception he could find peace of mind.

A few days later, torn between disappointment and relief, Grania wrote a note to Roderick. "Please destroy this as soon as you have read it. Something has happened, so that you'd better not come here for a while. I can't explain now, but someday I will. Please under-stand."

She printed his address on the envelope, and made Christmas shopping her excuse for going to Oban. She posted her letter there, so that it would not bear a Mull postmark, then she bought some more cards and calendars, and baubles for the Christmas tree.

Roderick sent them a Christmas card, but although he had dinner with the Ameses at Caraig Lodge on Boxing Day, he didn't call at the castle.

The New Year heralded the death of a dearly-loved king, and the brief reign of his successor. Grania and Roderick met sometimes at the various events on Mull, ploughing matches, agricultural and horticultural shows, sheep-dog trials. Nothing was said about the note or its contents. They were never alone.

Robert still regretted the crudity of his accusation about what had taken place in the boat house, but he was convinced that by ridiculing Roderick he had undermined any romantic notions Grania may have felt about him. There was no talk now about blood-ties, and kith and kin.

Evelyn's mother died in December, and Robert made her funeral his excuse for keeping Grania in London until after Christmas, so that they heard the abdication speech of King Edward VIII on their wireless at Lowndes Square. Grania then demanded a holiday in Italy, and Robert found himself sitting through a number of operas at La Scala, Milan. He didn't learn how to appreciate music, but he found that *prime donne* could be surprisingly attractive.

By March, they were back at Kilcaraig, and then came the excitement and the bonfires on the night of the 12th May, when King George VI and his lovely Scottish Elizabeth were crowned in Westminster Abbey. The bonfire that raged on the top of Ben Caraig was kept going for most of the night, until by morning it was out of control, and tore through the heather, so that the day of May 13th saw all the able-bodied men and women beating out the flames with the sacks which they managed to keep wet, because fortunately there were many bogs in which they could be soaked.

"That's a coronation we won't forget," an exhausted Grania, covered in soot, announced as she helped to make tea for the fire fighters in the village hall. It was a coronation nobody was likely to forget, because from that time the threat of war, which had been creeping up, became very real indeed. By the following year, Hitler was demanding just a little bit more territory, and by autumn it looked as if he was going to be given peace at any price.

"Thank God," Robert had said when the Munich agreement was announced. "We aren't ready for war."

"I've never felt so humiliated," Grania had stormed. "I'm ashamed to be British."

In a year's time, she had no cause for shame any more. She left Chrissie and Angus and Willie in charge at Kilcaraig, because cook had retired, the new cook had joined the A.T.S., Duncan MacPhail was in the Air Force, and Robert had to be in London.

"You'll be safer in Mull," he said when she arrived at Lowndes Square, but he knew he pleaded in vain. Marian had left her hat shop and was working in a factory, Evelyn had joined the W.V.S., and because Diana's husband was now in the Air Force, and Helen's in the Navy, the two girls had joined together to help run a crèche.

Grania, mercilessly using her influential friends, was soon proudly wearing the uniform of an ambulance driver. She was part of the war-effort, and she had at last found a worthwhile reason for living. Over there, across the channel, Roderick was somewhere in Europe. Rumour had it that he had been seconded for special duties and was not with his regiment, but there was no means of knowing what was false and what was true. One thing was sure – the quiet first winter of the war would break into something quite different in the spring.

Nicholas Danvers had been put in charge of a home for incurables near Oxford. He had been too long out of the medical profession to be able to serve as a doctor with the armed forces, but he set to work with vigour to bring his old skills up to date.

Mr. Ames died shortly after the first Christmas of the war. Grania, training for her ambulance driving, couldn't leave London to attend his funeral, but Robert went to Mull. There he found everything calm and peaceful, as he had expected it to be.

The funeral was carried out with the mixture of homeliness and dignity, which made a Highland funeral almost a joyful occasion. The coffin was placed in the drawing-room of Caraig Lodge, where the minister conducted a short service. It was then carried shoulder-high to the burial ground. Mrs. Ames, following Highland custom, did not accompany it, but remained in the house with the women mourners, who would stay with her until the burial had taken place and they were joined by their menfolk.

Robert, walking behind the coffin, noted how efficiently the men stepped in and took it in turns to get under it, to help carry their friend. Some of these men would have dug the grave, and then would help to fill it with earth, and it would be the loving hands of friends that would pat the green swatch of turf back into place, and tuck it in as if it were an eiderdown. The Ameses had been in Mull since before the first world war. He had been told that at first they were regarded with suspicion, but they had adapted themselves to the life of the islanders, and now were loved and respected as he knew he himself was not. He had bought an estate, but he could not buy the affection of the people.

He was given one of the eight cords which were attached to the coffin, and he helped to lower it into the grave. It was a privilege to be on the cords – he had learnt that much while he lived here.

Some day, this would be happening to him. He tried to picture it, but he found he couldn't. The thought of his death frightened him because of what would happen to Grania. Then he saw old Lachlan MacLachlan standing beside him. Lachlan, who years ago had been threatened that he would occupy the first layer in the new addition to the burial ground. People lived long in these parts; to die at seventy was to be cut off in one's prime, and he felt reassured, for Lachlan must be in his eighties, and Donald MacBean, years older, was still alive and mentally alert.

There was a tot of whisky and cheese and biscuits for all who attended the burial. They stood outside the gate in little groups, partaking of the food and drink, and talking in normal voices of weather and crops, for life went on.

Michael, his blind eyes tearless, was staring at the sky, as if he could see there the hope of a future that the grave had seemed to deny. Robert, seeing him, thought that when Mrs. Ames died, Michael must be asked to make his home at the castle. Grania was fond of him, she would want it that way.

Then he remembered that other man of whom Grania had been fond. Fate had removed him from the scene, perhaps for ever. *Curses come home to roost*, Chrissie would say. He shivered, and abruptly he left the mourners and went to his car, which he had strategically placed nearby before the service. It was small, and he had to drive it himself, but a petrol allowance was one of his perquisites for his comfortable role of providing weapons that would help to win the war.

He called at Caraig Lodge to offer a last word of condolence to Mrs. Ames. The next day he returned to London.

*   *   *

Spring came, and with it the catastrophes that everyone in their hearts had expected. Robert knew a great deal more about what was happening in France than he could say to anybody, even to Grania.

One day he was having lunch with her in his club. She had been out since early morning, because she was on shift work, although at present all the work she was doing was routine care of the ambulances, and a routine guard on them in case they might be sabotaged. Coffee had just been served, when he remembered that the mail had been delivered after Grania had gone out that morning. One of the letters had a Mull postmark. He handed it across the table to her. It was from Mrs. MacPhail of Caraig Farm, and it described what the villagers were doing for the war effort, and how Mull was to be registered as an area of special security, and how they were all being issued with special identity cards, bearing the photograph of the holder, just like having a passport. It made her feel important, she wrote, but she had no idea what the security was about. She completed her letter with a list of the people to whom she sent her regards, and Grania was about to fold it, when she saw there was a postscript over the page.

"We were all very sorry to hear that Captain Lamont is reported missing, believed killed. It is a terrible war."

Robert, who had listened attentively to the letter as Grania read out the list of people to receive regards, was gratified that his name was among them. Then he looked across at her, and saw that she was slumped, her head on the table, her silky curls wet with spilt coffee. He took the letter out of her hand, and saw the postscript.

So Roderick mattered as much as this to her. Over the years, he had been lulled into believing that what had seemed to be a blossoming romance between his wife and Roderick had resolved itself into a casual friendship. Grania had shown no particular desire to speak about, or to write to Roderick. She hadn't talked of him, but her thoughts must have been obsessed by him.

He watched helplessly as the waiter and the inevitable first-aider set to work to revive his unconscious wife. Presently she was sitting upright, white as death, but able to apologize for the spilt coffee, as if spilt coffee mattered, but it was always trifles on which a bemused mind would fasten.

She sipped the brandy someone had thrust at her, and the colour began to return to her cheeks. "I'll find him for you," Robert told her. "It will be all right." He had said the same to Marian, when she had been burgled, and it had been all right.

"Roderick," Grania said. "Thank you."

Robert wondered if she knew to whom she was speaking, or if she just had to say that name. And was she thanking Roderick for what he had been in the past, or himself for what he would do in the future?

"I'll trace him," Robert said, altering the meaning of his earlier assurance. She had come to her senses now.

"When you trace him you could find that he's dead," she said.

He did not have to answer her. They both knew that this was perfectly true.

28

The calamity that had struck the Fifty-First Division during those first days of June was to deal a severe blow to the population of the Highlands, for nearly every family had a relation or a friend in one of its battalions. On Mull, households both great and small were awaiting news of the Argyll and Sutherland Highlanders, cut off while holding a rearguard position at St. Valery, but in the chaos that followed Dunkirk it was taking time to trace the missing to prison camps or graves.

Roderick Lamont, who lived at Tormore, had given the name of his brother, who lived in Cape Town, as his next of kin. That made Robert's attempts to find him even more difficult, and already he knew himself to be struggling against his will to do anything about it at all. Time would reveal what had happened, but because he had told Grania he would help, he pestered everyone he knew for information, from the Prime Minister downwards.

Grania went daily to her ambulance station. She never mentioned Roderick, and was inclined to dismiss her fainting attack at the club as a mixture of tiredness and of heat.

Robert telephoned Nicholas to ask his advice. "She's like an automaton," he said. "She wakes up and gets through the day, and goes to bed, and I suspect doesn't sleep, and she shows no interest in anything. If the raids start, she'll be in no fit state to drive her ambulance."

"She'll be all right when she knows what's happened," Nicholas said. "And if the bombs drop, she'll rise to the occasion like everyone else. Grania isn't the only woman in Britain under strain. There are millions of them, and you'll see how dependable they'll be when they're needed."

Robert replaced the receiver, feeling rebuffed. Grania was not one of millions, she was his wife, his possession, but not his toy any more. Those days of delight were over. He had ignored her taunts about buying her, and had won back her confidence after the episodes when jealousy and desire had driven him to the brink of brutality, but now he knew that even if she ever emerged from her present state of apathy, he could not force himself upon her again. She had perhaps been acting a part since he had first made love to her, had felt her rigid fear melt into submission, and then into response. The early days of their honeymoon had been difficult days for him, because he had been careful to take gradually what he had longed to take by storm. The play-acting was all over now. Almost he was thankful. When the war ended, if ever it did, and Roderick came marching home, he would find a very different Grania from the girl he had left behind him, and Grania would find a very different Roderick. He pulled himself together, remembering that he had to find out if there was Roderick alive to be found. This time he dialled the War Office.

It was Grania who was the first to hear what had happened to Roderick. She had left her ambulance station, and was walking along the embankment towards Vauxhall Bridge Road, when she met Mrs. Wright, who was being towed along by a Golden Labrador dog. The Wrights had left Mull a few years ago, but they kept in touch with some of the friends they had made on the island.

"Grania Dutton!" screamed Mrs. Wright. "I've been hunting the telephone directory for you. I've heard from Jessie MacQuarrie, who's helping on the telephone exchange at Tobermory, that Roderick Lamont is a P.O.W. He was badly wounded, but no lost limbs. I knew you would want to know." Her sharp eyes watched for the joy her news would give Grania, but Grania merely stroked the Labrador's head and said dully, "I'm glad. Robert had been trying to trace him. It's been awful, what has happened to so many of our friends."

This disinterested response did not match up with the reports of a romance between Grania and Roderick that the Wrights had been receiving from Mull. But Grania Dutton did not look the same. Her uniform partly accounted for that of course, but her eyes were tired, her face drawn and pale. Quickly calculating, Mrs. Wright guessed her age as twenty-seven. She looked older than that. They exchanged brief accounts of the war work they were doing. Mrs Wright was helping in a Citizens' Advice Bureau, and she congratulated Grania on having undertaken what would in time be dangerous, difficult work. "I like it," was all Grania had to say.

"You won't when the bombs come down."

"No, I suppose I won't."

"When will you be going back to Kilcaraig?"

"When it's all over, I suppose."

Mrs. Wright gave up. She had hoped for an invitation to Lowndes

Square, but that obviously was not forthcoming. With promises to telephone and to meet again, Grania continued on her way, while Mrs. Wright returned to her flat to tell her husband that she had met Grania Dutton, who looked weary and listless, and didn't seem to be interested that Roderick Lamont was alive and would soon be well.

"She's weary and listless because she has an ardent husband, and a lover she believed to be killed," he said, moving along the sofa to make way for her dog. "She'll not jump for joy in front of you, knowing Mull would hear of it within the half hour. The tidings won't be very glad for poor Robert. In his secret heart, he must have hoped that one rival had been removed from the fray."

Grania took a bus to Victoria Station, but walked the rest of the way home. She wanted to think, and to know how to tell Robert what she had heard. He would not believe that she had fortuitously run into Mrs. Wright. He would think she was following her own line of enquiry. He did not trust her at all.

There was no need for an explanation, because he was out when she let herself into the flat, and he had left a note for her, giving the same information she had just heard, but he had added "There's no need to worry. It was a stomach wound and severe shock, but he is now out of danger."

She changed out of her uniform into a silk dress. She wanted to go out, to the cinema, to the theatre, to anywhere that would take her mind off herself. She had never been introspective, but for so long now, so very long, she could think only "What am I going to do?" She heard Robert's key in the lock, and quickly picked up a book. She looked absorbed in it when he came into the sitting-room. He had expected her to come to him, happy and grateful because she had read his note.

"Thank you for letting me know about Roderick," she said. "Perhaps you can write to him now, and arrange for Red Cross parcels."

Robert kissed her forehead. He wanted to kiss her mouth. "I'll find out about the parcels. But he'll expect letters from you, not me. It wouldn't be natural for me to write."

"But you will, please, on behalf of us both. Otherwise people will talk."

"What people? And hasn't there been enough talking already? You've been looking like a widow for weeks now. Do you think nobody has noticed? Or talked?" He could see that she wanted to cry. He could see, too, how easily she controlled herself. For years he had believed in those facile tears.

She stood up. She made no excuses, no denial. "I'll get supper," she said, and left the room.

Robert had wanted to take her out to dinner, and to a cinema, anything rather than spend the evening alone with her in the flat. He followed her to the kitchen, where he half expected to find her in tears after all. She was standing on tiptoe, fetching a pan from the rack over the cooker.

"We'll go to Hatchett's," he said. "Tonight's a night for celebrating." As he spoke, the air-raid siren sounded the alert. She pushed back the pan.

"Yes, let's go to Hatchett's. I'm not on duty, and it's so noisy there that we won't hear the raid."

There was no raid over London that night. The All Clear sounded before they left the flat, but it gave them something to talk about to start off the evening, and by the end of it they had joined up with some people they knew, so it was a sort of celebration after all. It was to be their last for some time, because soon the air raids were a regular nightly occurrence, and lasted most of the day as well. Grania was kept busy driving her ambulance, while Robert combined fire-watching at night with increasing productivity in armaments by day. Nicholas was proved to have been right. Grania had no difficulty in showing that she was capable of doing her very responsible job.

Just before Christmas, there was a letter from Roderick. He was grateful for their letters and for the parcels. He would look forward to more news from them both. They must take care of themselves and he hoped they would soon be able to return to Kilcaraig.

Marian's flat received a direct hit before his next letter came. She moved to Cranston Terrace, to Nicholas's house, part of which had been converted into flats. She read the letter Grania showed her.

"Thank you for the parcels. I shall look forward to having more news of you both. I wonder when you are going back to Kilcaraig."

"He's not very communicative," Marian said, handing back the letter. "Being a prisoner of war must be extra hard for him. He's so accustomed to being free from all ties." She watched Grania fold the letter and return it to her handbag.

"I wonder what she does with it," she thought. "Does it go in her jewel-case, or in the litter bin?" When next she saw Nicholas, she asked him what he thought.

"She'll give it to Robert. Their letters and parcels are joint affairs. I don't know who they're supposed to be fooling, but perhaps it's as well Roderick is regularly reminded that Grania has a husband."

He noticed that Marian's cuffs were frayed, and he remembered the first time he had met her, at Craignure Inn, over a quarter of a century ago. She noticed and laughed. "My things went up with a bang! Remember? And this suit is my sole good possession, put on especially for you. Frayed, but elegant. Not like these awful utility clothes that cost coupons as well as money."

"We've known one another for a long time," he said. "I was worried about you for a while. I thought you were getting bitter."

"What! Me?" She seemed genuinely surprised. "I went through a spell of envying Grania. Silly, wasn't it? I wouldn't have Robert if he was the last man alive. He's making a wreck of Grania. I think she'd crack up if she didn't have her ambulance work to keep her going. She badly needs a holiday. Roderick's right, she needs to be at Kilcaraig."

Grania's next visit to Kilcaraig took place sooner than anyone had anticipated. She was driving her ambulance during the raid on Westminster on the night of May 10th. The next thing she knew was that she was somewhere very quiet, except for the twittering of birds and the buzzing of bees. This must be a hospital, because she was aware of the hospital smell, and the tramping of busy feet, and the heavy scent of flowers somewhere near her head. Gradually, as consciousness returned, without surprise or fear she became aware that she was blind.

Robert had spent every available moment of his time at her bedside ever since the bomb had dropped in front of her ambulance, and her body, still miraculously alive, had been transported to this hospital in Surrey.

He was with her now, and because she was swathed in bandages, he did not immediately notice that she was suffering the ebb and flow of returning consciousness. Then he saw her hand move to her face, as she tried to pull the bandages from her eyes. At once he was beside her, his hand on hers. "It's Robert," he said. She still tried to pull at the bandages. "Not yet, Grania. You'll be all right when the bandages come off."

"Who says so?"

"I do." The positive voice. The voice that had assured Marian that he would recover her stolen property, and he had. And that he would find Roderick.

"Is my face a dreadful mess?"

He had expected her to ask this, but not so soon. "You were very lucky," he said. "It could have been much worse."

Because she could not bear to hear any more, she pretended to lapse into unconsciousness again. As she expected, he left her and came back with a nurse.

"She spoke for a moment," he was saying. "She asked if she was blind. Then she asked if her face is in a mess."

The nurse, who knew that the sense of hearing is the last sense to go, replied briskly, for the sake of the patient, and not because of Robert at all. "She'll be fine. A little plastic surgery, and she'll be good as new. Then you can have her home."

Grania heard this, as she was meant to do, and as she had studied Red Cross nursing and first aid, she knew just why the nurse had spoken as she did. She continued to feign unconsciousness, and the medical staff knew what she was doing, and why. The reluctance to face the truth was commonplace, and it was too soon to remove the bandages anyhow. When that was done, she would know what would have to be achieved before she could be seen by other people without causing them embarrassment. She might even be pretty again.

It was Nicholas, who came several times, sometimes alone, sometimes with Marian, who decided the act had gone on long enough.

"When these bandages come off, which will be at the end of the week, you are going to see something that will surprise you so much that you won't care about having to have a wee bit of plastic surgery," he said.

Grania, forgetting that she was supposed to be unconscious, fell into the trap. "What would that be?" she asked.

"Marian is wearing a plain, gold band."

There was a chuckle from the other side of the bed, and Marian said "I'd moved into his house, and he thought the neighbours might talk, so he married me! Wonderful isn't it."

"It's so wonderful that I've proved my eyes can cry." Grania was trying to sit up, and was holding out her arms to them.

"Thank God there's been a happy ending for a Lamont at last." It was Robert's voice. Michael would have known he was in the room. Michael had years of practice. Grania hoped she would never need to practise at all. To cover up any awkward silence, Robert held Grania's hand and added, "And there will be a happy ending for you. I'll see to that, if it's the last thing I do."

"Now I know my face will be all right," Grania said. "You've never given me false hope, not in all the eight years we've been married." She thought about the baby she had never had, and hoped Robert wouldn't think about it too. Then she asked Marian when they had married, and why so secretly.

"Because we'd have felt old fools if everyone knew. But we did it properly, in church, and we'll have a party when next we go to Kilcaraig. We spent our honeymoon sitting around this hospital.

You see, of all days, we chose to get married on the Saturday you were injured!"

"Can I be unveiled with champagne on Friday," Grania asked. "Can you all be here, so that I can get plastered and not care if I'm now the Bride of Frankenstein?"

"Seems improbable," Nicholas said. "But I'll ask Doctor Thomas. We were at Edinburgh together. And don't go worrying about your face."

And so it was that the party was allowed. Doctor Thomas agreed with Nicholas that it might help the patient over the first shock of discovering that, although she would not be permanently disfigured, she had a long way to go.

The room had to be dim, because of her eyes, but she felt the bandages being gently removed, until her face felt cool and free. She kept her eyes closed, because she was afraid that when she opened them, there would be no difference. She heard the pop of a champagne cork, and the cold of a glass being placed in her hand. Her eyes flickered open. Robert was beside her, his arms round her shoulders. Nicholas and Marian, side by side, looked happy, but a little anxious. They were all looking at her.

"A mirror, please" Grania said. The nurse gave her a large hand-mirror. She held it before her face. Her hair had been clipped close to her head. The right side of her face was familiar. The left side of it looked like a jig-saw puzzle. The left side of her mouth had felt stiff. Now she knew why. She seemed to be covered in stitches.

"*Grandda*," she said. "My mother had second sight. *Grannda*." She handed back the mirror. "Whoever patched me up was very clever indeed. Please thank him. Could we have a little more light, please? I want to be sure I can really see." She smiled up at Robert. It was the right side of her face that was turned to him. Except for her cropped hair, she looked like herself. He didn't care what she looked like. His little love, he didn't care at all. He repeated what he had said several days ago.

"There will be a happy ending for you. I'll see to that, if it's the last thing I do."

There was a pop, as someone opened another bottle of champagne.

29

"Hello again! We're on the radio again!"

Grania turned up the wireless, and settled down to listen to Geraldo and his orchestra. She hoped that when the war ended he would receive an appropriate honour, for she would always associate his band with the blitz – the bombs raining down, the ambulance waiting to go out on call, and the cheerful music coming over the relay system in the air-raid shelter. Even here at Kilcaraig she needed cheering up. She still felt self-conscious about her face, and she dreaded the journey south, which she had to make at regular intervals, so that the left side of her face could be re-modelled to match the right.

Robert came into the library, followed by Chrissie with a tray of tea. She had made little cakes, but they looked very yellow, because they were made with dried egg, but they tasted all right.

"And so again, it's time for us to go again!"

"May we talk now?" Robert asked. Grania smiled her crooked smile and switched off the wireless. She liked to listen, but hated background music.

"I've been thinking," Robert said, "and wonder what you'll make of my idea."

She nodded, waiting for him to go on. He was looking tired, as if he had been doing his thinking all night as well as all day.

"You've been so well since you came back here," he said, "that I wondered if we could have other people here to recuperate. It would mean an awful upheaval, but it's an idea – if you can bear to have strangers about the place."

"It's a lovely idea," Grania said, hating the thought of it. "It's very selfish, having all this to one's self. But if it's to be a sort of convalescent home, we'll have to uproot the fitted carpets and put down something more practical." As she spoke, she could see the castle being less luxurious, more utility, more like it used to be. Having strangers here would have its compensations.

Back in London Marian and Nicholas visited her frequently in hospital. Nicholas was now doing relief work in a London practice, so that he could live at home. It was strange to think of them being married, yet stranger still that they had never thought of it before. They had always been good friends, and this was very evident now.

Grania wondered if they ever made love. She blushed at the thought. Nicholas was a bit older than Robert, and Robert was sixty, too old for making love. It must be that, because she didn't think her scarred face and thighs would put him off. He had lost interest in her in that way before the bomb fell in front of her ambulance. He had lost interest after he had heard that Roderick was reported missing.

"I'm thirty," she thought. "Now I'll just get older and duller. I'm not attractive any more." This feeling of melancholy was often with her. She couldn't even tell Michael how much she longed to be loved.

When she returned to Kilcaraig, she found that Robert's plans had been put into action. There was linoleum instead of carpets in the hall, and some of the more valuable pieces of antique furniture had changed places with some old castle junk that had been in the attics. The castle was becoming familiar again. It was home.

Robert was delighted with her obvious appreciation of what he had ordered to be done, but more still, he was delighted with her appearance. Even her smile was almost normal now. It had never struck him that she would think he had stopped loving her because her appearance had been so badly damaged. He had never made love to her since he had read the postscript of Mrs. MacPhail's letter, and his worst fears had been confirmed. That faint of Grania's had been nature's defence against unbearable shock. A few moments release, total oblivion, then the awakening to a new situation that had to be faced.

Roderick was the man she loved and wanted more than any other man. Knowing that, even her husband could only, in her eyes, be a substitute, an understudy. Robert had long suspected this was so, but he comforted himself, and saved his self-respect by giving her the benefit of the doubt. Grania, in his arms, was his wife. So long as he believed her relationship with Roderick Lamont was nothing more than the physical attraction of two people of similar age and background, he had been reasonably content. Now, with that fatal postscript, the situation had changed. Grania must, in her heart, dread his advances, and regard him as an intruder. Day and night he was tormented by the thoughts which assailed him. It was not the war that was wearing him out, it was the grief he felt for Grania.

She had been home for about a week, and he was, as usual, tucking her up in bed when she surprised him with a question.

"Does Roderick not write to us any more?"

"Not for a long time, no." When Roderick's letters had come, he had always given them to Grania, who showed them to Marian, and then returned them to him, as if to imply that they were of no special value to her.

"We still send parcels?"

"Of course."

They both thought about this, and Robert said "I haven't made any enquiries about them." He hesitated, not sure whether it was wise to go on, to put ideas into her head, ideas that would at this stage of the war, worry her. Then he went on. "It is almost regarded as a matter of honour for P.O.W.s to try to escape. That's why I don't want to ask questions."

She sat up straight, wide-eyed, frightened. Because she had lost colour, her scars showed. There was no make-up on to conceal them when she was in bed.

"What will they do if he escapes and gets caught?"

"Put him back. Geneva convention and all that."

"They don't obey rules."

His hand caressed the left side of her face, her scars. "I think they mostly do." He felt like a traitor saying it, because for Grania there was only black, no white or grey, about the enemy. "Anyhow, they know they're beaten. They'll want our prisoners to come out saying nice things about them."

Grania pondered this. "I never thought about his trying to escape."

Robert said, "I never thought about him not trying to do so. Perhaps I understood him better than you do, after all."

"After all what?" He had caught her off-guard.

"After all you have been to one another." He stood up, hoping she would say something, hoping for a denial. Grania was thinking that he would never believe her, would never understand how, in what seemed a lifetime ago, she and Roderick had guarded against physical contact.

She settled down under the bedclothes, and Robert kissed her cheek. "Goodnight," he said.

"Goodnight."

He left her, knowing that as soon as he was out of the room, she would be reading the sonnets in the shabby book she kept on her bedside table. He knew most of them by heart. He had always loved Shakespeare, although there were many of the sonnets he didn't think were good at all. He would like to ask Grania what she thought, but it wasn't the sort of thing she would expect him to ask, and she wouldn't know what to say. With just two doors and a bathroom between them, they each returned into their own private worlds of loneliness, amounting sometimes almost to despair.

By Christmas, there were fourteen extra men living at Kilcaraig Castle. All were now sound in wind and limb, but all had at some time been on the danger list, not only because of their wounds, but because of other horrors they had endured. Everyone guessed that they had been involved in some special sort of service, but everyone also knew that there were questions that could not be asked.

It had been easy to adapt the castle to accommodate what were to be known as Grania's soldiers, but it had taken Robert's skill and persuasion to win official approval for his establishment. Very soon it proved to be such a success that it was decided to build a Nissen hut in the field where Nicholas and Catriona had walked beside the barley.

Catriona had nibbled at an ear of barley here and there, and Nicholas had started the rumour that would shield her from gossip when her baby was born. Now men with spades were preparing the foundation for the hut, and telephone wires, not the breeze, carried the news that Grania, who hated change, had taken leave of her senses and was ruining the look of Kilcaraig.

"People are more important than places," Grania retorted, when Marian telephoned her from London.

"But the war's nearly over!"

"The aftermath hasn't even begun."

Robert heard the remarks as he went to the library and found Grania flouncing away from the telephone. He could see that her argument with Marian had been vehement. He watched, amazed, as she lit a cigarette, a Lucky Strike. Grania's soldiers were providers of many normally unobtainable luxuries.

"Marian's old-fashioned," Grania said. "She doesn't realize huts can be taken away as easily as they are built. We won't have a Nissen hut for ever. Some day we'll have barley again."

"They don't seem to grow it any more." He lowered himself into the big armchair and held out his arms to her. She hesitated, then went to him and knelt in front of him. Being here with him, in front of the fire, gave her a feeling of peace. Marian would be telling Nicholas, wrathfully, about the hut. She wondered if Nicholas would convey this peaceful feeling too.

"Grania, will you tell me something truly, from your heart?"

The sensation of peace left her, as if it had been switched off like a light. She fidgeted, and smoke got in her eyes. She tossed the cigarette into the fire.

"Is it about Roderick?" she asked.

"No, as a matter of fact, it is not." His tone was bitter. Her cheeks flamed, that she had spoken so thoughtlessly. She could feel her heart thumping. There was a time when a situation like this had always led to one remedy, with Robert half-punishing her, half-rewarding her for whatever she had done or said.

"What do you want to ask?" She tried, and failed to conceal the fear in her voice.

"You've answered me without me having to ask you." He didn't sound angry. He sounded hopeless and hurt, so it must have been something about Roderick, even if not directly so. She thought how the months had gone by, with no letter from him, no news of him. She had dreamed that one day she would see him coming up the drive, safe, free. Then she had reminded herself that he wouldn't come to her at Kilcaraig anyway, he would look for her in London, at Lowndes Square. He knew nothing of her injuries, for the letters Robert wrote had been carefully worded. A man in captivity is a man with a fertile mind. He had to be spared anxiety.

Robert still had his arm round her. He was deep in thought. She felt uncomfortable, but she didn't want to move, to make him think she was rejecting him, rebuffing him again. At last he said, "I think I should go back to London. I've been up here too long."

"I'll come with you. I would like to."

The suggestion obviously pleased him. "Only for a month or so," he said. "We'll give a party on your birthday. Marian and Nicholas will be able to come to it."

"I'll be thirty-one." Ten years ago, Roderick had kissed her. Ten whole years ago.

"You'll have owned Kilcaraig for ten years," Robert said, his thoughts on the same lines as her own. "Sometimes I think it was the most foolish present I could ever give you."

"Oh Robert, why?" She was hurt now. She had never abused her ownership of Kilcaraig.

"Because people are more important than things," he said. "Remember? You've just been talking to Marian."

He took her chin in his hand, and tilted her face up to his. He kissed her on the mouth, then fumbled with her pullover. "Not here!" she gasped, but he didn't seem to care.

It was all over when Chrissie came in with the tea, but her sharp eyes noted that the cushions were tossed off the huge sofa, and that Grania's eyes were shining. Robert, standing with his back to her, was looking at the portrait of Kilcaraig. Chrissie took it all in and repeated it to Angus.

"They're together again," was all she said.

"Aye," he said. "I know. I chust nearly went in with the peats."

30

Although she was not to know it at the time, Grania had entered into what was to be the happiest time of her life with Robert.

When they arrived at Lowndes Square, the change in the face of London was almost palpable. No more worrying about a chink in the black-out curtains, nor more fear of that chilling alert from the air-raid sirens, no more startling horror of awareness when a rocket dropped within earshot. No more fear.

She found that she could talk to Robert, ask his advice, listen to him. She was becoming his companion, and sometimes he made love to her, but gently and kindly, as in the early days of their marriage. That wild moment in the library at Kilcaraig had established her physical need of him, not as a substitute for the man she loved, or because he had bought her, but because she was fond of him. He was content with that.

Diana's husband, who had survived the Battle of Britain as a fighter pilot, was now a flying instructor in Canada, and Charles Maitland was now in command of a mine sweeper, but his letters to Helen were no longer about the war, they were about the life awaiting them when he was demobilized. The bombed cities of Britain would be needing architects, and there would be plenty of work for him to do.

Evelyn, seeing the end of her work with the W.V.S. in sight was attending bridge classes as a preparation for adjusting to a world at peace. Grania visited her from time to time, out of a sense of duty. She and the family had drifted almost totally apart.

Robert was out for most of the day, and war work continued for their friends, so that Grania spent a lot of her time alone.

One afternoon she was sitting in Kensington Gardens, working at the sampler she had started to embroider before the war. Overhead, the transport planes were flying home the prisoners of war, who were being re-united with their families, some of them after nearly six years in captivity. Adrian Ferguson had been one of these. He had presented himself at Lowndes Square nearly a week ago, surprising

Grania, who had heard that he had been reported missing, believed killed at Anzio.

"How did you get away?" she asked, when her exclamations of incredulity and joy were over.

"There was nothing to it," he said. "The guards just left and we walked out."

"And what of those who escaped and joined the resistance?"

"Caught between various crossfires, the poor things. Not all of them of course. Depends where they were."

Then Robert joined them and she could ask no more questions.

Now she was grudging Adrian his health and his strength and his freedom in her anxiety over Roderick. She folded her embroidery into its bag and left the park, making a slight detour in order to pass the Albert Memorial. She had not forgotten that part of it was built of Tormore granite.

When she reached home there was still an "Out of Order" notice tied to the lift door. Climbing the stairs was only an irritation for her, but for Robert it was an ordeal, and he would arrive on the third floor breathless and puce in the face. She had only time to put away her embroidery and tidy her hair when she heard his key in the door.

"You're early," she said, taking his brief-case from him. He nodded, unable to speak for a moment; then we went into the sitting-room and sank onto the sofa. She poured out some brandy for him and left him to drink it while she changed her dress. When she went back to him, he was standing by the window, overlooking the square.

"If you're going to light the victory bonfire at Kilcaraig, we should be preparing to go up there in a day or two," he said, his voice normal, the breathlessness gone.

"As soon as that?" She sat beside him, with her arm across his shoulder. "Is this premonition or fact?"

"A bit of both." He picked up her free hand, her left hand, and instinctively rubbed his fingers on her wedding ring. "I have news of Roderick."

"Yes?" She wet her lips, but he could not see her face.

"He made his way through Europe by speaking Gaelic, which of course no one could understand. They'd think it a dialect of some sort, with so many migrant workers around. Then he attached himself to the Maquis and is known to be alive and well. But he won't be coming back yet. He won't walk into this flat the way Adrian Ferguson did."

"So hostilities are over, but not for him." She had to say something. She had to sound cool and calm, and not particularly interested.

"When you see him again he'll be changed, Grania. He's not a gilly doo kare doo any more."

She smiled at his attempt to pronounce Gaelic. She didn't notice his use of the present tense. She stood up. "Thank you for telling me." She touched her cheek, the scar still livid under the make-up. "None of us are quite what we were six years ago. Now I'm going to get supper. We'll have it here on a tray, and then we'll go to bed."

He knew wnat she meant. Sometimes they slept together in her bed, but always for companionship, never for making love. She wanted to be sure that there would be no love-making tonight.

Later, when she was asleep, he propped up on his elbow. Seeing her there in the moonlight he thought of the Shakespeare sonnets in that book beside her bed, and of the stricken look on her face whenever Roderick's name was mentioned.

> "Let me not to the marriage of true minds
> Admit impediments ... ."

True minds. Impediments.

He lay awake for a long time, thinking about her, making up his mind what he should do. At last he fell asleep.

Two days later they left for Mull, and Grania's soldiers, who were already dwindling in numbers, formed a guard of honour to welcome them as they rattled up to the castle in their rusty little car.

Marian telephoned on VE Day to report that she and Nicholas had been doing all the right things. They had been to Parliament Square, where they had heard Churchill's declaration of peace being broadcast, and they were just off to join the crowds outside Buckingham Palace, to show loyalty to their monarch. She admitted that the celebrations had fallen rather flat when compared with the spontaneous joy and sudden excitement of Armistice Day in 1918. The pain of bereavement which she must have felt at the loss of her fiancé had been forgotten, and Grania took heart in the knowledge that even the most bitter of grief came to an end at last.

Michael seldom came to the castle now because his mother was frail and needed to have him beside her. His sister Nancy, like Diana and Helen, had virtually severed her connection with Mull, but Robert, who had for so long been embarrassed by Michael's blindness, now sought his company quite often, walking slowly through the pine trees and up the brae to Caraig Lodge. Grania never knew what they talked about, but she was thankful that Robert had someone in whom he could confide.

In August the bonfire blazed again, celebrating victory over

Japan, and the final end of the war. Tea and dumpling were consumed halfway up Ben Caraig, and when the fire died down there was dancing in the village hall. Grania's soldiers, who represented several different nationalities, added to the fun, and there was American square-dancing as well as the hokey-cokey and other innovations which the war had brought about.

"You'll not be dancing the foursome tonight, Sir Robert?" Mrs. MacPhail asked, as she poured tea into his cup during the interval.

"My dancing days are over," he smiled, his eyes upon Grania, who was surrounded by soldiers. He sipped his tea and longed for bed, but a sing-song was starting, and he felt obliged to stay for a while, even to mouth words and try to join in.

> "We'll meet again,
> Don't know where, don't know when,
> But I know we'll meet again some sunny day . . ."

The grandfather clock in the hall was striking two when Grania and he arrived home. Grania told him to sleep on in the morning, but he said he would prefer to get up as he had always done.

She tapped on his door on her way downstairs for breakfast. He called to her that he would join her presently, but when she had finished her first cup of coffee he had still not appeared.

Concealing her anxiety from Chrissie, she went upstairs. Robert was half dressed, slumped on the bed, breathing stertorously. She thought, "Don't panic", hurried downstairs and asked Chrissie to telephone for Doctor MacColl, as Sir Robert was not well. She returned to the bedroom and knelt by the bed. She was still kneeling there half an hour later when Doctor MacColl arrived, bringing with him the District Nurse. Chrissie had not been deceived by Grania's calm instructions, and the doctor had known what to expect.

Robert lived for three days, but never regained consciousness.

Marian and Nicholas had come to Mull immediately, and Evelyn arrived in time for the funeral. Mr. Goddard, Robert's lawyer, came to attend to legal matters, and on the evening of the funeral the members of the family gathered in the library while he read the will. Grania, pale but dry-eyed sat bolt upright in her grandfather's chair. She had, as Marian had done before her, followed the coffin to the grave that afternoon. She still could not believe that Robert was dead.

"This last will and testament was not drawn up by me," Mr. Goddard was saying to them. "It is dated May the third of this year, and it is written in his own handwriting. It does not, under Scottish law, need to be witnessed."

He then read the document spread out before him. Much of it must have been copied by Robert from his previous will, because of the formal way in which it was worded. He had been both thoughtful and generous. Nobody was forgotten, and amounts left to the charities he had supported were lavish. He had even remembered to make a permanent arrangement for the upkeep of the village hall. Marian was to receive the residue of his estate. She didn't quite know what that meant, but it sounded wrong. Then she remembered Death Duties and decided that the residue would not amount to a great deal.

Grania listened, but not attentively. She could not think of the amount of money involved. Acquisity. Then she became aware that out of all these names, her own had not been mentioned.

Mr. Goddard cleared his throat and read the last paragraph.

"I have already given to my wife, Grania Lamont, the castle and lands of Kilcaraig, and a sum of money which will ensure that she will never be in want. She will understand the reason why I have not allotted to her any additional impediments. She has a legal right to contest this will." Robert had signed his name, and had written the date.

Grania rose from the huge armchair, bowed to Mr. Goddard, and addressed the others. "I expect you will want to talk together. If you will excuse me, I will leave you as the matter no longer concerns me. Please understand that I would never, never contest Robert's will."

She left the room, her head held high, the personification of dignity and breeding. Grania Lamont of Kilcaraig.

When she had closed the door behind her, there was a long, sickening silence in the room.

31

Within twenty-four hours, from Tobermory to Iona Ferry, and even in the far corners of the island, Calgary, Tavool, and Croggan, the people of Mull were gathering in groups to discuss the startling news that Sir Robert Dutton had disinherited his wife. They were profoundly shocked. Grania was a popular person, and what was more important, she was a Lamont of Kilcaraig. She belonged to the island. Disbelief mingled with anger as individual ideas about the cause and effect of the outrage were tossed into the cauldron of conversations.

The people of Kilcaraig set about their daily work silent, embarrassed, betrayed. The piles of flowers on Sir Robert's grave seemed to mock them. The castle on the hill looked cold and sinister, instead of the symbol of protection it used to be. Nobody had emerged since the lawyer left early in the morning to catch the boat to Oban. Nobody knew how the contents of the will had leaked out, or how the rumours had spread so quickly. Some people on the estate hid even from themselves the fear that they now felt for their future, fear of what would happen to them when someone new took over at Kilcaraig.

The people most immediately concerned, Grania, Marian, Nicholas and Evelyn had no idea that anyone but themselves knew the terms of the will. Mr. Goddard had left after a very early breakfast, and was driven to Craignure by Angus. Grania had not appeared until nearly lunch-time, when she summoned them to the library. She came straight to the point.

"One of you has suggested that you pool part of what you have been given, and share it out with me. Please don't think I'm ungrateful, but it's out of the question. It would be, even if Robert had left me penniless. In fact, he made Kilcaraig over to me when I was twenty-one, and later gave me an investment worth over forty thousand pounds. I won't starve. And I want you to know that whatever happens I will keep Kilcaraig, the castle, the land, and the people."

"You can't do that on the interest of even forty thousand pounds." This was Evelyn. The others looked at her as if her interruption were indecent. Grania, sorry for her, smiled, a little crooked smile that struck each one of them like an arrow in the heart.

"My grandfather never had money like that," she said. She avoided adding, "Neither did your husband", because Evelyn had sold Kilcaraig the minute Ian had died. "I've talked to Chrissie and Angus and Willie," Grania went on. "They will all stay with me. Robert, as you know, has given them what they so rightly deserve. I think really he has thought of everything, and of everyone."

For one moment, the tearful Grania nearly broke through this calm, self-assured woman whose presence dominated the room. She controlled herself and finished. "I'll go to the post office this afternoon. The people will be gathered there waiting for the mail. I want them to know from me what has happened. I don't want rumours raging round Mull like a heather fire in dry, windy weather." Again she tried to smile. "It's maybe in the breeze already – a breeze that'll be a hurricane by the time it gets to Iona!"

Chrissie came in with a tray of drinks. Chrissie, who one forgot because she was so much a part of Kilcaraig. She signed to Grania that she wanted to speak to her. Grania went over to her, moving the glasses on the tray around, to give herself a reason for being there.

"Johnnie came up from the village," Chrissie said in an undertone. "They're saying you don't own Kilcaraig any more. It will be all over Mull."

"How?" What a silly question. As if anyone could know how rumours began. Grania turned to face the others. "Help yourselves to drinks. I'm going down to the village now. I can't even wait until the afternoon. The breeze has beaten me to it."

She refused offers to accompany her. She chose to walk. They saw her, wearing her suede coat, her Wellington boots, and the green headscarf Marian had given her for her birthday, cutting through the woods to the road. She was over the humpy bridge before anyone spoke.

"Her grandfather would be proud of her," Marian said.

"Where's Roderick Lamont?" Evelyn asked. "I take it he's the villain of the piece. He must have been Grania's lover."

Nicholas could have hit her. How, he wondered, had Grania survived being brought up by this conscientious, but utterly unimaginative and relentless woman.

"Grania hasn't set eyes on him for years," he said. "If they had been lovers, it would have been before the war. Robert took a long time before he changed his will!"

"He gave her Kilcaraig when she was twenty-one," Evelyn persisted. "We don't know when he added the forty thousand. Some years ago, I think." She could remember noticing a time when Grania had seemed to be more independent, more free with Robert's money. "What he had already given her, he couldn't take back, no matter what he later discovered about her."

Nicholas said nothing more. Unlike Marian, he knew what the residue of a will meant. Grania had been deprived of a fortune.

While they were talking about her, Grania had reached the village. Everyone seemed to have gathered in the post office. They made way for her to reach the counter, and old Lachlan MacLachlan wheezed at her, "It's chust a shame, Miss Grania. We're talking about it, and it's chust a shame."

Grania put her arms round his grimy neck, and kissed his bristly cheek. "You've said exactly what I needed," she told him. "Because

I didn't know how to tell you all. I've owned Kilcaraig since I was twenty-one and please try to get the true story wafted through Mull. My husband gave me all I need to keep it going, so please, no more worries for anyone." She addressed the postmistress. "Say what I've said to everyone who comes in here. And tell them they must not be accusing my husband of treating me badly. He has been very kind to me indeed. I understand his will. I was married to him, and I understand."

It was only then that her composure crumbled. Mrs. MacPhail was nearest to her and took her in her arms while she wept. Everyone else murmured words of sympathy, unembarrassed, because they had known her all her life, and would continue to know her now, because she would never part with Kilcaraig. Tucked away in the minds of most of them was the hope that Roderick Lamont would some day come back into her life. Not yet. Not until it was decent for him to do so, but back he must come, because they all needed him now as much as she did.

Grania telephoned from Caraig Lodge to tell Chrissie not to wait for her, as she was having a bowl of soup, and cheese and biscuits with the Ameses. She had wanted to tell Michael and his mother all that had taken place.

Michael walked with her as far as the gate of the castle. He asked her, "You say you understand Robert's will, do you really understand, Grania?"

"He said so in the will," she replied. "So I must say I do."

"But do you really?"

"I think some day I shall. I don't think he would spite me from the grave. I think there was a reason for writing that paragraph the way he did."

They had reached the gate. "Go on thinking about it," Michael said. "Because when you told me about it during lunch, I thought at once I could explain it all. But Robert would rather you understood him yourself. He loved you very much."

As Grania went on up to the castle, she could hear Michael tapping his way along the ground, back to his home.

During the months that followed, no one guessed how difficult it was for Grania to keep up appearances. She knew that however false the original rumour had proved to be there were some people who believed that she had been tarred and feathered and were waiting to see how soon her lover would install himself in the castle.

Robert's death had been widely reported in the press, and Grania dealt personally with every letter of condolence that was delivered to the castle. It was on Christmas Eve that she received a letter from

Roderick. It was kind, but formal, and had been written in Cape Town.

"I have been repatriated at last," he concluded. "I'll let you know if ever I return to Mull."

She sighed, and tucked the letter into her handbag. Her acknowledgement might well prove to be her last contact with him.

That first Christmas of peace was strangely subdued. Grania did not attend such festivities as there were in the village hall, but the MacPhails, whose youngest son had been killed on the Normandy beaches, brought in the New Year with her at the castle. They needed one another's support.

Grania spent Easter in London with Marian and Nicholas, and she attended Adrian Ferguson's wedding. He married Alison at last, Alison with whom he had philandered years ago, and who had remained faithful to him during the years of his captivity.

When Grania made her return journey to Mull, she ate mince and mashed potatoes and cabbage in the dining saloon of the *Lochinvar*, and heard from the steward that Roderick Lamont was back at Tormore. She managed to eat the mince, and then the cold rice pudding which followed. Duncan MacPhail met her with the car at Craignure, and as he drove her home, he said nothing about Roderick Lamont. Clearly he considered that the subject was taboo.

At first she hoped daily that Roderick, having heard she was back at home, which he was bound to do, would telephone, but nothing happened. She built up a resistance to him, determined to avoid him, afraid to go to Oban for the day in case she met him on the boat.

She was kept fully occupied in and around the castle, and as Michael Ames said nothing more about the will, she almost stopped thinking about it. Robert had wanted to convey something to her, of that she was sure, but she had not understood what that something could be.

Angus climbed about the roof, carefully patching up the slates, but the rain came in all the same, right down to the dining-room. A copper pot was placed near the window to catch the drips, and Chrissie put a picture in front of the damp patch by the library door.

"What we need is another pair of hands in this place," she said to Grania. "There's altogether too much to do."

Marian and Nicholas had made the same observation when they stayed at the castle during August. Grania knew what they were hinting at, but it was no good. If Roderick wanted her, he would come and tell her so, no matter what anyone thought about it.

217

It was a September afternoon, pouring with rain. Grania was sitting disconsolately in the drawing-room, where the fire was lighted today in an attempt to combat the damp. She had been embroidering a sampler to match the one she had started before the war and had meant to exhibit in the Mull and Morvern Show. She folded it away, and wandered over to the piano. It had not been tuned this year. She winced when she struck a chord, but she saw the sheet of music, so sat down and fumbled through the accompaniment, then in a small voice she sang –

> "*My bonnie dubh ciar-dubh!*
> Let sharp tongues assail thee,
> One heart will not fail thee
> That knows to be true.
> *Dubh ciar-dubh! dubh ciar-dubh!*
> Though poor, poor thou be,
> No rich man can please me,
> Like thee, love, like thee."

A tear dropped onto the damp piano. She shut the lid, so that the strings jangled, as they had done years ago, after her grandfather's funeral. It was more than the strings that jangled. She felt as if something had tugged at her memory, stirring it up, bringing to mind what she had long forgotten.

"*There will be a happy ending for you. I'll see to that, if it's the last thing I do.*"

Robert was not referring to her face, and her scars. He was talking about Roderick. And it was the last thing he did do.

Trembling, she ran upstairs, remembering something she had often noticed, but had not taken to heart. She leafed through the book of Shakespeare's sonnets, until she came to number one hundred and sixteen.

"Let me not to the marriage of true minds
Admit *impediments*."

The word had been very faintly underlined and signed R.D.

Without further thought, she ran downstairs to the cloakroom, flung on her mackintosh, and called to Chrissie that she was going out, and not to worry when she came back. Then she fled to the garage, and was in the car and down the drive before Chrissie could stop her. She drove faster than she had ever driven before, rattling three times over the cattle grids where once there had been gates. She had to slow down to negotiate the sharp left-hand turn into the Glen road, then she was off again at speed, the rushes in the middle of the road scraping the bottom of the car.

The rain was lashing down so fast that the windscreen wipers could not prevent her vision from being blurred, but by the time she reached the top of Loch Scridain, and was on the Iona road, she could see it was clearing in the west. There would be a sunset tonight in Tormore Bay, on the right-hand side on the way to Iona.

When she reached the horse-shoe shaped village of Bunessan, she nearly turned back. She was pinning her hopes on such flimsy evidence. If she completed her journey, she could be facing a rebuff that would be recounted through the island in a matter of days. She had to risk it, she had to go on.

The village at Iona ferry looked deserted, but she knew there would be interested, probably sympathetic, eyes watching as she parked her car, and made her way down the slope, past the little burial ground, then up the back of Tormore, up to the granite quarries. She had forgotten to change her shoes, and although her heels were not very high, she kept stumbling.

She was panting when she reached the top of the quarries, and she stood among the huge piles of granite, looking down to where she could see Roderick's cottage, with its view of the pier and Tormore Bay. She felt her knees had deserted her as she made her way down the steep slope, avoiding tripping over the disused railway lines. She had thought she might hear the sound of bagpipes when she was at the top of the hill, but when she listened, there was no sound at all. But now she heard them. He was tuning up. He was at home.

She reached his door and knocked hard, in case he would start playing and not hear her at all. She knew she was dishevelled. Her hair was soaking wet, her make-up was washed off, and her ridiculous shoes were squelching with wet. She was about to knock again when he opened the door. He held out his arms to her. He said, "At last. I thought you were never going to come."

She was enfolded by him. He pushed the door shut with his foot, then helped her out of her wet mackintosh, and hung it near the fire to dry. Immediately she was back in his arms.

"Why didn't you come to me?" she asked.

"I promised Robert that I'd leave you to make the first move. He was fatalistic about dying. He said none of his family had lived much longer than sixty, and that if you wanted something badly enough you would do anything to get it. But I told him that you'd never get me if you were worth acquisity, because my pride is stronger than my love. So he said he'd fix that for me, and he did."

"When did all this happen?"

"In London. I ran into him quite by accident. He hauled me off to his club, and because he was obviously reliable I told him a little of what I was doing. Not much. Official secrets act and all that. But it convinced him that I'd be a suitable person to take care of you."

"So he left us to each other," she said.

"That's right." He was stroking her hair. "And I'll have you know that I'm not a pauper. I'll help you with Kilcaraig."

"Let's not talk about money. It's nuisancy stuff to own."

"If you talk baby-talk, I won't marry you!"

"I'm going to talk baby-talk because I want an heir!"

He burst out laughing and hugged her to him. "Grania, you're incorrigible. I believe it's not me you want at all. You just want to ensure the continuity of the Lamonts at Kilcaraig."

"And isn't that really what love is all about?" she asked.

That evening, the sunset was like a flame, lighting the sea, the hills, the granite. Inside the cottage overlooking Tormore Bay, two people had fulfilled their heart's desire.

Part Two
1968–1975

THE SILVER LINK

True love's the gift which God has given
To man alone beneath the heaven;
It is not fantasy's hot fire
Whose wishes soon as granted fly;
It liveth not in fierce desire,
With dead desire it does not die;
It is the secret sympathy
The silver link, the silken tie,
Which heart to heart and mind to mind
In body and in soul can bind

> from *The Lay of the Last Minstrel*
> by Sir Walter Scott

32

"There's only one place fit for Rorie to live in, and that's a bull-pen."

Grania Lamont was sitting at the dressing table of her hotel bedroom in London, combing out her tangled, silky curls, and she was referring to her second son, younger than his brother by a merciful half-hour, and already a problem because of his feckless nature and irresistible charm.

The twins were twenty years old. Niall, the elder, was tall, handsome, intelligent, and industrious. He showed a wide and discerning appreciation of the arts, coupled with an ability to excel in any activity country life required of him. He was fulfilment of his parents' dreams of the heir who would one day inherit Kilcaraig, its castle, its land and its people.

Roderick, who knew every inflection of Grania's voice, recognized that she was trying to conceal her very real anxiety under her flippant remark. He was shaving in the bathroom, but could see her reflection in the mirror. Her loveliness had not diminished with the passing years, nor had his love for her. There could never be two people with a love story like their own, but he wanted at least a second-best one for his three children.

"I was a terrible wolf myself before I met you," he said. "Rorie takes after me. He'll settle down."

"We shouldn't have arranged for him to go to the Sorbonne. It was asking for trouble."

"My darling, we did it because you were afraid of becoming a possessive mama. Remember?" As he came out of the bathroom, he saw her take a tiny jewel case out of her handbag. She fingered her pearls, then chose a diamond brooch, which she pinned onto her grey chiffon dress.

In the early days of their marriage, he had simmered with secret jealousy over the jewellery which Robert Dutton had lavished upon her, but gradually her first husband had faded from his memory, and he hoped also from hers. Running Kilcaraig for her, and keeping a watchful, if ignorant, eye on the Dutton fortunes, upon which the future of the estate depended, had kept him fully occupied, and his book about the French Resistance had been an unexpected success. It was written under a pseudonym, so caused him minimal embarrassment, but gave him financial independence, an important factor in maintaining his self-respect.

He stood behind her, admiring her in the mirror. She leaned back against him.

"Please read the letter again," she said.

It had been forwarded by dear old Chrissie, who ruled Kilcaraig in their absence, and who would have wanted to make sure that Rorie's letter would reach his parents as quickly as possible. It would not have occurred to her that its contents could threaten their enjoyment of their evening at the opera, planned long ago, as soon as they had heard that Isabella Connelli was to sing at Covent Garden. They had heard her in *Lucia di Lammermoor* in Milan, and in *The Pearl Fishers* in Paris. Her *Traviata* should be an exhilarating experience. Now, suddenly, they were confronted with her in a new and disturbing dimension.

"Darlings," Rorie had written. "I've just come back to Paris to collect my possessions and bid farewell to the Sorbonne. I've been in Rome for a week, and I did all the right things, like kissing St. Peter's toe, and a lot of the wrong things, most of which I won't tell you about, but one I just can't keep to myself. I've collected Isabella Connelli! I met her at the de Stefani party, the one they always lay on to demonstrate to clod-hoppers like myself that Italy has all that's needed to please the senses – and they have a point! Anyway, there was La Connelli, looking like something out of this world. How limited my vocabulary is – there's Eton for you! I approached her with trembling knees, thinking of all the skilled seducers who have failed to get as far as kissing the hem of her dress. I was wishing I'd worn my kilt – the exhibitionist in me screams out for notice – so when I got within earshot, I addressed her in Gaelic. It worked like a charm. She almost dropped her glass of champagne, and I held her attention, and the attention of the whole room, while we talked in Gaelic, although she would call it Irish, of the sweet mystery of life that brought me from Mull and her from Skibareen – don't know how to spell it – together in the heart of Rome. Two days later – never mind what happened during those two days – I got to know her rather well. That can mean anything, as you know! We flew together to Paris. She went on to London, and you'll be seeing her on Friday, when she takes London by storm, as she undoubtedly will.

"I'm showing remarkable restraint by not coming to London immediately, but Niall is with me now, and we've been to the Louvre and Notre Dame, and I'm showing him some of the more delectable eating places I've discovered, which will help him through his stint at the Sorbonne.

"Alas he can offer me no such consolations when I take his place in Cirencester. I view the two years ahead of me there with dread. What can I learn from an Agricultural College that I couldn't learn better at Kilcaraig? Niall says I will, but then he always sees the bright side of things.

"I'll spend a few days in London before I come home. I must see Aunt Marian and various other friends, and maybe I'll be able to be with Her again.

"I do hope she enchants you as much as she does me. I'll be seeing you soon. Have a good holiday. Your loving black sheep – Rorie"

Roderick returned the letter to its envelope, and replaced it in his wallet.

"The young of today have no scruples. To seduce a woman is improper. To boast of it is indefensible. I'm ashamed of him," he said.

"She's at least ten years older than him," Grania retorted. "He's an incident in her glittering life, while she could be important to him. He's been a fan of hers for years. She had no right to do this to him. He could get dreadfully hurt."

"Which might be salutory." Roderick knew that Grania would defend Rorie. If anyone was hurt, it would be her. He handed her mink stole to her.

"You'll give him a good lecture when he comes home," she said. "He'll listen to you."

When they walked through the lounge, they were unaware of the admiring glances which followed them. In their early fifties, they were still an eye-catching couple, and to some people vaguely familiar, because there were times when their photographs appeared in the glossy magazines to be thumbed through in doctors' and dentists' waiting-rooms.

While they waited for their car, Roderick bought an evening paper. On the front page was a picture of the crowds who had slept in Floral Street in order to hear Connelli sing.

"I don't think a lecture is going to reform Rorie," he said. "If what we think is true, he's won the jack-pot."

Grania took the paper from him and tossed it into a nearby litter bin.

*   *   *

While her parents were preparing to go to Covent Garden, their daughter Catriona, who was in boarding-school at Cambray College in the Cotswolds, struggled with an algebra problem and thought about them.

Catriona was fifteen. She had short, dark, silky curls, slate-grey eyes, and a beautiful little figure. She was an exact replica of her mother, just as Rorie was an exact replica of his father. Niall alone was different, although he bore a strong family resemblance to both of his parents. He was special. Catriona adored him. She would hate forever the woman who would ultimately marry him, and deprive the family of his company, and eventually of Kilcaraig Castle.

Even now, Catriona was experiencing the conflicts which arise when people love one another, and property is inherited, and some-time, sooner or later, the familiar way of life would have to undergo a change.

*   *   *

Adrian Ferguson, Q.C., arrived home late from the Central Criminal Court. He had particularly wanted to be in good time tonight because he was taking his family to *La Traviata*, but Sir George Watson had wanted to discuss the Bolton affair with him, and he depended too much on George to be able to tell him that another time would do. Talking to Sir George had been a bit of an anti-climax, because the Old Bailey grapevine would not yet have conveyed to him how well Adrian had conducted his case. Juries were hard to convince these days, but he had held this one in the palm of his hand, and Jinx Lewis had gone down for the long stretch he so richly deserved.

His wife, Alison, wearing a house-coat, was waiting for him in the drawing-room of their house in Victoria Road, Kensington. She gave him a perfunctory kiss on the cheek and told him she had a stiff neck, and was threatened with a cold. For years she had alibied on ailments when she didn't want to do something.

"There'll still be four of you," she said. "Stewart's turned up unexpectedly this afternoon. I don't think he does any work at the Sorbonne, thanks to the influence of Rorie Lamont. But at least he's not protesting about accompanying his sisters tonight."

Stewart was twenty-one. His sister Pauline was sixteen, and Mary was fourteen. The girls had never been to an opera before.

Alison followed Adrian upstairs, and talked to him while he changed. He recounted what had happened at the Old Bailey, and she gave him her dutiful attention while she manicured her nails.

When he was ready, he found his daughters and Stewart waiting for him in the hall. The girls were giggling and excited, preening themselves in their party dresses, and he noted with relief that Stewart had shaved off his beard and was wearing conventional clothes, in place of the lurid shirts and jeans he had favoured for months.

"We'll be kept out for the first act if we don't arrive in time," Adrian told them as he helped them into the car.

Alison waved to them from the drawing-room window; then she settled down to do her crossword puzzle and enjoy a bit of peace.

*   *   *

Josanne Murray lived with her parents in a large flat in an old fashioned block off the Kensington High Street. Every day she caught a 52 bus which bore her to Victoria. Her office was in the Vauxhall Bridge Road, where her boss dictated letters to her about pensions. She was a very small cog in a very large industrial machine, and she was reminded of the importance of her work every year at the annual meeting of office staff which preceded the Christmas party. Josanne was unconvinced of her importance, but she did enjoy the party, held always in one of the most luxurious hotels in London. It was the one occasion in the year when reality equalled, sometimes even surpassed, her day-dreams.

Her father was William Murray, a chartered accountant whose air of preoccupation seemed to show that his mind was never far from the problems his clients presented to him. He was a very good accountant and was well rewarded for the unstinting service and advice he offered, but he was a prudent man and his daughter gained little help through his affluence, apart from a very comfortable home. She dreamed of being daddy's darling, over-indulged, and at times sitting on his knee, pouring out her secrets, and being given sound and always acceptable advice. William Murray was tall, slim, and meticulously dressed. His was not the sort of knee anyone would sit on, nor was his interest in his daughter sufficient to take his mind off his work for more than a few minutes. In her more practical moments, Josanne wondered how it was that he had ever married at all.

Her mother did nothing to solve the conundrum. Sybil Murray had been the Honourable Sybil Montfort, and she was a beautiful woman, but rigidly uncompromising. Josanne's inability to face the fact that there must have been a time and a place when these two people had, just for once, obeyed their natural instincts and in due course produced a child, led her to invent another fantasy. She must be adopted. She worked on this theory until enthusiasm spilt her story into the ears of a school friend, and soon it was all round the school that Josanne Murray was an adopted child, whose natural parents were so grand that their name must not be disclosed. This tale reached the ears of the headmistress. She summoned Josanne and extracted a tearful admission that the story was sheer invention, a pack of lies.

"Don't dare mention any of this to your parents," the headmistress had admonished her. "If they ever heard it, think how distressed they would be. Virtually, you have tried to disown them."

When Josanne had left the study, the headmistress picked up the dossier concerning her reports. Over-imaginative, over-sensitive, she was the only child of parents who had borne her late in life, and who openly resented the fact that she was a girl. She felt infinitely sorry for her.

Today Josanne had woken up in a state of excited anticipation. She had bought herself a ticket for the Royal Opera House at Covent Garden, and she was to hear Isabella Connelli singing *La Traviata*. She had bought all Connelli's records, and had collected her photographs and any reference to her in the papers. This was to be Connelli's first visit to London. Her beautiful voice was coupled with her beautiful appearance. She had Titian hair, green eyes and a lovely figure. She was already a legend on the continent, and the darling of the Metropolitan Opera House in New York. Her debut in London had been the talk of the season.

"Please God, don't let her get a cold," Josanne had prayed. All these months of anticipation could be in vain if a London chill caught the throat of her beloved.

Her parents believed that she was going to an extra night-class, and spending the rest of the evening with her friend, Hope Garnett. She had not dared to tell them about the opera, because they would query the price she had paid for her ticket and would never believe that she was going alone, preferring not to break the spell of the music by having to indulge in small-talk during the intervals.

She had come home from the office by taxi, to give herself time to brush her dark hair until it shone. She wore it in a long page-boy style, which suited her oval face, with its clear skin, good features, wide blue eyes, and well defined mouth. Her figure was neat and her legs shapely. Her great grief was that she had to wear spectacles for reading, which meant always at the office, and even tonight she would need them for reading the programme.

The telephone rang. She could hear her mother answering it, which gave her a chance to call out that she was off to her night-class. She let herself out of the flat.

*   *   *

In her dressing room at the Royal Opera House, Isabella Connelli was having the final touches put to her dress while she fought to control the mounting terror that always gripped her before a performance, and particularly before singing Violetta, which was a very demanding role.

That morning, during a brief rehearsal, she had been upset when Paolo Bardini had snapped at her, "Can't you do what I tell you? Are you deaf?"

Bardini always had this effect on her. He could use words that struck like a whiplash, but it was under his baton that she gave of her best, knowing that he noticed her weak moments and could cover up for her, guide her, inspire her. He was becoming necessary to her, and it was part of a carefully considered plan that he was to conduct her first appearance at Covent Garden.

For twelve years she had been preparing for tonight. To be acclaimed in London was to receive the accolade, not because the audience or the critics were more discerning, but because it was the nearest great opera house to Ireland, where she had been born.

Tonight, Rorie Lamont's parents would be in the audience. He was twenty. She was thirty. Already she was afraid of what had happened in Rome.

She sprayed her throat again, and prayed that her voice would last out until the final ecstatic gasp as Violetta experienced the freedom from pain that was death.

33

Josanne travelled by underground to Covent Garden. When she reached the Opera House, she had time to look at the stage door, not because anyone important would be going in as late as this, but it was exciting to think who had passed that way earlier.

Someone was practising a scale in a dressing-room. Connelli? No, she thought not. She made her way into the theatre and claimed her seat, which was in the front row of the balcony stalls and had cost her more than she could afford, but she could lean over and study the audience through her opera-glasses.

People used to wear magnificent clothes and jewels, she had been told. That was long ago, before the war, and now some of the people even in the boxes, were not in evening dress at all.

The flash of diamonds caught her eye, and she saw a lovely woman in grey chiffon, accompanied by the sort of man who could have been a film star twenty years ago. Other people were looking at them. They were somehow familiar to her, but now she saw Adrian Ferguson, Q.C., being ushered into a box, with what must be his family. She knew him by sight, because sometimes she went to the Old Bailey with Hope Garnett, and had seen him in action, looking and sounding like the actor his profession presumably required him to be.

Rapturous applause. Bardini had emerged, and had taken control of the orchestra and of the whole packed auditorium. Josanne sat back, enraptured. Presently, she would be seeing Violetta – Connelli herself. But very soon she was aware only of the prelude, thrilling, with its sense of heart-beat and awe.

The curtains parted to a ripple of applause, reaching a crescendo as Violetta moved into the centre of the stage, but Bardini knew how to handle the impact Connelli had upon her audience. Her voice would silence its exuberance. Violetta greeted guests as if she was really glad to see them, but for a moment it seemed as if she would break down and faint. Connelli was a cosummate actress, as well as a beautiful woman and a great singer. Even the music critics stopped thinking about the clever things they were going to write. They listened instead.

*   *   *

Grania and Roderick met Adrian Ferguson in the crush-bar during the first interval. Grania had spotted Adrian in his box as soon as she had settled in her seat in the stalls.

"Stewart's being noble and coping with his sisters while I get something to sustain me for the next act," Adrian said. He was being sustained by a double brandy.

"Where's Alison?" Roderick asked.

"She has a stiff neck and thinks she's starting a cold." Adrian sipped his brandy, his mind far away from Alison. "Don't you think there's something melancholy about a performance like the one we've just seen? It's so sublime yet so ephemeral. I'd like to wrap her up in cellophane and take her home."

"I think Rorie took her home, but not in cellophane," Grania said. "I'm very worried."

"I'm very envious!" Roderick said, but he added, on a serious note, "I think he's blowing up a brief encounter into a dazzling and improbable romance. Have a word with him if you can. You're his godfather. You may be able to influence him in private before you have to defend him in court!"

"As bad as that?"

"Judge for yourself." Roderick could say no more. Other friends had seen them, and kept them talking until the warning signal sounded, and they returned to their seats.

*   *   *

Josanne lost count of the number of curtain calls, because at first she had been too much carried away by the exquisite performance of Connelli to start counting the appearances she made in acknowledgement of the applause. Surrounded by the bouquets handed onto the stage, Connelli bowed to her audience, looking grateful and natural, having dropped the role of Violetta, who, being dead, could not have been standing there, even looking pale and wan.

At last she shook her head, gestured to them that she was tired, and amazingly, the applause died down. A night to remember, and it was all over.

Josanne joined the crowd making its way out of the theatre, and debated whether or not to go to the stage door. She decided against doing so, as she was late already and her parents would be thinking that she and Hope Garnett were spending too much time after their night-class sitting around and drinking frothy coffee. They might even ask Hope, next time they saw her, what they'd been doing. Hope was a bad liar, and would admit that she knew nothing at all about being out on that Friday evening. Josanne was caught so much unaware that all she knew was that she was in the gutter, wet and muddy, with her headscarf somehow landed on the bonnet of a car. Willing hands were helping her to her feet, and she was being reprimanded as well as being consoled. The driver of the car, white-faced, had pushed his way through the knot of people, apologizing, and not trying to blame her for what she knew was her own fault.

"She's not hurt," somebody said. A few disappointed spectators moved away.

"I walked in front of you," Josanne admitted. "I was in a daze. I'm all right."

"I ll have you checked up by a doctor, then I'll run you home."

Obediently she got into the car, recognizing that it was Adrian Ferguson's car she had failed to notice when she crossed the street. She was shaking. She tried to conceal the fact from him, but her teeth were chattering and it was impossible. She managed to say urgently – "I must get home. My parents think I've been at a night-class. I've been to *Traviata*."

"Is there anything wrong with that?" His voice was kind and cool and reassuring.

"My parents would think so."

"Were you there alone?"

"I always go to the opera alone. I get bemused. I can't talk to people." She was still shivering. "I live in Maybank Court, off Kensington High Street. And please, I can't go to a doctor. There isn't time and I'm all right." Now I'm going to cry, she thought in horror. "I must get home."

Adrian could see that she was very young, very pretty and very frightened. He asked her name and then said, "Where do you go for your night-classes?"

"Oxford Street. But there wasn't one tonight. I made that up. And I said afterwards I'd be with my friend – my girl friend."

She was knotting and un-knotting her hands, her knuckles white. She was in a bad way, not because she'd been hit by a car, but because she was afraid of her parents. Adrian was touched by her distress.

"I'll talk to your parents," he said.

"No!" There was panic in her voice.

"You'll have to tell them something, so it had better be good. Won't you leave it to me?"

The offer was coming from one of Britain's leading Q.C.s. She knew this, although he hadn't said who he was. Seeing him in court had convinced her of that.

"I'll leave it to you," she said meekly.

When they stepped into the brightly-lit vestibule at Maybank Court, it was obvious that Josanne would have to admit to an accident. She was muddy, her stockings torn, her hair bedraggled. She stood beside Adrian Ferguson in the lift. He was wearing a dinner-jacket, and looked like an advertisement for an expensive brand of cigarette. He rang the door-bell of the flat, and the palpitating Josanne moved beside him, as if for protection. It was her father who opened the door, and Adrian quickly introduced himself. Josanne's plight became apparent.

"Mr. Murray? Your daughter's not hurt, but I've made her horribly muddy, so I insisted on bringing her home."

A puzzled William Murray backed into the flat and invited them to follow. Sybil appeared from the drawing-room, and recognized Adrian Ferguson immediately. One glimpse of her parents was enough to explain to Adrian why their daughter had been so much afraid.

"I cut the corner, and she got the full benefit of the water that had accumulated in the gutter. I'm so ashamed. I had to come and tell you myself." He turned to Josanne. "You'll have to send your suit to the cleaners and buy new stockings, and don't say you won't, because I insist." He was smiling, and he had a winning smile. Josanne had never seen him smile in court.

"Get changed," Sybil Murray snapped to Josanne. "And you'll have a drink, Mr. Ferguson. It was so kind of you to bother bringing my daughter home. I expect she was day-dreaming and not looking where she was going."

Josanne fled to her bedroom, and she heard the drawing-room door close. She was still trembling, but she changed from her muddy suit, which was drip-dry anyway, although he wouldn't have noticed that, and she put on the blue dress she would have worn to the opera, had she not pretended she was going to night-class.

When she joined them in the drawing-room, her parents looked more animated than she had ever seen them. Adrian Ferguson at once rose to his feet, so that even her father stood up and offered her a drink.

"Brandy," Adrian replied for her. "I gave her a fright." He was exaggerating the incident, and in some way this allayed her parents' fears, so that they were not asking her the questions she had expected. How? Where had it happened. Where was Hope? Perhaps she would have to face all that tomorrow, Saturday, with no escape to the office.

Her father gave her some brandy, just a little. Her hand shook when she took the glass, but he didn't notice. She sat on the edge of a chair, and felt a bit better after a few sips.

"I've been to *Traviata*," Adrian was saying. "I took my son and two daughters, and sent them off to Rule's for supper. My wife isn't well, so I was going straight home. Then this happened." He smiled across at Josanne. "Do you like opera?"

"I love it." This was safe. Her parents heard her record-player. They knew the sort of music she liked to hear.

"I have a box for *The Barber of Seville* next Wednesday. Connelli is singing. Would you care to join my family?"

This morning she had been a humdrum bespectacled girl, in a

humdrum office. Tonight she felt that a Fairy Godmother had waved a wand, and transported her to Fairyland.

That magical performance, so stunning that she had taken leave of her senses and could have been killed! And now an invitation to repeat the rapture of hearing Isabella Connelli sing. She flushed scarlet and looked from one parent to the other.

"May I accept?"

"It's a very lavish recompense for a trifling accident!" Sybil Murray actually smiled. "Of course you'll accept." She turned to Adrian. "We hear Connelli screeching *Una voce poco fa* night and day on Josanne's record-player. I prefer Rosina sung by a mezzo myself. Who sang Alfredo tonight?"

Josanne very nearly answered – "Costa", but stopped herself in time. She exchanged a quick, meaningful glance with Adrian Ferguson who said, "Costa". She was in league with someone, someone who loved opera, and knew what it was to be afraid of the consequence of disobedience. She was experiencing for the first time in her life the blissful sensation of being understood.

She had no idea, as she sat there with her glass in her hand, that tonight a trivial incident, involving a little bit of mud, was to alter the whole fabric of her life.

Adrian Ferguson was leaving. Her parents were thanking him, and she roused herself to say goodbye.

"I'll collect you on Wednesday at about seven o'clock," he said to her. "We'll have supper afterwards." He turned to Sybil. "We consist of myself, my son, my two daughters and my godson, Rorie Lamont." As he spoke, he remembered what the Lamonts had told him in the crush-bar, and resolved to lecture Rorie before he introduced him to this pretty girl.

When he had gone, her parents spoke appreciatively of Adrian Ferguson, almost congratulating Josanne on having acquired him under such unusual circumstances.

It was the happiest night of her life, in all her twenty years.

34

Rorie Lamont had telephoned Adrian Ferguson as soon as he arrived in London, and had been asked to lunch at Simpson's. This in itself was ominous. It meant that they would run less chance of meeting friends than if they had lunched at one of Adrian's clubs. It also indicated that Adrian had been warned about his escapades on the continent, and of the claim he had hinted at in that shameful, facetious letter he had sent off so light-heartedly to his parents. He adored his family. They had always shared everything, their joys and sorrows, hopes and disappointments, but a little reticence would be necessary now that he was a student, not a schoolboy, a man of the world, not a shy youth shivering on the brink of experience.

The roast beef was all that one would expect it to be, the wine chosen by Adrian who was a connoisseur, had loosened Rorie's tongue, as it was meant to do, and without the interruptions of greetings from friends, the choice of venue had proved to be the right one. While they were eating, they talked of impersonal things, politics and polo, Wimbledon and Lord's. Now, with the coffee, they had got onto the subject of the theatre, and Rorie knew where this was going to lead to, so he said it himself.

"I'm immersed in opera. It's been growing on me ever since you took me to hear Callas when I was fifteen. Now it's a passion that's taken possesion of me. I wish I could sing."

Adrian knew that all the Lamonts were musical, and that Rorie had a pleasant baritone voice. "Well, now that you have finished with the Sorbonne, when you've completed your course at the Agricultural College you could study music."

This was unexpected. Rorie had thought Adrian would grasp the opportunity to deliver a lecture, not give the sort of advice he most wanted to hear.

"I'll be about a hundred by the time I'm qualified, according to the plans my parents have made for me."

"You'll be a mere twenty-two, and you'll have learnt the difference between loving music enough to make it your life's work, and loving musicians in a way that does little credit either to you or to them. I'm speaking in the plural because to name any particular woman in this context is the essence of bad taste, as you should have known when you wrote that disgraceful and degrading letter home."

"There's no need for you to address the jury! I already stand condemned out of my own pen." Rorie spoke sulkily, staring into his coffee, which was as black as his future appeared to be. "I wrote while I was in a state of euphoria. I didn't expect my parents to tell anyone else about it, not even you."

"I met them unexpectedly at *Traviata*. They had only just received your letter, and they were worried, picturing you having to face a libel action. It doesn't seem to strike you that you're claiming to have seduced, or have been seduced by one of the most publicized women in the world. What sort of story do you think the newspapers could make of this, even if it were true?"

Rorie knew that he was being offered the chance to recant, to dismiss the episode as an invention, based on wishful thinking. He would be branded as a fool and a liar, but that would soon be forgotten, lumped together with other minor mistakes of the past. Honesty, caution, guilt, pride, jostled for a place in his reply. "I didn't invent it. I can't back-pedal on what happened – it's too important to be dismissed as a fable."

In the silence which followed Adrian thought about this young man sitting opposite to him. With his sturdy body, black hair, and Highland blue eyes he was born to dazzle and allure, even if he had been a pauper. But he was not a pauper, for his Aunt Marian, finding that the residue of Robert Dutton's will was not the small change but the bulk of his estate, had divided the fortune that was left to her equally, and with only limited safeguards, into the hands of Grania's three children. She believed it was what she was meant to do. The union of their Celtic Twilight temperament with the affluence which flowed from the Dutton industrial empire was accepted by the Lamonts with a cool disinterest that was the eighth wonder of the world.

It was the senior partner of Adrian's firm who had handled the intricacies of Robert Dutton's will, but after old Mr. Goddard died, the Lamont file was passed on to Adrian. It epitomized the wizardry of the man who had controlled his wife during his lifetime, and now manipulated the family purse-strings even from the grave.

"Isabella Connelli's voice is far too valuable an asset to be put at risk," Adrian said at last. "Because of her astonishing talent she is big business, and there are those that will see that she stays that way.

What happened to her chief protector, Maestro Grandi, while you were storming her citadel in Rome?"

"He was in bed with 'flu. He joined her in Paris. He thinks I've just got a schoolboy crush on her, so he doesn't bother about me."

"And isn't he right?"

"He's not right, and Isabella knows it. She understands." Rorie drank the dregs of his coffee, which was cold. "When I watched her on the stage, she was a gorgeous woman with a heavenly voice. But now I know her and I love her and I'd die for her."

Adrian sighed. He knew the pain of young love, sharp but sweetened with hope. He signed to the waiter for his bill, then he said, "I'm taking Stewart and the girls to *The Barber of Seville* tomorrow night. Would you like to join us? Your parents will think I'm compounding a felony, but I think infatuations are better worked through than stifled. There'll be another girl there – Josanne Murray. I picked her up in the gutter! Ask her about that when you see her."

"Is she being produced to take my mind off Isabella?" Rorie asked, gratitude giving way to suspicion.

"I may be an old fuddy-duddy, but I'm not stupid. I'll fetch you from Lowndes Square just before seven. And if your Aunt Marian wants to come, there'll be room for her in the box."

They parted in the Strand. Rorie watched Adrian thread his way through the traffic, then turn towards the Law Courts. He had been decent about Isabella, had not laid on the ridicule too thick, but he had made his point. A *diva*'s romance with a student would make a great story for the newspapers, but the possible risks couldn't alter the situation.

He walked disconsolately towards Charing Cross. He couldn't understand why he had chased Isabella round every opera house in Europe, yet had failed to apply for tickets for her first season in London. There was a great deal about himself that he couldn't understand, and the greatest of these was the mystery of her submission to him.

Suddenly resolute, he hailed a taxi and gave the address of Connelli's hotel. Progress was slow, and he was grateful for every red, delaying light, for he had no idea how he would be received, or what he would say to her if he found himself in her presence again. Pride compelled him to complete his journey instead of thumping on the glass and asking the driver to take him somewhere else.

He stammered when he asked for her at the reception desk, and he was told she was out. He didn't believe it. More likely, she was in the arms of the Maestro during this, her hour of siesta. Torn between relief, jealousy, and disappointment, he asked the florist to send a spray of white camellias up to her room. He signed the card, "In homage, R. L." – and as he sealed the envelope, he was uncomfortably aware that she might not recognize the initials.

Then he went to the cinema.

*   *   *

Josanne had never been in a box before, and was disappointed with the view of the stage, but its nearness was a compensation. In spite of the large orchestra, she felt she could almost touch the performers, and she was intrigued by the close view of Connelli, wetting her lips with a deliberate action before she burst into the vocal acrobatics required of her marvellous, limpid voice. A glimpse of the human touch behind the artistry and skill.

The young man beside her, whose name she hadn't taken in, had told her that he knew Connelli. He called her Isabella, and said that he had talked to her on the telephone that very afternoon. She supposed it must be true. She had stepped into a new world, where make-believe was fact. Josanne was immensely happy.

Connelli's performance, sparkling, yet sensitive, portrayed the freshness and youth of Rosina. The critics would find no fault with her when they came down to earth after the final curtain. Whenever she sang, wherever she went, it was always the same. The old niggles about her gestures, her mannerisms, even sometimes her costumes, were never mentioned any more. Nothing mattered except the flawless, heavenly voice.

Adrian had booked a table at Rule's for supper. Josanne found that she couldn't eat very much, because being with other people hadn't changed her after-opera feeling, as if her spirit had deserted her and she was hovering in some never-never-land of music.

"Josanne." Her name broke through her thoughts. "Now I know why I found you in the gutter. You're out of this world, aren't you?" Adrian Ferguson was speaking from across the table.

She laughed, and told Rorie what had happened after *La Traviata*.

'You're fey," he told her. "Not suitable for wandering around London. You'll have to come to Mull, where there aren't any gutters to fall into, or road-hogs to mow you down."

They talked about Mull, especially about Kilcaraig. Twelve thousand acres seemed to Josanne to be a vast amount of land to own, but Rorie assured her that it wasn't considered so, by Highland standards, and that like most estates it had become very run-down and dilapidated.

"My twin brother and I are taking it in turn to study agriculture and languages," he said. "In due course, we'll reclaim hundreds of acres of rushes and bracken, and we'll be able to tell land-hungry foreigners what we think of them when they cast their greedy eyes on Kilcaraig, their cheque books in their hands."

"So your parents have a point, when they send you off to learn foreign languages?" Her eyes sparkled. "I thought maybe they just wanted you to learn the facts of life a long way from home!"

Rorie's interest was awakened. He had thought this pretty girl could be a pious little prig. "You'll come to Mull some day. You'll see it for yourself." And he patted her hand.

He sounded as if he meant it. A few days ago Josanne had been sitting as a nonentity in an obscure seat at the opera. Tonight she had been in a box, and perhaps other girls had studied her through their opera-glasses and wondered who she was.

Adrian asked her if she would take Pauline and Mary to a concert at the Albert Hall, a task which his wife disliked and one he could seldom perform. Her eager acceptance of the suggestion brought them all back to the subject of music, which quickly became a discussion between herself and Rorie about opera in general and Connelli in particular.

When she went home that night Josanne knew that a different way of life was opening up to her. She would never have to invent extra night-classes any more.

35

Josanne was called to the telephone at her office. Mr. Painter, her boss, did not encourage personal calls, but he was smiling as she came to his desk and took the receiver from his hand.

"Miss Murray," she said in a clear, crisp voice, wanting Mr. Painter to be impressed by her efficiency. She managed to continue to look cool and unruffled when she heard that it was Rorie Lamont on the line, and what he had to say.

"My Great-Aunt Marian's having a small supper party on Sunday evening, just for us opera lovers. Can you come?"

Josanne had thought that she must have bored Rorie, rhapsodizing over opera as she had done. Evidently the reverse had been the case. "I'd love to come but –", she swallowed. Rorie would despise her for what she had to admit. "My parents expect me to spend

Sunday evenings with them. It's become a sort of tradition that I do."

"No problem. They'll come too. I'll give them a ring. The Fergusons are coming and Isabella Connelli will be there. That's what it's all about. My aunt wants to meet her."

"How on earth did your aunt get her to accept?" Josanne gasped in astonishment.

"When you meet my aunt, you'll understand! It wouldn't surprise me if she invited Herbert von Karajan along for tea!"

When Josanne replaced the receiver, she found that Mr. Painter was still smiling benevolently upon her.

"That was Mr. Rorie, wasn't it?" he asked, and seeing Josanne's look of surprise, he added "If you read our reports, you would know that he is one of our directors. All the Lamonts are."

She still looked puzzled. "Did you not know that Mrs. Lamont's first husband was Sir Robert Dutton? What is the name of this company?"

"Carnsworth, Prior, and Dutton." She remembered the talk she had been given when she joined the firm. Carnsworth and Prior were long defunct. "Dutton, Dutton and Dutton," she had been told. "Get that name into your head, because there isn't anything from a pin to an oil-well that the name Dutton doesn't in some way control."

"For Dutton, read Lamont," Mr. Painter said. "But mercifully, the Lamonts leave the affairs of their empire in the hands of those who know how to run it. You are a very small cog in a vast machine . . ."

She had heard it all before at the Christmas pep talk. She had never imagined that she would meet a member of the family that kept the wheels of the vast machine turning – Rorie Lamont, whom she thought of as a schoolboy. Rorie's family – not ordinary people at all.

She sat at her desk, staring blankly at her typewriter. When her mother's influence had helped her to get a job here, she had told her of the immense prospects that lay ahead for her if she did well in the office. There were branches in New York, San Francisco, Tokyo, Sydney, everywhere in the world. She would someday be able to transfer to one of the branches of her choice, and would be able to travel widely, through her connection with the Dutton empire. For some weeks, lately, she had been watching advertisements in the evening papers to see if she could find a more interesting job. She must have been insane!

She struck a wrong key on the typewriter, and hit a question mark instead of a K. Smiling, she removed the sheet of paper and replaced it with another, but she tore off the scrap with a question mark and put it in her note-case.

Accidentally, she had struck the sign that most appropriately summed up her confused, excited state of mind.

*   *   *

Marian Danvers was putting the final touches to the preparations for her party, annoyed with herself that she had changed too soon, and that a wisp of hair was tickling the back of her neck. It had escaped from the tiny and invisible hairpins inserted by the hairdresser at Harrods.

She had moved to the flat in Lowndes Square left to her by Robert Dutton only two years ago, after Nicholas had died from a long and crippling illness. She still missed him immensely. That war-time wedding, when on an impulse they had behaved like immature children, instead of mature, middle-aged friends, had proved to be the start of a new and unbelievably happy period in her life. Now, when she saw romantic love fade into boredom and infidelity, she thought of the prosaic way in which she had accepted Nicholas's half-faltering proposal of marriage.

"We know each other well. We like one another. We've lived our lives and loved our loves. Isn't it time we settled down?"

And she had laughed and said "yes", and they had chosen May the 10th for their wedding. On that night, the biggest air-raid on Westminster had taken place, both of them were kept on duty, and by the morning the news of Grania's injuries had reached them. During the weeks that followed she had discovered just how desperately she needed Nicholas's support. Secretly, often, she needed him still.

The door-bell rang, Marian jammed the errant strand of hair into place, and Rorie went off to admit the first guests.

They were the Murrays, and Josanne was at once at ease in the presence of Rorie's Great-Aunt Marian, who was such a delightful blend of sophistication and Highland hospitality. The flat was beautifully furnished in a mixture of loved, familiar things, and antiques that would be the envy of collectors, a taste which she was later to find reflected in the castle at Kilcaraig.

Rorie had been right about there being no problem in persuading Josanne's parents to come to the party, and now, to her relief, she found that her mother recognized Marian Danvers from some long-ago house party where they had both been guests.

"I never realized you were married to Nicholas Danvers," Sybil Murray said. "I loved his style. I've read all his books."

Josanne had never before seen her mother look so glowing, so enthusiastic. It was as if she had taken on a new personality when she came through the drawing-room door.

They had just settled down with their drinks when the door bell rang, and Rorie went off to admit the Fergusons, who came in force. Alison looked elegant in a dress of deep blue silk, which she wore with a flourish, the self-possessed wife of a distinguished man.

Stewart and Rorie were soon together, exchanging anecdotes about their student life at the Sorbonne, while Josanne, drinking sherry, drifted towards Pauline and Mary, feeling she had a duty to be with them.

"I've been told not to ask for her autograph, or suggest that she sings," Mary grumbled, and was rewarded with a snappy, "I should think not," from Pauline, whose excitement had made her irritable.

While the girls were bickering about etiquette, Isabella Connelli and Maestro Grandi, her manager, were waiting for the lift. Isabella's insistence that she would accept this invitation from the elderly aunt of a youthful fan had taken some explaining, but she had convinced the Maestro that a small party in a private house in London would be a new experience for both of them. He had been in a mood to grant her anything she asked. She had hit London like a tornado, and the critics in their different ways had prophesied that Connelli, born in obscurity in Ireland, would one day make musical history. She was not another Patti, or another Jenny Lind, another Melba. She was the first Connelli.

The lift was an old fashioned one, creaking as it bore them upwards. Under her light-hearted chatter, Isabella was feeling the familiar nervous tension that always preceded an encounter with the public, be it a roomful of people or a packed auditorium. And tonight was special. Tonight she was going to see Rorie again

The Maestro bowed her out of the lift with a flourish and pressed the bell of the flat. Rorie opened the door.

"*Ciamar a tha thu?*" he smiled, holding out his hand.

"*Tha gu math,*" she replied.

"*Ciamar a tha thu?*" said the Maestro. "You see, I speak the Irish too."

They were laughing as they entered the drawing-room, and to Josanne it seemed as if a spotlight had turned onto Connelli. There she stood, her green dress picking out the green in her eyes, her glowing hair beautifully styled, her aura of fame clinging to her in the Knightsbridge flat.

Soon Marian was making the introductions with her enviable informality and ease, and presently Connelli was sitting on the sofa,

242

drinking tomato juice and congratulating Adrian on his success at the Old Bailey. Rorie must have briefed her about the people she would meet, and what would be the right thing to say. She was used to taking direction and would play her part faultlessly.

The Maestro, with an eye for a pretty woman, made straight for Alison, who talked to him in abominable Italian until Marian ushered them into the dining-room for the buffet supper which she had so lavishly prepared. The table had been pushed to one side, and the chairs were arranged so that they could sit in groups and eat, when they had helped themselves to what they wanted.

"I can't stop gawping at her," Stewart said to Josanne. He was perched on the arm of her chair, and was eating lobster mayonnaise. He had drunk a considerable amount of champagne. "Do you think Rorie really brought it off with her, or is he just boasting?"

"Brought what off?" Josanne asked.

"It doesn't matter," Stewart said awkwardly. He was too inexperienced to know how to extricate himself from an ill-chosen remark.

Understanding dawned on Josanne. She felt shocked, but didn't want him to think her a prude. "They don't seem to be taking any particular notice of each other," she said.

"That's what I meant," Stewart said. "Studied indifference is unnatural. It's because of him that she's here."

Connelli was holding court, gesticulating as she instinctively acted what she was saying, making William Murray and the Ferguson girls laugh. Rorie had his back to her and was talking to Sybil, while Alison was still with the Maestro, but talking English now, so that he could understand what she was saying. Adrian was moving closer to Connelli's chair, a glass of champagne in his hand, and determination in his eyes. Marian appeared to be unobtrusively everywhere. Stewart signed to her to join them, and he made her sit down to eat.

"Stewart, if you just take a wee look round you may find where I wriggled out of my shoes," Marian said. "I'll need them when I shepherd you all back to the drawing-room."

The shoes were under the table, and the Maestro knelt down to help her into them. He remarked on the neatness of her feet, while Alison told him about Cinderella and the glass slipper. He beamed at her, delighted, pretending he had never heard the story before.

"Do you ever feel you are part of a fairy-tale?" Adrian said to Connelli. He had achieved his coveted position and was beside her now.

She was picking at a wishbone. She held it out to him and he hooked his little finger round it, but it was too slippery to break, so they had to give up. He wiped her hand with his handkerchief, relishing the loveliness of her.

"Do you ever feel that the clock will strike and you'll wake up to find that your phenomenal rise to fame is part of a dream?" he persisted.

She considered this, her head tilted to one side, revealing a tiny mole close to her right ear. He wondered how many men had kissed that mole.

"Jetting round the world, constantly changing climates and clocks is often more like a nightmare," she said. "But Maestro Grandi does ensure that I stay for several weeks at most places where I sing. I almost lived in a suitcase before I became established, but that's a thing of the past." She laughed her pretty laugh which was music in itself. "I'm certainly glad I'm not still in a grocer's shop in Skibbereen, terrified of snicking off the tip of my fingers in a bacon machine."

Everyone knew that she had served in a shop before the Maestro discovered her. It was a story the journalists loved to write about.

Rorie came up to her, offering her a choice of tipsy pudding, or strawberries and cream. She accepted the strawberries, and kept her face averted as he handed the plate to her. Colour crept up her neck. Adrian, watching her, saw the effect Rorie had on her, knew that Rorie's claim could be true.

Rorie did not linger. "Coffee in the drawing-room," he said and piled up a tray of dishes to take into the kitchen, where Marian's daily help was doing the washing up.

Someone was playing a Chopin waltz. Isabella brushed the crumbs from her dress, and Adrian followed her to the drawing-room, where Stewart stopped abruptly and rose from the piano stool. Isabella smiled at him and asked him to continue to play, then she sat on the sofa, Adrian still beside her, not caring that he was monopolizing her.

William Murray pulled up a chair, and asked her about her singing. She answered readily, happily, sipping black coffee and exchanging reminiscences with the Maestro.

Stewart had stopped playing and had swivelled round on the piano stool to listen to her. The girls sat on the floor, Josanne drinking in every word, unable to believe that she was almost at the feet of her heroine, fascinated by this peep behind the scenes.

"Don't get the idea that it's all fun and laughter," Isabella said. "It's immensely hard work. Physically and mentally one has to be in perfect condition, and emotional stress can affect the voice."

"Doesn't gazing into someone's eyes and singing love duets get

244

you all steamed up?" Pauline asked. She had a secret passion for Carlo Costa, who so often sang with Connelli.

Isabella shook her head, amused. "Sometimes there's quite a tussle between stage lovers when they try to get the better of one another taking curtain calls. Wherever I sing, I refuse completely to take curtain calls between acts, which annoys some singers very much."

"Now that you've reached the summit, what next?" Sybil asked, characteristically brusque.

"There's always another summit ahead, and the possibility of an avalanche! I've still a very long way to go."

"To Isolde?" Stewart asked. He had read that the role was one which all sopranos dreamed about, and he hoped it wasn't a silly question to put to a coloratura soprano, who had only recently moved to singing more dramatic parts.

"I want to achieve Isolde without losing what I already possess," Isabella said kindly. "It's my ambition, and you're very clever to have sensed it."

She saw that her reply had pleased him, and she added, "It's going to take a long time. I don't want to be a burnt out case by the time I'm forty."

Looking round the room, seeing them all watching her, she realized that only the Maestro belonged to her world. These people were her audience, separated from her by a heavy curtain which just for a while had become a flimsy, revealing veil.

Sybil said, "Sooner or later you'll have to face the years of decline. Time takes care of that. What'll you do with the rest of your life?" Josanne winced at her mother's intrusive question.

Adrian could see Connelli stiffen.

"I'm making the best of the time I have," she said quietly. "Family ties have never existed for me, or ever can exist. It means no home, ever. No husband, ever. The singing years are too precious to allow for other commitments. Some people manage it, but I can't. And when it's all over? I don't know. I don't know at all." Her eyes were anxious, visualizing a future that was blank and hopeless.

"Is such dedication worth the cost?" Rorie asked.

"I love to sing. But the cost? There's no way of counting it because I'll never know what I've missed." She was looking at him, communicating something more than words. Then she turned to the Maestro. "I know something I'll miss, if you don't make arrangements about it soon. The Wexford Festival. When, please, will you fix for me to sing there?"

The Maestro shrugged and raised his hands in a gesture of despair.

"The great opera houses of the world clamour for her, and all she thinks about is Wexford. *Carissima*, you shall have your lollipop. Somehow I will fit in Wexford."

He walked over to her and touched her shoulder, briefly possessive. Marian, who considered that Isabella had been put on display for long enough, created a diversion by pouring out more coffee. Soon she had tossed the ball of conversation round the room, restoring balance and enabling Isabella to talk to Rorie if she wished, but she didn't attempt to do so. She asked Stewart to play the piano some more, and after a while, perhaps because they had been talking about Ireland, he had them all singing *An Irish Lullaby*. Gradually they stopped because Connelli was singing too, softly, for the love of it, not thinking of herself as special at all. "Too-ra-loo-ra-loo-ra, that's an Irish lullaby."

They were dabbing at their eyes when it was over.

"That's all wrong," she said. "You shouldn't be crying. You should be asleep!"

"Which you should be," the Maestro said. "Early to bed on free nights is our unbreakable rule."

"Early to bed with who?" Stewart whispered to Rorie, who pretended not to hear.

When they had all gone, Rorie and Marian bumped up the cushions in the drawing-room, and commented that there were no ashtrays to empty. No one had smoked.

"Out of deference to our *diva*, I suppose," Marian said. "Under that gentleness, there's a burning ambition to get just what she said she wanted, and quite obviously she's going to succeed. Nothing will be allowed to get in her way."

"I'm in love with her. It will last forever."

"That's what first love always feels like." Her heart ached for him, but she could do nothing to help. "No home ever. No husband, ever. You got the message? It was intended specially for you."

Yes, he had got the message, spoken in that soft voice, her accent a curious mixture of all the languages she knew.

"For a moment she held my hand."

He regretted these words as soon as they were uttered. That had been a private moment. Again, his impulse to boast had betrayed her. Had she known he had written to his parents about her, talked of her to Adrian, hinted of conquests to Stewart, she would never have come to the party, would never want to see him again.

Marian gave him a long look. "Rorie, don't play with fire. It isn't necessarily you who will get burnt."

She kissed him goodnight and left him to consider her warning.

Rorie stood by the sofa, stroking the place where Isabella's arm had rested. The moment of physical contact had meant so much. Just her hand, but it expressed his affection for her, and had shown that she was not indifferent to him.

He must see her alone before he went to Kilcaraig to face his parents' interrogation. If he telephoned, she would talk to him – he had discovered that – but she might not agree to meet him. Her hotel was close to Kensington Gardens, because she loved the Peter Pan statue, and the Albert Memorial, and she always stayed near the places that had fascinated her when she was poor. She had confided this to him when she lay in his arms during those relaxed intervals in bed in Rome. In retrospect, those intervals were even more exquisite and intimate in memory than were the moments of physical discovery and passion that preceded them.

He wrote her a note. He would deliver it to her hotel in the morning. If he meant anything to her at all, she would surely comply with his request.

There was still a light shining under Aunt Marian's door when at last he went to bed.

36

Isabella Connelli sat in the window of her hotel bedroom, brushing her hair and looking at the stars, because she had switched off the light. She knew nothing of astronomy – which were planets and which were not – but some shone more brightly than others and had done so for millions of years. Any human achievement dwindled to nothing when one considered the stars.

She thought about the party. Nice people, kind people, who had accepted her as one of themselves. No flash photographs, no autographs, and a room like a stage set, but the furniture was real, not to be pushed into the wings and covered in dust sheets until the next performance.

Rorie's aunt had kissed her goodnight, had held her in her arms and kissed her, as if she were her child; but Rorie had said his aunt had no children of her own and had lavished her maternal love upon his mother. Rorie had said a great deal as she lay in his arms that night in Rome, but tonight he had said almost nothing at all. His blue eyes had held hers, and he had pressed her hand, firmly and gently, possessive yet discreet.

Rorie had told her about his parents and his brother and his sister, and about Kilcaraig Castle, which was not really a castle at all, but a comfortable house, his home.

Home. Her own had been a convent near Cork, where she had been taken into the care of the Sisters when she was a toddler, and it had been discovered that her little brother had died of starvation.

It was when she was sixteen years old that she sang the part of Mary Magdalene in an Easter play produced by the nuns to raise money for their convent. She was working then in that grocer's shop in Skibbereen, where she had been born, but the convent was the only home that she knew, and she went back there for Christmas and Easter and when they needed extra help, especially with singing. She loved to sing.

The Easter play marked the beginning of a new life, because the impresario, Maestro Grandi, was in the audience. He heard her, he sought her out, and after much wrangling, first with the nuns and later with higher authorities, it was agreed that she could go to Italy, to live with the Maestro and his wife, and learn how to become a singer.

Now she recalled the day she had arrived, trembling, at the Imperial Hotel in Cork, her suitcase packed neatly with the best clothes she could afford. Twenty minutes later, the Maestro's wife had mortified her by tipping the contents onto the bed, exclaiming that a cardboard suitcase was not the fitting luggage for a girl who would one day become a *prima donna*. Her most intimate garments lay before her, even the packet of Kotex which she had wrapped in a petticoat, for fear of embarrassment if her luggage were opened by the customs officials.

She had said nothing. She had learnt never to raise her voice, never to protest or complain. On the following day, she left for the airport, terror in her heart, and in her hand a large fibre-glass case concealing all those precious garments with their supermarket labels.

Almost insensible as the result of air-sickness and home-sickness, she had settled in the Maestro's house in Genoa. His wife, who had seemed to be an insensitive dragon, now proved that she too had merely been suffering from nerves over the responsibility her husband's enthusiasm had laid upon her. Childless herself, the care of a young and talented girl was a formidable undertaking. Singing lessons began, but the Maestro very soon insisted that the right person to teach her worked in Milan, so to Milan they must go.

Meekly, Isabel packed her case. Awe-struck, she presented herself for instruction to the *prima donna* who had once enchanted audiences all over the world, and who now accepted a few very special students.

"Sing!" she had been commanded.

She sang *The Famine Song*, she knew not why.

"I'll accept you," she was told.

It was three months before she was allowed to sing again, three months of doing exercises, and learning how to breathe, and lying on the floor while her mentor stood on her abdomen to ensure that her muscles were strong and correctly used.

Sometimes, in the middle of a lesson, she would be whisked off to look at a museum, or to buy a new dress. Her faltering Italian was becoming fluent, and her music lessons were the joy of her life. When at last she was allowed to sing, even the scales and arpeggios indicated the sound which would one day bring audience after audience to its feet.

She was eighteen when she sang the name part in *Lucia di Lammermoor* in a small provincial opera house. She had stood on the stage transfixed while the *bravos* rang in her ears. This taught her that there was a personal price to pay for success, and she was to discover that jealousy and malice would go hand-in-hand with acclaim.

Engagements were now offered to her, but wisdom prevailed, and her training continued, interspersed with occasional appearances in minor roles, to give her experience. Gradually Isabel Connell from Skibbereen became known as Isabella Connelli. Then came the day when Bardini himself auditioned her for the season he was to conduct at the San Carlo Opera House in Naples.

The careful preparation was over. From a small part, sung offstage, she was summoned at short notice to deputize in the role of *La Sonnambula*. She created a sensation, was hailed as a phenomenon.

Inevitably, her knowledge of life progressed with her music. Her first lover was a German tenor, whom she met when she was a Flower Maiden in *Parsifal*. She found the experience embarrassing, painful and messy, but instinct urged her to try again. Repressed by years of self-control, delight always eluded her, but she knew how to act a pleasure she was unable to feel. Until that night in Rome.

The thought of Rorie nagged at her like toothache, or worse, like the earache she always endured whenever she travelled by air. The only other person who could throw her into this sort of turmoil was Bardini, who could destroy her self-confidence, yet his every word increased her dependence on him.

She knelt in front of her crucifix, as the nuns had taught her to do. She was never any good at praying, but she kept up the habit, and hoped her brief and jumbled thoughts made sense to God, in whom she believed profoundly.

The pinnacle of her profession, maybe, but always that threat of an avalanche. A breakdown in health. Love. A boy, the touch of whose hand could cause her acute sensual pain.

She lay awake for a long time, and she was still troubled when she fell asleep.

* * *

On the morning after the party, Marian had just finished her bath when Alison telephoned to thank her, and to rhapsodize about the Maestro. She had just rung off, when Adrian came on the line, speaking from his office.

"As a matter of interest, how did you get Connelli to come?" he asked.

"I told her the truth. I'm an aged fan who can't get out a great deal, and my great-nephew met her and admires her very much, so please would she come. And she came."

Adrian laughed. "I might have known you'd use the direct approach, and get away with it!"

"Adrian, I'm worried about her. She's a simple person, friendly and affectionate, yet her life is a time-table, planned for years ahead. She meekly accepts that she's dedicated wholly to singing. She's not allowed to be human."

There was a momentary silence, and she thought that the telephone was dead. Then Adrian said, "I think the situation is a lot more delicate and more dangerous than I had expected. Be careful what you say to Grania. She's not easily fooled, and she'll fight like a tiger-cat to protect her young from trouble. She'll see Rorie as the victim of a spoilt and unscrupulous woman, and for that he has only himself to blame. By the end of the summer, he may believe it himself. He's very young."

"And Isabella?"

"That coloratura comet will leave the turbulence behind as she hurtles into outer space. Destiny. Leave her to heaven."

Marian was left with the receiver buzzing in her hand. She had never before heard Adrian speak in such a fanciful way. Star dust in his eyes.

An hour later, she went out to post her letter to Grania. It was factual, and she had not tried to gloss over the impact of having a famous *prima donna* in her drawing-room, but she did describe the charm of Josanne Murray, whom Adrian had introduced to Rorie just at a time when a diversion was so much needed. She hoped she wasn't sowing seeds of trouble for Josanne in the future. She genuinely liked the girl.

When she returned to the flat, she found her daily woman, Mrs. Grant, re-arranging the party flowers, so that the silver rose bowl would be available for the bouquet of red roses that had been delivered by special messenger. With it was a polite and carefully worded letter of thanks, and there was also a card attached to the roses. "To Aunt Marian, from Isabella with love." A timid expression of affection from a woman who was adored by millions, but belonged to no one. She put the letter and the card in her desk, then changed her mind and went to her bedroom, where she kept the Family Bible.

There were special pages where Lamont births, marriages, and deaths were recorded. Some of the earlier entries were yellow, almost indecipherable with age. She pushed the card and the letter between those pages and then returned the Bible to its shelf.

*   *   *

Rorie was waiting at the Round Pond in Kensington Gardens. He had left a note at Isabella's hotel, telling her that he would be there between three and five o'clock. He had watched nannies and children and model boats, and had seen fights between some of London's most fashionable dogs.

He was beginning to lose hope. The touch of her hand could have been a gesture of friendship, nothing more. He traced back all the contacts he had with her since that marvellous, incredible night, and they amounted to very little. Apart from a couple of telephone conversations, there had only been the flight to Paris, surrounded as always by opera people, who laughed and talked and made him feel young and gauche and angry. He had wanted to cry out to them, "I've been her lover". He didn't of course, but he had written to his parents, and he was sickened now by what he had said. Adrian was right, it degraded something that was special. He had betrayed Isabella.

That night in Rome, the de Stefanis' party had been held in the hotel where she was staying. His knowledge of Gaelic had enabled him to keep her all to himself, although he was aware of the amused looks exchanged by the guests among the glittering throng.

If she knew he was palpitating with fright, she didn't show it. He told her about Kilcaraig, and she told him some of her memories of Skibbereen. When she said goodnight to her friends, he escorted her to the lift, and it was then natural for him to accompany her to her apartment.

251

She was surprised to find she had to search in her handbag for her key. She had expected Motti, her dresser and general assistant to be waiting for her. The door opened into a large sitting-room, and there was a note for her on a table. It was from Motti, who was afraid she was starting a cold, so had retired to bed before she could hand on any germs.

Isabella had read the note while Rorie closed the door behind him. Then, feeling like a screen villain, he had slipped the bolt. She didn't notice. She offered him a drink, which he refused. She held out her hand to bid him goodnight, and he caught her arm and jerked her to him. Then he kissed her. After the first few moments, when she resisted him as if she were made of steel, she relaxed, her arms hanging limply at her sides, her breath coming in small, quick gasps.

He undid the fastener of her dress, which he eased over her shoulders, then he kissed her smooth bare shoulders. After that, he rocked her in his arms. She remained limp, unresisting, like a rag doll. When he released her, she stood with her back against the door. Her eyes were closed. She could be acting a part in an opera.

Then she said, "How old are you?"

He replied, "I'm twenty".

She opened her eyes and gave him a long look. She went towards the bedroom. He followed her, and caught her by the shoulders.

"Is there a telephone in there?" he asked.

"Yes. I am not going to use it."

She opened a cupboard and tossed him a bathrobe, then she went into the bathroom. When she emerged, she was wearing a green silk wrap, and he had put on the bathrobe.

She stood by the bathroom door, hugging herself, avoiding looking at him. He pulled the pillows down the bed, so that they would be under her shoulders, not her head, then he took off the bathrobe and spread it on the bed. He held out his arms to her.

She went to him, as if under some compulsion. He kissed her again and again, fondling her. When he was sure of her response, he edged her closer to the bed. As she lay down, he could feel her heart hammering under her breast.

"Turn off the light," she said.

"No. You are too beautiful to be in the dark."

His thoughts were still on that night in Rome when he saw her coming towards him. She was wearing a green linen suit, a headscarf, and sun-glasses. It was half-past four.

"I'm sorry that I kept you waiting," she said. "I did a recording session this morning, and Motti made me rest this afternoon. I fell asleep."

He had met Motti, an abbreviation of her surname, Mottram, in Rome. She was a brisk young woman, not at all a motherly type, and she had been a nurse in Dublin before she managed to get the job as dresser to Connelli. She was discreet, and she took her responsibilities very seriously. Rorie guessed that she probably knew about their hours of love.

"Does the Maestro suspect anything?" he asked.

"No, no," Isabella said in alarm. "If he did, I wouldn't be here. He thinks you're too young for me, and he's right. I have to meet him at the opera house at six. I don't know why. No more singing for me until Wednesday."

They walked aimlessly. She kept her head down, afraid of being recognized. "It only needs one person to ask for my autograph, and they pop up endlessly," she said. "It's like looking at the sky. You soon have everyone in the street doing it."

"You don't have to apologize to me because people admire you!"

"Many of them don't know who I am until they see what name I've written on their scrap of paper. It's all that television, and now my film." The screen version of *The Barber of Seville* had just been released. "I hate publicity. I could curl up and die."

"Then you're in the wrong job."

"I'm a singer. I love to sing, but on a stage, to a live audience. I don't want my voice to be messed about by engineers, and posted off in parcels all over the world."

"You don't mind making records."

"That's different. People who buy my records love music. Often they've heard me on the stage, and want something to remember me by. I can understand that. Some day, they may listen to a scratchy record of me singing, and feel awe-struck, as I do when I hear Caruso."

She was thinking aloud, saying what she knew to be the truth. "I shouldn't be here with you now. I could be recognized. I don't want your name linked with mine in a gossip column."

"Why not?"

"Because you are twenty, and I'm thirty, and there's no future for us, which you know as well as I do." They stood still, thinking of their predicament. She added, "I don't want you to be disgraced".

"Disgraced! By you!"

She bit her lip, frowning, as if trying to see into the future. "What I was saying last night is true. Singing has to come first."

"You won't always be able to sing. Your voice can't last as long as your life. Mrs. Murray was blunt, but she was right."

"I am nothing when I can't sing. I'm not even very responsive to love-making, as you have discovered."

Yes, he had discovered that, and the discovery had enabled him to give her joy, when she had expected fear and shame. They had made love, and they had talked, and they had made love.

"What are we going to do about it?" he asked. "When can we be alone again?"

"We can't. You know we can't. Nobody must ever find out about us."

He had told his parents. Adrian knew. And Marian. He was sick with the thought of how he had betrayed her. He said, "There can be no one else for me now, except you".

She shook her head. She was not going to offer any hope for the future.

"If ever you need me, if ever you change your mind, I'll always come to you. You'll never know how ashamed I am over the way I treated you that night, but I'm thankful too, because without that, I'd never have found the person that is you. Now I'm going to love you forever, and nothing, ever, will change my love."

"It's been said before, by millions of people all through the centuries." They had reached the Round Pond again, and the model yachts gave them an excuse to stand together, pretending they were watching. "My father stabbed my mother. He was drunk. She didn't die, they both died later, after we were taken away from them to be cared for by the Sisters. He had wanted to be a priest. All his life he had wanted that, but he met her when she was dancing with a travelling company in Bandon. After that, he cared nothing for his vocation, only for her. He would love her forever. That 'forever' didn't last very long. I sing about love, but I don't believe in it. I want you to know, because I want you to know the sort of person I really am. I come from a squalid background. I don't want to spoil your life. No one else knows what I've told you." She thought about it, then shrugged. "I suppose it's all in some musty file in a Welfare Office. It would make a good newspaper story, if the dancer and the would-be priest motif weren't so corny that people would think it had been made up."

"But it's true?"

"Yes, it's true." She turned away from him walking quickly, ashamed of the truth she had revealed. It was meant to be her goodbye. He caught up with her after a few paces.

"Isabella, what you've told me has nothing at all to do with you!"

"They were my parents. You, of all people, know what that means."

254

"What's bred in the bone comes out in the flesh," Rorie quoted. He had heard it all his life. A commonplace saying. "Is it that worry, as much as your singing, that has ruled marriage out of your life?"

She didn't answer. They walked on in silence until they reached the park gates. Then she said, "I've written to your aunt. It was so kind of her to have me to her party. The Sisters taught me how to say thank you. I can't help my hand-writing, but the letter won't let you down."

She was apologizing for herself, as if by relating to him that pitiful fragment of her life she had forgotten that she had gone a long way since she was born in abject poverty to drunken parents in Skibbereen.

He hailed a taxi. She would not allow him to accompany her to Covent Garden, claiming that in London the freedom to travel alone was one of her special treats. They shook hands.

He watched her taxi until it was swallowed up in the traffic and hidden from sight.

37

Rorie drove from London to Oban during the night, and caught the mid-day car ferry to Mull. As he left the Craignure pier, he remembered to cast a nostalgic look at the old jetty where a few years ago the ferry-boat brought the passengers and the mail and even the animals from the steamer to the shore. In those days cars were off loaded at Salen or Tobermory, and life had been leisurely and he had been young. He was afraid of what progress was going to do to the island, but as he passed the inn where Marian had first met Nicholas Danvers, it stood out as a solid link with the security of the past. Though a little larger now, it looked unaltered, and it was easy to picture how it was when carriages, not cars, were parked outside its welcoming doors.

His engine purred as he negotiated the bends in the narrow road, which was being re-surfaced but not widened. At one point, he pulled up to talk to the roadmen who were leaning on their spades, waiting for the flow of cars from the boat to pass by and allow tnem to get on with their work. These were local maintenance men, and he knew them all by name, but conversation with them was brief, because the driver in the car behind hooted impatiently, and he had to move on. Tourists could never grasp that on Mull there was always plenty of time.

The top of Ben More was shrouded in mist, but the sun was shining, highlighting the heather and the bracken in the Glen. When he turned left onto the Kilcaraig road, no other vehicle followed him, but the stream of cars climbed steadily westward, heading for Iona Ferry, and finally disappearing round the shoulder of the mountain. He could feel the rushes in the middle of the road brushing against the car, and this was a sound that used to thrill him, being the prelude to his arrival home. But not today. Today he was apprehensive about his reception, and anxious about Isabella who was flying to Hamburg and who hated journeys by air.

As he approached the Kilcaraig boundary cattle-grid, he saw that Catriona was sitting on a boulder, waiting for him. He hardly recognized her. She had taken on the contours of a woman during the last few months, and as she greeted him and bundled into the car beside him, he was almost overpowered by the scent in which she was drenched. He bit back a comment. She was growing up and had reached a self-conscious, sensitive age. Rorie had a very kind heart.

"Pull into a lay-by – I want to have a talk with you before we get home," she said, propping the little gun that had once been her mother's against her seat. She had been shooting hoodie-crows, and two of them were tied to a nearby fence as a warning to their mates. She was a very good shot.

Rorie switched off the engine, but remained in the middle of the road. "Nothing will come along," he said.

"We can't be sure of that any more. There's some sort of a land survey going on, and people with measuring devices and tripods creep about the place. We're going to be developed."

"How? Why? When?" But he wasn't really interested. Catriona's ability to exaggerate was well-known.

"Niall's had to go to Tobermory today to some meeting about it. That's why he's not around to greet you, and it serves you right for philandering in London when you should have come home."

"What else?"

"Michael's gone grumbling off to stay with his sister. You haven't got him to act as a buffer when you're set on to about getting involved with Connelli. I'm thrilled to bits about your glamorous pick-up, but Papa is shocked that you've bragged about it, while Mama is terrified you'll want to bring her here, and we'll have the press all over the place, and candid-camera shots of her in her bath."

256

"We've always been encouraged to bring our friends home," Rorie said. He had pictured himself walking through the heather with Isabella, the breeze blowing through her hair, as she laughed and relaxed and forgot the fetters of her fame. "Even the Royals can picnic in peace on Mull."

"The Royals are given a respect that wouldn't be accorded to a *prima donna*," Catriona said, obviously quoting someone else. "There's an article about her in *Trendy*. She's become a cult, and is liable to be kidnapped, so don't fly with her any more. You could be hi-jacked."

"I suppose you hand on this rubbish to Mama," Rorie said, suppressing the fear that her words had aroused.

"I'm realistic. Like Mama, I can see the snags. But whatever will be will be, and that should give you hope." She leaned against him and patted his arm. "Where is the girl of your dreams now? And did you really think she'd be allowed to come to Kilcaraig?"

Rorie switched on the engine. "She's doing some guest appearances in Germany, followed by a concert tour in Australia. Then on to New York for a season at the Met. No, I didn't expect her to come here, partly because she works too hard."

"She's a mechanical song-bird that has to keep going until the spring runs down," Catriona said, as they moved forward. "That's what Uncle Adrian wrote after he met her."

"Away!" Rorie's astonishment almost landed him in the ditch. "What else did he say?"

"Least said soonest mended, or words to that effect. But Mama and Papa won't take any notice. You'll have a grilling when you get home."

They stopped at the village, because it was traditional for a home-coming Lamont to be greeted first at the post office. A number of people had gathered there, and as Rorie laughingly kissed the women and shook hands with the men, his old sense of joy returned. He belonged here, was part of Kilcaraig, and if he were wise he would live at Caraig Lodge, with his wife and children, just as his mother planned he would do. A little later, as they crossed the bumpy bridge, he slowed down, so that he could glimpse the Lodge. It had the dead look of an empty house, but it would be let to tenants during the stalking season.

"Someday, you'll carry your bride over that threshold," Catriona said, following his thoughts. "Cheer up. When you're over your opera-mania, there'll be some nice suitable girl to take her place. Josanne Murray, for instance. She has Aunt Marian's unqualified approval. It's only a matter of putting up the banns!"

They were through the rusty iron gateway and had pulled up at the castle before Rorie could utter an indignant reply.

*　　　*　　　*

The hall with its wide spiral staircase was shabbier than he had remembered it, and the huge tapestry, showing scenes of Kilcaraig, had been moved onto the wall between the drawing-room and the library, in order to hide the patch of damp which had grown altogether too conspicuous.

Grania managed to explain this as she kissed him and helped him to extricate himself from the bouncing welcome of the dogs. Chrissie emerged from the kitchen, her hands covered in flour, to scold him for catching such an early boat, for he must have driven too fast, but she too kissed him, and told him to hurry up with his unpacking, as she was making scones, and would serve tea in the library as soon as they were ready.

He went upstairs with Grania, who sat on his bed and watched him unpack. He told her about the journey and whom he had seen on the boat. There was a time when he would have known all the passengers, just as they would all have known him, but every year brought new residents and more tourists, so that the natives were beginning to feel like strangers in their own land. He expanded on this theme, wanting to keep the conversation on impersonal grounds. For the first time in his life, he felt awkward, being alone with his mother, but he heard his father's footsteps on the landing, and he knew from experience that what was to be said would be dealt with immediately, as had happened when he brought home a bad school report.

"She's a bit low-slung for Mull," Roderick said, sitting beside Grania on the bed and referring to Rorie's new car. "I expect she eats up the miles between Paris and Milan and Rome."

"You're not wasting any time, are you?" Rorie said, arranging ties on the rail in his cupboard.

"Time is something you seem to have on your hands," Roderick replied. "Do you ever do any work at the Sorbonne?"

"I speak French in France, German in Germany, Italian in Italy, and Spanish in Spain." Rorie had a natural flair for languages.

"And Gaelic in Rome," his mother said.

"That was just a gimmick," he replied uncomfortably. He was standing by the cupboard, wishing he had a chair to sit on. A slave of fashion during the last few years, he had banished the best of his furniture to the attics, preferring the enormous cushions he bought at Habitat, but now he would feel undignified if he had to sit on the floor.

"*Fior no breug, millear bean leis,*" Roderick said. "I take it you know what that means?"

"True or false, it can injure a woman," Rorie translated. It was exactly what he had been thinking ever since he posted that letter. "When I wrote to you, I didn't expect you to hand on the information to anyone else."

"Adrian is your godfather. Even if his duties in that respect are long past, he's a close family friend, and if anyone can get through to you that some relationships will lead to trouble, he can." Roderick's eyes were on the suitcase. A photograph of Isabella stared at him from a plastic frame. "You've played around too much with women. They can't be collected like stamps, with a shout of triumph if you acquire a rarity like a penny black."

"I never meant to suggest anything like that. I've always adored Isabella on the stage. Meeting her at a party was an almost unbelievable stroke of luck. And some sort of compulsion drew us to one another. I'll never understand the sequence of events – how it was I saw her up to her room, or how I was alone with her. Normally she's never, never alone."

Grania stood up. "I don't want to hear the squalid details of this affair. She's a woman ten years older than you and loaded with experience. She could have kept things under control if she'd wanted to. Don't try to be gallant and take the blame for what happened. She may be the world's greatest singer, but she must also be a round-heeled tramp. I'm going to help Chrissie get the tea, and after you two have had a talk I don't want to hear that woman's name again, except in the context of her profession, which I realize is unavoidable."

Rorie opened the door for her, and she brushed past him. She was almost crying, and he had never seen her so upset.

"You see what you've done?" Roderick said.

Rorie sat on the bed beside him, where Grania had been. From this angle he could see the photograph lying in his suitcase. Isabella's smile was as artificial as the cheap frame. There had been stark terror in her eyes in that room in Rome, but not for long. "It wasn't her fault, Papa. You must believe me. I behaved outrageously towards her, but she was afraid of resisting me – a struggle could have meant publicity. I knew that. I knew it was a sort of blackmail."

"Or a seduction that was so crude that it amounted to rape." Roderick waited to allow the full implication of what he had said to sink in. It was terrifying. Rorie, his son.

Rorie stood up, collected some underwear from his case, and folded them into a drawer. He avoided touching the photograph, but was conscious of it, as if Isabella herself were in the room. "She didn't want me to face the humiliation of failure. She's infinitely kind," he said.

"And very quickly forgiving. Doesn't that strike you as odd?" Roderick clutched at the straw of credibility. Grania could be right, and Rorie the victim, not the villain, in this affair.

"Astonishing perhaps, but not odd. She doesn't understand her feelings, but she knows something has happened to her that's never happened before." She had experienced her first orgasm. He couldn't tell his father that. "I'm in love with her. I think it's possible that she's in love with me. But she won't recognize that until she discovers that her life can't always be arranged for her by other people, and her emotions only allowed to be unleashed under the direction of Bardini's baton."

Adrian Ferguson had written something of the kind in his letter, but with pity, not with the venom that Rorie was showing now. Naturally not. Adrian didn't imagine himself to be in love. Roderick addressed Rorie's back, for he was putting socks in one drawer and shirts in another. "What do you propose to do about it?"

"Marry her when her singing days are done."

"You aren't going to waste your life on her, surely!"

"You didn't think the ten years or so that you waited for Mama were wasted."

"Mama was married to a man thirty years older than herself. It was likely that he'd die before she did. It may sound ghoulish and calculating now, but it didn't at the time. There's no comparison between what happened to me then, and what is happening to you now."

Rorie was thinking that he would wait double, treble, that time for Isabella. Some day her beauty would fade, her voice no longer enchant. She would be faced with loneliness and old age, and the obstacle of his youth would become an advantage, for when she needed him at the end of her life, he would be there to love her and take care of her, to make up to her for all she had lost personally when she became the property of the whole world.

Roderick, watching his son, knew that he was having sentimental thoughts, and he was worried. During the reckless days of his own youth, he had never become involved with a woman who was the cynosure of all eyes. Even if Rorie were older, and Isabella were younger it was an impossible match. They belonged to different backgrounds, different worlds. Their coming together was an unfortunate trick of fate, but the explanation could be that this had been a moment of weakness and self-indulgence in two people.

260

Misconduct was the word that was once used. It was a good word. A pity that permissiveness had made it out of date.

Roderick rose to his feet rather stiffly. His war wound troubled him still, more than he would admit. "So be it. Time will soon smooth out your difficulties, but it might take a long time. Try to spare your mother anxiety, and don't be upset by what she says. She's trying to protect you from being hurt, just as I try to protect you."

"If Mama wants to make me happy, she can help me. She can meet Isabella and judge for herself. Then she would change her mind."

Roderick left him to finish his unpacking. The love of a young man for an older woman was neither strange nor new, and was seldom lasting. Rorie looked so much the outdoor man, tough and strong, yet he was the most vulnerable member of the family, because his interests were in music, poetry and art. Now all these were fused together in a tangible way. Music, poetry, art. Isabella Connelli, who was the personification of them all.

Tea would be waiting downstairs, so would Grania, needing his reassurance and his guidance in helping Rorie through this crisis in his life. Her reaction would be less intense if it were Niall who had made this unfortunate misalliance. She would always resent the women in Rorie's life, no matter who they were.

As he crossed the hall, he winced with pain, but he must spare her the worry of hearing his unmistakeable limp.

*   *   *

There were candles on the table for dinner, and Catriona had put on a long dress in celebration of the homecoming feast Chrissie had prepared. Rorie was wearing his kilt, as he and Niall always did when they were at home, and except for the few minutes during the six o'clock news, when he had listened to the radio, fearing an announcement of an aeroplane crash, everything was as normal as Lamont family life could be.

Niall was indignant about the meeting in Tobermory, where he was shown how Kilcaraig would be improved if more acres were given over to forestry, and greater thought given to the management of deer.

"I suppose it makes sense. There's your children's children to think about," Roderick said. "I can't really see the land reclaimed and cultivated the way you want it to be. Weather, population, everything's against it, but there's gold in them there hills." He smiled across at Rorie, who prided himself on his knowledge of deer.

"Hungry Europe cries for venison, and there are sportsmen who will pay handsomely for providing it."

"They'll be shot by our own poachers. I can't see Sandy MacPherson sitting idly by as foreigners with telescopic lens rob him of our deer," Niall said.

"I'm sick of venison," Catriona said, ladling rowan jelly onto her plate. "Rorie's children will all be making fortunes on the operatic stage, and we'll be basking in a life of luxury from the royalties that pour in from his wife's records. We're a united family. We expect a share of the lolly when he nets that fabulous fish."

No one took any notice of her, and the talk moved on to plans and suggestions about the upkeep of the estate, Niall and Rorie arguing about the amount of paint that would be needed to put two coats on to the barn roof, while Grania talked across them to Roderick, working out dates for dinner parties that wouldn't clash with other Mull social events.

When Grania and Catriona went together to the drawing-room, a formality they still observed in the fashion of the more civilized past, Grania said "Being provocative is tiresome and can be dangerous. Don't do it again."

Catriona felt more chastened than she would have done if she had been roundly scolded and sent off to bed.

"I'm sorry," she said, and turned on the radio as her mother poured out the coffee. Connelli's unmistakeable voice filled the room.

"Don't turn it off," Grania said wearily. "We're going to have to learn to live with it. And no one can deny the beauty of it. Not even me."

The *Queen of the Night* ended in its crash of thunder, and the ordinary sound of an ordinary voice took its place.

38

Josanne was not sure if she was imagining it, but her parents appeared to be far more human after Aunt Marian's party. They had both enjoyed it, and she felt that they had greater respect for her, now that she had shown she was capable of making wholly acceptable friends.

Rorie had sent her a picture postcard of Duart Castle, and had scribbled on the back of it, "You'll see this when you come to Mull". For some unaccountable reason, he hadn't forgotten the invitation which he had issued so light-heartedly during supper at Rule's. She had brought the postcard to the office, and had fixed it with a drawing pin to the wall beside her desk, along with the pictures of Majorca, Ibiza and Malta, which she had received from members of the staff who were on holiday.

She had forgotten how awful London was in August, with hot pavements, and weary tourists cluttering up the buses during the rush hours. She had taken her holiday early this year, lured into doing so by an advertisement about April in Paris. It had sounded lovely, but it had rained a good deal, and was now almost forgotten.

Her parents were in Scotland, and she enjoyed having the flat to herself. She could turn up her record-player as loud as she liked, and could play the same record over and over again, which she never dared to do unless she was alone. During the lunch hour, she had bought the new recording of *La Traviata* with Connelli as Violetta, Costa as Alfredo, Silvano as Papa Germont, and with Bardini, of course, as conductor.

The picture of Connelli on the box was beautiful, but the notes that came with the libretto gave little information about her which was not already known. Connelli refused to be interviewed either in the press, or on radio or television. The Maestro probably knew how to maintain an air of mystery about her, how to keep the public intrigued.

Mr. Painter came into the office. He had been at a meeting all afternoon. Finding her alone, with a neat pile of letters awaiting his signature, he told her he would see to them himself, and that she could go home.

"You'll avoid the crowds," he said, indicating the box of records. "You don't want to risk Connelli in a crowded bus!"

He watched her tidy her desk methodically, and check through the pile of letters before handing them to him. She was completely reliable. He had never known a secretary who worked so well. He hoped she wouldn't think he bestowed special favours on her because she was a friend of the Lamonts.

She crossed Vauxhall Bridge Road, and bought an evening paper at Victoria Station. The stop-press caught her eye.

Connelli's tour of Australia cancelled due to illness.

That was all, but it was enough to make her decide to take a taxi to Aunt Marian's address, in the hope of finding out what was wrong.

Marian was delighted to see her. It had been a very diffident Josanne who had called in to thank her for the party, but a few days later she had called again, and now Marian found that she looked forward to Josanne's company. They had tea together, with pancakes and oatcakes and scones and slices of cold dumpling, because Marian had never lost the habit of providing what had always been available at Kilcaraig.

"I won't have to make supper tonight," Josanne said. She had told Marian about *La Traviata* and the treat that was in store for her when she got home; then Marian told her that she had talked to Isabella on the telephone. She was suffering from a severe cold, and had been advised to take a long rest.

"She's always under pressure, the poor little soul," Marian said. "My husband was a doctor before he became a novelist, and he was a good psychologist before the jargon tossed around these days had even been invented. He knew about stress and repression. Emotional problems can affect health. I've warned Rorie. He can prattle about Isabella as much as he pleases, but she has to keep her thoughts to herself."

"He's told her he loves her. Surely that's balm for hurt minds," Josanne said, unconsciously revealing her own sense of deprivation.

"There's a time and a place for everything, and the outpourings of youthful ardour are best left to the close season, if such a thing exists in the world of opera!"

"Do you often talk to Madame Connelli on the telephone?" Josanne asked, lapsing into the form of address which for some reason the newspapers applied to this particular *diva*.

Marian pursed her lips and pushed back an errant lock of hair. "I'm as bad as Rorie. I say too much, but I've only said it to you, and you're reliable. Yes, I talk to her quite often. I've appointed myself her honorary aunt."

When Josanne left Lowndes Square, she did so with a new sense of importance. Aunt Marian was Isabella Connelli's friend, as well as hers. She foresaw none of the complications that would arise as a result of being embroiled in the family affairs of the Lamonts.

She settled down to a blissful evening, listening to her records, while unknown to her Marian waited impatiently for a further telephone call from Milan.

*   *   *

Rorie left Kilcaraig in September, and he telephoned Josanne from Cirencester to tell her that he had started at the Agricultural College, but proposed to spend most of his weekends with Aunt Marian.

264

"Does she know?" Josanne asked suspiciously. As Rorie had never attended the Sorbonne for more than a few days at a time when he was in Paris, it seemed unlikely that he would settle down in Gloucestershire.

During the weeks that followed, Josanne became increasingly disappointed because she heard nothing more from him, a point which would not escape the notice of her mother, who was always around whenever the telephone rang. Then one day came a picture postcard of the Eiffel Tower. Rorie had written on it, "I'm over in Paris for a few days to see Niall". Josanne wasn't deceived. Connelli's recovery from her illness had been much publicized, and she was singing *The Daughter of the Regiment* at the Paris opera.

"I don't expect you'll see him again until the office Christmas party," Sybil said sourly.

"Rorie's never been to the office party. If he had, I'd have seen him there ages ago!" But Josanne resolved to buy herself a new dress for the occasion.

In December, Connelli was back at the Milan Scala, singing her first *Norma*. Josanne knew that this was another step up the ladder that would one day lead to the coveted role of *Isolde*, and she scanned the review pages of all the newspapers and magazines that she could find. As usual, Connelli had come up to the expectations of audience and critics alike. Every fresh triumph must remove her a degree further from Rorie. Josanne wondered if Rorie realized this, and Aunt Marian could throw no light on the matter. "He saw her a wee bit in Paris, but he's back in Cirencester now, as good as gold," was all that she would say.

Sybil had been right about Rorie attending the Carnworth, Prior and Dutton party.

Josanne noticed him as soon as she arrived at Grosvenor House, but she hid herself among groups of people from the office, hoping he wouldn't see her. The dress she had bought was plain and black, and her parents had protested that she was far too young for that style. Seeing herself in the looking-glass, she hadn't agreed with them. She felt it enhanced her ethereal look, and at the same time gave her dignity, but at the sight of Rorie, her knees had turned to water.

"Shall we dance?"

He was standing in front of her, bronzed and smiling, and her friends were watching her with envy. He led her towards the dance floor.

During supper he said, "You're coming to Kilcaraig for the New Year, aren't you?"

"I haven't been asked," she stammered.

"Yes, you have. I know my mother wrote to you, because I was with her. She came to see me at Circencester and I posted the letter myself."

"I didn't receive it."

"I expect I gave the wrong address," he said cheerfully. "You'll come just the same. We're expecting you, and it's time you met the rest of the family."

Josanne could picture his home. A castle in the Highlands, surrounded by mountains, heather and lochs. Deer looking like the Monarch of the Glen poised in strategic places, and flights of wild geese honking overhead.

The sound of the bagpipes would be wafted in the light wind, and dinner would be eaten in a dining-hall, its walls covered with trophies. The men would wear kilts, and when they toasted the Queen, they would toss their wine glasses over their shoulders, smashing them so that they could never be used again for a lesser purpose.

She caught Rorie's eye. He was watching her, amused. "What was that long think about?" he asked.

Surprised at herself, she told him. He roared with laughter, an infectious laugh, so that people next to him joined in.

"That settles it. You'll come, even if only to shatter your illusions. And if anyone tosses their wine glasses over their shoulder, there'll be hell to pay, because they're Waterford and Mama is very fond of them! Come, we'll go and ask your parents right away."

"They'll never allow it. They'll be in bed. They'll be furious."

But Rorie laughed and steered her towards the exit.

Her parents were in bed, but they were not furious at all. Dazed, Sybil sat in her dressing-gown and listened to Rorie talking to his mother on the telephone, while William poured himself another brandy, and smiled at his nervous daughter. When Sybil was handed the telephone, all she could say was "Yes", and "How kind of you". Then she rang off and exclaimed, "I couldn't refuse that! Mrs. Lamont has chartered a plane to fly you from Glasgow to Mull on New Year's Eve. Just imagine that! And you'll be returned the same way on New Year's Day. You'll have to miss one day in the office, so you'll need Mr. Painter's permission, but obviously there won't be any difficulty about that."

Rorie wanted her to go back with him to the party, but Josanne had had enough excitement. She saw him out of the flat, her parents for once staying in the drawing-room instead of hovering in the hall.

"Do you always get your way so easily?" she asked him. He smiled a smile that made her heart miss a beat.

"I almost always do – in the end," he said, and he bounded down the stairs, not bothering to wait for the lift.

39

During the few days that followed the party, Josanne went out with Rorie several times, to a theatre or a concert, then on to dinner. She knew by instinct that he would never look upon her as other than a friend, but it was a special sort of friendship, because he could confide in her about Isabella.

He had been indignant when the flowers and letters he sent to Isabella had been acknowledged by a printed slip, bearing a facsimile of her signature, but the Maestro was always pleasant to him on the telephone, and there came a day when he was allowed to talk to her himself. After that, there had been other telephone conversations, and when she had recovered and was singing again, he had seen her in Paris.

He implied that they were together at a party. Josanne guessed that they were together, but alone. Rorie didn't elaborate. He had learnt how to be discreet, and he had also learnt how to dissemble. Isabella had suffered from a severe cold, with its aftermath of catarrh, enemy of any singer. It could be that the explanation was true.

Marian spent Christmas at Kilcaraig, and Rorie flew south with her immediately afterwards, so that he was able to collect Josanne from Maybank Court on New Year's Eve for the flight back to Scotland.

A few weeks ago the Murrays would not have believed it possible for anyone to board an aeroplane as unconcernedly as they themselves boarded a bus, but they had come to accept Rorie as a different species from anyone they had met before. Sybil made no attempt to conceal her surprise that Josanne had struck up such an astonishing friendship, while William sipped his brandy and hoped it wasn't going to end in tears. Sometime he might have to take action, but not yet. Playing the father, heavy or otherwise, was a role he preferred, if possible, to avoid.

The flight to Glasgow was without incident, but the tiny plane that flew them to Mull was rather bumpy, and Josanne sucked barley sugar as they skimmed over mountains and lochs, and a strip of sea that looked like blue ribbon.

The little airfield on Mull had been cleared of the sheep and cows that usually grazed it, but Josanne knew nothing of this as she climbed out of the plane, and was greeted by Rorie's twin. Niall's eyes were dark grey, not blue, and he was a little taller and a little more slender than his brother, but he had Rorie's fascinating smile, and she loved the swing of his kilt as he led her to his car. It was a modest little estate car, not a limousine the size of a hearse, as she had expected. She was soon to learn that there was nothing ostentatious about the Lamonts.

At a command from Niall, the collie that was occupying the front seat made way for her. She sat back contentedly while the cases were squeezed in among the packs of fertilizer and hen food that Niall had collected from Tobermory. Then Niall was beside her, and they lurched across the rough ground which separated them from the road, Rorie perched uncomplainingly on a large tin of paint, because of the back seat being folded away to convert the car into a van.

Her first impression of Mull was its wildness, its grandeur, and its desolation. That this twisting one-track road was the main road leading to Iona Ferry seemed to her to be quite extraordinary, but she realized that there was very little traffic and that even during the tourist season the passing-places, marked by black-and-white painted posts, must have proved to be adequate. Here and there, sheep wandered across the road, and at one point she gasped with pleasure, because there were deer, staring at them, motionless but alert, on the mountain-side.

"Your Monarch of the Glen," Rorie said. "They're stuffed, and they're usually only on display for tourists!"

Josanne laughed as the deer bounded out of sight.

"If you believe what Rorie tells you, you'll believe anything," Niall said, turning to her for a moment with that marvellous smile. "I'm not usually so silent, but driving on these roads means a great deal of concentration. We never know what's going to leap in front of the car."

Rorie made up for Niall's silence. He kept up a running commentary, showing points of interest where there appeared to be nothing but bracken and heather, shimmering lochs, and menacing mountains. He knew every stick and stone of the place, all of its history and its legends, but his remarks were made lightly, arousing interest, not treating her to a lecture.

268

The road had become very twisty, and she realized that she was beginning to feel sick, and she had finished her barley sugar on the plane. She stifled a yawn, and prayed that Kilcaraig was not as far away as she feared. Then Niall pulled into a lay-by, leaned across her and opened the door. She scrambled out, and managed to walk a few yards away before the worst happened. When she returned Niall handed her a bundle of tissues.

"Feeling better?"

"How did you guess?"

"When my little sister starts to yawn, I stop. And we weren't being callous. We didn't come and cherish you, because there are moments in life when one prefers to be alone!"

Josanne felt relief from tension, as if it were sawdust spilling out of a doll. This man had a quality she had never known before, an ability to make her feel wholly at ease. She wouldn't even have cared if he had seen her being sick.

"You're very kind," she said.

"You're welcome!" he replied, and she saw that there were lights twinkling in the distance, lost for a moment as they rounded a bend, then back there ahead with a large house on a hill, outlined in the dusk, a light in every window, the traditional Highland welcome she had known she would receive.

The burn under the bumpy bridge was in full spate after heavy rain, and the trees dripped on the car as they drove slowly up the mossy drive, but the castle door was wide open, and there were people gathered to greet them in the porch.

Catriona Lamont ran out to open the car door, and Grania Lamont greeted Josanne with an embrace. Josanne recognized that her hostess, now wearing a pullover and skirt, was the woman in grey chiffon she had seen at the opera in what seemed like a world away. She was introduced to Rorie's father, and she wondered how she could have failed to guess at the relationship. The similarity to Rorie was almost absurd.

"*Ceud mile failte.* A hundred thousand welcomes. I'm Chrissie, and I look after you all." The white-haired woman about whom Rorie had talked so much ushered her into the hall, and Catriona showed her up to her bedroom.

"Tea will be in the library," she said. "Straight across the hall, at the foot of the stairs. Michael Ames will be there. He's blind – world war one – but that doesn't worry him, so you mustn't let it worry you either. That door leads to your bathroom. No need to avoid squeaky floorboards if you want to go to the loo during the night! Central heating isn't hot enough at this time of year – kick the electric fire if it doesn't work." Catriona demonstrated the kick, and the element glowed red. "That's MacNeill tartan you're wearing. Where did it come from?" She spoke with admiration, not impertinence.

"Off the peg at Harrods,"-Josanne replied, taking her literally. Then she remembered the Highland obsession with genealogy. "My mother's mother was a MacNeill of Ardcross."

"Away! Then you must be related to us. Mama's father was a MacNeill of Ardcross, but he never married her mother. It's a closely guarded family secret."

"Then you shouldn't have told me."

"Everyone knows. Mama's the only one who pretends the great deception worked. It's impossible to keep secrets in Mull." She began to leave the room, but turned back at the door. "I'll wait for you if you hate going into a room full of strangers."

Josanne smiled. "It's all right," and strangely, she meant it. Her new-found self-confidence would last at least until she returned to London. She began to unpack, then she went to inspect her bathroom, with its sunken bath and gold dolphin taps and bidet. It was clearly a relic of Robert Dutton's regime.

Back in her bedroom, she heard a deep sigh, and discovered that a young black labrador dog had hidden under the bed. He had chewed up a pair of tights and some cleansing tissues. Laughing, she took him by the collar, and led him down the stairs.

*　　　*　　　*

Roderick Lamont was playing the bagpipes for an eightsome reel, and Josanne, who had been disappointed when she was told not to wear a long dress, knew the reason why, now that she was being whirled round by Donald MacPhail from Caraig Farm, who had marvellously strong arms. Next, it was Niall who was swinging her, then back to Donald. What an evening it had been!

Tea in the library was on the Aunt Marian scale, scones, pancakes, fruit cake, while she sat in the place of honour, the huge Kilcaraig chair, once occupied by the old Laird of Kilcaraig, Grania's grandfather. He was long dead, but watched them from his portrait on the wall, his blue eyes smiling their approval.

Mrs. Lamont had been right about Michael Ames. Rorie had described Josanne to him, and he had laughed and added, "She must have beautiful legs, or you wouldn't have asked her here, Rorie!" He turned to Josanne, as if he could see her. "There'll be some competition tonight! That poor Lucas girl will break her heart when she sees the opposition Rorie's imported."

The Lucas family came to dinner. They had bought Duff, the

small estate near Tobermory, and Margaret Lucas made it patently obvious that Michael's observation had been correct. She was being swung around by Rorie now, but this energetic dancing was frustrating for a girl wanting to be held in a man's arms.

When the reel was over, Josanne, hot and laughing, sat down beside Michael Ames, who was on one of the benches that lined the walls, his imagination following the activities of the packed village hall.

"Niall tells me you dance beautifully," he said.

"So does he. And he's a wonderful piper. So is Rorie. What an amazing family they are."

Even Catriona could play the accordion, or bang out a Hesitation Waltz on the piano. For years Josanne had despised amateur talent, but here in this hall, bright with decorations and a big Christmas tree, she had discovered what talent was, amateur or otherwise. She had heard Gaelic songs sung by local people, as they should be sung, and had heard piping that would put many a professional to shame.

The children were playing a traditional game which involved a lot of singing and miming, under the amiable and concealed direction of their teacher, while the adults watched and admired. Josanne had been struck by the natural acceptance of the young at this adult function, and could see Chrissie across the room, hugging a toddler who was sitting on her knee; then her attention was diverted to the ladies of the Women's Rural Institute, who emerged from a side room with heavily laden trays of sandwiches and cakes, and with baskets of cups for tea. She saw how deftly Michael helped himself to a cup, and held it out to be filled with tea from a huge kettle, and milk from a big enamel jug. The children were now settled at two trestle tables, which had been pushed into the centre of the room, and Niall and Rorie were helping them to pull their crackers, and put on their paper hats.

The arrival of the New Year was heralded by a roll on the drums, and a trumpet fanfare was played by a young soldier from the Argyll and Sutherland Highlanders, who was home on leave. After that, there were handshakes and kissings, and more handshakes, with everyone knowing one another, and making Josanne feel that she was part of one enormous Kilcaraig family. Finally, *Auld Lang Syne* was sung, properly, with no hands crossed until "Here's a hand, my trusty friend" was reached. Josanne had remembered that this was the correct way to do it, and a little thrill of pleasure ran through her when she realized that when she did cross hands, it was Niall and Rorie who were on either side of her.

The Lamonts and their guest stayed for one more dance, then

they left with the Lucas family who had a long drive ahead of them to Duff.

Back at the castle, they sat round the peat fire in the drawing-room, and toasted the New Year in Roderick's favourite brand of whisky. Catriona was sleepy, but refused to go to bed until Aunt Marian had telephoned her customary greetings. They could hardly hear what she said, because somehow she had got hold of a piper for her party, and the Lowndes Square flat was reverberating to the strains of *Scotland the Brave*.

"Shall I wake the household if I get up early tomorrow and go for a walk?" Josanne asked. "I'd love to have a look round the place."

"It won't be daylight until about eight," Grania said. "But if you'd like to explore, there will be time for you to go out after breakfast. Do wrap up warmly."

Half an hour later, Josanne was in bed, and had fallen asleep almost the moment her head touched the pillow. She woke up at seven the next morning, dressed, and went downstairs. There was no sign of life in the house, but she looked into the kitchen and found that there was a coffee pot on the Aga. Someone would have gone out to see to the aminals. She had a cup of coffee. She would have breakfast when she got back from her walk.

It was still dark when she went outside, but not too dark to see where she was going. She walked round to the back of the house, past the walled garden, and along a footpath which led up to the hill. Very soon, she had reached a peat-stack. She decided to climb a little higher, so that she could still see the castle, but would also have a view of the rising sun shimmering on Loch Caraig.

Across a field, on the far side of the burn, she could make out the village hall, scene of last night's festivities. Lights were snapping on in the row of cottages and in the post office and the manse, but the church and the school remained dark and almost invisible. The silence was so complete that her ears buzzed.

She leant against a boulder, inhaling the scent of peat, which clung upon the air. It was then that she saw it, something flickering white, something making a squelching sound that disturbed the silence. It must be a bird, perhaps a heron. Alert, she narrowed her eyes and tried to make out what it was.

Very suddenly a breeze whipped up, tousling her hair and blowing her skirt above her knees, as if some invisible hand had pressed the button of a wind-machine. She shivered, put her hands in the pockets of her wind-cheater, then she saw the movement again, something too substantial to be a bird. She moved forward to get a closer view, and in the grey light which preceded dawn she realized that she was seeing the swishy tail of a Highland cow which had sunk into a bog, every frantic effort to extricate itself serving only to increase its plight.

She was wearing the brown brogues in which she proposed to travel, and as she picked her way towards the cow, each step brought her ankle deep into the squelchy, peaty moss. When she reached the cow, she saw that it appeared to be in the last stages of exhaustion; tears were coursing down the side of its face. She had never known that an animal could cry, but she did know that there was nothing on earth she could do to rescue the poor beast from its plight.

There were lights on now all over the castle and throughout the village, but there was not a soul in sight. She patted the cow and gave an ineffectual tug at one of its horns; then she shouted "Help", startling herself by the urgency and the sound of her voice, despairing that it would be carried away from human habitation by the wind. Then, in the distance, she saw a figure walking along the village street, and she realized it was someone who was tapping with a stick. Michael Ames. Michael Ames, who, being blind, would probably have cultivated his other senses to a marked degree. If anyone could hear her, he could.

When she was a child, the hall-porter at Maybank Court had shown her how he whistled for a taxi. She tried this now, putting her fingers into her mouth, and blowing hard. She was astonished by the sound she made.

Instantly Michael Ames stood still, and listened.

Josanne whistled again. The only white thing she possessed was her pants. She removed her shoes and tights with lightening speed, whistled again, and waved them; then she remembered the futility of if all. Michael was blind. He could hear but not see her.

She watched him turn away. Almost sobbing, she stood by the cow, her pants in her hand, and her shoes and tights lying beside the bog. A few minutes later, Niall Lamont found her, still rooted to the spot, holding tightly to the horns of the cow, as if by so doing she could prevent the head from sinking under the water.

"You'll catch your death!" Niall exclaimed. "Go straight back to the house. There's more help coming. Michael alerted the Manse, and the minister phoned through."

Her teeth were chattering. She tried to answer him but couldn't.

"Put on your pants," he said, and laughed. Suddenly the fear and tension were broken, and she could laugh too. She wriggled into her pants and tights while Niall made soothing noises to the cow, and the sound of voices came closer and closer.

There were six in the rescue party. Roderick and Rorie Lamont were two of them, and Catriona, carrying a can of something, brought up the rear.

Josanne watched the operation, too fascinated to be cold. The man attached ropes to the cow, and with the skill which was the result of years of experience, they eased her out of the bog. She lay on her side and was rubbed vigorously with sacks, while Catriona spooned the concoction from the can into the cow's mouth.

"It's oatmeal laced with whisky," she explained to Josanne.

"She'll be all right now, she'll be great altogether," someone said. Then Josanne felt an arm across her shoulders.

"You won't be great altogether. You'll be dead if you don't get into a hot bath quickly." It was Niall, and he gave her a little push towards Catriona. "Take care of her," he said. "Our heroine has saved Dougie MacColl's best cow."

Grania was waiting for her at the castle, and Chrissie, seeing the bedraggled figure, ran straight upstairs to prepare a bath for her.

Later that morning, having luxuriated in the green foam produced by Catriona's best bath-salts, and having borrowed a pair of Catriona's shoes, Rorie drove her to the MacPhails' farm, south of Kilcaraig, to pay a traditional New Year's Day visit, and to enjoy a *sensation*, which proved to be a tot of whisky. Shortbread and ginger cake were also provided, and when they left, she was given a pound of fresh butter, stamped with a thistle pattern, to take back to London. She received a second pat of butter when they visited the MacGillivrays' croft, but she managed to refuse, with tact, the offer of a hen from Sandy MacPherson who stood at his cottage door, prepared to wring its neck there and then.

Before returning to the castle for an early lunch, they did a short detour, so that Rorie could point out the ruined village of Caraig, and the shell of what had once been a prosperous farm house. "Niall dreams of restoring it all one day, making a shooting lodge out of the farm house, and using the profits to subsidize the cottages for islanders who can't pay fancy prices for a place of their own. We're both romantics in our different ways. I don't know which of us is the most unrealistic!"

They stopped at the post office-cum-general-store, which was closed because of the New Year's holiday, but a number of people were gathered outside, and Josanne found herself being shaken by the hand, and congratulated on her show of commonsense over the cow. The people implied, although they didn't say it, that for a girl from London she was quite remarkable. The cow, she was assured, was in Dougie MacColl's cow shed, none the worse for her mishap.

Niall was to accompany her on the flight to Glasgow. She was rather in awe of him, not exactly scared of him, but not at ease with him, as she was with Rorie. Yet this morning he had been gentle. The touch of his hand had conveyed a marvellous sense of assurance, and his laugh, when he saw her white pants, was infectious and warm.

Catriona went to the air strip with them, so that Rorie wouldn't be alone when he drove home.

Grania, turning back into the house after waving them off, said to Roderick, "Marian was right about that girl. She's got what it takes."

"What it takes for what?" he asked, smiling, knowing so well the way her mind worked.

"For Kilcaraig," Grania said.

Roderick took her in his arms, and pressed his lips to hers. Over all the years, she had not changed one little bit.

40

Rorie telephoned Josanne from Cirencester. He asked her if she was going to the Caledonian Ball in May. She said – yes, she was – which he said was a pity, as his parents were taking a party, and they would like her to come with them.

His end of the telephone had sounded very noisy. He must have been in a public place. Her end was even worse, because she was in the sitting-room at home, and both her parents were with her, ostensibly reading, but naturally listening to all she had to say. She didn't blame them for that. Everyone listened to telephone conversations, even those they professed not to hear.

"Was he inviting you to something?" her mother asked.

"The Caledonian Ball."

"You never told me you were going to it. Who with?"

Josanne wanted to escape from the room. She wanted to scream, or cry, or kick something. She was a fool. She had completely lost her head, and had deprived herself of a wonderful experience. She adored the Caledonian Ball, and to go to it with the Lamonts would be another daydream come true.

"I asked you who you are going with."

"I'm not."

"Then why did you say you were?"

"Because I don't want always to be beholden to the Lamonts."

"He wouldn't have asked you if he didn't want you," Sybil said. She would keep to the subject all evening, annoyed that Josanne was not going to be seen out and having a good time, maddened that her only daughter was incapable of maintaining a friendship with anyone worth knowing. Her only lasting companion was that dull girl, Hope Garnett.

"He'll find out you weren't going when he sees you're not there," her father said.

"I'll say that I had a cold, or something." She must somehow get out of the room before doing something shameful like crying. "Please don't go on about it. I just don't want to go with him."

Her father shrugged and picked up his book.

Josanne went to her bedroom, and flinging on her coat, she tied on a headscarf, then left the flat, slamming the front door, so that her parents would know she'd gone out.

She did some window shopping in Kensington High Street, wandering past the big stores, and on to the smaller ones, jewellers and lingerie shops; then she turned back and bought an evening paper outside the Underground Station.

She thought about going to a film, but felt she couldn't walk out of the flat and disappear for hours without telling her parents where she was going. Sometimes, when she was upset about something, she went for a walk, never more than that. She decided to telephone home if she found something she wanted to see. She managed to open the paper and a photograph of Isabella Connelli caught her eye. She was to sing Tosca on television tonight.

Josanne almost ran home. As she entered the flat, she called to her parents to switch on B.B.C. 2. She need not have been in a panic, because it was only the second act that was to be transmitted.

She was ignored when she went back into the sitting-room, but the television had been turned on, and a picture of dolphins at play was silently flickering on the screen. The untouched copy of the *Radio Times* was on a table with other magazines. Josanne made a mental note that she must always look through it. It would have been the last misery of a wretched day if she had discovered tomorrow what she could have seen tonight.

She read the short notes about the plot, then the larger ones about Connelli's astonishing career. She had read about that many times before, but tonight millions of people would be seeing for the first time a performance that was unsurpassable, and hearing a voice that was unique. She adjusted the sound and picture, and sat expectantly in front of the set; her parents doggedly read their books, but after the first few compelling introductory bars, William put his aside, and he too watched the screen.

"Please turn it down, I can't concentrate," Sybil said. Josanne took no notice. Isabella was singing off-stage. Soon she would be on camera, thinking of the conductor and the prompter, and of not tripping over her train, or kneeling on a drawing pin. These little anecdotes about her life on the operatic stage had added a new dimension to Josanne's enjoyment, but now Isabella was there before her, commanding, gorgeous, and very soon not Isabella at all, but Tosca suffering, anguished, pleading.

Sybil put her book down. "You wouldn't think, when we met her at the party, that she could make so much noise," she said. William winced, but Josanne didn't hear. She was lost in the beauty of it all.

"I can't understand why you refused that invitation," Sybil said, the moment the act was over, and the credits were being shown on the screen. "It's thanks to Rorie Lamont that we met Connelli. They know so many interesting people."

"I can't keep on accepting hospitality and never returning it," Josanne said, coming back to reality with a bump. She had often said this before. She had always been discouraged from inviting her friends home.

"But we're going to have a party. Your father and I were talking about it while you were sulking off for that walk. You know quite a lot of young people now. There's the Lamont twins, and Stewart Ferguson, and those men you meet at the Young Conservatives, and your cousin Hector MacNeill."

"Mother, I haven't set eyes on him since I was about two! We can't scrounge round inviting remote acquaintances!"

"It won't be a large party," Sybil said, exasperated. "Hector's mother wrote on her Christmas card that now he's in the Navy, he's sometimes in London. We should have asked him here long ago."

Josanne could think of nothing to say. She hoped that her parents would have changed their minds by the morning, but there she was wrong, and the first she heard about the arrangements that were being made was three weeks later, when she received another telephone call from Rorie.

"What happened to you at the Caledonian Ball?" he asked.

"I had a cold."

"Bad luck." He didn't press the point. The ball was not as important to him as it was to her. "Anyway, we're all coming to your party, Mama and Papa, as well as Niall and myself. It was so good of you to ask Michael. He can't come, but he was so pleased that you thought about him."

There was no one in the sitting-room tonight. Josanne remembered not to say "When is the party?" – he would know that she had not been consulted, and would guess how embarrassed she must be. She didn't know that she had ever told her parents Michael's surname. They must have looked in her address book, where she kept her Christmas card list.

Rorie would think the line had gone dead, but after a pause, he said, "Isabella can't manage it".

Josanne stifled a gasp. "Does she know who we are?" She couldn't pretend she knew about this.

"Of course she knows. She often talks about Aunt Marian's party. She goes to dazzling functions, clad in mink and diamonds, and full of witty, flirtatious badinage, but not to small friendly affairs like that. It's sickening that she can't come. Mama and Papa would have to meet her, and then their objections would vanish."

"It's your own fault they're against her. You shouldn't have told them about her." She wanted to keep the subject of the party in abeyance until she found out when it was to be, and what had been planned.

"Don't you start! I've had it all for months from Niall. He's a dark horse. He'd never write a letter that would injure anyone's reputation."

Josanne could believe this. "Does she know you've set off this whispering campaign about her?"

"Of course she doesn't. I didn't mean to set it off. It just happened."

"It wouldn't have happened if you hadn't been in such a hurry to brag about her. You must never, never, in a fit of conscience, admit to her what you've done. Being so famous makes it much worse for her. A pedestal can so easily become a pillory."

"You do sometimes come out with statements that make me squirm."

"That's what I meant to do."

When he had rung off, she wondered how she had been able to keep up a conversation with him, she had been so shocked over the disclosure about the party. She felt ashamed, but when her parents came home she managed to thank them for the arrangements they had made, and as the appointed date approached, she found to her surprise that she was feeling excited.

There was to be a buffet supper in the flat, run by a team of caterers, and then the younger guests were to go to "Toni's", a very respectable, very fashionable club.

Josanne's pale blue dress had been designed and made for her by a leading couturier. As she waited in the sitting-room, which had been transformed into a spacious salon, beautifully decorated with flowers, she could see herself in a long mirror, and she liked what she saw. She felt pretty, oh so pretty, like the girl in the song.

Earlier, a cablegram of good wishes had been received from Isabella Connelli, who was in Buenos Aires. Josanne put it on the mantelpiece. It would make a talking point.

To her relief, Rorie was one of the first to arrive. "I thought you might need a helping hand to warm people up at the beginning," he said to Josanne. "I'm never at a loss when talking to gorgeous girls, but no one tonight will look more gorgeous than you do." His smile was kindly and admiring. He was a very nice person. She sipped her champagne and watched his progress round the room, but soon she had forgotten about Rorie, because she was too busy receiving the flow of guests, among them Aunt Marian, and Roderick and Grania, who would lend colour to any gathering.

Niall arrived with the Fergusons, having flown from Paris with Stewart, who was still at the Sorbonne. Josanne felt an unexpected pang of annoyance that he should be with Pauline Ferguson right at the start of the evening. Mary had been too young to be invited.

Hector MacNeill was the last guest to arrive. He had come from Portsmouth, and Josanne was proud of him. He was tall and good-looking, with the blue eyes she associated with people who spent their lives gazing out to sea. He teased her about the last time they had met, which was when they had shared a bath twenty years ago.

During supper, everyone was mingling happily and the Connelli telegram had been spotted, and was being handed round like a trophy.

"Our pin-up *prima donna*," Hector said. "She's all over the ward-room walls, delicious and decolletée. It's astonishing that an opera star should become top of the pops!"

Rorie kept up a look of studied indifference, but Josanne knew that he would be noting every word that was said.

"She's a very nice person," she said, fearing that her cousin might launch into the sort of anecdotes sailors could tell, and Rorie had better not hear.

There were sixteen of them at the table reserved at "Toni's", and Niall, who had organized them into cars and taxis, now looked after the seating arrangements, so that Josanne had no responsibility for anything, and could concentrate on enjoying herself. She did. All her misgivings were forgotten as she laughed and talked and danced.

It was daylight when they left the club, and it was Niall who drove her home. He complimented her on her appearance, and on the way she had acted as hostess, with such assurance and charm.

"But I'm hideously shy," she said. "I always feel I must flash shyness, like those lights on ambulances and breakdown vans. Besides, you did all the hard work for me. You and Rorie and Hector MacNeill."

"There was nothing to do, it was all so well planned."

"I was afraid you'd find my friends very dull." She smiled at him as he pulled up in front of Maybank Court. She knew she was safe with Niall. She seldom went out with men, but when she did, they all seemed to expect the goodnight kiss they never received from her.

He said goodbye to her outside the double mahogany doors at the flat, then, astonishingly, he kissed a lock of her hair. "That's something to remember me by," he said, and in a moment she had shut the door behind her, and could hear him running down the stairs. It was just friendship, but it was touching and refreshing.

She tip-toed into the flat which was now completely restored to order. She went to her parents' door wanting to thank them for the party, and to apologize for having been so tiresome in the past. Then she heard her mother speak.

"She looked quite pretty tonight. She might get herself a husband after all."

Josanne shrank away and went to her bedroom. She had felt pretty, oh so pretty. Now she saw that she was just an ordinary girl, with a shiny nose, messed up hair, and eyes that were pink because she hadn't been wearing her spectacles. Her lipstick had worn off. Only her dress was lovely. It was all over, and she was a drab girl who might get a husband after all. After all.

41

A whole year had passed since Adrian Ferguson had knocked Josanne into the gutter, and had introduced her to people who had so much affected her life.

Connelli was to sing five times at Covent Garden, and Adrian had booked his usual box for two performances, inviting Josanne to join his family as before. She studied the publicity leaflet. Connelli as

Mimi in *La Bohème*, and as Adina in *L'Elisir D'Amore*. Finally as Violetta in *La Traviata* for one performance. Adrian hadn't booked for that. She longed to see it again, but after what had happened last year, she didn't dare to use subterfuge, and by the time she had changed her mind, it was too late. The Personal Column in *The Times* was full of people wanting to hear Connelli.

One day she arrived home from the office to find nobody in the flat. She remembered that her parents were having drinks with friends, which would mean a late meal. She decided to wash her hair.

She looked in the oven. Something in a casserole was being kept hot, and there was fruit salad and cream. Nothing for her to do.

When she heard the telephone, she didn't know for how long it had been ringing, because the water had been making such a noise in her ears. She hated answering the phone and hoped it would stop before she reached it. She wound a towel round her head, lifted the receiver, and gave her number.

"May I please speak to Miss Josanne Murray?" It was a woman's voice. The accent was peculiar.

"Speaking."

"This is Isabella Connelli." Josanne nearly dropped the telephone. This must be a joke. "Rorie Lamont asked me to get in touch with you." There was a pause. Josanne waited for one of the Ferguson girls to burst out laughing, but the voice continued. "He told me you are going to *La Bohème* tomorrow night – is that correct?"

"Yes, I'm going with friends."

"He didn't say that. He said you usually go alone. I wanted to tell you that it's cancelled for tomorrow night. I can't appear, so there's no sense in putting it on." She said it without a trace of vanity. She was stating an obvious fact.

"Are you ill?" Josanne was still suspicious.

A little laugh, a very distinctive laugh. "No, only indisposed. Flying gives me earache, and I seem to have a double dose of jet-lag. I expect another performance will be arranged. Please tell your friends. It will be in the papers, what they should do." On the telephone, her curious mixture of Italian and Irish accent was more pronounced. It sounded like someone trying to disguise her voice. Perhaps it was a joke after all.

"I'm sorry about your earache. You're too nice to be ill."

"You are most kind." That was Connelli for sure. "I'm just sorry to disappoint people. I hate doing this."

"I'll see you in *L'Elisir D'Amore* on Wednesday," Josanne said, not wanting to ring off.

"And *Traviata*?"

"No, I couldn't get seats for that." It was nearly true.

"I can fix that. I have a box for Rorie's parents, who were bringing a blind friend, but they can't come. Mrs. Danvers will bring him instead. There will be plenty of room for you. I think Rorie will be there, and his brother. I'll telephone Mrs. Danvers about it."

Josanne could hear her parents come into the flat. They had paused in the hall to hear what she was saying.

"It's terribly kind of you to bother." Her mother was in the sitting-room now, signing who is it? Josanne shook her head, not wanting to miss anything Connelli said, for she spoke so softly.

"I hope you'll enjoy *L'Elisir* and that you will see *Bohème*. I'm sure it will be arranged. And oh – I hear that your party was lovely. It was most kind of you to ask me to it. Thank you very much." She rang off.

"You shouldn't be answering the telephone with wet hair. You could get electrocuted." Sybil said. "Who was that?"

"Isabella Connelli." She had hoped her mother would be impressed. She wasn't. "She's arranging for me to see *La Traviata*, and she can't appear tomorrow night in *La Bohème* – so it's cancelled. I'll let the Fergusons know."

"Hasn't she got an understudy?"

"No, mother, there could be no understudy for Connelli." Josanne didn't know if this was the technical truth, however factual it might be.

"I wonder why she bothered to ring you? It's bound to be in the papers."

"Rorie asked her to."

"So he's still involved with her! That won't please his mother. She's worried about his being infatuated with such an unsuitable woman. But I wish you had reminded me about Covent Garden – I'd like to see her on the stage."

"I thought you didn't like sopranos."

"She's different," Sybil said, which was absolutely true.

*   *   *

Josanne did see *La Bohème*, because the other performances were switched so that Connelli could make the advertised number of appearances.

She had enjoyed the fun of *L'Elisir D'Amore*, but watching the death of Mimi was an unforgettable experience. She had heard the expression "not a dry eye in the house". Now she had witnessed it.

Somehow Bardini had kept control of the performance when

outbursts of applause threatened to interrupt some of the scenes, and the audience showed its appreciation when he joined the principals for the curtain calls. As always, it was Connelli who brought everyone to their feet.

"I can't believe she's real, even though I've met her," Pauline murmured when at last they left the box. Josanne was thinking the same thing. Connelli was a person whose talent set her apart from other people. It was sad, but true.

They found Grania, with Niall and Rorie, in the foyer. Grania's eyes were still glistening with tears.

"I'm never coming to an unhappy opera again," she said. "Roderick very sensibly desisted. We've cancelled *Traviata*, as we have to go back to Kilcaraig for the Red Cross sale. I haven't yet recovered from having my heart wrung out last year!"

"I'm going in Mrs. Danvers' box," Josanne said. She thought it unwise to mention Connelli's telephone call. "Rorie says that Michael Ames is coming specially from Kilcaraig. I'll be able to help to look after him."

"She's good with people and cows!" Niall laughed.

They were being jostled, and Grania pulled her stole around her, preparing to go outside. She paused and said, "Where are you going for your holidays, Josanne?"

Josanne invented a package tour of Norway.

"Nonsense, you'll come to Kilcaraig. Fix it up with Niall. Rorie won't remember. He has other things on his mind."

Josanne, confused, thanked her. Then, on an impulse, she said in a small, shy voice, "Mrs. Lamont?"

"Yes."

"Please don't be hard on her. All over the world people go home mopping up their tears because she's so marvellous. It's awful that she has no one at all of her own flesh and blood to care for her."

"Poor little Orphan Annie," Grania retorted in a voice of ice.

Josanne followed the Fergusons to their car.

*   *   *

During the next few days, Josanne expected to receive a letter from Grania, giving some reason why she could not, after all, spend her holidays at Kilcaraig. She should never have put in that appeal on behalf of Isabella Connelli. It was a family affair, nothing at all to do with her. She was about to make belated plans for the package holiday, when Rorie telephoned and invited her to dinner.

They dined at one of his many clubs. He helped her to choose what she wanted to eat and drink, and with Rorie there was never the agony of being worried about choosing something too expensive.

As soon as the ordering was done, Rorie brought out his diary, and it was arranged that she would spend the last two weeks of August at Kilcaraig. A great peace descended on her. She really was going back.

They talked a great deal about opera, but not at all about Isabella until they were having coffee. Then Rorie said, "She's spending the weekend at a stately home in Suffolk – target of an earl this time. I pretend I'm not worried, but I'm chewing my finger-nails".

"She must be wooed all over the globe. You're only worried because you happen to know about this. Besides, what she said at the party must apply to everyone."

"Until she falls in love." He didn't say that she didn't believe in love. She didn't believe in it because she had never experienced it. But she could fall in love one day, even though it wrecked her design for living.

"Rorie, I can understand your parents being so worried. You've set your sights on someone rather unusual, you must admit. But what does Niall think?"

"I don't know. Niall's inscrutable, even with me. But he's very determined and I know for certain that he'll never love in vain."

Josanne could imagine this. There was a disturbing aloofness about Niall that she found very attractive. Even on that flight to Glasgow, although she had enjoyed his company, she had left him with the feeling that he would always keep something in reserve. He would never talk, as Rorie did, about the girl he loved.

"When you see her standing there on the stage, with the audience thundering applause, don't you think you are crying for the moon? And who is the person you claim to love? Do you know her, or do you love the excitement, the enchantment, of the great *diva*?"

Rorie laughed. "Last time I saw Isabella, which was yesterday, she was wearing black tights and a leotard, with a wrap-around skirt, which is her rehearsal gear. She was walking up and down the room, hugging herself the way she does when she's nervous or concentrating. Then, at a sign from the répétiteur who coaches them in their parts, she was standing under a naked electric light bulb, looking like a waif and singing like someone straight out of heaven. The voice is the *diva* who stirs up rapturous applause. The person is the near-waif, Isabella. It's the person I love."

"It's a phantom you love. A creation of your imagination. Perhaps that's what we all do, and wake up with a shock to find reality."

"My parents have stood the test of time," Rorie said. "They know it can happen. They should believe it can happen to me."

"They loved one another," Josanne said. "If Isabella loved you, do you think they'd care about her background, or her age, or her fame, or anything at all? Don't you think what they are really trying to do is to prevent you from breaking your heart?"

He was silent, playing with a coffee spoon, trying to make it float on top of the cream.

"She very nearly loves me," he said at last.

"Isn't that like very nearly having measles? It really means nothing at all."

"If you're exposed enough to measles, you'll get them all right! Unless you've had them, or been immunized, and love isn't like that."

"Isn't it?" she said.

They were still arguing about it when he paid the bill.

During his supper party after *La Traviata*, Michael Ames said that this was the best outing he had been to since he saw *Chu Chin Chow* in 1916.

"The standard of singing was higher tonight," he told them. "And although there's a lot to be said for *The Cobbler's Song*, it doesn't compare with Verdi! Tonight isn't just an outing – it's an experience."

He had sat at the back of the box, with Marian, Josanne, and the twins in front of him. There was no need for him to try to see the stage.

Rorie's records had made him familiar with the score of the opera, and with Connelli's voice, but he admitted that hearing her in the flesh was even more moving, more entrancing, than listening to her on records. Aunt Marian had been so enthusiastic, and her applause so uninhibited, that Niall had to tell her to keep quiet, or she would receive a nasty look from Bardini.

"It's just as well Isabella decided not to come with us," she said, looking round the Savoy Grill. "She's so conspicuous, poor little soul, and she must be very tired. Even putting on all that make-up must take it out of her. She put some on me. Have you noticed how young I look?"

"Were you in her dressing-room?" Rorie asked, surprised.

"I went round with the flowers Michael bought her, and to thank her for getting us the box. I asked for her, and they let me in – no fuss at all." She beamed at Rorie. "And I met that nice conductor you said would be cross with me if I made a noise."

"What was he doing there?"

"Just sitting watching her putting on her make-up. What do you think he'd be doing in her dressing-room. especially with Motti and me and all those mirrors everywhere!"

Rorie scowled. Bardini always saw the soloists before a performance, but there was no need for him to watch Isabella dress. He himself had never been in her dressing-room. She had never suggested that he went there. She never gave him any kind of encouragement at all.

Josanne was making an effort to talk. Niall must find her very dull. He wouldn't understand how she felt after an opera. She was exhausted, almost as if she had sung every part herself. She caught his eyes. He smiled. He had a wonderful smile, lighting up his whole face.

"I'm being boring," he said. "I've seen a real, live Violetta, and I've watched her die. I'm emotionally disturbed!"

"So you feel like I do," she said, and she didn't try to speak again for quite some time. Michael and Marian and Rorie kept talking light nonsense, but she and Niall ate their steaks, and wallowed in their memory of the music.

Another piece of the human jigsaw puzzle had been fitted into its place.

42

Josanne travelled overnight to Crianlarich, and when she awoke in the morning, the train was chugging uphill, and there were mountains on either side. She leaned out of the window to feel the nip in the air and inhale the glorious scent of the Highlands.

Rorie was waiting for her at the lovely little station, and she felt proud as he helped her from the carriage and carried her cases down the long flight of steps leading to the lane where he had parked his car.

"Shout if you feel sick," he said, fastening her seat-belt. "I'm not observant like Niall."

She soon discovered that she had nothing to fear. Rorie drove carefully and well, and there was none of the swaying and constant gear changes that had been the cause of the trouble before.

"Did you get that sun tan in Mull?" she asked.

"I've been in Italy for a week. I spent last night at Inverary. It's all dove-tailed neatly with meeting you here today." He accelerated past a lorry, then said, "I stayed with the de Stefanis at their place on Lake Como."

"Aren't they the people who collect art treasures? And was she one of them?"

"She was one of them."

They drove for a long way in silence, each thinking their own thoughts, but neither of them embarrassed. There were road works as they approached Loch Awe, and the light changed to red just as they reached it. It would be a long time before the single-lane traffic allowed it to change to green again. Rorie switched off the ignition and lit a cigarette.

"You'll have seen a lot of Isabella," Josanne said. He could take this as a question or as a statement, whichever he liked.

"A moderate amount."

"What went wrong?" She was sure that something had, and that he wanted to talk about it. Rorie always wanted to talk about Isabella.

"She played her allotted part in her usual faultless way. She looked gorgeous, said all the right, charming things and was the *prima donna* of everyone's expectations. The Maestro beamed his satisfaction, and I lurked in the background thinking I should punctuate her performance with an occasional *bravo*. She's a chameleon – she changes her style according to her surroundings."

"Isn't that what she's supposed to do? Adapting to her audience is part of her job. The charming, friendly person we met at Aunt Marian's flat, the glamorous creature on display for the art collector and his friends. A different person must emerge when you're alone with her. A person nearer to the truth."

"I'm intoxicated by her, I'm jealous of her friends, I'm grateful when she flashes me a smile. I love her, but I don't know what I love, and her feelings for me can only be a sort of lust."

The light changed to green, and he drove forward cautiously over the newly tarred strip of road. They had reached a finished surface when he said, "We walked in the garden together, and we messed about in a boat on the lake. We danced in the evening, and then, like all the others, I held her in my arms. That was all. That was almost all. Now she's in Munich, appropriately singing Manon. I sometimes wish I could go into a monastery like des Grieux!"

Josanne gave him a quick look. His jaw was set, but his eyes, steadily on the road, betrayed nothing. By the end of two weeks, his natural craving to share his thoughts might compel him to confide in her. Time would tell.

The picture postcard beauty of Oban became apparent as soon as they drove down the curving hill into the town. There was time to do some shopping before they drove on board the Mull car ferry, and they had lunch in the cafeteria before going up on deck. To the north, Ben Nevis glittered in the sun. The sea was an unbelievable shade of blue, and on Mull Ben More stood out in sharp relief. Near it, but invisible, was Kilcaraig. As the boat approached Craignure, Duart Castle seemed to rise out of the rocks of Mull, and this was the sign that it was time to go down to the car-deck, and prepare to drive ashore.

They had nearly reached the Kilcaraig boundary fence when Rorie said, "I've been having Catriona trouble. She's discovered that she's pretty and shapely, and that she can bowl men over like ninepins, if she gives her mind to it."

They rattled over the cattle-grid, and he pointed to the boulder where at one time Catriona used to wait for home-coming members of the family. "She chatted up a hiker over there, and I suspect she gave him the full treatment. Anyhow, he got out of hand, and if I hadn't driven up I don't know what would have happened. He belted off when he saw me, leaving her with a torn blouse and her jeans ripped open. She was terribly shaken. I managed to smuggle her home, so Mama and Papa haven't found out."

"Surely you should have told them? The man shouldn't have been allowed to get away with it."

"It would do no good, and would only cause a scandal."

"Whatever sort of man would do a thing like that?"

A green dress, and green eyes wide with terror, but later closed in ecstasy. "I don't know," Rorie said. "I just don't know at all."

They swung left, over the bridge, past Caraig Lodge, and Josanne received a heart-warming welcome at the castle, and was shown up to the bedroom she had occupied at the New Year.

Last time, it was almost dark when she arrived, but today the sun was shining, and she had a glorious view across the field and the barn to the village, with Loch Caraig and the mountains as a background. She stood by the window, which she would not be able to open, as the sash-cords were broken. The Lamonts were a puzzle, aeroplanes when they were in the mood, yet not enough money to keep their castle in good repair.

She turned to her bookcase, and found that someone had been very thoughtful in making a selection that would appeal to her. Opera, lives of composers, poetry, and even some miniature scores. For lighter entertainment, there were thrillers from one of the book-clubs and rows of paperbacks. Then she remembered that tea would be ready, and that she hadn't yet seen Michael Ames. She went downstairs.

Michael heard her come into the room.

"Last time we met, you were standing us a gorgeous supper after *Traviata*," she said, accepting the cigarette that he offered her because she thought it was so clever of him to put his hand straight into the box.

"And the following day, Connelli came to see Marian, for whom she seems to have developed a deep affection." There was a hint of sarcasm in his voice. "I found her disturbing, ill at ease. I suppose she knows she's playing havoc with Rorie, but his bank balance and his obvious virility must attract her. You'd think with her legions of admirers she could survive without using a boy like him."

Josanne was deeply shocked. "I think she's a darling person, so thoughtful and kind." It was difficult to rebuke a blind man.

"That's what Marian thinks. Mercifully his parents see the threat she is to Rorie, and indirectly to all the family. A scandal could break at any moment. Rorie doesn't see it that way. Try to get it through to him. He might listen to you."

"Peace of mind these days means turning a deaf ear and a blind eye to other people's problems." Niall had come in. There was a smudge of oil on his cheek because he had been changing a tyre. "Don't get mixed up in the Rorie-Connelli drama. It's such stuff as dreams are made on. I expect this advice comes too late, and you've been making sympathetic noises all the way from Crianlarich!" He brushed his hand across his face, enlarging the smudge. "I'm covered in oil. I'll have to apply paraffin." He turned abruptly, his kilt swinging as it would at a dance.

When the door had closed behind him Josanne said, "Mr. Ames, will you explain something that you mentioned just now. Rorie seems to have money to burn . . ." She stopped sharply. She must sound like her mother, who could make such awkward remarks.

Michael drew on his cigarette, then he said "Robert Dutton made provision for his wife during her life-time, but left her nothing under his will. He left the flat in Lowndes Square and the residue to Marian. She, typically, thought that meant the loose change. When she found she had virtually scooped the pool, she salted it away until it was obvious that Grania had completed her family, and then she divided what she had between the three of them. Grania and Roderick won't touch a penny of it. Hence the mixture of rags and riches. Does that answer your question?"

"I should never have asked it," Josanne said.

"Now that you're involved in the family, it's something you might as well know."

She could feel herself growing scarlet. Thank God Michael couldn't see her. "I'm not involved. I don't even know them very well, except for Rorie, and he doesn't count." By adding that, she had made matters worse, but Michael laughed.

"It's Grania who decides who counts in this household," he said "If she didn't like you, you wouldn't be here."

*　　*　　*

It was typical August weather, bright sunshine changing suddenly to dark clouds and rain, and on one night there was a gale, screaming round the roof-tops, and flattening the corn which grew on what had once been the Nissen field.

Josanne found that Catriona never left Niall's side, so it was Rorie who taught her how to cast, using a match box on the lawn to represent a fish, and later taking her out in the boat, laughing as she tried to row and succeeded only in moving round in circles on Loch Caraig.

They attended sheep dog trials at Duff, and a regatta at Tobermory, and Josanne helped Mrs. Craig, the postmistress, with the produce stall in aid of the Women's Rural Institute at the sale of work held in Kilcaraig village hall. In London, she had always felt like an outcast. At Kilcaraig she felt she was at home.

One day Rorie took her to Tormore Bay. They approached it, not by boat, but on foot, climbing up the hill from Iona Ferry, and stopping on top of the granite quarry to get their breath back, and admire the view.

Josanne clicked her camera, knowing that she could never catch this magnificence on a little strip of film, but she managed to include Rorie in the foreground of a seascape, his kilt and his hair ruffled by the breeze, his brown arms raised to shield his eyes from the sun. Presently, he took her hand and led her down the old rail track, through granite and heather, to the disused pier.

He pointed at the cottage on a ledge, overlooking the pink rocks, the white sand, and the sea. "That's where Papa lived when he came here to escape from the cares of the world. Then he met Mama, and for a while his cares doubled, but it had a happy ending, as you can see. Some people get their heart's desire."

"And what happened about you, Rorie? What happened when you were at Lake Como?"

"You will have noticed that particular subject is taboo."

"Nothing is taboo with me. I'm not family."

They sat on a granite slab that had been ready for shipment to some faraway place when the quarries were closed at the beginning of the century. Seagulls wheeled overhead, and a patient heron, still as a statue, waited to catch an unsuspecting fish. Rorie was picking lichen off the slab. "Nothing much happened," he said. "Isabella's a song-bird on display in a gilded cage. She's on display, but the Maestro holds the key. He allows her a degree of freedom, knowing that after a flutter around she'll be beating with her wings to get back, because the cage is her security. She must be protected from anything that could threaten her design for living. Such as falling in love."

"Are you sure it isn't you who have taken fright, who wants her safely locked up in that cage?" she asked.

"I love her, and I'm too young to cope with her. I could only admit that to you."

He left her to think about this. He walked down to the crumbling pier, and stood gazing at the water. Shoals of tiny fish were swimming around, as they had done in Lake Como. He and Isabella had watched them as they leaned on the balustrade at the foot of the de Stefanis' garden. They had talked quietly together of nothing in particular. He was wearing bathing trunks. She was in a long-sleeved voluminous dress, that buttoned up to the neck, and she wore a sun hat, as she had to be protected from being sunburnt. Some of their friends were sun bathing nearby.

Isabella pulled at his arm, and gradually they moved towards the flowering shrubs that were part of the beauty of the garden. They were scarcely into the bushes, when she caught at his wrist.

"Now!" she said. "Please, Rorie, now!" Her green eyes were fixed on him, demanding him. She sank onto the ground, almost pulling him on top of her.

"Somebody might see us," he said.

"I don't care," she gasped, and suddenly he didn't care either. But nobody disturbed them.

Afterwards, watching her, cool and serene, surrounded by their friends, and playing her usual role as *diva*, he thought about her there in the garden, responding in a frenzy to his touch. The wild-cat woman in the bushes bore no resemblance to the diffident woman in that Rome hotel.

On the following day, they were sitting at a table by the swimming-pool, watching the antics of some of the others. Isabella never went into the water. She looked demure in a cotton dress.

He said to her, "How often do you make love in the bushes?"

She caught her breath, startled, then retorted "How often do you?"

He put his hand over hers, believing in her. "May I come to your room tonight? I won't let anyone know. We can have privacy and comfort."

She turned her head away, wanting to conceal her embarrassment. "I'm not in a condition for anything like that for a few days," she said.

He pressed her hand. "My precious love, I don't think of such ordinary functions happening to you."

She smiled, still embarrassed, but grateful. A wave of affection passed between them, far more binding than had been that moment of physical ecstasy. But the Maestro was coming towards them. Rorie released her hand. Two days later, she left for Munich to sing in *The Magic Flute*, and he flew home, to find that as soon as he arrived there, his confidence in her had become doubts. It had been an infinite relief to him that he had been able to speak of her to Josanne. Unlike Niall, he needed to confide in somebody, somebody reliable. He had learnt a great deal as a result of having written that bragging letter.

Josanne was beside him now, as if she had timed exactly how long he wanted to be alone.

"I've been thinking about love," she said. "I expect you have too. You can't love a person *but*. You can only love a person *because*. If you love Isabella, it's because she's the person she is. It's an unqualified acceptance, and anything else isn't love. If you love her, but she's too old for you, or too famous, or too lustful, that isn't love because it can't possibly last. It's desire. Think about it, and you'll come up with the right answer."

He took her hand, and they climbed to the top of the quarry. A last look at Iona across the strip of sea, then down the grassy slopes, and round the hill to the place where they had parked the car.

Ten days ago, Josanne would have felt devastated, had she made a statement like that, and received no reply. Now it didn't matter. She had made her point. It might be of help. She left it at that.

They had driven several miles when he said, "I love her because she's all the things she is, good and bad, known and unknown to me. What you've said has given me my answer, but it leaves me with another question. How do I make her love me back?"

"Answer that, and you'll have solved most of the problems of mankind," she said.

He gave her a quick look, but left it at that. He had done enough soul-searching for one day.

43

Josanne was in the post office, writing the postcards she was sending to a number of people she had forgotten about at the beginning of her holiday.

"I'll be back home before they're delivered," she said to Mrs. Craig, who was sitting behind the counter, knitting. On the shop side of the partition, the Minister's wife, Mrs. Allan, was buying her messages, which Josanne had found was the word used to describe the shopping.

Rorie had walked down to the village with her, and had mumbled something about remembering an urgent telephone call he must make. He went into the call-box, which was beside the post office, close to the Manse gate, and Josanne was wasting as much time as she could over her postcards, because she guessed that Rorie's call would be long distance, and one he didn't want to make from the castle.

She was right about that. Rorie, holding the receiver, looked through the glass, which was getting steamed up by his breath. A few people had gathered for a gossip close to the bumpy bridge; apart from that, the village was deserted, but everyone would know he was in the call-box, and would probably guess why.

At last the gentle, Highland voice of the operator in the local exchange told him that his call to Milan was through.

"Rorie?" The way Isabella said his name conveyed a note of urgency, but she waited long enough for him to say, "Yes, it's me".

"Rorie, I must see you. I must see you at once."

"What's happened?"

"I can't tell you on the telephone, but it's desperately important to me."

"Is it a baby?" His reaction was masculine and immediate. For a moment she sounded dazed.

"Of course it isn't. You know that. But I must talk to you,

please." She waited a moment and repeated, "Please". She knew just how to reach the heart with a single word.

"When do you leave Italy?"

"The day after tomorrow. A couple of nights in New York, then Chicago."

"I can't possibly get to Milan before then."

"I'll be in Chicago for two weeks." Her voice was breathy, expectant.

"Isabella, I can't nip across the Atlantic at a moment's notice." (*Mama, I'm off to Chicago for a few days. You'll hardly notice I'm gone. I'll be back before the Mountstephans come to stay.*) "It would be very difficult to leave here just now. Very difficult indeed."

"You said you'd come if I needed you. I need you now. Please."

Isabella pleading with him. Isabella whom he loved more than life itself.

"Very well, I'll come." (*How, in heaven's name, how?*) "I'll come next week."

His misgivings, his hesitation, had carried over these hundreds of miles. The urgency left her voice, and she said, almost wearily, "It doesn't matter, it can wait". She went on to tell him her schedule, which would end at the Metropolitan Opera House before Christmas. She would, as usual, be back at La Scala in December.

Rorie answered her in monosyllables, confused by her sudden change of mood, worried because of what he would have to say to his mother, regretting the impulse which had prompted him to put through the call.

As soon as Josanne saw him enter the post office, she knew by his expression that something had upset him, but in a moment he was all smiles, greeting Mrs. Craig as if he hadn't seen her for years, and joking with Mrs. Allan and with Effie, who worked in the shop. Josanne pitied him, and wondered how much of his cheerfulness was part of an act.

She stopped fumbling with the stamps, and handed her post-cards over the counter. Rorie bought her a packet of conversation lozenges before they left the shop. She chose a bright pink one to suck. It was heart-shaped, and "I Love You" was written on it in purple.

They stopped to talk to the group of people at the bridge, then they made their way back to the castle. Walking up the drive was a very different matter from walking down it, but Josanne knew that Rorie's silence was not due to lack of breath.

"Has something gone wrong?" she asked. It was unkind not to give him the chance to tell her.

"I'm in a quandary. Isabella wants me to fly over to see her in Chicago."

"In Chicago!" Accustomed though Isabella must be to Rorie chasing round Europe whenever he wanted to do so, this was an astounding request. "What on earth does she want you for? I thought she was careful not to draw attention to your – well – your friendship with her."

They were close to the castle. "I said I'd go next week. I don't see how I can, yet I know how fragile is her belief in human integrity. If I fail her now, I'll never face her again. Never again."

"Can't she write about whatever is worrying her?"

"She knows she can never commit her thoughts to paper."

The studded door, which long ago had impressed Robert Dutton, was open. They went into the hall, where Grania was on the top of a stepladder, adjusting the Kilcaraig tapestry. She had evidently moved it along the wall, to cover up a new patch of damp.

When she saw them, she climbed down the ladder and said to Josanne, "It's not a thing of beauty, but it's interesting and serves a useful purpose."

Josanne laughed. She knew about the leaking roof, and on rainy days she had helped to put out receptacles to catch the drips.

She examined the tapestry now. "Who started it?" she asked.

"My great-grandmother. It was supposed to be just the house, but my grandmother added to it. You can see how she did her stitches backwards. Then my mother put in the trees, each one representing a member of the family. Their initials are stitched in very neatly, but as you know, she died, so there isn't a tree for me or any of the rest of us. Aunt Marian cobbled in some background. Someday perhaps I'll manage to bring it up to date."

Rorie stood beside his mother, looking at the tapestry. His likeness to his father was almost uncanny, and probably explained why he was so obviously Grania's favourite child.

"Make Catriona do it as a holiday task," he said. "It'll keep her occupied on rainy days and spare us those God-awful pop groups that deafen us on her record-player."

"When you were sixteen, you treated us to the Beatles. You hadn't progressed to the dulcet tones of Connelli and the like." She smiled up at him and patted his arm. "When you put away the ladder, will you give Willie a hand with the lawn. We don't want the place to look like a wilderness when the Mountstephans come next week."

Next week Rorie would be going to Chicago. Now was his chance to tell her so. Josanne murmured that she must go and see to her packing, but Grania steered her towards the kitchen.

"Chrissie says you want to learn to make scones," she said. "Why don't you have a try now? We can have them for tea. You don't want to be cooking tomorrow, your last day here."

The scones were a success, and they did have them for tea. Josanne saw that Michael knew by the feel of the pots which one contained honey and which one jam. Nothing was left to chance where Michael was concerned, everything was done in a way that would make life easy for him.

That night it rained, so after dinner, instead of fishing on Loch Caraig, they gathered in the drawing-room, and played the piano and sang as the Lamonts had done for generations.

Josanne packed before she went to bed. She wanted to be absolutely free tomorrow to do whatever she liked. Most of all she wanted somehow to have Niall all to herself. She could not delude herself any longer. She had fallen idiotically, hopelessly in love with him.

*   *   *

Goodbyes had been said all round the district. Josanne's suitcase was packed, and Catriona had given her a smart bag made of a shiny material in which to put the pats of butter and other presents which had been handed to her. Sandy MacPherson's hen was not going to be tied onto her luggage, as he had suggested, because it was now being cooked as part of the special farewell dinner which Grania had arranged.

"You don't want to go home, do you?" Michael asked, finding her alone in the library. During the past two weeks she had told him quite a lot about her parents and her home.

"I've never been so happy in my life as I've been here." There was a catch in her voice as she said it. She took her glass of sherry over to the window. She felt that if she stayed close to Michael he would read what was in her mind as easily as he read his braille books. He would discover her secret about Niall.

Catriona came in, breathless because she had been chasing a sheep out of the walled garden, then Rorie appeared, followed by his parents. There were all seated at dinner when Niall joined them, his spaniel Kenny puffing after him, all covered in burrs. Nial apologized for being late. He had been repairing the thatch on the MacBeans' cottage.

"Nobody's lived in it for years," he said to Josanne. "But we want to preserve it if possible. It's almost unique."

Josanne had taken photographs of the cottage, with its rounded walls and slanted wooden chimney. It was difficult to believe that anyone had ever lived in it, but Roderick assured her that he used to visit it himself, and had stored up a wealth of Highland memories from stories told to him by old Donald MacBean.

"They don't teach one how to thatch at Cirencester," Rorie said. He had always considered that two years spent at an agricultural college were a waste of time for a Highland landowner. The prospect of returning there in two weeks' time was a gloomy one.

"They don't teach you anything anywhere because you're never there," Catriona teased.

"I've scarcely stirred out of Cirencester. Ask Josanne. She knows!" Rorie said heatedly, but Josanne, who was beside him, had been asked by Niall if she would like to go half way up Ben Caraig with him, for the weather promised a spectacular sunset. She finished dinner in a daze, merely putting in a word here and there, to keep up appearances.

When she and Grania and Catriona went to the drawing-room for coffee, she expected Catriona to say that she would like to see the sunset too, but instead she scrabbled in a cupboard, looking for the chess board, because her father had challenged her to a game.

*   *   *

Niall guided Josanne through clumps of heather, avoiding the treacherous bogs, which were marked by bog cotton, the white fluff that was nature's warning of ground that looked safe until one sank into it, knee deep or more. They were close to the place where the cow had been rescued on that dark morning. Josanne had not thought then how important Niall would become to her. Her love, the first love of her life.

He paused, and held out his hand to her. "It's a bit of a pull up here. I'll help you." His grip was sure and steady and in a little while they had reached a plateau by the waterfall. Josanne sat on a boulder, and Niall made a fan for her out of bracken, to keep away the midges. The scent of heather and bog-myrtle was almost intoxicating, and the water thundered behind them.

Below was the castle, and lower still the village, with its church and school and row of cottages and ugly village hall. The doctor's house on the brae stood exposed to every wind that blew, but Caraig Lodge was hidden by the trees. A wisp of smoke rose from the chimney of the Manse, which stood back from the hub of village life, tucked in beside the post office, its garden separated from the grave-yard by a low stone dyke.

The MacPhails' farm, to the south, was neat and well-managed, and the croft cottages adequately fenced, though here and there an old bedstead replaced a broken gate, or a rusty car disintegrated where it had ground to a halt. Prosperity with a dash of chaos, Highland style.

"When you look at all this, don't you feel you own the Promised Land?" Josanne asked.

"When I look at it I wonder how long we can protect it from progress, which threatens to close our school, and to channel our people into Council houses. The planners are upon us, and the new Highland Clearances have begun. We're responsible for protecting the place and the people. When Papa and Mama are too old to cope, the burden will fall on me. Without Rorie to help me, I don't know how I'll manage."

"Is there a living for both of you on the estate? Assuming that you'll have wives and children to support."

"Yes, it needs the backing of two families. What I mean is, when Catriona marries, as I expect she will, her share of the Dutton capital goes with her. I can't see Rorie settling here, and that's not just because of his fantasy over Isabella. Mother adores him. She'd fight like a tiger-cat to protect and control him. He knows instinctively that one of these days he'll have to succumb, to be a dutiful son under her thumb, or break away."

Josanne was astonished, yet touched, that Niall had spoken to her so candidly. Under a serene surface, the Lamonts had their problems, like any other family. She flicked with her fan, but the midges continued to give her their relentless attention.

"Has he said anything to you about Chicago?" she asked. If Rorie had said nothing, she could turn the question somehow. She wouldn't betray him.

"He's told me," Niall said. "I'm not advising him either way. It's all part of the Mama-Isabella conflict, and it remains to be seen who wins this round."

The sky was changing from crimson to gold, so that the valley and the three lochs gleamed in burnished splendour before sinking into darkness.

They watched in silence, a shared experience. Then Niall snapped the beam of his torch into the darkness, and guided her carefully down the hill. They had reached the walled garden before she became aware of Kenny, who had been at Niall's heels all the time. Dogs understood fidelity, even if in the end it meant pain and death.

Not like people, all conflict and worry, wrong decisions, and endless regrets.

She put her Wellington boots in the cloakroom. Grania told her that she should leave them there, because she would need them again next year. Josanne accepted the invitation with gratitude, but she felt in her heart that Niall's courtesy concealed his indifference to her, and feeling as she did, she could never come back.

★   ★   ★

Catriona waved Josanne off in the morning, then she set out with her camera to take snapshots of the wild life of Mull. Chrissie had given her a picnic pack, consisting of the things she most liked to eat – cheese sandwiches, fruit cake, an apple and a Mars Bar. There was also a plastic cup, so that if she wanted to, she could drink from a burn.

She climbed above the house, then turned north. If she continued long enough, she would get to the main road running through Glen More, but her intention was to climb gradually up the mountain. She would have to be very patient if she was going to get the photographs which would be of interest to the village people next time she gave a slide show in the village hall in aid of a charity.

Now and again, she stopped to admire the view. All her life she had looked at Mull at different times and at different seasons, and all her life it had never grown stale, never ceased to enchant her. She could see a bus far away in the distance, over in the Glen road, and it was followed by a number of cars. Traffic was getting heavier every summer season; a few years ago, she would have recognized most of the vehicles she saw on the road.

She came to a burn, which raced down the mountain side. She decided to settle there, quiet as a mouse, and see if suitable wild life would present itself. She set her film, and kept her camera in her hand, so that if anything were to appear, she could raise it and take her picture without sending whatever it was scampering away.

Her patience was rewarded more quickly than she had expected, and she got a beautiful shot of a field mouse. Contented, she flicked the film lever and prepared for the next shot.

Snap. She nearly missed the rabbit, but if it hadn't moved, it would make a good picture, sitting on its haunches eating a blade of grass.

She was startled, then frozen with fright, when a man's voice said, "I've been watching you for quite a time. Did you get a good picture?"

Catriona's stomach lurched in fright. She hung her head and

fiddled with her camera. If she pretended not to hear him, he might go. She didn't want to look up and see him. Rorie had told her not to wander off by herself. She was miles away from the road. No car and no cattle-grid could rescue her this time. The rustle of the heather indicated that he was moving nearer.

She put her hand to her mouth to stifle the scream she knew she must not utter. They strangled you if you screamed.

"I'm sorry – I think I startled you." She could see his feet. He was wearing brogues and kilt stockings. "Do you live here?" he asked.

"No. I live at Norwich." She had never been to Norwich in her life.

"Do you know the Armstrongs – Caroline and Crispin?"

Caroline and Crispin! He must be joking! No she didn't think she knew the Armstrongs. Her family had only recently moved to Norwich.

"That's the Lamont tartan," he said. "Family, or off the peg?"

"Off the peg," she said. "From Harrods."

"I thought it had a Harrods look," he said. He sat down beside her and she saw that he was wearing a kilt. At first this reassured her, then it terrified her, remembering the jokes her brothers made about kilts. She gave him a cautious, sidelong look. He was handsome, nearly as handsome as Niall, but his hair was light brown. He turned his head and she hastily looked down again.

"What's your name?" he asked. The other man hadn't asked her name. Her name didn't matter to him, only her body.

"Celia Brown," she said.

"How strange. I thought it was Catriona Lamont." She could feel his amused look as she turned crimson. She thought of denying it, but this would be pointless.

"Why did you pretend?" she asked.

"I didn't pretend anything. I only asked some civil questions, and got some rather odd answers. Why are you incognito?"

She still hung her head. "I don't like talking to strange men."

"I'm terribly sorry." He sounded as if he meant it. "Would you like me to leave you?"

"No, please, unless you have designs on me!"

He laughed, but not unkindly. "I'd like a photograph of you sitting here in the heather. Is that all right?"

She looked at him properly now. He had dark blue eyes. There was nothing that could remind her of that other man.

She tilted up her chin while he took the photograph, then he took another one.

"I'll send you copies when they're ready."

"Thank you very much. You know my address!" She indicated her picnic. "Would you like to share my lunch with me?"

He took a sandwich to keep her company while she ate the rest. They talked about their common interest, photography, and they talked about music, and found that they both liked reading poetry. At last he looked at his watch and said he must be going, as he had to catch the Craignure bus in the Glen at the Kilcaraig road-end.

She shook hands when they said goodbye, and she thanked him for being such pleasant company. He had gone some distance and was just a tiny figure fading into the heather, when she realized that she hadn't asked him his name. But she knew his tartan. He had never got that kilt off the peg – it fitted him too well.

She decided not to mention him to her family.

*　　　*　　　*

Rorie was in his room, listening to *A fors e lui* through headphones. Isabella would be in New York now, and somehow he would have to make up his mind as to whether or not to join her.

Niall was filling in several pages of the diary which he kept locked in a drawer. He recorded his thoughts as well as his deeds, so it was a very private document indeed.

Catriona was sitting up in bed writing a sonnet to a stranger with navy-blue eyes. She had written A.B.A.B.C.D.C.D.E.F.E.F.G.G. at the end of fourteen lines, and all she had to do was to fill in some words, properly scanned.

Michael Ames was reading a new thriller, his finger returning at times to feel words which seemed to be even more shocking when written in braille.

Grania and Roderick lay in the darkness, listening to the ticking of the alarm-clock, which was set for six-thirty. Even when the twins were at home, Roderick liked to make an early start. They had exhausted the subject of Rorie and Isabella, at least for one more day.

In her bedroom at Maybank Court, Josanne had given up trying to sleep. She was thinking of Niall and the sunset over Kilcaraig, and she was hating the roof-tops and chimneys that were now her everlasting view.

Some four thousand miles away, the doctor said to the Maestro, "She'll sleep now. She should be all right by morning." And Isabella Connelli, whose voice was insured for half a million dollars, sank into oblivion.

44

A few days after returning to London, Josanne went to see Aunt Marian. She showed her the holiday snapshots which, as she had expected, weren't very good. Rorie at Tormore was under-exposed, and a shot of Niall on the tractor caught only the back of his head. The landscapes were minute and blurred.

She found it easy to chat about Kilcaraig to Aunt Marian, who asked questions about everyone, but not questions of a searching nature. Josanne felt that confidences would be welcome, but not wrung out of her.

It was from Aunt Marian that she heard about Isabella's illness. "There was only a tiny bit about it in the papers," Marian said. "You would easily have missed it. They don't want a fuss, after the cancellation of the Australian tour last year. She's back in Italy, recuperating at her villa in Ravello. It was a short, sharp attack, and although she's missed Chicago, she'll be singing at San Francisco as arranged."

So she was not in Chicago. Her illness had solved that problem for Rorie.

"Has Rorie gone to Italy?" Josanne asked.

Aunt Marian looked surprised. "Not that I know of." She shook her head. "I don't think he'd chase off from Kilcaraig. It was different when he was in Paris, or when he's at Cirencester, but his parents have a steadying influence. So has Niall." She buttered a scone, her lips pursed in thought. "I might take a wee trip to Ravello myself. I've seen pictures of her villa, perched high up on the mountains above Amalfi, with a beautiful view of the Mediterranean."

"Does she live there alone?"

"She has Motti and the servants. It's her bolt-hole, and the Maestro is there a good deal."

"The Maestro's wife must be very broad-minded!"

"I don't know. We never talk about that." But Aunt Marian said it with a smile. She always treated Josanne as an equal, thus bridging the gap in their years, and making friendship with her so valuable and so secure.

Towards the end of September, Josanne was typing a report which was to be put before the Board of Directors on the following day, when Mr. Painter called her over to the telephone. Only Rorie ever contacted her in the office.

It was not Rorie, it was Niall. "I'm in London for a few days. When can I see you?" he asked.

She thought of an excuse, inventing a night-class for that evening, but failing inspiration for the following day.

"I'll fetch you from the office at five-thirty tomorrow," he said.

"No, please don't come here. Mr. Painter's the only person who knows I know you."

She heard him laugh. "All right, I won't disgrace you! I'll meet you at Victoria Station, at the Continental Departure board. Five-forty-five, and don't worry if you have to be late."

When she put down the receiver, Mr. Painter asked her if she was feeling ill.

"I would like to speak to you privately, please," she said. Her mind was made up now. There was only one possible solution to a problem that made her feel as upset as she did now.

Mr. Painter offered her a chair, and put up the "engaged" notice on the door. He was puzzled. It had been Mr. Niall she had spoken to, not Mr. Rorie. But she had been at Kilcaraig for her holiday, and it would be round about now that she would begin to worry if anything had gone wrong.

"Tell me what I can do for you, my dear," he said in the gentle kindly voice of her father in her daydreams.

She sat up straight, twisting her handkerchief in her hands, incapable of speech. Then to his and to her own dismay, she burst into tears.

*　　*　　*

Although she arrived early at Victoria Station, Josanne found that Niall had got there first. He looked strange in trousers, now that she was accustomed to seeing him in a kilt.

"We'll go to Aunt Marian's flat," he said, leading her to the taxi rank. "It's far too early for dinner, and Marian has remembered a bed-ridden friend in urgent need of help. In other words, she knows we'll want to be alone."

This was the very last thing Josanne wanted, but she had no choice in the matter.

The flat was airy and smelled of flowers. The mantelpiece in the drawing-room was covered with invitations, most of them bearing a tick of acceptance. Aunt Marian was always in demand, but was never needed more than now. Josanne sank onto the sofa, where Isabella and Adrian had sat on the night of the party, and she asked after the family and Chrissie and the dogs and the postman and the cats, while Niall poured out drinks, and accounted for other members of the community including the doctor and his wife, the District Nurse, and Mrs. Craig for good measure. He could understand Josanne's prattling nervousness. He expected her to have much to say to him before the evening was over.

He sat on the sofa beside her and raised his glass. "*Slainte*."

She smiled and responded. Then she sipped her drink, coughed, and sipped again. "What have you put in it?" she asked.

"Nothing that will make you say anything you may regret. You're safe with me."

She relaxed. It was true. She was safe with him.

"First, a message from Rorie," he said. "He decided against Chicago, which was just as well. There'd have been a God-awful row about it, and she wasn't there anyway."

"She's in Italy."

"And Rorie's at Cirencester. He sent her the usual offerings, flowers and so on, which were acknowledged with a printed slip. He's realized at last that he's merely a name on her mailing list, the same as all her fans. I don't think he'll try to get in touch with her any more."

"So he doesn't love her after all."

"She's not a very suitable person to love."

"Can anyone decide who is a suitable person to love?" She turned on Niall, her eyes snapping. "A short time ago, he'd have gone through hell for her."

"Why does it upset you so much?" Niall was baffled. He thought he had given her good news.

Josanne stared at her glass. She could hear Rorie's voice saying "*If I fail her now, I'll never face her again. Never again*". She sighed, disappointed. "It was such a romantic romance," she said.

Niall re-filled her glass. Whatever had prompted her to speak to Mr. Painter, it was obviously nothing to do with Rorie. Niall experienced the sense of relief that is only apparent when an unexpectedly heavy burden has been carried almost unnoticed until it is taken away.

They dined at an Angus Steak House, and by the time coffee was served, Josanne had recovered from the potion which he had concocted for her. She had barely touched her wine.

They had not reverted to the subject of Rorie and Isabella, but they had put the world to rights over the soup, had condemned a number of politicians to a degrading end during the main course, and had settled down to the subjects they both enjoyed, music and literature, over the biscuits and cheese.

Suddenly Niall said, "Why do you want to transfer to our branch at Sydney or Hong Kong?"

"So Mr. Painter has told you?"

"I saw him at a meeting this morning."

Of course. She had typed the report which he was to give to the Board of Directors.

"Life at home has become rather tricky. I can't move to another address in London without hurting my parents' feelings. Besides, I want to see the world." It was the explanation she had given to Mr. Painter, who had tactfully not asked her why her request had to be accompanied by tears. She hoped Niall had not been told of the shaming exhibition she had made of herself.

"Do you really want to go so very far away? Wouldn't you be happier in New York – the Met and all that. And our branch in Manhattan is a show-piece. Very prestigious!"

"So I've heard. I wouldn't aim so high!"

Niall poured out some more coffee from the Cona, which he had asked to be left on the table. "It so happens that the boss of our Export department has a secretary who wants to do a year in London. Work permits and so on can easily be arranged, if you'll agree to do a swop."

"I don't want preferential treatment or influence," Josanne said suspiciously, and this was true. She wanted to escape from the Lamonts, not to become more indebted to them.

"Nothing like that, it would be most unprofessional," Niall said, in his best imitation of Adrian, who could be pompous at times.

"I'll have to think about it," Josanne said. Sky-scrapers, tugboats on the Hudson, the Statue of Liberty, and the Metropolitan Opera House, which she still visualized on Broadway! It was too good to be true, but it had its drawbacks. New York was only a few hours' flight away.

"There are too many flies in Australia, and the wrong sort of music in Hong Kong," Niall said, using the arguments he thought might appeal to her most. He omitted the lure of Isabella at the Met. In the circumstances, that might even put her off.

When he drove her back to Maybank Court, Josanne's future was almost decided, but she asked him not to say anything to her parents until she had slept on her decision. She was not a person who could be rushed into something she might later regret.

He watched her, docile and self-effacing, sipping tonic-water under the parental eye. By the time he returned to Lowndes Square, he had come to the conclusion that the reason she had given for requesting a transfer was genuine. She just could not be herself in her own home any more. He said so to Aunt Marian, who had waited up for him. She gave him cocoa, which she always had done when the children had been out at night. She forgot that it didn't mix with wine, but he managed to pour some of it onto a plant when she wasn't looking.

"Sydney or Hong Kong was a lot of nonsense," Marian said. "She'll choose New York, you'll see, and you'll be able to nip over and see her, no bother."

"What would I want to do that for?"

"Flying round the world is part and parcel of your education at the Sorbonne, if Rorie's anything to go by, the wretched boy." She took the empty mug from him. "I'll just say this. Think hard before you arrange anything that could ultimately damage you or anyone else. If the Maestro had left that poor little soul alone, she would have married her postman at Skibbereen, and she'd be a lot happier than she is now." She marched off to the kitchen, and he could hear her rinsing out the mug under a running tap.

A postman at Skibbereen, first of many loves perhaps. Niall felt strangely touched, wondering what sort of confidences had passed between Isabella and Aunt Marian on those rare occasions when they were alone together. But he took the warning to heart. One could overdo the string-pulling and become hopelessly tangled up.

In Cirencester, Rorie ticked off another day in his diary. Three hundred and thirty-eight to go before he completed his course. After that, he had no idea what he would do, neither did he care.

*　　　*　　　*

William and Sybil accepted Josanne's decision to work in New York with resignation, almost with relief. Her father gave her a cheque to ensure that the quality of her clothes would be a credit to Britain, while Sybil made arrangements for her to share a flat with three other girls at an address off Sixth Avenue.

"Susan Knight works for the United Nations," she said. "Her parents suggested this as soon as they heard you were going to Manhattan. It'll be nice for you to be with a girl who has the same background as yourself."

Josanne complied with the arrangement, although the Knights

belonged to Sybil's horsey past, and she thought it unlikely that she would find anything in common with their daughter. She had to live somewhere. Anywhere would do.

There were formalities to go through, papers to be filled in, blood tests to be carried out, but the reputation of Carnsworth, Prior and Dutton made all that an easy matter.

As Christmas approached, Niall telephoned from Paris to ask her for a progress report, and to give her the names and addresses of friends she must contact in various parts of the States. She was to work for George Hawtrey, who was a charmer, and whose wife looked crisp and elegant and alarmingly smart. But that was all camouflage, for she had a heart of gold. "She'll be a shoulder for you to cry on if you're homesick," he said.

"There's no fear of that," Josanne said, fighting down an impulse to ask him if he would be in London before he went home to Kilcaraig on holiday, but he merely wished her luck, and said casually that he would write some time.

Rorie came from Cirencester one evening, and took her to a theatre and to dinner at Toni's. He gave her an account of his life at the agricultural college which made her laugh, but he avoided any reference to Isabella. This omission hung over them all evening like a pall. She was glad when it was time to say goodnight.

She spent Christmas Day at home and went to a pantomime with the Fergusons on Boxing Day. Aunt Marian had them all in for drinks on New Year's Eve, and she took her turn to shout good wishes on the telephone to Kilcaraig, remembering, as she did so, every detail of her visit there a year ago.

Two weeks later, she was deposited at Heathrow by her father, and the great adventure had begun. A new life in the New World, offering excitement and opportunity, yet filling her with dread. Her body was held securely by her seat-belt, but at the moment of take-off, she knew that she had left her heart behind.

45

The cab driver pulled up outside the sleazy red-brick building off Sixth Avenue which was to be Josanne's home for the next twelve months. The janitor, white teeth flashing in his black face, lugged her cases up three flights of stairs and let her into the apartment. He handed her the key and accepted with alacrity the unexpectedly generous tip before leaving her in her strange surroundings, where there was not so much as a note of welcome awaiting her in the hall.

The sound of a dripping tap led her to the kitchen, where there was a pile of unwashed dishes in the sink. The living-room next door was large and untidy, but the ceiling-high bookcases were filled, and a record-player was on a table, under which were piles of carelessly stacked records, many of them not in their sleeves.

She tried two bedrooms, one of which reeked of stale tobacco from the cigarette ends which filled an ashtray beside the unmade bed. Then she found her own room, dull and dusty, but offering possibilities when her heavy luggage with her books and records arrived. There were a number of letters on a tray on her dressing-table, and someone had arranged flowers in a chipped vase.

After the freezing cold outside, the apartment was as warm as an oven, so the central-heating must work. She took off her sheepskin coat and hung it in the closet; then she went to the window, scarcely able to believe that this magnificent man-made sky-line really was Manhattan, and that when darkness came she would see it in the glittering glory, so familiar in travel posters.

She had been in the States for four weeks, and had been met at Washington by friends of the Lamonts, who were strangers to her, but only for about five minutes, because she was instantly plunged into the whirl of kindness that was American hospitality. It was the start of a holiday of a lifetime, as she progressed from place to place, friend to friend, showered with admiration until her natural timidity gave way to self-confidence. It was at her own request that she had made the last stage of her journey, from Philadelphia to New York, by herself. She had seen films of girls arriving unaccompanied at Grand Central Station, dazed and lonely, but they ended up, after many vicissitudes, in the right arms for the final kiss. Social success had not diminished her daydreams, and every night in bed she wrote an imaginary letter to Niall, telling him all the events of her crowded day, all her thoughts.

Now, sitting at the window and composing such a letter, she was reminded of the real ones waiting her attention. She took them over to her bed and opened them at random. Most were good-luck cards from girls in the London office. One was from Hope Garnett, who scribbled across it how much she was missed at night-classes, and the Ferguson girls had sent a postcard from Adelboden, where they were on a ski-ing holiday. Aunt Marian wrote a friendly note, enclosing a cheque, and Grania Lamont wrote briefly but sympath-etically, understanding the loneliness she would feel until she had settled into her new job.

Almost unconsciously, she had put off opening the envelope addressed in Niall's writing, hoping he would have written a dream letter to her, but all it contained was a picture of a cow, and a message, dutiful and polite, wishing her success. Tears of disap-pointment pricked her eyes. Distance had not added enchantment to Niall's view of her. She ripped open Rorie's letter, but heard the front-door opening, so she laid it aside and went into the hall.

She was greeted by a tall girl with a mop of tousled hair and a wide smile, who introduced herself as Amelia Court from Hartford, Connecticut. She worked for Macy's and was sorry that the apartment was in such a mess, but they had held a party last night, intended as a welcome for Josanne, but there had been a mistake about the date of her arrival. She chattered on, sometimes asking questions but never waiting for an answer, until Nan Bradley arrived, carrying a large bag of groceries and complaining about the delay on the subway. She had wiry black hair, red cheeks, and terrible legs, painfully revealed by her mini-skirt, but her eyes were kind, and as Josanne helped her to unload the frozen and canned foods onto the kitchen table, she said that she worked in the art department of an advertising agency, and that she had painted the murals in the living-room.

"I was in a depressive state at the time," she explained. "You may have thought they were just daubs on the wall. I'll change them now that I've taken up Yoga."

During the months to come Josanne was to hear a great deal about psychology and about various forms of meditation which required a complicated routine of diet, if they were to be properly applied. She was saved from immediate enlightenment by the noisy arrival of Susan Knight.

Susan was all charm and gush. She had long, mouse-coloured hair and slightly prominent teeth, so that she spoke with a lisp, but her figure was exquisite. The slanting hazel eyes were all that was needed to complete the feline qualities of a man-eater. *If I were a cat, I would arch my back and spit* Josanne registered for the make-believe letter to Niall which she composed in her head every night, but she shook the proffered hand with a semblance of warmth, and went to the living-room with Susan, who kicked off her shoes and tossed her coat onto a chair.

"I'm sorry our party last night misfired," she said. "What's more, I have to go out tonight – I've been talked into a dinner-date with a creep Amelia invited here last night." She called into the hall. "Fix us some coffee, Amelia, and bring it to me in the bathroom. I must have a quick shower."

"It's your turn to make the supper," Nan said accusingly.

Susan ignored her. She said to Josanne, "You study Italian and German at night-classes, instead of going to parties, and you aren't interested in men. Your mother told my parents all about you."

"I expect my parents know as little about me as yours know about you," Josanne replied.

Nan suppressed a giggle, and Susan cast a deadly look at her and then marched out of the room.

"She's angry!" Nan hissed. "She thinks we've been gossiping about her. She's terrified you'll be reporting back to London about her love life."

"I wouldn't do that, and it's none of my business anyway."

"It's your business all right! We have to turn out of here every Saturday afternoon, two until seven, to leave the coast clear for her steady."

"Is he on shift-work or something?"

"He's a guitarist. Quite well-known. He plays in the night-spots. She likes being mysterious about him, so we don't ask questions."

Amelia came in, carrying two mugs of coffee. Steam followed her into the room. Evidently Susan showered with the bathroom door open.

"She's collected Warner!" Amelia said indignantly.

"No loss. She's right about him being a creep," Nan said consolingly.

"He's a *rich* creep. And he's taken the trouble to track her down at work. She doesn't want him – she just wants to show she can grab our men." Still grumbling, she returned to the kitchen. Susan would be waiting for her coffee.

Josanne was trying to make out the smudges on the wall, which she could now see were meant to be pictures. She had heard that girls who shared flats bickered over their men friends and she had no intention of becoming involved.

"Is it true that you aren't interested in men?" Nan asked. She must have been thinking about this for some time.

"I won't pay for dinner-dates with a goodnight kiss, if that's what you mean."

"You'll have to give a lot more than that if you're going to have a good time."

"Then I'm in for a bad time."

"Don't you mind?"

"Not awfully. There's lots of things I enjoy which have nothing to do with men. For a start, I have the whole of New York to discover."

"You'll find you can't do that on your own."

In London, she could go to Covent Garden by herself. This might not be possible at the Met. "I'll have to see," she said.

"Susan can be a frightful bitch, but she does have her uses. She collects the men, and we get her leavings," Nan explained.

"From what I've heard, she gets your findings."

Nan considered this, then she said, "I don't think it will apply to you. We all had the impression you were dull and bespectacled. But you're not. You're pretty. Amelia and I are no competition, so we're allowed to stay here. The pretty ones always go. She tortures them out."

"How?"

"You'll see."

With this grim warning in her ears, Josanne went to her bedroom to unpack. As she passed the bathroom, she could see Amelia talking to Susan, whose naked body was reflected in the steam-hazed mirror. She closed the door of her own room, and sank onto the bed. Rorie's letter, half out of its envelope, was lying on the pillow. With an odd feeling of reluctance she opened it and read his words of good wishes, of advice, and of consolation. Somehow he had assessed just how she would feel at this minute, and he wrote with sympathy and insight. It was the letter of a wise man, not of a boy. Then she turned over the page.

"You'll think I was very craven when I didn't mention Isabella the night I saw you. I couldn't. I would have wept, to the embarrassment of both of us," he wrote. "The illness which prevented her from reaching Chicago acted as a kind of reprieve for me. Mama is right, and our lives can never blend. Like the gods from Valhalla, she comes to earth occasionally to dazzle poor mortals like me. If there was any substance in her appeal to me, I've failed her. If it was just a passing hysteria, she will have forgotten it by now. One thing is sure, I'll never face her again."

He signed himself "Yours bitterly, Rorie," and he added a post-script; "As you know, she's Lucia at the Met just now."

She sighed, folded the letter away, and waited until she heard Susan leave, escorted by Amelia's perfidious friend, then she went to the kitchen and offered to cook spaghetti bolognese for supper.

*   *   *

In the New Metropolitan Opera House, Isabella Connelli and Paolo Bardini shared one of those moments of rapport which made their partnership so rewarding. Silvano's baritone broke through the tumultuous applause, and the rumble of disappointment died away as *Lucia di Lammermoor* continued, uninterrupted by an encore.

Isabella wet her lips and swallowed, alert, ready for her next cue. Her voice, when it came, was strong and crystal clear, so that Bardini allowed the orchestra to reach the full crescendo he had rehearsed so carefully.

He was soaking with sweat, and as usual had to change his shirt during the intermission. Emotion as much as exertion did this to him, and it was always the same when he was in the orchestra pit and Isabella was on the stage.

He knew, as no one else did, that her survival as a singer depended largely on his skill.

★   ★   ★

While Susan was entertaining her guitarist friend on Saturday afternoon, Nan and Amelia whisked Josanne round Manhattan on a sight-seeing trip. She had to remind herself that she was no country bumpkin, that she was accustomed to living a sophisticated life in the heart of London, but the speed and the noise of New York caught her unawares, both exciting her and alarming her. Exhausted, her head spinning, she asked to be shown the building on Madison Avenue which housed the firm of Carnsworth, Prior and Dutton.

It rose to the sky in glossy splendour. She could hardly believe her eyes. Niall had told her that the branch was prestigious, but he hadn't prepared her for this.

"I'll never dare go into it on Monday," she said, staring upwards, fighting the sensation that all these sky-scrapers were going to tumble down on top of her.

"You'll be okay. You'll get V.I.P. treatment because your Lamont friends are friends of your boss."

Only her mother could have disclosed this information, but Josanne pushed it out of her mind. She had plenty to think about without worrying over what was written in letters between London, Susan Knight's parents, and New York.

George Hawtrey himself was waiting to welcome her when she stepped out of the elevator which had taken her to the eighteenth floor. She recognized him easily from Niall's description, and his smile and friendliness soon put her at her ease. Her office, with its large desk and miniature telephone switchboard was the first indication of the importance of her job, and all that talk about being a small cog in a large machine had been meaningless until she found herself being introduced to the people with whom she would be working during the coming year. George Hawtrey knew them all, knew all about them. She could see that here efficiency and friendship went hand in hand. She was in a marvellous job, and it was Niall who had done this for her.

"Don't be scared about making mistakes. You will at first. Just tell me about them, and I'll help to put them right." And with these words of reassurance, George left her to her own devices. The typists who worked in her outer office would give her any help she needed.

During the afternoon, Mrs. Hawtrey telephoned to ask her round for drinks, so when she left the building she was escorted by her boss, and driven in his Cadillac to his home on Park Avenue. She felt more like a member of the Royal Family than like a secretary at the end of her first day in a new job.

Virginia Hawtrey, although smart and jangling with costume jewellery, had the knack of overcoming shyness in a young girl, and soon Josanne had told her as much as was prudent about the apartment and girls who lived in it.

"You'll soon be making friends of your own. For a start, you must come to dinner next week. We'll fix it, and I think I can produce someone you're really going to like," Virginia said, exchanging a conspiratorial glance with her husband.

The Hawtreys dropped her off at home on their way to a dinner engagement. Susan Knight, watching them from the window, saw the blue Cadillac draw up, and a tall man escort Josanne across the sidewalk, which shone in the full glare of the street light. She fled to the sitting-room and settled herself artistically on the sofa, with a book of poems in her hand.

When Josanne came into the apartment, she was alone.

"Where's the boy-friend?" Susan asked, tossing the book aside.

"I wouldn't let him come upstairs."

"Who is he?"

"My boss."

"Quick work, isn't it?"

"I do it with mirrors." She laughed at Susan's look of incredulity, but it set the pattern of their relationship, because Susan reckoned that girls who were driven around in Cadillacs could not be ignored, might even be worth cultivating. At breakfast the next day, she was grudgingly amiable, and within a few days she had stopped complaining when Josanne insisted on locking the bathroom door. She noted that Amelia and Nan were modifying their usually spicy language. It could be that Josanne's old-fashioned ways were attractive to men.

On the following Friday night, Josanne left a note in the hall saying she would not be back for dinner, and on Saturday morning she was evasive about where she had been, but she asked Amelia and Nan to go to a film with her in the afternoon, to be followed by supper in an Italian restaurant. She had accepted that Susan must be allowed the freedom of the flat on Saturday afternoons.

When they returned, there was no one at home, but Susan's door was open, and the unmade bed and the ash-trays piled high with cigarette ends told their own tale.

"Smoking that amount can't give them much time to do anything else," Josanne said tartly, shutting the door. Then she saw that Amelia was examining a bouquet of flowers in cellophane wrapping which lay on the hall table.

"*To Josanne, looking forward to Thursday, Desmond.*," Amelia read out. "Jesus! Susan'll be furiously jealous. Who's Desmond?"

"A friend of the Hawtreys. I met him there at dinner last night."

"What's happening on Thursday?"

"He's taking me to the Met. *Lucia di Lammermoor* with Connelli."

"You quiet mouse, you haven't wasted any time getting dated!" Amelia held the flowers against herself like a bridal bouquet, and admired herself in the mirror. "Opera's far too highbrow for me. But I've seen Connelli on television, and I can see why she has them stampeding up the aisles." She handed the flowers to Josanne, who went to the kitchen to arrange them.

Desmond Drayton had been one of the three guests, besides herself, who had dined with the Hawtreys. They had told him of her passion for opera, and he had wasted no time in introducing the subject. When he heard that she had met Isabella Connelli, he had at first been incredulous, then touchingly envious. She had to tell him about Aunt Marian's party over and over again, like telling a fairy story to a child. When he asked her to go to *Lucia di Lammermoor* with him, she accepted readily, not only because of the opera, but because she liked him.

The sound of gun-fire ripped through the flat as the television play came to an end. There followed the genuine bang of the front door. Susan was back, complaining that her afternoon had been ruined by the messenger delivering Josanne's flowers.

"I'll tell the men who shower me with bouquets not to do so on Saturday afternoons," Josanne said. Then she relented, because Susan, with her make-up smeared and her hair awry, looked more as if she had been walking the streets than being entertained to dinner by a guitarist about to begin his evening's work. She held out the bowl of flowers. "Put them in your bedroom. They'll drown the smell of tobacco."

Susan hesitated, so she went into the bedroom herself and put the bowl on the bedside table. Some sort of revulsion prevented her from offering to help make up the dishevelled bed.

46

In spite of its opulence, the New Metropolitan had none of the atmosphere Josanne had always associated with an opera house, but she supposed that one day it would acquire its own character. People would boast that they had heard Connelli sing there, and *prime donne* of the future would look into the mirror of the star dressing-room and know that once that heart-shaped face, those green eyes, the Titian hair, had been reflected there.

Tonight, watching her on the stage projecting the anguish of *Lucia* into the packed auditorium, Josanne was transported into the drama of despair and treachery that was being enacted before her, and during the intermissions Desmond Drayton was blissfully of the same mind as herself, not wanting to talk very much.

It was not until it was all over that she saw the change in Isabella. The glorious voice, the superb acting, could be taken for granted, but the curtain calls lacked the light-hearted spontaneity that had always been evident in the past. The singer who acknowledged the applause was *Lucia*, not Connelli. She was clinging to her role instead of casting it off as she used to when the curtain came down.

"Are you going backstage to see her?" Desmond asked eagerly.

"She doesn't receive visitors in her dressing-room."

He looked crestfallen. "I thought they all held court and drank champagne into the small hours."

"She isn't like anyone else." This was absolutely true.

"Will you hand in a note, just to thank her?"

She was about to refuse, when Desmond produced a sheet of paper so neatly folded that he must have prepared it in advance, and Josanne, using her handbag to press on, hating to do it, feeling foolish, managed to write;

"Dear Madame Connelli,
   I have just had the joy of hearing you sing. I am with a friend who wants to join me in thanking you for such beauty. You may not remember me, but we met at Mrs. Danvers' party in London.

I am now working in the New York branch of my firm. I was very
sorry about your illness, but we know, because we have heard
you, that your recovery is complete. Take care of yourself for
everyone's sake.

Yours sincerely,
Josanne Murray"

She thought it was a very poor effort, but she showed it to
Desmond, who read it with approval; then they pushed their way
through the waiting crowds and handed it in at the stage door.

On the following day, she was in her office reading through a
number of letters which were ready for George's signature, when the
telephone rang. It was Mrs. Mottram, Motti, her strong Cork accent
untainted by the years she had spent in Italy.

"I'm speaking on behalf of Madame Connelli. She was most
touched that you wrote to her, and she would like to see you. She's
free this evening, and we're at the Waldorf-Astoria, a bit hemmed in
by police, I'm afraid. It's a kidnapping threat. It doesn't really worry
us, but it worries the police. Will half seven suit you? Briano – that's
Madame's driver – will collect you from where you live. You'd
rather come by yourself? Very well, but he'll meet you when you
arrive, and show you to Madame's suite."

Josanne, frozen with dismay, had made suitable remarks between
the sentences. There could be only one reason for the invitation and
that was Rorie. Isabella would want news of him, and there was
nothing on earth she could say.

*   *   *

Josanne set off early for the Waldorf-Astoria, knowing that there
were many lounges where she could lurk until it was time for her
appointment.

Here she was mistaken. As soon as she crossed the threshold, she
was barred by a dark man who looked like a brigand but addressed
her by name.

"Briano, at your service," he said. "I take you to Madame
Connelli's suite."

"I'm too early."

"No matter. Come!"

If she had fallen into the hands of the Mafia there was nothing she
could do about it, because even the elevator attendant treated her
with deference as he whizzed her upwards. She kept a careful eye on
the brigand's hands, but there was no flash of steel, only a bright and
winning smile on his dark, handsome face. They had reached a very
high floor when he bowed her into a wide corridor, their footsteps

falling soundlessly in the thick carpet. He stopped at a door and beat a tattoo which must surely be a code, for it was opened almost immediately by a woman who could only be Motti. His duty fulfilled, the brigand vanished, doubtless to mount guard somewhere near at hand, alert, stiletto in hand.

As she divested herself of her coat in an ante-room, Josanne stammered her apologies for being so early, knowing that at this hour the absence of other coats was not at all ominous.

"We're all by ourselves," Motti said amiably, apparently using the Royal plural. "Madame Connelli was very glad to hear from you because Mrs. Danvers has asked her to get in touch with you, but she forgot to give your address."

So that was the explanation! To Aunt Marian, friends were friends, be they *divas* or typists. But Marian was Rorie's aunt, and she herself was Rorie's friend, and she might have to put in about an hour without mentioning his name. Relief mingled with apprehension.

The next she knew, Motti had coughed a professional cough, and had thrown open the door of an adjoining room.

Her first impression was of the panoramic view of Manhattan seen through the picture windows, then of the flowers which were arranged in groups everywhere, like in a florist's shop. Isabella Connelli was sitting at a table, signing photographs of herself, and it was as if a spotlight had been turned on to her as she stood up, holding out her hand, smiling, her green house-coat and her disarranged hair giving an impression of informality arranged by a skilful stage-director. She even staggered slightly as she moved, steadying herself against the table.

"I've got cramp," she said. "I've been asked for a thousand of these, and I've only about a hundred more to do." She pushed the photographs aside, and offered Josanne a chair. "I'll put cigarettes beside you because I always forget to offer them to people. And Motti will deal with the champagne. If there's something else you'd prefer, do say so. There's a *gorgeous* concoction the bar-tender has invented called *Cabaletta Connelli*. You're welcome to try it, but it had me almost insensible after the first few sips!" She was talking quickly, with the extraordinary accent Rorie raved about, ugly yet fascinating at the same time. And she was nervous, far more nervous than Josanne.

"You'll just sit down and relax. And Miss Murray can have anything she likes – except that elixir that gave us a headache for a week." And Motti settled Isabella on a chaise-longue, with her feet up, before she turned her attention to a bottle of champagne.

In a very short time the pale gold liquid had worked its magic.

Josanne told Isabella of her tour of the States, of the weird ways of her flatmates, and of the joy of working for George Hawtrey. She even confessed her surprise that within a few days of her arrival in New York she had met a man who had invited her out to dinner.

"He was with me last night," she said. "He's an adoring fan of yours, and I expect that's the reason why he bothers with me at all!"

Isabella was a good listener, knowing when to allow a few moments' silence, and when a little prompting was needed.

She had changed a great deal since Aunt Marian's party less than two years ago. She looked older than she had done then, and that she was pale and tired was visible even under her make-up. A gentle person, restful and kind, not formidable or alarming at all.

Motti came in with a menu, and Josanne, exclaiming that she had only come for a drink, was quickly silenced. She sank back into her chair.

"I'm alone tonight," Isabella said. "The Maestro usually has dinner with me, but he's at *Rigoletto*. Lisa Verini's singing Gilda, and he's interested. She has a lovely voice." She sounded wistful, recognizing the ephemeral nature of her art. "She's taken over from me for this season. *Lucia* is all I'm allowed to sing – for a little while."

"If I booked for you and got her, I'd want my money back!"

Isabella smiled. "The change was made before the box office opened. But I expect that's what people said about me, when I replaced a singer who'd fallen ill. One person's misfortune is another's opportunity."

"Nobody can ever, ever replace you."

"Nobody can ever, ever replace anyone. We're all unique, in our different ways. It just happens that I love to sing and people love to hear me."

"And when will they hear you in Wexford?"

She looked surprised. "In Wexford? Oh, of course – the Maestro's lollipop. I go there in October, but I'll be all over the world before then." She had lost interest in Wexford, like a child who had waited too long for a promised treat.

Motti served dinner from a trolley which was brought to the door. She stood over Isabella, coaxing her to eat, addressing her as Madame Connelli, which Josanne thought was strangely formal. These two women must have spent hours together, alone, for years and years.

She noted that Isabella ate chocolate gateau without persuasion, and this prompted her to produce the chocolate mints she had brought as a gift when Motti brought the coffee tray and left it on a table between them.

"You are most kind." Isabella undid the packet delightedly, as if she had never received a box of chocolates before. "Like most singers, I have to watch my weight, but just now I may eat what I like, and I love these."

"You're terribly thin. What has been the matter with you?" As soon as she said it Josanne regretted it. She had sounded like her mother, almost rude.

Isabella folded the wrapper from her chocolate mint into the shape of a tiny boat, and put it carefully on the coffee tray. Josanne thought she was going to ignore the question, but then she said "I had some sort of virus infection. I felt ill before I boarded the plane for New York. I was worried about something – in a state of panic. Flying away offered a silly means of escape. The next thing I knew, I was back in Italy, being pumped full of antibiotics. The cure was worse than the malady, so far as I was concerned. But at least I recovered my voice!"

"We were worried about your life, not your voice."

"That's not important. I'm not worth anything unless I can sing." But she was laughing, not inviting sympathy. "I'm so cossetted that I'm practically under house-arrest. I'm confined to this hotel and to the Lincoln Center, but on previous trips I used to have a house on Long Island for my days off. And I loved going to the shops, and walking in Central Park. I even borrowed toddlers so that I could go to the Children's Zoo. And there was Coney Island, carousels and hoop-la. I won a plaster giraffe which I carted round as a mascot for years, until I knocked it off my dressing-table and it smashed to smithereens." She frowned now, remembering the freedom of the past. "Could be there's something in superstition. It's ever since then that I've been pushed around so that I can hardly call my soul my own." She stood up suddenly and walked over to the window, hugging herself, the light of a giant gyrating advertisement changing the colour of her face. "Last night, for a ghastly moment, I couldn't remember which opera I was singing. Then I saw the blood on my dress and knew that I was going on for the mad scene in *Lucia*. It was all over in a second, but like a nightmare it seemed to last for ages."

"It didn't show on the stage."

"It wouldn't matter on the stage. I was supposed to be mad. It's when I'm mad and not on the stage that I get worried." She shivered and returned to the chaise-longue, arranging her house-coat carefully, so that her lovely legs were covered. "It's all this travel, I suppose. One gets disorientated. Tell me now – what brought you to New York? Aunt Marian tells me a lot about you. She misses your visits. She's really, truly interested in us all."

Josanne could not resist the candid eyes, the gentle suggestion

319

that a bond existed between them because they shared an honorary aunt. She admitted that it was the threat of a hopeless love-affair that had made her ask for that transfer. 'He's tall, dark, and handsome. Every woman's dream-man. I hadn't a chance with him, so I fled."

"There's a psychological reason why some people's instinct is to run away. Did you know that? But at least you had a practical reason. Did it work?"

"In a way it's made it worse. I think about him all the time, and I write imaginary letters to him every night before I go to sleep."

"What sort of letters?"

"Not love-letters. Nothing like that. Things like the excitement of seeing the Statue of Liberty, and the sudden pang of home-sickness in the middle of Washington Square."

"A substitute for crying yourself to sleep."

"I'd never do that. I'm not the crying type."

"Tears that run down the cheeks bring relief. Tears that are bottled up pour into the heart, solidify, turn it to stone. I didn't invent that. It's out of an opera, like most of my thinking is. But it could be true."

She handed the box of chocolate mints to Josanne. There were only two left. They each took one, and Isabella added another little paper boat to the row on the coffee tray. Then she said, "Some day you should write that letter and mail it. It can't do any harm, and it might do some good."

"I'd never dare! And it would make nonsense of the extremes I've gone to in order to avoid him."

"Being in love has nothing to do with sense, so don't let that worry you!" But she was not going to pursue the matter. She led on to talk about opera singers, past and present, a subject that fascinated Josanne and was a safe refuge for them both.

When she left, Josanne had acquired two signed photographs, one for herself and one for Desmond Drayton; also a little piece of hair, intended for Desmond, but as she tucked it into her wallet she thought it unlikely that she would part with it. Motti accompanied her to the elevator, and the brigand drove her home through the crowded streets of Manhattan night-life.

There were party noises when she reached the apartment. When she joined the others in the cigarette-hazed living-room, she found them grouped around the floor surrounded by empty coffee-cups, half-filled glasses, and an assortment of empty bottles. A record-player was blaring a popular song, and Susan was wound round a young man whose hair was as long as her own.

Josanne slopped some wine into a used glass, and curled up on a chair. Nobody asked her where she had been, and by tomorrow no one would care.

At the Waldorf-Astoria Isabella Connelli put her signature to the last of the photographs, and piled them into a box. When Motti came to order her to bed she was staring at the smiling pictures of herself, and the tears were pouring into her heart.

47

Josanne wrote to Rorie.

"I have had supper with Isabella. Had I known that I was going to see her I'd have asked you if you wanted to write to her, and I could have given her your letter, so that at least you would know she had received it. She is an adorable person, and she looks tired and ill, not at all like a goddess from Valhalla. She is giving a concert in the Carnegie Hall at the end of April. Do you want me to do anything about it?"

Rorie replied; "Thank you for your offer about the letter. There is nothing for me to write about. I hope you enjoy the concert. Bardini, of course, is conducting."

These lines, at the end of a long, newsy letter, were his last words on the subject. She decided not to mention Isabella to him again.

Her heavy luggage had arrived, so that now she was surrounded with the books and records she loved most. She introduced Desmond Drayton to her flatmates, but he dated none of them, although he often took her out, lavishing gratitude upon her because of the photograph of Connelli, which was now in a silver frame by his bedside. He had not been told about the lock of hair.

The weather was getting warmer, and the need to keep out of the apartment on Saturday afternoons was less trying, because instead of spending hours in the cinema, there was the whole of New York to see. When Desmond was with her, as he often was, there were places she could explore where she would not have dared to go alone.

One Saturday early in April, he took her to Coney Island. It was far larger and more exciting than she had pictured it, and she rode on carousels and clung to him on the switch-back, and won a plaster gnome at hoop-la. That night, she wrote to Niall and told him all about it. A week later she received a reply. He wrote, as she had done, of things that had interested or amused him, and he asked her to write again. She did.

On the eve of the Connelli concert she received a second letter. He had spent the weekend in London, and had seen Rorie, who now seldom left Cirencester, morosely making the most of the time that was left to him there. He concluded, "If only Aunt Marian would phase out Isabella as resolutely as he has done I think he'd be happier. It's not easy for him while those links remain."

Josanne took the hint. She had written a letter of good wishes for the concert to Isabella, and had added as a postscript, "I have done as you suggested. I wrote that letter and he's replied. I am very grateful to you and always will be, even if it comes to nothing".

She had meant to hand in her note at the Waldorf-Astoria, and it was still in her handbag when she read Niall's letter. If she was going to make any progress with him she could not afford to have any links with Isabella, so she tore it up into tiny pieces and flushed them down the lavatory.

Rorie had said that concerts terrified Isabella, making her feel vulnerable and exposed. As she took her seat beside Desmond Drayton at Carnegie Hall, Josanne thought about that, and wondered what Isabella was feeling now, waiting there with the Maestro and Bardini, surrounded no doubt by flowers and good wishes, and knowing that thousands of people were anticipating her magic, and a few of them would be happy to detect some flaw in her performance.

Isabella wore a plain, white dress, her only ornament an emerald brooch, catching the green of her eyes. She looked beautiful, and she looked diffident, smiling at Bardini, then at the audience, offering herself, wanting to please them. She had to wait while Bardini allowed time for the tumultuous greeting to die down, but she bowed several times, her lips moving as she uttered, unheard, her thanks. Then the pianist played the first few bars of *Doretta's Song* from Puccini's *La Rondine*, the orchestra joined in, and she began to sing.

"That audience was composed of New York's upper crust, yet they were as uproarious as any crowd at a pop concert," Desmond said afterwards, as he and Josanne had supper at their favourite Chinese restaurant.

It was true. From the first moment, Connelli had captivated her audience, and when she acknowledged its applause she conveyed the impression that she, too, shared its pleasure. It was as if each individual mattered personally to her, was her friend. It was an inspired performance, and its culmination in an almost unknown song by Benjamin Britten was a masterpiece of programme planning, for what appeared to be yet another encore soothed the audience into silence, and they were left with the wistful request – *Tell Me the Truth About Love*. This time, when she left the stage, they knew Connelli would not come back. Josanne recalled her evening with Isabella. That talk of panic and disorientation had been intended, she was sure, for Rorie. It would explain that telephone call, perhaps re-kindle his interest and arouse his sympathy. Isabella had been counting on Josanne to pass the information on to him, as she certainly would have done, had she not established a pen-friendship with Niall. Isabella had no idea that the dream-man they had been talking about was Rorie's twin brother, so that in offering advice, she had severed what could be a valuable link with Rorie.

"You're unusually quiet tonight," Desmond said towards the end of supper. He knew how silent Josanne would be when she had been listening to music.

"I'm thinking of the truth about love. It's probably the most selfish emotion there is. It makes people treacherous and unscrupulous." But she would say no more, for she was not sure what she meant.

The following day was Saturday, and because she was still in a state of euphoria, she forgot about the ban on returning to the apartment in the afternoon after her shopping. She had reached her bedroom when she remembered, and was about to tiptoe to the door, when Susan emerged from the bathroom, a towel wound turban-like round her head. When she saw Josanne, she stood still, rigid, as if she had seen a ghost.

"I'm sorry if I startled you," Josanne said. "I forgot it was Saturday." There was water dripping down Susan's neck. Josanne asked the obvious question, "What's happened to the boyfriend?"

She could see that there would be no answer. She went to the kitchen and made tea. She took the tray to the living-room, where Susan was listlessly brushing her hair, helping it to dry.

"How long have you been spending Saturday afternoons alone?" She handed Susan a cup of tea. "Is this the first time, or has it happened before?"

"He said he would come every Saturday. It lasted for three weeks. I couldn't tell the others it had ended so soon. I was so proud of him. He's a very well-known guitarist, though you're too high-brow to bother about that."

Susan was in tears, her face blotchy. She was not weeping for a lost love but for her hurt pride, her deception being found out.

"You won't tell the others, will you?" she said. It was all that really mattered to her.

"Of course I won't. Just tell them that you kicked him out because all that smoke got in your eyes. It could easily be true."

Josanne left her to finish her cry while she washed up. When she returned, Susan's hair was dry, but her face was still wet. She was fiddling with the knobs on the television set. The name Connelli boomed into the room.

"Hold it!" Josanne said. It was the end of a news item. Isabella was holding the arm of a bronzed property tycoon. She was spending a few days in California before returning to Europe after her sensational concert tour.

"The only pretending she has to do is that she doesn't go to bed with all her millionaires," Susan said. She saw Josanne's jaw tighten. She had seen the rows of Connelli records in Josanne's room. "You're lucky she's still alive. There was that drug overdose a year ago, and last August an abortion."

Josanne was used to hearing stories about Isabella, but nothing of this sort. "Where did this sordid gossip come from?" she managed to say.

"I've got a boyfriend who's in the chorus at the Met. He told me some things that don't bear repeating, such as the close relationship between Connelli and the Irishwoman who's supposed to be her dresser. She's as kinky as they come. Don't look so shocked. Surely you can admire her voice without having to believe all that nauseating stuff about how angelic she is?"

There was a short silence, while Josanne thought about that prolonged cold, Aunt Marian's anxiety, Grania Lamont's hostility, and Rorie's sudden change of heart. Then she said evenly, "People do like to open the sewers of their minds upon the famous. There's not a word of truth in what you've said. I know her fairly well. To know her is to know it isn't true".

"You've been remarkably secretive about your friendship! With her reputation and your indifference to men, you'd better watch it, or some funny things will be getting said about you too."

Josanne's fingers were stinging. She had never slapped anyone's face before, but instead of relieving her feelings it made her feel sick.

Susan was rubbing her face, astounded, yet shaken into realizing the enormity of what she had said.

Josanne went to the door. "I'm going out. When I come back, I don't want an apology for your disgusting allegations. I don't want ever to hear another word about it again. I'm sorry I slapped you. No, that isn't true. I wish I'd done it sooner, and a great deal harder." Then she collected her handbag from her bedroom, and ignoring all the warnings she had been given about walking alone in side streets, she found that she was close to the Hudson river.

She stood for a long time, watching the tug-boats and the slow progress of a ship making for the open sea. Her head throbbed and she was still trembling. Nagging in her brain, like an engine that would not stop, was the thought that the ugly rumours could be true. They explained so much. They could be true.

True or false, it could injure a woman. Chrissie had taught her this in English and in Gaelic.

Sick at heart, she turned and made her way home.

*   *   *

During the suffocating heat of the New York summer, Grania wrote to tell Josanne that Michael Ames had died, peacefully and happily, after a short illness. Niall and Rorie had come to Mull for the funeral, so had Aunt Marian, who remembered him when he first arrived at Kilcaraig, his eyes full of fun, loving everybody and everything he saw.

"You will not be surprised to hear that we're buying Caraig Lodge and all the land that goes with it," Grania wrote. "Michael wanted to leave it to us, but mercifully he spoke to my husband about it, and was reminded that his sister has a family now. We didn't want anyone to feel deprived after his death, and this he understood. He always understood. I shall miss him dreadfully."

Josanne folded the letter away. Michael, more than anyone, was the person in whom Grania Lamont confided, especially her worries over Rorie and Isabella. And he had never come under Isabella's spell. His misgivings were there from the start.

Niall wrote frequently now. Rorie had been accepted as a student at the Royal College of Music, an arrangement which apparently caused his parents no surprise. Catriona was to attend a secretarial college in London when she left school, so both she and Rorie would live with Aunt Marian. Meantime, Morag MacKinnon, who belonged to Kilcaraig and was a retired nurse, had moved to the flat in Lowndes Square to give Aunt Marian the little extra help she needed. Niall became expansive about this, thinking out the future, and how age and inflation were going to affect them all. His letters, from being factual, were becoming personal and self-revealing. Josanne unconsciously replied to him in a similar style.

She spent a wonderful holiday with friends of the Hawtreys in California, and when she returned to New York, letters had accumulated for her, but only one of them was from Niall. She was eager now for closer contact with him, not just for thoughts committed to flimsy sheets of paper. When she and Niall met again, they could find that they were strangers, and Isabella's well-meant advice would have been in vain.

Isabella. She was still there in Josanne's mind, like an uneasy wraith, a poltergeist. She was singing *Norma* and *Linda di Chamounix* all over Europe, as if to prove to the world that her voice and her versality were unimpaired by her illness, yet these engagements must have been made long before her illness struck.

Peace was maintained between Josanne and Susan since that dreadful Saturday afternoon, but Josanne knew that nothing could repair the damage that had been done.

She was repelled by what she had heard, and she felt guilty that the spoken word could influence her feelings so much more strongly than the personality of Isabella herself. She longed to ask Niall for his opinion, but it was not a suitable subject for a letter. In the meantime, Isabella's records remained on their shelf, and the photograph in its drawer, under the jewel-case that contained the lock of hair.

One evening, she was working late in the office. The air-conditioning was an encouragement to stay at her desk instead of going out into the street. Her hands were sticky, and she had to tear up the letter she had typed because it was smudged, and nothing must leave the office that was less than perfect.

The buzzer sounded. She picked up the receiver. It was Reception, asking if she was still in the office. "I won't be long now," she said. "Don't lock me in. And thank you for remembering me."

She returned the receiver to its cradle, and he said "Josanne".

She swung round in her chair. Niall was standing by the door to the outer office. He looked mature, not the boy she had left behind last winter.

She stood up, her new-found assurance draining out of her. She was wearing a neat navy-blue dress and her hair, as always, was immaculate, but she was wearing her spectacles.

They shook hands. He was cool. She was aware of her stickiness.

"Do you always work as late as this?" he asked.

"I'm goaded into it by all those pep talks we had back home." She realized that there was a catch in her voice, and hoped he wouldn't notice. "You didn't tell me you were coming over," she added quickly.

"I came on an impulse." He half moved towards her, then changed his mind. "I want to take you out to dinner. The girl in that sleazy flat you share told me she thought you'd be free."

That would be Susan, trying to imply that she was a social failure.

"I'm out a lot, but you're in luck tonight." She stood awkwardly, her hand on the back of her chair. Her eyes slid to the typewriter.

"Forget that letter, it can wait until tomorrow."

"I can't, George Hawtrey wants it," she faltered. "But I suppose you can countermand it – you're the boss!"

"Thank you for reminding me of that. I've come to talk to you about your work. You have very good reports."

"Sent by George Hawtrey, in Top Secret envelopes, I suppose!" It was the only correspondence she didn't deal with herself. As she spoke, her heart sank. It could be the truth. This could just be a business visit after all.

"Do you feel like changing your job?"

She looked round the office, thinking of George and the other people who had helped her so much from the moment she arrived.

"I'd rather not, please. But my contract ends in January. I'll have to go where I'm told. What do you want me to do?"

"Marry me."

"Niall!" She sank onto the little chair and swivelled it towards him. He was still standing close to the main door. She hadn't even asked him to sit down.

"This hasn't happened as I had meant it to do," he said, his own voice strained. "I suppose things don't. But when you asked for a transfer, I thought you had fallen for Rorie. Girls always do. But I was puzzled when you sounded disappointed when he gave up Isabella – yet you went on writing to him. Then suddenly, out of the blue, you wrote to me, and I feel we have got to know one another rather well." He was leaning back against the door, and she could see the pulse beating in his cheek. Her eyes were riveted on him. "I think it was seeing you beside that cow, with those absurd little frilly pants in your hand. . . . This is a damned silly way to propose, but I've never done it before. Shall we go and have dinner? Maybe I'll talk you into it by the end of the evening."

She stood up and said "Niall" again, then she was in his arms, feeling his heart thudding against her breast, feeling his lips crush hers. The telephone rang, but still they kissed. At last he released her.

"Answer that – it's never going to stop."

It was Reception, reminding her of the time.

"This little cog is holding up the whole machine," he said, fondling her hair.

"I must go home and change."

"Stay as you are. I know a Hungarian restaurant that caters specially for lovers. Flowers, candles, music, everything that puts you in the mood. Then we'll go to the Sheraton and I'll show you the wonderful view from my window."

"I seem to have heard that one before!"

The Hungarian restaurant was the perfect prelude to the night. He drove her there in the company car kept specially for V.I.P.s and she was reminded of that first day in the office as he led her to the parking lot. Now it would be V.I.P. treatment all the time, a side of Niall's life she had least thought about.

His suite at the Sheraton was filled with flowers, and there was champagne waiting in an ice bucket, just as there had been at the Waldorf-Astoria. Even now she could not forget Isabella.

"You must have been very sure I'd come," she said.

"I wasn't. But if you hadn't, you wouldn't have known that I'd prepared for you."

She sat on the chaise-longue, as Isabella had done, with her feet up. "Does that stuff we had at dinner mix all right with champagne?" she asked.

"That stuff was okay. It doesn't matter whether they mix or not. I'll take care of you. I'll always take care of you. You've nothing to be scared about any more."

They were on to their second bottle when he said he must telephone Kilcaraig.

"You'll give them a fright. It must be about four in the morning back home."

"They'll think someone's found a cow in a bog!"

"Will they be angry about us?"

"Of course not. They'll be thrilled. You're just right for Kilcaraig."

"I'm not marrying Kilcaraig. I'm marrying you."

"It's the same thing."

It was a long call, because Grania had to be woken up, and then she talked while Roderick fetched a bottle of champagne from the cellar. From thousands of miles apart they drank to their future together.

When they rang off, Josanne said, "Why are your parents so wonderful to me, when they utterly reject Isabella?"

"You make sense. She doesn't."

"Is that the only reason?"

"What else could it be?"

At last she poured it all out to him, all that Susan had said. "It's not that I didn't know these things happen – I'm not that stupid – but it's creepy when it's someone I admire so much. Aunt Marian wouldn't understand about it, but it's different for your mother, your family, for Rorie."

"Isabella's love-life isn't our problem, and I'm not having her spoil things for us now."

Even Broadway was beginning to sleep when he drove her home. She tip-toed to her room, undressed in the dark, and flopped into bed for what remained of that magical night.

48

The flat in Maybank Court had an elegance which Josanne had never appreciated when she lived there before.

Her parents had met her at Heathrow Airport, and everything had been planned to make her homecoming both exciting and memorable. William and Sybil could at last feel proud of their daughter. Ever since they had received her telephone call from New York two weeks ago they had been preparing for today. Her bedroom was newly papered and painted, and a magnificent new record-player had replaced the old one that used to be in a corner, hidden by her bed.

"An engagement present," her father said. "We've missed so much hearing the operas you used to listen to day and night. We're glad to have you back."

He sounded as if he meant it. The engagement had not yet been formally announced, but Sybil had told friends, and a pile of letters of good wishes awaited her.

"The Fergusons are coming in for drinks tomorrow evening," Sybil said. "It's all thanks to them that this has happened." She didn't add how good it was of them to have bothered with her. Josanne felt she wouldn't be hearing that any more.

She had asked Niall not to see her on her first day home. She had expected to be overwhelmed by her old sense of inferiority when she was back with her parents, and she had not wanted him to witness it. By tomorrow, she would have adapted to her surroundings. But already she knew that her fears were unfounded. Eight months in New York had given her a measure of self-confidence which she would never have achieved had she remained in London.

On the morning after her arrival she overslept, and her mother brought her breakfast on a tray. As she had expected, the arrangements for the wedding had been worked out in detail. It was to take place in April in St. Mary Abbots, or St. Paul's Knightsbridge if she preferred, and the reception would be in the Hyde Park Hotel. The bridesmaids would wear yellow, the colour of spring, and Josanne's dress would be made by any couturier of her choice.

She ate her egg, and listened to her mother talking; then she said, "I want to be married at Kilcaraig. I hate the thought of a London wedding, and I'm going to live there all my life. The Lamonts always go to the village church."

"But you're Church of England," Sybil replied. She had pictured it all – the choir, the red carpet, the photographers, and her daughter the bride of one of the richest men in Britain.

"The Lamonts are Church of Scotland," Josanne said. "I'll be just as validly married in their church. It's what I want. I've talked to Niall about it, and he says it's entirely up to us. If you're determined on a London wedding, I'll have one, but it's not what I want." She bit into a slice of toast, smothered in marmalade. She was feeling unexpectedly emotional, and wasn't thinking what she was doing. Sybil saw this, and dreaded the embarrassment of a sentimental scene.

"We'll talk to Daddy," she said soothingly. "I'm sure we both want you to have a really happy day, but it's most unusual for a bride to be married from the bridegroom's home."

Josanne could see that she would have it her way if she pressed on now. "We want to be married before Christmas. Once the place and date are settled, choosing a few clothes won't take long."

"Marry in haste, repent at leisure," Sybil said, unconsciously quoting the nanny who had dominated her life in the nursery days at Montfort Hall. It was a school now. It had been a perfect setting for her wedding reception after her marriage to William all those years ago. Taxes had driven her family from the home it had occupied for centuries. The Lamonts, too, had been forced to sell Kilcaraig, and it had taken Grania's resourcefulness to restore it to the Lamonts. Josanne's future mother-in-law was someone to be reckoned with.

"How are you going to get on with Niall's mother?" she asked.

"I'm very fond of her. It should be all right."

"Under that charm, she's as hard as nails, and you'll be living right beside her, at Caraig Lodge."

Josanne considered this remark. Her mother may already have heard something of Grania's plans.

"Niall and I are going to live in the castle. His parents are moving to Caraig Lodge. They want it that way. Niall will take over the responsibility of running the estate."

"It won't work," Sybil said. "The Lamonts will be interfering – directing you from Caraig Lodge, and resenting you being in the castle when they are virtually in a dower house."

"It's their choice, and nobody will interfere with Niall." Josanne now knew she had won. The wedding would be at Kilcaraig, and it would take place in October. If she handled this carefully, her mother would think she had decided on it all herself.

Sybil took the tray, but paused at the door. "What's going to happen to Rorie? Where's he going to live?"

"With us, of course; it's his home."

"And when he marries, do you become a communal menage? Are you going to enjoy sharing your kitchen with Isabella Connelli?"

Josanne laughed. "Mother, you're out of date. That affair is all over, much to my regret. I can't think of anything nicer than to have Connelli about the place. But I just won't be drawn into taking sides." But her mother hadn't heard the last sentence, because she had closed the door.

Josanne got up, and when she was soaking in her bath, she thought about Rorie. Her mother was right. Nobody knew what would happen to him. One sure thing was that he would never settle down in Kilcaraig. He would want to have music. He would want Isabella. Whatever he liked to say at present, she would bet a dollar to a doughnut it wasn't the end of the affair.

*   *   *

Rorie was in the library at Kilcaraig. He had arrived the previous day, and had brought with him a number of newspaper reports of Niall's forthcoming marriage. There were some photographs of Niall and Josanne, and the "Town Talk" of the *Chronicle* reported an October wedding at Kilcaraig, followed by a honeymoon in the Mediterranean on a yacht lent by friends. The reporter must have talked to Niall, because the information was accurate. The yacht belonged to the Mountstephans, who were in oil and shipping, and who were the only friends they had who owned such luxury.

Catriona had skimmed through the pages, and had dismissed them with disdain. She had been sullen and unyielding ever since she had heard of the engagement. Even Niall had been unable to soften her and persuade her to accept the inevitable.

"She seemed to be so nice," she had said, as if Josanne were committing some enormity in marrying Catriona's brother. It was useless to point out to her that soon she would be in London, at a secretarial college, and that later she would be doing a job, and would at any rate be living less at Kilcaraig, where changes were bound to take place as the years went by.

Seeing it all in print brought home to her that it really was true. Josanne Murray would rule at Kilcaraig, and she and her parents would be relegated to live at Caraig Lodge. At seventeen years of age she could look to a bleak future, and the knowledge that all she loved, even her home, would now belong to the past. Niall was her special person. She had thought he felt the same about her. She felt hollow, broken, finished. She wished she were dead.

The evenings were drawing in now, and by the time of the nine o'clock news it was getting dark. Television reception was poor that night, but Rorie managed to see the black faces of Commonwealth politicians, and the white shirts of cricketers somewhere or other. He was not interested in the news. He was not interested in anything, although he feigned enthusiasm over Niall's engagement. He understood how Catriona felt, but he was able to conceal his misery. He had plenty of practice, and Catriona had none.

His parents were over at Caraig Lodge, measuring for curtains and carpets, in preparation for the great upheaval which would take place when Niall and his bride went off for their honeymoon. They would return after Christmas, to find the castle redecorated, and Mama and Papa would be installed at Caraig Lodge. Rorie was to keep his room at the castle. Josanne wanted this, and it would be unkind of him to point out that it was of no interest to him where his home might be.

He switched off the television, and went through to the kitchen to ask Chrissie if she knew where Catriona could be. Chrissie was sitting on the big chair by the Aga, which she now occupied a great deal, as her rheumatism was troubling her. It was becoming her throne, from which she ruled the household. Cathy, her niece, was shaping well under her watchful eye. Continuity had been established at Kilcaraig Castle.

Chrissie said she had seen Catriona go out immediately after dinner. She was probably at Caraig Lodge, helping her parents paint, but when Grania and Roderick came home, Catriona wasn't with them.

Anxious, but not wanting to worry his parents, Rorie muttered an excuse and went outside. He had not gone far when he saw Flush, the spaniel, sniffing along the ground a few yards ahead of Catriona. As she came close to Rorie, she averted her head. He could see that she had been crying. He held out his handkerchief.

She wiped her eyes and blew her nose. "My world has fallen apart," she said. "I'll never be happy again."

"That makes two of us," Rorie said.

"I'm going to hide my broken heart under a mask of cheerfulness. I'm going to be nice to Josanne, because I'll do anything on earth for Niall. Even that."

"Very commendable!"

They had reached the house. Rorie opened the back door, and told her to run upstairs and wash the tear-stains from her face.

Then he joined his parents in the library.

*   *   *

Isabella Connelli was sitting on the terrace of her villa at Ravello. She was having a few days' rest and she was studying *The Marriage of Figaro* because she was to sing the Countess at the Salzburg Festival next season. It was not a new role – she had sung it before.

A copy of *The Times* was on the table in front of her, and the Maestro had marked an engagement announcement for her attention. Josanne Murray was to marry Niall Lamont. It would have been Niall she was talking about that night at the Waldorf-Astoria. No wonder the plan to have first-hand news of Rorie had failed. She thought wryly of how she had hoped to introduce the subject lightly, not showing much interest. She had practised the inflections as if she were rehearsing for an important performance at a gala first night, but when it came to the point, her courage had failed. To refer to Kilcaraig, to the Lamonts, to Rorie had withered in her throat, dried up like an amateur who had over-learnt a single line.

Write that letter and mail it. The advice she was incapable of applying to herself might have been partly responsible for this happy ending. She would like to think so. She would never know.

This was one of her bad days, when everything seemed bleak. She longed to talk to someone who would care about what was going to happen to her, not just to her voice. She had thought Rorie would care, but he had not even given her a chance to tell him. She had brought it on herself. She had made an exhibition of herself there among the shrubs beside Lake Como. Her skin prickled with the shame of it. She richly deserved the humiliation of the rejection she had received from her disenchanted lover. She was too old for such antics. She should have had more sense.

She picked up her pen and wrote a letter.

"Dear Josanne, I have seen the announcement of your engagement to Niall Lamont, and I want you to know how happy I am for you. He is a very fortunate young man.

When I was in New York in April and you didn't contact me, I wondered if your heart had pulled you homeward sooner than you expected. It looks as if it had. Please accept my good wishes for the future of you both.

Yours sincerely,
Isabella Connelli"

The signature was beautiful, the rest written in that copy-book, spidery writing, betraying her lack of education. The Maestro had said to her, "Don't write letters. They could end up in a museum and disgrace you. Use the telephone, if you must communicate with someone, otherwise put your thoughts down on paper, then tear them up. They don't matter to anyone but you, so you don't want them preserved for posterity."

She had obeyed the Maestro. She only wrote letters to the Sisters, because letters to them would never end up in a museum, and she knew better than to write her thoughts, as they would realize how deeply she was disturbed, and how sad.

She re-read her letter, and thought how awful it would look in the eyes of Niall and Rorie and all the other Lamonts. They might even think she was being cunning and using Josanne as a means of stirring Rorie's conscience, so that he would feel guilty about her, and be obliged to contact her again.

She tore up the letter and threw the fragments onto a flower bed. Then she put a match to them – dust to dust and ashes to ashes. She sucked at her tongue to stifle her tears.

As the flames flickered, she returned to the score of *The Marriage of Figaro*, concentrating, trying to suppress the fear that had such a hold on her. If she could share it with someone it would not be so bad. If she could tell Rorie – but he didn't want to know. She was back on the treadmill of her thoughts, round and round, until the music took possession of her mind, and she found her one infallible refuge from despair.

49

Rorie drove Catriona to London in the Volvo he had bought during the summer. Grania and Roderick waved them off from Kilcaraig with some apprehension, but Rorie was a careful driver, and they knew he could be trusted in the care of his sister.

Niall would marry Josanne in the village church in October, and preparations for the wedding had delayed both Rorie and Catriona from presenting themselves at their respective places of education at the beginning of term. Catriona looked forward to living in London with Aunt Marian, but not to attending a secretarial college. Rorie, who had longed to study music since he was a child, now believed that all he would achieve would be a constant reminder of Isabella, practising her scales, studying her roles, living the life he had wanted to share with her, but from which he had now cut himself off completely.

Catriona had seemed suddenly to grow up. She talked of the future with a realism that surprised him. After her year in London, she would spend a year at Grenoble, and then she would want to travel and see the world.

"I won't be at Kilcaraig much, anyway," she said. "And we must both be a blessing, not a burden, to Aunt Marian."

Grania and Roderick had tried to prevail on Marian to live at Kilcaraig, so that in due course she would end her life where she had begun it.

"I could live to be a hundred, and think how awful that would be for you," she had said. "I'm staying in London, but you'll bury me at Kilcaraig in a coffin. I don't want to be sent home in a wee poke."

It was getting late when they arrived at Lowndes Square. Marian had been looking out for them for some time, but had reminded herself about punctures, and running out of petrol. She found it difficult to realize that the journey from Oban to London now took hours, not days.

"Your room, Catriona," she said, leading the way along a wide passage, and opening a door. There was a divan, and two sag-bags, a record-player, a tape recorder, and stereo speakers fixed to the wall. There was also a typewriter on a proper office table, to act as a reminder that the room was intended for work as well as leisure. It was a dream room for a girl of seventeen.

"Your room's next door," she said to Rorie, when she had extricated herself from Catriona's grateful hug. "Nothing trendy for you – you're a big boy now!"

There was a handsome bed, an antique bureau, two armchairs, and there was a grand piano. On it was a photograph of Isabella. It was signed, "To Aunt Marian from Isabella Connelli, with love and thanks".

Rorie picked it up and looked at it, his face expressionless.

"How did you get this?" he asked.

"She gave it to me last time she was in London."

Marian studied the photograph. It was very much a publicity photograph, careful laughter, even in her eyes. "If you don't want it here, I'll take it away, but her picture is all over the place, so having this shouldn't make any difference, and I think she'd like to be here." She bustled off to see if Morag was ready with the supper.

Catriona examined it. "I think it's a shame that I've never met her. I'm going to call on her next time she's in London."

"You'll do nothing of the sort. She'd be very much embarrassed. She wouldn't know what to say to you at all."

"I'd know what to say to her, but I'm not telling." With that, she went to her room, with its sag-bags and its stereo equipment, and in a few moments, Isabella's voice, singing *Caro Nome* flooded the flat.

When the record came to an end, Catriona came back and said, "I shouldn't have done that, and I won't call on her if you don't want me to, but I think our family, turning its back on someone who can sing like that proves that we're in-bred, or for some reason or other crazy. We should be worshipping her at her shrine, instead of kicking her in the teeth. There, I've said it. I'm on her side, but I won't mention her any more. I think supper's ready."

He followed her to the dining-room. What she had said was true. They were all insane, but none so insane as he. He had held her in his arms, had possessed her, had pledged his undying love, yet when she needed him she had appealed to him in vain.

The door bell rang. It was Niall and Josanne, who had been to a cinema. Catriona hadn't seen Josanne since her return from New York. She greeted her with loving enthusiasm to the surprise and pleasure of Niall, and she admired the huge solitaire diamond engagement ring.

"You are lucky," she said. "I'm longing to get married and have people looking up to me. And I want passionate kisses, and love bites and all the things you read about in women's magazines."

This Catriona must have forgotten the fright she once had in the heather, when offered just such an experience. Rorie chose this moment to remind her again of the two snapshots of herself, sent anonymously, which she had tried to hide from him. She laughed.

"I was minding my own business, taking photographs of rabbits, and a gorgeous young man came and took some snaps of me. I didn't tell anyone, because you'd all think I'd been philandering, which I wasn't. It was a romantic and exciting experience which fizzled out because he hadn't even the decency to write me a wee note when he sent the pictures."

"So you don't know who he was?"

"I'll find out some day, and I'll marry him and wear a great big diamond ring."

Aunt Marian signed. "I'm afraid, Catriona, that you have a long way to go. You look grown up, but you're just a baby after all."

"I'm nearly as old as Mama was when she first married, and that turned out all right, although it was Kilcaraig that she loved, and not poor Robert Dutton. But it's the man I love, and I've written a sonnet to prove it. It's a tear-jerker, and shows how deeply emotional I am inside. Come and see my room, Josanne. It's all cushions and stereo, and you can pour out all your secrets to my understanding heart."

"What's happened to her?" Niall asked, as soon as Catriona and Josanne had gone. "She was furious when I arrived back from New York. She said she'd give Josanne hell when she saw her."

"Commonsense has prevailed," Rorie said. "Come to my room – I've something to show you."

Niall looked at the photograph of Isabella, then replaced it on the piano. "Isn't it better to let sleeping *prime donne* lie?" he said.

Rorie placed it in a drawer in the bureau. "There!" he said. "Out of sight and out of mind. She won't be visiting Aunt Marian now that we are here. Tell me how the wedding plans are going. I hear there's to be a marquee for the overflow from the church. Kilcaraig will take on the gala appearance of the Mull and Morvern Agricultural Show!"

While they talked, they could hear Catriona playing a Connelli record to Josanne. It was one of a group of love songs she was to sing at a concert during the Wexford Festival. Rorie had read about it in the newspapers.

"She's getting the lollipop the Maestro promised her," he said. "And she's singing Zerlina in *Fra Diavolo* – it's a role she loves. She'll enjoy Wexford. She's wanted to go there so very much."

Niall sighed. Rorie was thinking only of Isabella, not of the forthcoming marriage at all.

* * *

The choice of Kilcaraig as the setting for the wedding relieved the Murrays of a great deal of worry and expense.

The Lamonts arranged that an hotel normally only open during the tourist season, would accommodate the guests who had to travel to Mull. Hope Garnett was unable to be a bridesmaid, because Adrian Ferguson had used his influence to get her a job in Paris, and she would be too new there to ask for time off for the wedding, but Josanne secured the services of Pauline and Mary Ferguson, and decided that, with Catriona, she had enough of a retinue for the small church.

She and her parents were to spend the night before the wedding with the Lucas family at Duff. Grania's two sisters, Diana and Helen, were to stay at the castle, which they had always disliked and seldom visited, but duty compelled them to come on this occasion, representing, as it were, their own families, all of whom were now married. Niall, Rorie and Catriona were united in their relief that only what they called the lesser aunts would be staying at the castle. They had always disliked their cousins.

The MacNeills, once of Ardcross, were also staying with them. Hector MacNeill, on leave from the Navy, was to be one of the ushers. That Josanne's family had been the link re-establishing the old Lamont-MacNeill friendship was one of the fascinating side-effects of the marriage.

"I'll be glad when it's all over," Chrissie told Catriona, as they made Aunt Marian's bed on the eve of the wedding. Only Chrissie knew how to be sure it was properly aired and tucked in the way Marian liked it. "You'll be the next to go, and I'll see you have a grand banquet, and an even bigger bride's-cake – if I'm spared."

MacBrayne's Road Transport had delivered crates at the village hall; one contained the cake, but it was so large that it was said in the district that yet another Scotfast house was to be built on Mull.

The Fergusons arrived with Marian on the afternoon boat, and assured Niall that he had not been jilted, because his bride was now on her way to Duff. Pauline and Mary made straight for their bedroom, and soon were busy with face-cream and curlers, giggling

338

together because Josanne's gorgeous cousin Hector was to be there. Mary had never met him, but Pauline had talked of him ever since Josanne's party nearly eighteen months ago.

Marian was indignant when it was suggested that she went straight to bed. She settled herself in the drawing-room, drank whisky, and made sure that all those who had assembled were mixing well, and getting to know one another.

Hector MacNeill had crossed with his parents on the small ferry-boat from Lochaline. He had gone straight to the village hall with Rorie to make sure that everything was in order for the reception, and to check that the closed-circuit television from the church to the overflow congregation in the marquee would work properly. In the village, all eyes were on Ben More. There they could find the answer to their questions about tomorrow's weather. It would be fine and dry.

Catriona came downstairs, wearing her Lamont tartan dress with its white collar. She looked smart and demure as she helped her parents to hand round the drinks and to talk to the lesser aunts. Mary Ferguson had arranged herself on the sofa, with her brown velvet dress spread becomingly about her, and Pauline had chosen to sit on the piano stool, looking as if she were about to play. All she needed was a rose in her hair, and she would be suitable for the cover of an old-fashioned chocolate box. Catriona hoped they wouldn't have to keep their poses until they got cramp, when she heard a familiar voice behind her.

"Miss Celia Brown – how's Norwich?"

"You!" she said, her eyes brilliant with indignation.

All eyes in the room were upon them. He was laughing down at her, his dark blue eyes, about which she had written a sonnet, missing none of her confusion.

"I didn't know that the far-out cousin Hector could be you," she said. "How silly, because I knew you were wearing the MacNeill tartan, and that your kilt was made for you, not off the peg."

He was wearing it now. He was all she remembered him to be, only more so. *I'll marry him, and I'll wear a big diamond ring*, she had said. She smiled at him, because there was brown-velvet clad opposition sitting there on the sofa, and a girl who should be wearing a rose in her hair was at the piano, so a winning smile was needed before she paid attention to anything else. He greeted everyone in the room politely; then he brought his drink over to where she was sitting, and he sat on the arm of her chair.

Marian watched the pantomime. She had seen it all before – a Catriona Lamont meeting a Hector MacNeill for the first time, and him a Roman Catholic. It had happened just like this, over sixty years ago, when her sister had met this young man's grandfather, and it had ended in tragedy, because people were more bigoted in those days.

The wheel had come full circle. But this time there must be a happy ending. A sentimental tear fell into her whisky. She fingered her glass, needing another drink.

50

The *Lapwing* lay at anchor in the bay, and the little town of Amalfi with its terraces and vineyards seemed to beckon to them to come and savour its delights.

Josanne and Niall were standing on the deck, and had taken it in turns to view the whole wonderful panorama through their binoculars. They had been married for three weeks, and last night had experienced their first quarrel, because Josanne wanted to go on shore, and Niall did not.

"You'll be wanting to look at Ravello, and it's like spying on her," he said. "She won't be there at this time of year anyway."

"So there can be no harm in going there."

So it had gone on, a silly argument, which had ended with both of them lying in bed, their noses in their separate books, though neither of them was reading. Finally Niall had tossed his aside and snapped off his light.

"Isabella's a menace," he said. "She's kept our family quarrelling for years, and now she's messing up our honeymoon."

"She doesn't know we're here. She doesn't know why we've all turned against her. I don't think any of us knows, and when I say us I mean me, too, because I've been sucked into this affair just because I'm now a Lamont. She's been so kind to me. From her giddy heights she had no need to spend a whole evening entertaining a typist in New York. But she did."

"Because she wanted to get a line on Rorie."

"If that's so, it could only be because she's in love with him. Don't tell me she's ten years older, and all that. It happens. If she feels about Rorie like I feel about you, she must be suffering, as I would do if I didn't have you."

"If she had Rorie, she might be quarrelling with him over a trifle, like you're doing with me!"

"She'd rather be quarrelling with him than have no contact with him at all. She'd rather be finished with him through a quarrel, than for no apparent reason. I don't believe she was given her letters when she was ill. Rorie had no right to be bullied by you all into dropping her without so much as an *arrivederci*."

There was silence. She looked at Niall, who was doing a bad imitation of being asleep. If there had been other passengers on the yacht, their raised voices would have been overheard. She didn't know where the crew slept. The captain wouldn't hear them.

"I'm going on shore tomorrow. I'm going up that perilous road to Ravello. And I'll see the villa where Connelli relaxes, when she isn't singing or travelling. Then I'm going to start obeying you, like I promised three weeks ago."

The sleeping Niall laughed. "You're going to start obeying me right now!" he said. "Put that book away. The advice pages in Catriona's dreadful magazines would all tell us not to sleep on a quarrel."

Now, on the deck, Niall said, "Do we head for Sorrento, or do you really want to go ashore?"

"I want to go ashore, but we head for Sorrento. You're right – we can't spy on her. If Rorie is expected to show no interest in her, neither can we." She moved closer to him. Nothing and nobody mattered to her at this moment but her husband. She might regret it later that she had not seen Amalfi and Ravello, but there would come another day. She would become used to knowing that if she wanted to travel, she could do so. She would get used to being the wife of a millionaire.

There would be letters for them at Sorrento, letters about the wedding.

It had been a lovely evening, Kilcaraig golden, like the rest of Mull in October. Thanks to the ladies of the Women's Rural Institute, everything had gone smoothly.

The church, beautifully decorated, had been filled with more people than had ever packed into its pews before, and the Minister had conducted the service in such a manner that it was almost indistinguishable from the one they would have had in a church in London.

The three bridesmaids had looked lovely in their primrose yellow dresses, a colour which had worried Josanne, until she saw for herself that her mother's choice had been right. The professional organist worked wonders with the music, and there had been no need for a choir, for the people of Kilcaraig were musical by nature, putting their hearts and their intelligence into their rendering of the hymns and the metrical psalm. Then there had been the march to the nearby village hall, led by Duncan MacKinnon, who was Kilcaraig's finest piper, and who had even won medals at the Mod, the Gaelic Eisteddfod.

There was room for everyone at the banquet, even for the overflow who had watched the closed-circuit television in the marquee, and Rorie had excelled as best man, had told witty stories when he made his speech, and had read out the innumerable telegrams, only once fumbling and losing his place, but even that he had turned into a joke which had everyone shrieking with laughter.

Niall's speech had been brief, but was a sincere pledge of himself and his wife – laughter and applause – to the people of Kilcaraig.

"We'll protect you from progress," he had promised, and this was received with stamping feet and cheers, because Mull had come under the eyes of the developers, and indignation and resentment were surging round the island as the carpet-baggers moved in.

When the banquet was over, the tables were quickly folded away, and the floor swept, ready for the dancing to begin, to the music of Anda Campbell's band, one of the finest in the west of Scotland.

Josanne and her husband led the Grand March, and Aunt Marian, from her vantage point on the platform, saw that Catriona and Hector were together, and knew that it would be they who would be leading the Grand March in the not too distant future. She hoped she'd be spared to see it.

The festivities had continued all night, but the bride and bridegroom left at two in the morning. Their destination was not an hotel for the night, but the cottage at Tormore Bay. The ferryman had preceded them from the dance, so as to take them the short distance by sea, instead of having them stumbling over the hill in the dark.

On the following morning, they left by helicopter from the car park at Iona Ferry, from there on to Glasgow, then by plane to Venice, where the Mountstephans' yacht, the *Lapwing*, awaited them.

A dream honeymoon for a girl who had been told all her life that she was a nuisance, a bother, a disappointment, not of interest to anyone at all. She knew that she had been a wonderful bride, not just a girl in a beautiful dress and veil. She had come, like a shooting star, into the atmosphere that would forever be her own.

*   *   *

While Josanne and Niall stood on the deck and reached their decision about Amalfi, Isabella Connelli leaned on a parapet overlooking the bay. She had been studying the yacht through her binoculars. She knew the *Lapwing*. It belonged to friends of Rorie's, he had told her so during one of their brief encounters when he had thought he loved her. Perhaps it was the honeymoon yacht. It could be.

She had seen the yacht as she was being driven down to Amalfi. The car had turned one of the perilous corners on the twisting road when she called to Briano to stop. He slowed down carefully, and pulled on to the left side of the road, thinking it safer to face approaching vehicles than to be rammed from behind.

Isabella kept binoculars in the car because she liked looking out to sea. In the off-season, she could enjoy Amalfi. The people knew who she was, but they were used to her, and would never ask for her autograph or try to photograph her.

The *Lapwing* was a diesel yacht, with beautiful lines which Isabella could appreciate, although she knew nothing of those things. She knew very little about anything except singing. She knew a lot about that.

"You're too young for *Isolde*," Bardini had told her. "Your voice is a treasure too valuable to risk. In a few years' time . . ."

He had said the same about *Tosca* in the days when she sang only light coloratura roles. Then came *La Traviata*, learnt in a hurry to replace a *prima donna* who had fallen ill. This had proved the versatility and strength of her voice, and had swept her into stardom; then, through other roles, to super-stardom.

Somebody had said, "So much to do, so little time to do it". Whoever that person was must have felt as she did now – that time was running out.

The yacht was weighing anchor. It would be lovely to be at sea, even in November, provided that it was calm, as it was today. To be away from it all, from the perpetual strain of sounding right and looking right, remembering always the people who had put their trust in her, had recognized her unique quality, and had enabled her to learn how to make a gift of it to all the world.

Briano called to her that they had better move. She took no notice, lost in her thoughts.

As he watched her standing there, gazing out to sea, looking as she did in *Madam Butterfly*, he thought how good it was of Almighty God to design that this precious life was to be in his care.

He sounded the horn, and she awoke from her reverie, and smilingly returned to the car. She was always smiling, always kind. She sat in the back seat because it was safer, but she was usually ready to talk, and when they didn't talk, he sang. Sometimes she sang with him, so there he was, Briano Campi, carolling duets with Connelli herself, as they cruised along the highway.

He pulled up near the landing-stage where the boats sailed to Capri, but she didn't leave the car. "I've changed my mind," she said. "I want to go home."

It had happened before like this. She was restless not capricious. She didn't seem to know what she wanted to do, but she still came to Ravello whenever she had a few free days, although what was ideal in the summer was freezing in the winter.

He loved her. He would like to make love to her. He envied the Maestro, and sometimes there were other men, about whom the Maestro knew nothing. But Briano knew, because it was his job to do so. There was one man, a special one. When she was with that man, she was different, glowing, happy. Then he had gone, and he hadn't come back.

Briano negotiated the terrifying hairpin bends, his hand on the horn, until the car screeched to a halt in front of the villa. There was a blue sports car with a G.B. plate parked outside. She had jumped out and approached it before Briano could even leave his seat, then he saw her hesitate as two tourists accosted her for her autograph. Tourists in November! But she smiled and signed their books and talked to them for a few minutes. When he had garaged the car, he could hear her in the villa, practising her scales, like any beginner in any school of music.

*   *   *

Catriona and Rorie had taken a week off for the wedding. Now they were back in London, and Marian, no worse for the journey and all the excitement, heard stereo sounds from Catriona's room, and the click of a typewriter, in rhythm with the heavy beat of the drums and the guitars. Rorie, in his room next door, was busy with his scales and arpeggios, his voice developing as time went by. The occupants of the neighbouring flats must be stone deaf, or unusually tolerant. Marian felt sure she should be looking for somewhere else to live, such as a tent in the middle of Hyde Park.

Life was dull now, with the wedding over, and a picture of Capri on the mantelpiece to prove that the yacht was still afloat in the November Mediterranean sea.

Catriona had laughed when she was teased about Hector MacNeill, and had pointed out that she wasn't marrying anybody until she had a certificate to prove that she was capable of earning a living if marriage didn't measure up to her very high standards. She would come into her inheritance on her eighteenth birthday, but, like her brothers, she made it clear that she was not going to squander what had been entrusted to her. She had confided to Marian that, if she married Hector – and it was a very big if – as he was a Roman Catholic, and in the Navy with a wife in every port, she would do as her mother had done and acquire his home, if ever it was back on the market. Mama had to marry the owner of Kilcaraig to get it back. She would get back Ardcross House merely by writing a cheque.

Rorie, his photograph of Isabella smiling at him on the piano, was astonished that he was so far ahead of his fellow students in technique. It must be because he had learnt so much from watching her. He turned on his tape-recorder and listened to himself. It was not bad, not bad at all. In fact, it was very good indeed. He let it run while he opened the drawer where he kept Isabella's picture when it was not on the piano, and he took out the telegram she had sent to Mr. and Mrs. Niall Lamont.

"Wishing you every happiness on your wedding day and in the future. Isabella."

He could not have read it out in front of all those people, even though she had used only her Christian name. In the isolation of her fame, she had wanted to show that she was remembering them, but tried to convey this without causing embarrassment. He had lost his head and fumbled, and turned the incident into a joke. He had not read out her telegram. He had failed her again.

He closed the piano, returned Isabella to her drawer with her telegram, and picked up his book. But every single page was imprinted with her face.

51

As the first anniversary of their wedding day drew near, Niall and Josanne woke up to find a gale blowing, and rain drumming against the window.

"South-west," Niall said. "If it had been like this last year, we'd have been having fits!"

All day, people were to compare the weather with that of last year. In the post office, Euphie MacLean draped her dripping headscarf in front of the electric radiator, and unfurling her copy of the *Oban*

Times, read the announcement everyone in the village had been waiting for. Catriona Lamont was to marry Hector MacNeill. There was a news item too, and a photograph of Catriona, but not of Hector, who was somewhere at sea. Everyone knew him, for he often came to Kilcaraig when he was on leave, even when Catriona was not at home, and the only reservations anyone had was over his religion. With the funny beliefs milling around these days, at least the poor soul was Christian.

Katy McPherson, reading over Euphie's shoulder, was thinking that the Women's Rural Institute would again be invited to see to the catering. She was the president of the Kilcaraig branch this year, and would make sure that her members equalled, if not excelled, the banquet they had prepared last October.

Josanne came into the post office, water pouring off her oilskin coat. Her sou'wester was in her hand.

"We're very pleased about it, Mistress Lamont," Katy said. "And I'm thinking you'll be needing us to do the reception."

"After all you did for us last year, I know Mama will want you to do it again, if you can face such hard work so soon," Josanne said.

"Two weddings in the family. That means a third to come," Sandy MacPherson said portentously. The rule of three was usually applied only to funerals.

The shop was filling up now, because Josanne had been seen coming down from the castle, and everyone wanted to talk to her about the engagement.

"Catriona planned this before she went to Grenoble," Josanne said. "She wanted the notice to go into the *Oban Times* as near as possible to the date of our anniversary. It'll be in the London *Times* too, and other papers." She called through to the post office section, "Is Colin home on leave, Mrs. Craig?" In the excitement over the engagement, she had not forgotten that Mrs. Craig had been looking forward for weeks to seeing her son.

"Yes, Colin's home on leave. He helped Lachy sort the letters," Mrs. Craig said. "There were several for you, and one was from Mr. Rorie. He's just gone up to Caraig Lodge to visit your family. It's a wonder you didn't meet him on your way down."

Josanne hoped Colin wouldn't mention Rorie's letter to Mama. Rorie wrote home so seldom now.

The rain had stopped when she left the shop. She went to the church, where Niall was mending the organ. It was suffering from age and damp, and he was lying on the floor, tinkering at something with an oil-can. She sat in a pew and told him about the letter from Rorie.

346

"The first for months. Perhaps he's remembered our anniversary."
He tried the pedal with his hand. It didn't squeak any more. "This is
the new organ, installed before I was born. We need a *new* new
organ."

He stood up, and dusted down his kilt. Then he sat in the pew
beside her, his arm round her shoulders. A year ago on Saturday,
they had stood together, and had made their vows to have and to
hold from this day forward. It was a tremendous promise to make. It
meant taking on the responsibility for the happiness of another
human being.

"If I asked you to marry me now, would you still say yes?"

"I never did say yes. I said *Niall*, but you thought I meant it as yes,
which is just as well, because that's what I did mean, but I wouldn't
have dared to say it, in case I had heard you wrong."

"What a complicated mind you have."

"I wasn't very sure of myself in those days." She turned and
looked at him, then she kissed the oily smudge on his cheek. "I love
you so much I don't know how I ever lived without you."

They walked together up the hill to the castle. The trees dripped
on them, and it was still blustery and cold. They could see Grania in
the sun-room at Caraig Lodge, and she waved at them. She and
Roderick had moved there while Niall and Josanne were on their
honeymoon, so that when they returned, they had found the castle
in perfect condition, after an invasion of painters and decorators.
Roderick and Grania informed them that Caraig Lodge was the
dream house of their old age, so much smaller and warmer than the
castle.

Catriona had elected to have a bedroom in both houses, which she
said was good for her ego. Rorie still retained his own room at the
castle, and he had used it when he came home for his duty visit at
Easter.

They opened their letters in the library. The faithful Hope Garnett
had remembered their anniversary; so had the Fergusons, and
Josanne put their cards on the table she had cleared for the purpose.
They had received a number of cards, sent a little early to allow
for postal delays. Catriona's, sent a week ago, was written in
French.

"Listen to this," Niall said, and he read to her Rorie's letter.

"Dear Josanne and Niall,
    You will be celebrating on Saturday having spent a whole year
together. I know it has been a happy one for you both, and I hope
there will be many more to come.

So Catriona has landed her Hector! He's going to have his hands full. She's taken her pop records with her to Grenoble, and Aunt Marian threatens to buy some replacements, because she's missing the din so much!

You'll be astonished to hear that I've been chosen to sing a duet at a students' concert to be held in December. My partner is pretty, but as one so often finds with sopranos, in her lower register she sounds as if she is singing into a jug.

I kept away from Covent Garden during the summer, but last night I couldn't resist Isabella's concert at the Festival Hall. It meant a black market ticket, and a seat miles away from the stage, but in the introduction to the first song, her eyes met mine. She knew I was there, in that vast hall, and she knows, as I do, that the bond that binds us is as strong as it ever was, in spite of everything. I don't know what to do, but I'll find a way somehow, somewhere, to put right the mess I've made of the past.

Please don't tell Mama about this letter. In fact, destroy it. I'll regret sending it the minute I've posted it, I expect.

Much love to you both – Rorie"

Niall handed the letter to Josanne. She read it through, then looked at him. He nodded. She threw it in the fire.

Grania was in the hall. She called to them, and came into the library. "Colin Craig was over," she said. "He says there's a letter from Rorie."

"There was," Josanne said. "Like an idiot, I burnt it with its envelope. It was congratulating us on our year together, and telling us that he's to sing in a concert in December."

Grania made a show of looking at the cards arranged on the table. "I suppose he's dreaming that one day he'll be singing at La Scala with You Know Who."

"I don't think that Rorie day-dreams any more." Niall's words lacked conviction.

"I'll get coffee," Josanne said quickly. "It'll have to be Instant." She left the room. She always tried to give Niall and his mother a little time together, but today she was in a hurry. Luckily, the kettle on the Aga was on the boil, and Cathy set mugs on a tray, while Chrissie spooned the powdered coffee into a jug.

There was silence in the library when Josanne returned with the tray. Grania would have been wanting to know exactly what was said in that letter, and Niall would have been avoiding a direct answer. He was not good at dissembling.

"I won't have any myself," Josanne said, putting the tray on a table beside Grania. "I've been a bit squeamish lately in the morning. Draw your own conclusions!"

Niall knew that she had said it now, in front of his mother, to take her mind off Rorie's letter. She certainly succeeded, and Grania wanted to telephone Roderick right away.

"Please, Mama, it could just be indigestion," Josanne said.

"It's not, it's our first grandchild." But Grania drank her coffee, and afterwards, the three of them went to tell Roderick.

They were laughing, Rorie forgotten, by the time they reached Caraig Lodge.

*　　*　　*

After a rehearsal for the students' concert, Rorie asked Sylvia Leeming if she would like a drink. They went to the Hyde Park Hotel, where he listened to her analysing every nuance, every breath of their duet. An earnest young woman, whose good looks were not matched with the degree of talent she would need if she were to become an opera singer, Rorie found that he had to choose his words carefully when she asked him to criticize her work. The truth would be too hard for her to bear, and even faint praise would encourage an ambition which was doomed to failure.

The lounge was filling up with people, as the shops and offices began to close, and Sylvia was on to her third gin and tonic. Rorie managed to look at his watch, without letting her see his impatience. He had told Aunt Marian he would be home before seven, as Morag MacKinnon was having supper with friends, and although she did not at all mind being alone in the flat at night, Rorie minded. He felt responsible for her, in spite of her independence.

Release came when Sylvia remembered that she had a job as a baby-sitter that evening. Rorie drove her to an address in Bayswater, then he spent a long time finding somewhere to park near Lowndes Square. When at last he reached the flat and tried to get his key into the lock, he found that the safety catch had been engaged, so he had to ring the bell.

Aunt Marian came to the door. "I thought you'd gone gallivanting off somewhere," she said, propelling him towards the sitting-room. "I'll be with you in a minute. I just want to see what's going on in the oven."

Isabella was standing by the window. Her hat and her handbag were on the sofa, and she had kicked off her shoes. She looked small in her stockinged feet, and her face was a mask. She stared at Rorie, just as if she had never seen him before.

He took a step towards her, then hesitated. His diffidence disarmed her. She smiled and held out both her hands.

"Aunt Marian asked me to come," she said. He had forgotten her accent, that curious mixture of all the languages she spoke, none of them correctly. "I told her I had seen you at the concert, and somehow, after that, I told her everything about me." She shivéred. "We'll talk about that some other time. I don't want to go through it all over again tonight."

Rorie, cupping her hands in his, looked down at her, then he kissed her gently on her temple. He was incapable of speech.

"Please don't be upset," she said. "I made an idiotic request to you when I was in a state of panic. It's all worked out now – the panic, I mean. You couldn't have done anything for me anyhow. Don't let it worry you any more."

"Isabella!" He buried his face in her hair.

Aunt Marian came noisily into the room. Rorie held on to Isabella, who remained limply in his arms.

"I'm a meddlesome old woman," Marian said. "I just couldn't bear to see two people whom I love so much pining away, and me doing nothing about it. Don't think that meeting one another tonight is going to solve all your problems, like thè end of a fairy tale. It solves nothing, but now you can really get to know one another again. Dinner's ready, and I'll need you to uncork the wine, Rorie. I hope it isn't frozen hard. I popped it into the deep-freeze to chill it and forgot about it."

Isabella put on her shoes, then she went to Marian's room to repair her make-up, and tidý her hair. She looked like the *prima donna* she was when she joined Rorie and his aunt in the dining-room, but Rorie knew, with relief, that something that had divided them was gone forever. She was no longer a *diva* on a pedestal, she was the woman he loved.

They ate the chicken and mushroom casserole which Morag had prepared, and they drank the white wine which Marian had bought as a special offer in a supermarket, and which she had thawed under a hot tap; then they had apple crumble and cream. They talked of music, and of Isabella's second season at Wexford, which was imminent. Only at the end of dinner did Isabella say why she was still in London, and not in Ireland with the Maestro.

"I have to see a Harley Street specialist tomorrow," she said. "I wanted a second opinion from someone a long way from Milan, and I don't want any newspaper reporters to find out about it. Too much has been said about my health. Too much, too soon."

Rorie looked up quickly, but he caught Marian's warning shake of the head, so he did not pursue the matter.

After dinner, Isabella sang for them for a while, relaxed and happy doing the thing she most enjoyed. At half-past ten, Briano arrived with her Mercedes, to drive her back to her hotel.

"Shall I see you tomorrow?" Rorie asked.

She nodded. "After the doctor. In Aunt Marian's flat."

She sank back into a corner as Briano closed the door of the car.

*   *   *

Rorie had driven Isabella to Heathrow, and he was waiting with her in the V.I.P. lounge. There was nothing left to say to one another. Everything that could be said had been said.

Isabella had seen the specialist in the morning, then she had lunch with the Italian Ambassador at the Connaught Hotel. She wanted to draw attention to herself, and to her robust state of health. Afterwards, she went to Marian's flat, where Rorie was waiting for her. Marian had gone to Harrods to help Morag choose a hat.

As soon as she knew that she was alone with him, Rorie was to see the change of character which had so baffled him during the telephone call begging him to go to Chicago. She had arrived at the flat, apparently in the best of spirits, yet a moment later she was sitting stiffly on the sofa, twisting her hands, the personification of despair. Years later, he was to find that the best method of helping her was that used by a priest when confronted by a tongue-tied penitent. He asked questions, and she answered yes or no. At the end of the ordeal, she was in his arms, shivery and wretched, incapable of the relief of tears.

He didn't try to comfort her with smooth words of hope. She needed wisdom and courage and a constructive solution to dispel her fears. She needed him to show his love for her, not by smothering her with kisses, but by letting her know the strength of his support.

Now, at the airport, she was checking through her handbag, making sure that she had her passport and face-powder, making sure that people would think she looked upon this as she did any other journey, part of her normal routine.

"I should have kept Motti with me, instead of sending her with Briano and the car," she said. "They'll be in Liverpool by now." There would be no Mercedes to meet her at Dublin Airport.

"The Maestro will be meeting you."

"I hope he isn't recognized. He loves to collect crowds. He thinks it's good publicity when I get mobbed."

"Before you go back to Milan, will you be sure and visit Cork?"

351

"Of course I will. I'll be seeing the Sisters."

The Sisters. Her home. The only home she knew.

"Please ask Briano to drive you round the highways and byways. I'm looking for a Georgian house with a farm attached. You find one and I'll buy it."

"Who for?"

"For us."

She closed her handbag with a snap. "I've already told you, you must be sensible. I never accept engagements for more than two years ahead. Not any engagements of any kind."

"You dedicate yourself to your singing. I'll take care of the rest."

Her flight number was called. They shook hands, and she joined the other passengers who were making their way to the exit for the Dublin plane. Someone asked for her autograph, then someone else. She smiled and talked, moving away from him. She never failed her public. Tonight she would tell the Maestro of her predicament, but no one else, not yet. She glanced over her shoulder when she reached the gate, flashed him a smile, and was gone.

He went to his car. The remark about the Georgian house near Cork had been made just to say something that would hint at a future. Now he would give it serious thought. A farm. Cows, pigs, hens, beautiful surroundings, charming people. His years at Cirencester would not have been wasted, and his life at Kilcaraig was a natural preparation for an Irish farm. He was learning Isabella's language of song. He would learn how to read scores, as other people read books, the way she did. When she was ready, she would enter into a new kind of happiness.

A plane roared overhead. It could be her plane. She would have fastened her seat-belt and fondled the rosary beads in her pocket.

"They're better than a seat belt if you run into trouble," she had said. She could be right. It was a side of her life he must explore.

He was waiting at the red lights near the North End Road when her Aer Lingus plane touched down at Dublin Airport.

52

The ladies of Kilcaraig were knitting and knitting. The chest-of-drawers in the night nursery at the castle was full to overflowing with beautiful baby clothes.

Every day, Josanne opened each drawer and took out the tiny garments to stroke them and admire them and memorize who had made what, because although she had listed everything in a book, she wanted to know at a glance to whom she should feel grateful when her baby was wearing the so-lovingly provided clothes.

Rorie and Catriona came home for Christmas and the New Year. Rorie stayed at the castle, in the room that had always been his, while Catriona stayed at Caraig Lodge, though she cast longing eyes at the sag-bags and other comforts of her former room.

It was too cold for Marian to travel north, but she was installed in the Fergusons' comfortable spare-room, so that Morag MacKinnon was free to go home to her family during the holiday period.

Josanne had often invited her parents to come to the castle, but they always found some excuse, and eventually she gave up trying. She had been to London from time to time to see them, hating every moment of it, and worried sometimes by her father's addiction to brandy, but she mostly found that she was amused by them, rather than being nervous or strained.

The presence of Rorie had a curious effect on Grania. She could find nothing to say to him, her favourite, her most adored son. He talked about music in a general way, and he spoke of the students' concert, which he had forbidden any member of his family to attend, but he made it clear that he had no intention of taking up singing professionally. He avoided any mention of his plans for the future.

When the holiday was over, Rorie and Catriona set off south together, but Catriona was to stop off at Edinburgh, to spend a few days with her future parents-in-law.

"No problem," she said, settling herself beside him in the Volvo. "They like me and I like them, and my only worry is that I won't like Hector when I see him again, because I've forgotten so much about him, and he'll find me inadequate after all those eastern ladies who have interesting insides."

"What have you been reading now?" sighed Rorie.

"*True Stories from the Seraglio*. Audrey Harris's father bought it in Port Said. I've learnt a lot at Grenoble." She brooded about what she had learnt for a little while, then she said, "Tell me, honest and true, did lovely exciting things happen between you and Isabella when crafty old Aunt Marian reunited you?"

"Sorry to disappoint you. Nothing happened at all."

"Whose fault was that?"

"It wasn't a fault, it was on purpose. There are two sorts of intimacy, physical and spiritual. Sometimes one is more important than the other. That's how it was with us. We had a lot of spiritual sorting out to do."

"I don't think you mean spiritual-holy," she said.

"No, I don't mean that at all."

They covered several miles.

"Rorie, you are going to marry her, aren't you? When?"

"When her singing days are done."

"That could mean a long wait." She glanced at him, but he didn't reply. A straight bit of road was coming up, and he was preparing to make use of it. They sped past a lorry.

"There's an unusually strong, unbreakable link binding you two together," she said, suddenly older, as if serious thoughts were hiding inside her flippant, student mind.

"We will be very happy," he said.

"Even without a song?"

"Isabella will never be without a song. She is a song."

He had tea with the MacNeills in their flat in Moray Place. Then he left them, giving them the opportunity to discover more about Catriona. He would drive faster, now that he was by himself, but he was careful. Isabella needed him. He had to stay alive.

A.R.C.M. would look good after his name, but he wasn't sure if he could complete the course. It depended how soon he would need that Georgian house in Ireland. It was all a matter of time.

At the castle, Josanne helped to strip Rorie's bed and to tidy up his room. She picked up his Bible, which he had forgotten. Something fluttered out of it. It was a telegram. She read the message, then she went to find Niall. He was in the library, waiting to hear the farming news. She showed it to him, and he switched off the radio.

"How nice of her to have remembered us," he said. "No wonder Rorie fumbled his lines when he found this in front of him."

Josanne sat in the Kilcaraig chair. Its height was comfortable for her. Her baby was active now, and she wasn't sick any more.

"Isn't it time all the hostility was over? Can't Mama be told that she has a straight choice – Rorie and Isabella, or no Rorie at all?"

"Let's have no more talk about choice. No either or. Let nature take its course, as it will do in the end, anyhow."

"What end?"

"When Isabella has that plain gold band on her finger, all will be forgiven, and Mama will take her to her heart."

"Will Isabella be so forgiving? She's a V.I.P. who has been insulted by our family for years."

"She'll do whatever Rorie wants to make him happy."

"In that case, she should marry him now, and stop stringing him along, as if he were someone of whom she's ashamed."

"She has her reasons, and Rorie understands."

Josanne gave him a quick little look. Rorie must still confide in Niall. She was glad of this, for there was no jealousy in her.

She picked up her sewing, and with her tongue protruding as she concentrated, she stitched ribbons onto the matinee jacket she herself had knitted for her baby.

Niall watched her proudly. His wife, the mother of his son, the heir to Kilcaraig. He kissed her bowed head, then he went out to work in the fields.

*   *   *

One blustery day towards the end of February, Josanne gave birth to a still-born daughter.

Her labour pains had begun during the night, but she didn't want to wake the sleeping Niall, believing that she had eaten something that had disagreed with her. Her baby was expected in May.

When Niall woke up at seven, he found her already up, standing by the window, and supporting herself by holding onto the back of a chair. She knew now it was not indigestion. He helped her to bed, then telephoned for the doctor.

Twenty-four hours later, she awakened from a muzzy state of mingled sleep and limbo. Niall was sitting by her bedside, and she knew that the little creature who had shared her body for nearly seven months would now have been buried in a grave somewhere in the ground near Kilcaraig church.

Niall saw that she was awake, kissed her forehead, and asked if she would like a cup of tea. She nodded.

The nurse came forward, not the dear, familiar District Nurse, but an efficient stranger.

"We'll move her to the other room now," she said to Niall. "It's difficult to nurse her in this huge bed."

The huge bed had been the birth-place of Niall and Rorie, and later of Catriona, and of many generations of Lamonts before them. Josanne was too weak even to shake her head, but if Niall allowed her to be moved, she would never have any faith in him again.

Grania brought her tea in an invalid cup, and held it to her lips. After a few sips, she closed her eyes. There were two Granias, one each side of the bed. This confused her. In a little while, she was asleep again.

Catriona, whom Josanne had mistaken for the other Grania, kept a vigil at the bedside all night. She had flown from Grenoble as soon as Roderick had telephoned to say that Josanne was in labour. The ambulance had been cancelled, to spare her the distress of being in the maternity hospital in Oban, where other mothers would have babies, and she would have none. Catriona was determined that Josanne would not be moved from her own familiar surroundings. She would guard the bed until Niall, dazed with anxiety and grief, could assert himself and protect his wife from the unimaginative care of Nurse Bacon.

She had her way. Josanne was not moved, but she lay listless and unresponsive. She turned her face away when she was offered food. Then Sybil and William arrived from London to pay a fleeting visit to their daughter in her plight.

"Cheer up, darling. It's not as if it were a boy," Sybil said, consolingly.

"She was a girl." These were the first words Josanne had uttered since the anaesthetic had silenced her cries forty hours ago. "Please go away. Come back some other time. Catriona, send them away."

Afterwards, Catriona was to look back on that evening with both sadness and pride. She grieved for Josanne, but for Sybil and William too, who had wanted a grandson, and who couldn't help being insensitive.

The moment they were out of the room, Josanne was in tears, gulping, terrible tears, while Niall sat helplessly looking on, knowing that this was a necessary prelude to her recovery. Then she slept, while downstairs Grania explained that Niall had baptised the baby, naming her Catriona, and that Mr. Allan had performed a brief but beautiful burial service, as the little body was laid in the grave of her ancestors.

Rorie, in London, knew better than to try to hide from Aunt

Marian what was happening at Kilcaraig, but like most old people, she accepted death, even the death of a baby, as a fact of life, an episode that caused anguish, but in due course there were compensations. No one, not even a fragile baby, lived in vain. She read the metrical version of the twenty-third psalm aloud to Rorie. Then she dried her eyes and asked for tea. She was practical, and she had faith.

*   *   *

Isabella had told the Maestro about Harley Street, then she told him about Rorie. Emotional always, he had wept, and he held her in his arms as a father would hold a daughter, not as a man would embrace his mistress. It was the end of their association, but the beginning of a new kind of friendship. A tiny bit of the burden of anxiety was eased from her mind. A milestone was passed.

From then on, the Maestro and his wife made a point of parading Rorie as their friend. Whenever he came to Milan, or to Rome or wherever Isabella was singing, he would accompany them to the opera, be with them at parties. It was rumoured that the music student from London was one of the Maestro's latest protégés. The Maestro's philandering with pretty women was too well-known for his interest in Rorie to be misunderstood, and it enabled Rorie and Isabella to have what they both needed most, time to be together, unremarked by either the public or the press.

The day after she heard about Josanne's baby, Isabella was rehearsing with Bardini.

"Will you do something for me?" he asked.

She looked up, surprised. "For you?"

He struck a chord, then another, then a few bars of the *Liebestod*.

"I want you to sing it with the Philharmonic in the Albert Hall. And perhaps later at the Edinburgh Festival?" He struck another chord. "I don't care where you sing it, so long as you do."

She sank onto the sofa the rehearsal room provided for exhausted singers. "You said it will be years before I can sing Isolde."

"There aren't going to be so many years, are there, Isabella?" He saw the colour drain from her face. He felt infinite tenderness towards her. She stared at him, her green eyes fixed on him imploringly.

"How did you know?"

He leaned over, and laid his hand on her. "I am a conductor," he said. "It's my job to make a study of those who depend on me. I'll help you all I can. Remember that. Learn the *Liebestod*, then we'll talk some more."

He saw her to the door, and watched as she walked along the corridor, hugging herself, the personification of desolation. Then he returned to the rehearsal room.

53

As soon as she was allowed out of bed, Josanne went to the nursery and systematically wrapped the baby clothes in moth-proof packages.

"We'll be needing them," she said to Niall. "I'm never again going to accept myself as a failure. I lived with that until I married you. And now I've failed you and the family, but I won't give in. I'm determined there will be an heir for Kilcaraig."

He saw the Josanne he had first known and loved. She made these little declarations, suddenly pouring out what was in her heart. He watched her take up another little packet, and place it neatly in a drawer.

"I married you for yourself. I didn't marry you to produce an heir. You mustn't ever think that. If need be, we'll leave that to Rorie."

"Rorie's embroiled with Isabella all over again, and she'll be past child-bearing by the time her singing days are done. So it will have to be me." She was surprised at the resentment she felt at the thought of Isabella – Isabella, whom she had adored, whose records she still treasured. The voice was sublime, would always be unique, no matter what other voices might flood the world with music as time went by, but the person was an enigma. She could understand how Grania felt. Isabella wanted a youthful toy, not a husband, and out of all the world she had chosen Rorie.

"It'll have to be me," she repeated, folding a lacy shawl, tears welling into her eyes.

She made her first appearance in the village three weeks after the death of her baby, and on that Sunday she went to church. The minister offered a special prayer for her, which had her terrified she would cry, but she appreciated his kindness, and later, with the understanding handshakes of the people of Kilcaraig, she knew how much they accepted her, looked to her to follow the Lamont tradition, to be the matriarch of them all, as Grania had become.

In May, everyone thought about the baby that should be born at the castle, but was already lying there in the burial ground, and by November, Josanne knew that she was pregnant again.

Rorie came home dutifully at Christmas, bringing Catriona, who would stay at Kilcaraig until her marriage in June.

"I hope Chrissie and Aunt Marian live until it's all over," she said to Josanne. "I don't mean I'm afraid they'll mistime dying and spoil all the arrangements. I just want them to be there – that's all."

"So there's still to be a wedding in June? I thought it was all off, because you don't know one another any more!"

"It's all on again, because in Hector's last letter he said not knowing one another will be a great advantage. It will be like an arranged marriage, and they work out very well. I think that's true. We're always seeing Indian ladies looking woeful, because they can't import fiancés they've never even met." She stroked her engagement ring. "I said I'd marry the man in the heather, and have a huge diamond ring. I couldn't go back on that, now could I?"

Josanne never knew how to take Catriona's changes in mood. Sometimes she seemed so childish and feather-brained, yet it was she more than anyone else who had understood her feelings, had helped her through the loss of her baby.

They were checking through the linen that was piled high on the shelves of the airing room. Josanne worked on, happy in the knowledge that if Catriona needed her help or advice about her approaching marriage, she would say so. Probably Catriona had more experience of men than she had herself, because the only man in her life had been Niall.

As if following her thoughts, Catriona said, "I'm putting a cassette of *Try a Little Tenderness* under our pillow on my wedding night. It might have a subliminal effect on Hector, now that he's been in all these places where girls wear garters, and black bras, and sequins on their navels."

"I don't think you have anything to worry about," Josanne said, not sure if Catriona was speaking entirely in fun. "Hector is a very kind person, very chivalrous. You'll be all right."

"Most of my chums have been liberated," Catriona said. "I never fancied any of the chaps, or I'd have been liberated too. But I suppose it's better this way. Hector will know how pure I am, and not niggle about whether or not I've had a murky past." She held up a towel, which was embroidered with Rorie's name in chain stitch. "I made this for him when I was nine. Funny how Rorie always protected me from the assaults of his friends, when he used to be such a ram himself."

359

"Used to be?"

"He leads the life of a monk," she said. "Except, of course, when he's with Isabella."

While Josanne and Catriona were talking in the linen room, Rorie was on a tractor, dumping mounds of manure systematically over the Nissen field.

Before he left Kilcaraig, he would have to break it to his parents that he had decided to change course again, and revert to farming. He would have to admit that he had already bought a farm. He would have to tell them that his life in future belonged to Isabella, but he couldn't tell them the whole truth. Isabella didn't want that yet, and he would respect her wishes. He would never fail her again.

Oblivious of the sound of the tractor, he plodded on with his work, not needing to concentrate because he had done it so often before. Instead, he remembered Wexford.

*   *   *

It had been Isabella's third Wexford Festival. She had prevailed upon the Maestro to accept the invitation to return, although Bardini protested that it was a mistake to make her presence there a matter of routine. She would not go back there next year. She might never go back there again. Because of the special circumstances, she had her way.

Now she was installed in her usual hotel, while Briano prowled around, to make sure that everyone knew who he was, and why. The Maestro and his wife were staying in the same hotel, but Bardini's headquarters were in Dublin. His wife cared more for shopping than for music.

Rorie Lamont was a guest in the ramshackle but welcoming home of his friends, Sean and Mary O'Hara, who knew about Isabella, and who lived only a few miles from Wexford.

"I've acquired a halo," Isabella said, as he drove her out to spend an afternoon with them. "People are saying that they were mistaken about me and the Maestro. They guess, rightly, that he's interested in Lisa Verini. He likes them young." Verini was singing Musetta in *La Bohème*. "They watch my Mimi, to see if I try to detract from her performance on the stage!"

"They'll be saying things about you and Bardini instead. Your *Liebestod* has put all sorts of ideas into people's heads, including mine." He waited for her to deny it.

After a pause, she said "He still shouts at me. I would hate him to start revering me. I would feel that I had died already, and that he was conducting my requiem. And Rorie, I'm so well now, I think it's all been a mistake. Do you think it's all a mistake?"

He could feel her eyes upon him. There were little pigs on the road. They must have escaped from somewhere. He drove carefully to avoid them, and she was fascinated, exclaiming at their pink skin and curly tails. She didn't press for a reply.

The O'Haras were out when they reached the house. He took her straight to his room. Later, she lay beside him in bed, the sheet pulled neatly up to her chin.

"Your modesty is the most tantalizing thing about you," he said. "If you weren't covered up, I would dress now, and we would both look prim when the O'Haras get back."

She wriggled. The sheet slipped a little, revealing her bare shoulder. She gave a litle cry as he turned upon her, crushing her, ravishing her, delighting her.

They were asleep when the O'Haras arrived, but the sound of the car awoke them. Rorie went into the adjoining bathroom to dress. Isabella waited in bed until he was ready to go downstairs.

"I'll bring you some tea," he said.

She shook her head. Her hair was spread on the pillow, like a Titian halo.

"Tell them I was tired out, and you made me sleep. It's perfectly true. Please – I'll sleep some more." She closed her eyes. He had exhausted her.

Briano fetched her after dinner. She was to sing in a concert the next day, then she had two free days before *Bohème* again.

"We'll look for the Georgian farm," Rorie said. "Briano can drive us, and we'll drop you off for a while to see the Sisters."

"You can come to them too."

"No, I'd feel guilty. Like Mama, they'd welcome me as your husband, or even as the man you're going to marry, but not as your lover. They wouldn't approve of that at all."

They were walking slowly towards the waiting car. The O'Haras always left them alone as much as they could.

Isabella opened her handbag, and took out a scroll, kept folded by a rubber band. "It's messy but readable," she said. "It's one of the encores I sang at the Festival Hall, the concert that brought us together again. I composed it myself."

He opened it. She was right. It was messy, but he recognized it at once, some lines from Sir Walter Scott's *Lay of the Last Minstrel*, set to an enchanting waltz.

"True love's the gift that God has given," he hummed. She put up her hand to stop him, and he saw that she felt shy. It was the first time she had revealed to him what she really felt about him in her heart. He put the scroll in his pocket, but kept his hand on it tightly, as if he feared that it would be spirited away.

She got quickly into the back seat of the car. Briano made sure that she was comfortable, ignoring Rorie, whom he thought was a blackguard, a bounder, a cad. These words he had looked up in his English dictionary when he was planning to plunge a stiletto into that faithless heart.

On her first free day, they drove to Cork. She saw the Sisters while Rorie saw a house agent. Then they drove round the by-ways in search of the Georgian house described as needing some repair. They found it, the sale notice hanging drunkenly from a board. A farm of nettles and mess and neglect, but the house was not a ruin yet, not quite. It was called Clonbracken, and they loved it on sight.

On her second free day, they bought it.

"We'll be happy ever after here," Rorie said, as they stood in the overgrown garden. In the distance, a church bell tolled the Angelus. Isabella crossed herself and bowed her head, her lips moving. Then she looked up and smiled.

"I hope you'll be happy ever after," she said, stressing the pronoun.

Briano drove them back to Wexford.

*　　*　　*

"You've bought it, Rorie, so there isn't anything for us to say." Roderick had seen the photographs of the house, the plans of the fields and the out-buildings, and had listened to Rorie's ideas about how he would restore it. The farm had been left divided between three members of a family. Legal disputes had reduced it to its present state. No one had wanted it, they preferred to sell it and share the cash.

"Have you finished with music? Is it farming now, and for how long? Will you still have to flit around every opera house where she sings?" Grania always had to avoid naming Isabella.

"I want to make it my home, and I want your approval. That's all. We all know there isn't work for me here." His eyes pricked. His artistic temperament would be easier to manage if he looked artistic, instead of like the strapping kilted figure of an athlete about to toss the caber at any Highland Games.

"Niall thinks it's a good idea," he added. Niall was the sensible one. They listened to Niall.

"Would you like Mama and me to fly over with you and have a look at it? We could do with a few days' break before we start to plan Catriona's wedding." Roderick remembered that terrible sensation, the yearning of the heart for the seemingly impossible. He guessed that Isabella figured somewhere in the plan. Rorie had been with her at Wexford. She might even want to see him settled. She could be as much embarrassed by his attentions as were his family. He had said this to Grania in private. He waited for her reaction now.

"What we think about it will make no difference to what Rorie does about it," she said, as if Rorie wasn't there. "But I'd like a few days off. We might as well go there as anywhere else."

With this grudging acquiescence, it was arranged. Rorie felt he had come out of the discussion lightly. They hadn't cross-examined him about where Isabella fitted in. They wanted to avoid that as much as he did, because he didn't know the answer.

Amazingly, when they arrived at Clonbracken a week later, it was Grania who fell in love with the house. She scrambled round it, exclaiming at the rat-holes, and at the marks where water had poured down the interior walls, and she admired, nostalgically, the rusty kitchen range. There had been one like that at Kilcaraig when she was a child. She shared Rorie's vision. This would be a dream house for a family. If anything could cure him of his desire for that woman, it would be this.

She and Roderick returned to Kilcaraig with a sense of triumph. Rorie would follow, when he had seen about architects and builders, and when he was needed for the wedding.

*   *   *

Aunt Marian came to Mull in May, and once she was back in her own bedroom, she forgot about Lowndes Square, so it was easy to convince her that she had been away on a holiday and had now come home.

"Oh, it's good to be in one's own bed again," she said. "And it's good that Catriona's marrying Hector. I always thought people made too much fuss about religious barriers." She knew that Catriona was her great-niece, and that this Hector was the other Hector's grandson, but the past and the present were merging, and it was too complicated to sort them out.

If Catriona was nervous as she made her vows to the man she professed not to know, she didn't show it. She was a lovely bride, standing there in her white satin dress, beside Hector in his MacNeill tartan kilt, the pages similarly clad, and lined up nearby on the right.

The reception was arranged in the same way that Niall and Josanne's had been, by the ladies of the Women's Rural Institute, and when the naval lieutenant who was the best man read the telegrams, he made no mistakes. Rorie, sitting at the top table, trying to look happy, recalled the telegram he had failed to read. He had never owned up about that to Isabella.

Niall was keeping a watchful eye on Josanne. She had lost a second baby, in early pregnancy this time. He knew she believed herself to be a failure, that she was slipping back into being the unsure, self-conscious girl he had first known. She would escape to her day-dreams, withdrawing into herself, fearing physical love. Not again, she had told him. She could never endure to lose another baby again.

The young priest who had assisted at the marriage ceremony played the accordion so well that some members of the community decided there must be something to be said for the Roman Catholic religion after all. Chrissie and Marian talked together about the past and the present and their hopes for the future, and they thought about Michael Ames and Angus, and others who would like to be present if they had been spared.

After Catriona and Hector had driven off amid cheers and hootings and clanging of ironmongery on the first stage of their honeymoon, and the dance had resumed, Grania caught at Rorie's sleeve and beckoned him outside.

It was a beautiful night, with the scent of June in the air. They walked together towards Loch Caraig, silver in the moonlight.

"I've seen Niall married, and I've seen Catriona married. What about you, Rorie?"

"My time will come." He fingered the lace round his cuff. He was in full dress because of the wedding.

"When her voice is on the decline, and she can't reach the high notes any more. When she's past child-bearing. Kilcaraig needs an heir."

"No man can be sure that his wife will bear him a son."

"Her glamour won't survive the intimacy of marriage. You'll be burdened with an ageing beauty, dwelling on her glorious past and hating the thing she has become. She'll never be content to live on a farm in County Cork, the applause still ringing in her ears, and nothing to listen to but the birds and the bees."

They stood by the loch, among the bluebells and bracken. A light breeze kept the midges away. There was very little darkness at this time of year.

"Mama, she would be very content with that, but she hasn't made up her mind about the future. She wants to do what is right for us both."

"She should have thought of that before she developed the habit of going to bed with you." A pause. "How many men do you share her with?"

"Millions. The people who love to hear her sing." He stared straight ahead, seeing the loch and the moon and seething with anger. Her words reflected what he himself had believed, still sometimes believed. He wanted to shout the truth about Isabella. His mother's kindness would overcome her prejudice. Or her anxiety might increase it.

"You wouldn't talk about her like that if you knew her," he said, his voice betraying nothing of his anguish.

"You can't expect me to receive your mistress, or your paramour, or whatever is the appropriate description of a woman who enjoys the flattery of young men." Her distress was boiling into rage. Rorie, her son. "If she proves me wrong, if she marries you, I'll welcome her into the family, as I've done with Josanne and Hector. I'd do that for you, Rorie."

"You are most kind."

She didn't recognize the phrase, but she caught the sarcasm. She had brought him here to make peace with him, but instead she had widened the gulf between them. She shivered and turned away.

They walked slowly and silently back to the festivities in the hall.

54

The people of Kilcaraig were rejoicing.

The castle lights had sprung on at four o'clock in the morning, and Sandy MacPherson, who, being sleepless, had got up to make himself a cup to tea, stood by the cracked window of his cottage and saw the lights go on in the doctor's house, then at Caraig Lodge, and he guessed that the district nurse too would be aroused. Mistress Niall was due to leave for Edinburgh for her confinement the following day, but the heir, who must surely be the reason for all this activity, must have decided to be born at Kilcaraig.

And so it proved to be. By morning, everyone was up and about, some apprehensive, remembering what had happened before, others convinced that third time was lucky. By breakfast time, the longed for announcement, artistically framed in blue, was on display in the post office window. Roderick Niall Lamont, weighing eight and a half pounds. had arrived and he and his mother were both well.

Up at the castle, Josanne lay back in the Kilcaraig bed, tired by her untimely but surprisingly easy exertions. Niall sat on a chair close to her, and between them was their son in his cot. The district nurse was bustling about in the adjoining bathroom. Grania had gone back to Caraig Lodge, and Chrissie was dispensing tea in the kitchen to the first of the callers, who would be bringing gifts and good wishes throughout the day.

"I've never felt so proud." Niall said.

"And I've never felt so happy." Josanne stretched out her hand and touched his. He leaned over, kissed the baby's downy head, then kissed her on the mouth.

When the nurse returned to the room, he was gazing into the cot, and Josanne was pretending to be asleep, but there was a conspiratorial smile upon her face. She had been determined to have the baby at Kilcaraig, and somehow had got away with faking dates just a little. Tonight there would be a bonfire on Ben Caraig, and she would see the glow for herself. She would see the fireworks display, and she would hear the people as they tramped past the castle on their way back from the bonfire, to the celebration that would take place in the village hall.

Roderick Niall yawned, squirmed, and made a sucking noise. Niall, glad of the chance, picked him up and placed him in Josanne's arms.

During the weeks that followed, Josanne resolved on breast-feeding her son, struggled with some of the difficulties of motherhood, worried that he was over-fed, under-fed, or deficient in some way. Grania, remembering her own fears, could reassure and encourage her, and in so doing the two women drew nearer together in understanding. Aunt Marian, whose greatest delight lay in singing Gaelic songs to her great-grand-nephew, could always be relied upon to put in a wise or amusing remark in time of crisis. On one such occasion, a tiny, grabbing hand had reached out and broken her string of beads, and the baby swallowed one of them. Josanne, horror-struck, talked of X-rays, while Marian placidly explained the wisdom of leaving such matters to nature. Roddie survived and Josanne learnt the folly of panic.

"I hope he doesn't disturb you tonight," Josanne said to Nanny one evening. The heir to Kilcaraig was six months old, and had given them all a noisy day because he was cutting his first teeth. "And I wish you'd join us for dinner. It's only a family celebration of our wedding anniversary, and we'd love you to be there."

"Thank you, Mistress Lamont, but I'd rather eat by the fire in my sitting-room, and watch the telly."

Josanne wanted to watch television too, but it would not be possible, not tonight.

She left the nursery, and changed into the long, blue dress Niall admired so much. He hadn't come in yet. He was probably at Caraig Lodge, and would bring his parents to the castle in his car.

It was more than seven years since Adrian Ferguson had knocked her into the gutter in Covent Garden, and had introduced her to the Lamonts. Seven glorious years. No, not all glorious. The deaths of her two babies were still painful memories, the one no less than the other, for they had been loved from the moment of their conception, and would be loved in her heart for as long as she lived. And there was the rift with Rorie, which had become almost complete now that he lived in County Cork, in the renovated farmhouse none of them ever visited.

Something had happened when he had been home for Catriona's wedding, something had been said that had put an end to his ever returning again. He had made the alterations to the house, and the reclamation of the farm his excuse at first, but over two years was a long time never to be able to come to Kilcaraig. He always found time for Salzburg and all the other places in Europe where Connelli appeared.

By coincidence, tonight was special for Isabella Connelli too. It was the twentieth anniversary of her first appearance on the stage, when, as a girl of eighteen, she had sung *Lucia di Lammermoor* in that small, provincial opera house. To mark the occasion, *La Traviata*, which was one of her most popular roles, was to be transmitted from La Scala, Milan, throughout Europe, and would be bounced by satellite across the world. She had come a long way since she had talked about summits and avalanches in Aunt Marian's flat.

Josanne had heard her sing the *Liebestod* at the Edinburgh Festival. It was like a trailer for the marvel that was to come when she would sing Isolde at Bayreuth. When it was over, Bardini had stood on the rostrum, Connelli on the platform, surrounded by the orchestra, all of them frozen into position. For a long minute, there was silence. Nothing could follow that consummation of love. When at last the audience broke into applause, it was as if each one of them was under a spell.

She thought of it now. Connelli at the summit, a person set apart. And tonight, because of Grania coming to dinner, the television set at the castle must not be turned on.

367

She went downstairs, and found Marian in the drawing-room, sitting in the Kilcaraig chair.

"Niall moved it here from the library, so that I can watch the television in comfort," she said. She tapped the *Radio Times*, which was spread on her knees. "Isabella isn't smiling," she said, referring to the coloured picture on the cover. It was true. There was a pretty tilt to the head, but the eyes were anxious. She was in the character of Violetta, a Violetta whose smiling days were done.

"We won't be able to watch it," Josanne said, whispering although there was no one around to hear her. "I don't want to upset Mama."

"If we don't watch it, think how much it'll upset *me*. She used to come and see me when she was in London, the poor little soul." Marian could vividly remember what had happened long ago, but not what happened yesterday. "I sent her a telegram today. Twenty years singing means not many singing years left, a bitter-sweet celebration for her. Even Isabella is subject to wear and tear."

"In another few years, she may deign to marry Rorie," Grania said. Josanne, but not Aunt Marian, had seen her come into the room.

"That's what I was thinking," Marian said. "And isn't this a splendid opportunity for you to put an end to the hostility that's made so much misery over so many years?"

"Roderick tells me that you want us to send her a telegram. It's absurd."

"I had hoped that for once you'd see Rorie's point of view. Will nothing ever change that one-track mind of yours?"

Josanne poured out the drinks, a whisky for Marian, sherry for Grania. She handed them their glasses, feeling the battle of wills that was being fought out in the room.

"She hasn't been able to break with Rorie, any more than he could break with her. She's never brought scandal upon us, and, but for family opposition, I believe she might have married him long ago." Marian sipped her whisky, nicely iced the way she liked it. "A wee telephone call could put so much right."

"A telephone call! Marian, it's years too late!"

"It's never too late, until we're dead," Marian said. She was the nearest to the grave of any of them. To say so now would be blackmail.

Grania stood by the fireplace, drumming her fingers on the mantelpiece. Roderick came in, limping a little, his old war-wound hurting. His hair, once black as ebony, was grey, his face lined, his blue eyes tired. He smiled at her and held out his hand.

"Grania?"

She sighed. "I can see that this is a conspiracy. Very well. We'll try to get Milan. We'll use the office telephone. I'll talk to Rorie. He can hand on our felicitations, or whatever I'm supposed to say!"

Niall, who was at the door, stood aside to let them pass. "I left the number for them," he said to Marian. "A very successful operation wouldn't you say?"

"Why was I excluded?" Josanne asked.

"If it had misfired, you would have joined Isabella in the dog-house!"

The call did go through, and Grania spoke to Rorie. "She couldn't come to the phone, thank God," she said when it was over, but her cheeks were flushed and her eyes sparkled. She was happier than they had seen her for years. "Rorie says that tonight is an ordeal for her. Aren't these people temperamental! She must know that when it comes to singing, she can't fail."

Catriona telephoned after dinner to remind them to watch *Traviata*. She was in Edinburgh, staying with Hector's parents while he was at sea.

Josanne made sure that baby Roddy was sleeping, then she joined the others in the drawing-room.

The people of Kilcaraig, the MacPhails at their farm, the Allans at the Manse, the doctor and his wife, Mrs. Craig at the post office, and all the ladies of the Women's Rural Institute, with their families and friends, gathered in front of their television sets. They all knew that there was some special connection between Isabella Connelli and the Lamonts. Some said that she was Mr. Rorie's fancy lady.

The prelude to *La Traviata* throbbed to its conclusion. The curtains rose. Violetta moved to the centre of the stage to greet her guests.

Absorbed in their different thought processes, Europe watched.

* * *

At La Scala, Milan, Rorie stood at the back of his box. It was the last act of *La Traviata*, and it was running late, because the audience frequently held up the action with their applause. Bardini's skill kept the orchestra and the singers together, and Isabella had never sung more exquisitely. The telephone call from Kilcaraig had come through just at the moment when it was most needed, when her nerves had threatened to snap under the strain of what was to happen tonight.

Immediately after the final curtain, he left the auditorium. He wasn't waiting for the curtain calls, as he had arranged with Motti that he would be in the dressing-room when Isabella returned there.

It was a break with tradition. This was the first time he had been in her dressing-room during a performance, for her insistence on solitude had never wavered.

Motti was waiting for him, looking anxious. Tonight there would be speeches, and the stage would be filled with flowers as Isabella murmured *grazie*, and showed the right degree of emotion expected by a *prima donna* who was celebrating her twentieth anniversary. She would keep up her act until the final curtain. She never failed her audience, not even if her heart was breaking.

After what seemed to be an eternity, she almost flung herself into the dressing-room; then she stopped, bewildered, when she saw Rorie reflected in the mirrors. He held out his arms to her. She threw herself at him, weeping convulsively. He had never, since he met her, seen her cry, except on the stage.

Motti had left them alone, but she now returned to the room. "You'll have to take another call."

Isabella drew away from Rorie, saw her tear-stained face, mopped it with tissues, applied some powder and joined the escort who awaited her. When at last she returned, she looked worn and spent. No more tears.

Bardini came in to say goodnight. She was sitting at her table, rubbing cold cream on her face. He touched her shoulder, then kissed her hair and turned and left the room.

Rorie stayed with her while she changed. She was scarcely aware of him, as Motti unfastened her buttons, and then helped her into her dress. Her mind was numb now. She had survived tonight, had shared in the excitement felt by the rest of the cast on this, her special night. It would be days before they knew the full significance of it all.

Motti was bundling things into her suitcases. There were two large ones, and a trunk for her costumes, but they would be packed away tomorrow morning. Motti was not coming on the yacht.

"I'm ready," she said to Rorie. She looked every inch a *diva*; usually muffled against the chill, there would be no need tonight for such precautions, but she would act her part for as long as she was able. Tomorrow she would be on the Mountstephans' yacht, bound for Ireland, and the newspapers would state that she was cruising in the Mediterranean, taking a short autumn holiday. They would expect her back by the first week in December. She was part of the scene on gala occasions at the Scala.

The press reporters were very kind. With their sixth sense they knew that there was a story at hand, but Connelli had always been courteous and helpful to them, and in this time of her greatest need they respected her right to privacy. She would be well away before the news was released – news that would knock the current crisis out of the headlines.

Tonight was not going to be a night of love. She wanted Rorie to be with her to comfort her, to hold her, to keep her alive while she faced the first terrible hours of readjustment which she must make moment after moment, over relentless weeks and months and years.

She said "goodnight" to Motti, no more.

The audience had dispersed after the safety curtain was lowered, but vast crowds had gathered outside for a glimpse of her. Briano stood by her car, unruffled, like a sentry on duty. She paused to smile and wave, then she sank into her seat, Rorie following swiftly to her side. There would be sharp eyes which would see that her companion on this night of nights had never before appeared with her in public.

Briano drove carefully through this throng, who would believe that her destination was some exotic party, given in her honour, but his instructions had been to take her on the road to the south. She would spend what remained of the night in a villa belonging to friends, and in the morning he would drive her to Santa Margherita.

Even he was unaware that she had sung in public for the last time in her life.

55

During the first few days at sea, Isabella spent most of her time sitting on a deck chair and reading the score of *Tristan and Isolde*. Christopher Mountstephan, his wife and his sister, knew that this was a major crisis in her life, which she must solve in her own way. The only other guests on board the yacht were the Maestro and his wife. The Maestro had supported Isabella through the early turmoil of her years as a singer, and could not be dispensed with yet, not until she was able to recognize that it was on Rorie Lamont that she had elected to rely, that it was he who would hold her life and her happiness in his hands.

Sometimes Rorie sat with her. Mostly she ignored him, intent on learning the role of Isolde, although she knew she could never now sing it. Bardini had given her what he could, the experience of the *Liebestod*. Unwittingly, he had increased her sense of loss.

Rorie didn't want her to think of him as a life guard, but he was well aware of her almost irresistible urge to end her life. The sea was so inviting, it could all be over long before the yacht could be stopped, or anything done to save her.

That night in the villa, she had slept, exhausted after the gruelling ordeal of her last appearance on the stage. It was Bardini who had persuaded her to give up her struggle, knowing with what courage she had faced every audience. She gave always of her best, but one day that best would fail. He wanted to spare her that. If anything went wrong it would break her heart. And his.

Her cabin was next to Margaret Mountstephan's, and Rorie knew that Margaret was not sleeping, because at night she stayed awake, alert, fearing that in the darkness and dread Isabella would give way to her despair. Rorie himself only slept in snatches. He would not sleep peacefully again until he had her at his side, his love for as long as she lived.

She pushed the score aside, and turned to him. "Any news?" she asked. The Maestro would release a press announcement of her retirement.

"It won't happen until you're safely at the convent."

"I want to hear it myself. Then I'll believe that it's true."

"It is true, Isabella."

"I used to talk a lot of nonsense about the gift to me of my voice . . . on the effect it had on my life. And all the time, I've not been heading for a destination, but for limbo."

She bit her lip, struggling against tears. "Did you say anything to your mother that would make her relent, feel sorry for me, so that she telephoned her good wishes that night?"

"I said nothing. The family will hear the announcement when the world hears it."

"Did it have to be now? Couldn't it have waited for a little while longer?"

"We've talked about this before." They had talked about it over and over again. She had agreed on the wisdom of the step she had taken now.

Her hair was blowing in the breeze. She was thirty-eight years old. She looked older, drawn and perplexed.

"We can have children. You love children." If they waited much longer, there could be no children.

"And they'll grow up to love and to hate, to kiss and destroy. They'll grow up to be people, people like you and like me, and like your parents, messing up every good thing that God has given, and if they don't mess it up for themselves, He'll do it for them. Like He has for me. I don't think I believe in Him any more."

She spoke with passion. She had said it all before, but he knew she had not yet convinced herself that she was speaking the truth. He knew that in her state of desolation she would cling to her faith, and the Sisters at the convent would know the right things to say to her.

Margaret Mountstephan came onto the deck with a tray of beef tea.

"Elevenses, P. & O. style," she said. "Eat well and often today. The Bay of Biscay tomorrow, and although we have stabilizers, we're not going to be very keen about food."

"When do we get to the Bay of Biscay?" Isabella asked.

"Tomorrow," Rorie said. "Stoke up, you've a grisly few hours ahead of you." Isabella turned to look at him, and smiled.

"When you've seen me being sea-sick, you'll know what a thin veil all that star quality charisma has been! I'm an awful sailor. I really should never travel at all."

She sipped the soup. Margaret exchanged a look with Rorie, and left them together. Rorie leaned over, and picked up the score of *Tristan and Isolde*.

"Show me how you do it," he said. "It's fascinating. I've watched you at it for years."

"I know it all in my head, like Beethoven. And it's more rewarding than reading Tolstoy, and getting in a muddle with everyone's names."

Rorie had told her that she was uneducated, and she had tried to improve her mind, but she had not tried very hard.

"Set it to music," she had said. "And I'll have it right, every nuance of it." He hadn't bothered her about her education after that.

It was very rough indeed in the Bay of Biscay. The Maestro and his wife were confined to their cabins, where they wished that the yacht would sink. Rorie was confined to Isabella's cabin, where he proved that his devotion to her had nothing to do with her charisma.

He gave her champagne, assuring her that it tasted the same coming up as it did going down. This was true, as it never stopped down long enough to be anything but champagne.

It was during the night that the sea became calm.

"I want to go up on deck," Isabella said. "I feel revolting and degraded, and I must breathe some fresh air."

Rorie made her put a coat over her nightdress. She looked a mess, like a refugee from some horrible accident. Her hair was tangled, and she still had a green tinge about her face. They went up on deck, and stood together, watching the night sky and trying to identify the stars. Years ago she had done this, and it had made her realize how tiny and unimportant she was.

Rorie put his arm round her shoulders. "When are you going to marry me, Isabella?"

She pressed herself against him, her arms round his neck. "I love you, Rorie. I love you. It's been said over the centuries, and it will go on being said, because the mystery of love is greater than the mystery of death."

She had sung about it often; now she knew it to be true. Her hands touched his face, and felt his tears. "My love, I have to marry you, because there isn't anything else I can do. It's our love story. It's our score."

She was standing there, bedraggled and soured by sickness. Rorie wiped away the tears he would have been ashamed for anyone else to see. He hadn't shaved for twenty-four hours. His hair, like hers, was a mess.

"We'll never be more sordid than we are now," she said.

"It makes a start." He put his arm round her, and steered her to the companion-way. "And so to bed. We'll have a few hours' sleep, and I'll buy you a ring when we get to Cobh."

"In Cork. There's more choice, and they'll be more expensive." They were happy, whispering together, because the others in their cabins were asleep. When she was settled in her bunk, he kissed her goodnight. His fears were over. Now he would sleep, knowing that she was safe.

*　　*　　*

The announcement was made during the nine o'clock news. Grania and Roderick had gone over to the castle for coffee, as they often did after dinner, and Niall had nearly forgotten to switch on the television, so they missed the headlines.

Afterwards, none of them could remember how it was worded, because it had come as such a shock – that Isabella Connelli had announced her retirement. She had been compelled at last to accept that the tremendous pressures under which she worked were too much. There must be no more travel, no more stress. She must have peace.

There followed scenes from some of the popular operas in which she had appeared, *Rigoletto*, *La Bohème*, *Tosca*, and finally *La Traviata*, transmitted to a world-wide audience only a week ago. She had given the performance of a lifetime, the last performance of her

374

lifetime. It was predicted that her voice, feather-light in coloratura, but able to meet the demands of her dramatic roles, would be venerated for all time. She had never married, and was now resting at the convent near Cork, where she had been brought up.

It was an obituary notice. All it needed was some form of R.I.P. at the end.

"Rorie must have known when I rang him," Grania said. "He should have warned us about it. Isabella's singing days are over a good ten years too soon."

"He wouldn't think we'd care." Roderick recalled the years that had passed. When illness struck her, not one of them had expressed regret. Their only thought had been to preserve Rorie from an entanglement that could break his heart, and to protect Kilcaraig from publicity that could spoil the quality of its life.

Marian, sitting in the Kilcaraig chair, said nothing. Josanne had been watching her, and she was sure that the news had come as no surprise to her. She had known of the urgent need to accept Isabella.

Niall offered to telephone Rorie immediately.

"She'll marry him now," Grania said, resigned and sad. She could recall distinctly the words she had used to Rorie on the night of Catriona's wedding. *An ageing woman, brooding over her glorious past, hating the thing she has now become.* A young woman, forced to give up what was the core, the purpose of her life.

"The poor little soul. Yes, telephone Rorie. There may be something we could do to help."

The telephone call was unproductive. It was answered by a man with a strong Cork accent who said that Mr. Lamont would be out until half-ten, but he would write down a message. Niall dictated a few words, asking Rorie to telephone the castle as soon as he came home. He could hear, by the heavy breathing, that what he was saying was being written down.

Grania and Roderick stayed until half-past eleven, but no call came through from Cork. Niall drove them the short distance from the castle to Caraig Lodge, and when they had gone, Josanne quietly put through another call to Clonbracken House. She was alone in the drawing-room because Aunt Marian always went to bed by ten.

The telephone rang and rang. There was no reply. She managed to replace the receiver just before Niall came back into the room.

*   *   *

When Rorie got home, he read the message Paddy O'Sullivan had written out for him. He thought for a while, then he tore it up. He would telephone Kilcaraig, but not tonight.

He turned his attention to the list of people who had telephoned. Isabella had given the Clonbracken House number to her friends, not wanting the Sisters to be deluged with telephone calls. Paddy had faced real difficulties here, but had done his best, making some of the Central European names into artistic but unrecognizable squiggles. Others, though inaccurate, made sense. Pa Varotty, Sholty, Fraynay, Carrageen were among the names of the superstars. A host of others proved to him what he had already known. Connelli, the person, was loved by her colleagues. They would be suffering for her now, and they wanted her to know it.

The decision that she should stay at the convent had been a wise one. There she was protected from press and public alike, and, as the Mother Superior had pointed out to her, she was in the midst of the people best equipped to understand her special needs.

"We've helped her through the temper tantrums that could have ruined her life," Mother Donovan said. "She has learnt to control herself. Now she must learn to give free expression to what she feels. It will be a distressing sight. We know how to look after her. It's our job."

It was only after he had bought Clonbracken House that he found the Sisters specialized in the care of maladjusted children. Isabella had never told him that.

"She's a very docile person. I've never seen her throw a temperament," he said.

"You will see it now. She has to take the first stage to a new kind of life. She's going to cry out for the old, feel helpless, cheated, and rebellious. Leave her to us, but come here any time you wish, because you will have to learn how to handle her too."

He had been at the convent tonight, to see the nine o'clock news. He saw Isabella calmly watching herself. She listened to what was being said about her, and like the rest of them, she waited for the R.I.P. When it wasn't said, she said it herself, first of all quietly, thoughtfully, then rising to a crescendo of screaming, as if she had been struck suddenly by the horrifying finality of what she had heard. She was like one possessed. She had sunk to her knees by the chair where she was sitting, covering her ears, as if to keep out the words she had already heard. She had beaten with her fists on the chair, she had appealed to, then abused, Almighty God, and had finally wept on and on, uncontrollably. At last, she had fallen asleep, slumped where she was, her head on the chair, her breathing still rasping, as if her lungs and her veins had become an amalgam of pain.

Mother Donovan and the other nuns present had gestured at him not to touch her. He sat paralysed, watching this display of mental anguish. It was after eleven when he left for home, assured that Isabella must not be disturbed. Two nuns would remain with her. He could come and see her in the morning.

When the telephone rang at eleven forty-five, he didn't reply. He could stand no more tonight.

He lay awake. Tomorrow he would have to face Isabella, and what he had seen had made him afraid of her. He had been afraid for her for long enough. To be afraid of her was a new and daunting emotion. He couldn't be responsible for someone who behaved as she had done tonight. The woman he loved was a different being from that unharnessed fury he had left behind him at the convent. She was fit only for a cell, a padded cell. The Maestro was on the yacht, now heading for Scotland. Had he been in Cork, Rorie would have gone to him now, and asked him how he could escape from a situation he knew he was unable to handle. Daylight was creeping through the curtains when he fell into an uneasy sleep.

He left for the convent immediately after breakfast. He dreaded meeting Mother Donovan, who would read his thoughts as easily as she read a book. She was in her office, waiting for him.

"You haven't slept," she said. "It's very alarming at first, but you'll get used to it, and it won't happen very often. Two of the nuns were able to put her to bed, so when she wakes up she'll be in her own cell. She won't remember much of what happened, so you needn't be afraid about that."

So she knew he was afraid. She didn't know the nature of the fear.

"If, after you've seen her, you feel you can't cope with her, talk to Father Malachy about it. He'll explain to her in a way she'll understand, and she knows she's safe with us. It may be some time before she can pull herself together, but she will."

He left the convent, and set off to find Father Malachy at the presbytery. He had known the priest since he first bought Clonbracken House. He had told him that he wanted to be received into the Roman Catholic church, because he hoped to marry a woman who was an ardent Catholic, so he must share her faith.

"You can't share her faith. It's not a secondhand commodity, to be handed over without even reading the small print. It must be your faith," Father Malachy had said. "I can instruct you in it, but I can't give it to you. What I tell you can only be accepted by you if you believe what I tell you is true."

Today he told the priest what had happened last night, of his shame at finding that his reaction to Isabella's display was of repugnance rather than pity.

"It's a bit of a shock, when we see another being stripped of all pretence, of that veneer that makes up decency and respectability. The Sisters are trained for this, you aren't. But you've been privileged to witness something very intimate and special, far more so than seeing her without her clothes on."

Father Malachy was clearly not shocked at all. Nothing shocked him, nothing surprised him.

Rorie walked round the room. There was a crucifix over the door, a statue of the Sacred Heart by the window, and on the desk a picture of Father Malachy with his family on the day he was ordained. He had committed his life to the priesthood, was responsible for thousands of individuals, not just one. And he didn't complain.

"I want to marry her as soon as possible," he said, returning to a chair by the desk.

"Do you believe you can make up for all she has lost?"

"Father, if I believed that I would be a megalomaniac. But I'll love her forever, and that's the next best thing."

Father Malachy was doodling on his blotting-paper. He was drawing rabbits. Rorie could see him adding their ears, and their bobbly tails.

"I'll receive you on Saturday evening," he said. "It's a private ceremony, but you can bring her if you wish. You'll have to make your confession. Talk to her about that. She's very bad at it herself, but she tries, and nobody can do more than that."

Rorie almost ran to the convent, which was a few hundred yards away. He had forgotten that a short time ago he had been frightened of seeing Isabella again. He found her in the garden, looking pale but composed.

"Isabella, I'm going to be received," he said. "And you're to rehearse me for my confession."

"Good heavens, now I really am going to learn about life!" she said, and they laughed and laughed, hugging one another.

The Sisters were walking in the garden. It was their time for recreation. They saw them, and they heard them and exchanged smiles.

Jubilate Domine. It was going to be all right.

56

Grania was sitting in the sun-room at Caraig Lodge, watching the rain. Every now and again, the telephone gave a little tinkle, because the linesmen were repairing the damage done during last night's storm. It had to happen now, when they were all waiting for Rorie to telephone. If he had done so last night, it would have been all right. It was two o'clock in the morning when a branch of the doctor's sycamore tree had brought down the wires, and disrupted telephone communication between Kilcaraig and the rest of the world.

Today's post had brought a letter from Rorie. It had been written on the *Lapwing*, and posted at Cobh. He thanked Grania for her telephone call. She would know by the time she received his letter why the performance of *La Traviata* had been such an ordeal, and why the good wishes of the family were so well timed. For the first time for years, he was the Rorie she knew, her son, pouring out his thoughts to her.

"Isabella will be with the Sisters at first, going through a necessary period of adjustment," he wrote. "Her condition has been deteriorating for years, but with care the outlook isn't hopeless. I will be able to give her that care, because at last she has agreed to marry me.

"Please understand, Mama, that she couldn't do that before. She had to fulfil her vocation, knowing, as she did, how it would all have to end. She has been wonderfully brave. We both know that the future won't be easy, and that we are going to depend a great deal on one another and on our friends. Please will you help us? Will you try to love Isabella? May I some day bring her home?"

When Roderick came in, breathless because he had been to the village and was now feeling the steepness of the brae, he found her twisting the envelope in her hands. The letter was on her lap. He picked it up and read it.

"We made that telephone call just in time," he said. "If we'd waited another day, the news would have been out, and any friendly move from us would have been interpreted as pity."

She nodded, unable to speak. He pressed her shoulder, loving her as he had done unfailingly all these years. Then he saw that the rest of the mail lay untouched on the table beside her. There was *The Times*, and *Country Life*, and some bills. There was also a letter, addressed in spidery hand-writing, with an Eire stamp and a Cork postmark. He opened it, and read it to her.

"Dear Mrs. Lamont,

It was most kind of you to telephone me when I sang my last *Traviata*. Your good wishes were a great help to me.

I have known for some time that I would have to give up. The strain had become too much for me, and for those working with me.

I am sorry that I have caused you so much distress over my association with your son. I never meant it to happen, and I hope that some day you will forgive me for marrying him, and that I will never give him reason to regret it, in spite of the difficulties that lie ahead.

Please may he go home sometimes? He misses you very much. I will try very hard to be a good wife.

                    Yours sincerely,
                    Isabella Connelli"

He handed the letter to Grania, but she shook her head. Her eyes were swimming. "I can't see," she said.

"It's taken this pitiful attempt at self-expression for both of us to see what should have been obvious. Isabella and Rorie belong to each other. They're just like us."

"She doesn't say what's wrong with her, neither does Rorie, so what sort of a life do they expect to live together?"

"There may be a truth they can't yet face. That's where we can help."

There was a gust of wind as the outer door opened to admit Josanne. They hadn't seen her approaching. She pushed the door shut, and saw the letter in Roderick's hand. Then she saw Grania's expression.

"News?" she asked. Roderick handed her Isabella's letter. She read it through, and handed it back. "She means what she says about Rorie. She expects you to accept him, but not her. She'll learn a lot from us all about being a family, about being loved."

She sensed that Grania would give anything she could to turn back the pages of the years, and delete all the animosity she had felt towards Isabella, even towards Rorie.

"I came here to tell you that our telephone has been repaired, but yours won't be sorted until this afternoon," she said. "Come and have coffee, and you can call Rorie. You'll feel much better when you've talked to him. So will he."

Grania put on the cape which someone had left behind at Caraig Lodge. She used it in emergencies, and they called it the Psychic Tourist Cape, because that's what she looked like when she wore it. The three of them struggled against the wind to the castle, where coffee was ready for them in the library. Chrissie, from her chair by the Aga, saw to it that Cathy kept up the Kilcaraig tradition of service.

Niall, who had been in the Nissen field, joined them. He, too, was restless and anxious, waiting to hear from Rorie. He and Josanne had talked about Isabella's retirement for half the night, while the storm raged and the telephone wires came down. He went to the office with Grania to help her put through her call.

Left alone with Roderick, Josanne said, "Papa, she wouldn't surely marry Rorie if she were fatally ill – but she wouldn't give up singing unless she had to. Singing is her life. What do you make of it?"

"Illness can be crippling, not fatal," he said. "Rorie won't say anything on the telephone, or in a letter, because he'll be afraid of what might leak out. We've got to face the fact that for a while the eyes and ears of the world will be upon us. Isabella's private avalanche will get even more publicity than her twenty glorious years have done."

He was pacing about the room, forgetting the pain in his leg in his anxiety over Grania, and what she would be saying to Rorie now, and what she might be hearing.

When she returned, she was smiling. Rorie had been trying to ring them all morning. He'd guessed they'd had storm damage. He was cagey, but managed to say that he would marry Isabella quietly in the convent chapel one day next week. When the tumult of the news had died down, he would bring her to Kilcaraig.

"I don't care about the razzamatazz any more, I just want them home. And at last I've talked to Isabella. She has such a soft voice, you wouldn't believe it possible she could produce all those decibels when she sings! We didn't say much, just enough to lay a foundation for the future, as if the past had never happened at all." She sighed and laid her head on Roderick's shoulder. "I don't know how you've put up with me all these years."

"Don't you?" he said.

Josanne almost tip-toed from the room. She met Niall in the hall, and pulling his handkerchief from his pocket, she dabbed her eyes

381

and said, "Your parents' love for one another has reduced me to sentimental tears!"

*　　*　　*

The quiet wedding of Isabella Connelli and Rorie Lamont received full press coverage. They appeared on the television news, and Rorie handled the interview with charm and tact, while Isabella looked radiant, and murmured how kind everybody had been.

At the castle, and at Caraig Lodge, the family was taken by surprise. They had not expected this to be of worldwide interest. They were not accustomed to having a celebrity in the family.

On the following day, there were newspaper accounts that caused some consternation, and Mrs. Craig decided to hide the *Daily Messenger* under the counter, because she objected to the banner headline – DIVA WEDS JET-SET PLAYBOY. One surmise ran through most of the accounts. Connelli's retirement was due to a heart condition which was nothing to do with her state of health. It was hoped that in due course the darling of the operatic world would be back on the stage to enchant them again.

By midday, the press reporters had swarmed upon Kilcaraig, and in the village questions were asked and answered while tea, coffee and whisky flowed.

"We need a drawbridge, and guns on the boundary," Niall grumbled to Josanne. He had been photographed on his tractor in the Nissen field, and he suspected he would appear under a caption about Connelli marrying a crofter. Earlier, Grania, with a set smile on her face, and holding Flush by his collar, had posed for a picture outside the studded door of the castle. She would look like the wife of a Conservative candidate in a bye-election. Roderick had hidden in the MacPhails' barn, with a book and a bottle of whisky, and was prepared to remain there for weeks if need be, rather than be described as the Laird of Kilcaraig, who had been too disdainful ever even to have met his future daughter-in-law.

Marian prudently stayed in bed until the last of the press cars had gone.

"On earth what are they going to say about us all?" she asked.

She need not have worried. Glowing accounts appeared about the Lamonts and the people of Kilcaraig, and it was predicted that Connelli would soon regain her health when in the midst of the friendship and hospitality of these wonderful islanders.

"We'll be invaded by tourists," Grania moaned.

"Mrs. Craig has let a room to that nice reporter from *The Sunday*

Special for two weeks in August," Josanne said. "And old Sandy is thinking of doing up his bothy for self-catering holidays."

"And I've seen off an awful man from Leeds who had the nerve to ask for land for a chalet development," Niall told them, still flushed and angry from the encounter.

The Oban tourist office mercifully was closed. It would have done a roaring out-of-season trade.

*   *   *

While Kilcaraig wallowed in the limelight, Isabella and Rorie had disappeared.

Motti was installed as housekeeper at Clonbracken, and a lifetime of experience enabled her to ward off the press without offending anyone. She managed to conceal the fact that the bride and bridegroom were spending their honeymoon in their own home. Its fifty acres, much of it woodland, allowed them to go out walking among the trees or by the lake. They had done this so often before, furtively stealing moments together, but now the trees were their own trees, the lake was their own lake, and the beautiful Georgian house their own home, which they would enjoy in privacy once the hue and cry died down.

By the middle of November, life at Kilcaraig was back to normal, and Rorie telephoned several times a week, but he remained careful in what he said. Isabella was well, so well that she felt she had given up the stage unnecessarily.

"She doesn't seem to mind," he said to Roderick. "She isn't yearning for past glories. Almost it's frightening, like a lull before a storm."

The storm broke soon, and the press was quick to report it. Connelli was ill, seriously ill, as was apparent by the number of nurses at Clonbracken House; and the doctors who were treating her came from further than Cork. Grania offered to fly to Ireland, but Rorie assured her that there was no need. Isabella had been smitten by the virus infection which had caused a stir some years ago, but she was responding well to treatment. She would be up and about by Christmas, and Grania was relieved to know that her first meeting with her daughter-in-law would not have to take place over a sickbed.

It was Catriona who suggested that the family should get together for the New Year.

"Hector will be on leave," she wrote, "and if Isabella is fit to travel, she can convalesce with all of us around to cherish her. We'll give her a new lease of life."

And so it was arranged. Catriona and Hector arrived the day after Boxing Day. They occupied Catriona's old bedroom, which was large enough to take two beds, now that the sag-bags had been disposed of at a jumble sale in aid of the Tobermory Games.

Rorie and Isabella had crossed from Cork on the car-ferry, and were being driven to Mull by Briano. They were breaking the journey near Penrith, where they would spend a couple of nights with the Mountstephans. This was more than a means of seeing their friends, it was a way of avoiding publicity.

Catriona helped to put the finishing touches to the bedroom that Josanne was preparing for Rorie and his bride.

"I slept here when I first came to Kilcaraig," Josanne said, remembering the puppy that had eaten her tights. The puppy was the mature dog now, Flush, and he was breathing heavily, asleep under the bed.

A piano had been installed in what should have been a dressing-room, and Rorie's records had been neatly arranged there.

Catriona stood at the door, looking at the adjoining room. She was wearing a maternity dress, to disguise her thickening waist, although her longed-for baby wasn't due for another five months. "They can make love and they can make music. I hope they'll be happy. Matrimony is such a very difficult state."

"There's too many partings for you and Hector," Josanne said.

"I'm hoping to change all that." Catriona fiddled with the flowers which Josanne had arranged. "Ardcross House is supposed to be coming on the market. I'm going to buy it, and we can run it as a guest-house or something. Hector can leave the Navy, and the MacNeills will be back where they belong."

"Don't do anything without consulting Hector," Josanne said, knowing full well that such counsel would fall on deaf ears. "Men don't like to be beholden to their wives."

Catriona mumbled something unintelligible, and picking up a duster, she went downstairs. Josanne followed.

*　　　*　　　*

The lights were switched on in every room in the castle. It was the same at Caraig Lodge, and all over Kilcaraig. In each house and even in the church and village hall the lights blazed a Highland welcome for Mr. Rorie and his bride. Some of the menfolk had toiled up Ben Caraig and the moment the car was seen approaching from the Glen road, a match would be put to the paraffin-soaked bonfire that had been prepared.

The family had collected in the drawing-room at the castle. Niall and Hector were talking about bagpipe tunes, using the curious jargon known to both of them. Roderick was sitting by the fire with Catriona, who preferred the floor, at his feet. Aunt Marian was in the Kilcaraig chair, alert and excited. She knew exactly what was happening.

Grania stayed near the door, ready to go into the hall as soon as the travellers arrived. Josanne had asked her to be hostess for this evening, knowing that it was important for Isabella to be greeted first by her mother-in-law. In the kitchen, Chrissie was preparing to receive Briano. She had been practising her fractured Italian on Cathy, to whom she had issued a warning about the fickleness of Italian males.

Josanne was standing in the window, watching for the lights of the car, and wondering how often she had kept this vigil for family home-comings. She could scarcely remember the days before she lived at the castle. They were swallowed up in memories and no longer felt like part of her life.

"I can't believe it's true," Catriona said. "She should start singing off-stage, like in *Bohème* and *Tosca* and so on."

"Watch it!" Hector said. "This isn't an opera. This is real life and we may be in for a shock. Perhaps she has nothing to sing about any more."

They were all of the same mind, joyful anticipation mingled with dread.

"There are lights now," Josanne called. Grania went into the hall, but Josanne stayed by the window until the car drew up at the door, then she sat on the sofa, shivering, in spite of the blazing fire.

There was a muffled sound of voices, then Roderick went out to greet Rorie and be introduced to Isabella.

"He'll go upstairs and wake His Lordship," Josanne said despairingly. She could never keep Roderick away from his grandson.

When Grania returned, she showed no sign of the emotion she felt. "You've made their room look gorgeous," she said to Josanne. "And Rorie is like a schoolboy, going through his records, while Isabella is saying all the right things about the view, though in the gloaming there isn't a lot of it to see. But the lights everywhere are marvellous, and the bonfire is as big as the one we had for the Coronation."

The sound of young Roderick awake drowned the sound of Isabella and Rorie coming downstairs. There they were, in the room, with Isabella wearing a pullover and the Lamont tartan skirt which Grania had sent her for Christmas. She bowed to them all, not a *prima donna* taking a curtain-call, but a diffident woman meeting her husband's family in their home for the first time. Then she saw Aunt Marian, and in a moment was embracing her, murmuring endearments, loving her. Aunt Marian had always been kind to her.

Rorie touched her shoulder, and gestured to her to sit on the sofa. She obliged, looking up at him a little anxiously. Grania sat beside her and pressed her hand.

"You're cold," she said. "Put more peat on the fire, Catriona. We don't want Isabella catching her death. I'm afraid Roddy is being brought down to meet his new aunt." The roars drew slowly nearer.

Isabella smiled, and stood up, holding out her hands to take the baby. He recognized a stranger, and his screams increased, but she took him over to the window, and sat on a chair, rocking him in her arms.

Rorie, standing by the mantelpiece, watched her lovingly. "I've just been explaining to Mama and Papa," he said. "Isabella is deaf. It's been happening gradually for years. It's the result of damage that happened when she was a baby. It's worse at present, since her last illness, but there's always been a great improvement after a while." She smiled across at him. "She knows what I'm saying. She's been learning to lip-read, and she's used to keeping a careful eye on her conductor."

The momentary shocked silence was broken by a fresh outburst from Roddy. Isabella stood up, patting him and singing – "Too-ra-loo-ra-loo-ra, that's an Irish lullaby."

Her glorious voice floated round the room. The baby closed his eyes and very soon he slept. Cuddling him, she brought him close to the fire. "I can still be useful," she said.

Josanne sensed the importance of this moment. There must be no show of pity, or embarrassment.

"Years ago, you told us that the correct reaction to that lullaby should be sleep," she said, speaking carefully and looking straight at Isabella. "You've proved your point, but you'll find you have a very demanding audience. Please be sure you have an unlimited supply of encores!"

Isabella laughed, the lovely laugh that was part of her fame. They were not going to treat her as an oddity. They would tease her and help her, and she would belong to a family. Perhaps some day she would hold a baby of her own in her arms. She turned to Rorie.

"It's strange," she said. "I feel like Violetta at the end of *Traviata*. The suffering is over. I am joyful, re-born. But she died, and I am beginning to live."

Part Three
1978

SONG WITHOUT END

57

The removal van outside the Manse had come from England. It bore the names "Tucker and Dolman" in big, black letters painted on a psychedelic background, which looked incongruous there, under the old sycamore tree that darkened the dining-room window and threatened to crash down during the many winter gales. The new people would probably remove the tree. They would alter the character of the house, and paint the window-frames blue, and put up a notice stating that they sold honey or vegetables or craft-work of some sort. Incomers always did, or so thought old Sandy MacPherson as he ambled out of the post office, and retrieved the bicycle which he had propped against the Manse gate-post.

Because the village had developed naturally, the Kilcaraig post office and general store divided the Manse from the church. Behind it was the burial ground, its lichen-covered grave-stones tilting with age in the peaty soil. The only visible change in the village since the turn of the century had been the replacing of the thatched roofs on the row of cottages with slates, and the building of the village hall.

Sandy could remember the opening of the hall, back in the early thirties. There were more people around in those days, before television gave them ideas and lured them off to the world which lay across the strip of sea which separated Mull from the mainland.

Now everyone expected to own a car and a washing-machine, but in his youth, Sandy had tramped blankets in tubs full of soapy water, which were carried down to the banks of Loch Caraig for that purpose every spring. The children of today, who ran about the school playground, didn't know how progress had denied them the joy of tramping the winter grime out of the blankets, of experiencing the wonderful feeling of grass under their bare feet, or the prickle of heather, or the scrunch of the sandy road.

Mrs. Craig watched through the little side window, behind the counter in the post office. She could see that Sandy was hoping to pick up what information he could about the new people at the Manse, but she could not see the removal van because, as the house stood back from the road, only the gate-posts and hedge were visible to her.

The Manse had been empty for nearly six months, although it seemed only yesterday that they had all gathered in the village hall for Mr. Allan's farewell *ceilidh*. He had been given a radio and a cheque, and there was a Celtic brooch for his wife, while regrets and appreciations were expressed in speeches, long and short, witty and sad. Then the dancing began, and the men slipped outside now and again for a wee drop of something more interesting than tea. The Allans would be missed, and the decision of the Kirk authorities to sell the Manse had come as a bitter blow to the people of Kilcaraig.

A Lamont of the past had given the land to the Church of Scotland more than a century ago, when it could not have been foreseen that dwindling congregations would render church buildings redundant.

Now the Manse, with its garden adjacent to the burial ground, would no longer house a Minister. In future, the services in the tiny church would be conducted by visiting preachers, and Mrs. Craig had agreed to set aside a room in her flat above the post office especially for their use.

In her privileged position, Mrs. Craig knew more than most people about the transactions over the Manse. It had been advertised in the *Oban Times*, and people had looked at it, some out of curiosity, others among the growing number of those who were tired of city life, wanting to get away from it all, but the building was too large for retirement, yet too small as a source of income. Four bedrooms, three living-rooms, and vast kitchen quarters were costly to keep heated and repaired, and as a boarding-house it would not be a viable proposition at all. There were no apparent buyers, but there was much comment that the Lamonts, who owned the rest of Kilcaraig, did not avail themselves of the opportunity to regain what had once been their own property. When Caraig Lodge had been put on the market after Mrs. Ames' death, the Lamonts had snapped it up without hesitation.

There was activity behind the screen which divided the post office from the village store. The children always came in on Saturday afternoons to spend their pocket money, and Euphie, behind the counter, would be giving good-natured advice about how to get the best value for their money.

Lachy MacDougall came in, his round as postman completed for the day. It had been a long round, because there had been official envelopes for everyone in the place, probably something to do with the electors' register, or the rates, and Lachy would have to call at every house, even going across the fields to MacKinnon's croft, where Morag lived with her brother, now that his wife had died.

"The Manse people have come," he said, handing in the letters he had been given to post.

"Just their furniture," Mrs. Craig said. She was the only person in the village, apart from the Lamonts, who knew anything at all about the Manse. She knew everything that went on, because as postmistress the incoming and the outgoing mail went through her hands. She recognized the writing on the envelopes, could identify even those that were typed, but secrets were safe with her. She never spoke of those things, not even to her son Colin, who was living with her for a while.

"There's a letter for Mrs. Sedley, care of the post office," Lachy said, slapping it down on the counter. "I had it in the MacPhails' pack by mistake. It will be for the Manse." It was said as a fact, but it was intended as a question. Mrs. Craig relented.

"That's right. I know the forwarding address." She knew it was a house near Sevenoaks, but she didn't re-address the letter under Lachy's eye. She had entered into the spirit of secrecy that hung over the new owner of the Manse.

She could see through the main window that Mrs. Niall was crossing the burn on her way from the castle, which was no longer screened from the road, now that the last of the fir trees had been cut down. The pink granite peeping through the ivy that covered it created a warm and friendly effect, but Sandy MacPherson had considered the removal of the trees as an act of vandalism. He had liked the air of mystery which the trees had bestowed on the house. He was still there at the manse gate. He would be hoping that someone knowledgeable would come off the afternoon boat-bus. Anyone who had been to Oban for the day could invariably pick up news of what was happening at Kilcaraig, often such information being totally unknown to the people who lived their lives in the place.

Josanne Lamont looked in at the post office to say that she was going to see how the removal van was getting on at the Manse. She alone, and of course Grania Lamont, could be allowed to show a womanly interest in the domestic activities on the estate, even though the Manse was not Lamont property.

"You got your Mothercare parcel," Mrs. Craig said. She knew Josanne was worried that Roddy's feet were suddenly cramped into his shoes. There had been a talk about children's feet at a meeting of the Women's Rural Institute, and Josanne was now president of the local branch.

"Thank heavens for that. Now, may I borrow your Book sometime please?" Josanne said. She referred to Mrs. Craig's mail-order catalogue, which covered everything from a mixing-bowl to an out-board motor, with clothes and shoes and household goods besides. "I want bunk beds for the nursery. Anne's getting too big for her cot."

The birth of Anne ten months ago had caused some concern in the village over the choice of names. Like most Highland people, the Lamonts respected the use of family names, and it would have been a courtesy to call the child after her maternal grandmother, but Josanne had rebelled at the thought of a Sybil Lamont at Kilcaraig, and her feeling for her mother had never been other than dutiful.

It was not until the people had sat in the tiny church and had seen the baby held over the font in the arms of Mr. Allan, who baptized her with the names of Anne Catriona Murray that tradition was seen to be upheld. Josanne's parents who came unwillingly to Kilcaraig for the occasion, returned home to London with the satisfaction of knowing that their name, Murray, had been incorporated, as it had been when Roderick was baptized in the same church, at the same font, just over three years ago. They were not interested in their granddaughter. They felt pride, but not affection towards their grandson. William Murray found increasing consolation in the brandy bottle, and Sybil Murray basked in the knowledge that her daughter had made a suitable marriage, and was not a bother to her any more. Josanne, chatting to Mrs. Craig in the post office, was fully occupied in caring about her family and Kilcaraig. Life before marriage to Niall was behind her, like an uncomfortable dream.

Mrs. Craig called up the stairs to Colin to bring down the catalogue. Josanne could hear footsteps overhead.

"Any news?" she asked. The post office was empty, although there was activity still in the general store.

"He's hoping for an interview next week."

Colin Craig had become a marine engineer, thanks to his own hard work and the unfailing support of his mother. Redundancy had forced him to return to Kilcaraig, humiliated by what he regarded as failure, and worried that living in such a remote place would weigh against his chances of finding another job.

"Perhaps you'll persuade him to let Niall help," Josanne said. Colin had refused any suggestion that the Lamonts should use their influence on his behalf. First pride, then obstinacy, compelled him to reject their offer.

"I'll speak to him again," Mrs. Craig said, without hope, but then Colin had appeared with the big catalogue in his hands.

"I'll take it up to the castle," he said to Josanne. "It's too heavy for you to carry – I see you walked down."

"Jogged," Josanne corrected him. "I got as far as the bridge, when I decided I was about to have a heart-attack! Weight-watching is going to be the death of me!"

She accepted Colin's offer. Niall was at home today, trying to balance the books, and to work out how the Dutton millions were going to be stretched to meet the ever-rising cost of running an estate that devoured income and produced nothing. Niall might take this opportunity to talk to Colin about an idea that had been simmering in his mind for a long time.

"I'm off to investigate the Manse," she told Colin. "I'll know by the furniture what sort of people to expect. Kilcaraig's slipping – not a thing discovered about them, when by now we should know every detail, right down to what sort of tranquillizers they take!"

She left the post office with Colin, then watched him walk briskly towards the bridge, tall, handsome, a credit to his widowed mother, who had been a MacKinnon from Kilcaraig before her marriage. His father was a major in the Royal Marines, but he had been killed towards the end of the war. Mrs. Craig had received that Government Priority telegram on the morning of the day Colin was born. She was living in Deal at the time, but the Lamonts brought her back home to Kilcaraig, and in due course arranged for the post office to be made available for her. They could understand why her son felt reluctant about accepting further help from them all.

The furniture removers were carrying a Sheraton table into the Manse, watched by a group of school-children, and by Sandy MacPherson, who was now half way up the short drive, still holding onto his bicycle. Josanne stopped to talk to him before she went up to the house.

"Will you be finished in time to catch the boat?" she asked the foreman. There was no means of leaving the island on a Sunday.

He told her they had almost finished. They had been asked only to put the furniture into the house, not to arrange it anywhere.

"I'm Mrs. Lamont, I come from the castle," Josanne said, wanting to identify herself and hoping they wouldn't think she was putting on airs. She held out her hand, and the foreman sheepishly shook it, then the two men who had deposited the table in the house shook hands with her also. Years ago, she had found the Highland hand-shake a remarkable formality, performed as it was on every occasion. Now she didn't even pause to think that these men might consider her odd.

"We can give you a meal any time at all," she said. "There isn't a hotel round here, and you must be famished."

They refused the meal, but invited her into the house to share their sandwiches. She sat on an elegant Queen Anne chair, while the men sat in a row on a sofa. A grand piano was in a corner of the room, piled high with cardboard boxes. Josanne made a mental note to try to come back and remove them after the men had gone. They couldn't be doing much good to the piano.

"You came from Kent?" she asked. The address and telephone number were in the small print at the side of the van.

"Near Sevenoaks. This is only part of the load. The rest will follow when he's dead."

Josanne looked up from her cheese sandwich. "When he's dead? You mean the man who's coming here?" Funny people came to the island now, but she'd never heard of a house being prepared for a corpse. She must have heard wrong. The foreman saw her confusion.

"It's his wife coming. She'll be his widow by then. He's had a stroke and been ill for years. It's only a matter of time." He wiped his hands on his trousers and indicated that it was time he got back to work.

Josanne wished them safe home, and returned hastily to the castle to tell Niall about the macabre set-up at the Manse.

"Away!" he said, leaning back in his office chair so that he could see her beautiful legs. She was sitting on the edge of his desk.

"The ghoulish lady is waiting for him to breathe his last, then she'll dash up here to arrange the furniture before the stuff they've left behind comes – his bed, I suppose. And maybe his coffin!"

"No room in the burial ground," Niall said, and they both laughed, then Niall suggested, "Maybe she'll bring his ashes up here in a wee box!"

Josanne was suddenly serious. "When the Manse was up for sale, we should have put in an offer for it."

"What with?"

"Rorie would have helped, if you'd told him about it in time. He said so. And it's the only part of Kilcaraig that doesn't belong to us."

"Rorie and Isabella have a son now. We can't be propped up by them." He added, "Besides, it'll be getting sold again in a few years' time. Incomers don't settle long in Mull. Here today, and away yesterday, as the missionary said." The missionary was Gaelic-speaking, unused to English, and he had said it from the pulpit many years ago, before any of them were born. The saying had become legendary.

"Some of them stay," Josanne said, thinking of the Ameses, who, despite a cool reception, had fitted so admirably into the Kilcaraig way of life.

"We'll be prepared to welcome a widow with superb furniture, judging by what you've told me, and an urgent need to get away from the scene of her husband's demise. Maybe she has her reasons."

"I think it's all horribly sinister, and the thought of it gives me the creeps."

Niall left the desk, and took his wife in his arms. "Josanne, your imagination leads you to all sorts of strange ideas. With luck, we'll find a bossy individual who'll run all your committees for you, and you'll have more time for me and the children. Come to the nursery now. We haven't been with them all day, and they'll help you to forget your forebodings about the mysterious occupant of the Manse!"

In a country house near Sevenoaks in Kent, the figure in the bed pressed the hand that held his. Three tiny, almost imperceptible movements. He wanted water.

His wife rose, and presently she held the glass to his lips.

58

Rorie Lamont drove along the rough road that led to Clonbracken Farm.

Home is the place where your heart is, they said. For him, home was the place where his wife was – an hotel, a railway carriage, a car. Her presence gave him all he would ever need of content.

The road had been under repair ever since he bought the farm six years ago. Now and again, workmen came along and put up notices, and looked busy with tar and a steam-roller for a day or two, then they went away because the money allotted by the government had run out. This never surprised Rorie. He was used to the ways of Celtic people, having been reared at Kilcaraig, and in County Cork the haphazard ways of authority equalled that of the Island of Mull. That they would never conform to anything was the only thing about them that was predictable.

He had to get out of the car to open the farm gate. The house was screened by trees, and nobody would have seen him coming, because he was earlier home than he had expected. He kept a careful watch on the donkey who was at the far side of the field, but who could be through the gate and on the road in the twinkling of an eye. A big sow with her piglets was snuffling close to the fence. Isabella must have forgotten to close the gate leading to the pig sties. Forgotten on purpose. She was far too sentimental to be a farmer's wife, caring more for the liberty of the animals than for the kind of meat they would eventually produce. Eventually was the right word for it – when they dropped dead from old age, because she, with her Titian hair and green eyes and unbelievable beauty had never allowed a beast to go to the slaughter-house from the day she arrived at Clonbracken as a bride. His heart soared as he drove towards her. Tesoro mio, he thought. *Ich liebe dich, joy of my heart.* In any language, his feeling for Isabella remained the same – undying love.

The Georgian house glowed warmly in the setting sun. Tosca, the spaniel, lay across the front door like a sentinel, but she moved aside to let her master pass. She would have bitten a stranger, or the postman.

Isabella's shoes were lying in the middle of the hall, where she had kicked them off, and her cardigan was dumped on the oak settle. Motti must still be in Cork, for she unfailingly tidied up after her mistress, not caring that the *prima donna assoluta*, whom she had dressed with such care in every great opera house, was now merely a farmer's wife whose life consisted of her husband and her child and her household.

The drawing-room door was open, but there were no signs of disarray. Isabella hadn't been there. Then he heard the piano in the music-room upstairs. She had her back to him, and was fingering an enchanting tune that was emerging as a waltz. He stood in the doorway, and almost immediately she turned round. She had felt him, but because of her deafness, she had not heard him approach.

They embraced as if they had been parted for years. Rorie had left the farm only that morning.

"Composing?" he asked.

She nodded. "Silly little songs. Product of a silly little mind. I wish I'd listened to you years ago when you told me to read Tolstoy. Then I might be composing operas, instead of writing ditties for the convent Christmas play!" She was still faithful to the Sisters in the Convent of the Five Wounds, never allowing it to be forgotten that they had cared for her when she was a destitute child.

"Your ditties have been sung in the Albert Hall," he said.

"My friends are most kind." She turned away from him, and her fingers were on the piano keys again.

"Isabella, will you sing for me now?"

"What do you want me to sing?"

His heart leapt. She had heard him. Her hearing-aid was helping, although she hated wearing it.

"Sing any of your little lollipops about love," he said, remembering how he used to listen to her in the concert halls, tossing off the encores as if she were handing out bouquets, a technique that had won her a personal affection, which matched the acclaim of the opera audiences.

Her voice had lost none of its magic. Rorie thought of the waste it was that only he could hear her, when all over the world people still wrote about her, demanded re-issues of her recordings, grieved at the loss of her talent, which was so matchless, so unique. After a while, he joined in with her, for he loved to boast that he now partnered the great Connelli in duets.

The room was becoming dark when they sang the words by Sir Walter Scott, which she herself had set to music. It had become especially their own, their signature tune, because it had carried them through those grim days when his family had rejected her. They both knew, although they never said it, that she was still regarded as an embarrassment, not because of her disability, but because of her fame.

She played the introduction, then they sang –

> "True love's the gift which God has given
> To man alone beneath the heaven;
> It is not fantasy's hot fire
> Whose wishes soon as granted fly;
> It liveth not in fierce desire,
> In dead desire it does not die;
> It is the secret sympathy
> The silver link, the silken tie,
> Which heart to heart and mind to mind
> In body and in soul can bind."

She turned and leaned against him. "Will you remember those words always, forever, whatever happens?"

She was referring to those dark moments, when despair took hold of her, when the loss of her life of music swamped all other thoughts, and she was locked in the purgatory of her misery, refusing food, sleep, life itself if she could find a way to end it. It didn't happen often, but when it did, Rorie knew, as she did, what it was to experience the dark night of the soul.

He pressed her close to him. Her hand fiddled with the lobe of her ear, and fear welled up in him like bile. He knew that gesture, saw it as the prelude to the agonizing bouts of ear-ache from which she suffered. Over the years, the curative drugs lost their potency. After each attack of pain, her hearing was further impaired, but always he would love her and hold her to him as he was doing now.

"I will always remember," he said. A little shiver ran through her body. He repeated it. "I will always remember." He gave her a moment to let the reassurance sink in, then he said, "You left your shoes and your cardigan in the hall. Did the nuns only teach you paters and aves?"

"They taught me how to be tidy, too. And how to cook." She laughed. When the cook was out, she gave Rorie fish fingers, frozen peas and potato croquettes, followed by tinned fruit. "I'll get Francesca to give me lessons. Benedict will soon be getting sophisticated food, and Bridget won't always be around to feed him."

The beautiful red-headed daughter Rorie had dreamed of possessing had turned out to be red-headed all right, but a boy who at present showed little other resemblance to his mother. Rorie had hidden his disappointment from Isabella, who thought her son was the most wonderful creature ever to be born. She had concealed from Rorie that all through her pregnancy she had been terrified of producing a baby that was malformed or mentally retarded. She had been approaching forty, old to be having her first child.

"Benedict will thrive on frozen food and pork from pigs that have died of heart-failure." He kissed the mole which was just behind her right ear. "When you did your round of the pig sties, you didn't shut the gate."

"So Brunhilde got into the big field," Isabella said. "She likes it there. The others are quite content to wallow in the mud, but her thoughts are on higher things."

"Living up to her name?"

"Wagner's Brunhilde finished up on a funeral pyre. Ours will be buried decently in a grave. No smoked bacon from Clonbracken Farm."

She stood up, small in her stockinged feet, she who had trod the stage as Tosca, Violetta, Norma, electrifying her audience with the impact of her beauty and her voice. The invisible hearing-aid was very visible indeed from this angle. Again she caressed her ear.

"Is it uncomfortable?" Rorie asked. She didn't answer, and he saw that she held the tiny device in her hand. He embraced her again, stroking her hair, pouring into her the warmth of his love.

There was nothing else he could do.

*　　　*　　　*

While Rorie and Isabella were talking about pigs at Clonbracken, Rorie's parents were talking about survival at Kilcaraig.

"Josanne says her instincts have alerted her to the worries Niall is trying to hide from her," Grania said. They were in the sun-room at Caraig Lodge. When they had bought the house, thereby restoring it as part of their estate, they had meant to demolish this addition, which ill-suited the style of rugged Scottish architecture, which the family always referred to as Presbyterian Gabled. Time passed, and due to Highland procrastination, the sun-room was allowed to remain. Now its usefulness had been proved, for it was warm and commanded an excellent view of all that was going on in the village.

"The mammoth repairs that had to be done to the roof last year must have cost a fortune," Roderick said. "Pity they couldn't get it off the insurance." A gale had ripped off slates and caused considerable havoc, but the insurance premium had not been increased for years, so compensation had been infinitesimal.

"If it isn't the roof, it's the windows. Or the floors." Grania had discovered long ago just how much it cost to keep the castle in a state of reasonable repair. On this storm-swept island, nothing remained intact for long.

"I can't see it as a guest-house. It would drive Niall up the wall." Roderick ran his hand through his hair, still thick, but now iron grey. "The Dutton empire is going to have to do a lot of expansion if Kilcaraig is to remain the rich man's toy it has become."

"I don't understand about inflation," Grania said, as she always said when reference was made to Carnworth, Prior and Dutton, which kept Kilcaraig out of the hands of the receiver. She thought for a while then she said, "When I was a child and my grandfather was alive, we never had a halfpenny to spend on anything, yet we kept going, with quite a staff of servants, and innumerable men paid to work on the estate. Everyone was content and happy. Nobody starved."

"Times have changed."

They had indeed. Now there was Chrissie in the kitchen, to rule Cathy from her arm chair, and there was a few hours' help on two days a week from a couple of women who came up from the village. No shepherd to pay, because Niall saw to the sheep, while Angie Campbell looked after the cows and did many other jobs besides. At seed time and harvest, everyone helped everyone. That was traditional, and the only things that had changed there were the sophisticated machines which had replaced the scythes and horse-drawn ploughs.

"There's Nanny to pay," Grania said. "And Morag MacKinnon when she can come." Morag divided her time between her widowed brother and the care of Great-Aunt Marian, who now lived permanently at the castle.

"They can't economize more than they do," Roderick said. "Josanne's marvellous, the way she copes with everything. I wonder if Rorie has any idea how difficult things have become?"

"It would never occur to him, and the children would die rather than tell him!" Grania always referred to her family as the children when she was worried, as if she were still responsible for them, still protecting them from the threat of anything that might cause them anxiety or distress.

Roderick leaned forward and clasped her hand over his. The little brown spots of age were on her skin, her lovely neck showed the passing of time, but she was still beautiful, she would always be beautiful in his eyes.

"Rorie, who was our greatest anxiety, is the one who has come off so well. When I think of the sleepless nights we had over Rorie I wish we were all endowed with second-sight. It would save so much worry," he said.

"I sometimes wonder how things really have worked out with him and Isabella," Grania said. "He needs a proper career. Clonbracken is only a pastime, and although he breeds pigs, he never seems to sell them. I don't know what he does with all their progeny."

"Briano takes them to market when Isabella is safely away at Ravello. He told me so. He drives them there himself."

Briano had gone into voluntary exile when Connelli retired. If he could no longer be chauffeur to the world's greatest *prima donna*, he could at least be around with his stiletto to see that she came to no harm. He installed his wife, Francesca, and the children born to him in and out of wedlock at Clonbracken, where they settled happily, and learned to speak English with an Irish brogue.

"Isabella's records must be a permanent gold-mine," Grania said after some reflection. "No money problems there."

She left unsaid what both of them were thinking. Catriona, who resembled Grania so closely, and whose marriage had appeared to be so perfect, was in trouble for buying Hector's old home, with a view to turning it into a guest-house. Instead of winning his gratitude, he had been furious with her for acting without consulting him, and had resented being indebted to his wife for the very roof over his head. He had moved into Ardcross House only to save the family name, his as well as hers, from scandal. He remained in the Navy, and spent very little time at home.

"The Kirk will have made a mint out of the sale of the Manse." Roderick's voice broke into her thoughts. This topic was never far from their minds. "Not that I grudge the money that'll probably pay some impoverished minister's stipend."

"If it had belonged to Niall, its sale would have been a useful addition to the castle kitty." Grania picked up the binoculars which were always kept near at hand, and trained them on the Manse.

"If it had belonged to Niall, he wouldn't sell it. So it would be just another house to keep in good repair, and eat into capital!"

Grania smiled and handed the binoculars to him. "I hadn't thought of that. I wish someone had been appointed to light fires in it. Three weeks since the furniture came, and we've had all that rain."

Roderick was focusing on the Manse. "Niall has the key," he said. "One can't light fires in other people's houses. If they don't come by the end of the month, maybe they'll wait until the spring. No one in their right mind would move to Mull in November."

"No one in their right mind would buy an outlandish house they've never seen."

Roderick caught his breath. "A car's turned into the drive. Not a car I recognize. I can't see it now because the sycamore tree's in the way. Our talking of it must have willed it here!"

Grania stood up, screwing up her eyes against the setting sun. As she did so, a light snapped on in the Manse, then another one.

The telephone rang. Knowing who it would be, Grania picked up the receiver.

"Mama," Josanne said. "There's a light in the Manse. They've arrived."

59

The naked light bulb revealed the piled up furniture in a way that made it look grotesque. The house smelled of damp, and a branch of the sycamore tree was brushing on the window, making an eerie sound.

The girl stood still, frozen with apprehension.

"It'll be all right when we've moved some of the packing cases, and lighted a fire," the woman said, her voice cool and calm, beautifully modulated.

"I'll get the cases from the car." The girl was glad to escape outside, to the setting sun, and the nearness of the post office, just there at the end of the drive. Then she saw the burial ground over the hedge and was sick with fear again. She undid the boot of the car.

Inside the house, the woman saw that the removal men had done their best to leave some sort of order behind them. They had guessed which would be the sitting-room, and which the dining-room, and had put down the Persian carpets accordingly. They had placed an electric fire in the grate of one room. Thankfully she switched it on, and its glow transformed the room. She could hear the girl bumping the cases into the hall, and she felt guilty.

"Shirley, you were right – we should have stayed at an hotel," she said, taking one of the cases and looking at it, dazed, as if she had never seen it before.

Shirley Morris said nothing. She went back to the car and hauled out two more cases. The picnic basket contained all they would need for an evening meal, so that, too, she carried into the house.

Mrs. Sedley had gone to the kitchen, where the table was surrounded by packing-cases, but there were two chairs, side by side, where they could sit to eat. A tap in the scullery was dripping, and she nearly screamed when she saw a mouse creep silently across the floor. Suddenly she laughed, and Shirley came and stood looking at her, not knowing what to say.

"I've seen a mouse. I was going to stand on a chair and scream, like women are always supposed to do. How silly to be afraid of anything so small," she said.

"They're creepy," and Shirley turned and went back to the car. She heard the telephone ring, sounding hollow and peculiar, and it was a long time before it stopped, but after she returned to the hall, she could hear Mrs. Sedley speaking, so she had not ignored it. Maybe it had been difficult to locate which room it was in, because of the empty, echoing house.

"That was Mrs. Lamont from the castle. They own this estate," Mrs. Sedley explained. "She saw our lights and wondered if she could do anything to help. She offered us dinner, even bedrooms." She saw the momentary glimmer of hope in Shirley's eyes, and said quickly – "I refused. We can't start off by imposing ourselves upon strangers".

"We haven't seen the bedrooms yet," Shirley said pointedly.

"I'll go upstairs and look. Switch on the kettle. The men have left it by the electric cooker. How thoughtful they've been."

She was grateful. She was kind, and she was beautiful. Shirley had got the job through an advertisement in *The Lady*, but after two weeks in her company, she knew no more about Mrs. Sedley than she had when they first met for an interview in the lounge of the

Goring Hotel near Victoria Station in London. To be companion-help to a woman who was moving to a house she had never seen, situated in a remote village on the Island of Mull had sounded both daunting and exciting. She had accepted the offer, partly because the salary was far above anything that she had expected, and partly because there was something compelling about this middle-aged woman with violet eyes and greying black hair, whose figure put the slouching younger generation to shame.

"My husband can communicate with me by pressing my hand. We've evolved a sort of morse code," she had said during that interview. "I've got to get home as soon as possible, so I can't offer you tea or anything. Please eat somewhere, and enjoy your evening in the West End." Then she gave Shirley four five-pound notes, insisting that she spend them.

"When do you want me to come?" Shirley had asked.

"I'll let you know. It won't be until he's dead, but your salary will start immediately, plus whatever you pay for your room and so on at Cricklewood."

When she stood up to go, Shirley noted with approval the beautifully cut linen suit. As she left the hotel, she put on dark glasses, although there was not any sun.

The summons to go to Sevenoaks arrived a week later. Mrs. Sedley must have known how close to death her husband had been. The funeral was over when Shirley arrived, and Mrs. Sedley was composed, but still showed signs of grief. Surprising, because she had been tied to a sick-bed for seven long years, and could be excused if she regarded her widowhood as a release from captivity.

The large, rambling house in the overgrown garden had every kind of luxury, and there was a maid, who brought Shirley her morning tea, but although she had never experienced such an opulent way of life, she was struck by its unreality. It was like living in a museum, the staff like waxworks, the books in the library unused, the records unplayed. If she had any home to go to, she would have taken fright and gone there, but she had no fixed address, and had drifted round from job to job, and from place to place ever since she left the university. Mrs. Sedley had asked her no questions about her past.

"I've switched on the fire in your bedroom and draped the bed-clothes in front of it," Mrs. Sedley told her now. "I've plugged in your electric blanket, so at least you'll be warm in bed. The packing-cases were very well labelled. I found the things at once. Thank you."

Cautiously, Shirley went upstairs. There was a bedside light on a packing-case, and a chair beside the fire. Mrs. Sedley had tried to make the few articles of furniture look welcoming, had even unfurled a mat, one that had been in the hall at Sevenoaks. Touched, Shirley experienced the familiar surge of affection which this strange, withdrawn woman aroused in her.

She crossed the passage and looked at the other room. Mrs. Sedley had made no attempt to prepare her own bed.

Shirley opened the big cardboard box, and arranged the sheets to air by the electric fire, then she found the plug and fixed the bedside light. When she went downstairs, Mrs. Sedley had made the tea, and had laid the table as best she could with the picnic cups and plates. There was cold chicken and salad, still in a polythene bag, and there was toast with butter, and cheese.

"We'll manage," Mrs. Sedley smiled. "It won't seem so awful tomorrow. You'll be all right."

Surprisingly, Shirley found that she had to blink away her threatened tears. Always Mrs. Sedley thought of her comfort, not of her own. She was so beautiful, yet so remote. And she never asked questions.

They ate their supper as the wind rose and the whole house creaked.

*　　*　　*

"I asked them to come over to dinner, and to spend the night, but they refused," Josanne told Niall, who had come in from the fields, and was sitting on the sofa in front of the library fire. He had piled it high with peat, despite Josanne's warning that the chimney needed cleaning, and he could burn the castle down. "She has a very attractive voice. And she sounded sane!"

"They'll freeze in that cold house, with never a fire in it since the Minister left," Aunt Marian said. She was sitting in the Kilcaraig chair, and had taken a lively interest in what was going on at the Manse. Now in her mid-eighties, she was not as alert as she used to be, but her hearing was good, and she could still read, even when she had mislaid her spectacles.

Josanne was watching Niall with interest, as he rolled a cigarette and gazed into the fire. He seldom smoked, unless he had something on his mind.

"Has Adrian anything to do with this woman buying the Manse?" she asked. She would always be indebted to Adrian Ferguson for introducing her to the Lamonts. He had been knighted in the Birthday Honours, which had proved to be an instant cure for Alison's hypochondria.

"What made you ask that?" Niall said. Josanne was standing by the mantelpiece, her figure thickened a little with motherhood, but still lovely in his eyes, her sleek, page-boy hair worn just as it had been when first they met ten years ago.

She turned to him, her big blue eyes searching his face, as if for a clue, then she smiled. "I read you like a book. Adrian had telephoned several times, and you've never told me what about. But you showed an interest in the Manse after the Allans left, and I knew you weren't snooping around it with a view to buying it for ourselves."

"If Adrian had put someone on to it, I hope it was an innocent client, and not a guilty one. I suppose it's all the same to him! A job's a job, and he takes on what interests him, but it's not all the same to us at Kilcaraig. We have enough weirdies around without providing a refuge for poisoners," Marian said.

Josanne laughed. "Adrian says he never defends the guilty."

"He's an advocate, not a judge. What fool is going to hire a top Q.C. and tell him he's done it! He'd say he hadn't done it, then leave Adrian to work out the alibis." Marian thumped a copy of *Famous Trials* which was on the table beside her. "I've learnt a lot about crime, since Cathy bought me all those paperbacks in Oban." She leaned back in her chair, closed her eyes, and appeared to be asleep, but Niall and Josanne knew that she was merely registering that she had said her say, and the subject didn't interest her any more.

It was when they were changing for dinner that Niall told Josanne about Mrs. Sedley.

"Adrian made me vow silence, so I suppose this is a breach of confidence," he said. "Now she's here, I think you should know about her. Adrian helped her through legal difficulties years ago, before he became such a pundit in criminal cases. Aunt Marian obviously thinks she's the nurse he defended in the Crale poisoning case." It had been a spectacular victory for Adrian, but not a popular one, as the public had found the nurse patently guilty before the trial had even begun.

"How do we know she's not that one?" Josanne shared Aunt Marian's misgivings.

"Because she was at her husband's bedside nursing him through a stroke. She has a water-tight alibi!" He took a slip of paper from his wallet and handed it to Josanne. It was a cutting from *The Times*, and it read "Sedley. On October 8th, peacefully in his home in Kent, Paul Michael Sedley. Funeral private, no flowers or letters, please".

"What an extraordinary notice! His widow's craving for anonymity is pathological! Please Niall, come clean. Just what has Adrian told you about this woman?"

"Not a great deal. Only that she wants to live her life in a quiet village, miles from anywhere. He heard about the Manse from us, and thought that if she was going to forsake the world, she'd better do so in a place where someone responsible would keep an eye on her." He added defensively, "I had no part in the negotiations. That was seen to by her solicitors, and the Kirk."

Josanne was brushing her hair vigorously, to make it shine the way Niall liked it. "Adrian must know there's no escape in any village. If she wants to get lost, she should do it in London or Tokyo! Here, all eyes are upon her." She walked over to the window and saw the lights in the village. The uncurtained windows of the Manse were ablaze with light. "Whether they know it or not, they're giving themselves a Highland welcome. Niall, let's switch on all our lights. She may be peculiar, but she may also be anguished and need cheering up. I should have thought of it before."

It took some time to go all round the castle, but it was done, and they could see that Mama and Papa at Caraig Lodge had followed their example. There was a light in every window.

Mrs. Sedley stood at the front-door with Shirley, and she knew why the lights shone so brightly.

"A Highland welcome – how kind of them," she said. "My grandmother told me about it. She was born at Kilcaraig."

She had never mentioned her connection with the place before, and almost as if she regretted it, she added quickly, "I like that sycamore. It must darken the dining-room, but it touches the house as if in an embrace."

Puzzled, Shirley followed her back into the eerie hall.

60

Josanne stopped on the bridge over the burn, leaned over the wall, and watched the water racing towards Loch Caraig. Niall had told her that she should look in at the Manse on her way to the shop, and she had agreed, not wanting him to know that even after all these years she found it an ordeal to have to visit a stranger, unless he was at her side. This stranger in particular alarmed her, although she tried to suppress the wilder ideas that crossed her over-imaginative mind.

The calm voice which had answered the telephone last night should have reassured her, but her anxiety remained.

She looked across to the row of cottages that faced the burn. Mrs. Cameron was shaking out a mat, and Duncan MacLean was removing the dead heads of flowers from his gold and bronze strip of autumn garden. Behind the village, the fields were light green, the crops now safely stored in barns, and Loch Caraig glimmered in the background, towered over by the mountains austere in their beauty.

Above her, on her left, was the castle, and close to it Caraig Lodge, each backed by the plantation of young fir trees which now covered the lower slopes of Ben Caraig. Every day she saw this familiar scene in a new way, transformed under the changing lights of a Highland sky, but this morning the people in the Manse had awoken to see it for the first time. She hoped they were as enraptured by it as she had once been, still was, when she wasn't feeling afraid, and trying to think out ways of introducing herself without sounding stuck-up and patronizing. She forced herself to cross the road, waved at Mrs. Craig who was at the side window of the post office, and knocked at the door of the Manse.

It was opened by a slim girl with long blonde hair, who was wearing the sweater and slacks that were the prevailing fashion of the younger generation. Josanne had expected a much older woman, and, disconcerted, she stammered out that she had telephoned last night, adding uncomfortably that she was Mrs. Niall Lamont from the castle.

The girl tossed back her hair, gave her an appraising look, and invited her to come in. Josanne refused, suppressed an urge to turn and run, and managed to say, "You'll be busy getting your furniture into place. We just wanted Mrs. Sedley to know that we can provide two stalwart men to heave things around and do anything else that's necessary. Are you her daughter?" As soon as she said this, she knew she sounded like her mother.

"I'm a Girl Friday. I'm paid to help. I'll fetch Mrs. Sedley." There was unmistakeable hostility in the girl's tone, but as she spoke, footsteps echoed on the uncarpeted landing, and Mrs. Sedley came downstairs.

Josanne was conscious of the feeling that this had happened before. This lovely, graceful woman, with wide violet eyes, dark hair, and an almost apologetic smile, was a familiar figure of the past. But the extended hand was in hers, and the sensation of time remembered was gone.

"You'll be Mrs. Lamont – I recognized your voice. It was so kind of you to telephone last night, and to give us that glorious Highland

welcome. I've heard about it, but I never expected to receive one!"
Mrs. Sedley laid her hand on the girl's shoulder. "This is Shirley
Morris, who has come to help me. It's a formidable undertaking,
because she doesn't know me, neither of us knew this place, and
there's several miles of Atlantic ocean to cross if she wants to flee to
the mainland."

Shirley Morris managed a flicker of a smile, but Josanne restrained
a natural impulse to shake hands with her, fearing a rebuff.
Protesting, she allowed Mrs. Sedley to show her into the kitchen,
where order had already been achieved.

"Tea, or instant coffee?" Mrs. Sedley switched on the electric
kettle, while Shirley Morris produced a tray, which she set with cups
and saucers from the big walled cupboard.

"Tea, please, and nothing to eat. I'm counting the calories!"
Josanne looked round the kitchen with approval. The cream walls,
which had yellowed with age during the Allans' occupation, had
been painted white, and an oil-fired cooker had replaced the old
kitchen range. The workmen who had come from the mainland as
soon as the Allans had left had been a talking point in the village, but
it was accepted that some minor improvements would be carried out
on a house that was to be put up for sale. The real changes would
happen when the new owners arrived, eager to transform their
Highland homestead into the sort of house they had known and
loved somewhere over the border, for it was people from the south
who invariably bought houses on Mull.

While they waited for the kettle to boil, Mrs. Sedley told Josanne
that she had been warned about the resentment she could stir up in
the local community, who saw in every newcomer a threat to their
way of life, and even their most cherished traditions undergoing
subtle change. Josanne guessed that the warning had come from
Adrian Ferguson, but she thought that this woman, who wanted to
put her past behind her, would not welcome the instant discovery of
a mutual friend.

"We had a charming visitor just after breakfast," Mrs Sedley was
saying, as Shirley put the tray on the table, and pushed a jug of milk
towards Josanne. "He was convinced that we would cut down the
sycamore tree, and that we'd do spinning and weaving or pottery
under some Government grant. But I think we made it clear that we
had no sinister intentions. Anyway, he came back later with a sack of
peat, and offered to help in the garden." She looked over at Shirley,
who was absorbed in cutting slices of gingerbread, and was not going
to be drawn into the conversation.

"That would be Sandy MacPherson," Josanne said. "He's a

seaman who retired to the cottage of his childhood, and nothing escapes his vigilant eye. He's an arch conservationist, and a splendid but erratic worker. He'll do wonders with odd jobs, but don't employ him full-time." Had she been alone with Mrs. Sedley, she would have added that Sandy went in for bouts of heavy drinking, but she would say nothing of the kind in front of this intensely shy or intensely disagreeable girl. Mrs. Sedley would soon find these things out for herself.

"We'll buy everything from the village store, or from the butcher's van that calls once a week." When Mrs. Sedley smiled, her face lit up, and her expression showed pride that she had learnt her lesson so well. "We'll use the mobile bank, and we won't put a notice that we've got something to sell!"

"I can see that Sandy's done his stuff well, but I'll give you a useful list I've made out, as I don't expect he did that! Telephone numbers such as the doctor and the vet, and the people you'll need in real emergencies – when the electricity fails or the telephone lines blow down – and you've lost half your roof in a storm!" She saw that she had caught Shirley's startled attention, so she added, "Always have candles in the house, and keep your oil-lamps trimmed. I see the Allans remembered to leave some for you." There was a row of lamps and some enamel candlesticks on a shelf above the dresser. "My husband ordered things for you, so you'll find coal and a tin of paraffin in the outhouse. I'm glad old Sandy thought about the peat. We burn it a lot, and it smells so lovely."

When she stood up to go, she walked over to the window which overlooked the bedraggled garden. The trees were bare of leaves and on the south boundary the grave-stones were visible through the thinning hedge. The only splash of colour was the ribbons on the dead wreaths on old Mrs. MacLachlan's week-old grave.

"I hope that doesn't give you the creeps," she said.

"I'm not afraid of the dead."

"Only a few months ago there was a well-stocked vegetable patch, and raspberries and gooseberries, and a wide border of flowers. In the spring, there'll be thousands of daffodils, and in June there will be yellow irises, and bluebells beside Loch Caraig, just across that field. You've no idea how beautiful it's going to be," Josanne said.

"It's beautiful now. The colouring, brilliant green grass, and bronze bracken. And last night, there were deer crossing the road in front of our car. They bounded up the mountainside and made us feel as if we'd wandered into a nature reserve. It was difficult to concentrate on driving, wasn't it, Shirley?"

There was no reply. Shirley had her back to them, and was running the water, preparing to wash the few cups.

Mrs. Sedley saw Josanne to the front door. The sycamore creaked ominously in the rising wind, and one side of the garage door had blown open, revealing piles of packing-cases. The car was in the drive where it had been left last night.

The offer of help having been gladly accepted, Josanne said that she would ask Angus Campbell and his friend Murdoch Coll to come over soon. "They'll bring sandwiches, so don't worry about food," she said. "But tea would be welcome, and a wee dram, if you have whisky with you. And do please telephone if there's anything at all we can do to help. My husband can turn his hand to anything." Josanne paused for breath. She was thankful there was no Shirley Morris to hear her sounding like the Lady of the Manor giving orders about her serfs. "And Mrs. Sedley – this is a big adventure for you. I hope it will be a happy one." She swallowed and touched the smooth hand, a hand not fashioned to push furniture around, and lay fires and throw out ashes. "You must come to dinner soon. It won't be a party. I don't expect you feel like that just now." It was the nearest she could get to expressing sympathy. She was extraordinarily touched by this woman, so much younger than she had expected, vulnerable somehow under the cool dignity, and saddled with a totally unsuitable companion, who would be out of the house and back to the mainland as soon as she found it was dark by tea-time, and that gales could rip the slates off the roof.

She scarcely heard Mrs. Sedley's murmured thanks. She turned at the gate to wave, and Mrs. Sedley waved back, standing there, framed in the doorway, a strikingly familiar figure, yet someone Josanne had never seen until that day.

She went to the post office to tell Mrs. Craig as much as it was prudent to report about the new people at the Manse.

*　　*　　*

Shirley Morris tidied the kitchen and waited for Mrs. Sedley to return to the house to reprimand her for being rude. She knew the routine. She had been through it many times before with Aunt Deborah, until she could stand no more and had packed her few possessions and moved to lodgings. She could not explain to anyone what she could not understand herelf – the resentment she felt that her lot in life was always to be a subsidiary one, doing what she was told, expected almost to drop a bob-curtsey when addressed by that young madam from the castle, who had come along to patronize her.

She heard Mrs. Sedley go upstairs. She would be planning what to say and how to say it, and the end of it for herself would be a seat on the boat-bus and a ticket back to London.

Afraid to leave the kitchen in case she ran into Mrs. Sedley and precipitated her fate, she went into the wreck of a garden, and surveyed all that would have to be done before it was restored to order. On the other side of the hedge, the tombstones tilted at angles, their foundations sinking slowly into the peaty soil, but it was life, not death, of which she suddenly became aware as a flight of grey geese cried their way in perfect V-shaped formation overhead. She was staring up at the sky, so that when Mrs. Sedley called to her from the back-door she could hardly see her, because she was blinded by the light.

"Shirley, will you be brave and go to the shop?" Mrs. Sedley held out a basket. "I've made a list of everything I can think of, but look around and add anything you like. Ask if we can open an account. In case we can't, I've given you my wallet."

She had placed the wallet in the basket, which she handed to Shirley. "We'll give the men a bumper high tea at six. We'll show them that we know a little about Highland hospitality." There was not a hint of coolness or of pique in her voice.

The gate which separated the back garden from the front creaked as Shirley pushed it open. She must oil it. The short drive was covered in weeds, and the car was dirty. She must clean it. There were many, many things she could do if she settled here. If.

She walked past the post office, past the church, small and unadorned, past a row of houses, and the school. She stopped at the village hall, which had a notice about a Halloween party and a list of social activities; a badminton club, a piping class, a Scottish dancing class, rifle shooting instruction available on application at the castle.

She was thoughtful as she retraced her steps. Across the road from the church, close to the burn, was the pink granite obelisk of the War Memorial. She went over to look at it, and stared, appalled that two world wars could have deprived this small community of so many men. She read the inscription – *The Flowers of the Forest*. Campbells, Lamonts, MacDonalds, MacCormicks, MacKechnies, MacKinnons, MacPhails, MacPhersons, the list went on and on, the repetition of surnames typical of the area in which these people had lived.

A tractor chugged past and the driver waved at her. She waved back, bemused. Then she remembered that she had been sent out on an errand. She picked up her basket, tilted up her chin, and swaggered to the shop.

The woman in the post office section gave her a curt "Good

411

morning", and went on with paper work of some sort, but the girl in the shopping area was helpful and was able to provide her with goods she would never have expected to find in a village store – red peppers, avocado pears, grapes. She bought far more than the items on her list, and returned, laden, to the Manse.

There was a battered blue van parked behind the car, so she knew that the two stalwart men had arrived.

There was no sign of Mrs. Sedley, but the bumps and bangs from upstairs indicated that she would be telling the men where to put the heavier furniture.

She unpacked the basket, also the carrier bag she had been given for the overflow, and stacked the contents on the table. The wallet was at the bottom of the basket, untouched, because it had been assumed that Mrs. Sedley would want to open an account. When she picked it up, some notes, carelessly pushed in, fluttered to the ground. She gathered them into a neat wad, and pushed them into one of the flaps, but it stuck. She felt with her finger, and hooked out a piece of cardboard, which she was about to throw away when she saw that on the reverse side was a photograph, evidently cut from a group of people. Just a head and shoulders of a man with a strong, kind face, an arresting face. Shirley studied it. It had been cut out carefuly and glued onto the cardboard, but this man was not Mr. Sedley, whose photographs she had seen at Sevenoaks. She pushed it back carefully, just as she had found it, and replaced the wallet in the basket, which she left with the groceries for Mrs. Sedley to deal with as she wished.

There was no private conversation with anyone that afternoon. When Shirley took a tray of tea and sandwiches upstairs to the men, they grunted their thanks, too busy moving a wardrobe to take any notice of her. She left the tray on a dressing-table, and set another one for Mrs. Sedley, whom she could see was kneeling in the dining-room, surrounded by sheets of newspaper from the packing-cases filled with ornaments, which the men had brought in from the garage. There was no room on the table for a tray, so Shirley put it beside her on the floor.

Mrs. Sedley sat back on her heels, brushing a dusty hand across her forehead. "Where's your tea, Shirley?"

"I'm going to make pancakes and scones. I'll take the men some from time to time, and I'll hang the curtains." She waited, wondering if Mrs. Sedley would countermand her plans, but all she got was a smile and a word of thanks. She returned to the kitchen, and she had to store the groceries away herself, because she needed the table, but Mrs. Sedley wouldn't mind. There would be no checking of the shopping-list, no exclamations about the price of things, or about the unnecessary additions she had chosen.

Some day, she would get used to this tranquil attitude to life. Some day – if she lasted. She kneaded at the dough, while the men banged and bumped around upstairs.

*   *   *

"You're a great baker altogether," Angus Campbell complimented Shirley, when he had eaten his third scone. He and Murdoch Coll were talkative now, fortified by the glasses of whisky which had been replenished periodically during the afternoon.

By six o'clock they were all tired and hungry, and every room in the house was habitable, although it would be a few days before the dining-room table was cleared of its piles of pictures and ornaments.

Shirley had provided black pudding and fried potatoes, as well as bacon and eggs, and had noted with delight Mrs. Sedley had eaten as heartily as had the two men.

"You'll be staying here a while, seeing you've brought a grand-piano," Murdoch observed. He spread plum jam on his pancake, thankful there was a choice between that and raspberry, which would be painful under the plate of a man who had false teeth. This young girl seemed to think of everthing.

"Is that regarded as a sign of permanency?" Mrs. Sedley asked.

"They come and they go," he said, looking at her with interest. "You are the first to come to Kilcaraig. There's not been a house for sale here since the Ameses bought Caraig Lodge, before the first world war. When they all died, the Lamonts bought it back."

"We thought maybe they'd buy this back too. It would make a nice holiday home for Mr. Rorie." Angus was saying what everyone in Kilcaraig thought about the sale of the Manse.

"Mr. Rorie?"

"Mr. Niall's twin brother. He married that fillum star, and they live in Ireland."

"And there's Catriona, the sister. She married Hector MacNeill of Ardcross. That's on the mainland. She doesn't see much of him because he's in the Navy, the poor soul." Murdoch wanted it known that he, too, could account for the Lamont family, and regretted their lack of foresight in failing to obtain another house for their expanding family. "They've a nice wee son," he added, to press home the point. "So's Mr. Rorie, but we've not seen him yet. It's a long way to bring a baby from Ireland, and could be there are other reasons besides."

Mrs. Sedley let the dark hints pass. It sounded as if all was not well, either at Ardcross or in Ireland. "So the elder Lamonts moved to Caraig Lodge when their son Niall married the girl we met today." She wanted to sort out the family, but to hear no gossip about them.

"That's right. Mr. Lamont was badly wounded in the last war, though you wouldn't think so now, except for his wee limp. He's Mrs. Lamont's second husband. Her first was Sir Robert Dutton, who bought Kilcaraig, where she was born and bred, so of course she had to marry him to get it back." Murdoch washed down this highly practical explanation with a few mouthfuls of sweet tea, and accepted another cup. "They're a great family, the Lamonts. You're lucky to get a home here, I'm telling you, Mrs. Sedley."

"Mr. Coll, you make me feel guilty, an impostor!"

"Mistress Sedley, I'm thinking that if all the incomers were as pretty-looking and as nice as you, there would be nothing for us to grumble about at all, at all," Angus said gallantly.

Mrs. Sedley blushed, a real blush, right down her neck, and she laughed at Angus, looking ravishingly beautiful, wasted on a Manse kitchen, with only two men and a girl to see her.

When the men had gone, loud in their praise of the house, its occupants, and the brand of whisky, Mrs. Sedley and Shirley watched the tail-lights of the van as it rattled off towards the castle.

"Mrs. Sedley, I'm sorry I was rude to Mrs. Lamont this morning. I couldn't help it." Shirley forced out the words she had been working on all day.

"That's all right. One covers up for shyness in all sorts of ways."

That was all. No scolding, no recriminations. Shirley followed Mrs. Sedley back to the dining-room, and they worked in comfortable, contented silence until the ornaments had been unpacked.

61

As soon as she returned from her visit to the Manse, Josanne telephoned Caraig Lodge, and said to Grania, "I have my report to make. Will you dine here tonight on our stew, or shall we come to you for yours?"

"You'll come to us, and it's mince," Grania said.

They were eating it now, made as only Mrs. Coll could cook it, with onions and oatmeal and a herb which she gathered mysteriously in the peat-moss. Her head popped through the serving-hatch from time to time, to ask if they wanted anything, or to join in the more interesting snatches of conversation that came to her ears. As she had expected, young Mrs. Niall described the new occupants of the Manse, but it was not until afterwards, when they were having coffee in the drawing-room, that Josanne gave a full account of her visit.

"I had that I-have-been-here-before feeling when I saw Mrs. Sedley coming downstairs in the manse. Don't look like that, Niall. I'm not being fey. I know I've been there dozens of times before, but this was different. Mrs. Sedley is a lovely woman, and I'm afraid not at all the type who will relieve me of some of my committees, and other aspects of life which I find such a burden." She sat on the hearth-rug, leaning against the sofa, where an ancient spaniel slept. "What bothers me is her companion, a hippy-looking girl who took against me on sight, and who will probably flounce off home after the first gale."

"Which will dispense with that problem," Grania said, scooping her toy poodle on to her knee, and being rewarded with a sharp nip. "Skittles, if you were an Alsatian, you'd have to be put down."

"I saw a slender young blonde coming out of the post office," Niall said.

Josanne thumped his knee reproachfully. He had squeezed on to the sofa beside the spaniel. "She's quite attractive, in a sort of way. I'm terrified Colin Craig will fall for her, and cause a furore, breaking his mother's heart, and setting everyone against us for opening the door to drop-outs."

"She's not a drop-out if she's working for Mrs. Sedley." Roderick had been training his binoculars on the Manse. He, too, had seen the shapely blonde girl walk through the village before going into the shop, and he had seen Mrs. Sedley standing in the doorway. He liked what he saw.

"The word drop-out has painful undertones at present," Grania said. Mrs. Craig had been in to see them on the previous night, and had told them how bitterly Colin was feeling his enforced idleness. "Niall, you really should get hold of Rorie, and tell him about the plan you're hatching. It could be such a help to Colin if you can get it off the ground."

"And it could have the lot of us bankrupt if it misfires," Niall said. He knew what his mother was thinking, although she would never say it. The scheme would be pea-nuts to Isabella, if she became interested. Every record she had made was becoming a golden disc.

"It's time Rorie and Isabella came here with Benedict. People will be thinking there's something wrong with him. Catriona brought Iain home when he was only three weeks old." Great Aunt-Marian had been very quiet during dinner, but she was alerted by the mention of Isabella's name. She had always loved Isabella, even during those terrible years when the rest of the family had feared a total eclipse if such a comet were to marry Rorie. "If I were younger, I'd do go over to Clonbracken and see him for myself." This was directed at Niall, although she knew it was unjust. He had far too much to do to be able to pay even a flying visit to Ireland, and Josanne felt tied to Kilcaraig until Anne was a little bit older.

"It's easy for Catriona to bring Iain from Ardcross," Niall said. "Bringing Benedict from Clonbracken is a formidable thought, as Isabella's not allowed to fly. Babies have so much clobber. So does Isabella, when it comes to that. But I'll talk to Rorie. I'll see what can be done."

Grania, leaning back in the rocking-chair she had adopted as a suitable seat for a grandmother, closed her eyes and listened as the conversation swung from people to places, and back to the new-comers at the Manse. While Josanne and Niall tried to work out a way in which Mrs. Sedley could be invited to dinner without her young companion, Grania's thoughts turned to Benedict, whom Rorie and Isabella thought was the world's most remarkable baby, while she and Roderick shared the fear that he had inherited his mother's deafness.

When Isabella last came to Kilcaraig she had not been well but had claimed that she was suffering from morning-sickness, not from the effects of her journey.

All the family had dined together at the castle that night, and afterwards Isabella was sitting by the window in the drawing-room, trying to crochet something, absorbed in what she was doing. Some-how the rest of them got on to the subject of family names. All male Lamonts of Kilcaraig were Roderick or Niall or Iain, and they were laughing about the importance of maintaining tradition, despite the confusion it sometimes caused, when they became aware that Isabella was staring across at them, compelling them to look at her, and to be silent.

"My father's name was Benedict," she said.

Not one of them had given her a thought. Worse, not one of them, not even Rorie, had remembered that she could pick up only scraps of what they were saying. Always kind and affectionate, she laughingly ripped her crochet, and asked Grania to start it for her again, as she was incapable of making the first little chain. She had

416

not meant her decision to sound like a rebuke, but her intention was clear. The baby, if a son, would be Benedict. And the seeds of doubt were thus sown in Grania's mind. She confided to Roderick that Isabella had always claimed that her deafness had been the belated result of her father's ill-treatment of her as a baby. That she should want her son to be named after such a man was inconceivable. She must have invented the story, preferring its dramatic content to the truth that she carried a congenital defect.

Grania had been at Clonbracken for Benedict's birth. She spent fourteen hours with Rorie, who clung to her in anguish, as he had done when he was a small boy in trouble. His resentment over her years of opposition to his marriage was forgotten as she kept his mind away from what was happening to his wife behind the sound-proof walls of the music-room which, aptly, had been prepared as the birth place of the diva's baby.

It was only when he saw Isabella, pale, triumphant, and inordinately proud of the fat, red-headed son she held in her arms that Grania realized that she would be capable of loving as well as of pitying this woman, who had for so long been her nightmare. Her relief that it was all safely over was almost as great as Rorie's, and she could hug Isabella in an upsurge of motherly love. She returned to Kilcaraig, happier than she had been for years, but the weeks and months slipped by, and excuses and postponements kept Rorie from bringing his son to be introduced to his native land. The old suspicions took hold of her, and she knew that her love for Isabella had been short-lived, and she was soured with fear about the child.

"Mama, you may be a granny, but you don't have to behave like one." Niall's voice broke into her thoughts.

"I wasn't asleep," she said. "And you can't invite Mrs. Sedley without the girl. It would be extremely rude and unkind."

They all laughed. They had come to that conclusion long ago.

Now it was time for them to go home, but Aunt Marian was insisting on walking.

"You treat me as if I were an old woman," she grumbled. She loved the night air, and there would be a full moon, when it could be seen through the clouds. "I like the path through the woods, and I've brought my torch." She flashed it to prove it. "If I can't walk a quarter of a mile on a November night, I'm fit only to be put in the burial ground, and those poor souls won't want a grave opened for a wee while, not until they've settled into the Manse."

Josanne helped her into her coat while she talked, and Mrs. Coll brought her a hot-water bottle for the five minutes she would spend in the car. Marian accepted it with good grace, knowing it was intended as a kindness, not an insult. She kissed Grania and Roderick goodnight, and warned them to put the guard in front of the fire, and to pull out the television wall-plug before they went to bed; then she walked briskly through the sun-room, to show that she still had her faculties in spite of all their mollycoddling.

"I believe she too thinks there's something wrong with Benedict," Grania said, as the tail-lights of the car disappeared behind the trees.

"I guessed that was what you were brooding over while we were talking about the Manse," Roderick said. "You can never keep your thoughts away from Rorie. Now, why should that be?"

"Because he's very much like you," she said, and raised her mouth to his.

They stood there in the sun-room, and Shirley Morris, gazing into the night, saw the silhouette of their embrace. She had thought that the old Lamonts lived at Caraig Lodge. They must have young people staying there, lucky young people who were in love and knew how to show it.

With a little pang of envy, she turned away from her window and snuggled into her warm and very comfortable bed.

*   *   *

Colin Craig parked his car in the small quarry that was used by the county road-men for filling in the pot-holes in the main road. The track to Caraig village was full of them, because nothing but tractors ever came this way, or had done for many years. Caraig village had been deserted for some time, because the newer village of Kilcaraig offered more amenities, being beside the school and the church, and close to the castle, and water was available in a piped supply, not collected in buckets from a well.

It had poured with rain during the night. The top of Ben More was invisible, and heavy clouds were scudding across the sky from the north-west. Soon it would be raining again.

He picked his way over the puddles and reached the old smiddy, the fireplace still discernible among the fallen stones. He climbed over the dead bracken which now carpeted the floor, and so through to the first house, the slates from its roof lying where they had fallen when the supporting beams finally crumbled away. Brambles clawed at his duffel-coat, and a tangle of barbed wire ripped a hole in his sock.

He thumped the walls, solid stone walls three feet deep, then he climbed through the place where there had once been a window, past a rowan tree, and into the next cottage.

418

The blonde girl was sitting on a rusty piece of a broken threshing-machine. She had a sketching pad and a pencil in her hand, and she sat bolt upright, alert, and frightened. She would have heard him approaching her.

"I'm very sorry I startled you," he said, and he held out his hand. "I'm Colin Craig, your next-door-neighbour. I thought I'd seen a ghost. Nobody ever comes here now."

"You do. So do I. We're here!"

He smiled, towering over her. She had seen him yesterday from her bedroom window and had wondered who he was.

"You've walked a long way," he said.

"I was given a lift as far as the farm."

"That would be Peter MacPhail." Colin pulled out a packet of cigarettes.

"I don't smoke." She tossed back her hair. She was wearing a blue duffel-coat over her jeans, and the silk scarf she had knotted at her neck was the same shade of blue as her eyes, the same shade as his own eyes. "Please tell me about this place," she said.

He showed her over the village. Ten cottages, all of them with walled gardens and pig-sties and other out-houses. The farmhouse was a little distance away, looking gaunt and lonely, but it was protected from the north by trees.

"Why did they let it fall down?"

"*They* were the Lamonts. They couldn't afford to keep up houses that nobody wanted to live in."

"So they weren't shipping people like cattle off to Canada?"

He whistled. "Say that to anyone here, and they'll boil you in oil! You've chosen to live in one of the few places where the landowners care more for their tenants than they do for themselves."

"I haven't chosen to live here. I'm paid to do so for a while. And how does this relic of the feudal system work, now that the serfs are educated and pay income-tax, and can even fill in their own forms?"

"I'll bet you a dollar to a doughnut you won't talk rubbish like that when you've lived here for a while. There's going to be a plump at any minute. I'll run you home in my car, and if you're a good girl, I'll accept your invitation to come in and have a cup of tea."

So it was that Shirley Morris, who had been at Kilcaraig for less than two days, arrived at the Manse with an escort who was six foot two, and had shoulders that indicated he could toss a caber the length of Loch Caraig.

Shirley, accustomed to the freezing inhospitality of her aunt, was both scared and apologetic as she introduced Colin Craig to Mrs. Sedley, but the smile that greeted him reminded her yet again of her employer's unfailing graciousness and charm. The firelight flickered on the silver tea pot as they ate scones and fruit cake in the drawing-room, and Colin complimented them on the speed with which they had made the room so attractive.

"Angus Campbell told us about the piano," he said. "No ornaments on it, so which one of you plays?"

Mrs. Sedley looked enquiringly at Shirley.

"Before I took to going to discos, I used to manage a few easy pieces, and I played the organ in our village church during school holidays, or when the organist was ill." Shirley went to the piano and played a few bars of *The Blue Danube*.

Colin followed her with his eyes. "And where was that?"

"In Cornwall, but I was born in London. I'm a mongrel, if ever there was one. I'm not a true blue anything, not like all you people, with your ancestry traced back to antiquity."

He laughed and said, "You've got a lot to learn about people, but first, you must get rid of that chip on your shoulder. It doesn't suit you, not one little bit." He turned to Mrs. Sedley. "We covered a lot of ground, back there in the ruined village. You'd think we had known one another for years!"

When he had gone, Shirley washed up while Mrs. Sedley put the remains of the cakes and scones away in their tin boxes.

"He said the old Lamonts are the only people living at Caraig Lodge, besides someone who works for them," Shirley said. "It was young people I saw embracing last night. The house must be haunted and I was seeing ghosts."

"Lovers don't always have to be young."

"It's indecent for lovers to be old." But she paused, frowning there beside the sink. "Colin says that old Mr. Lamont was something terribly secret during the war, and he won the Croix de Guerre, and Mrs. Lamont drove an ambulance and had plastic surgery on her face. But he says they're still a wonderful looking couple. Everyone seems to venerate the Lamonts, and that girl who called yesterday is very shy and not stuck-up at all." She sighed, and pushed her hair away from her face. "I expect they think dreadful things about me, like I've been thinking about them. And they could be right. Mrs. Sedley, why did you give me this job? You took an awful lot on trust. Why did you do it?"

Mrs. Sedley shook her head, incapable of speech, and Shirley saw that her eyes were bright with tears.

"I talk too much," Shirley said. "And I'm being impertinent, but you'll forgive me because you're the nicest person I've ever met. I'll put the pie in the oven, and there's time for a game of Scrabble before supper. Just you go and get out the box. It's in the bottom drawer of the chest."

Mrs. Sedley left her, and Shirley leaned against the sink, her mind in a whirl of incomprehension. She had never felt like this before, and she had given an order to a woman who was years her senior, as well as being her employer. But she was sure it was the right thing to do. She had inadvertently stirred up some painful memory, said something that hurt, and she had acted on impulse to avoid causing further distress.

She remembered to put the pie in the oven before she went to the sitting-room, where Mrs. Sedley had prepared the card-table, with the letters arranged face-downwards, ready for the draw. She smiled at Shirley as if nothing at all had happened, and they began their game.

They ate the pie beside the fire, as the dining-room table was still stacked with ornaments, then they returned to their Scrabble. At ten o'clock Shirley went upstairs to turn down the beds and switch on the electric blankets.

She had never been in Mrs. Sedley's bedroom at Sevenoaks, because there had been a maid to attend to such things, and last night they had still been under camping conditions, but now she could admire the thick carpet, the colour of milky coffee, which was so right with the antique furniture, made during a period of grace and elegance, unlike the heavy oak chairs and tables, with legs like old-fashioned barley sugar, which she had lived with for so long in her aunt's house.

The bed was a narrow divan, incongruous, almost screaming its virtue and simplicity to any would-be lover. Mrs. Sedley was past lovers. She must be at least fifty. But she was beautiful, and she kept a photograph of a young man in her wallet.

When she switched on the blanket, she put the night-dress where it, too, would warm up. It was exquisitely made, far too beautiful to be worn by someone who would never be seen in it by anyone else. She fingered it lovingly, then turned her attention to the writing-bureau, which was by the window. Mrs. Sedley could write her letters and look across at the trees and the castle and Ben Caraig. In the morning, she would see the glory of the rising sun. Shirley pulled up a chair and sat at the bureau.

Her hand crept onto the inlaid wood, and she followed the pattern with her fingers; then she leaned over and began to open the flap. She glimpsed some letters and a diary, then she closed it quickly and left the room, slamming the door behind her. Mrs. Sedley would have heard her footsteps overhead, and would wonder why she had lingered there for so long. She would not believe that she was only admiring beautiful things, wishing she had not wasted twenty-three years of her life.

She went to her room and turned on her own blanket, then, like a child afraid of the dark, panic overcame her, and she ran to the comfort of the lights downstairs.

62

"Would you like us to have someone to meet you when you come to dinner on Friday, or would you prefer just family?" Josanne asked Mrs. Sedley. The invitation had been given and accepted by telephone, but on the way to the post office, Josanne had seen Mrs. Sedley cleaning her car, so she thought it was more friendly to stop and talk, rather than merely wave from the road.

"I'd like just family, please." Mrs. Sedley had been asked a direct question, and had given a direct reply. It was easy to see that she would always be decisive without being officious. She was a person who was accustomed to being in command of a situation, accustomed to giving and receiving respect.

"You'll soon be able to put your car under cover." Josanne could see that there were only a few packing-cases left in the garage.

"It takes ages to unpack books. If they aren't arranged properly from the start, they stay higglety-pigglety for ever."

It was a week since the green car had arrived at the Manse, a week during which Shirley, who had seemed to be so sullen, had become a familiar sight in the village, for it was she who always called at the shop on her way back from her afternoon walk. Mrs. Sedley had not been beyond the garden gate, as far as anyone could see, but Sandy delivered good accounts of her. She had engaged him as general handy-man, and the village buzzed with the news, at first incredulous, until they saw that he had mended his jacket and washed his shirt. He trundled past now with a wheelbarrow filled with manure, and he saluted Josanne, calling out a greeting in Gaelic. Mrs. Sedley waited until he had gone through the dividing gate into the back garden before she explained to Josanne that she had offered him the job because he had shown signs of doing it anyhow.

"I'm not an amateur do-gooder who thinks she can mend broken reeds," she said. "If he has a drinking bout, he'll have a job to come back to when he sobers up. He's mended the washer on the kitchen tap, and removed two dead rats from our out-house." She smiled, suddenly radiant. "People like him can keep people like me from being driven to drink, so it's well worth having a part-time worker on a full-time pay-roll."

Shirley came out of the house, holding a grey kitten in her arms. Josanne went over to stroke it, and identified it as having originated at the castle.

"Sandy MacPherson says we'll have to have it dressed. We didn't know what he meant at first!" Shirley said, smiling. Mrs. Sedley or the Mull air had brought about a personality change during the last few days.

"It's a job for the vet. Quick, painless, very frustrating for the cat, but a necessity for you. I suppose you know what sex it is?"

"No, we've called it Bliss." She hesitated. "Would you like some coffee? I'm just going to put the kettle on."

Josanne refused, as she was expected back at home, but she stayed and talked for a while, being aware that just as her own shyness sometimes made her sound patronizing, it could be that Shirley's shyness made her sound hostile. Mrs. Sedley's judgement may not have been so misplaced after all. When she left them for the post office, she began to look forward to Friday night.

Colin was behind the counter. His mother had gone to Oban for the day to have her eyes tested.

"She'll find Papa on the boat. He's gone grumbling off to the dentist, terrified of the drill. We've been telling him he's lucky to have his own teeth, with his seventieth birthday looming ahead." She handed a parcel over the counter and exclaimed in disbelief when she heard what the postage to Cork would cost.

"It's a pram set for Benedict," she said. "He must have dozens of them, but Aunt Marian loves to knit them."

"And when are we going to see him?" Colin franked the parcel and tossed it into the mail-bag that would go on the boat-bus the next morning. He asked the question automatically. Like the rest of the people he had given up expecting to see Rorie and his family at Kilcaraig.

"I'm trying to fix a family reunion for the New Year," Josanne said boldly. "Hector MacNeill hopes to be on leave, and Catriona keeps telling us she wants to bring Iain back, now that he can run around and take an interest in things." Iain was two and a half years old. "He's a lovely little boy. He needs a brother or a sister. It's a wretched situation, as you know very well." She glanced over her shoulder. Some people had come into the shop. She lowered her voice. "Have you decided anything about the matter you discussed with Niall?"

"I'll have to think it over. I'll not do it unless I think it'll work."

She left the post office. She had meant to ask him what he thought of Shirley because tongues were wagging after he had driven her home in the rain on her very first day in Kilcaraig. It was perhaps just as well that Mrs. Sedley had preferred to meet only members of the family at dinner. An obvious person to invite would have been Colin, but it would have looked like match-making in the eyes of the outraged local community.

Marian MacGillivray was coming towards her, pushing a pram. Josanne stopped to admire the new baby, and slipped the traditional silver coin under the blanket, thankful to discover that she had a fifty-pence piece in her pocket.

"Another pupil for the school," she said. It was break-time, and the children were shouting at one another, playing a game of tig. The axe was poised to fall upon the building that had prepared seamen, doctors, lawyers and others to make their way in the world, but the education authorities were relentlessly playing the role of Pied Piper, and were determined to remove the children from their homes, to be taught and made alien to their own way of life.

"By the time he's five, there won't be a school here," Mrs. MacGillivray said resignedly. She knew, as they all did, that pleas and protests would fall on deaf bureaucratic ears.

"We'll go on fighting," Josanne said with an optimism she didn't feel. The way things were going at present, there would be no Kilcaraig, at any rate not Kilcaraig as they knew it now.

She walked through the woods to the castle. She could hear Roddy calling to Nanny. He would be collecting fir-cones, while Anne watched from her pram. She loved her children, but she was very glad that Nanny was with them for most of the day. According to Rorie, Isabella was never far from Benedict – Benedict, the wonder-baby who cut his teeth without a murmur at a far earlier age than Roddy and Anne had done. Benedict, who had no feeding problems, and who never cried. Benedict, who might already be deaf, and if he was deaf, he wouldn't learn to talk. She shivered at the thought. She was deeply ashamed at the jealousy she felt when she looked at the innumerable snapshots of the laughing, chubby face, which were enclosed with the glowing reports of his progress.

She found Niall in the Nissen field close to the castle. He was not working, but standing staring ahead of him, and he beckoned to her to join him.

"The Nissen huts went when they were no longer needed," he said. "What would you feel about building holiday chalets here instead?"

Josanne gasped, not believing her own ears. "You can't be serious! You, of all people, to suggest ruining the appearance of the place, the whole way of life, defacing Kilcaraig!"

He turned to her now, and held her by the shoulders. "Josanne, we have two children. We could have more. We can't go on fighting against the future. Development is here to stay, and the sooner we grasp the fact and cash in on it, the better."

She pulled away from him, her cheeks burning, tears in her eyes. "I've just been talking to Colin Craig. He says he's considering your proposition about restoring Caraig village. It could become a dream village, that would attract the right sort of people, and make sense. I don't believe for a moment that he'd unite with you in order to destroy Kilcaraig. I don't believe he'd be so calculating and wicked. I don't know how you can even suggest such an outrageous plan."

She almost ran to the house, leaving Niall to watch her retreating figure. He was smiling.

Thank God, he thought. She feels as passionately as I do. The staggeringly high offer he had received from a property developer had been lying in his file for the past ten days. Now he knew how to answer it. Relieved, he followed her to the house.

*　　　*　　　*

"I'm not going to dine with you," Aunt Marian said on Friday morning. "Four members of the family to give the new people the once-over are quite enough. Besides, I'm so forgetful that I'll ask after Adrian and embarrass the poor woman you say is too pretty to be a criminal."

So it was that she ate a specially prepared supper served on a tray in her bedroom, while the candles flickered over the silver and Waterford glass on the mahogany table in the dining-room.

Even Chrissie had to admit that Cathy excelled herself in the dinner she produced, and Niall Lamont had chosen the best wines from the cellar, thinking that this was an occasion which invited something better than plonk.

He wore his second-best jacket with his kilt, and watched Josanne struggle with the zip of the blue crêpe dress she had worn for informal dinner parties for years. She had never replaced it because Niall loved it, but after tonight she might have to do something about her clothes. She prophesied that Mrs. Sedley would wear a simple black dress in the new fashionable length, while Shirley would wear a glittering blouse over her blue jeans. She had been right about Mrs. Sedley, but not about Shirley, who had glided into the drawing room in a mauve kaftan, which showed off her figure, while her hair was swept up in an Edwardian style. Carefully applied make-up had transformed her pale, unremarkable face into a thing of beauty.

"Mrs. Sedley dressed me up," she said to Josanne, as she sat by the fire, a glass of sherry in one hand and a cigarette in the other. She had taken it as she thought it might add to her new-found poise. "It belongs to her. I haven't any evening clothes."

Grania and Roderick arrived almost immediately after the green car from the Manse had drawn up at the castle, and Josanne, always an apparently serene hostess, felt the relief of having her mother-in-law to support her through what could have been a difficult evening. Entertaining strangers, one of whom had broken with her past, could have been an ordeal. As it was, there had been light-hearted, easy talk, and Mrs. Sedley had shown that she was capable of laughter. Roderick, who sat next to her at dinner, made no attempt to conceal his admiration, while Grania watched from across the table, her grey eyes registering amusement, with an undertone of pique.

Afterwards, when Roderick and Niall were left to their masculine conversation and their drinks, Mrs. Sedley walked round the drawing-room, looking at the ornaments, turning them over sometimes to find out where they were made.

"I see you go in for Meissen," she said.

"And also *A Present from Torquay*," Josanne said. "I'm told that all your possessions are beautiful."

"We had no children." This apparently explained everything. She moved on, and paused in front of the miniature of Isabella, which Rorie had sent to them last Christmas.

"Surely that's Connelli?"

"Yes," Grania said. "My daughter-in-law."

Mrs. Sedley swung round and faced her. "Do you mean that your son married Isabella Connelli?"

"I thought everyone knew," Grania laughed. "We all feel as if we'd been branded."

Mrs. Sedley turned back to the picture. "I thought she'd married an Irishman. It shows how out of touch I've been for the past few years." She spoke slowly, puzzled, searching her mind for what she should have known, but had somehow passed her by. Then she went over to the fire. Shirley was sitting on the rug, cuddling Grania's poodle.

"When you asked me to come to Kilcaraig, the first person I thought about was Connelli," Shirley said. "There was reams about her marriage, and pictures of the village, and I was thrilled that I might see her. I watched her in *Salome* on television. We did it for a giggle, me and some friends, because we thought she might strip off all her veils. She didn't, but she got us all hooked. It's the most high-brow programme I've ever seen."

"I knew she had sung *Salome*. It didn't seem possible, but I suppose hers was an unlimited talent." Mrs. Sedley was staring into the fire, seeing far more than peat and flames. "I first heard her sing the voice of the Falcon in *Die Frau Ohne Schatten*. That's another Strauss opera, Shirley, but not high-brow at all. It's a fairy story about an Empress who can't have a baby unless she acquires a shadow. The Falcon is sung off-stage, but even so Connelli stopped the show. It was the same," she paused as if surprised by her own memory, then she finished, "it was the same wherever she sang. You must be very proud of her, Mrs. Lamont, and very sad for her too."

"She still sings for us. We're hoping she'll come here for the New Year. Of course we don't know – and never like to ask – how much her hearing has deteriorated, but if she can, she'll be singing at the ceilidh in the village hall. The people adore her. She sings Gaelic songs unaccompanied, which probably makes it easier for her." Grania could always be enthusiastic about Isabella's voice, whatever reservations she felt about Isabella herself.

"Don't people throng to look at her?" Shirley asked.

"Goodness, no. They'd think it dreadfully rude. Tourists are different, but then she's never been here in the tourist season."

When the men joined them, Roderick gave Mrs. Sedley his full attention, and Niall concentrated on Shirley, who told him that all through dinner she had felt like a character in a Bonnie Prince Charlie film. "Women's Lib should do something about men in kilts. You put us women in the shade," she said. She touched his kilt. "Lamont tartan, of course. I wish I were entitled to a tartan."

"You can always marry a tartan," Niall said. "I'll give you a book about the clans, and then you can choose your men friends carefully, according to your favourite colour scheme!"

"But there's right tartans and wrong ones, aren't there? Depending on whether one was a Jacobite or not."

"That, Miss Morris, is a subject which can rouse such intense feelings that you'll find yourself fighting the battle of Culloden all over again." Niall was greatly amused by this girl, who liked to pretend she was a lightweight nonentity.

It was nearly midnight when the green car, with Shirley at the wheel, lurched down the drive through torrential rain. Roderick and Grania stood in the porch with Niall and Josanne. They would see by the head-lights when the car reached the Manse.

"We'll have to go. They mustn't think we're lurking here to chew them up," Grania said. The poodle, shivering, was tucked under her arm.

"That's the most fascinating woman I've met for years. *Green leaves in a darkened chamber*."

"Roderick, I'm not having you wax lyrical over another woman at your time of life. It's the seventy year itch! You'll please take me to London, and buy me some expensive clothes, and we'll make Adrian tell us all about this enchantress he's landed in our midst."

They hurried to their car through the rain, laughing together, and soon their lights could be seen swinging round the sharp right bend into the drive of Caraig Lodge.

"I'm still convinced I've seen her before," Josanne said when she and Niall had kissed the sleeping children, and seen the reassuring gleam of light under Nanny's flatlet door. "Perhaps she's a rich millionairess, planted here by crafty old Adrian to save our bacon." She still felt indignant when she remembered how Niall had teased her over the chalet scheme.

Niall put his arm through hers, and guided her to their bedroom. "He may be up to something, but I don't think it's that," he said, knowing how wildly imaginative Josanne could be. He could understand Josanne's conviction that she had seen Mrs. Sedley before, for so had he. Somewhere before, but he could not remember where or when.

In the Manse, Margaret Sedley stood at her bedroom window. She had switched off her light. The rain cascaded down, and there were still lights on at Caraig Lodge and at the castle.

She could not believe what she had heard tonight, but she must believe it, for it was true.

She could hear Shirley's radio playing softly in the room across the landing. *Love is the sweetest thing*. The sound faded away, turned lower. Shirley had looked lovely tonight. *The oldest, yet the latest thing*. She could just make it out. Shirley would be afraid of disturbing her. She was an amazingly thoughtful girl. *Love is a song without end*. Nothing could disturb her like the discovery she had made tonight.

She had come here to get away from it all, and in two weeks it was catching up with her.

She took a sleeping-pill before she got into bed.

428

63

Mrs. Sedley telephoned Josanne on the following morning, to thank her for dinner. Josanne was in the library, systematically looking through the books in the music section. She was sure she was being stupid, but the voice on the telephone goaded her into further action. She had a duster beside her, to justify her search. Some of the books had not been touched for years.

Song Without End. A portrait in words and pictures of Isabella Connelli by Richard Smythe. Josanne flicked through it. The photographs were attractive, but the information scant. Richard Smythe, who was a renowned critic, must have compiled his information quickly, to get the book on the market as fast as he could, while Connelli's sudden withdrawal from the operatic stage was hot news. There would be other books about that brief and illustrious career. There would be book after book, but none of the authors would know the real Isabella. Nobody knew her. Not even Rorie.

She replaced it, took out another, and gave it a perfunctory wipe with her duster. It fell open at an illustration, and she gave a little gasp.

La Bohème. Mimi on the staircase leading to Rudolfo's squalid studio. Mrs. Sedley standing on the uncarpeted staircase at the Manse. The similarity was amazing, and it explained that sensation of experience repeated. She read the caption. Mara Sevilla, whose Mimi had added to her laurels at La Scala, Milan.

Josanne turned to the index. There were several references to Mara Sevilla, mentioning the roles she had sung. Madam Butterfly and Manon. The Empress in *Die Frau Ohne Schatten*. They had talked of that opera last night. Josanne, in her days when she was an opera fan, had bought the records, although she had never seen it. She put the book aside to show to Niall when he came home. He would know that she had not been claiming to be fey, she really had reason to believe that it had happened before. The proof was here in the photograph. She heard Chrissie helping Aunt Marian downstairs, so she put aside her duster and pulled the big chair closer to the fire.

"I've been hearing all about last night," Marian said, settling herself and her knitting and her detective story in the chair. "Grania telephoned me. She says Cathy's cooking is nearly as good as Chrissie's. Personally, I'm impressed by Lobster Thermidor, but I prefer mince!"

Chrissie petted her, rearranged a kirbigrip in the once-chestnut coloured hair, and returned to the kitchen.

Josanne handed the book to Marian. "This is why I thought I'd seen Mrs. Sedley before."

Marian examined the picture. "Grania says Roderick has a roving eye for the first time since she met him! If that's what he's looking at, I'm not surprised! Mara Sevilla was a lovely singer, but the battlefield of the operatic stage was too much for her. A pity. Her *Manon* was enchanting."

When Lachy arrived with the mail, there were two book-club books, a parcel that was obviously a gramophone record, several newspapers, and some letters. One of them was for Marian from Isabella. Josanne knew better than to ask about it. The correspondence between Marian and Isabella had gone on for years, but it was always conducted in secret, and Marian had stipulated that if any letters survived her death they must be destroyed, unread. If anyone knew the real Isabella it was Aunt Marian, but she would never write a book.

In the afternoon, Josanne took the children to Caraig village in the car. It was a place full of interest and excitement for Roddy, who played among the ruins, imitating the bangs and crashes he saw and heard all too often on television news programmes. Josanne had to carry Anne, who couldn't walk yet, although she could stand for long enough to give her mother a rest from time to time. Progress was slow, but Josanne managed to inspect the ten cottages carefully. She didn't venture as far as the farm.

The idea could become a success, or it could be madness. With the tourist season so short because of the weather, winter lettings would be necessary, and the sort of people who wanted to rent stalking would be unlikely to want to live in a village, within earshot of their neighbours' radios, with unreliable television reception, and with erratic weather that could change from peaceful sunshine to storm-force winds within a matter of minutes.

Niall had worked it all out on paper, and had explained it to her. There were so many difficulties to be overcome, starting with the planning authorities, but she could understand his enthusiasm. It would be fascinating to see life again in this deserted place, the visitors would not be a nuisance to the islanders, the cottages would be solid and suitable, not a row of tawdry eye-sores, and the island shops, garages – even the distant hotels – would benefit. Provided the scheme appealed to the right sort of people. That was the difficulty. And it might not appeal to anyone, which would be the calamity Niall so much feared.

"Ma-ma-ma." When Anne said that, it meant misery. "Da Da" was her happy sound. Josanne cuddled her and kissed the pink, cold cheek. She called to Roddy to come, but there was no reply. He would be hiding somewhere. She went with Anne and waited for him in the car, tooting the horn occasionally, to remind him that he could not play around in the ruins for the whole of the wintry afternoon. He came at last, emitting a sound which she supposed was meant to be an aeroplane. She wondered if Isabella would be able to hear Benedict when he was as old as Roddy was now. She wondered how much Isabella could hear. She even wondered if the whole thing was a mammoth hoax, because Isabella Connelli, like Mara Sevilla, had found the battlefield of opera too much of a strain, and had invented her own theatrical way of opting out of it all.

"I'm bad-minded," she thought, driving very slowly over the pot-holes onto what passed as the main road to Kilcaraig. Life could never be revived here. She felt depressed, answering Roddy's questions automatically, worried about the future, not only for the children but for everyone on the estate. A few years ago it would have been impossible to imagine what taxation would do to people like themselves. Destructive, crippling, personal punishment because Carnsworth, Prior and Dutton was an international financial success.

The lights were on in the cottages when they reached the village, and she could see that the shop and post office were full of people. She had slowed down as they passed the War Memorial. There was a time when she used to forget that small, almost unnoticeable tribute the Lamont family paid to the dead of two world wars. On Remembrance Sunday, the whole community would gather before it, and an ex-serviceman would place a wreath of poppies against it, and then Mrs. MacColl would lay a wreath from the Women's Rural Institute. After that, two of the school-children, proud that they had been selected, would add their posy of Haig poppies, wired together by themselves. After the silence, Papa would play *The Flowers of the Forest* on the pipes, and all who were able, many of them now old and bent, would wear their medals.

To fail Kilcaraig would be to betray the dead. Patriotism and sentiment were mingled as she drove up to the castle, Roddy's shrill little voice telling her about the lion he had seen among the ruins. Thankfully, she handed the children over to Nanny. She didn't lack love for them, she lacked patience.

She could smell buttered toast as Cathy took the tea-tray through to the library. Niall would be home at any moment now. Niall and loving companionship. She changed her shoes, brushed her hair, powdered her nose, and prayed for a miracle. Somehow a way must be found to ensure that Kilcaraig survived.

Mrs. Sedley made her first appearance in public at the brief War Memorial service. She stood close to Mrs. Craig, with Shirley at her side – Shirley wearing a skirt under her black oilskins, for it was still pouring with rain. Colin, standing on the church side of the obelisk, admired her shapely legs, and thought what a waste it was that she usually wore trousers. Then his attention turned to the ceremony, as Niall Lamont read the seemingly endless Roll of Honour. When it was over – the silence, the short prayers, the laying of the wreaths, and the playing of the lament – he went across to Shirley.

"I'm going to Iona tomorrow. Would you like to come with me?"

"I won't have to cross the ocean in a cockle-shell?"

He laughed. "Not in a cockle-shell. In a very reliable motor boat, with two ferrymen who have the sea in their blood. You'll be quite safe. New terminals are being built, so that larger vessels can be used to cope with the increasing number of tourists. I'm interested in their construction, and I expect you'd like to go over and see Iona Abbey."

Shirley glanced over at Mrs. Sedley, who was talking to the Caraig Lodge Lamonts. "It's very kind of you, but it would mean being out for quite a long time. I never leave her for more than an hour or so." She swallowed and paused, not wanting him to think she was being neurotically conscientious. "There's still a lot of books to unpack. Please ask me another time."

Josanne, talking to Mrs. MacLean, had overhead the conversation.

"I'll come over to the Manse in the morning," she said. "I'd love to help unpack the books, and I'll make Mrs. Sedley come to lunch with us. Aunt Marian's longing to meet her."

So it was arranged. But when Colin went up to the flat over the post office, he found his mother waiting for him in the sitting-room, the light of battle in her eye.

"What possessed you to ask that girl to go out with you tomorrow? You'll be the talk of the place."

"It's a friendly gesture, that's all."

Mrs. Craig removed the Earl Haig poppies from her lapel, and carefully fixed them in the frame of her husband's photograph. They would remain there for a year, until the next Remembrance Sunday came round, when they would be replaced by new poppies.

"We all know these drifters who come to Mull. We see them on the boats, with their long, straggly skirts, and their haversacks on their backs, and before you know it, they're living with some man or other in a caravan, and getting themselves onto the Council housing lists, priority because they're homeless!"

"Mother, we can't generalize." Colin knew that his mother was saying what he had often said. "Besides, this girl came here in a job. Mrs. Sedley is obviously respectable. She wouldn't employ a drifter."

Mrs. Craig shrugged. "We know nothing about her either. It's not like you to behave in such an impossible way. I suppose you'll want to take a picnic with you. The thermos flasks will probably be fusty. Bring them to me and I'll give them a good rinse."

Colin knew his mother. She had made her point, but she wouldn't nag him about it. He was beginning to wonder, in fact, why he had committed himself to going to Iona Abbey when all he wanted to do was to watch the dredging that was being done in preparation for building the new jetty.

On the following day, he waited until he saw Josanne arriving at the Manse, then he collected Shirley, who was wearing a windcheater and a skirt, and carrying an oil-skin coat over her arm. She had a map and a book on bird-watching in her hand. She was regarding this as an educational, not a romantic, experience.

Mrs. Sedley asked him to drive carefully, and to be back before dark, sounding like any mother concerned about the welfare of her daughter; then she and Josanne waved until his little grey Renault had disappeared round the bend beyond the brae on which the doctor's house was perched.

Sandy MacPherson had put the two packing-cases in the hall, and had prised them open. Mrs. Sedley worked on one of them, Josanne on the other, both of them silent, intent on what they were doing, but Josanne, who tended to be embarrassed by silence when she was with people she didn't know, felt only contentment. *Green leaves in a darkened chamber*. Roderick had been right about Rupert Brooke's poem. It described Mrs. Sedley exactly.

Sandy brought in a full packing-case, and removed the empty ones. They all stopped for coffee at eleven, then they worked on until the shelves were almost filled. When it was nearly time to go to the castle for lunch, Mrs. Sedley went upstairs to tidy herself, while Josanne insisted on completing what she was doing. She went into the sitting-room with another pile of books in her arms. They were a miscellaneous collection, all the others having been kept together, packed under relevant subjects. Then she saw that these were more personal, probably kept in Mrs. Sedley's bedroom. A Bible, a devotional book, attractively bound but evidently not much read, an India paper edition of *The Oxford Book of English Verse*, and Sir Thomas Beecham's *A Mingled Chime*. She opened this and saw written on the fly-leaf, "Mara. Thanks for the memory. P".

Trembling, she closed it and pushed it into the middle of the pile, then she went upstairs, somehow making her legs work although her knees seemed to be missing. Mrs. Sedley's bedroom door was open, and she was brushing her hair. The likeness to that photograph, which had seemed to be a coincidence, was now unmistakeable.

"These look like bedroom books – Bibles and things," Josanne said, putting them on the bedside table. Mrs. Sedley gave them a disinterested glance and thanked her. A few minutes later, Josanne drove her to the castle, and introduced her to Aunt Marian, who would be feeling fresh at this time of day, her memory under control. She wouldn't talk about Adrian Ferguson, or ask awkward questions.

Niall joined them for lunch, and it was nearly tea-time before Mrs, Sedley said she must go home, so that she could welcome Shirley back from her first jaunt on the island. She wanted to walk, but Niall took her by the arm and led her to his car.

"Adrian knew what he was about when he manipulated her here," Aunt Marian said. "The crafty old fox! Give the fire a good poke, Josanne, and don't say anything to Niall. If she wants anonymity, she must be allowed to attempt it."

"How did you guess?" Josanne was astonished, although she had known Aunt Marian for all these years.

"I recognized her the minute she walked into the room."

Josanne told her about the photograph, and of the words written at the front of the book. "Mara could be an abbreviation of Margaret, but the double coincidence was too great," she said. "But why make any mystery about it? There's nothing disreputable about being an opera-singer – rather the reverse."

"I expect she has her reasons," Aunt Marian said, with the finality Josanne knew so well.

"Paul was her husband. P. sounds like someone else," Josanne said, but there was no reply. She stood by the window, watching the pale gold sky under the autumn sun darken steadily into night. She saw the lights of the car leaving the Manse, then they snapped off outside the post office. Niall would be waiting to see Colin Craig, to talk to him again about what she now recognized as the Master Plan.

She drew the curtains, and went over to the music section of the bookcase. *The Dictionary of Opera* had been her joy when she was a young fan, but she hadn't looked at it for ages.

Sevilla, Mara. Born 12th July 1928. Australian soprano of Italian origin. Studied Rome, Santa Cecilia. Debut on Italian TV as Mimi 1950. Stage debut Spoleto as Manon 1951. NY Met 1952. Dallas, San Francisco, Chicago, Buenos Aires. La Scala Milan from 1957. An actress-singer of quality, famed for her lyric roles, until her early retirement due to ill-health. R.

She replaced the dictionary. These potted biographies obviously omitted any reference to a private life, husband or children, but R. meant that Mara Sevilla had at some time made records. Josanne knew she had none of them. For years, the only soprano she had cared about was Isabella Connelli, beside whom all the others paled into insignificance. Isabella would have heard of Mara Sevilla. And Isabella was coming to Kilcaraig for the New Year.

She tip-toed over to the fire. Marian, sitting bolt upright in her chair, with a book held in her hand, was fast asleep.

At the Manse, Mrs. Sedley sat at her writing-bureau in her bedroom. Niall Lamont had refused to come in when he brought her home, but she had done some skilful questioning during the few minutes she had been with him in the car. His twin brother, Rorie, lived at Clonbracken Farm, Clonbracken, County Cork.

She wrote her address on the top of a sheet of paper. There had not yet been time for a die to be made for her letter-heading.

"Dear Madame Connelli," she began. Then she thought for some time before she wrote the letter. It covered nearly two pages, and when she read it through it was not very satisfactory, but it would have to do. Laboriously, she typed the envelope, having to do several as she made so many mistakes, then she took the letter to the post box outside the post office. She had just returned to the Manse when Colin's car came round the bend and into the village.

She was sitting in the drawing-room reading when Shirley came into the house.

64

While Mrs. Craig was kept busy in the post office, and while Colin and Shirley exchanged reminiscences as they ate their lunch in the car and watched the reconstruction work being carried out at Iona Ferry, Catriona MacNeill was typing menus in the little room on the first floor of Ardcross House, which she had converted into an office.

Her desk was by the window, and she had a beautiful view across the sea to the mountains of Mull. There were clouds obscuring the top of Ben More. She could picture the valley with its three lochs, and Kilcaraig, where everyone would be living their normal, happy lives. Probably Josanne and Niall would be having coffee with Mama and Papa, either at the castle or at Caraig Lodge. She would give anything she possessed to be with them now.

She saw the Misses Taylor crossing the lawn in front of the house. They would climb the stile and make for the woods, and they would bring back fir-cones to throw onto the blazing log fire which always burned in the square front hall. It was one of the features of Ardcross House, and partly accounted for the fact that the short Highland tourist season could be extended into the winter. There had been an article about Christmas at Ardcross in the *Scottish Field*, and as a result bookings had poured in, particularly from Americans, and from people wanting yule logs and snow and the sort of jollifications they had seen depicted on Christmas cards.

"God Almighty, are we never to have the house to ourselves!" Hector had said when he had last come home on leave. His fury that Catriona had bought Ardcross House without a word of warning to him had never really cooled down.

He came home to see Iain. He made that very clear when, having spent as much time as possible with his son during the day, he had eaten dinner almost in silence with his wife, had watched television until bed-time, and then had buried his nose in a book the moment he got into bed. They had not yet agreed to move into separate bedrooms. It was necessary that their marriage should appear to be successful, for neither of them could face that, after such a romantic and promising start, it had failed.

"Don't do anything without consulting Hector," Josanne had said. "Men don't like to be beholden to their wives." Adrian Ferguson had issued a similar warning, but Catriona had been set on what she wanted to do, had been so sure that Hector's delight at owning Ardcross would sweep all other considerations aside.

Isabella had much more money than Rorie. Rorie himself was the first to say so, and with pride, not showing any sense of inferiority. Theirs was a real marriage, a truly shared relationship. In a way they reminded Catriona of Mama and Papa, which brought her back to the misery of being here on her own, when home was not much more than rowing distance away.

"Mrs. MacNeill, the man from the Wine Company is here. He'll have to have your order now, or he won't be able to get the crates to you by Christmas." Marilyn Coleman poked her head round the door. She and her sister Jane came from Australia, and had been helping Catriona to run Ardcross for the past year. They would soon be going home, and she would have to find replacements for them.

She found the wine list in her desk drawer. Hector had ticked off what they would need. Unasked, he had done at least that for her. Gratefully, she took it downstairs to the sales representative, who had been given coffee, and who was waiting for her in the staff sitting-room.

In the nearby kitchen, the washing-machine chugged and thumped and screamed in its disconcerting way as it dealt with the laundry, and during its rare moments of silence, the electric mixer whirled into action.

Catriona, curled up in her chair, sucked a pencil and tried to sound business-like, while the man wrote things on his order form, and thought how devastatingly pretty she was, and how odd her husband must be to neglect her so.

When he had gone, it was time to prepare the light lunch, which was served to the few paying guests during the winter. In the summer, lunch packs were dealt out, to be eaten on the shore, or on the mountain-sides. Catriona never knew which task she least liked to do.

Iain returned from his walk. He came slowly into the kitchen, holding the grubby shawl from which he refused to be separated. His nose was running and he was pale, not like a child who spent most of his days out of doors.

"Where's Veronique?" Catriona asked.

He shook his head. If he said he knew where she was, he would be told to go to her.

Catriona pressed the button on the liquidizer, and yesterday's vegetables were transformed into today's soup.

Iain stayed on, watching her. She ignored him because her mind was on other things.

*   *   *

"You didn't eat much," Mrs. Craig said as she emptied the picnic basket.

"We did a lot of talking."

He helped to stow away the left-over cakes into tins, and he put the cornish pasties into the deep-freeze.

"She comes from Cornwall," he said. He was obviously not going to be questioned, so he gave a brief account of what Shirley had told him about herself. Her father had been a master at Mill Hill School. Her mother had died when she was seven, so she had been sent off to live with her mother's sister, a maiden lady who lived near Truro. Her father re-married when she was twelve and at boarding-school, but the holidays soon established a hate-relationship with her step-mother, so that her return to Aunt Deborah seemed to be the only sensible solution.

She did well at school and continued her education at the University of Exeter, but although she left with a good degree, she could not find work. Finding her home-life intolerable, with her aunt's endless criticism and interference, she found it was humiliating to live on social security in lodgings, so she had taken anything that came along; washing dishes at an hotel, being a home-help to the bad-tempered and niggardly widow of a stockbroker, being a children's nurse to a theatrical couple who thrived on brawls. Changing jobs became a habit, even when the jobs were reasonably pleasant ones. Then, out of the blue, she had seen the advertisement in *The Lady*, which had brought her to Mrs. Sedley and ultimately to Mull.

"Oh, the poor little soul," Mrs. Craig said, relenting. "If it's all true, she might not be such a bad thing after all. But she's too young for you. You can't get away from that. She's far too young."

"I'm a drifter without a job," Colin said. "I'm in no position to think about marrying this girl, or any other girl. Besides, I hardly know her."

He went to his room. He knew he had distressed his mother with his reference to unemployment, and he had spoken of marriage, a subject he had always avoided raising at home. He could imagine the sort of standards his mother would expect to find in his wife, and he had never wanted to give the matter his serious thought. He had discovered that many of the women he met were prepared to enjoy a love affair without setting their sights on marriage.

Shirley was different. He had seen so little of her, yet he recognized in her something disturbing, an awakening of emotions he had never experienced before. He felt gentleness, protectiveness, a desire for permanency which must surely be the early warning signals that even he could fall in love.

He looked out of his window, the little side window from which he could just see the Manse. There were lights on in both of the front bedrooms. Mrs. Sedley and Shirley always changed and tidied themselves for dinner. He drew his curtain, excluding that view, and turned his attention to the main window, from which he could see Caraig Lodge and the castle and Ben Caraig. None of the curtains were drawn and all the lights were on at the castle. A Highland welcome for someone, or perhaps a dinner-party. The Lamonts were renowned for their hospitality, and no one would suspect Niall's nagging anxiety about the future.

If Colin could help in any way, he would. Planning the re-birth of a village was a strange occupation for a marine engineer, but what Niall needed was someone with vision, who knew and understood the place.

The smell of bacon wafted up the stairs as his mother prepared high tea. When he had sorted out the Lamonts' affairs, he would be able to consider his future, work out what he could do to make his own life worthwhile.

The wind was rising, and he tapped the barometer as he went downstairs. The needle swung towards storm. He hoped that they had their lamps trimmed and their candles ready at the Manse, for anything could happen during the night.

*　　*　　*

Mrs Sedley had prepared the dinner and had set the table, when an animated Shirley returned home. Colin had refused to come in for a drink, saying that it would make him late for high tea.

"I had a lovely time at the castle." Mrs. Sedley poured out two glasses of sherry, and carried the tray to the sitting-room. "Everyone is so relaxed, and Aunt Marian has marvellous stories to tell about the place and the people. I was wishing I had a cassette recorder with me. And now tell me about you."

439

Shirley described the motor-boat trip to Iona, and the Abbey with its pink granite walls and its green marble altar, the precincts beautifully restored.

On the way home, they had stopped for a while at a bay a few miles along the road, where countless seals, looking like Labrador dogs, had been swimming around in the water. She had seen oyster-catchers, and had taken photographs of a heron, and as they drove through the Glen road, she had seen a herd of deer.

"I suppose I'll get used to it some day, but at present it takes my breath away."

"So you don't feel lonely, so far away from everything?"

"Mrs. Sedley, I've never been so happy in all my life."

She had little to say about Colin, except that he had been a good companion. Mrs. Sedley found nothing significant in this. She didn't see a budding romance in every encounter between a girl and a man, as the village people tended to do.

They too noticed the rising wind when they were changing for dinner, and by the time they went to bed the sycamore tree was bashing against the Manse, the slates on the roof were rattling, and they could hardly hear one another speak because of the force of the gale. Shirley took Bliss upstairs with her, and found that Mrs. Sedley had placed an oil lamp on her dressing-table, and a candle. She had taken her instructions to heart and was ready for all contingencies.

Shirley was asleep when the lights snapped out at two o'clock in the morning, but Mrs. Sedley was still awake. She turned up the wick of her oil lamp and lay there in the graceful, subdued light, thinking and thinking.

Isabella Connelli would have her letter any time now. The thought of what she had written made her feel empty and afraid.

Making contact with Isabella had been so necessary, yet it stirred up many memories, many anxieties. She should try to be practical, pay more attention to her affairs, see about making a will.

Where are you now? she thought. Where are you now. She would never know, this side of the grave. Her lawyers might be able to trace him when it was all over, and she was well out of the way.

She fell asleep without turning down her lamp. In the morning, the telephone, like the electricity, was dead, but Niall came down from the castle, and Colin came from next door, and Sandy MacPherson brought planks of wood, because he had noticed that some damage had been done to the Manse shed.

"Do you always look after one another like this?" Mrs. Sedley asked. She had produced a bottle of whisky and some glasses. She had gathered that this was customary when people came in un-expectedly, no matter what the time of day.

"Och, it's nothing," Niall said, tossing back his whisky. He had other calls to make.

Colin left with him, and Sandy went off to see to the shed.

"A short time ago, I'd have jeered at the Lord of the Manor for coming down to see to the well-being of his serfs," Shirley said. "Now, I don't even feel grateful to him. I just feel comfortable that he does his job so well."

By lunch time, the electricity cables had been repaired, and when Shirley went into the shop, Mrs. Craig asked her if she had enjoyed Iona, and offered her a cup of tea.

Shirley realized that in a small way she had been accepted at Kilcaraig.

65

Rorie found Isabella in the music-room. She was sitting in an armchair, earphones on her head, listening to a record. Benedict was on her knee, contentedly asleep, his sturdy legs resting on the arm of the chair, his chubby cheek against her breast. His hair was brighter than hers, but it would darken as time went by. When Isabella's hair turned grey, as some day it would, Benedict's would serve as a reminder of the way she looked tonight.

For a while he stood watching them, the perfect picture of a mother and her son, the perfect fulfilment of his dreams. His wife. His son.

He walked into her line of vision. He was careful never to alarm her, for once he had put his hand over her eyes, teasing her, to draw attention to his presence, and she had been terrified. Only then did he realize that the kidnapping threats which had been part of her life during the days of her greatness had worried her in a way she never had admitted. She had always shrugged them off as nonsense, and he had believed her. She had acted so many things she didn't feel in the past, sometimes he wondered if she ever acted now. He hoped not. He hoped he shared her life as totally as she shared his.

She took off the earphones and put them on the table beside her. He could now hear that she had been listening to the mad scene from

Lucia di Lammermoor, sung by Lisa Verini. He pushed the button on the record-player to *reject*. It clicked to a halt, then his arms were round her shoulders, his lips kissing her neck, her temple, her eyes. Benedict stirred, but cuddled up more closely, soothed by the beat of her heart.

"Why listen to Lisa Verini when you could be listening to yourself?" he said, using his lips carefully. She was watching his face.

"Because I hear much more than music. I hear crackles and hums. The penalty of deafness, which few people understand. I'd rather have the sound of her spoilt than the sound of me." She laughed up at him, her green eyes dancing.

"How have you got hold of Benedict at this hour of the day?"

"Bridget's gone to Confession." Bridget, who was nanny, was very devout.

"Josanne says that we won't need Bridget at Kilcaraig. She says her nanny can cope with him. It would give Bridget the chance to go home to Ballybunion for the New Year."

"Bridget doesn't want to go to Ballybunion. She'd rather look after one Benedict than about eight little brothers and sisters. Besides, Benedict needs her. She's his substitute mother, and he mustn't grow up to be insecure." She stroked Benedict's hair. "I wish I could look after him all the time myself, but now that he can crawl my eyes aren't enough. I need ears that hear." There was the smallest catch in her voice. Only Rorie knew how she hated to speak of her deafness, how much she feared pity. "I hope I didn't wean him too soon. Chinese babies are breast-fed until they're about two."

Rorie smiled and let it pass. Isabella read countless books on child psychology, and knew how to select the methods that pleased her most. Benedict's total dependence upon her as his larder had, because of modern methods, been short-lived, and when she watched Bridget spooning meat and vegetables into his eager little mouth, it was she and not he who felt deprived.

Rorie pulled up a chair, so that he was close to her, able to look at her, feast upon her, marvel that she belonged to him.

"When we get back from Kilcaraig, I hope the Maestro will be able to come here for a few days, or I could go to Italy to see him. I don't altogether approve of his still handling your financial affairs."

"He understands the arts and crafts of show-business," she said. "It needs different handling from your Carnsworth, Prior and Dutton."

Rorie was still a director of the industrial empire and sometimes he went to London for board meetings. "Your assets outweigh mine by about a hundred to one," he said.

"Then why worry about the Maestro? If he's doing so well for me obviously I'm in safe hands."

"I resent the fact that you were quite literally in his hands."

"Delayed action doesn't suit you, Rorie. We've both been through a few hands, one way and another, but not any more. Besides, now that women are liberated, they have as much right to indulge in sexual experiments as men." She broke off as he leaned forward and held out his wallet to her. Dazed, she took it from him.

"Look at the innermost pocket."

She pulled out a small cellophane envelope. Inside it were some red hairs.

"Yours," he said.

She shook her head.

He laughed. "Pubic hair."

Colour rushed to her cheeks and down her neck. "I never gave you that," she stammered.

"Like kisses, all the more more precious because they were stolen! That very first time, when we were together in Rome. Afterwards, when I watched you on the stage, and heard the roars of your audience, I would finger those hairs as if I had the koh-i-noor diamond in my pocket."

"Rorie, you're disgusting!"

"Isabella, you passionate, red-haired minx, you're basically such a modest little prude that I sometimes think the Maestro was nothing more than a father-figure, and your other lovers sheer invention."

"*Prenez-garde!*"

Benedict, wide-eyed, was gazing at his father.

"He can hear, but he doesn't understand," Rorie said.

Benedict gave a contented snort and cuddled up to his mother again.

"I don't think your mama really believes that he can hear properly," Isabella said wistfully. "She never could understand why I wanted to call him Benedict."

"He's obviously all right. You've nothing to fear." When he saw his mother at the New Year, he would ask her how Isabella had got hold of such ideas.

Benedict stiffened, alert, his lips drooping, then Bridget appeared to collect him for his supper. He whimpered when he was taken from his mother, but quietened by the time the door was shut. He loved Bridget.

"He heard her footsteps – I didn't," Rorie said, secretly ashamed at his own sense of relief. Isabella was looking away from him. She wasn't wearing her hearing-aid. He leaned over to her, caught her chin in his hands and turned her face towards him. There was no need now for words. She responded to him, as she always had done, and it was a while later, as they lay together on the bear-skin rug that he said to her, "It's unseemly to make love on the music room floor".

She caressed his ear. "Making love is unseemly anywhere. The position is ridiculous and the whole invention crude. I wonder why God created it this way." She sat up and wriggled into her panties deftly, tantalizingly, like a strip-tease act working backwards. "Rorie, while I was listening to Lisa a little while ago, I thought about my own singing days, of people sleeping in the streets outside opera-houses and concert halls all over the world, so that they could hear me. I was thinking of them standing and clapping and shouting their *bravos* until it seemed their lungs would burst, yet all the time all I cared about was the music I could make, the joy of singing. When my hearing fades totally, as some day it will, I'll even be unable to sing a lullaby for Benedict. Will you remember always that I'm grateful for all I've lost, because I've gained so much more than ever I possessed – Benedict and you." She turned to him, nestling against him, ready for more love. "I'm not good at saying things, only at singing, but all that I've said now is true. Will you remember always, no matter what happens?"

"I'll always remember." He held her tightly in his arms, knowing that she was speaking the truth from her heart, but remembering also her black moments, when nothing mattered to her but her loss of music.

They were both tired out and a little dishevelled when they went upstairs to say goodnight to Benedict. He stood up, holding onto the bars of his cot, smelling of soap and baby-powder, and laughing his pleasure at seeing them.

Isabella sang to him, and Rorie did *This Little Piggie*; then Isabella produced her rosary beads, imitation mother-of-pearl, given to her by the Sisters at the convent for her First Communion. When in later years her jewel-box overflowed with emeralds and diamonds, these beads remained her most treasured possession. Benedict listened quietly for a few minutes, liking the rhythm, not under-standing the words, then he joined in with a few la-las, and was rewarded with a cuddle and a kiss.

When he was tucked up, he would croon himself to sleep. He was never any trouble.

It was not until after dinner that Isabella told Rorie what had been uppermost in her mind all day. "I've had an unexpected link with the past," she said. "I want your help, because someone I care about is having to realize that anonymity is something the famous will have to look for in vain."

He settled in the big leather arm-chair by the music-room fire, and she sat on the bear-skin rug, leaning against his legs.

"I'm going to do a lot more talking," she said. "It's easy for you to listen, because you don't have to strain to hear." She took hold of his hand, needing as always the comfort of contact with him.

Then she told him about Mara.

*   *   *

"You know the first part of this," Isabella said. "When I sang in *Lucia di Lammermoor* at the age of eighteen, and the audience went wild about me, I thought I was an established star. My singing teacher and the Maestro had other ideas!"

They made her continue with her singing lessons, but she was allowed occasionally to appear in small, insignificant roles. One day she was told that there was to be an audition for the part of the Falcon in *Die Frau Ohne Schatten*. On discovering that this consisted of a few lines sung off-stage, she was indignant and lost no time in telling the Maestro what she thought of his suggestion.

"Paolo Bardini will be the conductor. Mara Sevilla is the Empress. The production is for the San Carlo at Naples," he said crushingly.

Isabella protested no more. The audition took place in one of the rehearsal rooms adjoining Bardini's house. Always a perfectionist, he liked a production in the making to take place close to him, so that he could supervize it himself. Awestruck, Isabella took her place among the other young women who waited to be heard by him, for the soloists were to be chosen by the great man himself.

Her name was the first to be called. Bardini, at the piano, hardly looked up when she entered the room. Nettled, she tucked her roll of music under her arm and broke into an unaccompanied Irish folk-song. Bardini allowed her to sing it through, then, still without looking at her, he said. "I don't want to hear anyone else. Tell them to go home."

She faced the others with the unwelcome message, and a few days later she was in the hands of the répétiteur and the chorus-master, for although she had already studied the role, she was learning what it was like to begin at the bottom and work her way up. Then came the day when the principals were to join the lesser lights. Bardini himself had taken over. An excited Isabella was at last in the presence of the great singers she had so far seen only from a remote seat in the gallery.

She had longed to see Mara Sevilla in close-up, and she was not

445

disappointed. Her idol was as lovely off-stage as she was on. She had charm, and a fascinating aloofness. During the first few days, Isabella heard her sing, heard her try to correct a tendency to scoop on to her top notes before she had worked into a role, recognized that she herself was immune to the difficulties of voice production that even the great encountered. She was so absorbed in listening that she had forgotten that she, too, would be expected to sing her falcon part.

When her name was called, she was smitten horrifyingly with stage-fright. She saw Sevilla's encouraging smile. She smiled back and sang.

There was a ripple of applause when she finished, and Mara Sevilla beckoned to her, and asked her please to go to one of the small rehearsal-rooms afterwards, because it was so lovely that she wanted a private encore. Isabella almost dropped a bob-curtsey before she scuttled back to her seat.

Sevilla, as the Empress, took her place beside the piano. She exchanged a few words with Bardini and began to sing.

The door of the studio burst open. The man who stood there was tall, handsome, white with rage.

"Where were you this afternoon?" he called across the room, addressing Mara Sevilla. Bardini slewed round on the piano-stool and stared.

"I was at the hairdresser." Sevilla's voice was calm, but her face was ashen.

"Which one?"

"Antonio's."

"What time?"

"I don't know."

"Don't be absurd. Of course you know."

So it went on, question and answer, while the onlookers froze like a fresco against the wall.

Bardini brought a sharp end to the interrogation. He crashed a chord on the piano, and asked for a repetition of the falcon's song. Isabella was surprised, but she was already an actress in the making. She went over to the piano as Mara Sevilla sank down on a nearby chair, her inquisitor departing as abruptly as he had arrived.

Isabella sang. When she had finished, Bardini dismissed the others, but flipping through the score, asked her to stay for a few minutes.

"Are you going to sing to Madame Sevilla now?" he asked.

"I can't. She must be dreadfully upset."

"She'll be more upset if you don't go to her. Say nothing about what has just happened. Just sing. That was her husband, and there are times when he chooses to demonstrate his power over her. Publicly humiliating her does something to his ego."

"And hers?"

"Some people are masochists." Impatient, he could see that she didn't understand him. He directed her to a room along the corridor.

Mara Sevilla was at the piano, calm, as if nothing had happened. Isabella sang her falcon song, then one of Moore's Irish Melodies, this time accompanying herself. Sevilla stood by the window, staring out of it. She appeared at first not to have noticed when Isabella stopped singing, then she turned round, her face expressionless.

"You know you're special, don't you? You can't sing like that and not know. Don't ever let personal involvement get in your way. You possess a talent too marvellous to be put at risk."

It was the only time she was ever alone with Sevilla, but these words made a lasting impression. Her falcon at Naples ensured that she would never sing the role again, for there were to be no more small, off-stage parts for Connelli. She progressed to Hamburg, Paris, Rome, Milan, as always, adding to her repertoire, and in New York she sang the Empress herself, worried that the little off-stage falcon chirped so inadequately.

By then she was an established star, absorbed in her work, unaware that fame was separating her from her former friends and colleagues. She was singing Violetta at San Francisco when she heard that Sevilla's husband had engaged once too often in his merciless tormenting. There were various rumours about how the marriage had come to an end, but Isabella had not taken in the garbled accounts that were told to her.

"She never reappeared, not on the stage, anyhow," Isabella concluded. "I should have cared enough about her to ask what became of her, but I never held court in my dressing-room and gossiped. I just somehow let other people's lives pass me by."

"Who was the heel of a husband?" Rorie asked.

"Paul Sedley. An English businessman. In spite of all that he did to her, she was in love with him, and she proved that in the end." Isabella opened her handbag and brought out a letter. "From Mara Sevilla. Received today. Please tell me how to answer it."

He opened the letter and whistled when he saw the address. Then he read aloud;

"Dear Madame Connelli,

You will be surprised to hear from me, and still more surprised to see my address. It was only when I came to live here that I discovered this house is on the estate owned by your husband's family.

The news of your early retirement through ill-health came as a great shock to me. I wanted to write to you, but there are some situations in life for which there are no words. I hear now of your happiness with your husband in Ireland, and maybe your personal gain makes up for the loss to the world of your marvellous voice.

You will know that I gave up singing many years ago, and you will perhaps have heard accounts of that ghastly night at Stresa. These may be garbled, because those closest to the truth would have the least to say. By being with my husband during the last years of his life I like to believe I have in some way made up to him for the misery he must have gone through, but retribution strikes in many ways.

When I came here, I thought I could live out my life in a place where no one would know anything about me. I realize now that consequences should be faced, not dodged, but having made my break with the past, I haven't the courage to look back.

Please, when you come here, will you pretend not to know me? It shouldn't be difficult. I seldom go out and you will be absorbed by your family.

This letter is badly expressed because it has been milling over in my mind, and the more I think, the more confused I become. I am in your hands. To be recognized by you will be to have the whole world look at me again, because, as I told you years ago, you are special and an old acquaintance of yours would go straight under the microscope. It isn't your fault that you have gained undying fame.

This is not the ramblings of a distorted mind, so please take me seriously, no matter what you may have heard.

Yours sincerely,

Margaret Sedley. (Mara Sevilla)"

Rorie folded the letter and handed it back to her. "What a tangled web we weave. It's a small world, and all that. Was she at Stresa when she was carried off into oblivion, or is she referring to some other drama?"

"I don't know. She obviously thinks I do. But whatever happened, it wrecked her career, though evidently not her marriage."

"Did you ever think of asking Paolo Bardini about her? Or is it a fable that conductors have a special relationship with their *prime donne*?" Rorie had always regarded the friendship between Isabella and Bardini with suspicion.

"Paolo was particularly reticent about Mara Sevilla. I had my ideas about that." Isabella considered the letter, still held in her hand. "This was written in great distress. Please draft a reply for me. I can't write letters. I can't even spell."

"You must do it yourself, woman to woman, heart to heart. I have an idea that like God you'll not give her what she asks for, but something much better."

He watched her at her writing bureau, scraping with her pen, her tongue protruding between her lips in her effort to concentrate. She had left her shoes on the rug and her handbag, open, on a chair. There was a toffee paper beside her on the floor.

From time to time he spelt a word for her, writing it on a scrap of paper. Difficulty. Modelled. Focused. Affliction. Then she stopped asking, writing hard and fast. Entranced, he waited until she had finished. She read it through carefully, placed it in an envelope, sealed it, then pencilled in the name and address.

"Motti will type that bit for me in the morning," she said. "I feel like a secret agent! But Mrs. Craig and Lachy both know my writing so well."

She fixed her hearing-aid, took out her sewing, and sat opposite him, ready for an evening of domestic small-talk, the farm, the pigs, and Benedict, the little threads that bound them closer together as each day passed. His life began and ended with Isabella. His mother thought it was all sex, and that some day he would tire of her.

"Isabella, what'll we do when we're too old to make love?"

She was trying to thread a needle with a gadget Motti had given her, but she couldn't get even the needle-threader into the eye of the needle. "Making love and loving are two totally different things until two people like us come together. Consummation is a tremendous experience and happens over and over again, but when it stops happening it's still there, for ever and ever, like when the voice fails there's still a song in the heart." She paused and sighed. "It's deep in our consciousness, far deeper than physical pleasure, because it can never come to an end."

"Where did you get all that from?" he asked.

"I did a lot of research when I was studying the *Liebestod*. It's necessary if you are to understand Wagner. Please will you thread this needle. I'm sorry I've made it all so soggy."

Enchanted, he obeyed.

66

Shirley stood at the sitting-room window watching Mrs. Sedley trying to light a bonfire. She had built it very carefully, using firelighters, but she was on to her second box of matches. Wearing an old mackintosh, with a scarf tied over her head, she still managed to look beautiful, and Shirley was fascinated by her.

They had dined at Caraig Lodge, and the doctor's wife, Mrs Fraser, had been to tea. There was a notice up in the post office about the Christmas party to be held in the village hall; then would come the New Year festivities, which appeared to continue until about the middle of January.

Whenever he met them, Colin was friendly enough, but he had not invited Shirley out again. His mother still offered her a cup of tea, if she was having one herself behind the post office counter, and they talked in a stilted way about the weather, and about whatever happened to be the headline news.

Sandy MacPherson, who was digging the vegetable patch, put down his spade, took the matches from Mrs. Sedley, and soon the bonfire was blazing, but the wind began to rise, and Shirley went into the garden to help retrieve the pieces of paper that were blowing around, some of them alight.

"No post yet?" Mrs. Sedley asked.

"The roads are icy and the post-bus is delayed." Shirley had heard this a few minutes ago in the shop. Mrs. Sedley always waited eagerly for the post, although there were seldom any letters. Christmas cards were pouring into the castle. Shirley had seen them on display, and she hoped her aunt in Cornwall would remember her. One card was better than none at all.

"If the roads are bad tomorrow, you mustn't go to Oban." Mrs. Sedley had ordered a music-centre, and it was ready to be collected. She thought it too fragile a package to be brought by the big red Cal-Mac delivery van.

"Colin Craig says there's a thaw coming." He too had been in the post office this morning.

They returned to the house for coffee, keeping a watch on the bonfire; Sandy left them from time to time to poke it and control it.

"I'll make a bird-table," he said when he came back for the third time. "That cat's after the robin. You'll need to put the crumbs up high, not on the ground. And I told you to have it dressed. It's going to have kittens."

"We over-feed it."

"It's never food made it the shape it is!"

They knew that he was right. Sandy had a wealth of knowledge about animals, flowers, and vegetables, and they knew that they had acquired a treasure, provided he could be kept off the bottle. The New Year would have its difficulties for him. Sometimes Mrs. Sedley talked of going away for two or three weeks after Christmas, but she never said when they would go, and Shirley had an idea that she would feel responsible for Sandy, and prefer to stay near him, not leave him to his whisky and his fate.

When Lachy arrived, he was heavily laden. There were parcels of Christmas presents they had ordered by post, and there were magazines, newspapers and bills. The bonfire had burnt itself out, and Sandy had nearly finished his digging for the day. Mrs. Sedley had restricted his work-hours to mornings only, because of his age, but he was given a hot dinner before he mounted his bicycle for home.

Mrs. Sedley left Shirley in the kitchen and took her parcels and letters up to her bedroom. For a long time she held a typed envelope with an Eire stamp in her hand. The postmark was Dublin. She put it in her writing-bureau, not wanting to read it until she could be sure of being alone for a long time, and opened the other letters, none of them personal or important. The parcels contained oddments that could be set aside and used as needed, for she was unsure about to whom she should give presents, apart from Shirley and Sandy, but she had ordered a jig-saw puzzle for Aunt Marian, who said she enjoyed them. She and the castle children must certainly be given something for Christmas.

Josanne looked in at tea-time to say that Rorie and Isabella and Benedict were coming for the New Year, weather permitting, health permitting, and all the usual provisos.

"I don't count on it," she said. "They're always coming, but somehow they never arrive."

"If they do come, will she sing to us?" Shirley asked.

"She will if she's able to. Her hearing varies a lot. It seems to flare up and subside, and there are side-effects one scarcely notices – dizziness and so on. She must feel pretty wretched at times."

"Will she have droves of reporters sleuthing her?" This was Mrs.

Sedley, who could picture the effect of a visit from Isabella Connelli would have in any part of the world.

"All the hullabaloo is over. She's left in peace." Josanne was on the way to the gate when she added casually, "Catriona is coming too, and bringing Iain. We don't know about Hector. He may not get leave." Hector had been posted to the Admiralty, and because of the guest-house, Catriona could not be with him in London. There must be a lot of gossip about the estrangement, but the newcomers at the Manse would be unlikely to have heard it yet.

Shirley was to be up early the next morning to catch the boat for Oban, so she went to bed shortly after ten o'clock, with the kitten which had all too soon become a cat tucked under her arm. She had checked the tyre pressures and had topped up the battery, and put petrol in the car. Colin Craig had told her that she should be able to cope with simple car maintenance, and she was determined to be able to turn her hand to anything. She wanted to be useful, for it was one way to be needed, and she wanted that most of all.

Mrs. Sedley went to her bedroom and closed the door. It was idiotic to be panic-stricken at the thought of reading that letter, but her hands were shaking, and she felt sick when she at last retrieved it from the pigeon-hole in her bureau. The fact that it was typed, and posted in Dublin proved at least that Isabella knew about village life, would know that kindly Mrs. Craig couldn't fail to recognize her hand-writing and the postmark, had it been sent from Clonbracken.

Wearing the night-dress Shirley had admired so much, with its matching dressing-gown, Mrs. Sedley pulled a chair close to the electric fire, and tore open the envelope.

"Dear Madame Sevilla," Isabella had written in the untidy copy-book style of which she was so much ashamed. "I was astonished to see your address, and it is wonderful to have a letter from you, although I am sorry that it is a letter you must have found very difficult to write.

"Of course I will do as you ask, and will not tell anyone at all about you, except my husband who shares everything with me. When I come to Kilcaraig, I will be sure to see you, because at that time of year, everyone visits everyone else, and you, a stranger, will be particularly cared for so that you won't feel lonely or left out. Everyone knows that I find it easier to manage when I have only one person to talk to, so there will be no difficulty in seeing you alone. I would like that very much, if you wish it. I am sorry that I am so ignorant, but I don't know what happened at Stresa, though it sounds as if I should have heard. I knew you left your husband and had given up singing. I am ashamed that I never troubled to find out what had become of you, for I always admired you so much and modelled myself on you with social graces and in acting and things.

"As I write this, the thought comes to me that Josanne Lamont is a great opera fan. All the family tease her about this and say she should go in for 'Mastermind', but she is so shy she would say 'pass' if asked her own name! Does she know who you are? I ask this not to alarm you, but because I have found that things one most fears turn out not to matter very much after all. I thought people knowing about my deafness would be so terrible, worse even than the affliction, but now it doesn't matter, as I have my husband and my son, and will always hear music inside my head, even when I can't sing any more.

"I hate to be pitied. So must you which is perhaps why you prefer to draw a vale over the past. When we have talked, you may change your mind. Will you talk to me? It would be a grate privallage.

    With sincere affection,
      Isabella Lamont"

Mrs. Sedley sat with the letter in her hand. She could picture the effort it had been, and the use of a dictionary, abandoned as the message it conveyed became more personal and urgent.

She drew back her curtains. There were still lights on at the castle and in Caraig Lodge, and she could see by the gleam reflected from the puddles in the road that the village people had not yet gone to sleep. They kept late hours, visiting one another, exchanging news and views, although some of them, like Sandy, spent all the time they could watching television.

She was a fool to enclose herself in her little world, ashamed even of that part of her life of which she should have been proud. Sir Adrian Ferguson had assured her that she would be happy at Kilcaraig, and he had been right, but he had also told her that he couldn't guarantee that her real identity would never emerge.

She re-read Isabella Connelli's letter before she switched off her light. That little chirping falcon had wisdom as well as beauty and an unsurpassable gift for song. She lay awake for a long time, thinking but not worrying.

What Rorie had said was true. Isabella, left to herself, had known exactly how to strike the right note.

*   *   *

Shirley fixed the plug for the music-centre, but panicked when the time came to switch it on to see if it would work, so she telephoned Niall Lamont, as everyone in the place did when they were in any kind of difficulty. Within an hour he was at the Manse.

Aunt Marian came with him, proud that she had won a battle with the family, who thought that she should never leave the castle fireside during the winter. She sat with Mrs. Sedley by the drawing-room fire, while Niall and Shirley bumped about next door, rearranging the furniture, and fitting the loud-speakers as inconspicuously as possible against the walls.

"Gramophones aren't the pleasure they used to be," Marian said when she had admired the room and complimented Mrs. Sedley on her good taste. "We had a wooden thing that wound up and could be taken anywhere. We would sit in the middle of Loch Caraig, while Ian, my brother, fished and we listened to Harry Lauder or George Grossmith, who were the pop stars of the day. We thought we were very trendy – though the word hadn't been invented in those days."

Mrs. Sedley was piecing together Marian Danvers' life, from being a carefree young madcap, to the octogenarian she had become. She would never grow old, not if she lived to be a hundred.

"I've talked a lot about me. Tell me about you, please Margaret. And although I wear tights and read the porn that passes now as novels, I don't call people by their Christian names until I've known them for a little while. But you don't mind, do you? Margaret is such a graceful name."

Margaret Sedley smiled her rare smile. "I suppose I must be formal and forbidding, because I find that rather than address me by my Christian name, people avoid calling me anything at all. My husband was unconscious for years, and he hadn't lived in Kent long when he was taken ill, so close friends were non-existent. We travelled a great deal. We never really had any roots."

She was spared elaborating on the past by the burst of song from next door. The sound was turned down quickly, for it could have been heard as far as the post office, but the strains of *Dove Sono* continued to throb through the walls.

"Such a sad song, when one thinks of happy little Rosina in *The Barber of Seville* turning into that droopy Countess in *The Marriage of Figaro*," Marian said.

"That's life. Romantic beginnings and miserable outcomes," Margaret replied, but lightly, tossing it off as a platitude, and leading Aunt Marian into further chatter until the record had ended.

Niall appeared, his kilt dusty and his hands filthy. "Shirley is making tea for us all, and I'm off to clean myself up. All is in order, and you'll have plenty of music from now on. Mrs. Sedley, may I borrow some of your old records? You have such gems in that pile."

"Borrow anything you like."

"I like old records best," Aunt Marian said, thinking of Lotte Lehmann and Frida Leider, before the advent of Connelli.

When they left, Niall helped her into the car and handed her the box of records.

"Don't bother to return them," Margaret said. "We've been ordering records galore, and we'll need all the space for them we can get."

When they were back in the house, Shirley demonstrated the new toy, switching from radio to record-player and cassette.

"I hope they'll return those discs," she said. "There's some I haven't tried yet, by old singers that I've never heard of. Dino Capiro, Mara Sevilla, Anton Fane."

"You would have heard of them if they'd been worth remembering. Connelli's record won't be forgotten, not in a million years."

To prove her point, Mrs. Sedley slit open one of the cellophane-wrapped boxes of new records, and handed Shirley the latest Isabella Connelli album. It was called *Encores and Lollipops*, and had been compiled from live performances during the peak years of her singing.

There was laughter in the voice, and wistfulness, and tragedy, each song touching the heart, conveying just the right mood.

They listened to every record. There were four of them, and when the recital was over, it was time for bed.

"I'll hear her in my dreams," Shirley said, carefully returning the records to their album. "They're all so lovely, but I liked the waltz best, the one about the silver link, the silken tie."

"She wrote it herself." Mrs. Sedley had been reading the programme notes. "I.M. Connell. That's a name I'll look out for. Perhaps she wrote other songs as well."

She sang it softly under her breath, as she dried the coffee cups which Shirley had washed up, and Shirley, putting dish-cloths to steep in suddy water, paused and listened, and was surprised at the beauty and accuracy of what she heard.

67

Grania Lamont was in the walled garden at Caraig Lodge, busy with her secateurs. Christmas was only a week away, and Josanne had come over to help her tidy up the straggling remains of the flower borders which had been a riot of colour until the November gales destroyed them. She held out a Christmas rose to Josanne.

"Hellebore Niger, and I've enough to decorate the church. It'll give me something to talk about when we dine with those awful Claytons."

The Claytons had bought Duff when the Lucas family left Mull. Mrs. Clayton was a dedicated gardener who always referred to flowers by their Latin names. Her husband kept bees and sold honey.

Josanne, back aching, put down her clippers and examined the rose. "Can you spare me some for Isabella's bedroom when they come for the New Year?"

"If they come," Grania said, attacking another plant with her secateurs. "I'm not really expecting them. They often cancel at the last minute."

This was true, and in her heart Josanne hoped that they would cancel again. She had never been able to get used to the idea that Isabella was her sister-in-law, and she found her presence disturbing, raising as it did both awe and pity. But she knew that Grania yearned to see Rorie, and everyone wanted to see Benedict.

"Her *Hansel and Gretel* is one of the Christmas attractions on television," she said. "It'll be shown before she arrives here. Years ago, she said that she hated her voice being edited and tampered with, and distributed in boxes all over the world. Now it's her means of survival, the only way people like Shirley Morris will be able to assess her true greatness."

Grania put the last of the flowers into her trug, and wiped her hands on her ancient mackintosh. She never could garden in gloves. "People like Shirley Morris are more interested in watching pop groups than opera singers. Besides, she's better occupied in filling the blank years in Mrs. Sedley's life than in mugging up culture that will all wash off after she moves to her next job."

If Grania had identified Mara Sevilla, she was not going to say so.

Josanne took the trug from her and helped to stow away the gardening implements, while they reverted to the subject of Catriona's marriage, which was a subject of perpetual anxiety to both of them.

"I've said and thought many hard things about Isabella," Grania said as they went into the house. "Now I'm more at ease with her than I am with my own daughter. Josanne, make the best of your children while they're young. Your hopes and plans for them will not work out. Niall's the only one who has made sense out of his life." She smiled her crooked little smile and touched Josanne's shoulder. "I knew you were right for him as soon as I met you. It was so important for him to marry a girl who would understand Kilcaraig."

When she walked through the woods to the castle, Josanne thought about Grania's words. There was a time when she would have been shattered at the thought of Niall being manipulated by his mother, Niall, who had always appeared to be so detached and self-sufficient. Now it didn't matter. The marriage of convenience had proved to be a love-match, and how it was brought about was no longer of any interest to her.

The pine needles were soft under her feet and she was startled when she met Mrs. Sedley walking silently towards her in the gloaming, leading Grania's poodle on a string.

"Aunt Marian asked me to return her to Mrs. Lamont. She followed Nanny and the children and Chrissie has been stuffing her with titbits all afternoon." Mrs. Sedley often looked in on Aunt Marian, and she loved playing with Roddy and Anne, who managed to break through her reserve, revealing a glimpse of the person she had been before she froze into the recluse she had become.

"Skittles is a wanderer," Josanne said, knowing that the poodle would have returned home of her own accord, and that Aunt Marian had seized upon an excuse to make Mrs. Sedley call at Caraig Lodge. "Mama's on her own, as Papa is at Tobermory for the Island Council meeting. She'd love to see you, and Mrs. Coll has baked new bread, but I couldn't stay for tea." She paused, then said "Will you be going to the Midnight Service on Christmas Eve? There's no minister, but the older children will read the lessons, and there'll be lots of carols. It's really lovely. Papa has arranged it, and he's hoping for a good turnout."

Mrs. Sedley hesitated, and Josanne wished she hadn't mentioned the service. The first Christmas of widowhood must be very trying.

Mrs. Sedley replied that she was sure Shirley would be there, then Skittles created a diversion by yapping and pulling on her string because she had realized she was within sight and smell of home. She stood on her hind legs, and Mrs. Sedley allowed the tiny ball of wool to tow her to the side gate which led to the Lodge garden.

When she reached the castle, Josanne went straight to the library, where Aunt Marian was casting on stitches for a shawl. She must know that someone was expecting a baby. She always knew that before anyone else did, often before even the mother herself did.

"Catriona telephoned. Hector's coming here with her for the New Year, so the family rift won't be exposed just yet, unless the island is already buzzing with it." She was proud that she had reported the telephone call. These things tended to slip her memory. "She's very grateful that Nanny will cope with Iain, for it means the *au pair* can go back to France for a week. Poor little Iain has enough to confuse him without having to learn French as well as English." She disregarded the fact that she and Chrissie were making sure that Roddy and Anne would grow up knowing the rudiments of Gaelic.

"Mama thinks Isabella and Rorie won't come after all."

"They'll come. Isabella has promised me. They're breaking the journey with the Mountstephans in what Cumberland was before those idiotic know-alls messed up the map."

Isabella's letters to Aunt Marian were more explicit and more reliable than were her letters to anyone else. Josanne unfastened the buttons of her coat, thinking aloud. "That means Briano to drive them and Bridget to look after Benedict, and Motti to boss us all around."

"Motti isn't coming. There'll be an upsurge of fan-mail after *Hansel and Gretel*, so she's staying at Clonbracken to cope with it. At any rate, that's the explanation Isabella's given. I think myself that the poor little soul feels that her retinue forms a wedge between herself and the family."

This meant that Marian knew it was so. It was natural that Isabella would find the adjustment to becoming an ordinary person was a difficult process. Marian counted her stitches, then added, "Margaret spent most of the afternoon with me. She's far more relaxed. She's looking forward to meeting Isabella."

"Who will recognize her immediately. She must know that," Josanne said.

Marian was counting again and did not reply.

"Has she told you who she is?" Josanne asked.

"Twenty-four, twenty-five, twenty-six . . . Ask no questions and

I'll tell you no lies!" But Aunt Marian had that secretive smile that Josanne knew so well. "I just pointed out to her that she has a very pretty voice and that she should practise a bit. It's a pity when a gift of God is wasted."

"Aunt Marian!"

The needles clicked for a minute. "We weren't talking much about her, we were talking about Shirley, who seems to be a typical example of unemployable youth, lacking purpose or ambition. But Margaret says she's not like that – she's made of good stuff, but has sometimes picked up wrong ideas. What we used to call an inferiority complex. Margaret didn't think about stranding her here, with no one of her own age-group or interests to be friendly with. And she's afraid she's a bit smitten with Colin Craig, and disappointed that he hasn't bothered with her any more."

"My mother used to talk about the men I knew not bothering with me. But Niall was lurking all the time! We can't judge what's going on in someone else's head." Josanne was emptying her coat pockets, pulling out some tissues, a few soda-mints, a screwed up card of aspirin, and a mangled packet of elastoplast. She threw them in the fire. "These accumulate. I keep them for emergencies," she said.

They watched the multi-coloured flames, which licked round this unusual fuel.

"The strange oddments people carry around with them," Marian said. "It's a pity worn-out memories can't be tossed into a fire and reduced to ashes. It would be such a helpful solution."

"Solution to what, Aunt Marian? What has Mrs. Sedley really been saying to you?"

"It isn't what she has said, but what she hasn't said that I'm thinking about. When you're as old as I am, you'll find out more about people by what they don't say, rather than by what they do."

Josanne had reached the door on the way to the cloakroom. She stopped and asked, "Do you think Mrs. Sedley was having an affair with Adrian Ferguson during the years when Alison was carrying on about her aches and pains?"

"Mercy, Josanne! What gave you that idea?"

"He's gone to such immense trouble to put her where she'll get the sort of friendship she needs. He must know who she really is. He's an inveterate opera fan, and he's still a consultant to his old firm, and we know they're her lawyers."

"And they've made sure that the new occupant of the Manse didn't arrive with plans to turn it into a tea-room or a souvenir shop." Marian ostentatiously studied her pattern. The commercialism that was creeping into Mull distressed her very much, and she was suspicious of Niall's plans for Caraig village. Development of any sort was something she had hoped would never touch Kilcaraig.

Josanne hung her coat in the cloakroom, brushed her hair, then went up the nursery to play with the children. Nanny, impervious to noise, was sewing, and Niall was on his knees, roaring round playing tigers. Dutifully Josanne joined in.

Alone in the library, Aunt Marian took the packet which she had hidden in her knitting-bag, unfolded a typescript, and read the next instalment of the vivid, exciting saga which she received week after week. It looked so unremarkable in its buff envelope that nobody ever commented when, along with *The Times* and other letters, Lachy brought it up to the castle and left it on the table in the hall.

She would be seeing Hector at the New Year. She would have to convince him that his was no ordinary talent, no run-of-the-mill piece of fiction. She knew about writers. She had been married to one, and she had known that he was good.

Nicholas Danvers. Doctor Danvers, whom she had met in the Inn at Craignure, and who had loved Catriona. Not Hector's Catriona, but the real Catriona, the Catriona who belonged to her life with Papa, and with the laughing-eyed Andrew Sinclair, who had been her first love, and her only romantic love. Dear kind Nicholas, who had shared her experience of utter bereavement, so had always understood.

She nodded off to sleep, but first she tucked the manuscript away, for even when she became muddled and drowsy, she was careful never to betray the confidences that were committed to her care.

* * *

Christmas had come and gone. Margaret Sedley and Shirley attended the Christmas service at midnight, listened to the Christmas story, read haltingly but beautifully by the school-children, and they joined in the carols. Afterwards, as everyone streamed out of the church, they greeted one another with the age-old salutation, and kissed even strangers in the dark.

On Christmas morning, Mrs. Sedley gave Shirley a cashmere pullover, and a Black Watch tartan skirt. What was even more precious than the presents was the card that went with them. "To Shirley, with love from Aunt Margaret." Shirley gave Mrs. Sedley a very finely knitted stole which she had worked on secretly for weeks. She demonstrated that it would go through a wedding-ring, a ring which Mrs. Sedley unhesitatingly removed from her finger for the experiment.

The doctor and his wife, the school-mistress, the district nurse,

460

Mrs. Craig and Colin, as well as Mrs. Sedley and Shirley were among the guests at the castle on Christmas night. Aunt Marian, wearing a paper crown, pronounced it the best Christmas of her life, a statement she had made every year for as long as anyone could remember. Earlier in the day, she had been at the party attended by all the children of Kilcaraig, and she had clapped her hands and sung *Jingle Bells* until Niall, in his Santa Claus attire, made his traditional appearance with a sack of toys on his back.

On Boxing Day, there was the Women's Rural Institute party in the village hall, and this time Santa Claus, whose voice resembled that of Colin Craig, distributed more presents off the Christmas tree to the children. Grania banged out *The Grand Old Duke of York* to start off the dancing, and Roddy spilled orange squash all over Anne's frilly dress. Everyone was happy, and nobody but the infuriated Josanne heard her screams.

Shirley, helping with the children, was flushed with pride as she frequently referred to her Aunt Margaret, who was spending the evening with Mrs. Danvers. Chrissie and wisdom had prevailed upon Marian to forego the party, so that she would not be over-tired when the rest of the family descended on her later in the week. The arrangement also provided an excuse for Mrs. Sedley to stay away from an occasion which could be considered an unsuitable jollification for a woman so recently widowed.

A few days later saw the arrival of the MacNeills, their roof-rack piled high with a pram and a tricycle. Catriona extricated herself from the luggage with which she was surrounded at the back of the car, and a reluctant Iain, trying to bury his face in her skirt, was pushed forward to be greeted by the people who had gathered outside the post office. Hector left the car running, a clear indication that the stop was to be a brief one. He and Catriona had both lost weight, both looked ill at ease, and Iain, clinging to his mother, was the surest indication that all was not well at Ardcross.

"It's a shame," a villager said to Mrs. Craig. "If ever I saw two people meant for one another, it was those two, and just look at them now!"

Mrs. Craig made an evasive reply, well schooled in the art of keeping her thoughts to herself, but afterwards she remarked to Colin that everyone in the castle would be relieved, when Rorie and his family arrived the next day. In the past, Isabella herself had created tensions. Now she would be a welcome diversion from this wretched-looking trio.

On the following afternoon, it was Rorie who drove through the village, slowing down nearly to a halt outside the post office, but tooting his greeting, because everyone would know that his wife could not be expected to talk to a crowd of people all at the same time. She sat beside him, muffled in furs, with a chiffon headscarf keeping her glorious Titian hair under control, and she smiled, and waved, delight in her eyes, because there was an audience she knew and loved, and she would visit each one of them in their homes, and drink their teas, and not care when she had to say – "I'm sorry" – and make them repeat almost everything they said.

The car had turned away, heading for the bumpy bridge, when a small figure sitting between Briano and Bridget became visible, bouncing in his seat and turning round to wave excitedly at them all. Benedict. Rorie as he had looked as a baby, but a Rorie with red hair and a personality that projected right through the rear window and into their hearts.

Margaret Sedley and Shirley watched them discreetly from the landing window.

"Aunt Margaret, although she's hardly visible, she exudes glamour," Shirley said. "A person who looks like she does doesn't need to be able to sing."

"And a person who sings as she does is in no need of any looks at all," Margaret said. "But there's more to her even than that. She's unspeakably kind." She turned away from the window, because the car had disappeared up the castle drive. Shirley stayed where she was, the question she longed to ask unspoken. "How do you know?"

A pattern was forming in her mind, but she would do no sleuthing, and she could be wrong.

Up at the castle, Rorie brought the car to a smooth halt in front of the open, welcoming door.

* * *

Roderick and Grania had joined the rest of the family in the hall of the castle to welcome them. Hector and Catriona stood together, a little distance away from the others, Iain clinging to his mother's skirt.

Isabella carried Benedict into the house, a happy, smiling Benedict, holding out his arms as if he were bestowing a blessing on them all. He was snatched by his grandfather, and Grania waited for his howls to begin, but he rubbed his face against his grandfather's cheek, and roared with laughter at the strange, rough feel.

Isabella kissed each member of the family, while Josanne decided that she had lost none of her charisma, and she was suddenly shy of this woman who was to be part of their lives for the next ten days. She watched as Isabella took Benedict from his grandfather and put

462

him on the floor while she introduced Bridget to Chrissie, who would take her to the nursery to meet Nanny. Briano was unpacking the car, talking Italian to Cathy, who understood not a word he was saying, but was nevertheless pleased with what she heard.

The next moment, Josanne saw that Benedict had crawled halfway upstairs. She exclaimed, and stepped forward to rescue him, but he turned quickly, to make sure everyone had seen how clever he was, over-balanced, and somersaulted to the bottom, where he sat, dazed but smiling, rubbing his head, as Isabella went over to him, picked him up gently, and kissed his fat cheek.

"No panic," Rorie said. "Isabella's psychology book says they yell when they see us being frightened, not by being hurt. Isabella's made a study of it, and she's the boss!"

"It seems to work," Josanne said, thinking of the roars emitted by Roddy or Anne if anything went wrong.

Benedict, alert, was looking over his mother's shoulder at his father. He had green eyes as well as red hair. Isabella's colouring. Rorie's shape. He smiled at Catriona, who impulsively took him in her arms.

"Baby!" Iain said, staring at the intruder, and then he, too, smiled. "Nursery," he said. Catriona bent down, letting him prod Benedict, who showed no objection to being treated like a doll.

"That's right – nursery," Bridget said, removing Benedict and carrying him upstairs, followed by Iain and Chrissie.

"Doesn't he mind being moved from one person to another," Josanne asked, addressing Isabella and talking slowly. She could see the glinting stud of the hearing-aid fixed behind Isabella's ear.

"Benedict doesn't mind anything. He's very secure. That's immensely important. It's something we all need, but babies need it most of all." She leaned against Rorie, looking up at him. He put his arm round her shoulder, holding her as if he held all that was most precious in the whole wide world in his arms. "We've been a bit over-anxious, afraid of exposing Benedict to a chill that would affect his hearing. That's why we didn't bring him here sooner. You've nothing to worry about. He's flourishing – as you can see for yourselves."

She had read between the lines of their letters. She had known and shared in their anxiety. Now she turned to the Kilcaraig tapestry that covered the damp patch on the wall. "Someone's filled in a bit of embroidery. Is that Anne and Benedict who've been added to the family group?"

"Aunt Marian did that specially for you when we took it down for the pre-Christmas cleaning," Josanne said. "She's waiting for you in the library. She wanted to have you all to herself."

Isabella flung off the sable coat and tossed it to Rorie. Then she crossed the hall like an eager child, and they could hear the Gaelic greetings as she was gathered into Aunt Marian's arms.

*　　*　　*

On the following afternoon, when Bridget pushed Benedict up to the castle in his pram, she said to Nanny, "There's a small fortune in silver coins collected under his mattress. Thanks be to God he didn't swallow the fivepenny piece!"

Nanny, retrieving a toy Anne had thrown out of her pram, pretended not to hear. Benedict could have swallowed a number of coins before he had been seen conveying one to his mouth. He was old enough to grasp at the traditional offerings that were slipped into his pram by people who were seeing him for the first time.

Grania, in the sun-room at Caraig Lodge, saw the two nannies and the children parading through the village, Iain lagging a little bit behind, so that every few seconds the procession was held up, waiting for him. She loved her grandchildren, all four of them, but she specially loved Benedict, Rorie's son. Rorie, her special child, whom she scarcely knew any more.

All day she had hoped he would tear himself away from Isabella and come and see her. It was a vain hope, for last night at dinner it was evident that Isabella depended on him as her interpreter. She could understand what he said, as she could understand no one else, and time would show if it was really tiredness after the journey that had affected her hearing so badly. When Rorie came to Caraig Lodge, Isabella would come too, so Grania decided dejectedly that she would go to the village hall and help Roderick and Niall. They were refurbishing the Christmas decorations for the party to be held on New Year's Eve.

She was about to leave the house when she saw Rorie and Isabella and Catriona approaching the bumpy bridge. They stopped to talk to the nannies and the children for a few minutes, but when they reached the Lodge gates, Rorie turned up the drive, and Catriona and Isabella went on to the village.

Grania's heart raced. He had come. She could talk to him alone.

"Mama, me darlin'. I've come to cadge tea and sympathy. Catriona's been detailed to drag some girl called Shirley off for a walk, while Isabella does the round of visits, starting with the newcomer at the Manse."

464

"Why begin with her?" Grania asked, nettled.

"They're old acquaintances. It's Top Secret, but ask Mrs. Coll to put the kettle on, then I'll tell you all about it."

Which he did.

68

"The last time I spoke to you, I had sung my falcon song and you told me I mustn't let personal involvement get in my way." Isabella's eyes were shining. Catriona had wasted no time in effecting introductions and removing Shirley for a walk, and now that she was alone with Mara, Isabella found she was not smitten with the shyness she had dreaded. Their roles had been changed, by necessity or by choice, and while Mara was as cool as ever, she was no longer unapproachable. "I had a crush on you in those days. I longed to ask for your autograph, but I didn't dare. Madame Sevilla, please will you give it to me before I go home?"

"Madame Connelli, I'll be delighted, so long as you'll give me yours!" They laughed, the years that had separated them now drawing them together in the bond of shared experience.

Isabella slid onto the floor and leaned against the armchair on which she had been sitting. Her hearing-aid glittered in the firelight.

"I think I guessed right, about Josanne recognizing you," she said. "She was very tactful about fixing for me to come and see you."

"I wonder how much she knows?"

"How much is there to know?"

Mara sat on the sofa opposite Isabella. "How much can you hear?" she asked.

Isabella carefully removed her hearing-aid. "Try me."

Mara asked her some questions about her life in Ireland, her husband, her son. Isabella answered her easily.

"If everyone spoke like you, I'd forget I'm deaf," she said. "They shout at me, and it jars. Then I get flustered and can't hear anything at all." She was fiddling with her hearing-aid. Mara leaned over and took it from her, putting it out of reach on the mantelpiece. Isabella smiled her satisfaction. She knew she had passed her test.

"We haven't very long," she said. "Please tell me everything you can. I'll try not to interrupt." She rested her chin on her hand and settled down to listen. The firelight playing on her face erased the little marks of time and pain. She looked like a child.

Mara, deeply troubled, began. "You may remember that my husband was an antique-dealer."

"I knew he was very rich," Isabella said.

"Collectors relied on his judgement, and he travelled all over the world looking for the treasures other people coveted. Then one night, he came to the opera in Rome, and he forgot about antiques for other people. Instead, he coveted me, for himself."

"So collectors were right about his judgement!"

Mara smiled, less in acknowledgement of the compliment than in relief that Isabella was genuinely able to hear.

"He always knew how to get what he wanted. I was singing Manon and he wangled his way into my dressing-room. That wasn't difficult because, unlike you, I used it as a salon rather than as a sacristy."

"I was always deaf in one ear. When people crowded round me, I was afraid they'd find me out," Isabella said defensively. "Please go on."

"It was a lightning romance. My parents flew over from Melbourne for the wedding. My father was Italian. My mother's roots were here in Kilcaraig. My grandmother was born on that farm that's now a ruin, south of Loch Caraig."

There was a diversion while Isabella explained that if Mara had roots in Kilcaraig, she was not an incomer, and she should make sure that everyone knew it, but Mara was adamant.

"I don't want anyone to dig into my past. It was the one snag that worried me when Adrian Ferguson coaxed me into coming here."

Her parents had run a small-time restaurant, but they had burning ambitions for their daughter, and it was they who urged her to take part in the singing competition which was to lead her to Europe, and ultimately to Milan.

"They never knew what a battlefield I had entered when I won that competition! Mercifully, they only saw the successful side, and when I married a rich and eligible Englishman, their happiness was complete. They died before the cracks began to show."

Isabella was watching Mara's hands, fidgeting, twisting at the corner of a cushion, fiddling with an ash-tray. "What sort of cracks?" she prompted.

"Paul treated me as if I were an *objet d'art*. He guarded me jealously, and mistrusted me whenever I was away from him. That was our difficulty – he was compelled to travel, and so was I. We were often apart, but there was a kind of delirium when we were reunited."

466

"So that side of it was all right," Isabella said cautiously.

"That side of things was what our marriage was all about. We had little else in common. I learnt to my cost the truth of the saying that after four years of marriage one's husband should be one's best friend."

"Mine is," Isabella said, unable to resist it, but she immediately regretted what must sound like boasting, and she added, "What about children?"

"No children. I wanted them, but Paul didn't. He loved to display me. The enthusiasm of the audience meant much more to him than it did to me. Gradually, as I became better known, he became even prouder of me, and he liked to demonstrate that he owned me. It started in small ways, but it built up into the sort of exhibition you saw. He chose to strike where it hurt most – in front of my friends, or members of the company. Afterwards, there would be a marvellous reconciliation of the sort you can imagine! When you sang to me in the studio that day, I couldn't tell you that he would make up for it as soon as I got home."

"I wondered about that," Isabella said. "I was hoping you'd kick him out of bed!"

Mara was aware that Isabella was an actress who knew all the tricks of the trade. She could detect tension, just as she could express it. She would realize that the difficult part was coming, a part that was so painful, yet must sound so trivial in the telling.

"You were being mobbed in New York while I was singing Mimi in Milan. Paul was at an international conference about paraplegics at Stresa. He had a brother he adored who had died of polio – that was long before I met him – and his interest in helping victims had got him involved. He was asked to bring me along to a reception, as a *pièce de résistance* to dazzle the delegates, and I couldn't very well refuse, though I was revolted at the thought of being surrounded by gymnasts and basket-ball players and all those sweaty strength-through-joy sort of people who are part of the organization of such things."

"Healthy people tend to have a sort of revulsion about the handi-capped. It's based on an inner fear that it could happen to them."

"It wasn't the handicapped I found putting-off. It was the hearty ones."

"There's a Freudian explanation for that," the amateur psychologist observed.

"Our arrival at the party caused a stir, because I was a *prima donna*, and this impressed even those who never went near an opera. Champagne flowed, and the delegates, who represented all nations, tried valiantly to overcome the language barriers. Then someone asked me to sing. I made the usual excuses about saving my voice, and Paul, who wanted to show me off, was goaded into one of his bouts of mocking at me. I don't remember what he said. All I knew was that suddenly he was on the floor, and I was being swept off into the night and into a car."

"Didn't you think you were being kidnapped?" Isabella still remembered the fears which had haunted her in the days of her glory.

"I didn't think of anything at all, not even when I found myself sitting shivering in an hotel bedroom, while a broad-shouldered young man poured brandy into a tumbler and made me drink it all. He asked me if I knew the name of my tormentor, and when I said it was my husband, he stood there, shaking his head and repeating, 'This is a fine kettle of fish'. I can hear him still, as I did then. He spoke with a Welsh accent, and he said he was a physical training instructor, and his name was David Trevor. Then he gave me the key of the bedroom door, and said I must try to relax, while he went back to the reception to see what he could do to put things right. 'I don't want the police to think I'm a felon,' he said as he closed the door."

"So it wasn't a night of love," Isabella said, disappointed.

"It was a night of nightmare. But I suppose because of the brandy I slept, lying on the bed, not in it. I didn't even take off my shoes. David Trevor came to me in the morning, with a carrier-bag containing a dress he had bought somehow, and everything that a woman could possibly need in an emergency. The contents of that parcel were a practical indication of his character, although I didn't think about that at the time. He was meticulously thoughtful and kind."

"Although he had clobbered your husband?"

"Although he had set off what could have been an international incident! In fact, the fracas was hushed up. Paul had been felled but not hurt, and had risen to his feet with what dignity he could muster. He had driven straight back to Milan. Now I asked David to take me to him. It was the strangest journey of my life. Part of me was shaking with fright at the thought of facing Paul, and part of me experienced the serenity of having someone so calm and comforting at my side."

"That's what I feel like with Rorie," Isabella commented.

"I made him drop me off close to where I lived. I didn't want him to come up to our apartment and see a confrontation. In fact, there was none. The servants had been instructed not to let me in. One can't stand on one's own doorstep, pleading for admission." Mara went over to the window, turning her back on Isabella, re-living the humiliation of that day.

"Then what happened?" Isabella asked, after a long silence.

"I went down to the place where they collect the refuse. I sat for ages on a stair, until I heard someone come along. Then I did the only possible thing – I went to the Bardinis. I had to. They lived near, and I had no money and no clothes, only an evening-dress in a paper carrier. Constance was at home, and she could see at a glance that this was no ordinary matrimonial quarrel."

"She's American. They're good at psychology. I buy American psychology books because of Benedict," Isabella said, believing that a practical attitude would help Mara with her story now. "What did Constance do?" she asked.

"She fetched Paolo from his studio."

"Good heavens!" Isabella knew that to disturb Bardini in his studio was a crime.

"I was supposed to be singing at the Scala the following night. Obviously I was unfit to do so. But my husband refused even to see Bardini. I spent the night with the Bardinis in a borrowed nightdress. Then I remembered that I had sleeping pills in my handbag. I swallowed the lot."

She returned to the sofa and sat down wearily. "The next thing I knew, I was in an appropriate nursing-home in England. Paul had made the arrangements. I was there for months and months. I wouldn't talk to anyone. I seemed to be smitten with a kind of mental paralysis, and Paul never came near me." She looked at Isabella, and then round the room, as if she had lost her bearings.

"And what of your friends? Didn't any of them help you?"

"They didn't know where I was. Paul saw to that. But eventually David Trevor found me."

"And he came back into your life?"

"For a little while he became my life," Mara said quietly. She was shivering, as she had done in that bedroom in Stresa all those years ago.

Isabella stood up, collected her hearing-aid from the mantelpiece, and fixed it behind her ear. "You've said enough for one session. I'm to be here for another week." Impulsively, she caught Mara's shoulder, and kissed her hair, dark hair streaked with grey. "I heard the front-door bang. Catriona and Shirley must be back, so we'll have that panacea for all ills, a cup of tea." Her applied psychology had its effect. Mara relaxed.

Later, as she and Catriona were walking up the hill to the castle,

Catriona said, "I don't know what Mrs. Sedley was saying to you, but she looked as if she had seen a ghost."

"I think she had," Isabella said, her hearing-aid vibrating painfully. "It's therapy. It's good to tell of distressing episodes in our lives. It helps to resolve them. My psychology book says so. But it mustn't be overdone."

Catriona squeezed her arm. "Talking to you is therapy, no matter what about, or what the book says. You're the kindest person I've ever met."

But Isabella didn't hear her. Catriona's voice was pitched just a little too loud and too high.

* * *

Rorie drove Isabella and Aunt Marian from the castle at half-past eleven, and called at the Manse to collect Margaret Sedley, so that they would be in the village hall in time to welcome the New Year. Shirley had been at the party since it began, and would stay there until it ended.

Their arrival was greeted with cheers, and although she hung back a bit, Margaret knew that these people would be glad she had come. For the past few days it had been impossible to refuse the invitations to tea or coffee or a drink in their homes, and for the past few hours she had thought about what Isabella had said. She would love to claim her place in this community, but she would never have the courage.

Aunt Marian was ushered onto the platform, where she sat on the chair that had been painted gold, like a throne, when the Kilcaraig primary school won a shield in the Mull drama competition. She revelled in her moment of glory, recognizing everyone, remembering their names, even asking after individual members of their families whom she hadn't seen for years.

When the New Year was piped in, and they had all sung *Auld Lang Syne*, there was an expectant hush, and then Isabella walked onto the platform and stood beside the throne. She sang *An T-Eilean Muileach*, the song that specially belonged to Mull. Then there were other songs also in Gaelic, with everyone tapping their feet to the rhythm, and joining in the choruses.

Margaret Sedley watched her, marvelling at her loveliness, the perfection of her singing, her informality and ease. The little falcon, who had sung herself into the hearts of people all over the world was bewitching her small audience, just as effectively as she had always done in the great concert halls and opera houses.

"I'll end with a *Ninna Nana*, an Italian lullaby, and this one is

470

Benedict's special favourite," Isabella said, and she smiled across at Rorie, who stood close to the platform, never taking his eyes off her. She had to sing it twice, but the people were thoughtful and didn't press for more. A child ran forward and handed up a sprig of holly from the decorations in the hall, and Isabella leaned over to take it, laughing at the prickly tribute, as if it meant more to her than the bouquets that used to be piled round her feet.

When she left the platform, she sat beside Rorie, and momentarily she closed her eyes. Only Mara saw it, and only Mara recognized the instinctive sigh of relief that another performance was safely and successfully over. The change in circumstances had not reduced Isabella's professional conduct, nor undermined her courage. Mara, watching her, thought over her own paltry story of defeat. Other people had lived through marriage failures, nervous breakdowns, broken hearts. They didn't abandon their careers and wallow in their sense of shame.

Rorie touched her on the shoulder. "I'm taking Aunt Marian and Isabella home. I think they've had enough of party noises. Do you want to come too?"

"If you'll come in for a drink. Then I'll have a dark man as a first-footer. Isn't that the right way to start the New Year?"

Aunt Marian and Isabella chose to stay in the car while Rorie went into the house.

"*Slainte!*" he said, swallowing the neat whisky Mara had poured out for him. They were standing by the sideboard in the dining-room. "A happy New Year, Mara, and my wish for you is that your David will come back into your life."

"What has Isabella been telling you?"

"The truth. She always does. She's longing to know the rest of your story – what happened when he found you in that horrible place."

Mara could feel Rorie's deep blue eyes upon her. His whole being was a combination of strength and of gentleness. He had reminded her of David when he helped her into the car. "We lived together for a while. That was all. I've been making a mountain out of a molehill, and I'm ashamed."

"Didn't it work out?" he persisted.

"Paul had a stroke. He needed me, so I went to him."

"But after he died?"

"He was on his death-bed for seven years."

"You poor little soul," Rorie said, just as Aunt Marian, just as David would have said it. Then he kissed her lightly on the forehead, and joined the others in the car.

69

"This has been the best New Year I've ever experienced in my long and happy life," Aunt Marian said, and she sounded as if she meant it.

She was in the library with Josanne and Catriona and the children. Roddy and Anne were engaged in their game of tigers, from which they had not yet tired, and Iain was leaning against his mother's knee, sucking two fingers. Benedict was on the rug in front of the fire, his chubby legs stretched out before him as he banged a silver spoon against the coal shovel.

"They're too young to play together," Josanne said, worried at the lack of interest her children had shown in their cousins.

"Iain dotes on Benedict," Catriona said. "He keeps asking if we can take him home with us, just as if he were a Christmas present." She sounded wistful. It didn't need Isabella's psychology book to draw attention to Iain's insecurity. He always held on to someone, his mother or his father or Nanny, but most of all he clung to Benedict, showing unusual care and concern for this red-headed curiosity, whose laughter filled the nursery.

"Benedict is so uncomplicated. He eats anything one spoons into him." Last night, after the dancing was over, and she and Niall had at last switched off their light, Josanne had admitted that she was jealous of the impact Benedict had upon everyone. He seemed to have inherited the magnetic charm of his parents without even having to open his mouth and sing. Watching him now, happily absorbed in his occupation, she felt guilty. He was only a baby, not trying to win approval from anyone, just taking it for granted.

He leaned forward, preparing to get into a crawling position. Now he had to be watched, for he could move like lightning and there was no guard on the fire. Instinctively, Catriona put out her hand to protect him. He took it, smiling up at her, then he pulled himself to his feet, gurgling with pleasure.

Aunt Marian's beads were glittering at her throat. Benedict saw them and held out his arms. The next moment, he had tottered a few steps and was clutching at her lap.

"His first steps, in the very same place as his father took his! But he's terribly young to be walking!" Marian gathered the triumphant Benedict into her arms, kissing him and muttering endearments in Gaelic, while Josanne went to look for Isabella, to tell her of this important development in her son's life.

Isabella was in the music-room which had once been the dressing-room of the bedroom she now shared with Rorie. She snapped off her cassette recorder when Josanne came in.

"I'm so glad he went to Aunt Marian," she said after hearing of Benedict's achievement. "I'll have to write a ballad about it." She indicated the recorder. "Rorie and I provide an endless supply of songs and stories for him. Then, when we have to be away from him for a few days, as sometimes we must, he can hear us and know we're coming back."

"What do you record?"

"All sorts of things. Some are songs I've composed myself."

"Isabella, they must be worth a fortune!" Josanne thought of the crowds that used to camp in the streets when Isabella Connelli sang, and of the queues which even now formed outside the cinemas whenever a film she had made was shown. "They'll be worth a fortune," she repeated, thinking Isabella hadn't heard her.

"They aren't for money. They're never, never for money. They're our private bond with Benedict. They're only for him."

She replaced the recorder in its case and stowed the cassettes into their special carrier. When it was anything to do with music, Isabella was wholly methodical. Nobody in the world, not even Rorie, could take care of her music as scrupulously as she did herself.

She went downstairs with Josanne. Benedict's first steps had been proclaimed round the castle, and Chrissie and Cathy had left the New Year's Day dinner in the safety of the Aga, as they came to coax him into giving an encore. He saw his mother on the door-way, bounced on Aunt Marian's knee, and had fallen to the floor before she could put out a saving hand. Undaunted, he pulled himself up by her skirt, and shouting with joy, staggered towards the door.

Isabella moved forward to meet him, kneeling to gather him in her arms. Tears were streaming down her cheeks. Isabella who never cried, who quoted her psychology books about the disturbing effect a display of emotion could have upon a developing mind.

"Where's Rorie?" she said, taking her baby in her arms.

"I'm here, Isabella." He spoke softly, but she felt his presence.

"I'm the luckiest woman alive," she said, holding up her hand to touch Rorie, but still embracing Benedict. Then she whispered something to both of them, one of the secret, loving things she had committed to tape.

Iain let go of his mother, and walked resolutely towards his aunt.

"Mine," he said, pulling at Benedict's shoulders.

Isabella included him in her embrace. "Ours," she said, and he smiled, seeming to understand.

*   *   *

"They'll all be plastered by the time they get home," Grania said, referring to the men-folk, who had spent most of the day visiting the houses in Kilcaraig, to make sure that everyone would know that they were remembered on this first day of the year.

"Smashed is the fashionable word," Josanne said. "Next year it'll be something else. How quickly our language changes. No wonder the translators make such a mess of the Bible."

"Papa's hoping to knock sense into Hector about being so stupid over Catriona's money. He knew when he married her that she wouldn't be living on a naval officer's pay," Grania said.

"Hector hadn't reckoned that she'd buy a fourteen-bedroomed house, with all that it costs in upkeep, and expect him to give up his job and live in it. She thought it was a wonderful idea, buying back the family home. She didn't reckon with the MacNeill family pride." Josanne had often wondered if she could have done anything to stop Catriona from carrying out her misguided plan. But even Adrian Ferguson had failed to convince her of her folly.

"Papa once felt the same about Kilcaraig," Grania said. "He wanted me, but not my possessions, which he regarded as impediments." She smiled wryly. "Robert masterminded the plan which sorted all that out. We need someone like him to mastermind a solution to the Hector-Catriona conflict."

"Robert Dutton must have been a remarkable man." Since her marriage, Josanne had come to think of him as a person, not just as the awe-inspiring name that had brought prosperity to Carnsworth, Prior and Dutton.

"It was only after he died that I realized how little I knew him," Grania said. "I was a grabbing, selfish young woman, always wanting to manipulate people to suit my own ends. Like I did over Rorie. Do you know, I spent all yesterday afternoon with him, and he talked and talked, just as he always used to do before he met Isabella. But almost all the time he talked about Isabella. Josanne, he's blissfully happy. Can you understand it? The gilt has never worn off the gingerbread, her glamour hasn't been eclipsed by familiarity, the awful adjustments they've had to make have never robbed her of his patience or his respect."

They all knew of Isabella's savage moments of regret when her professional life had come to its premature end. Josanne and Niall had been at Covent Garden when she made her first appearance in the audience, a short time after her marriage. She had been given a standing ovation when she entered her box, of the kind she had been accustomed to at the end of a performance, and she had smiled and bowed her gratitude. But when they returned to the flat in Lowndes Square where they were all staying, she had become hysterical, the pent-up emotion of the last few hours spilling out in a torrent of protest and abuse.

"He adores her," Josanne said now, thinking of that night, and of how Rorie had soothed and cajoled and helped her to recover.

"She's his life. That's what I find so disturbing," Grania said.

Catriona came into the library. "Peace at last! I've left Isabella teaching Benedict the Rosary. Silly, isn't it? He's far too young, and it's such a waste of time."

She poured herself a large gin, and topped it with a dash of tonic. "Marilyn Coleman has just telephoned to say that the central heating isn't working, and Hector, of all people, took the call. He was in the office, writing one of his interminable reports to the Admiralty."

"What's the point of telling you about the central heating, when there's nothing you can do about it? Presumably someone local can cope."

"That's what Hector says, Mama. But what he means is that if we didn't have Ardcross, we wouldn't be tied to a guest-house from which there's no escape, not even for a few days!" She brushed her curls away from her forehead. She still looked like a school-girl, but one who had lost her zest for living.

She had poured out a second gin when they heard Chrissie helping Marian downstairs for the first dinner on the first day of the year that lay ahead.

*   *   *

As Grania had predicted, Roderick and Niall were more than usually cheerful when they sat down to dinner, and Hector concealed whatever chagrin he was feeling under his customary suave appearance. Rorie hadn't been on the New Year's Day round of Kilcaraig because of Isabella.

"I suppose you paid your respects to your green leaf in a darkened

475

chamber?" Grania said, addressing Roderick's back. He was carving the roast pork that was on the sideboard.

"My green leaf was holding court to every man that was capable of tottering to the Manse," he said. "I've never seen her so vivacious, or so tantalizing! And that splendid little Shirley was in the kitchen with Colin Craig, trying to revive Briano, who had found our native beverage and our wild dancing too much for him!"

"We dumped him in the car and brought him home. Chrissie's flow of Italian-Gaelic brought him to his senses *molto presto*, or whatever it is they say." Hector looked across the table at Catriona, hoping to see her smile. Her eyes were downcast as she helped herself to apple-sauce.

"Margaret loved meeting you, Isabella. She says she'll be seeing you again before you go away." Niall's use of Mrs. Sedley's Christian name showed the familiarity the New Year's celebrations had brought to the Manse.

"She'll see her tomorrow," Rorie said, answering for Isabella as he often did. As he often had to do.

"Isabella's going to sing to me after dinner. Just we two." Marian turned to Isabella. "I want some of the old songs, and Chrissie has put the sheet-music in the library. The rest of you can linger over your biscuits and cheese." She never ate cheese at night, and neither did Isabella.

By the time they reached dessert, Niall had led the conversation round to the re-building of Caraig village, explaining his ideas, seeing it as an act of restoration that would compensate to some extent for the monstrosities of chalets and bungalows that were cropping up like mushrooms in some parts of Mull.

"To make them as solid as they used to be will cost untold gold," Catriona said, her eyes avoiding Hector. Talk of money could plunge him into a state of simmering anger, rendering him sullen for days.

Isabella knew what they were talking about, and she caught the word gold. "I've achieved another golden disc. That should build a house or two or three," she said.

"But that's your money," Rorie said sharply, apparently outraged. "The restoration of Caraig is a family affair."

Isabella looked at him, surprised and hurt. "I'm family, aren't I? Who pays for what doesn't matter, if it's something that's sensible and right. I'll be very unhappy if you leave me out."

Aunt Marian saw Catriona glance at Hector. She rose majestically from her chair. "While you eat your cheese and plan for the future, Isabella and I will have music."

Isabella took her arm and they walked to the door through what was virtually a kilt-clad guard of honour. When they reached the library, Aunt Marian said, "You did that very well . . . Just the right touch".

"Rorie and I have rehearsed it for days! I hope the seed takes root. Men are so obstinate, but I think Hector may relent in the end."

She settled Marian in the Kilcaraig chair, with a footstool and the cap she was crocheting for Iain; then she turned to the sheets of music. She began with the *Eriskay Love-lilt*, and she could see that Marian was joining in the chorus, and then she sang *Caol Muile*, which was her own favourite song about Mull.

"Now sing *An Gille Dubh Ciar-Dubh*. You'll find it at the bottom of the pile. Grania keeps it in a special place because it's so precious, but she's lent it to us for tonight."

Isabella found the song, its pages yellow with age. *Catriona M. Lamont* was written on it, in fading ink. She read through the words, first in Gaelic, then in English. "The dark-haired youth. It reminds me of Rorie," she said.

"It reminded Grania of Roderick. Read the last verse."

> "My bonnie *dubh ciar-dubh*,
> Let sharp tongues assail thee,
> One heart will not fail thee
> That knows to be true.
> *Dubh ciar-dubh, dubh ciar-dubh*,
> Though poor, poor thou be,
> No rich man can please me,
> Like thee, love, like thee."

Isabella read it aloud. "Grania's ancient first husband couldn't have liked this one little bit!" she said.

"It caused a lot of trouble for quite a long time, but it brought about a happy ending. Sing it to me now, and I'll believe I'm in heaven."

Isabella wet her lips and sang.

She didn't hear Rorie open the door, but she knew that he was in the room. Then she saw that the rest of the family had gathered in the doorway, unable to resist listening to the enchantingly beautiful song.

They applauded when she finished, and she bowed to them, smiling, and then bowed, as if in homage, towards the Kilcaraig chair.

Aunt Marian was sitting with her crochet in her hands. Her face, in the firelight, was as smooth as a girl's. She was smiling.

She was dead.

70

Kilcaraig was yellow with daffodils. They blazed in front of the castle, and they lined the path up to Caraig Lodge. The Manse garden was full of them, and so was the burial ground. The willow-trees were covered in catkins, and there was the usual seasonal trouble with cows falling into bogs, wanting to eat the new grass that grew first at the edge of the water.

Lachy, when he delivered the mail, had told Shirley that March was a terrible month for gales, and as the daffodils were early, they could be flattened to the ground. So they were, but astonishingly they recovered, ready to be flattened by the next gale.

"There's a sermon in that, if I could think what it is," Margaret said, standing by the fence and looking at the grave-yard.

"Aunt Marian laughing at us, and telling us that to be laid low doesn't mean we won't rise again." Shirley's cheeks were pink with the exertion of spreading the load of sea-weed Angie Campbell had brought to them on his trailer. "It's funny, Aunt Margaret, but I've felt differently about death ever since I went to her funeral. It was all so natural and so happy, just the way she wanted it to be."

Aunt Marian had foreseen that she might die at an inconvenient time, and had left written instructions – no mourning, no cancellation of celebrations. It had been difficult to carry out her wishes, but somehow it had been done.

Isabella had at first shocked, then impressed, everyone by taking Benedict to see his Great-great Aunt Marian as she lay on her bed, still as a waxwork, calm and beautiful, a Lamont tartan plaid covering her up to her chin. Copying his mother, Benedict kissed the icy forehead, then went placidly off to play with his cousins. Isabella, having shown her son the dignity and inevitability of death, retired to her bedroom and was seen no more until after the funeral. At last she could give vent to her feelings, and she had Rorie to comfort her, but her tears brought on a recurrence of her agonizing ear-ache. She had not been able to hear the funeral service, held in the house, but she watched from the window as the coffin was carried shoulder-high down the hill to the burial-ground. Rorie stayed with her, knowing her need of him and knowing that Aunt Marian would have wished it. She had realized, even before he did, that he had become an inseparable part of Isabella's life.

Margaret stayed where she was for a while, thinking about death, how beautiful it could be, and how ugly. Shirley, humming quietly as she worked, could have seen very little of it, and had never experienced it as an amputation, the loss of a life that was part of oneself. But that could happen without death. It could happen when people were alive and apart. She pulled herself up. Ever since she had talked with Isabella, she had put self-pity behind her.

A lorry-load of bricks sped through the village. Work was beginning on the re-building of the cottages at Caraig village.

"Colin and Niall will be shivering there on the building site. I wonder what it feels like, watching a pipe dream become reality?" She had joined Shirley at the rose-bed and was kicking at the sea-weed, spreading it with the toe of her Wellington boot.

"Niall's pipe-dream is becoming reality so fast that Colin will soon be out of a job again," Shirley replied. Colin Craig had badgered the authorities into giving the necessary planning permission. Having accepted Niall's offer to act as overseer of the new development, he had used his powers of persuasion to cut through the red tape, and to speed the progress of the blue-prints through the council chambers. His greatest difficulty had been to convince the local people that this was a matter of private enterprise which would meet with their approval, and was not a government-backed venture which would be received with the utmost suspicion. There was always resistance to outside "interference".

Aunt Marian's death had established Margaret Sedley and Shirley as members of the community in a way that nothing else could have done. They had put up camp-beds in the Manse to help accommodate the numbers of people who had flocked to Mull for the funeral, and they had met MacColls and MacLeans and MacGillivrays and MacPhails and MacKinnons and others, who had been compelled to move to the mainland, and even as far afield as Canada, the United States, Australia, and New Zealand, in search of work. Some of them had found prosperity, others had managed to eke out an existence of some sort, but all were united by their common bond – Kilcaraig.

Sometimes, when the post office was closed on Wednesday afternoons, Mrs. Craig had taken to going to the Manse for afternoon tea, which consisted of sandwiches and cakes, instead of the more substantial tea that was served later, at about six o'clock. It was only after several such visits that she had broached the subject of Shirley, who now was often out of the house, shopping at Salen or Tobermory, or collecting wild flowers on Iona.

Margaret Sedley had sketched in as much as she could of Shirley's background, understanding Mrs. Craig's anxiety, and accepting her own responsibility for the fact that she had brought Colin and Shirley together.

"What I've never admitted to Shirley is that I asked her to come for an interview by mistake," Margaret said one day. "There were two applications from people called Morris. One was a woman of sixty-four, who sounded staid and probably suitable, but I sent the reply in the wrong S.A.E. and was confronted by Shirley. Something about her appealed to me. I felt that she was at the cross-roads, that she could get into the wrong set and go to the bad. Now I believe I was wrong about that, but right about her. She's a gem."

"She has a university degree. She should do something better with her life."

"People can't always do what they want to do. Your own son can't." Margaret felt nettled about criticism of Shirley, but as soon as she had said it, she regretted a remark that must sound brutal.

"Colin is doing what he likes now," Mrs. Craig said. "He's country born and bred. The Lamonts had always said he should study agriculture or estate management, but I had an idea that he'd do better as a marine engineer."

Margaret thought of that conversation now, as she watched Shirley, flushed and happy and absorbed, working on the rose-bed. Clearly the life she enjoyed did not depend upon a university degree.

"I'll go in and make the tea," Margaret said. Shirley nodded, and smiled approvingly of Margaret's distribution of the manure.

The kettle was boiling furiously, and the toast was burning when Shirley joined Margaret in the kitchen a short time later. She had spread the *Oban Times* on the table, and was reading it, oblivious of all else. Shirley laughed, threw the charred toast into the bin, put fresh slices in the toaster, and made the tea.

"When I first came here, I thought you never did anything wrong, Aunt Margaret. I thought you were perfection."

Margaret folded up the *Oban Times*, and put the tray on the table. After a moment of thought, she set it with cups and saucers instead of mugs. "I must have been a dreadful bore," she said.

"I realized fairly soon that after spending years looking after someone else, being kind and thoughtful had become a habit. You were impersonal, in a way, but never a bore."

They had tea in the drawing-room, sitting by the window, where they could see someone up a ladder doing something to the castle walls. Probably cropping back the ivy.

"Looking back, can you say what were the happiest days of your life?" Shirley asked, still thinking about the burnt toast, and the comments she had made, which a short time ago she would have considered to be outrageously impertinent.

Margaret stared out of the window, not seeing the castle or Ben Caraig any more, but seeing a housing scheme in the suburbs of Manchester. "It was spent in a bungalow, in a row of other bungalows, the sort that have unlined curtains and plastic gnomes in the gardens. They had names like *Hopalong* and *Justwetoo*. Ours was called *Nirvana*. It was written on a wooden disc that dangled over the door."

Shirley thought of the elegance of the house at Sevenoaks. The suburbs of Manchester must have been a long time ago, when love was new and beautiful and there was no inkling of the prosperity that lay ahead, before the drawn-out, sordid end.

"Nirvana is a beatific spiritual condition, attained by the extinction of desire," Shirley said. "I discovered that a few days ago when I was doing *The Times* crossword."

"I don't suppose the people who named our house knew about that," Margaret said, amused. "I don't think it was a very apt name. But it's attractive."

Another lorry rumbled by. It was followed by a car, the driver and the front-seat passenger dutifully wearing seat-belts.

"Tourists," Shirley said. "Summer's on the way."

"Prosperity," Margaret said. "So long as they use our shops and don't come here laden with provisions from their hometown supermarkets."

The car had stopped at the post office. Soon it would reverse and drive away, for there was little holiday accommodation available at Kilcaraig.

"It'll be a different matter when Caraig village is complete," Margaret said. "Aunt Marian was never convinced that we could be sure of getting the right sort of tenants."

"We can rely on Niall to see to that." Shirley had talked about this over and over with Colin. "We couldn't be in better hands."

The risk was enormous, and whether it would be for better or for worse, only time would tell.

*　　*　　*

Motti had been in Dublin for a week, and when she returned to Clonbracken she found the house badly in need of her attention.

Francesca could be relied on to produce perfect meals, but not to use a vacuum cleaner or touch a duster. Bridget considered the nursery to be the limit of her domestic activities, and it was Briano who had made some attempt to tidy the place when he wasn't busy with the car.

While she was away, Motti had been to see a friend in hospital. Long years ago she had been a ward sister before chance had brought her into contact with Isabella Connelli and she had abandoned everything in order to work for the world-famous singer.

In those days she had run Connelli's personal life, caring for her clothes and her surroundings, worshipping her, yet in a sense controlling her. Nobody could approach Connelli without first encountering Motti, who was a fierce guardian, over-protective, over-zealous, cramping, though she did not realize this, Connelli's ability to express herself as a woman, preventing her from discovering how to manage her fame. Now, as she saw the dead flowers in the vases, the accumulation of ash in the fireplaces, she realized that she was needed here. She could not go back to nursing, as that visit to the hospital had prompted her to do. Mrs. Lamont was a very different person from Madame Connelli. Mrs. Lamont had a husband to look after her, and Madame Connelli had only had Motti. But Mrs. Lamont needed someone to tidy up after her, just as Madame Connelli had done. No one else would be as indulgent, as untiring in her devotion. Motti went to the cupboard and brought out the vacuum cleaner. The hospital could do without her. Madame could not.

While Motti was resigning herself to a life far from the care of the sick, Isabella was preparing to take Benedict out in his pram. She could push him to the village, then let him walk. His progress was always slow, for he greeted everyone he met with his bewitching smile, and the apples and chocolates and packets of crisps that were thrust into his small hands were a source of amusement and of pride to her. He was one year and a month old, appropriately having been born on St. Valentine's Day.

Isabella was accepted with calm in the village now. People used to stare at her and whisper "Connelli". Often they asked for her autograph, or if they could take a photograph of her. It was only gradually that they discovered the malady which had driven her into early retirement was that she was deaf. Then she had to acknowledge their sympathy, but she never had to endure their amusement. For a famous *prima donna* to be deaf was recognized by all the world as a tragedy, nothing to laugh about. She had said so in her television appeal, which she undertook out of a strong sense of duty. Singing to people was one thing, speaking to millions with an accent she knew to be very weird was quite another.

The result of her appeal had been overpowering. The money had poured in, but it could be years and years before the real message she had wanted to impress upon her audience would reach their hearts. Deafness was more than a handicap. It could mean total isolation. It could wreck the personality. It was no laughing matter.

"Benedict, you'll sit down or I'll have to put you in your harness like a baby," she admonished him, as she pushed him down the drive, past the big field where Brunnhilde and her progeny roamed freely. Benedict's lips drooped for a moment, but he sat down and beamed at her, then he started his "la-la-la", inviting her to sing.

She had found singing difficult ever since the night of Aunt Marian's death. Everyone said it was a wonderful way to go, sitting there in her chair, listening to the songs she loved the best. Isabella didn't think so. When she died, she would want to be held in someone's arms. She wouldn't want to die alone in an armchair by the fireside. She would want to be close to Rorie.

"La-la-la." Peremptory now.

She opened the gate, and remembered to close it after her when she had pushed the pram through. Rorie never scolded her for her forgetfulness or untidiness, and every day she resolved to do better, to be the model wife she wanted to be. She was always procrastinating. She wanted to ask Mara to stay. She wanted to know how one tracked down a Welshman called David Trevor without letting anyone know she was on his trail.

"La-la-la-laa-la. La-la-la-laa-la," Benedict continued, seeing that his mother was ignoring him.

Isabella caught her breath. Out here, with no distraction, she could make out the tune. *"Child in a Manger, Infant of Mary."* They had sung it several times since they were at Kilcaraig, because although it had become the popular song *Morning Is Broken* the original words and the music were composed by natives of Mull.

She let him go on, not wanting to prompt him. He was like a record that had stuck, but he only needed a little help. When she joined with him, he could sing it all.

"La-la-la-laa-la," she began again. He bounced with pleasure and added his part. They had reached the end of the lane, and the village was round the corner. They would have to stop singing presently, because she couldn't go carolling through the street. Her voice always attracted attention, always had, perhaps it always would.

"Once more with feeling," she said to Benedict, as Bardini had so often said to her, then she turned the pram to cross the road.

She did not hear the car as it approached. When it hit the pram, her screams combined with the screaming of the brakes.

71

Rorie was heavy-lidded from want of sleep, but he would not leave Isabella's bedside. They had put her in a side-ward, the one usually used for the dying, because there had been nowhere else.

Benedict was fast asleep in Rorie's arms. He was covered in scratches from the bramble-bush into which he had been catapulted, but X-rays had shown that he was none the worse for his experience. It was the driver of the car who had come off badly, because he had slewed into the ditch, sustaining a broken nose, broken ribs, and a bad cut on the forehead.

Isabella stirred, moaning a little. She had been given an injection of some sort, to make her sleep at night, and this worried Rorie who would have preferred her to regain consciousness before she slept, so that she would know that Benedict was alive. He had been told about the screams, which brought people running out of shops and houses. Many of them had added their own screams when they saw the shattered pram.

It was a young man who had seen the baby in the bush and had shouted to the hysterical mother that he was all right, but he couldn't make her hear, he just could not make her hear. Then she had collapsed and the ambulance had arrived. Rorie, attending a meeting in Cork, was alerted, and he drove like one possessed to the hospital. He knew that his son was safe, but Isabella would not know this, and only he would be able to make her understand.

A nurse came in and found him slumped forward, his head resting on the bed, Benedict still sleeping in his arms. She touched Rorie gently and tried to remove Benedict.

"You can sleep in Sister's room," she said.

"No, I must stay with my wife. She's deaf. And I must keep our son."

All of the nursing staff knew the identity of the patient. They had been warned not to let a word about the accident get into the papers, until there had been time to warn the relatives, but despite precautions there was a photograph of the pram and of the unconscious Isabella in an evening paper, and the story was transmitted on the television news.

As dawn broke, there was a telephone call from Kilcaraig. Rorie knew that his mother would take action at the first opportunity. Now he was told that she was leaving Mull by the first boat. She could be in Cork by the afternoon. He needed her. In his shock, he had wanted to cry "Mummy, Mummy", as he had done as a child.

When Benedict was removed from the bush, he had cried "Mum, Mum", and then he had laughed because he saw her lying there, safe and sound, asleep. Now he woke up and saw her again, still asleep.

"Mum. Mum."

She stirred and opened her eyes.

"Mum. Mum." He held out his arms to her.

"No!" she said. "No!" And she turned her back on him, moaning.

"Isabella." Rorie tapped her shoulder and could feel her recoil. "Isabella. He's all right," he said, close to her ear.

Benedict's mouth was drooping. Never before in his life had he been rejected. He was dazed and looked to his father for action.

Rorie took one look at the child, bewildered, covered in scratches, trying not to cry. Incensed, he did what he had been taught to do to someone in hysterics. He slapped Isabella on the face. She sat up in bed, astonished, rubbing her cheek, while Benedict let out a roar that would penetrate even the deafest of ears. She didn't respond, she flung herself on her face, shaking as if she had a fever.

Rorie took the howling baby in his arms and left the room, while a nurse hurried towards him from the ward.

*   *   *

"Mama, what am I going to do?" It was evening. Grania had come straight to the hospital from the airport, and it was she who had organized an ambulance to take Isabella to Clonbracken. She knew that Motti had been a nurse, and she remembered from the war years very well how terrible could be the effect of shock.

"Be patient. Give her love."

"She won't touch Benedict."

"Rorie, she's terrified because of what she saw. Then Benedict, bruised and bloody, haunting her – accusing her."

"You mean she thinks he's a ghost? But that's sick!"

"She is sick, Rorie. You've heard of being sick with fright. That doesn't necessarily mean vomiting. It can mean the way Isabella is now."

"Will she recover?" His anguish was in his voice. Grania put her arm round his shoulder, comforting him as she did when he was a child.

"Of course she'll recover. It'll take a little while because as well as being in shock, she's deaf. We can't communicate with her as we should do, and we don't really know anything about her."

Rorie ran his fingers through his hair, like a stage gesture of despair. "I hit her," he said. "I slapped her face. Her father used to hit her when she was a baby. That's one of the few things I do know about her childhood, one of the few things she's remembered, because she couldn't possibly forget."

Grania felt herself stiffen, and guessed that Rorie was too much occupied with his thoughts to notice it. Isabella had spoken the truth about her father. He had done her irreparable damage, but she had loved him all the same. She had called her son after him.

"Isabella's a forgiving sort of person. She'll forgive you, when she knows the dreadful state of mind you were in."

Bridget appeared, holding Benedict by the hand. He crowed with pleasure when he saw his grandmother, and toddled towards her. Instinctively Grania recoiled, then held out her arms to receive him. She knew now what Isabella had felt like. The child's face was like pulp, but the wounds were superficial and would soon disappear.

"She couldn't bear to look at him because she couldn't bear the guilt," she said under her breath to Rorie. "Take him to her again, but take him in the dark."

"We're never in the dark. We sleep with the light on so that if she needs me, she can see what I say." Rorie thought of the first time he had slept with Isabella. It was as if it were a portent of what was to come. "*You are too beautiful to be in the dark.*" Then he had caressed her, knowing her shyness, yet seeing her urgent response.

Benedict looked from his grandmother to his father, sure that they were talking about his uncomfortable adventure, but unable to say anything about it. Confused, he put his thumb in his mouth and fell asleep.

Grania studied him, blood caked even on his eye-lashes. Then she said, "Go back to her now. You are the only person who can communicate with her properly. Explain to her that Benedict is hardly even hurt. He only looks a bit bloody and that will be over in a few days' time. And remember that the shock of finding him still alive is similar, in a way, to the shock of believing him dead."

Rorie went up to the bedroom, afraid of what he was going to find. Nobody knew, as he did, what Isabella was like when she was in the throes of anguish. Nobody knew how afraid he could be.

486

She had got out of bed and was sitting in front of her looking-glass. She didn't turn when he came into the room, but he knew she would feel him. She always did.

He put his hands gently on her shoulders, then kissed the cheek that he had slapped. "I'm sorry," he said.

She stared woodenly into the mirror.

"Isabella, it's all over now. It's all right. Benedict is downstairs with Mama. He thinks his adventure was a huge joke."

No reply.

Rorie released her, physically conscious of her misery.

She stood up and walked to the door. "I want to sleep in another room."

"Isabella! Isabella, I've said I'm sorry. I'm ashamed – I only wanted to rouse you, not to hurt you." He knew she didn't hear him because she didn't want to hear.

"I want to sleep in another room. The only thing I can do is sing. I can't cook. I can't sew. I can't keep the house tidy. I can't take care of my baby. I can only get him killed. I want to be alone. To sleep alone. To die alone." She sank to the ground, sobbing.

Rorie knelt down beside her, loving her, stroking her, broken by despair.

*   *   *

Grania returned almost immediately to Kilcaraig. Her presence at Clonbracken would irritate rather than console. Isabella and Rorie would be more at ease if they were left on their own. It was impossible for Rorie to cover up the morose mood into which Isabella was plunged.

Benedict sensed that being hurtled into a painful and prickly bed had in some way upset his mother. He had not meant to do anything wrong. His lips drooped as he played disconsolately with his bricks and waited to hear her footsteps approaching the nursery, but she never came.

Rorie had moved into a spare bedroom, temporarily he hoped. Every day, Isabella accepted a cup of tea in the morning, but refused breakfast. Then she would put on her dressing-gown and stay in her room. She refused to see the doctor when he came to call, and worse, she refused to see Father Malachy.

"What am I going to do?" Rorie asked the priest who had known her so well in the past, who still remained her friend and sometimes her confessor.

"Keep her with you, whatever happens, keep her with you. Her whole world is falling apart. Her career is finished. Aunt Marian, whom she adored, is dead. Because of her inadequacy her son could have been killed. Think about it, Rorie. Keep her with you, however difficult it may be."

"What else would you suggest I do with her?" Rorie spoke with the hollowness of fear in his breast.

"She'll want to go back to the Sisters. The convent gave her refuge in the past. She'll want to go home."

"This is her home, Father."

"She'll want to go home."

When Father Malachy had driven off in his rusty little car, Rorie went up to Isabella. She was lying on the bed, wearing her dressing-gown. She had not eaten her lunch. He tried to feed her, but she turned away from him. He took away the tray and gave it to Motti in the kitchen.

"She'll eat when she's hungry," Motti said, but he knew that she was as bewildered and anxious as he was himself.

It became the pattern of Isabella's life. She never put on anything but her dressing-gown, she picked at her meals, and she answered Rorie in monosyllables. She wore no make-up. She never went to the nursery, and when Benedict was brought to her, she gave him an absent-minded pat, but never a kiss, although he held up his face to her expectantly. Sometimes she said to Rorie, "I want to go home". Remembering Father Malachy's words, he ignored her request.

What puzzled him was that, although she ate virtually nothing, she was getting fat.

"She never sings," Motti said. "She always kept up her physical exercises, but now that's stopped, so her muscles are getting flabby. The same will be happening to her vocal chords."

"Motti, is she insane?"

Motti looked shocked. "You've seen her like this before, but only for brief spells. Between us all, we'll help her over it."

Isabella continued her brooding silence, and her figure spread under her dressing-gown, now visibly stretched across her hips.

It was weeks later, by accident, that Rorie found the sweet wrappings. Silver foil, toffee papers of every kind. They were stuffed into a box in her wardrobe. Isabella had always tended to drop things carelessly on the floor.

Rorie picked up the box and confronted her with it.

"Where did all these come from?"

She tossed up her chin defiantly. "Bridget buys me sweets. I ask her to. Is it a crime?"

"Why didn't you ask me – if you want them?"

"Because you don't love me any more."

488

"Isabella!" He had her by the shoulders, captive. She struggled for a moment, then stood stiffly, resisting him. "How can you think such a thing? You're my life. You know that I love you. Tell me you know."

She shook her head. She didn't know. She didn't even know what he had said. She only knew that years ago he had held her just like this. He had been a stranger then, but ten minutes later he had become her lover. Her hands dropped limply to her side. Her surrender. It had always been this way. Rorie picked her up in his arms, feeling the weight of her, she who had been light as a child, but he loved her more tenderly than he had loved her before. She had been lost and she was found.

He crushed her under him on the bed, her tangled red hair spread over the pillow, her breath coming in big, hungry gasps.

Motti, passing in the corridor, quietly closed the door.

72

Mrs. Craig was kept busy in the post office, because once Mrs. Rorie had recovered from the terrible shock of her experience everyone in the district wanted to send her "get well" cards and other good wishes, and to meet together to compare her replies. These she had written herself, each one of them worded differently, and none of the recipients realized what a task it had been, or how much she had appreciated their concern and kindness.

Grania had been to the hospital, and had visited the driver of the car before she left Cork. He was a British tourist who had been on a motoring holiday in Ireland.

"Worse than his physical injuries is his guilt and shock, but it wasn't his fault, it wasn't his fault at all," she told them in the post office, confirming the reports and reconstructions that had been in the newspapers. "It wasn't just that she didn't hear him. She didn't see him. She was so much absorbed in what she was doing that she just didn't look."

That was what Isabella had read in the newspapers, and it had increased her wretchedness, her agony and self-reproach. She had been so much absorbed in her singing that she just didn't look.

Catriona had been more upset by the mishap to Benedict than had any of the rest of the family. As soon as Rorie pronounced Isabella fit to receive visitors, she left Ardcross in the care of the two assistants who had replaced Marilyn and Jane when their year in Britain was over, and she left Iain in the care of Veronique. Then she flew to Cork.

Hector met her at the airport.

"You!" she said, as surprised to see him as she had been when she had met him at the castle on the eve of Niall and Josanne's wedding.

"Rorie suggested I came, so I got a couple of days' leave." He had not kissed her. His expression was impassive. He took her case from the customs officer and carried it to the car, Rorie's car.

She settled in the seat beside him, staring ahead of her, not knowing what to say.

"What have you done with all those people who clutter up your house?" he asked.

She told him what she had done. "They're all very nice about it, and they won't mind if standards drop a bit. I've learnt a lot about people since I've taken P.G.s. And it's our house, Hector, not mine. Please accept that, for Iain's sake, if for nothing else."

He drove on. He said nothing. When they reached Clonbracken, they had to negotiate the drive carefully because Brunhilde was lying across it and refused to move.

Rorie and Isabella were waiting for them at the front door, and Benedict tottered towards them, holding out his arms. His lips drooped when he saw that Iain wasn't with them, but he was snatched up in his uncle's arms, and swung onto his shoulders.

"He's been following Hector around like a puppy ever since he arrived yesterday," Isabella said, leading Catriona upstairs to her bedroom. It was a spacious room with twin beds. Hector's brushes were on a chest of drawers, and his brief-case was propped against a chair.

"I don't think people should pry into other people's belongings," Isabella said, indicating the brief-case. "But I do suggest that you have a look inside that. It's not full of Top Secret Admiralty papers. It may give you a talking point, which I'm afraid you both need just now, don't you?"

Catriona prodded the case with her toe. "I wouldn't dare touch it. Hector doesn't get furious. He just gets cold and moody and dark."

Isabella gave her a puzzled look. Perhaps she had not heard her. She looked round the room to make sure everything was in order, peered into the bathroom, and noted that the right number of towels were on the rail, and then said she must go and see how preparations for dinner were progressing. Isabella the *diva* could be Isabella the housewife when she was with Catriona, who was the only member of the family who had never seen her on the stage.

For two days, Benedict clung to Hector and Catriona clung to Isabella, who was almost always with Rorie, for the deterioration in her hearing was noticeable, and she rarely dispensed with her hearing-aid, and Rorie could communicate with her without trouble. In some strange way his dependence upon her was as great as hers upon him.

Hector and Catriona flew to London together, but they parted at Heathrow, and Catriona flew on to Scotland. She had arranged to spend a night at Kilcaraig to give a first-hand report of what was happening at Clonbracken, before she returned to Ardcross to sort out any problems which might have arisen during her three days' absence. Hector was right about one thing. Paying guests, however amiable, were a tie.

She had plenty to think about on her journey. She had examined the contents of Hector's brief-case, but had not dared to admit to him that she had done so. What she had discovered had opened up a whole new area of hope and encouragement for herself, for Hector, and for their marriage, and she found that Isabella had also recognized that this was so. It was how to approach the matter, how to use this information, that presented her with so many difficulties. She and Isabella agreed that Aunt Marian had been planning something for the benefit of the MacNeill family when she died.

Although she spent the night at Caraig Lodge, Catriona and her parents dined at the castle, and Catriona went over there early enough to be able to see the childen before they went to bed. She found Josanne with them in the nursery.

"Is Benedict as angelic at home as he was when he was here?" Josanne asked, having sorted out a dispute between Roddy and Anne over a toy tractor.

"He's always angelic, but at the same time he's well disciplined. I don't know how they do it. They can even take him out sailing. I wouldn't dare to take Iain. He'd fall overboard," Catriona said.

Rorie and Isabella had taken up sailing some two years ago. Hector had been summoned to Cork, ostensibly to be consulted by Rorie, but actually to give his support to the venture, which Roderick and Grania thought was madness in view of Isabella's disability, and her tendency to sea-sickness if there was a suggestion of a swell. But Isabella had discovered that there was a yacht for sale at Court-macsherry, and that it was called *Falcon*.

"It's a sturdy little sloop, heart of oak and all that – none of your fibre-glass for them!" Hector had reported. "There's a tiny galley, and a very primitive loo. I gave it my blessing because they obviously intended to buy it anyhow, and Rorie's a skilled yachtsman. He'll keep Isabella under control."

"I can't imagine Isabella sailing a boat," Josanne said to Catriona now. She had tried to do so herself and had failed.

"She doesn't," Catriona said. "She can learn the whole of an opera without any trouble, but Rorie can't din into her which side is port and which is starboard, or that a sheet is a rope and not a sail. So *Falcon* has a front and a back, a left and a right, and Isabella sits around looking decorative while Rorie does the work. She accepts that nautical language is one she'll never learn."

By the time the children were in bed, Grania and Roderick were having drinks with Niall in the library. Catriona asked for her customary gin and tonic, and she sat on the rug in front of the fire, soaking in the comfort and peace of the bygone days when she had taken happiness for granted, and had looked upon Josanne as the biggest threat to family harmony that she would ever encounter in her life.

It wasn't late when they returned to Caraig Lodge. She had undressed and was ready for bed when Grania came in to say goodnight to her. Catriona, slender under her Victorian-style night-dress, was sitting on a Chippendale chair, removing the varnish from her nails.

"You look exactly like the only photograph I ever saw of my mother," Grania said. "There's some very strong gene carried on our family."

"What happened to the photograph? I've never seen it."

"Oh, it perished years ago. It was destroyed." Grania tossed off the words, for that moment of truth was etched on her memory – the years of incomprehension that had followed, and the confrontation with Evelyn, without which her whole life could have been different.

She had come into this room tonight to talk to Catriona about what she saw as the gathering storm over Ardcross. The reminder of what a word out of place could lead to made her change her mind.

Catriona got into bed and picked up a book from her bedside table.

"Don't read all night," Grania said, moving forward to kiss her goodnight. "What are you reading?"

"They're sea stories, reprinted from an American magazine." Catriona turned over the pages and handed her the book.

"*The Loss of the Iolaire* by Lapwing," Grania read. "That's a true story. The *Iolaire* was bringing troops home on leave on New

Year's Day in 1919, and she foundered on the rocks as she approached Stornoway harbour. It was a terrible tragedy." Her eyes flickered down the page. "This is very vividly written, beautifully described."

"Hector wrote it," Catriona said. "Writing was always his hobby, and Lapwing was some silly pet-name when he was at prep-school. He always said he'd use it as a pen-name if he ever blossomed into print. But I didn't know he had. He didn't tell me."

"How did you find out?"

"From Isabella. Aunt Marian knew, and when Adrian Ferguson came for the funeral, he collected all her private documents, as she had asked him to do, and burnt Isabella's letters to her there and then, as you know. But there were bundles of manuscript, typewritten and unidentified, which he sent to Isabella because he thought they might be something to do with her, as they were all kept together."

Grania closed the book and gave it back to Catriona. "So Isabella was in the secret too!"

"Not really. She stumbled upon it when Benedict opened Hector's brief-case and some similar manuscripts fell out. She did the obvious and asked him about it. He wasn't annoyed. He gave her this book, but I didn't dare ask him about it. Isabella says I should tell him I know."

"I wouldn't pay much attention to Isabella's advice. You might consider it some time, when your domestic barometer is set fair."

"Which it won't be, unless I cave in and sell Ardcross, which I won't do. Never. It's Iain's home."

Grania recounted her conversation with Catriona when she and Roderick were in bed.

"We can't interfere," he said, stroking her hair, as he had always done when she lay worrying beside him. "She's talked to you now. That's a step in the right direction."

"But first she talked to Isabella of all people – Isabella who can't even hear properly what has been said."

There was no reply, but Grania knew that Roderick was thinking thoughts that he wouldn't express to her, because he wouldn't want to hurt her.

"I try so hard to love her," she said after a while.

He continued to stroke her hair until he knew by her breathing that she had fallen asleep peacefully, contentedly, the personal conflicts which she fought against daily temporarily overcome.

*   *   *

"I should have known by the way the wind was blowing, and by the colour of the sky," Shirley said to Colin Craig. He had picked her up at the Kilcaraig boundary cattle-grid, because she had gone for a walk unprepared for the downpour which had drenched her to the skin.

Colin had seen her set out, and had put petrol in the estate Landrover, ready to rescue her. He could read the weather as she could not.

"You've been here for nearly eight months," he said. "You've learnt a lot, but understanding the weather is maybe something that's inherited, like having the sea in your blood."

"And having an eye for a beast." She looked at him obliquely. He was driving very slowly, as if the Landrover was a delicate little car.

"What has that to do with it?"

"Niall Lamont says he's astonished at your judgement when you go to the cattle sales at Oban. He says you're wasted as an engineer. You should be a farmer. And breed stock that'll win gold medals at all the shows."

"There aren't gold medals at the shows, and Niall is far too cautious to say such things. You're getting imaginative, like his wife. Whenever she comes to see Caraig, she has fresh flights of fancy about the people who'll live there. She thinks the descendants of the people who survived the coffin-ships will return, and bring not only prosperity, but the ancient families back to Mull."

"That's not such a flight of fancy. Niall Lamont has had an enquiry from a MacQuarry in Australia who had read about the re-building of Caraig village in the *Oban Times*." Shirley could see Colin's face reflected in the wing mirror, and she knew that she had caught his attention.

"Who told you that?"

"Josanne, as a matter of fact. Ever since I went for a walk with Catriona MacNeill last Christmas, I've made some headway here. I'm no longer regarded as a pariah, but you've been too busy with your blueprints and your over-seeing even to notice."

"I heard you'd been to the Farmers' Dinner at Pennyghael with Peter MacPhail, and to a badminton tournament at Bunessan, and that you're often at Caraig Lodge and the castle."

"And where did you hear all that?"

"There's a lot of chat on the building-site. Most of the work is being done by local people." He let her think about that for a while, as a herd of cows was plodding homeward along the road, weaving from side to side, blocking the way. Then he said, "Now that you're spreading your wings, when will you be flying away?"

"I'll never leave Aunt Margaret."

"She thinks you're stagnating here."

"She's the one who's stagnating. She won't budge beyond the Kilcaraig boundaries."

"It's a curious twist of fate that brought her back here, where her forebears belong, to lick her wounds. But she'll pull out of that some day. The Manse is on a three-year lease. What then?"

"Who's been gossiping to you about her?"

"It's just the general talk. Memories are long here, and at the Remembrance Sunday service, she remarked that her grandmother was a MacDonald from Caraig Farm. After that it was all pieced together. One of the daughters had married an Italian and had emigrated with him to Australia. They had a daughter who become a quite well-known opera singer, Mara Sevilla. Your Aunt Margaret. She had a breakdown of some sort and retired. But she knew Sir Adrian Ferguson, who is trustee to whoever it is who bought the Manse. He arranged for her to rent it. So there you have it, in a nutshell."

"I don't believe a word of it!"

"If it's a lie I'm telling you, it's a lie I was given."

Shirley knew the expression well. It was a literal translation from the Gaelic.

"Will you please drop me off here? I'd rather walk now that the rain has stopped. I don't want to discuss Aunt Margaret's private affairs with you or with anyone else!"

He pulled into a lay-by, but she had jumped down from her seat before he could get round to open the door for her.

"See that you have a hot bath when you get home," he said. "We don't want you catching your death." He drove off, splashing her as his wheels sank into an enormous puddle.

She was crimson with vexation when she reached the Manse.

Margaret, who had been playing the piano and singing softly to herself, stopped as soon as she heard Shirley's footsteps on the stairs. Presently she heard the bath water running, and knew that she would be safe to practise singing for a little longer, until the screaming of the water re-filling the cistern in the attic stopped. She was tired of being so furtive, realizing that she was being neurotic and absurd. Isabella was almost certainly right. The things one most feared turned out not to matter very much after all.

Shirley came in, wearing a dressing-gown. Her hair was still wet from the rain. Margaret stiffened, but remained at the piano, apparently absent-mindedly fingering some scales.

"I went for a walk and got caught in that downpour and got

rescued by that horrible Colin Craig," Shirley said. "He hasn't looked at me for weeks. He's boorish and a gossip, and I hope he fries in hell!"

"He's been busy on the building-site."

"He's been busy prying into matters that are no affair of his. He'd never have picked up anything from his mother. She's the soul of discretion – everyone knows that." Shirley had moved over to the piano. "What was that you were singing just now? It was so lovely that I thought for a moment it was the radio."

Margaret's head was bent, but the colour was creeping over her neck. "It's one of Moore's *Irish Melodies*," she said. "*When Love Is Kind*."

"Love's never kind!" Shirley leaned over and read the words, pretending to be absorbed in them while her thoughts raced on. She should grasp this opportunity to repeat what Colin had said, what she herself had suspected for some time.

"Sing the rest – please, Aunt Margaret. Like you were doing just now."

Margaret struck a chord and sang very softly –

> "Love must, in short
> Keep fond and true
> Through good report,
> And evil too.
>
> Else here I swear
> Young love may go
> For aught I care –
> To Jericho!"

She gave full voice to the last line, and leaned back, laughing. "You can hear that I haven't sung for ages," she said.

"But you used to sing a lot, didn't you. Professionally?" She had taken the plunge. She waited for the denial.

"It was a long time ago." Margaret closed the song-book. "It's time to get supper, and I haven't fed Bliss."

"She'll come when she's hungry. She's asleep on my bed. Aunt Margaret – were you ever Mara Sevilla?"

Margaret was putting the song-book back in the cupboard where it belonged. "How long have you known?"

"I browse around in the library at the castle. At first I thought the photographs of her looked like you. Then one day, I saw your copy of *A Mingled Chime* in your bedroom, and the inscription inside – 'Mara. Thanks for the memory. P'."

496

"You worked it all out, didn't you?"

"I would never have told you, but that odious Colin has discovered part of it. Who you are, because the people on this island seem to trace their ancestry back to the apes!"

Margaret laughed. "I think your odious Colin has done me a good turn. I've been neurotic and absurd about the past. I've allowed a safety-curtain to divide two parts of my life. Now it's raised, and suddenly it doesn't matter any more." She paused to listen. There was a gentle scratching sound outside the door. "That's Bliss, honing with hunger, and I'm starving too." She opened the door carefully, and picked up Bliss, who covered her face with cat kisses.

Shirley saw that the episode was over without apologies or tears, thanks, perhaps, to the intervention of a little grey cat.

"Now that the truth is out, you must practise properly, and I do hope I'll be able to get those discs back from the castle – the ones you gave Aunt Marian," she said, and followed Margaret to the kitchen.

While Shirley spooned cat-food into a feeding bowl, and Bliss rubbed herself against her legs, purring loudly, Margaret was inspecting the casserole which was in the simmering oven of the Aga, and Colin Craig was standing at the side window in his bedroom. In the summer, with no lights on, it was impossible to know about the movements of the occupants of the Manse. Not that it mattered to him anyhow. Men approaching forty years old had better things to think about than a slip of a girl, whom he would never get to know, because of the binoculars that were focused upon him on the rare occasions when he met her.

He turned away from the window, brushed his hair, and added a few lines to the missive he had written to Rorie Lamont. He was becoming the confidante of all the members of the Lamont family, and sometimes their activities amounted to the nonsensities of a French farce. They were all so busy trying to help one another surreptitiously, yet inevitably the day would come when the truth leaked out.

As it had done over Mara Sevilla. He should never have said what he did. Shirley Morris was probably telling her all about it now, and she would be upset, and he had done a lot of harm just because he wanted to show off to a silly little girl.

There he was, back on the old, familiar theme.

He went downstairs and franked his letter himself, pushing it into the mail-bag. There was nothing secret about it, and his mother wouldn't ask questions, but his feeling of being under surveillance persisted.

He strolled outside and paused at the War Memorial. There was no one in sight, but there was a pleasant smell of peat, as fires were either being lighted or stoked up for a comfortable evening on this dank summer's day.

Grania, in her sun-room, put down the binoculars. "Colin Craig's having his evening moon-around," she said. "I think he had a brush with Shirley somewhere along the road. I saw him set out in the Landrover, and I saw him come back alone, and she followed a few minutes later, wet and bedraggled, so he must have passed her on the way."

Roderick looked up from his crossword. "Lovers' quarrel," he said.

"They don't know one another well enough for that. A few months ago, I'd have been livid at the thought of an incomer snatching an eligible local, but Margaret says she's pure gold, and she should know." She sat beside Roderick, helping him with his puzzle, so she didn't see that Shirley had emerged from the Manse and was walking, with Bliss at her heels, towards the War Memorial.

"I'm afraid I've been a bit scratchy," Shirley said as she approached Colin.

He swung round. He hadn't expected her to come to him. "And I've been a bit boorish," he said.

They walked along the road towards the village hall, and Bliss followed. Neither of them could think of anything to say, and when they spoke, they both spoke together. Their obvious self-consciousness made them laugh, and it was better after that. Bliss, seeing that they were going beyond the hall, gave an apologetic "prrrr", and made for home. She had walked far enough.

"Everyone will be watching us," Shirley said as they picked their way across the footpath that led to the banks of Loch Caraig.

"How much do you mind?"

"For myself, not at all. But it's different for you."

They stood by the loch, close to the place where Rorie had stood with his mother on the night of Catriona's wedding, and had finally realized that Isabella was the most important woman in his life.

Colin picked up a stone and tossed it skilfully. It skimmed across the loch and brought about agitated protests from a number of ducks who were hidden in the reeds.

Shirley moved closer to him. Someone must take the initiative.

"Let's go to the boat-house," she said.

"Temptress!"

"If you say so!"

He laughed and put his arm round her shoulders. "We'll go there but we won't go inside."

They walked along the marshy banks of the loch, pausing occasionally to examine the flowers or pebbles that caught their eye. They had nearly reached the boat-house when Colin tilted up Shirley's chin, and kissed her very gently on the mouth.

"You can do better than that," she said, her eyes shining.

He could and he did. She was breathless when he released her, and half amazed that she had thrown herself at him, when she should have lured him on to approach her in his own way, on his own terms.

It was becoming dark as they retraced their steps.

"I'm a tramp, and you think I'm cheap," she said, realizing that she was dishevelled, and that quarrelling with him came more naturally than kissing him.

"Time will tell what we think about one another when we know one another better," he said, with the wisdom of his forty years.

Satisfied that at least some sort of relationship had been established between them, Shirley returned home with him, finding Bliss waiting patiently at the bumpy bridge.

73

There were workmen at the Manse again, and this time they had come from the mainland, because they were doing a specialized job – sound-proofing the drawing-room.

"It has to be the drawing-room," Mara told Josanne. "There's no room for the piano in the sitting-room. And it must be very sound-proof – I couldn't bear to think that people going to the post office will hear me practising scales."

"You'll come up to us and make use of the music-room. It was fixed up for Isabella before we knew how little she'd be here. She'd love you to have it."

But Mara was adamant. She had admitted to Shirley just how much her voice had deteriorated during the past years. She wasn't going to risk anyone at all hearing what she sounded like on the cassette recorder they had bought through Mrs. Craig's Book.

Such people of Kilcaraig who had not already discovered her secret had accepted with their usual equanimity the fact that Mrs. Sedley had once been a singer of quite considerable renown. They would have been a great deal more impressed if they had heard that she had once won a medal at the Mod, the Gaelic Eisteddfod. Besides, they had Isabella Connelli. Compared with her, no singer was of any great consequence, nor ever would be.

"The owner of the house doesn't seem to care what you do with it," Shirley remarked one day, as she and Margaret and Sandy MacPherson were having coffee together in the kitchen.

"It's entirely in Sir Adrian Ferguson's hands. He has complete control," Margaret said.

"He's a nice, humble man, even if he's English," Sandy observed. He had never heard of the Race Relations Board.

"Ferguson's a Scottish name," Shirley pointed out.

"Oh well, he's not a Muileach." Sandy picked up his cap and made for the garden, where he was doing something mysterious to the compost heap. He turned back at the door. "That means he doesn't belong to Mull," he said, as if they didn't know.

A few days later, Rorie telephoned from Clonbracken. Shirley took the call, because Margaret was practising in the now completed drawing-room, whose walls were proof against all sound.

"I'll fetch Mrs. Sedley," she said.

"No, don't bother. We just want to ask you both to come to us for a couple of weeks in August. Margaret will probably need some persuading, so you can start working on her now."

"Having her doesn't mean you have to include me. Besides, there's the house to look after, and the cat to feed."

"Sandy will see to that. And we want you to come too. Isabella wants to thank you personally – she says you've helped Margaret over her identity hurdle, or words to that effect."

"What do you mean?"

"I haven't the faintest idea – I'm quoting Isabella! I suppose it means that Mara's no longer ashamed to admit that she can sing!"

Shirley repeated the telephone conversation when Margaret emerged from the drawing-room. She had chosen a bad moment, because Margaret had made a cassette recording of herself, and pronounced it dreadful.

"I can't go to Clonbracken. I haven't even been to Oban since I came here," she said.

"If you don't go, I can't go. I've never been to Ireland and stayed with a *prima donna* who breeds pigs."

"I don't suppose many people have. But I'll sleep on it."

She did, and in the morning she told Shirley that she would accept the invitation, and that Shirley had better borrow Mrs. Craig's Book, so that she could buy herself some new shoes and a pullover or two.

"It'll be wet, like here, but I expect a little warmer. I'll ask Niall to make our travelling arrangements. I can't cope with that sort of thing."

"I can," Shirley said, greatly relieved that she had won such an easy victory. "I worked at Thomas Cook during my knocking-around days. And I'll go and see Mrs. Craig right away."

She spent the afternoon looking through the mail-order book, and she had placed her order by tea-time. Margaret had gone up to the castle, so she had the house to herself. She went into the drawing-room and saw the cassette recorder placed on a chair close to the piano. She hestitated, longing to switch it on, but after a while she pulled the plug out of the wall socket. She had stumbled upon information about Mara Sevilla, but she had never deliberately spied on her.

She was reading when Margaret returned, covered in scratches, because she had called in at Caraig Lodge on her way home, and finding that Grania was trying to clip Skittles, she had offered to help.

"Grania's wondering what Rorie and Isabella are up to," she said, sitting on the sofa. "They're having Iain and Veronique to stay, and they've persuaded Catriona and Hector to have a holiday together in the flat in Lowndes Square, the one that used to belong to Aunt Marian. She left it as a pied-a-terre in London for the family, though Hector prefers to live in an hotel near the Admiralty."

"They'll have a sticky sort of holiday," Shirley said. Catriona hadn't said much about her marriage when they went on that walk together, but she had said enough to indicate that all was not well. Besides, there was the local gossip. No one could escape from knowing that.

"Maybe Isabella has picked up the art of bringing people together, based on the long talks she used to have with Aunt Marian. If she weren't so deaf, there might be a lot of good that she could do," Margaret said.

While they were talking at Kilcaraig, Hector was awaiting the arrival of Catriona at Lowndes Square, and was having much the same thoughts. It was reasonable for Isabella to have Iain to stay, because he adored Benedict, but it was not reasonable for her to coax and cajole, until she had forced him away from his bachelor comforts and Catriona away from her confounded paying-guests, in order to spend a holiday in London, which was no fit place to be in anyhow, in July – not for country people like themselves.

He had booked seats for three theatres, and in order to please her he was taking her the next night to see *Un Ballo in Maschera* at Covent Garden. It was the first opera he had ever seen, when a schoolboy on holiday in Milan with his parents, and he had expected to be bored to distraction by such a night of culture, but instead Verdi's music had entranced him, and he had been captivated by the cute little coloratura who had sung Oscar, the page. Isabella Connelli's name had meant nothing to him then, but now it was Isabella who could ask him gently on the telephone to give his wife a good holiday, just to please her. As if he could have refused!

He heard the taxi arrive, and waited for the creak of the lift. He should have gone downstairs to help Catriona with her luggage. He should have tried to look welcoming in some way, for she would be as nervous as he was, meeting him again after having written that ridiculous letter.

"I know you write fiction. Never mind how I know," she had added as a postscript to her usual stilted report on Iain's progress and the financial affairs of Ardcross House. "If you make a success, you can give up the Navy and buy Ardcross yourself. Then will you live here?"

He heard the lift door opening, and he went out to meet her on the landing. She was tugging at a suitcase, and her handbag had slid off her shoulder.

"Sorry I didn't come to carry this for you," he said, helping to disentangle her. "If you'd said what train you were catching, I'd have come to the station."

She pushed back an errant curl. She had changed so little since he first saw her, sitting there in the heather, her head tilted, her eyes downcast because she was afraid.

He brushed her cheek with his lips, and took her case and her carrier-bag, which was very sober-looking and smart and was labelled Jenner's.

She gasped when she saw the flat. It was filled with flowers.

"Isabella ordered a flowery bower," he said. "She seems to think it'll soften my heart over Ardcross, which I daresay it would have done, if you hadn't got it into your idiotic head that writing sea-stories for American magazines is going to line my pockets with gold."

"Uncle Nicholas did very well with his books, although he never made the top ten." She had not expected him to raise the subject immediately.

"There are more authors starving in garrets than there are eating at the Savoy," he replied. "That's where I'm taking you tonight. And for the rest of our holiday I want not another word about writing fiction or coping with paying-guests."

"You strike a hard bargain," she said, the old, mocking Catriona creeping into her voice.

He put his arms round her, held her close to him for a moment. Then he showed her to the bedroom which Aunt Marian used to occupy. He had chosen Rorie's old den for himself.

* * *

Josanne and Niall had dined at Caraig Lodge. It was a small dinner-party, and the few friends who had been there had left in convoy, after the fashion of such parties on Mull. Most had long distances to drive home, and when one got up to go, the others left too.

"I've been thinking of Catriona and Hector all evening," Grania said. "Isabella means well, thrusting them together, but I don't think it'll work."

"Isabella's good deeds have a way of paying dividends in the end," Roderick said. "Look what she did for Chrissie after Aunt Marian died."

Chrissie, who had loved and served Aunt Marian all her life, had been inconsolable, but Isabella arranged for her to go to the villa in Ravello with Morag MacKinnon for company, and Briano and the Mercedes at her disposal, so that they could stay cosily in the house on the hilltop, or tour Italy at will.

Chrissie and Morag had set off, sad and reluctant, but they had returned happy and restored, both claiming that the Italian sun had cured their rheumatism, although it had been particularly cold at Ravello at that time of year.

"I've never said that she isn't generous," Grania conceded now. "When they were here after Christmas, she asked Rorie to telephone every David Trevor he could find in the telephone directory. She was quite put out when he explained that it was impossible. I don't know what her idea was. Anyway nothing came of it because of Aunt Marian's death."

Aunt Marian's death. One of those big events against which, for years and years, everything else would be measured.

"Isabella can't telephone herself," Roderick said. "I think her hearing has deteriorated badly since the accident."

"Catriona says she's not too bad, though she wears her hearing aid much more. She's trying to lose weight. I can't imagine Isabella running to fat." Josanne had been shocked when Catriona had shown her some recent snapshots of Isabella.

"Singers always get fat," Grania said. "Rorie would still adore her if she was as fat as Brunnhilde."

"Brunnhilde is so called as a compliment to the pig, not as an insult to any *prima donna*. Isabella's mad about that animal. I think she's next in line to Rorie and Benedict in her affections!"

As she spoke, Grania felt the urge, the yearning, to go to Clonbracken, to try to be at ease with Isabella and happy with Rorie. Isabella would expect her to come without waiting for an invitation. But she would never, never invite herself there. She would never understand her ambivalent feelings about Isabella.

When they left the Lodge, Niall and Josanne walked through the pine trees to the castle. They were half way home when they discovered that Skittles had followed them. Instead of going back home herself, she would whimper at the castle all night, so there was nothing for it but to scoop her up and retrace their steps. They opened the sun-room door, and she shot into the house. They could hear her screaming and scratching at the drawing-room door; then they heard loving exclamations from Grania welcoming her in.

Their footsteps were soft on the pine needles. They saw that there were two people standing on the bumpy bridge, talking softly. Colin Craig and a woman. Not Shirley, someone taller than that.

"Mara," Josanne whispered, when they were out of earshot.

"An assignation?"

"Don't be silly. They'll be plotting about Ireland. I've a hunch that Colin's going to land up at Clonbracken too."

"Is this another of your day-dreams, darling?"

"It could be an Isabella day-dream. She loves to help on a romance. I know. Once upon a time, she gave some sound advice to me."

"And it worked?"

"You know it did!" She put her arm through his, and remembered to step over the snoring Flush as they entered the hall.

The grandfather clock ticked loudly under the Kilcaraig tapestry. When they reached their bedroom, there was no one on the bumpy bridge, but the upstairs lights were on in the post office and the Manse.

74

The first thing Mara and Shirley noticed about Isabella was that she had put on weight, and that she was wearing her hearing-aid.

"I became a compulsive sweet-eater after the accident," she told them on the evening of their arrival at Clonbracken. She didn't tell them that she had been a secret compulsive sweet-eater – only Rorie knew about that. "I gained a stone in less than three weeks. It's taken six for me to lose just a few pounds."

"Compulsive eating is a sign of insecurity. You were suffering from shock," Mara said, but Isabella heard not a word of it. She was asking about the journey, and about everyone at Kilcaraig, but they were sure she wasn't hearing their answers. Rorie was clever at repeating what they said without making it too obvious, and in some strange way she was able to understand him.

Bridget brought Benedict to see them before he went to bed. He was glowing with good health, his flaming hair almost matching his rosy cheeks, and he trotted round, holding up his arms and his face to be kissed. Shirley, who was shy of children, found herself cuddling this engaging little boy with a love that was fiercely maternal. If she could be guaranteed a baby like this, she would want a child of her own. Then came the big moment when Benedict went to his mother. He stood in front of her. "La-la-la."

She laughed, and pulling him onto her knee, she sang the Brahms lullaby. After a while, he joined in, every note perfect. The performance completed, he clapped himself vigorously and la-la-ed for more.

"No," Isabella said. "Bed."

His lips drooped. He looked up imploringly.

"Bed," she said.

Shirley waited for the screams to start. She was used to being around when the children were sent up to bed at the castle.

Benedict stared hard at his mother, holding her eyes, in a mute argument, then he laughed and scrambled off her knee. He gave a quick hug at his father's left leg, then he toddled off to the door, pausing for a moment to blow a kiss to them all.

"Rorie, I believe your son is going to prove that musical genius can be carried in the genes or chromosomes or whatever it is that makes Benedict a potential phenomenon, like his mother." Mara spoke as distinctly as she could without raising her voice, and she was rewarded by Isabella being the one to reply.

"He imitates me," she said. "I sang a lot when I was pregnant, just as I sang to him when I was feeding him. He drank in music with milk. It's environment, not heredity. But like me, he has absolute pitch. We had to change the bells on the little wheel he pushes round, because they were out of tune, and this upset him." Her expressive eyes were thoughtful, and she said sadly – "I can't hear the little bells any more, but I can still hear Benedict when he sings."

Rorie moved over to her, putting his arm across her shoulders. "When Benedict laughs, it's Isabella all over again. You'll hear plenty of that while you're here. He's a happy little boy." He exchanged a look with Isabella. For five long weeks, Benedict had not been a happy little boy. It must have seemed like eternity to his baby mind. "Music is as necessary to him as food," Rorie added, to cover up for the wave of nausea he felt at the recollection of that terrible time.

"We had glowing accounts of Iain's visit," Mara said, sensing some slight tension. She didn't have to be a psychologist to realize the devastating effect that accident must have had on them all.

"After a few days, he stopped clinging to Veronique, and played for hours with Benedict. It was a great success," Rorie said.

"But he's very insecure," Isabella put in. She was almost uncannily able to follow what Rorie said. Maybe that was because she never took her eyes off him. "He can't understand why his parents spend most of their lives apart. We hope their holiday in London will have solved a problem or two."

Mara knew from Grania that Catriona had telephoned when she got back to Ardcross, and had reported that the Lowndes Square flat was in good order, and that she and Hector had been to the theatre several times. Nothing more.

"We have one life, and don't we make a mess of it," Isabella said thoughtfully.

Shirley was moved almost to tears. She had learnt a lot about Isabella from Josanne's books on opera, and listening to her records had revealed, as nothing else could, the compelling perfection of her voice.

"It wasn't you who made a mess of it," she said, speaking as distinctly as she could, and she knew that Isabella had heard her, but the reply came as a surprise.

"I wasted years that I could have spent with Rorie. My sense of values was all wrong. Music first, Rorie second, when it should have been the other way round!" But she was smiling, as if relieved that fate had made her see her mistake before it was too late.

"My wasted years were listening to pop music instead of to you," Shirley said.

"You can make up for that by watching out for her films," Rorie said. He was never far from Isabella. "They appear from time to time, in cinemas as well as on television. I expect they're kept in safe storage, like the crown jewels."

During the days that followed, Isabella's dependence on Rorie was made manifestly clear. He knew when a statement had to be repeated or interpreted to her, and although Benedict was not confined to the nursery, it was Isabella, not Benedict, who held Rorie's hand when Mara and Shirley were shown over the farm.

"Only fifty acres of it, but I could do with a manager," Rorie said, pointing out the hen houses and pig sties. "When Colin Craig has finished being a property developer, perhaps I can lure him here. He's clearly a man of many parts, and he could have plenty of time to mess around in boats."

"That's why we asked him to join us here," Isabella said. "Though I'm afraid *Falcon* isn't much good to an engineer, because she hasn't got an engine." She turned to Shirley, who was putting on an act of studied indifference. Nobody had warned her that Colin was expected at Clonbracken. "You and Colin can experience the countryside together. You can kiss the Blarney Stone and get to know one another. People can think that they're attracted to one another, until they meet often enough to find it was a chemical reaction – nothing more."

"Isabella's psychology books make her sound rather blunt at times," Rorie said, seeing Shirley's discomfiture. "All the same, there's wisdom in women, especially in my wife." He still spoke with the pride of possession. He stooped to stroke the piglet which Benedict was holding by the tail. "We'll go sailing this afternoon, then you can show off a bit when he comes with us. Mara tells me you used to sail on the Norfolk Broads."

After lunch, they set off for Courtmacsherry, where they kept *Falcon*. They left Benedict behind because the cockpit was so small.

"He looks like a football in his life-jacket," Rorie said, as he helped his guests to fasten themselves into theirs. "He needs a safety-harness all the time. He's one man we don't want to lose overboard!"

"Is anyone likely to fall out?" Mara asked, seeing the size of the cockpit and low guard-rail on the tiny deck.

Isabella had leapt nimbly from the rubber dinghy, and she held out her hand to help Mara on board. Rorie would return to the jetty for Shirley. "You needn't be afraid. Just do what Rorie tells you. He's the skipper." Then she added proudly, "I'm the mate."

She certainly knew her drill, moving about easily in her shirt and shorts and plimsolls, looking like a schoolgirl instead of a woman of over forty years old. She had a band round her head to keep her hair out of her eyes, and she was covered in the freckles she had once avoided so carefully by keeping out of the sun.

"Some day we're going to sail until we can see nothing but horizon," she said, when they were under way and she could relax, sitting on the deck with her legs dangling into the cockpit.

"Some day we're going to do nothing of the sort." Rorie intoned it like a psalm, his hand on the tiller extension, his eye on a racing dinghy that was overtaking them on the port side.

"Some skippers are very inhibiting and unadventurous," she replied, in recitative. "When we're at sea, we sing to one another, and it's amazing what I can hear."

"Come down from there, I'm changing direction." Rorie spoke his order, not expecting Mara and Shirley to join in the domestic grand opera, but Isabella heard, slithered into the cockpit, and ducked her head. The boom swung over them and there was the slight dip as they turned to starboard.

"That thing once hit me and I went home with a black eye," Isabella said. "People must have thought we were having a barney at sea."

"A mutiny," Rorie amended, kissing his mate behind her left ear.

Mara leant over and touched Isabella's hand. "Will you sing me your falcon song?"

Isabella caught her breath, momentarily taken aback. Then she jumped onto the deck, leaned against the mast, and sang the falcon's agitated little song, just as she had done when she first met Mara all those years ago, and just as exquisitely.

"Sing your Empress part. It's only a few lines," she said.

Mara laughed and shook her head, and Isabella altered her tone and sang it herself, then reverted to the falcon's anxious chirp.

508

"It's absolutely beautiful." Shirley could hardly believe her ears.

The whole afternoon was absolutely beautiful, the blue of the sea, the green of the land in the distance, and the other little ships, looking like toys on a painted ocean. There was no need to say very much, and what was said got through to Isabella, as if the sea provided a special kind of amplifier.

"We'll have to make for home," Rorie said, looking at his watch.

Shirley had found it difficult to keep her eyes off him. She had always thought of him as a good-looking man, and now she saw him in his full virility, his powerful arms controlling the ship, caring for them all, protecting Isabella. "God! I could fall in love with him," she thought in horror. Horror because it would be such an utter waste of time.

Isabella was able to help with the manoeuvre that brought them round, beating against the wind.

"I don't understand it at all," Mara said. "We should be getting blown backwards."

"It's like a cake of soap," Isabella said. "Squeeze it and it'll jump forward. You must have done it dozens of times in your bath. The wind squeezes the sheets – I mean the sails – and that presses us forward. Rorie explained it all to me. He's even better than my book."

Isabella's book on sailing small ships was a worry to Rorie, who hid it from time to time, but she always found it. It was giving her ideas beyond her capabilities.

When they reached their mooring, Isabella made tea from a kettle that had not quite boiled on the calor gas stove in the minute galley, but the number of tea-bags she used ensured that it was a good shade of dark brown. They ate ginger biscuits, which they dipped in their tea, and these helped to disguise its bitter taste.

Isabella washed up while Rorie rowed Mara and Shirley to the shore, then he went back for her, and the sound of their laughter carried across the water.

"She dropped the tea-pot into the sea when she threw out the tea-bags," Rorie said as Isabella jumped onto the jetty, and turned to help him pull up the inflatable dinghy.

"Not for the first time," Isabella said smugly. "There's enough equipment to furnish a kitchen lying there under the sea. I expect some day we'll collect it. Everything eventually gets washed ashore."

They tied the dinghy to the roof-rack and Rorie drove them home.

When they got back to Clonbracken, Motti said that Mr. Colin Craig was sailing on the *Innisfallen* that night. He would be in Cork the next morning.

"And Paolo Bardini's arriving in the afternoon. He's flying over from Paris, just for a couple of nights," Isabella said.

"What have you been up to?" Rorie asked her sternly.

"I'm going to the nursery. I haven't seen Benedict for ages." She went upstairs, leaving him laughing in the hall.

"Paolo's visit will get in the papers," Mara said anxiously.

"Not here," Rorie assured her. "He often comes. The press are marvellously thoughtful about Isabella. They leave us blissfully alone. Bardini travels incognito when he isn't flying his own plane."

"Does he know I'm here?"

"Bardini? Of course he knows – that's why he's coming. Isabella thinks it's time a few ghosts were laid, and you'll find that she's right. She's always right about people. You'll see."

Mara sighed, resigned, and followed Isabella up to the nursery.

Benedict was sitting on the floor, playing with the jack-in-the-box she had brought him as a present. He undid the catch just as she entered the room, and his laughter as the head bobbed up at him greeted her with a warmth that would dispel the most worrying of thoughts.

Isabella was kneeling beside him, while Bridget was reading a serial story in a magazine.

Mara watched Benedict push the head back on its spring, into the box, fasten it carefully, then release it, finding its re-appearance just as funny as before.

"It's a wonderful present. It keeps him going for hours," Isabella said. "I thought toys nowadays were all space-ships and suchlike. You're clever to have found something so wholesome. I expect it's got some significance we don't recognize. Shutting away something that keeps popping up."

The head was being pressed back into the box – Benedict was absorbed in a feat which required all his concentration.

Mara leaned down and kissed the back of his neck. His hair was downy. He smelled of cleanliness and he radiated happiness.

"He's lucky that it's only a clown's head that pops up at him from the box," Mara said. "When he grows up, he'll have mental boxes concealing the heads of people that disturb him. We all have."

Bridget was absorbed in her serial, and Mara had spoken more to herself than to Isabella, but to her surprise Isabella had heard and understood. "You'll enjoy Bardini popping out of his box," she said. "Nothing disturbing in that."

Benedict's lips drooped when he saw that they were going to leave him. He ran over to the door, but Isabella smiled at him and

510

gestured that he must get out of the way. Staring at her, he smiled back and obeyed.

Sign language. He was learning to speak to his mother, because that was the way it was going to be in a few years' time.

75

Shirley could scarcely keep her eyes open during dinner, and Mara, who had also felt the soporific effect of the sea, told her to go early to bed.

Rorie said that he must shut himself in his den, and pretend to put into effect all the skills he had learnt about keeping accounts when he was at the agricultural college at Cirencester. Mara knew that he had been asked by Isabella to keep out of the way, and that the chapter of her life, begun at Christmas and brought to an abrupt end after Aunt Marian's death, would now have to be told.

She went to the music-room with Isabella, who curled up on the bear-skin rug, but this time she did not remove her hearing-aid. "Please go on where you left off," she said.

Mara was sitting in a leather armchair. She had brought a cup of Irish coffee with her. Isabella was making sure that her guests would have a true Irish holiday.

"Where did I get to?" she asked. Isabella, she thought, had been through so much since that day that she had probably forgotten most of the story anyhow.

"You'd gone to the Bardinis, and Paolo had been brought from a rehearsal to confront your other Paul, your husband." Isabella would never forget that part of the story. The enormity of disturbing Paolo Bardini in rehearsal was engraved on her mind. "Then you swallowed all those sleeping pills. Begin again from there."

Mara had to think for a few moments, to straighten out her tangled memories, for so long pushed to the back of her mind. Then, with a growing sense of relief, she told her tale.

"That bottle of pills offered the final solution, in the demented state I was in," she said. "You'll have to guess what happened next. So do I, for after a while all I knew was that I was sinking into the oblivion for which I had longed. But the unexpected happened, and I woke up."

She spoke without emotion, recounting something she could have read about in a book, something that was nothing at all to do with herself.

She had found herself in bed in a small room overlooking a large garden. There were people in the garden, wandering around, some of them in groups, some of them alone, but talking to themselves. There were two adult women on a see-saw. She saw them all day and every day, and they were always on the see-saw. They never even seemed to stop and eat.

She ate very little herself, and what she ate was fed to her, at first through a tube, straight into her stomach, then, because that was so uncomfortable and she had not the will to resist, she ate what she was given. When the doctors came to see her, she had nothing to say to them. She had taken pills and she was dead. Some day they would realize it, and leave her alone.

Then one day, he came. She heard his voice outside the door before he was shown into the room. She thought she was dreaming, but he stood there at the end of the bed with a box of chocolates and a bunch of flowers in his hands, and he wore a checked sports-jacket with very blocked out shoulders, and well-pressed flannel trousers. His hair, which was thick, was ruffled as if he had been running his hands through it, trying to tidy it up.

"Mr. Trevor has come to take you home," a nurse said briskly. "If you'll be a good girl, we'll soon have you ready for him. We're just getting your clothes from the store-room."

They always talked to her like that, as if she was a child, but she never answered them. She lay there, staring ahead of her, not answering now. Mr. Trevor couldn't take her away from here. It wouldn't be legal. It must be some sort of plot.

"Nurse, if we can be alone for a little while, I'll be able to explain what has been arranged. Then Mrs. Sedley might like to consider it." He walked over to her, put the flowers and the chocolates on the bed, and laid his hand on hers.

The nurse hesitated, then left them alone.

"I'm responsible for all of this," he said. "I've been trying to find you, but for a long time your husband wouldn't tell me where you were. At last I found out the name of his lawyers, and they've been very helpful. They wanted to get you away from here, and your husband has agreed that they do as they think fit. My mother lives in Caernarvon. She'll make you very welcome until you feel well enough to face the world again."

He pressed her hand. "I'll be outside the door. Call me if you need me, and I'll come to you."

She dressed as if she were an automaton, but her fingers were clumsy, and she could not fasten the zip of the skirt. She called, "David". It was the first word she had spoken for weeks, or maybe for months.

She would never remember the long drive to Wales. They drove through the night, and they seldom spoke at all. Then there was a small house, within sound of the sea, and a motherly woman who gave them breakfast and asked no questions. After that, there was the gradual return to normal life. First a word here and there, then an offer to help with the housework, then shopping, and having the minister of the Methodist church to tea.

David was not there. He had a job as physical-training instructor to a group of state schools in Manchester, but he came to see his mother at weekends, and he was home at the weekend when she died, quite suddenly, soon after she had come home from church. Now Mara could help David, as effectively as he had helped her. She dealt with all the Welsh uncles and aunts and cousins who came to the funeral. She had grown her hair, and she wore it in a bun, and she used no make-up. She was accepted as Mrs. Sedley, a widow who was going to marry David.

When the last of the plates of ham and tongue were finished, and the remains of the cakes tucked away in tins, she was alone in the little house with David, and the future faced them with a giant question-mark.

"Will you come and live with me?" he said humbly. "I'll be very honoured, and you can trust me not to take advantage of you. I obey the Book of the Rules." He meant the Bible, which he carried in his pocket.

The lilt of his accent was music in her ears. He had given her back her life, not just life, but a life that was worth living.

"I have a nice bungalow," he said. "It's called *Nirvana*. Two bedrooms, a lounge, kitchen and bathroom. Not a lot of work, and I'll keep the garden nice for you. The furniture is good fumed-oak, and the chairs are covered in moquette."

"And are there china geese on the walls?"

"How did you guess?" His eyes glowed with pleasure. "I'm afraid we'll have to be deceitful, for decency's sake, and say that you're my wife. But you'll be happy there, I promise you."

She was.

The wooden disc, flapping over the door, advertised to the postman and the rest of the world that the pebble-dashed walls housed *Nirvana*. And so it proved to be.

David's courtesy and kindness were unfailing. He went off for work at nine o'clock each morning, and he returned at five, usually with some small present for her, chocolates or flowers. Every month a cheque came to her from her husband's lawyers. It was for a small amount, but it covered her needs. She had shared a joint account with her husband, and what she received was only a very small amount of her own earnings, so that she was not beholden to him in any way. It was his lawyers who had made the arrangement, acting more on her behalf than on his.

David used the outside lavatory, even for shaving, so that he only used the bathroom on Wednesdays and Saturdays, when he had a bath at night after she had gone to bed.

At weekends, he worked in the garden, unless it rained, when they watched television together. They were polite to everyone, but were careful not to make friends, and this was easy, because their neighbours too were chary about starting friendships. On Sunday mornings, he went to chapel with his Book of the Rules under his arm, and he came home to roast beef and Yorkshire pudding, or a leg of lamb. She was a good cook.

They lived like this for some months, not talking a great deal, but getting to know one another. Then, just before Christmas, he went down with influenza. She looked after him, taking his temperature, giving him aspirin and hot drinks, and washing his pyjamas, which were soaked with sweat. When he recovered, she became ill, and she spent Christmas Day in bed. He took her temperature, gave her hot drinks, and washed her nightdress. She was well enough to wait up until midnight to bring in the New Year with him. They listened to the chimes of Big Ben, and they drank to each other and to absent friends in the red wine he had bought in the super-market.

That night he kissed her under the mistletoe, then he kissed her some more, but over on the moquette sofa, while the artificial flames flickered under the electric bars of the fire. He put aside his Book of Rules, and she slept in his arms.

It was nearly two years later that news came through of Paul Sedley's stroke. He was dying, but he was able to make it known that he wanted to see his wife. She had to go.

David didn't try to prevent her. He knew she had a duty she must perform.

"I'll soon be back," she said at the railway station.

"My little love." He always called her that.

When she reached the house near Sevenoaks, Paul recognized her, but she hardly recognized him because he was so pale and wizened. Her Nirvana had been his purgatory. She settled by his bedside and held his hand, wanting to give him a little happiness at the end.

The next day, he had a second stroke, leaving him deeply unconscious, but after a week he could communicate with her by pressing her hand. They evolved a morse code which somehow they both understood.

She wrote to David. "I can't say how long I'll be here, but I must stay for as long as he's alive."

David wrote to her. "I understand, but I don't know what to do. They think here that you're my wife, and that you've left me. They'll be wondering what sort of a rotter I am."

She could hear the lilt of his voice as she read his letter, and she knew that their Nirvana had come to an end.

"So that's the missing years," Mara said. "If I were a different sort of person, I'd have told my story in newspaper articles. I might even have written a book. Exhibitionists are lucky. They reap a rewarding relief."

"What became of him?"

"He left Manchester. He would be ashamed of what people were saying about him. Naturally we couldn't exchange letters, with me constantly beside my husband. It would have been indecent. So we lost touch. He would think it was his punishment for breaking the rules in his Book."

"That's the sort of thing that turns people against religion," Isabella said.

"No, it was his religion that gave him his goodness. I spoilt things for him. Another Eve. I hope he's found happiness with someone else, someone more suitable."

"You don't really mean that, Mara. You hope that he's missing you as much as you miss him. And someday he'll find you. Like the words in that song."

When Rorie appeared to tell them that it was after midnight, he found Mara slumped in her chair, asleep. Isabella signed to him not to disturb her, but Mara opened her eyes. "The audience stayed awake, and the performer fell asleep," she said.

"Nature's cure for stress, but that's all over now," Isabella said.

She was right. When they went to bed, Mara's head had hardly touched the pillow when she was asleep.

*   *   *

Colin Craig was at Clonbracken by lunch-time. He had chosen to come by sea, as he loved anything to do with ships, but the crossing to Cork had been very rough indeed.

In the afternoon, Shirley took him to kiss the Blarney Stone, while Mara argued with Isabella about the purpose of Bardini's visit.

"Naturally he wants to see you again, after all these years," Isabella said.

"You aren't telling him any rubbish about me singing again?"

"I'm not telling him any rubbish. I only speak the truth."

"So you *have* been telling him that I'm recovering my voice!"

"I've told him that you sing like a dream, like you always did. But even I'm not so silly as to think you'll return to the operatic stage."

"But you think you can entice me onto the concert platform! No, Isabella. A kind of vanity urged me to get back the talent I once had, but for home consumption only. I'll never, ever, sing to an audience again."

Isabella recounted the argument to Bardini, as Briano drove them from the airport. She had waited for him in the car, because while it was true that she was left in peace at Clonbracken, the crowds at the airport would recognize her. Isabella Connelli sang no more, but she was not forgotten, and there was always the risk that Bardini's incognito wouldn't work.

"She didn't seem to be worried about meeting me again?" Bardini asked. He knew how to modulate his voice to help Isabella to catch what he said.

"She's afraid you'll prevail upon her to sing in public. And she could do it, Paolo. You'll know that when you hear her. What's so important is that she'll get written about again, then he'll read it and find her. They'll be reunited and live happily ever after."

Bardini took her by the hand. "If he had wanted to, he'd have found her long ago. Sir Adrian Ferguson broke all sorts of professional rules when he let David Trevor know where to find her in that nursing home, and Adrian Ferguson is always in the news, easily traced by a Welshman whose sentimental heart wants to seek out an old love. He's younger than her, you know – quite a lot younger. He'll have a wife and children and a home in Caerphilly, or some place with an unpronounceable name . . ." He stopped because Isabella was staring at him appealingly, her green eyes trusting him, just as they had done during those last, terrible months when she had depended on his baton to shield her from the shame of her infirmity. It was his nerve, not hers, that had snapped. It was he who could stand it no more and had made her retire. He had to help her now.

"If it's humanly possible, I'll bring them together again, but it may not be in the way you plan it. There aren't often happy endings.

It isn't everyone who is as lucky as you." It was difficult to say this, thinking, as he did, of the pitiful waste her life had been, but his words had pleased her.

She bent down and kissed his hand. "Paolo, I used to be so scared of you! Now you're my second favourite man to Rorie."

It was the highest compliment she could pay him and he knew it.

Benedict was in the field with Rorie and Colin as they drove up to the house. He was sitting in the mud, cuddling a piglet, because the men had better things to do than to look after a small boy who could never come to harm among pigs.

Isabella hung back while Bardini went up to the house to meet Mara. Last time he had seen her, she was in a state of shock, and if his wife had not acted swiftly and sensibly, she would have been dead.

Mara was waiting for him in the drawing-room, apprehensive, aware of how much she had changed over the years. She knew what he looked like, had seen him often in the newspapers, and on the sleeves of his innumerable records.

"Mara!" She went to him gratefully. It was ten years since she had felt a man's embrace.

When Isabella joined them, they were laughing and talking of old times, picking up their friendship as if they had never been apart. She viewed her handiwork with satisfaction. Everything was fitting in with her master-plan, but there was still the final episode to be completed.

They took no notice of her, not even seeing her, so she left them to themselves, and went to find Rorie. She didn't have to look very far, for he was watching her from the verandah, anticipating her every move.

"Persevere," he said, noting that she was wearing her latest hearing-aid.

She misunderstood him, still thinking of Mara. "Paolo will do that all right. God moves in a mysterious way, but I'll go on badgering Him with my prayers."

517

76

It had poured with rain for weeks.

The buses splashed their way along the Glen road towards Iona Ferry in the morning, and they returned in the afternoon with their loads of day tourists, wearing wet clothes, their plastic hoods and dripping head-squares draped like bunting from the racks above them. Somehow they managed to enjoy themselves, and they had their guide books and picture-postcards and souvenirs to prove it.

Niall made the weather his excuse to take time off for fishing on Loch Caraig, and he watched the buses in the distance as they crept over the shoulder of Ben More. Now there were fifteen or more, besides the streams of cars and trailer-caravans that were disgorged from the roll-on roll-off car ferry several times a day, but not long ago five buses would have been a phenomenon.

Tourism had come and would increase every year. He had his moments of hating what was happening to Caraig village as much as he knew his parents, under their semblance of approval, hated it. Change was as objectionable to him as it was to them, but change there must be, and he had contrived that it would be channelled through his own controlling hands.

"Make the village really primitive. Thatched roofs and loos at the bottom of the garden. And oil lamps of course, and the daily trek to the well." Rorie, at the New Year, had accepted Niall's ideas with his usual enthusiasm, and had not lost heart when it was pointed out that to restore a village into what would virtually be a museum was a practical and financial impossibility.

"If they must have All Mod Cons, give the wretches a heated swimming-pool. It could be discreetly hidden in the ruins of the old barn." And to Rorie's surprise, his idea was incorporated in the plans which were now taking shape under the watchful eye of Colin Craig.

The butcher's van was approaching Kilcaraig. It came once

a week from Tobermory, and there would be people waiting for it when it came to a halt outside the Manse. In a year or two, it would continue its journey to Caraig village, and the holiday people would buy from it, just as the local people did. Holiday people who didn't support the local shops and local activities would find that they couldn't book accommodation if they tried to come back again.

It was an easy rule to make, but not an easy one to apply. People might not want to come back, after weeks of mist and rain and midges. But the right people would love it, whatever the weather – the wildlife, the beauty, the freedom of it all. There would be jobs for local people, maintenance men and gillies and gardeners, a whole new life rising out of the ruins. The see-saw of his feelings was still occupying his thoughts as a glance, not at his watch but at the sun shimmering through the rain-clouds, reminded him that it was time to go home.

He met Mara as he crossed the field towards the village, Mara flushed and worried because she had lost Skittles.

"That wretched poodle's slipped her collar. It's the last time I'll ever take her for a walk. Your mother will never forgive me if she's drowned in a bog."

"She'll be queuing up for the butcher. I saw his van," Niall said. Mara's hair was wet and windswept, her skirt clinging to her body. He had an almost irresistible desire to rip off her wind-cheater, and kiss her lovely mouth and find out what she was really like, because ever since she had been at Clonbracken, she had blossomed like some exotic, exciting flower.

He walked beside her, dismayed by his thoughts, understanding at last the emotion which had gripped Rorie when he met Isabella, and which had never been subdued with the passing of the years. Fierce desire. Good God! What on earth would Josanne think about that!

They cut through the burial ground, past the Lamont graves, where Aunt Marian's name was newly carved on the granite head-stone.

"She was always such a happy person," Mara said, pausing with him, never suspecting his thoughts. "It's no wonder Isabella nearly went round the bend when that accident followed so closely on her death."

"It wasn't Isabella I was worrying about, it was Rorie. You'd never believe how unsettled he used to be, how restless and unreliable. Being responsible for Isabella is the best thing that could have happened to him. I wish Mama could see it that way!"

He walked past her, close to her, and opened the gate that led into the Manse garden.

Shirley leaned out of the bathroom window, and called to them that she had found Skittles being fed by the butcher, and she had returned her to Caraig Lodge.

"That girl's a gem," Mara said. "She thinks of everything."

"What'll you do if she marries Colin?"

"I don't think it's as much if as when. She's on her feet now, and so am I. Our holiday at Clonbracken put the finishing touch on what started here at Kilcaraig." She smiled her wonderful smile. "Isabella's full of ideas about the future and I want to talk to you about it some time. She wants MacDonald's farm restored as a holiday home for the deaf. I think it's a wonderful idea. They'll see the beauty of the gales and not hear them! And I've my own personal reasons for being interested, as you well know."

They were standing near the back door, beside the rows of cauliflowers which Sandy MacPherson had coaxed into mammoth proportions.

"The Connelli-Sevilla Home?" he said, hardly taking in what she had said.

"Horrors, no! Just MacDonald's Farm, as it always was, but a farm with a difference. Now you'll come in and have a drink and forget about your responsibilities for a little while."

He handed her his basket of fish. "I must get home. These are all cleaned and ready and I expect I smell of them! I'll call in some other day when I don't feel squalid."

He left her there, looking after his retreating figure until he had shut the gate behind him. It was strange that he had never seemed to be a bit like Rorie, but now there was something about him which reminded her so much of his twin that it was almost uncanny.

She went into the house and called to Shirley that they would have trout, not mince, for dinner, and Niall walked up the castle drive with his fishing-rod in his hand, and his heart racing. He went in by the back door, tip-toeing like a naughty schoolboy, because he didn't want to talk to anyone until he had got a hold on himself and quelled the unruly feelings that had gripped him so absurdly. He paused when he reached the landing, and he could hear Josanne's voice, low and husky, reading to the children.

He poured some of her pine bath-salts into his bath, wanting to rid himself of more than the smell of fish. When he emerged, clean and refreshed, in his second-best kilt, Josanne had already changed and was in the library, helping herself to a drink.

520

"No fish?" she said, without looking at him.

"I gave them to Margaret. I met her looking for Skittles."

Josanne curled up in a chair. "Don't be like Rorie and develop a penchant for older women. No good can come of it. But I suppose there's nothing very romantic about a present of fish." She lit a cigarette. She very rarely smoked. "She's a different person since she went to Clonbracken. I don't think she and Bardini were talking music all the time they were together!"

Niall had never believed in thought-transference. Now he began to wonder if there was something in it. He sat opposite her in the Kilcaraig chair and wished he could talk to Aunt Marian.

"I'll take you to Clonbracken as soon as we've finished the harvest," he said. Josanne's hair was sleek. There were laughter-lines round her eyes and mouth, and she had been a wonderful wife. Clonbracken was a long way distant from temptation at the Manse.

"We'll see," Josanne said, thinking of the children and all the bonds that bound her to Kilcaraig, but she saw the flicker of disappointment on Niall's face. "If I can't go there, you can. You love being with Rorie, and Isabella doesn't alarm you as she does me."

They left it like that. There was plenty time for them to make up their minds when the harvest was gathered in.

*   *   *

It was a perfect day for sailing, enough wind to keep them moving, but not enough to cause any trouble. Isabella had to be watched, now that she was becoming more venturesome, but her turn at the tiller was over, and she stood in the cockpit, her hair blowing in the breeze, and her figure as neat as it had been when Rorie first met her. She was wearing jeans, tucked into her white socks, instead of her usual shorts.

"You look like Fidelio," he told her, and as he had hoped, it made her sing a snatch of an aria, but she gave it up shortly, having forgotten it.

"I never liked trouser roles," she said. "I always felt a fool singing love-duets with other women. But there was a time when I'd have given anything to sing Octavian to Mara's *Marshallin*. That was before I met her, when I had a crush on her."

"Does Paolo Bardini think she'll ever take a professional engagement again?"

"She wouldn't sing for him. She says she'll never sing for anybody. But it's the only way her professional name will ever be advertised again, and I'll bet anything that it would work out right."

"Isabella, aren't you betting against impossible odds?"

"I spent years and years yearning for you, only you. I know what it feels like to be parted from someone, when every moment of every day is a kind of *Liebestod*."

"Shall we give our automatic pilot a spell of duty?"

She knew his train of thought and knew what he meant.

"Just for a little while," she said. They were further from land than usual, and there was not another ship in sight. They made love that day, not in the saloon but on the deck.

The next time they sailed, and the next, they took Benedict with them. They still conversed with one another in song, and now he joined in, lustily, sometimes beating time.

"If he weren't my shape, I'd suspect he was Bardini Junior," Rorie said, watching his son poised on an imaginary rostrum.

"Conductors don't always sleep with their *prime donne*," Isabella said. "That's just an old wives' tale. Before you became my lover, sex was, for me, just an indecent duty. After you gave me up, it became a shameful necessity. In those days, Paolo Bardini would have terrified me frigid!"

"I tried to give you up because I thought it was hopeless. There was never another woman after you. There never could be. You are my heart's delight."

"Laa-la-la-la-laa." Benedict had been ignored for too long.

"You are my heart's delight," Isabella sang, hugging him. "Rorie, we'll have to be careful what we say. He can't talk, but he understands."

The three of them sang all the way back to the mooring, and Benedict beat time, looking puzzled sometimes when he had to stop because he had got it wrong.

"He's a genius," Rorie said.

"What else would you expect when he's our son!"

The genius slept all the way home, and it was the last time they took him on the yacht, because the seas were becoming too rough, and the October days were too cold.

*　　　*　　　*

"In another week or so, we'll have to be land-lubbers," Rorie said. He and Isabella were lying in the saloon. She nodded and shivered. It was chilly now to be naked, even for a short time, and they had felt the motion of the sea as their bodies united in their shared ecstasy.

"It would be a very unsuitable time to be sick," she said, wriggling into her shirt and shorts with the modesty that never failed to enchant him.

"You were bedraggled and sea-sick when I asked you to marry me. And you said 'the mystery of love is greater than the mystery of death'," he reminded her.

"I was quoting out of *Salome*, but now I know that it's true." She put her arms round his neck and kissed him with a gentleness that was somehow more intimate than passion.

"When we get back to our mooring, we'll put a little rum in our tea," he said.

"Splice the mainbrace," she laughed. It was the only nautical language she knew. He was fastening his life-jacket when he saw that she had forgotten hers, and had left it lying on the bunk. Then he felt the violent movement of the yacht, and appalled, he knew what had happened. He was in time to see Isabella spring to her feet as the boom, which she could not control, swung over her head.

"Sit down!" he shouted, but even had she been able to hear him, it was too late. She was struck savagely as it hurtled back in a terrifying gybe, and the next thing he knew *Falcon* had capsized. He could make out Isabella, quite close to him, in the sea.

He reached her easily, but found she had been stunned by the blow. He held her as he rolled on his back, and swam towards the dinghy, which was tossing in the waves, but free. He would be able to lift her on to it, and help would come soon, for the sudden squall would send all the little ships scurrying for the harbour.

"Isabella!" He held onto her with one arm, and onto the dinghy with the other.

"Isabella!" He tried again, his voice small against the sound of the sea. Somehow he managed to sing it.

There was a little gurgle in her throat, and he was ready to comfort her and to reassure her. The arm that held her was aching. She felt heavy, in spite of the lift of the sea. Then he knew why there was no response from her and what the little gurgle had been. He knew that she was dead.

He let go of the dinghy, and he managed to unfasten his life-jacket and work it off his shoulders.

As he let it go, he held her closely, tightly, in his arms.

* * *

The young man knew about the strand below him, but he was a student and wanted to study undisturbed by the tourists who sometimes discovered the sands, and stayed messing around and being a nuisance. He settled himself on the promontory, and took out his text-books. The sea-gulls wheeled overhead, and for a while he was absorbed by what he read.

He felt hungry, so he ate his bar of chocolate. Then he peered over the edge of the cliff, and saw, as he had expected, that someone had found the strand and was sun-bathing. He looked again, and saw that it was not one person but two who were lying there, holding onto one another in the act of love. Hastily he turned back to his book. He was no Peeping Tom.

An hour later, he felt it was time to go home. There was a glimmer of the setting sun creeping onto the horizon. He collected his books and snapped a thick rubber-band round them, then he peered over the cliff again. The couple were still there, but the sea was lapping round them for the tide was rising.

He froze as he saw that the man's face was covered by the woman's red hair. Their bodies were moving rhythmically in the tide.

He dropped his books and stumbled, whimpering, towards the road, but before he reached it, he met the men and knew at once what they were looking for. He pointed speechless, as his legs crumpled under him.

They caught him just before his head hit the ground.

77

A year ago, Kilcaraig had been invaded by press reporters and journalists, some of them kindly and thoughtful, others blatantly out to make the most of the tragedy which had happened at Courtmacsherry.

All that was over now, seldom talked about, but never for a moment forgotten.

Grania Lamont was in the sun-room at Caraig Lodge, glueing the story of Rorie and Isabella into a scrapbook, using articles and stories which had been selected from various magazines. It would be a more personal record to hand over to Benedict than would be the biographies and coffee-table books which were already proliferating. He would be able to read how his father had preferred to cling to his wife's dead body rather than to life itself.

The inquest had revealed that Isabella Connelli's death was due to a blow on the head, not from drowning. An inspection of *Falcon*, found capsized but afloat, had made it possible to reconstruct the accident, but not to explain why the life-jackets had not been worn on that fatal day. It was well-known that Rorie Lamont was a seasoned yachtsman, who took safety precautions very seriously indeed, but Isabella's book on sailing was produced in court, and it told its own story. She had tried to change direction in the wrong way, and at the wrong time, and she had panicked. Her life-jacket would not have saved her from the swing of the boom, but if her husband had been properly protected, he would have lived. That his death could have been of his own desire was glossed over, for there would be distressing overtones if suicide were suggested. Death by misadventure recorded a tidy ending to it all.

The burial, which was private, took place at Clonbracken, attended only by members of the Lamont family, and by some of the nuns who had been the nearest Isabella had ever known as next of kin. Bardini himself had delivered the eulogy at the requiem mass held in the Cathedral at Cork. His tribute to Rorie, whom he had known so little, was blended with his words about Isabella, whom he had known so well. They had died as they had lived, part of one another, and as the magnificent service drew to a close, even Grania had found some release from the anguish of her grief.

It was Mara who suggested the scrapbook, remembering, although she didn't say so, Isabella's own advice about re-tracing painful experiences instead of trying to suppress them, and Grania had assembled their life-story in reports and pictures and had now come to the tragedy at Courtmacsherry, which had been proclaimed in banner headlines in newspapers throughout the world.

Roderick had chosen which passages should be preserved and which were best forgotten, but he had included some of the accounts of the memorial services held even in tiny churches in outlandish places, where village choirs had hummed background music to a recording of Isabella singing the *Liebestod*. Although sentimental and tasteless, this was somehow touching and not to be ignored. Grania filled only two pages a day, partly because the glue had to be given time to dry, and partly because it was as much as she could endure.

She screwed the lid back onto the pot of paste, and her eyes flickered to the cuttings she would deal with during the next few days. She was nearly at the end of her task, and she could see a picture of Benedict at Ardcross on a Shetland pony. Josanne and Niall had wanted to have him at the castle, but Catriona had pointed out that as she and Hector were Roman Catholics, there would be fewer complications if Benedict were brought up by them. Iain already loved him as a brother, and Hector had resigned his commission, and was running Ardcross as a small farm. His writing remained his hobby, but sometimes he had the satisfaction of selling a story to a magazine. Tragedy had brought the MacNeills together as nothing else could have done.

It was only when the hammering stopped that Grania realized how noisy it had been. Roderick had taken up some floor-boards in the hall because Skittles, sniffing, had revealed not just a rat-hole but the control-room of a colony of rats. He stood beside her now, hammer in hand, looking at her work which would be dark and almost indecipherable until the paste dried.

"I forgot to tell you – Niall's gone over to Oban to collect Josanne's new car. He rang up about it last night." Roderick often forgot little things and wished he could forget important ones.

Grania received the information, as he had expected, in silence. During the few weeks before the events at Courtmacsherry, Niall had behaved in a wholly irresponsible way, characteristic of the youthful Rorie, but totally unlike himself. Margaret Sedley had become all too obviously the object of his admiration, and only because she handled the matter with the utmost delicacy and tact was his infatuation kept from the alert eyes of the villagers, and even from Josanne herself. But his parents had seen it. The catastrophe at Courtmacsherry had brought the matter to an abrupt end.

As the months passed and life gradually returned to normal, Niall had sub-consciously been making up for his aberration. He had bought Josanne new clothes, a very impressive music-centre, and now it was a new car.

"They can do with an extra car when the MacNeills are here," Grania said at last. She and Roderick had stayed at Ardcross for Christmas and New Year, having to break with the traditional family reunion at Kilcaraig, and they had returned there for Easter, but now Hector and Catriona and the children would be at Kilcaraig for the next few weeks. The first anniversary would be over when they returned to Ardcross, and Benedict would be around to bring comfort to his grandparents at the time when memories of the past would be stirred up all over again.

Catriona was expecting a baby in February, and Chrissie, sitting by the Aga in the castle kitchen, was knitting a layette, her rheumatic fingers still able to hold the needles, her mind as alert as ever it had been. She had accepted the death of Rorie and Isabella with the serenity of the very old. For her, the parting from those she loved would only be a very temporary affair.

"Grania, may I ask Mrs. Coll to make us coffee?" Mara had made her way up the brae without either Grania or Roderick seeing her. She was often at Caraig Lodge, and felt that it was part of her own home. Her handling of the Niall situation, though never mentioned, had cemented her friendship with Grania, and her involvement with Rorie and Isabella made her virtually one of the family.

She went to the kitchen and chatted until the kettle had boiled, and Mrs. Coll had poured water onto the instant coffee, then she took the tray to the sun-room. Roderick was still standing, and he drank his coffee that way, saying he was in a hurry to get on with his job, not wanting to admit that the old war-wound made it increasingly difficult for him to get in and out of a chair. When he had left them, Mara said "I want your advice. Truthful advice, not just polite".

She held out a letter. "The Connelli Memorial Concert that Bardini will conduct at the Albert Hall is being arranged. As you know, it's in aid of the deaf, and the artistes chosen will be from among her friends. He's asked me to take part."

"And of course you will!"

"But Grania, I'm not up to concert standard, and the very thought of facing an audience makes me sick with fright. I know I'm a silly old woman and everyone has forgotten about me years ago, but I can't forget."

"Bardini wouldn't ask you if he thought you weren't up to it. You've asked my advice. You'll do it because Isabella wants you to do it. If you refuse, you won't be failing Bardini or yourself, you'll be failing her. I know it, as surely as if she were telling it to me herself." And she did know it as surely as that.

"So I write and say yes?"

"You write and say 'of course'. And you'll remember that you'll be helping to make sure that MacDonald's Farm is maintained for all time for the purpose Isabella had in mind. You have a very personal part to play in that enterprise."

Mara had forgotten that the farm, already provided for in Isabella's will, would benefit from the concert.

"How strangely interwoven our lives are," she said resignedly. "It's as if everything were planned, a bit haphazard, like the Kilcaraig tapestry, but somehow the pattern makes sense in the end."

"So you'll do it?"

"I'll do it."

Grania went with her as far as the bumpy bridge, and was breathless when she returned to the house, feeling the climb up the brae. Mara was right, the pattern made sense in the end, but those who were still alive couldn't see it. Perhaps Rorie and Isabella understood it now. Perhaps they knew that tomorrow Benedict would be coming to Kilcaraig. It comforted her to be fanciful at times.

Roderick's hammering seemed to reverberate through the whole village. Skittles had taken refuge, trembling, in the broom-cupboard. Mrs. Coll found her there, gave her some brandy, and took her to Grania.

"We've enough troubles without the worry of neurotic dogs," she said, as Grania buried her face lovingly in that unkempt ball of wool, but she could smell the brandy and knew Mrs. Coll didn't mean a word she said.

Roderick called to her that he had hammered a nail into his hand. She fetched the first-aid box from the kitchen, as she had done hundreds of times. Small happenings never changed. Life went on.

*　　*　　*

While Grania and Mara were talking about the Connelli Memorial Concert, Josanne and Shirley were searching through Mrs. Craig's mail-order catalogue, looking for a skirt that would go with the Special Offer jacket which Shirley had ordered out of a Sunday newspaper.

"The weather in County Cork will be soggy, like it is here, but warmer, and man-made fibres will look all right. You'll need drip-dry, if you're going to be messing around with pigs," Josanne said.

Colin Craig's decision to move to Clonbracken had surprised no one. With Caraig village organized in a way that was working so well, there would be little else for him to do, except get in Niall Lamont's way. Some day, Benedict might want to live at Clonbracken, and it would need a reliable manager for many years to come. It was what Rorie and Isabella had wished, and they had both said so clearly in their wills.

Isabella had made generous provision for the upkeep of the convent in which she had been reared, and she had remembered musicians' charities, and the care of the deaf. She had thought of everything before she had put her signature to that document, only six months before her life was ended.

Benedict would receive the royalties from his mother's records, as well as the fortune Maestro Pietro Grandi had amassed for her. Many people had mistrusted the Maestro, believing that when he had discovered Connelli's talent he had also discovered Eldorado. So he had, but it was her Eldorado, not his. He took his fair share of the profits, nothing more, and after her death he directed that even that share must go to Benedict. The Maestro mourned Isabella as he would have mourned his own child. Nobody until then had realized how personal and deep was his devotion.

Death had revealed what was probably the only secret Rorie had ever kept during his life. When the Kirk had sold the Manse, it was he and Isabella who had bought it, to restore it to Kilcaraig. They had done so under the cover of a firm of lawyers, and they had entrusted its administration to Adrian Ferguson, not because of his legal connections, but because he was an old family friend.

"It was so obvious, when one thinks about it," Josanne had said to Niall. "It was too much of a coincidence that a stranger should have placed it in Adrian's care."

"It's easy to be wise after the event," Niall had replied, thinking of the many times he had resisted the temptation to ask for Rorie's help with the financial affairs of Kilcaraig. "Now it's ours, and when Mara tires of it, Adrian says he'll rent it from us as a holiday home for himself and his family. It's his way of keeping it in good repair. Some day Benedict may want it, or his children. It belongs to us, and we now have the security to be able to plan ahead."

"Why didn't they tell us?"

"Because they didn't want Mama to feel beholden to Isabella in any way. I'm only guessing, but that could be the truth."

Josanne often thought about that conversation, although by tacit consent she and Niall never tried to talk about it again. She was thinking of it now, as she turned over the pages of Mrs. Craig's mail order catalogue, helping Shirley to choose suitable clothes for her trousseau.

"You mustn't choose your wedding-dress from here. Everyone studies these catalogues. You must look stunning in something which nobody will recognize," she said.

"I'd like to be married in a registry office, with nobody there but your family and Aunt Margaret, and Colin's mother of course."

"Why?"

"Because so many people must be fuming that I'm marrying Colin."

"Plenty of people must have been fuming when I married Niall! Now, no more nonsense about plighting your troth in secret. Why, we're having the organ sorted so that the pedal won't squeak, and Mrs. MacPhail has ordered a dress from Jenner's. We're not going to be done out of a wedding that will cheer us all up." Josanne closed the book with a bang.

A whole year had gone by, but she felt she would never recover from her grief. Every morning she woke up believing it must be some terrible nightmare. Every day she reproached herself for the years in which she had ignored Isabella. The rest of the family must feel as she did, but they all put on an act to one another, pretending that there was no guilt or regrets in their grief. Isabella had been accepted as one of themselves after she had married Rorie, but it had never really worked. It never could work. She could never be an ordinary person, either in life or in death.

The telephone rang. It was Catriona, at Ardcross, to confirm that they would arrive tomorrow as planned. Bridget and the children would be left at Kilcaraig, while she and Hector went on holiday to Greece.

"We've got a Caruso in the family – I think I should warn you!" Catriona said. "Benedict can sing every song he hears on the radio, and his voice is a dream."

"God forbid!" Josanne said.

"Why? Benedict won't grow up to be deaf. We take proper care of him. Listen to him now –" She held the receiver so that Josanne could hear a faint "La-la-la", followed by a laugh, a very pretty laugh.

Somehow she managed to smile and to say to Shirley, "That laugh could have been Isabella's". But when she put down the receiver, she wept.

78

Hector and Catriona arrived at Kilcaraig in a Range-Rover stuffed to the roof with luggage. Bridget followed in the car she had bought with her legacy. She had bought many things besides that car.

Iain and Benedict, strapped into their respective chairs on the back seat, were conversing in the fluent language they both understood, though nobody else did.

Roderick and Grania had come to the castle to greet them, and Mara and Shirley were there too, because Josanne had asked them to make this not quite a family affair. All of them would be reminded of the first time Rorie had brought Isabella home as a bride, then of their return in triumph with Benedict, the wonderchild whom they had regarded with suspicion until they saw him and took him to their hearts.

The arrival of any member of the family was always the same, greetings and embracings, and the ecstatic welcome from an assortment of dogs. Benedict ignored his grandparents and made straight for Josanne's little Jack Russell terrier, hugging it, oblivious of everyone else.

"It's like a pig," Catriona said. "He has an incurable passion for pigs."

"Manners, Benedict," Hector ordered, and Benedict turned his attention dutifully to his grandparents. He was no longer chubby, because he had grown a great deal during the past few months, but his smile was radiant, and his "How do you do" was said with prim clarity. Then he saw Mara. He stared up at her, interested but puzzled. She knelt down and sang a few bars of the Brahms lullaby. He laughed delightedly, a memory stirring, but happy memory, nothing to upset him any more.

Mara went up to the nursery and talked to him while Bridget unpacked. She could hear Iain talking to his grandparents in the hall, words spilling out with such speed that they were barely comprehensible, but one thing was clear. He was not a shy, withdrawn little boy any more.

"Look!" Benedict tugged at Mara's dress. She looked. It was a pink velvet pig, rather grubby because he must have cuddled it a lot. "Brunhilde," he said. "Mummy made it." Mara took it and examined it, pretending just to be admiring it, but sure enough, it bore the signs of Isabella's lack of craftsmanship. It had been over-stitched where her inadequate efforts had failed, but its shape was right. She must have worked very hard to produce it.

"We found it in a drawer. She had made it for Christmas, God rest her soul," Bridget said.

"Look!"

A music-box now, another treasure.

Mara knelt on the floor and watched him haul his toys out of their case. Last of all came a broken cassette tape-recorder. It was still a precious possession, although its significance was long forgotten by him.

Mara had flown to Clonbracken with Grania and Roderick as soon as they knew of the accident. She had done so at Grania's request. No reason was given, none was needed. Grania and Roderick just could not face what lay ahead of them without added support.

During those first few days, it was Mara who had taken over the care of Benedict, for Bridget was beside herself with grief and in no fit state to be seen by him. Mara kept him confined to the nursery, while Motti dealt with the press reporters and photographers who had invaded the farm. Mara had learnt how to suppress her emotions, and the lesson of the years helped her now to appear calm and normal as she dressed and fed and cuddled the child. Bed-time was painful almost beyond endurance, because that was when she used the cassettes, prepared by Rorie and Isabella to keep Benedict happy when they were away from home for two or three days. .

She listened with Benedict to the stories of Brunhilde and her babies, told by Rorie, and to the songs, some of them composed by Isabella, because they referred to the daily happenings at Clonbracken. Always there was finally a lullaby, and when that was finished Benedict was invariably asleep.

After the fourth night, she had to revert to the first tape, then came the second. Ten bedtimes later, Benedict said "No" and thumped at the recorder, so she put it aside and sang to him herself. He listened, but his lips were drooping. He was beginning to understand.

It was Motti who found him one day sitting on the nursery floor, the broken recorder beside him, the precious recorded material trailing, thin and glistening like sea-weed, round the room. Benedict had made a good job of his destruction.

Motti, who until then had shown remarkable self-control, was incensed at the sight of this havoc, and was about to administer a mighty smacking to the wrecker, but Mara came into the room in time to avert a scene. She picked Benedict up in her arms, caressing him, fighting back her tears.

"Motti, he wants his parents. He thinks they're in the box."

Benedict recognized some of her words. He wriggled out of her arms and pulled his jack-in-the-box out of the toy-cupboard. "La-la," he said, looking up, apparently trying to make them understand.

"La-la," Mara replied, swallowing, her eyes flashing an appeal to Motti for help.

"Old MacDonald had a farm, Ee-aye, ee-aye, ay!" she sang. Soon Motti had caught what it was about, and put in the moo-moos and the quack-quacks, until Benedict joined in as well. The cassette recorder was not replaced, although Briano made a good job of splicing the tapes together. Benedict sucked his thumb as he lay in his cot, and his expression of resignation seemed to say – "Message received and understood."

Two weeks later, there was the flight to Glasgow, and the drive to Ardcross. Benedict crowed with joy when he found he was to share a room with Iain, his friend. He liked the big rambling house, and he enjoyed feeding the hens and the geese, and following Dougie, the gardener, with his little wheel-barrow, just like the one Iain had. There were visits, too, from Uncle Hector, who brought sweets and toys and laughter, and one day a large red delivery van drove up to the door, and he knew Aunt Catriona had fixed a welcoming flag to the pig-sty. Brunhilde and her latest family had come to their new home.

Mara went to stay at Ardcross and received a welcome almost as warm as Brunhilde had done.

On her first night there, she tucked the children up in bed, and she sang some nursery rhymes to Iain, then she stood by Benedict's cot and sang the Brahms lullaby. He stopped sucking his thumb and listened, then he sat up in bed and rocked in time to the music. Very soon he was joining in, his la-la soft and pure, with sometimes an attempt at a word. Then he cuddled up and fell asleep. Every night during her visit, Mara sang to him, and after she had gone, Catriona brought out her tape-recorder, and Benedict slept once more to the sound of his mother's voice, giving happiness not heartache, contentment not tears.

Now at Kilcaraig, Mara fondled the cobbled-up pig. "Where did you find this?" she asked Bridget.

"Motti found it. And other things besides. Cassettes, more than a dozen of them. Mrs. MacNeill has brought them here with her. She thinks you're the best person to listen to them, to know if they're the right sort of music for Benedict to hear. Mistress Lamont had prepared them for when he was older. She wouldn't have expected to leave him alone so soon." Bridget sighed and crossed herself. "It is the holy will of God. But I can't understand it, at all, at all."

Catriona and Hector set off for Greece on the following day, having given Mara the box of cassettes. Listening to them would be an ordeal she would have to face somehow, a little at a time. She told Shirley about it, and Shirley immediately offered to share the experience with her. Most evenings now, she was over at Mrs. Craig's. with Colin, because Mara preferred to have the house to herself when she practised. She was giving full voice now, surprising even herself at the volume she could produce, delighted instead of ashamed when she listened to the play-back on the recorder.

"I think I should listen to them alone, Shirley. These were meant to be for Benedict, and Catriona's right – Rorie and Isabella hadn't expected him to be so young when he received this very special legacy."

That same evening she settled down by the window in the sitting-room. The garden, so dank and overgrown when she had arrived two years ago, had taken on the golden shades of autumn, and the grass was short and green, the roses still in bloom. Across the hedge, the burial-ground looked peaceful, not depressing, and through the tomb-stones she could catch the glint of Loch Caraig across the field. Ben More was out of sight, but it would be clear to the summit. The sunset, when it came, would be beautiful.

She pressed the recorder into action, and heard the hiss of it before Isabella's voice invited Benedict to stop what he was doing and listen to her for a while – she had quite a lot to say. The informality and the reality brought Isabella into the room, then Rorie, talking naturally, sharing jokes and finally singing.

The burial-ground faded in the dusk, but the loch shimmered golden now in the setting sun. It was dark when she switched off the recorder. She replaced the four cassettes she had played in the box which contained the remaining ten. She would give them all to Grania tomorrow, for they belonged to the family, and there was no need for her to hear any more. She had heard all that was necessary, and it had brought her not sorrow but solace. Isabella and Rorie had expressed their thoughts and their dreams to their son, and in doing so had revealed all that had been exquisite in their lives together.

"I'm not another Mendelssohn, but listen to this." Isabella had laughed, and this had been a sea-song, catching the ripple, then the crashing of the waves. It might have been a forecast of their epitaph; instead it conveyed a sense of immortality in the constant surging of the sea. It was a masterpiece of its kind. Some day Benedict might decide to give it to the world.

When Shirley came home, she tip-toed cautiously into the house. She had not seen a light in Mara's bedroom, but the strip under the sitting-room door showed her that she was still up, although it was long past her usual bed-time. She hesitated, wondering if she could escape upstairs, because Mara would hate to be discovered looking weepy and upset, but Mara called to her. She had lighted a fire, and the tape-recorder and cassettes were neatly on a table. Mara had a tray of tea and biscuits beside her, and some ready-made meringues Euphie had recommended from the shop.

"Are you all right?" Shirley asked. Mara held out a cup of tea for her.

"I've emerged at last from a long, dark tunnel. The shameful episode at Stresa, the bitter-sweet years with David, tainted because they were stolen years and couldn't last, then Paul's long, gruesome illness. You see, I'm not even glossing over the sordidness of that any more! Then meeting you, and knowing Kilcaraig, and becoming gradually a person among other people, not an enclosed misery of myself. All that was being resolved when the tragedy of Rorie and Isabella struck. But I've listened to the tapes, only some of them, but enough to know that it wasn't tragedy. It was the complete fulfilment of two lives that had merged into one."

"But Mara, what about Benedict?"

"Benedict is a happy little boy, in a good home, surrounded by loving people. He has a God-given talent which he can use or abuse. That'll be up to him. But it's my belief that Isabella Connelli will make musical history in more ways than one. Benedict Lamont's glorious voice is one day going to take the world by storm." She went over to the window, and drew the curtains, shutting out the night. There was only a small reading-lamp in the room, so that the reflection of the flames could be seen dancing on the ceiling. "Isabella has composed songs that capture the beauty of everyday things. As the sounds of the world closed away from her, she wrote what she knew on manuscript paper. What she has written will never die. Her songs are a song without end."

She picked up the book she had been reading. Shirley knew the inscription – "Mara, thanks for the memory. P."

Mara stroked the book thoughtfully. "He rang this evening. He's worried in case I'll lose my nerve and back out of the concert. I hope I've reassured him. After hearing Isabella tonight, I couldn't let her down."

Shirley looked puzzled. "I thought your husband gave you that book."

"How strange. I never even thought of that. Paolo Bardini was my first love, long before he met Constance or I met Paul. It's wonderful now to look back on it all, and to say that 'we're just good friends'."

That night Mara slept peacefully and well for the first time since she had left David to go to her husband's sickbed. On the following morning, she gathered the last of the roses and put them on Aunt Marian's grave.

It was a thank-offering to a member of the family which had shown her the road back to happiness.

*　　*　　*

The Isabella Connelli Memorial Concert filled the Albert Hall to capacity, and every seat could have been sold many times over.

It was a surprisingly happy affair. Bardini had chosen the programme with impeccable taste, refusing to include anything that would suggest mawkishness or the banal. There was nothing that would awake painful memories, and the overture to *The Barber of Seville* set the style for the evening. The most prominent singers from the operatic world sang duets and quartets and sextets, so that as many as possible could pay their respects to the *diva* they had envied, sometimes resented, but had always admired.

Mara found that her dread of meeting the people from the past was wholly unfounded. She was welcomed among them, and the Maestro was there to help her through the rehearsal, which was necessarily brief, for the artistes had flown in from all over the world.

Bardini had cast her as the Marschallin in the final trio from *Der Rosenkavalier*. With the support of two famous voices, she had little to fear, and at the end of the evening, as she stood with the others, bouquets of flowers in her arms and bowing repeatedly to the prolonged applause, she re-discovered the exhilaration of success, and most of all the triumph of two people whose love-story had touched the hearts, not only of music-lovers, but the whole world.

Among that sea of faces in the hall would be the Lamonts, the MacNeills, the Fergusons, Briano from Italy, Motti from her hospital in Dublin, Shirley with Colin, and the people of Kilcaraig would be listening on their radios, for the concert was being broadcast that night, but not televised.

When at last she made her way to the artistes' room, Mara felt the first pang of disappointment. Letters and telegrams and flowers had been delivered to her all day, many from fans she would have thought would have forgotten her years ago. Her name had been in the papers, embarrassing her at first, then giving her excitement and hope, but that one precious link with the past was missing. She had not really expected him, but she wished with all her heart that he had come.

She found it easy to enter into the after-performance chatter of the artistes, the younger ones, like Lisa Verini, in awe of her, not daring to compliment her in case it would sound impertinent, but after a while she made her way to the conductor's room. Paolo Bardini had told her to come there when she could.

"Mara, is it to be the concert platform, or are you determined to resume your life of retirement?" he asked.

"I'm not going to be carried on a wave of vanity because I sang so well tonight. That was special, and will never happen again. You know that as well as I do."

"So it's Kilcaraig and the Manse?"

536

"After Shirley's married, I may look for somewhere else. Anything will do."

"Would you consider Cardiff? It's a very interesting job that I have there."

She swung round. He stood in the doorway, his jacket a little too blocked out, and the check too pronounced. His black hair was streaked with grey, but his eyes were as kindly, and his smile as engaging as ever.

"David!"

Paolo Bardini picked up his baton. "I'll leave you alone to talk things over. You must have quite a lot to say. But remember one thing. Isabella set her heart on this. She would consider it to be her greatest achievement."

He kissed Mara's hand, and went out into the night.

* * *

There was a furniture van outside the Manse. It was bright yellow, and had come all the way from Cardiff. Sandy MacPherson leaned on his bicycle, and watched the grandpiano being lifted down the steps. He was sorry that Mrs. Sedley had gone away, but Sir Adrian Ferguson had asked him to be caretaker, and to see that the house was in good order, and he was wondering if he could claim that he had been appointed factor to the Lamonts.

Mrs. Craig saw that Sandy was watching the removal van, just as he had done nearly three years ago, when Mrs. Sedley had become a mysterious stranger. Not Mrs. Sedley now, Mrs. Trevor, living in Cardiff in a house that sounded not at all suitable for her, but she had looked so happy last time she was at Kilcaraig, and the few pieces of furniture she was taking from the Manse would replace some of the veneered walnut her husband had described, in the vivid, beautiful phrases of the English-speaking Welsh.

She would visit Mrs. Trevor next time she went to Clonbracken. She usually went by rail and sea, for she hated flying, and there was always a welcome for her from Shirley. She was going to be a grandmother in August, if she was spared.

The children from the castle came into the shop. Benedict had grown tall enough to see over the counter. Euphie gave him five sugar-pigs for his tenpence. He handed one to Anne, then one to Roddy, because they were his hostess and his host, then he gave one to Iain. After some thought, he put one in his pocket, and came through the partition to give Mrs. Craig the last of his treasures. She accepted it with a smile. It was impossible to refuse Benedict anything, the child thrived on loving and giving. The pig in his pocket would be for Grania, his new little cousin, brought by the MacNeills to Kilcaraig for her christening, and too young to come to the shop.

"Watch the road," Mrs. Craig called after the children, when they left. She saw them do their road drill, holding hands, looking right, then left, then right again, but there was no traffic at this time of year, not until the boat bus arrived.

The torrential rain had turned the pot-holes in the road into pools, and now that the sun had made its first appearance of the day, it transformed the water into patches of shimmering nothingness.

People came and went, living out their joys and their sorrows, but Kilcaraig would always be the same.